Praise for
Freedom for a Change

"*Freedom for a Change* is a must read for any American who wants to see a restoration and revival of freedom. Timothy Baldwin's research and exposition of the principles of freedom come straight from the sources that America's founding fathers read and used. It is certainly time that America experiences this *Freedom for a Change!*"

> —JEROME CORSI, *New York Times* best-selling author of *The Obama Nation* and *Unfit for Command* (with co-author John O'Neill), Harvard graduate

"*Freedom for a Change* stands out among other books because of Baldwin's meticulous research, quotation, and documentation from the founding fathers' own writings, and from the sources they studied—Blackstone, Montesquieu, Locke, Grotius, Sidney, and above all, the Bible. Baldwin interacts with these sources and contrasts the original understanding of government with the usurpations of government officials today. Baldwin's analysis is clear, comprehensive, and convincing. To understand where America went wrong and what we Americans can do about it, *Freedom for a Change* is vital reading!"

> —JOHN EIDSMOE; Air Force Lieutenant Colonel, retired; teacher of constitutional law at Thomas Goode Jones School of Law in Montgomery, Alabama; author of several books, including, *Christianity and the Constitution: The Faith of Our Founding Fathers*

FREEDOM
—FOR A—
CHANGE

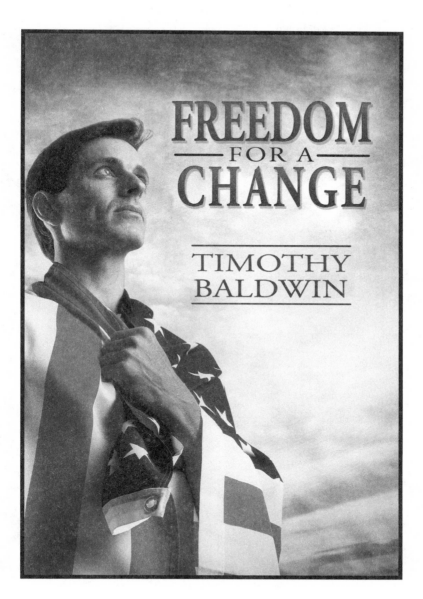

FREEDOM
—FOR A—
CHANGE

TIMOTHY BALDWIN

Agrapha Publishing

Orlando

Agrapha Publishing, Orlando 32835
© 2010 by Agrapha Publishing
All rights reserved. Published 2010
Printed in the United States of America

10   1

ISBN-13: 978-0-9843395-0-1 (CLOTH)
ISBN-10: 0-9843395-0-7 (CLOTH)

Library of Congress Control Number: 2009912700

Cover illustration and design by Steve Warner
Cover photo by Colin Anderson

This book is printed on acid-free paper.

ABOUT THE AUTHOR

Timothy N. Baldwin, JD, born in 1979, is the youngest of three children of Chuck and Connie Baldwin. Chuck Baldwin was the presidential candidate on the Constitution Party ticket in 2008 and the vice presidential candidate on the Constitution Party ticket in 2004. He is a syndicated columnist and founder and pastor of Crossroad Baptist Church in Pensacola, Florida. Without a doubt, Chuck Baldwin is the most influential person in the author's life.

Tim Baldwin graduated from the University of West Florida (UWF) with a bachelor of arts degree in 2001, where he majored in English and minored in political science. From UWF, Baldwin attended Cumberland School of Law at Samford University in Birmingham, Alabama, where he focused his studies on litigation and participated in trial team events, winning several awards and competitions. He graduated from Cumberland and received his juris doctor degree in 2004. Baldwin took the Florida Bar exam in June 2004, which he passed, and then received his license to practice law in October 2004.

After becoming licensed to practice law in Florida, Baldwin became a Florida state prosecutor in 2004 under former state attorney Curtis Golden and current state attorney William "Bill" Eddins. At the state attorney's office, he prosecuted thousands of both misdemeanor and felony crimes and tried scores of jury and judge trials during his two-and-a-half year career there. In 2006, Baldwin started his own law practice in Pensacola, Florida, where he now specializes in property management representation and represents numerous real estate property management companies in Northwest Florida.

Like his father, Baldwin believes in the spirit and principles that founded America, and he believes that to secure freedom for his posterity, knowledge, analysis, and action are required. He believes that there needs to be a resurrection and revival of the spirit of freedom in America, and to that end, he has written the book *Freedom for a Change*. It is his desire that each person reading this book will critically analyze America's current conditions and ask the necessary questions that will lead us to the conclusion of freedom once again.

To my dad, Chuck Baldwin, who has continually been an inspiration and guide to me. To my wife, Jennifer, who is truly a gift from God and my best friend. To my family, for all their support, love, and friendship. Most importantly, to my Savior and God, Jesus Christ, for the life, health, opportunities, and blessings He has given me my entire life.

CONTENTS

ACKNOWLEDGMENTS

Scripture quotations are taken from the following translations:

King James Version (KJV)
Modern King James Version (MKJV), courtesy of Soverign Grace
    Publishers
American Standard Version (ASV)
English Standard Version (ESV), courtesy of American Bible Society

FOREWORD

by *Charles E. Jones III*
Brigadier General, U.S. Air Force, retired

Author Timothy Baldwin studiously wrote *Freedom for a Change* with great wisdom, understanding, and insight as he developed and expounded a complete and comprehensive picture of what made America free and what it will take to keep it free. *Freedom for a Change* is a necessary read for all politicians, constitutional scholars, and freedom-first citizens.

America's citizens are being ruthlessly deceived by many politicians elected to public office and further by those who the politicians appoint to powerful, controlling political positions. Power and control do not satisfy the greed of some politicians in their endgame or quest for self-enrichment. Therefore, our freedoms are at great risk, and we see them taken away faster and more than ever before.

This republic has been in a severe crisis and will continue to rapidly decline into slavery until "we the people" come to understand the real meaning of the Constitution of the United States, the limited powers of the federal government, and the critical need to become responsible and active citizens of our respective states and the United States. We the people must all selflessly guard and preserve the freedoms that our forefathers fought to bequeath to their posterity.

When the contents of *Freedom for a Change* are digested and applied, they will undoubtedly play a large part in the recovery of our once great republic.

INTRODUCTION

On October 17, 2006, former self-proclaimed Christian, conservative, Republican president, G. W. Bush, signed into law the Military Commissions Act of 2006,[1] which denied the right of habeas corpus to detainees held under the act, a provision applicable even to American civilians if the executive branch of the United States deemed them to be an "unlawful enemy combatant." The act suggests that *unlawful enemy combatant* refers to any person "who, before, on, or after the date of the enactment of the Military Commissions Act of 2006, has been determined to be an unlawful enemy combatant by a Combatant Status Review Tribunal or another competent tribunal established under the authority of the President or the Secretary of Defense."

Under other synergizing legislation signed into law by G. W. Bush, such as the USA Patriot Act[2] and the Homegrown Terrorist Prevention Act,[3] American citizens have not only become targets of terrorist investigation but

---

1. *Military Commissions Act of 2006,* Public Law 109-366, HR 6166, 109th Cong., 2d sess. (October 17, 2006).

2. *USA Patriot Act of 2001.* Public Law 107-56, HR 2975, 3162, 3004, 107th Congress, 1st sess. (October 26, 2001).

3. *Homegrown Terrorist Prevention Act of 2007.* HR 1955, 110th Congress, 1st sess. (October 24, 2007).

have been denied the most fundamental right of Anglo-Saxon history—the right of habeas corpus. For many centuries, the right of habeas corpus has been held by Americans and their ancestors to be one of the most fundamental rights of mankind and enforceable by law, except in only very limited circumstances and conditions. Former U.S. supreme court justice Joseph Story described this right as follows: "It is justly...esteemed the great bulwark of personal liberty, and is grantable, as a matter or right, to the party imprisoned."[4] A self-proclaimed "Christian, conservative" notwithstanding, G. W. Bush signed into law the Military Commissions Act, jeopardizing the rights of American citizens secured by the Constitution of the United States of America. Fortunately, in a five-to-four decision, the United States Supreme Court recognized the unconstitutionality of this act and ruled that the suspension of habeas corpus as signed into law by former president Bush was unconstitutional, citing the Magna Carta of 1215 as a historical context for its decision.[5] But what if the U.S. Supreme Court had ruled differently? One vote would have changed the decision. What if President Obama (or subsequent presidents) were to begin a witch hunt in America under the "authority" of *War on Terror* in America? Who would be the victim of such a hunt? You, your family, or your friends? Who would care? Which citizens would recognize tyranny when touching it face to face? The issues regarding the tyrannical pursuits of America's federal government go much deeper and wider than the aforementioned example, as the assaults on freedom in America are as numerous as the ones enumerated in the Declaration of Independence and just as grievous. If the most fundamentally held convictions of freedom over hundreds of generations are now in jeopardy, what freedoms are not in jeopardy?

Many of "we the people" of the several (separate and distinct) states feel the cold metal shackles clamping tight around our ankles and the sound of the metal chains clanking as we drudge through society.[6] As a result of the oppression from the federal government (and, to some degree, the states

---

4. Joseph Story, *A Familiar Exposition of the Constitution of the United States: Containing a Brief Commentary* (New York: Harper & Brothers, 1868), 143.

5. *Boumediene v. Bush*, 553 U.S. ___, 128 S. Ct. 2229 (2008).

6. "In absolute monarchies indeed, as well as other governments of the world, the subjects have an appeal to the law, and judges to decide any controversies, and restrain any violence

respectively), the people have created a rising waive of resistance. So much so that to date, nearly half of the states in the union have proposed or passed state legislation reclaiming and re-invoking their sovereignty over the federal government under their respective state constitutions and the United States Constitution.[7] By the time you read this, there is no telling how many states will have joined this freedom movement. In addition, a continental congress has been scheduled to meet in Philadelphia in November 2009 to address the issues of reclaiming freedom and sovereignty from the federal government.[8] Never in American history since 1776 has this type of revolutionary action happened.

---

that may happen betwixt the subjects themselves, one amongst another. This every one thinks necessary, and believes he deserves to be thought a declared enemy to society and mankind, who should go about to take it away. But whether this be from a true love of mankind and society, and such a charity as we owe all one to another, there is reason to doubt: for this is no more than what every man, who loves his own power, profit, or greatness, may and naturally must do, keep those animals from hurting, or destroying one another, who labour and drudge only for his pleasure and advantage; and so are taken care of, not out of any love the master has for them, but love of himself, and the profit they bring him: for if it be asked, what security, what fence is there, in such a state, against the violence and oppression of this absolute ruler? The very question can scarce be borne. They are ready to tell you, that it deserves death only to ask after safety. Betwixt subject and subject, they will grant, there must be measures, laws and judges, for their mutual peace and security: but as for the ruler, he ought to be absolute, and is above all such circumstances; because he has power to do more hurt and wrong, it is right when he does it. To ask how you may be guarded from harm, or injury, on that side where the strongest hand is to do it, is presently the voice of faction and rebellion: as if when men quitting the state of nature entered into society, they agreed that all of them but one, should be under the restraint of laws, but that he should still retain all the liberty of the state of nature, increased with power, and made licentious by impunity. This is to think, that men are so foolish, that they take care to avoid what mischiefs may be done them by pole-cats, or foxes; but are content, nay, think it safety, to be devoured by lions." John Locke and C. B. Macpherson, ed., *Second Treatise of Government*, (Indianapolis: Hackett Publishing Company, Inc., 1980), 50.

7. Jerome R. Corsi, "Lawmakers in 20 States Move to Reclaim Sovereignty," *World Net Daily*, posted February 6, 2009, http://www.worldnetdaily.com/index.php?fa=PAGE. view&pageId=88218; Ernest Hancock, "21 States Claiming Sovereignty," *Freedom's Phoenix*, posted February 12, 2009, http://www.infowars.com/21-states-claiming-sovereignty/.

8. Jim Kouri, "New Continental Congress to Meet in Philadelphia," *News with Views*, posted February 8, 2009, http://www.newswithviews.com/NWV-News/news124.htm. Reference to the Continental Congress does not imply that this author, Timothy Baldwin, condones the particular Continental Congress mentioned.

So what are the reasons? Where is the proof of such a movement? The evidence proves that for many years the flames of tyranny have heated the American pot, with the surface appearing to be calm and still, but all the while a boiling movement has existed. Over the years, the heat increased and the brewing intensified. Now, the surface reveals the seriousness of the situation, to the point that even removing the flame completely would prove ineffectual in eliminating the fevering and overrunning boil. This effect is caused for good reason: we the people of the several states have shirked our responsibilities as overseers of federal action and power and have allowed the corruption and degradation of our constitutional compact—the United States Constitution. And while a freedom awakening is occurring, there is still much ignorance, lethargy, and confusion in America regarding true freedom.

There existed a pre-1787 presupposition that without the ratification of the U.S. Constitution larger colonies (e.g., Virginia, New York, and Pennsylvania) would overbear and overburden the smaller colonies (e.g., Rhode Island, New Jersey, and Delaware) because of this fact: "In the nature of sovereign power, an impatience of control, that disposes those who are invested with the exercise of it, to look with an evil eye upon all external attempts to restrain or direct its operation…This tendency is not difficult to be accounted for. It has its origin in the love of power."[9]

To form a more perfect union the states thought that their citizens' natural rights, happiness, and well-being would be best preserved through the union of the states, with the understanding that "the general government is not to be charged with the whole power of making and administering laws [and that its] jurisdiction is limited to certain enumerated objects…but which are not to be attained by the separate provisions of any."[10] Without a doubt and at this juncture, the union of the states is proving to be more detrimental to the natural rights of state citizens, state sovereignty, and the happiness and well-being of the people of the states individually in their sov-

9. Alexander Hamilton, "Federalist Paper 15," in, *The Federalist Papers: A Collection of Essays in Favour of the Constitution,* Alexander Hamilton, John Jay, and James Madison (Birmingham, AL: Cliff Road Books, 2006), 118.

10. Ibid., 106.

ereign capacities. Indeed, the love of power has created a monstrous federal government that has created overburdensome and overbearing pressure, the avoidance of which was attempted by the creation of the union in the first place.

Erroneously, party politics is the focus of many Americans, as we the people of the several states seek answers from a political party and not from the Constitution nor from ourselves as creators of our government. Evidence reveals that the same agenda has been promoted, consented to, advanced, and even demanded by politicians for decades—Republican and Democrat alike. How do we know this? Because the effect of both parties has been the same: more federal government, more federal controls, more federal regulations, more federal usurpation, more federal taxation, more federal corruption, less state control, less state influence, less state participation, less state independence, and less state power. Many Americans think that falling off the cliff of tyranny at fifty miles per hour is the only alternative to falling off the cliff at seventy-five miles per hour, not even thinking of how to activate the parachute for safe landing or to spread our wings to soar above it all. Similarly, many Americans believe that supporting and opposing one of the two major parties respectively is the only answer to restoring traditional values in America. But in the year 2009, we see that "Change We Can Believe In" in fact is just another ploy-slogan with more of the same agenda and propaganda.

Founding father James Wilson[11] compared freedom to a chain of links, which may be broken when attacked at its weakest points. It symbolized the joint effort, duty, and responsibility that each citizen and each state had to maintain the strength of freedom.[12] In America, what evidently is happening is that the chain used to restrain tyranny and promote freedom is being used

---

11. "James Wilson (September 14, 1742–August 21, 1798), was a Scottish lawyer, most notable as a signer of the United States Declaration of Independence. He was twice elected to the Continental Congress, a major force in the drafting of the United States Constitution, a leading legal theoretician, and one of the six original justices appointed by George Washington to the Supreme Court of the United States." "James Wilson," *Wikipedia*, (accessed May 5, 2009), http://en.wikipedia.org/wiki/James_Wilson.

12. Compiled by a member of the Philadelphia Bar, *American Oratory: Selections of Speeches from Eminent Americans*, (Philadelphia, PA: E. C. & J. Biddle, 1854), 5.

against us. The chain holding back tyranny seems to be either broken already or corroding with rust and decay. Freedom does not just exist; it takes the active understanding, participation, and preservation of society to secure it. Thomas Jefferson observed this fact stating, "The natural progress of things is for liberty to yield and government to gain ground."[13]

Thus, the questions become: do we understand liberty, do we know what it takes to secure it, and do we even want it? Freedom is delicate and fragile, and without the proper care, it will be destroyed with little effort from various sources. Of course, many claim to love freedom, but are they willing to set aside preconceptions to preserve it? Are they willing to endure the hardships that accompany it? Many claim they want their children to live in freedom, but are they willing to make the sacrifices now to secure it for posterity? Many claim that they know what it takes to maintain freedom, but America continually loses it.

The time has come in America to search the fundamentals of freedom and begin building again upon the foundations proven to secure freedom. Otherwise, the word *freedom* will simply be used as a pretense in attempts to convince the minds of citizens that no real action is required on their part, because all is well. To the end of freedom, however, citizens must actively engage truth, history, law, politics, and government administrators. Just as Patrick Henry said,

> I consider it as nothing less than a question of freedom or slavery; and in proportion to the magnitude of the subject ought to be the freedom of the debate. It is only in this way that we can hope to arrive at truth, and fulfill the great responsibility we hold to God and our country. Should I keep back my opinions at such a time, through fear of giving offence, I should consider myself as guilty of treason towards my country, and of an act of disloyalty toward the Majesty of Heaven, which I revere above all earthly kings.

Are we disposed to be of the number of those, who, having

---

13. Thomas Jefferson and John P. Foley, ed., *The Jeffersonian Cyclopedia, A Comprehensive Collection of the Views of Thomas Jefferson,* (New York and London: Funk & Wagnalls Co., 1900), 387.

eyes, see not, and having ears, hear not, the things which so nearly concern their temporal salvation? For my part, whatever anguish of spirit it may cost, I am willing to know the whole truth; to know the worse, and to provide for it.[14]

To enlighten and motivate the search for freedom once again this book was written, because "the most effectual means of preventing the perversion of power into tyranny are to illuminate...the minds of the people,"[15] as was articulated by Thomas Jefferson. While some would classify this book's approach as a Christian perspective, the fact is it was written with an American perspective, although the American ideal never imposed Christianity itself on anyone. Unfortunately, some believe that one should not actually use Christian ideology when arguing the facts, because they feel that to do so would turn off much of one's audience. However, in reality, this approach should not and does not exclude those who do not consider themselves Christian. The necessity of being a Christian in order to secure freedom is as it was during America's founding era; that is, "many, if not most, believed; yet none must."[16]

It must be understood, the Christian perspective is necessary to truly comprehending and appreciating the fullness and completeness of freedom as America has experienced it, not because freedom is about religion, but because freedom is about nature and nature's God. Anyone who desires to seek the truth of freedom must consider the foundation of freedom found in the creation of God, because the evidence overwhelmingly reveals that it is the basis upon which America was formed and sustained, "with roots both in classical philosophy and in holy scripture."[17]

Throughout America's history, legal scholars and historians have cited

---

14. Compiled by a member of the Philadelphia Bar, *American Oratory: Selections of Speeches from Eminent Americans,* (Philadelphia, PA: E. C. & J. Biddle, 1854), 13, 14.

15. Thomas Jefferson and John P. Foley, ed., *The Jeffersonian Cyclopedia, A Comprehensive Collection of the Views of Thomas Jefferson,* (New York and London: Funk & Wagnalls Co., 1900), 278.

16. John Meacham, *American Gospel: God, the Founding Fathers, and the Making of a Nation,* (New York, NY: Random House Trade Paperbacks, 2006), 11.

17. Meacham, *American Gospel,* 7.

the fact that America was founded upon Christian ideology when offering rationale and support for legal opinions and conclusions regarding interpretation of the Constitution and rules of law. They did so not because they wanted to force everyone to worship God as a Christian, but rather, they did so understanding that freedom is a gift of God found in His natural laws. One such case was the United States Supreme Court case of the Church of the Holy Trinity, where the Supreme Court stated the following:

> This is historically true. From the discovery of this continent to the present hour, there is a single voice making this affirmation...These are not individual sayings, declarations of private persons: they are organic utterances; they speak the voice of the entire people...These and many other matters which might be noticed, add a volume of unofficial declarations to the mass of organic utterances that this is a Christian nation.[18]

As John Meacham describes it, America's founders "believed themselves at work in the service of both God and man, not just one or the other."[19] Thus, you (the reader of this book) need not express a faith in Jesus Christ or even declare to be a Christian to understand, agree, and act upon the principles contained herein. However, you must acknowledge that the Christian perspective of natural and revealed laws of God formed the principles of this nation[20]—the nation that you likely claim to love.

Even those American founders who did not exhibit orthodox Christianity (like Thomas Paine, Thomas Jefferson,[21] and Benjamin Franklin[22]) all

---

18. *Church of the Holy Trinity Church v. U.S.,* 143 U.S. 457, 465, 470-471 (1892).

19. Meacham, *American Gospel,* 5.

20. Note: the word "*nation*" is used in this book for purposes of simplicity and familiarity. However, when referring to the United States of America, the truth must be acknowledged that the United States of America is *not* a nation as understood by America's founders, but rather, it is a *Confederate Republic,* composed of a league of independent and sovereign states and created by an accession of each of those states in their sovereign capacities.

21. David Barton, *Original Intent: The Courts, the Constitution, & Religion,* (Aledo, TX: WallBuilder Press, 1996), 144; Jefferson, *The Jeffersonian Cyclopedia,* 62.

22. Barton, *Original Intent,* 144.

accepted the Christian understanding of freedom and the influence of God's natural and revealed laws imparted to mankind regarding the rights of man. Moreover, they signed their names to a declaration of independence drafted on principles found in natural and revealed laws of God, and they sacrificed much—even their lives—for the sake of defending those principles. Now is not the time to segregate and shun the truth regarding freedom simply because you do not declare to be a Christian. Wisdom reveals that "there is no vice that doth so cover a man with shame as to be found false and perfidious."[23] Rather, now is the time to stand on the firm foundation of truth, which shall set you free.

Likewise, being a Christian does not necessarily mean that you understand, know, and apply the truths conducive to freedom. "A virtuous heretic shall be saved before a wicked Christian," said Benjamin Franklin.[24] However, now is not the time to reject the truth of freedom's principles for the sake of personal bias, motive, custom, or perception. It does not take a prophet to understand that

> these are the times that try men's souls…Tyranny, like hell, is not easily conquered: yet we have this consolation with us, that the harder the conflict, the more glorious the triumph. What we obtain too cheap, we esteem too lightly: 'tis dearness only that gives everything its value. Heaven knows how to set a proper price upon its goods; and it would be strange, indeed, if so celestial an article as freedom should not be highly rated.[25]

For the sake of freedom, it is incumbent upon freedom-loving Americans to grasp what made us free to begin with: natural law, revealed law, and compact law (the Constitution). Knowing that Jesus saves will not spare a

---

23. Sir Francis Bacon and Walter Worrall, ed., *The Essays or Counsels Civil and Moral,* (New York: E. P. Dutton & Co., first published 1597, newly written in 1625), 4.

24. Meacham, *American Gospel,* 28.

25. Thomas Paine and Mark Philip, ed., *Oxford World's Classics: Thomas Paine, Rights of Man, Common Sense and other Political Writings,* (Oxford, New York: Oxford University Press, 1995), 63.

nation from slavery. Knowing that individuals should be left alone and not harassed by government is not enough. Without an understanding of the fundamentals and their application in society and government, tyranny shall prevail and our posterity will know even less freedom than we do today—if not complete slavery.

You might agree that America's citizens have suffered evils at the hands of its government for many years. However, most Americans feel just as our founders did, that we should "suffer evils while evils are sufferable."[26] It behooves us then to prevent the evils from even taking place through peaceable means when possible. Indeed, I believe as Thomas Paine did that

> God will not give up a people to military destruction, or leave them unsupportedly to perish, who had so earnestly and so repeatedly fought to avoid the calamities of war, by every decent method which wisdom could invent. Neither [do] I...suppose that [God] has relinquished the government of the world, and given us up to the care of devils.[27]

At the same time, the truth contained herein reveals that America is perhaps teetering with the thought of consensual tyranny and voluntary slavery, the consequences of which are not unlike what Thomas Paine suggested in his day and will result in America being given up to the "care of devils."

Can we say, as Thomas Paine did, regarding our certainty of understanding freedom's principles: "My own line of reasoning is to myself, as strait and clear as a ray of light"[28]? Or are we "tossed to and fro with every wind of doctrine,"[29] not knowing which direction to take to gain the results of freedom? Will we have the principles of truth engrained in our minds and hearts to recognize and distinguish truth from falsehood? Can we say with boldness and reflect with understanding the principles regarding our relationship to government, such as:

---

26. Thomas Jefferson, *Declaration of Independence,* (See Appendix A).

27. Paine and Philip, ed., *Oxford World's Classics: Thomas Paine, Rights of Man, Common Sense and other Political Writings,* 64.

28. Ibid., 69.

29. Ephesians 4:14 (KJV).

Not all the treasures of the world...could have induced me to support an offensive war; for I think it murder: but if a thief break into my house—burn and destroy my property, and kill, or threaten to kill me and those that are in it, and to "bind me in all cases whatsoever," to his absolute will, am I to suffer it? What signifies it to me, whether he who does it is a king or a common man; my countryman or not my countryman; whether it is done by an individual villain or an army of them? If we reason to the root of things we shall find no difference; neither can any just cause be assigned, why we should punish in the one case and pardon in the other.

Let them call me rebel, and welcome; I feel no concern from it; but I should suffer the misery of devils, were I to make a whore of my soul, by swearing allegiance to one whose character is that of a sottish, stupid, stubborn, worthless, brutish man. I conceive likewise, a horrid idea in receiving the mercy from a being, who at the last day, shall be shrieking to the rocks and mountains to cover him, and fleeing with terror from the orphan, the widow, and the slain of America.[30]

Without such a conviction and understanding of freedom, "this is our situation...by cowardice and submission, the said choice of a variety of evils [will occur:] a ravaged country—a depopulated city—habitations without safety—and slavery without hope—our homes turned into barracks and bawdy-houses for Hessians—and a future race to provide for, whose fathers we shall doubt of! Look at this picture, and weep over it! And if there yet remains one thoughtless wretch, who believes it not, let him suffer unlamented."[31] The words of Thomas Paine still ring true today in America. Without "perseverance and fortitude,"[32] America will not enjoy the "prospect of a glorious issue [of freedom]."[33]

30. Paine and Philip, ed., *Oxford World's Classics: Thomas Paine, Rights of Man, Common Sense and other Political Writings*, 69.
31. Ibid., 71.
32. Ibid., 71.
33. Ibid., 71.

Thus, we must first do as our founders did when they won their independence and possessed a "new creation instructed to [their] hands."[34] We must reflect upon the truths, natures, principles, and philosophies that compose the new creation, and make it what it is, and "look back on the scenes we have passed, and learn from experience what is yet to be done."[35]

"The remembrance, then, of what is past, if it operates rightly, must inspire [America] with the most laudable of all ambition, that of adding to the fair fame she began with."[36] In other words, Americans should know where they came from so that they can add to the fame of freedom, such that we should "never be ashamed to tell [America's] birth, nor relate the stages which she rose to empire."[37]

---

34. Ibid., 72.
35. Ibid., 73.
36. Ibid., 73.
37. Ibid., 73.

1

THE STARTING POINT

The Thought Process

O ne thing is abundantly clear: we are not the same America that we once were. It is undeniable.[1] This fact means different things for different people. Some believe this difference in America to be a good thing. However, others believe this difference to be detrimental to God's gifts to mankind—life, liberty, and property. Of course, your answer depends on your perspective, your values, your beliefs, and your worldview. But can all perspectives be correct? Can the result of all perspectives lead to good? Undoubtedly, the ramifications of a nation's prevailing philosophies regarding society and government cannot be overstated. The accepted philosophies of a nation form the fixed perspective from which all outlooks, assumptions, and perspectives on human nature, government, and the world will be affected relative to every opinion about what thoughts, principles, policies, and maxims are "good" or "bad." Thus, given the philosophy adopted by a nation, one can predict much about that nation, including

---

1. "We're losing our country we grew up in…but what [does that] mean…It is this: America has undergone a cultural and social revolution. We are not the same country that we were in 1970 or even 1980. We are not the same people…No nation in history has gone through a demographic change of this magnitude in so short a time, and remained the same nation." Patrick J. Buchanan, *The Death of the West: How Dying Populations and Immigrant Invasions Imperil Our Country and Civilization,* (New York: St. Martin Press, 2002), 1–3.

its constitution, form of government, purposes of government, government administration, government leaders, and its citizens' submission and resistance to that government.

Everyone and indeed every nation have a philosophy.[2] The question is, however, from what source does that person establish and confirm his perspectives, assumptions, and premises—and ultimately his conclusions? It is common sense to understand that the sources one believes to be true will affect every aspect of that person's life—attitude, thoughts, and behavior. The most recognizable source for one's belief system is religion. Religion can be defined as "(1): the service and worship of God or the supernatural, (2) a personal set or institutionalized system of religious attitudes, beliefs, and practices, (3) a cause, principle, or system of beliefs held to with ardor and faith."[3]

Religion is not simply those people who go to church on Sunday at their local Baptist church, or their Jewish synagogue, or their Muslim mosque. Religion is believing there is no God; it is believing that all faiths are equal in the sight of God; it is rejecting any supernatural existence altogether; it is focusing only on the interests and values of humans as the ultimate authority in life. Religion is the system of beliefs that cause a person to act one way or another. Let it be known that simply having a hunger and thirst for truth is a religious practice. In short, religion is any belief system that has an impact on your mind, attitude, and behavior relative to truth. Furthermore, one's self-proclamation of being, say, Christian, does not necessarily mean that he believes and adopts all Christian philosophy but may in fact include a belief in humanist ideology, whether or not he is actually conscious of his adoption of such a belief. Thus, religion does not necessarily even mean the worship of God, but necessarily means a belief system which impacts behavior. We see the effect of religion in America's society and government every day unfolding before our eyes—and it is not pretty.

---

2. "Each society establishes its own moral code for its own time, and each man and woman has a right to do the same." Buchanan, *The Death of the West,* 52.

3. "Religion," *Dictionary.com,* (accessed May 5, 2009), http://dictionary.reference.com/browse/religion.

Consider that America has the highest number of self-proclaimed Christians of any nation on earth. In fact, some 85 percent of all Americans claim to be Christian.[4] That is around 224,457 million people!—a staggeringly high percentage of Americans. These are people who, if they believe in conformity with general Christian ideology, would prescribe to the following general tenets: God has prescribed right and wrong conduct in every area of life, His laws are above the laws of man, and mankind is obligated to conform its conduct to His will and laws. These Christians likely hold the belief that there is a law superior to man. While there are variations of beliefs within Christianity (the subject of which is not for this discussion), a large percentage of these Christians would declare with conviction that the Bible contains God's word, and that each person has an obligation to observe, know, and follow its direction, commands, and principles.

There would be no arguments from Christians when asked the question: does the Bible state that murder is wrong? Answer: Yes! Does the Bible say that adultery is wrong? Answer: Yes! Does the Bible provide a way for the salvation from your sins, allowing you to escape hell damnation? Answer: Yes! Does the Bible tell how people are to live? Answer: Yes! The answers are easy enough. In America, you can easily identify a Christian leader in just about every area of life—a leader who uses the Bible and biblical principles to proclaim the true and best way to live life.

For example, Dr. James Dobson in family matters and psychology may readily quote the following verses: "Train up a child in the way he should go: and when he is old, he will not depart from it."[5] And "Ye fathers, provoke not your children to wrath: but bring them up in the nurture and admonition of the Lord."[6] Dave Ramsey in financial matters[7] may have the following verses memorized, ready to recite at a moment's notice: "The LORD shall open unto thee his good treasure, the heaven to give the rain unto thy land in his season, and to bless

---

4. "Christian Statistics: The Largest Christian Populations," (accessed May 5, 2009), http://www.adherents.com/largecom/com_christian.html, citing, Russell Ash, *The Top 10 of Everything,* (New York: DK Publishing, 1997), 160–161.

5. Proverbs 22:6 (KJV).

6. Ephesians 6:4 (KJV).

7. Dave Ramsey, *The Total Money Makeover,* (Nashville, TN: Thomas Nelson, Inc., 2003).

all the work of thine hand: and thou shalt lend unto many nations, and thou shalt not borrow."[8] Or "Owe no man any thing, but to love one another."[9]

Likewise, Steve Arterburn, in personal and family issues, would likely have the following verses ready to explain and expound upon to a husband and wife who need professional counseling: "Husbands, love your wives, even as Christ also loved the church, and gave himself for it."[10] And the late Jerry Falwell on social and moral issues would be able to quote verbatim on national television these verses: "For this cause God gave them up unto vile affections: for even their women did change the natural use into that which is against nature: And likewise also the men, leaving the natural use of the woman, burned in their lust one toward another; men with men working that which is unseemly, and receiving in themselves that recompense of their error which was meet."[11]

Unashamedly, these Christian leaders would use the Bible as an authoritative source to proclaim the truth about life in their respective areas of expertise—and rightfully so. But does it stop at those types of issues? Ask yourself: what is the most impactful area of life in the entire world? The top three would have to be government, religion, and family—and for our discussion government is the focus. Think about it. What area of life is not touched by government (especially with the size of America's government today and the control asserted)? Everything we do is affected by government. Do you think that God has not already established His principles concerning government and a person's response and interaction to government? Is God not big enough to address *every* principle of life in His word and in His creation and reveal the manner and substance of its practice and use in daily life? If you do not think so little of God, then you must accept the fact that God has revealed the truth regarding these matters and that it is applicable today.

What I find perplexing in today's America is how hundreds of millions of Christians can—and will—acknowledge that God has addressed issues of, say, staying out of debt, treating your spouse with respect and love, the

---

8. Deuteronomy 28:12 (KJV).

9. Romans 13:8 (KJV).

10. Ephesians 5:25 (KJV).

11. Romans 1:26–27 (KJV).

creation of the world, the history of mankind (and even detailed genealogy of certain individuals including Jesus), the order and structure of a Christian church, the moral prescriptions and proscriptions of human behavior, and even the soul's very salvation from hell, yet the application of natural and revealed laws relating to our duties as Christians and truth lovers toward (or even against) government is misled, misunderstood, misapplied, or downright ignored. Do we desire to be ignorant on these matters? Please explain how such a disconnect makes any sense, especially for a Christian whose religion requires the belief in these principles. Of course, I never receive any biblical support for such a position, except maybe the misinterpreted, misapplied, and shallowly used Romans 13 argument of submission (which will be addressed herein and utterly undermined by God's word itself—among other truths) and other unsubstantiated rhetoric. Ironically, many nonbelievers possess more Christian values than Christians themselves do, as if the rocks are now crying out the truths of God's word.[12]

While engaging in discussion regarding governmental relations, policies, and philosophy, I have been surprised and, quite frankly, frustrated at the response I hear from most Christians regarding the state of affairs in our nation today. Common responses are:

Christians only need to worry about "clear-cut" biblical issues—like abortion and homosexuality.

Christians are required to submit to government, no matter what the government does, what regulations are imposed, what laws are executed, or what leaders say or how they act.

Our national condition is not as bad as you think.

There is nothing I can do about it.

Our country has no hope of restoration.

---

12. "[Jesus] answered, 'I tell you, if these were silent, the very stones would cry out.'" Luke 19:40 (ESV).

It's just politics.

There are many similar unfounded, unrealistic, and thoughtless responses. My all-time favorite response is probably this one: "No one is perfect; you cannot expect our leaders to be perfect." (Normally this is referring to a candidate running for office in their party who they know is less than worthy of office—a lesser of two evils.) They will even come back with the nonsensical follow up of, "Are you perfect?" Thus destroying all sense of logic, reasoning, and real discussion by establishing and proving the fact that I am not perfect, and therefore America should support a leader in our nation who demonstrates characteristics that are less than qualified and honorable.

Perhaps there is no arguing the Bible, the facts, history, and common sense to people who believe that those responses are adequate and actually address anything of substance, but if anyone is curious and sensitive to what truth is, they must address the matters of natural and revealed law discussed in America's history. God warns us about accepting false philosophies: "See to it that no one takes you captive by philosophy and empty deceit, according to human tradition, according to the elemental spirits of the world, and not according to Christ."[13] We must have *no* part of these vain philosophies: "Do not let my heart incline to any evil, to busy myself with wicked deeds in company with men who work iniquity, and let me not eat of their delicacies!"[14]

While some insist on arguing with non-responses regarding these matters of freedom, most agree that America is in serious trouble and that they are not satisfied with America's government. They know our nation is heading in the wrong direction; they fear what the future holds for them and their children; and they know the leaders of our nation—for the most part—do not follow the original intentions of our Constitution. Even while knowing this in theory, they demonstrate no power of understanding of how to invoke real change; they lack knowledge of the specific sources of our nation's founding and the philosophical and ideological foundation from which to demand change from their leaders; they act as if we are totally impotent to

---

13. Colossians 2:8 (ESV).
14. Psalm 141:4 (ESV).

insist on constitutional government from those whom we elect every two or four years. Ultimately, they contribute to the problems they complain about. Why is that? What has changed in the minds of Americans from the year 1776 to current times? Even more relevant, what authoritative sources are people who claim to love freedom relying on when they adopt and portray the philosophies previously expounded?

Are these the same people who believe that God is righteous, good, all-powerful, all-knowing, and that He created the universe and can actually save a person's soul from spending eternity in hell? Are these the same people who believe God can heal a body that is eaten up with cancer and who will actually lay hands on a dying person, praying that God will hear their prayer and heal the body—some even demanding in Jesus's name that the sickness leave the body of the sick? Are these the same people who believe God gave little David (later King David) the strength, skill, courage, and ability to kill the giant Goliath with a sling and stone? Are these the same people who believe God gave courage to the Hebrew boys Shadrach, Meshach, and Abednego to voluntarily be burned alive as a death penalty for not bowing their knee to the king, and then God miraculously prevented them from harm in the burning furnace (which was so hot that the guards throwing them in the fire died)? Are these the same people who believe God keeps His promises, and that His word is true? Are these the same people who believe that God will bless you with health, wealth, and riches if you set goals, establish a plan, go for your dreams, and speak them into reality? Are these the same people who teach their children that if you do right, God will bless you, and if you do wrong, God will not bless you? Are these the same people who believe there is right and wrong?

If so, then how can those same people look at America, look at our history, look at the natural and revealed laws of God, look at God's previous work and blessings in America, and have the attitude of vain and destructive philosophies, assumptions, and outlooks? Perhaps the reason is that Christians and Americans in general do not have the foggiest notion as to the principles that have undergirded and been the foundation of America's success, prosperity, and blessing. Even more basic than that, maybe they do not truly understand the very nature of man and God that has formed America's principles of government. Without virtue, knowledge, and action, no free republic can remain. Without the blessing and protection of God, no nation can exist. The fact is, the troubles, issues, and problems America faces today have already been addressed, expounded, discussed, debated, and experienced. Where are the seekers and doers of the truth on these matters?[15]

Can we not look more than two weeks into the past and future for the reasoning of our conclusions? Ecclesiastes 1:9 (ESV) says, "What has been is what will be, and what has been done is what will be done, and there is nothing new under the sun." Likewise and fortunately, the solutions for the problems we face today have been explored, attempted, and accomplished. For God's sake, why not study, know, and implement what has worked in the past to reform our nation and instead of accepting the failure of our country, demand the restoration of it! If you won't do it for your sake, then why not do it for the sake of your posterity?

Furthermore, for those who believe that America's founders were correct in their conclusions and implementations regarding government, from what basis do you resist, reject, or divert from the substance and form granted to their posterity? Indeed, "If [our founders] were wrong in their fundamentals concerning natural liberty, how could they be in the right when they built upon it? Or if they did mistake, how can they deserve to be cited? Or rather, why is such care taken to pervert their sense?"[16] In short, if our founding fathers were right concerning the natural laws of God, then we should follow their example and their lead; if they were wrong, we should depart from the pretentions that our form and principles of government (founded on natural law) are correct and institute a new government, as our Declaration of Independence declares we have the right to do, because freedom depends on it. It is time to get off the fence of ignorance and begin understanding what truly makes a nation free.

---

15. "Be doers of the word, and not hearers only, deceiving your own selves." James 1:22 (KJV).

16. Algernon Sidney, *Discourses on Government*, vol. 1, (Denmark: Dear and Andrews, 1805), 330.

2

THE FOUNDATION

Natural and Revealed Laws

irst and foremost, one must identify the foundation, authority, and success of freedom, which was demonstrated by America's founders. Like it or not, look no further than the natural and revealed laws of God. Much of the problem with those who declare to care about freedom and to be conservative is that they saturate themselves with modern politics and media (even conservative media) and do not study the foundational sources of society, government, justice, and law. Doing such only leaves people confused and frustrated. Thus, it must be established first that the Bible is the primary source from which all persons (especially Christians) must base their views concerning freedom and government. Without this fundamental precept established, such a person is "tossed to and fro with every wind of doctrine,"[1] which has been one of the contributing factors to the rise of our nation's moral, ethical, and legal problems.

The other equally important and authoritative foundational source of freedom is the natural laws of God. While this topic is not discussed much in the twenty-first century, the fact is natural law had a very large influence on the understanding of America's founders and, indeed, was the source of

---

1. Ephesians 4:14 (KJV).

law for hundreds of generations before God directly gave Moses His commandments. Can we say that no law existed on earth until God gave to Moses the Ten Commandments or until some established government passed legislation? Or can we say that no justice was ever demanded until the Old Testament was completed, or that there was no mercy until the New Testament was written? Absolutely not. The Bible reveals in the Old and New Testaments that natural laws existed at the creation of man and became more certain through God's revealed laws and through His prophets and apostles. This is confirmed over and over again through scriptures, including in Genesis 18:19 (ASV), where God chooses Abraham to be the father of the Jewish nation, partly because He knows that Abraham and his seed will do "righteousness and justice."[2] As is seen in this scripture, the concepts of justice and right and wrong existed well before the laws of God were given to Moses, which means that the laws of God were naturally incorporated into His creation. As will be discussed further herein, natural law (which is reflected and revealed in scriptures) exists on earth and in the hearts of mankind, and it is recognizable. Indeed, the truth is accessible, obtainable, and doable. "Know the truth, and the truth shall make you free."[3]

THE REVEALED LAWS OF GOD

So there would be no doubt regarding the inerrant quality of the Bible, God was certain to tell us that "all scripture is given by inspiration of God, and is profitable for doctrine, for reproof, for correction, for instruction in righteousness."[4] Unlike what former president G. W. Bush said,[5] *all* scripture is in fact inspired by God, meaning divinely breathed. This verse clearly estab-

---

2. "For I have known him, to the end that he may command his children and his household after him, that they may keep the way of Jehovah, to do righteousness and justice; to the end that Jehovah may bring upon Abraham that which he hath spoken of him." Genesis 18:19 (ASV).

3. John 8:32 (KJV).

4. Timothy 3:16 (KJV).

5. "Cynthia McFadden had President Bush on ABC's Nightline this past Monday. During the interview, McFadden asked Bush if the Bible was literally true. Now, acceptance of the Bible's literalness is one of conservative Christianity's most sacred doctrines. There is not a professor at PCC (or any other conservative Christian college or university) that would keep his

lishes the usefulness and function of all scripture: that is, it is profitable for *doctrine* (truth concerning man's relationship with God), for *reproof* (conviction), for *correction* (reformation), for *instruction* (education), and that all such uses are to accomplish righteousness—not only for the individual, but also for the family, community, and nation. Understand that "no prophecy of the scripture is of any private interpretation…for the prophecy came not in old time by the will of man: but holy men of God spoke as they were moved by the Holy Ghost."[6]

God's word is not an opinion, a clever thought, a lesson of history, or expounding worldly philosophy and enlightened thinking. Rather, it is the divinely breathed, inspired word of God moved by the Holy Ghost that gives power to those who study to show themselves approved unto God[7] and to those who are faithful to implement God's word for the conviction, education, and reformation of individual, family, community, and nation. Anything short of such use of God's word is to deny or to shirk its complete and absolute relevance to every area of people and nations.

Let us be clear: there is no other source from man or God any more sure or reliable than the Bible—even God's spoken word. Many people will claim, "God told me this" or "God told me that," almost gloating over the fact that God spoke to them audibly and directly. While we know that the Spirit of God can show truth to a person, give wisdom to a mind, and give sight to the blind, God has told us in His word that there is no surer word than the Bible itself— even God's audible words. Second Peter 1:17–21 (KJV) says the following:

> For [Jesus] received from God the Father honour and glory, when there came such a voice to him from the excellent glory, "This is my beloved Son, in whom I am well pleased." And this voice which came

---

or her job for a nano-second, if he or she even questioned the veracity of the Scriptures. Right? You know it's true! Most conservative Christians would even go so far as to say that one cannot be a born-again Christian who does not believe that the Bible is the infallible Word of God. Well, what was George Bush's response to McFadden's question? He said, 'You know. Probably not…No, I'm not a literalist.' Notice, Bush twice denied the veracity of the Scriptures." Chuck Baldwin, "Where Are Dobson and PCC Now?" *Chuck Baldwin Live, Talk Radio*, (December 12, 2008), http://www.chuckbaldwinlive.com/c2008/cbarchive_20081212.html.

6. Peter1:20–21 (KJV).

7. Timothy 2:15 (KJV).

from heaven we heard, when we were with him in the holy mount. We have also a more sure word of prophecy; whereunto ye do well that ye take heed, as unto a light that shineth in a dark place, until the day dawn, and the day star arise in your hearts: Knowing this first, that no prophecy of the scripture is of any private interpretation. For the prophecy came not in old time by the will of man: but holy men of God spake as they were moved by the Holy Ghost.

It is important to understand that the answers from God regarding our problems are not answers coming down from heaven in a loud voice; but rather the answers are found in the revealed laws of God—the "more sure word of prophecy." It is our guiding light and sure compass.

Purpose of the Revealed Laws of God

For Christians, the purpose of the Bible should be too obvious, and for the American patriot, the influence of the Bible must be acknowledged. If the Bible does not have life-changing and indeed nation-changing power, then any reference to it would seem ridiculous. But such is not the case, and America's founders obviously believed in the natural law and in the principles it revealed. Founding father John Adams declared the significance of the Bible in the founding of America.

> The general principles on which the fathers achieved independence were...the general principles of Christianity...I will avow that I then believed, and now believe, that those general principles of Christianity are as eternal and immutable as the existence and attributes of God; and that those principles of liberty are as unalterable as human nature.[8]

Indeed, God revealed His laws not only for man to obtain eternal life in heaven with Him, but also to obtain the fullest and most rewarding life here on "earth as it is in heaven"[9] as much as possible. Luke 4:4 (KJV) states,

---

8. Charles Francis Adams, *The Works of John Adams, Second President of the United States,* vol. 10. (Boston: Little, Brown, 1856), 45–46.

9. Matthew 6:10 (KJV).

"And Jesus answered him, saying, 'It is written, That man shall not live by bread alone, but by every word of God.'" Is it hard to believe that the physical and material considerations (the bread) are *not* what give and sustain life, but that it is by the complete word of God that men live, are sustained, and prosper?

Apparently many believe that knowing the verse John 3:16[10] will produce an everlasting freedom in America, or that understanding that God despises the killing of the innocents will somehow cause revival, understanding, and wisdom to spread like wildfire across our land. Such people are living in a world of their own and do not understand the fullness of God's word.[11] If knowing these things is indeed enough, pray tell where is the changing power of God in this nation, given the number of Christians in America?

The apostle Paul says in Romans 15:4 (MKJV), "For whatever things were written before were written for our learning, so that we through patience and comfort of the Scriptures might have hope." Not only do God's revealed laws give us the essentials of life but also of hope, meaning what is to come in the future. Seems easy, sounds simple—but evidently God's power has been removed from the church in America, and the influence of the church is barely felt in our nation, because for decades now America's trend continues in the same direction: over the cliff.

How is it that we live in a country full of Christians where abortion is legal and where over 1 million babies have been killed almost every year since 1973 after *Roe v. Wade*?[12] How is it that while there are millions of Christians in America, Judge Roy Moore, the former Alabama Supreme Court chief justice, was not only removed from his office for "continuing to acknowledge God"[13] in his public and official capacity but also was slaughtered (receiving only 35 percent of the vote[14]) at the polls when he ran against Governor Bob

---

10. "For God so loved the world, that he gave his only Son, that whoever believes in him should not perish but have eternal life." John 3:16 (ESV).

11. Acts 20:27 (KJV).

12. Author Unknown, "Trends in Abortion in the United States, 1973–2005," (Guttmacher Institute, January 2008), http://www.guttmacher.org/presentations/trends.pdf.

13. Chuck Baldwin, "Bill Pryor's Shocking Comments During Roy Moore's 'Trial,'" (November 18, 2003), http://www.chuckbaldwinlive.com/c2003/cbarchive_20031118.html.

14. "Bob Riley," *Bhamwiki*.com, (accessed May 5, 2009), http://www.bhamwiki.com/w/Bob_Riley.

Riley in the 2006 elections in the heart of the Bible Belt,[15] where supposedly thousands upon thousands of Christians and other religious people live? Apparently, Christians in Alabama do not feel such a man is worthy of public office, which again represents the depraved condition of America.

How is it that we have an army of God occupying America, but prayer—Christian prayer to be exact—is prohibited from public forum, creation is prevented from discussion, and the suggestion that Jesus is the only way to heaven is considered hate speech and intolerant in not only schools but also all government institutions? How is it that America is a "Christian nation,"[16] but Christians continue to elect presidents, congressmen, governors, sheriffs, county commissioners, and all other public ministers who promote, pass, and execute laws that strip our republic of independence and undermine the principles and philosophy that so many conservative Christians say they believe in? All the while, the voter is thinking that he is doing his civic duty and fighting the good fight, because the politician happens to have an "R" by his name. A nation just does not crumble without cause or reason. To suggest otherwise is to ignore God's revealed laws and historical facts. Thankfully, we had a few generations of men and women in early America who believed that "man shall not live by bread alone, but by every word of God."[17] Dare we follow their footsteps?

The Bible's Influence in America

An objective student or even casual reader of history would find the obvious influence that the Bible had in our nation's foundation and formation—from its nature, principle, and application, Christian ideology was its seed. A perhaps commonly known study by two professors, Donald S. Lutz and Charles S. Hyneman, revealed just how influential the Bible was to our nation. After reviewing an estimated fifteen thousand items and closely reading twenty-two

---

15. "The percentage of people who are 'non-religious' is only 6 percent." "Bible Belt," *Wikipedia*.org, (accessed May 5, 2009), http://en.wikipedia.org/wiki/Bible_Belt.

16. "[America] was once [a Christian nation], and a majority yet call themselves Christians. But our dominant culture should more accurately be called post-Christian, or anti-Christian, for the values it celebrates are the antithesis of what it used to mean to be a Christian." Buchanan, *The Death of the West*, 5–6.

17. Luke 4:4 (KJV).

hundred books, pamphlets, newspaper articles, and monographs with explicitly political content printed between 1760 and 1805, Lutz and Hyneman identified 3,154 references to other sources. The most often-cited source by the founding fathers was the Bible at 34 percent, with Enlightenment writers following at 22 percent, such as Baron Charles Montesquieu, William Blackstone, John Locke, and Hugo Grotius, and other very articulate and enlightened men. Other sources cited were the common law of England and, lastly, classical writers (such as Plato and Cicero) with significantly lower percentages of reference.[18]

With regard to the Enlightenment writers (which made up 22 percent of the citations), it becomes very apparent that much of their citations, references, and topics were in fact from the Bible, making the Bible's influence on our founders' philosophical views that much greater and significant. Thomas Jefferson observed the importance of the Enlightenment thinkers in the following:

> It is often said there have been shining examples of men of great abilities, in all businesses of life, without any other science than what they had gathered from conversation and intercourse with the world. But, who can say what these men would have been, had they started in the science on the shoulders of a Demosthenes or Cicero, of a Locke, or Bacon, or a Newton?[19]

The Enlightenment writers offer great insight into the thought processes and understandings of our founders as they took, many times, the Bible and elaborated the principles contained therein and how they relate to governmental, social, and human affairs. One such Enlightenment writer was Hugo Grotius, who was a famous Dutch lawyer, theologian, statesman, and poet and was called "the father of the modern code of nations" by James Madison.[20]

Grotius states a commonly held position amongst Enlightenment writers regarding man's duty to obey God. He says,

---

18. John Eidsmoe, *Christianity and the Constitution,* (Grand Rapids, MI: Baker Books, 1995), 51–52.

19. Jefferson, *The Jeffersonian Cyclopedia,* 1.

20. Eidsmoe, *Christianity and the Constitution,* 62.

We cannot grant without wickedness, that there is no God, or that
he bestows no regard on human affairs. But inasmuch as we are
assured of the contrary of this, partly by reason, partly by constant
tradition, confirmed by many arguments and by miracles attested
by all ages, it follows that God, as the author of our being, to whom
we owe ourselves and all that we have, is to be obeyed by us without
exception, especially since he has, in many ways, shown himself both
supremely good and supremely powerful: wherefore he is able to
bestow upon those who obey him the highest rewards.[21]

Enlightenment philosophers commonly used the duty to obey God in
their rationale concerning government, just as Grotius did in the preface
to his book, *The Rights of War and Peace,* which sets forth the logic and
rationale behind the positions he established in his book, all of which are
relevant to governments, nations, and citizens. Grotius further explains that
he uses God's word as a source for his conclusions by stating that "[t]he
books written by men inspired by God, or approved by them, I often use
as authority."[22] This expert on philosophical and theological study and their
application towards governmental and societal concerns believed and stated
that the inspired word of God was one of his authorities in stating his conclusions, and it was this philosophy that was repeatedly incorporated into
the very fabric of our nation. Using Grotius as just one example, a majority
of the Enlightenment writers concluded similarly. These were the men that
influenced America's founders, and their premises, rationale, and conclusions were largely adopted by America's founders, creating the foundation
of America.

One of the greatest founding fathers was John Jay. He was brilliant in
so many areas of life: intellect, history, spirit, bravery, military, and articula-
tion. He accomplished so much in his life that one wonders how it was even
possible (which can also be said of many other founding fathers). His contri-

---

21. Hugo Grotius and William Whewell, trans., *Hugo Grotius on the Rights of War and
Peace,* Book II, (Cambridge: University Press, 1853), xxvi.

22. Grotius, *Hugo Grotius on the Rights of War and Peace,* xxxvi.

bution to America's independence cannot be overstated. John Jay was a continental congressman from New York; he was an ambassador for the colonies during the American Revolution; he was a general in the continental army during the American Revolution; he was a United States congressman from New York; he became America's first United States Supreme Court chief justice; he was a signer of the Declaration of Independence; and the list goes on. Jay, and men like him, stated and reflected the same concepts regarding *both* the nature and principles of government which were articulated by the Enlightenment philosophers, theologians, and studiers of the law.

Like so many other founding fathers, Jay proclaimed that the truth concerning mankind comes from the Bible, and that the present and future state of mankind relies upon the Bible. "The Bible contains...the Divine revelations and dispensations respecting the present and future state of mankind."[23] Jay understood that the state of mankind depended upon and was contained in the Bible. Today, such a candidate for chief justice of the Supreme Court of the United States would be dismissed without consideration. But in fact, the Bible was used as the foundational reference and framework to form and describe the nature and the principles of the formation, function, and maintenance of America's government. This fact cannot be denied.

The Bible and Natural Law

Natural law today is more like an artifact placed in a glass bookcase for people to look at like a piece of art, covered in dust and not to be used. Perhaps it is worse than that. Perhaps most do not even know what it is. However, natural law is a vital element of not only God's revealed law but also America's foundation. Thomas Jefferson, the drafter of the Declaration of Independence, believed that "Man has been subjected by his Creator to the moral law, of which his feelings, or conscience as it is sometimes called, are the evidence with which his Creator has furnished him."[24] Of course,

---

23. William Jay, *The Life of John Jay,* vol. 1, (Bridgewater, Virginia: American Foundation Publications, 1833, reprinted 2000), 276.

24. Jefferson, *The Jeffersonian Cyclopedia,* 591.

this sentiment was shared by most American jurists throughout American jurisprudence.[25] In the *Origin of Government and Law in Connecticut*, Judge Jesse Root recognizes that "[our ancestor's] *common law* was derived from the *law of nature and of revelation*, which arise from the eternal fitness of things, which need only to be understood, to be submitted to; as they are themselves the highest authority."[26] Understand, common law previously contained and currently contains the rights of Englishmen and Americans. Common law is the rights of man, which we say we believe in today in America. But do we understand that common law was long and largely considered as follows:

> The perfection of reason, arising from the nature of God, of man, and of things, and from their relations, dependencies, and connections: It is universal and extends to all men, and to all combinations of men, in every possible situation; and embraces all cases and questions that can possibly arise; it is in itself perfect, clear and certain; it is immutable, and cannot be changed or altered, without altering the nature and relation of things;
>
> It is superior to all other laws and regulations, by it they are corrected and controlled; all positive laws are to be construed by it, and wherein they are opposed to it, they are void. It is immemorial, no memory runneth contrary of it; it is coexistent with the nature of man, and commensurate with his being; it is most energetic and coercive; for every one who violates its maxims and precepts are sure of feeling the weight of its sanctions.[27]

---

25. "[T]he law of nature stands as an eternal rule to all men, legislators as well as others. The rules that they make for other men's actions, must, as well as their own and other men's actions, be conformable to the law of nature, i.e. to the will of God, of which that is a declaration, and the fundamental law of nature being the preservation of mankind, no human sanction can be good, or valid against it." Locke and Macpherson, ed., *Second Treatise of Government*, 70–71.

26. Jesse Root, *Reports of Cases Adjudged in the Superior Court and Supreme Court of Errors from July, A.D. 1789, to June, A.D. 1793*, vol. 1, (Waterbury, CT: The Dissell Publishing Company, 1898), iv, (emphasis added).

27. Root, *Reports of Cases,* ix.

Put simply, common law is natural law which derives from God and which forms and formulates all human actions, behaviors, and laws and which is superior to any and all. It was this natural law that William Blackstone describes as being superior to all other laws.

> This law of nature, being coeval with mankind, and dictated by God himself, is of course superior in obligation to any other. It is binding over all the globe in all countries, and at all times: no human laws are of any validity, if contrary to this; and such of them as are valid derive all their force and all their authority, mediately or immediately, from this original.[28]

As Blackstone discusses in his *Commentaries,* one of the reasons that the Bible was so vital in the discussion of natural law among America's founding fathers was because they believed the Bible contained natural law. The question is not a matter of religion (as most would describe it today) at all and should not be confused as such, but it is a matter of justice: what is right and what is wrong, as established by God. How can government, whose purpose should be to pursue justice, be separate from the One who established right and wrong? The two—*Creator of Justice* and *right and wrong*—are inseparable. Consider this statement from Judge Jesse Root, which reflects the belief that natural law is contained in the Bible:

> The dignity of [natural law's] original, the sublimity of its principles, the purity, excellency and perpetuity of its precepts, are most clearly made known and delineated in the book of divine revelation; heaven and earth may pass away and all the systems and works of man sink into oblivion; but not a jot or title of this law shall ever fail. By this we are taught the dignity, the character, the rights and duties of man…This is the Magna Carta of all our natural and religious rights and liberties, and the only solid basis of our civil constitution and privileges.[29]

---

28. William Blackstone and William Draper Lewis, ed., *Commentaries on the Laws of England,* Bk. 1, (Philadelphia, PA: Geo T. Bisel Co., 1922), 31.

29. Root, *Reports of Cases,* x.

Judge Root clearly expresses the importance and the role that the Bible plays regarding the "rights and duties of man," because it is the "Magna Carta of all our natural and religious rights and liberties…the only solid basis of our civil constitution and privileges." Good luck trying to get even a Christian to understand this today. Be it known, the Bible itself reflects God's creation of natural law—both in the Old and New Testaments. Consider the apostle Paul's description of the Gentiles, who had not been given the law of God (through Moses and the prophets) but yet were held to the standard of natural law concerning the matters of right and wrong. Paul wrote, "For when Gentiles, who do not have the law, by nature do what the law requires, they are a law to themselves, even though they do not have the law. They show that the work of the law is written on their hearts, while their conscience also bears witness, and their conflicting thoughts accuse or even excuse them."[30] How can it be argued that the Gentiles had no justice, no law of right and wrong (and thus no responsibility to God and man) simply because God had not directly revealed to them His laws? Just as Paul describes, it cannot be argued. Rather, the Gentiles had a "law written in their hearts," which was the conscience of right and wrong as revealed in the nature of man, created by God.

This natural law is again confirmed by the apostle Paul in Romans 1:20 (ESV) when he states, "For his invisible attributes, namely, his eternal power and divine nature, have been clearly perceived, ever since the creation of the world, in the things that have been made. So they are without excuse." While some may attempt to use these verses to argue that the "natural law written in their hearts" respects the work of Christ and the need for salvation through Jesus, the Bible clearly says in Romans 10:14 (KJV) that nature alone is not enough to cause men to be "without excuse" regarding the knowledge of Christ. The apostle Paul says, "How then shall they call on [Jesus] in whom

---

30. Romans 2:14–15 (ESV). Note, enlightenment philosophers of the 1600s and 1700s used this verse (and others) as their support of natural laws of God. "[T]hese writers of the Stuart period were but elaborating the idea of Melanchthon a century earlier who, in defending natural law, said that he relied on the saying of St. Paul that the law is written in the human heart." Claude Halstead Van Tyne, *The Causes of the War of Independence*, Volume 1, (Boston, MA: Houghton Mifflin Company, 1922), 229.

they have not believed? And how shall they believe in [Jesus] of whom they have not heard? And how shall they hear without a preacher?"[31] Certainly, there is a distinction between the laws of God revealed to man in nature and man's ability to know of Jesus's salvation as revealed in nature, for if Jesus's salvation were revealed in nature, there would be no need for preachers and missionaries. Therefore, the natural law as described in Romans refers not to Jesus Himself but rather to the laws of nature and of nature's God—the natural rights of man: self-preservation, life, liberty, the pursuit of happiness, and property.

The Bible repeatedly confirms the existence of the natural laws of God—the laws of God created at the time of creation by the One who created the standard of right and wrong. If right and wrong did not exist at the time of creation, then why did God command Adam and Eve the following: "You may surely eat of every tree of the garden, but of the tree of the *knowledge of good and evil* you shall not eat, for in the day that you eat of it you shall surely die."[32] From the very conception of mankind at creation, God revealed to mankind that there existed good and evil. Indeed, Satan (in the form of a serpent) was at least partially correct when he tempted Eve to eat of the forbidden fruit, saying, "For God knows that when you eat of it your eyes will be opened, and you will be like God, *knowing good and evil.*"[33] Ever since that time, God has expected all of man to observe his natural laws, to which all humanity and nature are bound. These natural laws existed prior to any laws instituted by man, and even prior to the laws of God given to Moses.

God created man with the faculties to recognize the nature of God and the nature of man and to respond accordingly. The apostle Paul confirms this in Galatians 3, in which Paul acknowledges that standards of right and wrong existed upon creation and prior to the laws of Moses. He says, "What then is the law [as given to Moses]? *It was added because of transgressions.*"[34] Note that the written laws were added to what had already existed—including, the natural laws of God. How can there be transgressions except that

---

31. Romans 10:14 (KJV).
32. Genesis 2:16–17 (ESV) (emphasis added).
33. Genesis 3:5 (ESV) (emphasis added).
34. Galatians 3:19 (ASV) (emphasis added).

there be an existing standard of right and wrong? Infamous Bible commentator Matthew Henry observes that "the law, considered as the law of nature, is always in force, and still continues to be of use to convince men of sin."[35] God giving His laws directly to the nation of Israel no more nullified God's natural laws than did Jesus's coming to earth to provide mankind a means of justification and redemption to God (since no person is innocent under the enforcement of God's laws).[36] In fact, Jesus repeatedly referred to justice in the Gospels, including the following parable in Luke 18:1–8 (ESV):

> And [Jesus] told them a parable to the effect that they ought always to pray and not lose heart. He said, "In a certain city there was a *judge who neither feared God nor respected man.* And there was a widow in that city who kept coming to him and saying, *'Give me justice against my adversary.'* For a while he refused, but afterward he said to himself, 'Though I neither fear God nor respect man, yet because this widow keeps bothering me, I will give her justice, so that she will not beat me down by her continual coming.'" And the Lord said, "Hear what the unrighteous judge says. And will not God give justice to his elect, who cry to him day and night? Will he delay long over them? I tell you, he will give justice to them speedily. Nevertheless, when the Son of Man comes, will he find faith on earth?" (emphasis added)

If natural justice did not exist, then why did Jesus refer to it in this parable? Furthermore, the Old Testament and New Testament prophecies of Jesus proclaim that Jesus was to bring *justice* to every nation (Jew and Gentile)[37]—justice based upon the laws of God as He created them at

---

35. Matthew Henry and Samuel Palmerl, *An Exposition of the Old and New Testament,* vol. 6, (Philadelphia: Haswell, Barrington, 1838).

36. "Do we then overthrow the law by this faith? By no means! On the contrary, we uphold the law." Romans 3:31 (ESV).

37. "Behold my servant, whom I uphold, my chosen, in whom my soul delights; I have put my Spirit upon him; *he will bring forth justice to the nations.* He will not cry aloud or lift up his voice, or make it heard in the street; a bruised reed he will not break, and a faintly burning wick he will not quench; *he will faithfully bring forth justice.* He will not grow faint or be discouraged

the beginning of the world. And why would the Old Testament scriptures declare that one of Jesus's purposes was to bring *justice* to all nations? If the natural justice and laws of God did not exist, then why do the scriptures (Old and New Testaments) contain hundreds of references to justice, judgment, and equity, from the time of creation until the end of the world as we know it? If man did not have natural rights, then why did Jesus refer to the *evil* judge as being one who did not fear God or respect man? If people were not born with natural rights, then why did Jesus confirm that we were in fact born with natural rights when speaking of the woman who pleaded with the judge, "Give me justice"? Notice as well that Jesus joined the evil judge's lack of fearing God and his lack of the respect for man simultaneously. This lack of respect of man refers and speaks to the natural rights of man, which people join together in society by agreement to protect.[38] Certainly a government administrator who does not believe in the natural justice and laws of God would not place a man (under the subjection of government rulers) on a higher level than what God Himself deserves; such a ruler would not insist on respecting the rights of man as created by God, both of which (natural laws of God and natural rights of man) he does not believe in.

Furthermore, Jesus interestingly and tellingly connects the fear of God and respect of man to the implementation of justice—the essence of right and wrong. Very clearly, Jesus confirms that those who do not fear God and who do not respect the rights of man will not implement justice. Thus, the implementation of justice relates equally to God and man. The fact is, Jesus was simply reiterating about justice and laws what was already revealed to us

---

till he has established justice in the earth; and the coastlands wait for his law." Isaiah 42:1–4 (ESV), (emphasis added); "Behold, my servant whom I have chosen, my beloved with whom my soul is well pleased. I will put my Spirit upon him, and *he will proclaim justice to the Gentiles.*" Matthew 12:18 (ESV), (emphasis added).

38. "[M]en unite into societies, that they may have the united strength of the whole society to secure and defend their properties, and may have standing rules to bound it, by which every one may know what is his. To this end it is that men give up all their natural power to the society which they enter into, and the community put the legislative power into such hands as they think fit, with this trust, that they shall be governed by declared laws, or else their peace, quiet, and property will still be at the same uncertainty, as it was in the state of nature." Locke and Macpherson, ed., *Second Treatise of Government,* 70–71.

in the Old Testament, as in Ecclesiastes 3:16–17 (ESV), where God declares that justice and righteousness must prevail on earth. For when it does not, people become nothing more than animals.

> Moreover, I saw under the sun that in the place of justice, even there was wickedness, and in the place of righteousness, even there was wickedness. I said in my heart, God will judge the righteous and the wicked, for there is a time for every matter and for every work. I said in my heart with regard to the children of man that God is testing them that they may see that they themselves are but beasts.[39]

Here, the writer (Solomon) confirms that justice and righteousness are to exist in every place "under the sun" (as compared to "above the sun" where God sits as King of kings and where there is no injustice executed from His throne). This means the *entire world*—not just in places where God's chosen people lived (Israel), but in the Gentile nations too, where people lived who were not exposed to the direct, written, and spoken laws of God. As already shown of course, the Gentiles have the natural laws of God written in their hearts and are thus without excuse when it comes to passing this test revealed to us in Ecclesiastes.

Jesus confirms the truth of immutable justice and natural law in Luke 22:25–26 (ESV), where Jesus says to his disciples, "The kings of the Gentiles exercise lordship over them, and those in authority over them are called *benefactors.* But not so with you. Rather, let the greatest among you become as the youngest, and the leader as one who serves" (emphasis added).

Here, we see that Jesus recognizes that the leaders of Gentile governments were called *benefactors,* literally meaning in the Greek, "a worker of good."[40] Moreover, Jesus illustrates the ideal that government be the servant of man, and not the dictator over man. Thus, Jesus confirms not only the

---

39. "He who justifies the wicked and he who condemns the righteous are both alike an abomination to the LORD." Proverbs 17:15 (ESV). God clearly classifies those who do not execute righteous justice, but rather pervert it, as disgusting to God.

40. James Strong, *Strong's Exhaustive Concordance of the Bible,* (Peabody, MA: Hendrickson Publishers), 33.

notion that governments are only to be workers of good (see Romans 13), but also that all nations in the earth are to recognize what is right and wrong and incorporate justice into government's operation.

Furthermore, scripture reveals that at creation God separated the human race from the rest of the beasts on earth in that men are capable of knowing right from wrong and are capable of administering justice and righteousness in every God-ordained institution: individuals, families, churches, and government. If in fact these institutions (e.g., government) do not pass this test of God—whether or not they administer justice and righteousness—then Solomon tells us that humans might as well be animals, because all would be vanity without administering justice and righteousness.[41] Moreover, where justice is lacking in government, God is greatly displeased. "Truth is lacking, and he who departs from evil makes himself a prey. The LORD saw it, and *it displeased him that there was no justice.*"[42] To suggest that there are no natural laws of God or that Jesus nullified the natural laws of God or that the laws of God only existed in the nation of Israel beginning at the time of Moses is to state that no laws of God existed for any nation other than Israel, and no laws existed at all for any persons or nations until such time. To the contrary, God judged and judges and will judge all nations and persons according to the standards of natural law as revealed through God's creation. If this is true that God has established natural laws, then they existed in the past, they exist now, and they will exist in the future. They are immutable and unchangeable, and "he that doeth them shall live in them."[43] And for America, "this idea of natural laws...[became] a fundamental principle in American constitutional law."[44]

---

41. "For what happens to the children of man and what happens to the beasts is the same; as one dies, so dies the other. They all have the same breath, and man has no advantage over the beasts, for all is vanity. All go to one place. All are from the dust, and to dust all return. Who knows whether the spirit of man goes upward and the spirit of the beast goes down into the earth? So I saw that there is nothing better than that a man should rejoice in his work, for that is his lot. Who can bring him to see what will be after him?" Ecclesiastes 3:19–22 (ESV); "Man in his pomp yet without understanding is like the beasts that perish." Psalm 49:20 (ESV).

42. Isaiah 59:15 (ESV) (emphasis added).

43. Galatians 3:12 (ASV).

44. Halstead Van Tyne, *The Causes of the War of Independence*, 230.

However, understand that natural law is not simply one's subjective interpretation of right and wrong (meaning I do whatever I think is right, and you do likewise), but rather it is the law derived from God's creation, independent of one's interpretation or acknowledgment. *Black's Law Dictionary* defines natural law as "a philosophical system of legal and moral principles purportedly deriving from a universalized conception of human nature or divine justice rather than from legislative or judicial action; moral law embodied in principles of right and wrong."[45] This definition derives from the commonly held expressions of America's ancestors, as does the following view of natural law:

> We know that we have a property in our persons, in our powers and faculties, and in the fruits and effects of our industry, we know that we have a right to think and believe as we choose, to plan and pursue our own affairs and concerns; whatever we judge to be for our advantage, our interest or happiness, provided we do not interfere with any principle of truth or of reason and justice.
>
> We know the value of a good name, and the interest we have in it, we know that every man's peace and happiness is his own; nay more, when our persons are assaulted, our lives attacked, our liberties infringed, our reputation scandalized, or our property ravaged from us or spoiled; we feel the injury that is done to us, and by an irrepressible impulse of nature, resent the violation of our rights, and call upon the powerful arm of justice to administer redress.
>
> We also know that other men have the same rights, the same sensibility of injuries, when their rights are violated—this law is therefore evidenced both by the knowledge and the feelings of men. These ought to be the governing principles with all legislators in making laws, with all judges in construing and executing the laws, and with all citizens in observing and obeying them.[46]

---

45. Bryan A. Garner, ed., *Black's Law Dictionary,* Abridged Seventh Edition, (St. Paul, MN: West Group, 2000).

46. Root, *Reports of Cases,* xi.

Admittedly, natural law's implementation requires that man, who is finite and imperfect, use his reason, intellect, and logic; and as such, interpretations or applications may differ. In fact, the apostle Paul recognizes just how deep the laws of God are compared to human understanding, stating, "O the depth of the riches both of the wisdom and knowledge of God! How unsearchable are his judgments, and his ways past finding out!"[47] Regardless of our finite capacity to understand all natural laws, "the law exists the same,"[48] and the finite capacity of humans and subjective interpretation does not change nature (i.e., natural law). Thus, obtaining justice contained in natural law takes discipline, study, and persistence. Furthermore, that is why America's founders referred so often to biblical authority, because they believed the Bible contained natural law—not because they were trying to create a Christian nation, per se. Rather, they believed the natural and revealed laws of God contained the truth of justice and freedom.

By comparison, what subjective interpretation could change other natural laws, such as the laws of gravity or the laws of thermodynamics? The answer is obvious: none. However, one must still apply studious observation to the well-known and well-accepted functions of life. If one knows the general laws of gravity, such knowledge does not completely inform the observer of questions such as, "How can you get a plane to fly in the air?" and "How much force do you need to apply to this ball to get it to travel fifty yards?" and other more complicated equations that take into consideration natural laws in combination. In other words, principles derived from natural law may not always be simple, but they may and do require study, thought, logic, and solution, as the observance of nature does not reveal all answers to all questions regarding right and wrong. However, natural law can undoubtedly be discovered and does contain the truth relative to freedom.

The matter of natural law has been discussed for thousands of years, and as is clearly seen, the acknowledgment of the existence of the natural laws of God prevailed in America, just as founding father James Wilson states, "our ancestors were never inconsiderate enough to trust those rights, which God

---

47. Romans 11:33 (KJV).
48. Root, *Reports of Cases,* xi.

and nature had given them, unreservedly into the hands of their princes."[49] Likewise, it was the following notion that prevailed in America before and after its independence from Great Britain:

> Government and laws, have been erroneously considered, as originating in the prince or potentate, and the liberties and privileges enjoyed by their subjects as flowing from their free benignity and good will; for this cause the subjects exist only for their king; their lives, liberty and property are all devoted to his honor, pleasure and aggrandizement;
>
> Whereas, the truth, in fact is, that civil government is ordained of God, for the good of the people, and the Constitution they adopt, and the persons they appoint to bear rule over them, to make and to execute the laws, the Almighty recognizes to his ministers, acting under his authority, for the advancement of order, peace and happiness in society, by protecting its members in the quiet enjoyment of their natural and civil religious rights and liberties.[50]

"Guided by this religiously inspired idea of God-given rights, America has created the most inclusive, freest nation on earth,"[51] said John Meacham. It is undeniable that natural law played the most significant part in America's formation. Actually, its influence cannot be overstated. Philosophers, theologians, and founding fathers believed and recognized that human laws were to be a reflection of the laws already established by God in nature *and* as revealed in His word. They also recognized that man's observance of natural law may at times be difficult to determine, given the limited nature of man's capabilities to understand all of God's creation; which is why they appealed to and referred to God's direct revelation (the Bible) of His creation. This is why the acknowledgement of God, natural laws, and revealed laws had such a huge impact on our founders' understanding of the rights of man and the limitations of government and should have an equally substantial impact

---

49. Compiled by a Member of the Philadelphia Bar, *American Oratory,* 7.
50. Root, *Reports of Cases,* xv, xvi.
51. Meacham, *American Gospel,* 31.

on our society today. Of all people who should be concerned about knowing and accepting natural and revealed laws, it should be freedom-loving Americans—especially Christians.

DUTY TO STUDY NATURAL AND REVEALED LAWS

Whether you believe that the Bible is the infallible word of God, a great source for natural law principles, or an exceptional resource for principles incorporated into America, any belief in its validity creates a duty to study and understand it. For the Christian, we know that God's laws found in His word contain the truth and do not contradict natural law. In fact, there was not one founding father who did not appeal to the Bible or to the natural laws of God. There was not one atheist in the mix.[52] Regardless of their professions of faith in Jesus Christ, they all understood the importance of knowing and understanding the natural and revealed laws of God to form a free society. It is clear that our founders even read, studied, and adopted truths concerning God's natural and revealed laws. They did this through Enlightenment philosophers and theologians who described God's laws relative to nature and the Bible and their applications to man and government.

Enlightenment philosopher Algernon Sidney was a lieutenant general and cavalry officer under Cromwell and the Puritan forces in the English Civil War and served on the Council of the State of the Commonwealth under Cromwell's Protectorate in 1652. He was admired by republicans throughout the world and looked to as a martyr for the cause of liberty, and he was eventually convicted and beheaded for allegedly plotting to overthrow the pro-Catholic King Charles II.[53] Sidney's influence on America's ideology is just as clear as his proclamation concerning a citizen's duty to study the scriptures: "[There is a] necessity of searching the scriptures in order to know whether the things that are told them are true or false."[54] Once and if you have come to realize that the Bible is the most reliable and trustworthy source of truth, light, peace, hope, and happiness, it behooves

---

52. Barton, *Original Intent,* 143.
53. Eidsmoe, *Christianity and the Constitution,* 68, 69.
54. Sidney, *Discourses on Government,* 320, 321.

the Christian and freedom lover to study and know the scriptures, for how can "man live by every word of God"[55] if he does not know the word of God? How can man "obtain the hope through the scriptures"[56] if he does not know the scriptures?

BETTER TO NOT HAVE KNOWN THAN TO KNOW AND REJECT

The fact is, once you have been exposed to truth, wisdom, and understanding, any rejection of the same will only contribute to the more serious demise and destruction of those who reject it. Second Peter 2:21 (KJV) says, "It had been better for them not to have known the way of righteousness, than, after they have known it, to turn from the holy commandment delivered unto them." Seeking, knowing, understanding, and implementing truth is not a game. It is the most serious quest and task we have on this earth, especially living in what was once a Christian nation. The fact is God has made truth very obtainable for us. Luke 11:9 (KJV) confirms this: "Ask, and it shall be given you; seek, and ye shall find; knock, and it shall be opened unto you." It is clear, however, that before truth can be revealed, you must ask, meaning you must have the willingness to do what it takes to know truth. You must seek, meaning you must take active steps towards finding truth. You must knock, meaning once you have found the location of truth, you must be willing to accept whatever you find inside the door of truth. You do not accept truth on your terms and on your conditions any more than you accept the truth of gravity as you would believe it to be true.

IGNORANCE IS NO EXCUSE

The Bible is clear: we must take active steps to study truth and to act upon it. Second Timothy 2:15 (MJKV) says, "Study earnestly to present yourself approved to God, a workman that does not need to be ashamed, rightly dividing the Word of Truth." This thing of knowing the truth is no passive

---

55. Matthew 4:4 (KJV).
56. Romans 15:4 (KJV).

act. It requires active participation in all aspects. First, there is the *mental* aspect: study to show. Then, there is the *action* aspect: a workman. Finally, there is the *truth* aspect: rightly dividing. All are necessary, because the student is responsible for pursuing each aspect of knowing, and there is no excuse for ignorance. What good is knowledge without work? And indeed, what good is work without truth? Each element is necessary to understand fully the natural and revealed laws of God and how they apply to life.

In America, there is no excuse not to comply with the study requirement above. What nation has more access to the truth of God's laws? Acts 17:30 (MKJV) warns, "Truly, then, God overlooking the times of ignorance, now He strictly commands all men everywhere to repent." *Repent* literally means to think differently[57] in the Greek language. The excuse argument is undoubtedly not convincing (and is actually more shameful) in America, because our nation is the only nation in human history (with the exception of the nation of Israel whose laws were directly revealed by God) that has its roots directly saturated in the natural and revealed laws of God. Former United States Supreme Court justice Joseph Story states the same: "One of the beautiful boasts of our municipal jurisprudence is that Christianity is a part of the common law, from which it seeks the sanction of its rights, and by which it endeavors to regulate its doctrines."[58]

Harvard Professor Harold Berman clearly expresses the same notion as well: "The authors of the Constitution, including those who were very skeptical of the truth of traditional theistic religion, did not doubt that the validity of the legal system itself depended on the validity of religious faith, and more particularly of the Protestant Christian faith that predominated the new American Republic."[59] How has America at large gone from embracing and incorporating Christian ideology and philosophy into our governmental framework to firing anyone in the government who mentions Jesus's name in public under the "misled metaphor of separation of church and state"[60]?

---

57. Strong, *Strong's Exhaustive Concordance of the Bible,* 47.

58. Herbert Titus, *God, Man, and Law: the Biblical Principles,* (Oak Brook, Illinois: Third Printing, 1999), 38.

59. Titus, *God, Man, and Law: The Biblical Principles,* 19.

60. Barton, *Original Intent,* 43.

Is it because Democrats are evil and Republicans are good? Not hardly. Try looking a little deeper—actually, a lot deeper. Furthermore, simply having Christians in a nation does not preserve the nation from tyranny. For example, focusing on the hope that the government will not ban preachers from preaching against homosexuality does not even address the issue that actually makes a difference in society and government. Again, try looking a lot deeper and broader.

Let us be clear: ignorance is not a commodity America can afford any longer. There are already serious discussions regarding the collapse of the United States as we know it.[61] It is as if America has conducted itself like an irresponsible freshman college student, treating freedom like the college child would treat his parents' money: using it to fund irresponsible behavior with no thought to his decisions, spending, and future. It is as if America's founders deposited 1 trillion dollars into the bank account of freedom for their posterity, and for decades America has been spending billions upon billions frivolously, without making deposits of its own. Eventually, the freedom runs out and runs in the red. Unfortunately, most conservatives seem only to be concerned about being informed when a Democrat is in the White House. That ship will not sail any longer.

The Effect of Ignorance—Case in Point

The issue of abortion demands attention, but it is by no means the only salient issue facing an America in trouble. So let us explore the racket of ignorance this case in point reveals. As Pat Buchanan said, "After 1968, Republicans won more battles than they lost and did not lack political power. Polls showed the country was on their side of the barricades in the culture wars."[62] Indeed, over the past forty years, Republicans have largely controlled the White House, Congress, and the Supreme Court—yet abortions are consistently over 1 million per year, with reductions of such only being attributed to the wider use of contraceptives that are available. Let us be honest: Christians and conservatives would quantitatively prevent more

61. Joseph Farah, "The Breakup of the U.S.," *World Net Daily,* (posted January 13, 2009), http://www.worldnetdaily.com/index.php?fa=PAGE.view&pageId=84884.

62. Buchanan, *The Death of the West,* 206.

abortions (speaking solely of the federal government—as opposed to the state governments) in America not by voting for a Republican president who is pro-life, but by voting for perhaps a Democratic president who would promote the policy that contraceptives be free to the public, that children be mandated to take sex education classes, that children be provided family planning classes without parental consent, or that even provides for sterilization in women. Such a policy will have a greater impact on our fight for life than a self-proclaimed pro-life politician.

Republicans continue to chant the same cheer every two years: "We believe in right to life! Abortions are wrong! *Roe v. Wade* needs to be overturned! If only we can get conservative judges on the U.S. Supreme Court!" The effect: almost all of the pro-life voters listen to their words, get excited about their stance, and say, "Aren't Republicans great!" People vote for their party as if it is the ticket to salvation. Well, such a view is in complete contradiction to Thomas Jefferson, who detested party politics. This was evident by his statement, "If I could not go to heaven but with a party, I would not go there at all."[63] Still today, Republicans proclaim the same old rhetoric since former president Ronald Reagan in 1983, almost bribing or threatening Republican voters that if they do not vote for Republicans, then freedom has no chance, and all is lost. I hear Jeremiah 7:8 (ESV) ringing in my head: "Behold, you trust in deceptive words to no avail."

On the tenth anniversary of *Roe v. Wade*, President Reagan wrote the following article to the nation:

> Our nationwide policy of abortion-on-demand was neither voted for by our people nor enacted by our legislators—not a single State had such unrestricted abortion before the Supreme Court decreed it to be a national policy in 1973. But the consequences of this judicial decision are now obvious: since 1973, more than 15 million unborn children have had their lives snuffed out by legalized abortions...Make no mistake, abortion-on-demand is not a right granted by our Constitution. No serious scholar, including one

---

63. Jefferson, *The Jeffersonian Cyclopedia*, 677.

disposed to agree with the Court's result, has argued that the framers of the Constitution intended to create such a right...As an act of "raw judicial power"...the decision by the seven-man majority...has so far been made to stick. But the Court's decision has by no means settled the debate.[64]

Sure, it sounds great, and the late president Reagan certainly deserves respect for his position; but here we are twenty-five years after President Reagan's article and thirty-five years after *Roe v. Wade,* and nothing has changed—nothing! Yet, most pro-lifers still believe that voting for self-proclaimed pro-life candidates is the answer. This begs the question and brings up a very relevant point of politics and the citizen's approach to government: *what is your goal?* Think about it, the legal question is simply when does life begin? So who defines life? Well certainly the sovereigns of each state (that is, "We the People of the United States of America") can define life (through our state *and* federal legislators) to protect the most innocent in society, but for over thirty-five years such a simple task has not been done, with the exception of a few but growing number of states that have recently proposed and passed legislation defining life at conception and putting an end to abortion.[65] Congressman Ron Paul has repeatedly introduced The Sanctity of Human Life Act accomplishing the same effect.[66]

Most Americans who claim to be pro-life focus their political energy on changing the laws concerning abortion. Theoretically, as a result of changing the laws, you save the lives of innocent, unborn children. The alternate approach, however, is simply to focus directly on saving the lives of the innocent, unborn children by using more practical ways and means. In other words, if your only goal is to save lives, then why waste your time focusing on changing the laws when politicians have proven not to be very interested in

---

64. Ronald Reagan, "Abortion and the Conscience of the Nation," *Human Life Review,* Spring 1983.

65. Lawrence Jones, "7 States Seek Personhood Rights for Pre-Born," *The Christian Post Reporter,* February 21, 2009, http://christianpost.com/Society/Ethics_rights/2009/02/7-states-seek-personhood-rights-for-pre-born-21/index.html.

66. *The Sanctity of Human Life Act,* HR 2597, 110th Congress, (November 13, 2007).

the subject? Why not be more practical and pragmatic? Indeed, Democrats actually appear to be doing a better job at saving lives than Republicans, because at least with Democratic policies, birth control, sex education, and family planning result in fewer children being conceived, and thus thousands of babies are spared death through abortion.[67] Goal obtained! However, to conservatives such an approach would not likely feel or appear to be the right way to attain the goal. Thus, their goal cannot truly be said to be the pragmatism of merely saving lives, but rather the goal would be to reestablish the natural and legal right of every person to live without unjust interference. This latter focus has a much deeper philosophical implication and necessarily accounts for the natural laws of God.

This restated goal as just described indeed focuses on changing the laws and presumes its priority over the pragmatic goal of simply saving lives. Undoubtedly, this approach (whether or not with actual knowledge of its rationale) of most conservatives and Christians who advocate law change verses the practical approach of abortion reduction actually addresses not lives, per se, but the natural and revealed laws of right and wrong, the results of which are of course to protect the natural rights of man. If in fact the fundamental laws of right and wrong are more important than the pragmatic effect of saving lives, then the matter of right and wrong (i.e., justice) laws implemented in a nation does not stop at the issue of abortion, but includes the supreme law of the land entirely, fundamentally, and completely. This includes all philosophy, jurisprudence, and understanding from nature to principle; from principle to policy; from policy to law; and from law to procedure. If, however, lives are more important than laws, then how selfish and inconsiderate are those conservatives for putting their principle of voting for a pro-life candidate (which has proven to be ineffective) over the importance of the life of the innocent, unborn baby.

It is clear, however, that most conservatives, Christians, and right-wing Americans have chosen to believe (knowingly or not) that the goal of reestablishing natural justice is the better and more effective approach to saving lives

---

67. Nicholas D. Kristof, "Abortions, Condoms, and Bush," *The New York Times,* (November 5, 2006), http://select.nytimes.com/200v6/11/05/opinion/05kristof.html?_r=1.

(as would be argued for a long-term goal). If reestablishing justice is in fact our goal, it behooves us to understand what we are talking about, not for the sake of politics, but for the sake of righteousness; not as defined by man, but as defined by God through natural and revealed laws. The result of such an approach is this: where a nation seeks to implement not only good law but also correct principles based upon nature, then issues like, say, abortion will likely not even exist. The result: more freedom.

Thus, one cannot argue against and criticize as being selfish those citizens who have no faith in the same old approach of voting for Republicans or pro-life candidates—merely hoping and praying for the best. You cannot criticize those who propose that we who truly believe in natural justice and the natural and legal right of the unborn child to be protected by law try a different course of action from the one advocated for the past forty years, such as (using just one example out of many) voting for third-party candidates who understand and are willing to implement the natural and revealed laws of God. You cannot criticize those who suggest that we use alternative methods to accomplish these goals of natural justice and the right of life as found in nature, the Bible, and America's Constitution. To do so is to be like the foremen of the children of Israel who vehemently criticized Moses for telling Pharaoh, "Let my people go." They said against Moses, "The LORD look on you and judge, because you have made us stink in the sight of Pharaoh and his servants, and have put a sword in their hand to kill us."[68] Be it known, possessing the attitude that the foremen demonstrated towards Moses only shows your ignorance of the work that the deliverer attempts to effect upon a nation in slavery. Moreover, following the vain approaches of the past contributes to "Pharaoh's" mistreatment of the citizens, just as the citizens' failing to stand up and join the resistance against the Pharaoh contributes to the mistreatment. But be it known, it is no fault of Moses, who attempted to use more effective means than sloshing at snail pace through the slime and mud of tyrannical control.

Many conservatives (from laymen to leaders) would suggest that such an approach (as demonstrated by Moses) is ridiculous, wasting a vote, selfish,

---

68. Exodus 5:21 (ESV).

and puts principle before the life of the unborn; and that such an approach only contributes to the deaths of the innocent. First, tell that to Moses. Also, if the non-mainstream approach is in fact what some suggest, then pray tell how is it any worse than thinking that voting Republican is going to make any change in not only the laws of America but also the application of fundamental principles, as derived from natural and revealed law, which positive laws are supposed to be founded upon? Moreover, what reality is there in thinking that voting pro-life is going to awaken America's citizens and politicians regarding the revival of justice as understood by America's founders and as God has revealed in nature and in His word, from which America's principles and laws arose? Alternative approaches to voting for a lesser of two evils or Republican or pro-life candidate prove to be just as fruitful and are actually more meaningful in the overall scheme of society than the stale, ineffectual approaches of the past forty years, which conservative leaders and politicians have told us are the only way to make change.[69]

Pat Buchanan addressed this issue and makes the point clear that conservative voters have been duped by the Republican Party, because it no longer advocates and activates the conservative ideals that many claim to believe in. Instead, Republican candidates only make promises regarding what we believe in, knowing that our convictions will translate into votes—and thus, power. Buchanan notes their hypocrisy in the following:

The White House [of G. W. Bush] refused to step in while John Ashcroft was beaten bloody by Teddy Kennedy and the Democrats

---

69. "This election is about more than who gets what. It is about who we are. It is about what we believe; it is about what we stand for as Americans. There is a religious war going on in our country for the soul of America. It is a cultural war, as critical to the kind of nation we shall one day be as was the Cold War itself. And in that struggle for the soul of America, Clinton and Clinton are on the other side, and George Bush is on our side. And, so, we have to come home—and stand beside him." Buchanan, *The Death of the West*, 7. Juxtaposed to Pat Buchanan's criticism of the Republican party's failure to stand for true conservative values, he made the then-contemporary speech in the 1992 Republican National Convention at Houston, demonstrating the currently held, fallacious, die-hard loyalty to Republicans, as if they actually possessed the qualifications and convictions that would make America free once again. Former president Bush proved to be anything but a champion of freedom for us on our side. This loyalty has been proven to be faulty.

of the Judiciary Committee. Neither Mr. Bush nor his running mate attended the 2000 convention of the Christian Coalition...But he did make time in his campaign schedule to meet with the gay Republicans from the Log Cabin Club. When the Confederate battle flag became a blazing controversy, Governor Bush said it was for South Carolinians to decide. But, as soon as the primary was over, he ordered memorial plaques to Confederate war dead taken down from the Texas Supreme Court.

Not one speaker at the Republican convention in Philadelphia was allowed to defend the party's position on the defining moral issue of life. Yet Colin Powell was given prime time to lecture the party on its supposed hypocrisy in opposing affirmative action, and the chastened Republicans dutifully smiled through their public caning. On the social and moral issues that once defined Reaganism, the party has fled the field.[70]

Let us be honest with ourselves: for many years, conservatives have been deceived and shipped down the road of socialism, globalism, and hedonism for the sake of the interests of party politics. For those who are concerned more about freedom than politics, a different approach is necessary. The fact is, our study, approach, philosophy, understanding, and action must and should go much deeper than the shallow presumption that if I vote pro-life, then I am pleasing God and doing the right thing. God's natural and revealed laws contain the answers to this problem and all others, and we even have further guidance and help from the study of other sources of wisdom from our history. First, we must study, work, and rightly divide the truth. Then, once the individual and nation arrive at the truth, we must accept it and apply it. The truth shall set you free.[71] Once we are set free from the thought processes that enslave men, we must shine the light of truth on those who would "love darkness rather than light, because their deeds are evil."[72]

---

70. Buchanan, *The Death of the West*, 206.

71. John 8:32 (KJV).

72. "This is the judgment: the light has come into the world, and people loved the darkness rather than the light because their works were evil." John 3:19 (ESV); "This is the

PHILOSOPHY'S APPLICATION

Asking, seeking, knocking, and finding the truth necessarily means that the truth seeker is willing to change and will in fact be changed, firstly, in his mind. And when it comes to the formation, implementation, application, and preservation of a free nation, we must understand those fundamental truths "that are absolutely necessary to hold society together."[73] Once he finds truth, he must accept the fact that his way of thinking may not have been scriptural and thus needs changing. God created us and understands the importance and significance of the human mind. From the mind follows belief, and from belief follows action, and from action follows change. To be certain, thinking that something may or may not be true does not create belief or conviction. Put another way, "faith without works is dead."[74] Furthermore, believing something to be true but not taking action has no affect on and no meaning to anyone. Indeed, the devils believe in God, but so what? "You believe that there is one God, you do well; even the demons believe and tremble."[75] Likewise, acknowledgment of truth alone cannot create belief, as belief necessarily requires action. Thus, one's mind—or put in another term, philosophy—will dictate and control one's conduct in every situation in life, including politics.

Philosophy is a "system of ideas concerning this or a particular subject, a system of principles for the conduct of life."[76] If a man does not believe in the natural and revealed laws of God; does not believe in absolute standards of right and wrong; believes that his opinion regarding the issues of life is as authoritative as the next person's; believes that human conduct is simply a

---

message we have heard from him and proclaim to you, that God is light, and in him is no darkness at all. If we say we have fellowship with him while we walk in darkness, we lie and do not practice the truth." 1 John 1:5–6 (ESV).

73. John Locke, *An Essay Concerning Human Understanding,* vol. 1, (London: Oxford University, 1832), 42.

74. James 2:17, 20 (KJV).

75. James 2:19 (MJKV).

76. Eugene H. Ehrlich, Gorton Carruth, Joyce M. Hawkins, and Stuart Berg Flexner, *Oxford American Dictionary, Heald Colleges Edition* (New York: Harper Collins Publishers, 1982).

product of one's environment, random and regulated neurotic impulses, and desires; and believes that there are no eternal consequences for his decisions; such a philosophy will result in spontaneous, unprincipled actions simply controlled by natural self-preservation processes that are instinctive in any animal—the results of which will be a person living only for pleasure (i.e., hedonism). And as for his relationship to government, slavery or anarchy is much more likely. Similarly, a Christian who acknowledges that the Bible is God's inerrant word but does not actually believe it, meaning the Christian does not act upon it, such a person's philosophy will be controlled more by worldly, impetuous, emotional, and subjective perspectives. Such a Christian will not portray and carry out the power of God, which is only contained in seeking, finding, and performing truth.

Understanding the nature of the human mind as the Creator of it, God was certain to instruct us on the use and conditioning of our minds and the philosophical systems adopted by our minds. Mark 12:30 (MJKV) reiterates the first commandment as given to Moses in the Ten Commandments: "You shall love the Lord your God with all your heart, and with all your soul, and with all your mind, and with all your strength. This is the first commandment." If in fact you apply this first commandment of God, then you will perform your duties to God and man in compliance with this commandment. After all, God tells us, "Let us hear the conclusion of the whole matter: Fear God, and keep his commandments: for this is the whole duty of man."[77] Just as the asker, seeker, and knocker must first be willing to ask before he can know the truth, a person must first love God with all of his mind and actions before such a person can have a complete and sustaining philosophical transformation. Thus, a love for God is the starting point, but it is not sufficient to know God completely or His words of life and hope found in the scriptures.

Why, you may ask, is it not enough to love God? Because the human mind is "deceitful above all things, and desperately wicked"[78] and can be corrupted by worldly and ungodly philosophy—which may in fact come from persons you believe to be godly or good people. Jesus said this to the apostle Peter, as recorded in Mark 8:33 (MJKV), "Go behind Me, Satan! For you do

---

77. Ecclesiastes 12:13 (KJV).
78. Jeremiah 17:9 (KJV).

not mind the things of God, but of the things of men." Jesus said this after Peter told Him what he thought was a good thing—Peter's intentions were good. Speaking to the Christian church in Rome, Paul writes in Romans 12:2 (MKJV): "And do not be conformed to this world, but be transformed by the renewing of your mind, in order to prove by you what is that good and pleasing and perfect will of God." In the same book and to the same church Paul also states in Romans 1:28 (MJKV): "And even as they did not think fit to have God in their knowledge, God gave them over to a reprobate mind, to do the things not right."

Without question, those who come to know the truth of God's love can subsequently become the enemies of God by adopting a carnal philosophy and world belief system, "because the carnal mind is enmity against God, for it is not subject to the Law of God, neither indeed can it be."[79] It is clear that any person can adopt a philosophy that is completely and totally contrary to natural and revealed law and actually conduct himself contrary to those laws. Why else would there be a need for God to warn us of these dangers in scripture? These verses are warnings as well: "This I say therefore, and testify in the Lord, that you should not walk from now on as other nations walk, in the vanity of their mind;"[80] and "Be renewed in the spirit of your mind."[81]

God gives us many worldly philosophies from which to refrain: pride, fear, lust, world systems, envy, strife, jealousies, idol worship, faithlessness, greed, laziness, selfishness, irresponsibility, gluttony, and the list goes on. One must clearly identify not only the titles that worldly philosophy may be associated with, as in those just mentioned, but also their application— including government. One must be able to recognize, for example, that since God "has not given us the spirit of fear"[82] then all decisions based upon fear are of a worldly philosophy; that since we are "not to love the things of the world, neither the things that are in the world,"[83] then loving comfort, ease, and convenience more than truth is a worldly philosophy; that since

---

79. Romans 8:7 (MJKV).
80. Ephesians 4:17 (MJKV).
81. Ephesians 4:23 (KJV).
82. Timothy 1:7 (MJKV).
83. John 2:15 (KJV).

God commands every person to work diligently in "all that your hand finds to do,"[84] then any form of willful laziness to think, understand, and know the truth is a worldly philosophy.

Certainly, worldly philosophy has much more and deeper implications and applications than merely going to bars, listening to evil music, dressing immodestly, talking back to your parents, and voting for a pro-choice candidate. Worldly philosophy means failing to understand and implement all truth principles of God's word relative to all areas of life—including government. Ironically, one does not have to be a Christian to follow and understand the principles of God; and conversely, being a Christian does not necessarily mean that such a person follows God's laws and principles. Thus, God has described the necessity of renewing the mind and refraining from worldly philosophy.

America's history proves the influence of the Bible relative to matters of importance. America's founders were willing to ask, seek, and knock and were ready to open the door of truth regarding freedom in our nation. America today needs to renew its mind and reject the carnality of the worldly philosophical system. (Yes, the world is evil. "[Jesus] gave himself for our sins, that he might deliver us from this present evil world, according to the will of God and our Father."[85]) The only way to do so is to apply the truth in God's natural and revealed law to all of life, for what good is intent without action? Furthermore, we must recognize that God expects us to obey Him fully, completely, and willingly—blessings will follow accordingly.

---

84. Colossians 3:23 (KJV).
85. Galatians 1:4 (KJV).

3

RESPONSIBILITIES DERIVED
FROM NATURAL
AND REVEALED LAWS

Thomas Jefferson said, "Some have made the love of God the foundation of morality. This, too, is but a branch of our moral duties, which are generally divided into duties to God and duties to man."[1] It naturally follows that since natural and revealed laws contain truth, there are absolute rights and wrongs that men, as the creations of the Creator God, are subject to and responsible for. Thus, truth creates responsibility of man to man and of man to God. If there were no truth, there would be no responsibility to conform one's actions into any particular standard of thought and conduct: life would simply be to each his own—a philosophy adopted by many today (even Christians). The first responsibility to be addressed is one's responsibility to his fellow man. For the purpose of establishing basic and fundamental truths regarding responsibility, let us approach the following verses and their contextual application relative to freedom. For peace and freedom to exist in society, man must take his responsibility towards others seriously.

---

1. Jefferson, *The Jeffersonian Cyclopedia*, 592.

RESPONSIBILITY TO MAN

God desires that men live in peace with each other, for who can effectively raise and provide for a family, be productive in community, and establish and grow institutions of worship when the world is living in chaos, war, and distress? Jesus is called the "Prince of Peace."[2] Thus, ideally peace is God's will.[3] Thomas Jefferson recognized this duty to man (and to God) and observed the responsibility that each person has to do right to others, referring to Psalm 15 in the Bible: "I know nothing more moral, more sublime, more worthy of your preservation than David's description of the good man, in the 15th Psalm."[4] The following is Psalm 15 in its entirety:

> O LORD, who shall sojourn in your tent? Who shall dwell on your holy hill? He who walks blamelessly and does what is right and speaks truth in his heart; who does not slander with his tongue and does no evil to his neighbor, nor takes up a reproach against his friend; in whose eyes a vile person is despised, but who honors those who fear the LORD; who swears to his own hurt and does not change; who does not put out his money at interest and does not take a bribe against the innocent. He who does these things shall never be moved.[5]

In other words, treat others as you would have them treat you—the Golden Rule.[6] Let us be clear, the Bible has much more to say about man's responsibility to other men than it does towards government. The Bible does not say, "Do unto the government as you would have the government do

---

2. "For unto us a child is born, unto us a son is given: and the government shall be upon his shoulder: and his name shall be called Wonderful, Counsellor, The mighty God, The everlasting Father, The Prince of Peace." Isaiah 9:6 (KJV).

3. Did God create Adam in a state of war and chaos? No. He created him in perfect peace and expected Adam to work, provide for himself and his family, and to obey God's laws to maintain that peace.

4. Jefferson, *The Jeffersonian Cyclopedia,* 593.

5. Psalm 15:1–5 (ESV).

6. "Therefore all things, whatever you desire that men should do to you, do even so to them; for this is the Law and the Prophets." Matthew 7:12 (MJKV).

unto you." The Bible does not say, "Lay your life down for your government." The Bible does not say, "Sacrifice your family for the sake of government interest and power." The Bible clearly conditions man's duty of submission to government based upon God's purposes of government. Thus, where man has a duty towards other men to live in peace and harmony as much as possible,[7] what does this say of citizens who condone government behavior that contradicts the principles of peace and freedom? If peace and freedom depend on how the citizens of a nation hold their leaders accountable to God's standards of righteousness, can it be said that you are fulfilling your duty towards other men when you are indifferent, lethargic, and careless regarding the affairs of your state and nation? Moreover, do you forsake your duty to man when your duty of submission towards government interferes with the freedom and peace of your fellow man? No man lives as an island unto himself, but everyone must consider the rights of others regarding all relationships in life.

It is clear: God's word specifically instructs man to attempt to live in peace with other men, as it is good and acceptable in the sight of God. However, it is also clear that government has a lot to do with your ability to live in peace with others—not because they grant peace, but because they are to protect peace—and that government may actually hinder your ability to accomplish that goal. First Timothy 2:1-4 (ESV) says the following:

> First of all, then, I urge that supplications, prayers, intercessions, and thanksgivings be made for all people, for kings and all who are in high positions, that we may lead a peaceful and quiet life, godly and dignified in every way. This is good, and it is pleasing in the sight of God our Savior, who desires all people to be saved and to come to the knowledge of the truth.

Notice that we are to pray for all people and our leaders so that we may lead a peaceful and quiet life. Notice as well that living a peaceful and quiet life is good and pleasing in God's sight. God clearly states that our responsibility to attempt to live in peace with our fellow man is directly related to

---

7. "If possible, so far as it depends on you, live peaceably with all." Romans 12:18 (ESV).

society's rulers. This is no mystery, but it speaks directly to what has been the human experience since man was created. In other words, rulers over society have the power and ability to cause citizens not to live in peace and quiet, and therefore we should pray for such rulers—not for the sake of the rulers, but for our sake—so that we would be able to live a life of peace and quiet. And while our desire to live in peace with our fellow men is not for their benefit directly, our peace and quiet benefits society as a whole. And ultimately, our living in peace is not for our sole benefit, but for the glory of God. This is a circle of benefits and consequences stemming from peace.

Also notice in the same verses that we should give thanks for our rulers. Does this mean for *all* rulers? Absolutely not. Nowhere do we find in the Bible prayers from God's followers who praise God for an ungodly and evil ruler. The verse does not suggest that we should give thanks for rulers such as Adolf Hitler or other despots, but rather we should give thanks for the rulers who are helping preserve the peace and quiet—which is God's will. Such a ruler is acceptable in the sight of God, because it is "God our Savior who will have all men to be saved, and to come unto the knowledge of the truth."[8] Peace is God's primary way to facilitate that.

These verses draw a close connection and interdependence of peace and governmental rulers, in that living in peace with other men should be facilitated by their rulers. Thus, the responsibility that we have to our fellow man is to help ensure that takes place. What good is it to pray for governmental leaders who promote slavery? Is slavery the good and acceptable will of God? Absolutely not. Rather, the good and acceptable will of God is peace. Can it be said that peace comes with governmental leaders who ignore and trample over the rights of men? Again, no. Therefore, each person has a responsibility to others to preserve the good and acceptable form of government and rulers for the purpose of providing each person with the capability of leading a quiet and peaceable life for the salvation of mankind (both physically and spiritually). This ideology is reflected in God's command that we "love thy neighbor as thyself."[9] For what person who loves himself or his neighbor would desire that either one live in tyranny and anarchy? As a result of this

---

8. 1 Timothy 2:4 (KJV).
9. Matthew 5:43 (KJV).

responsibility, it behooves us to engage in the righteousness of government. It cannot be concluded that God's idea of a good citizen is one who simply allows government to be led by tyrants. Such an approach to government demonstrates a self-centered and selfish attitude. Rather, when we care about our family and our community and our nation, our prayers and actions affect rulers who will promote peace and happiness, not tyranny and suffering.

RESPONSIBILITY TO GOD

While the responsibility to our fellow man should create a desire to preserve and maintain a free and peaceable society, there is yet a responsibility much greater: our responsibility to God, our Creator. What God-fearing person would deny this? What Christian can disagree with the apostle Peter that "we are to obey God rather than man"?[10] So what does God demand from us? What responsibility do we have to God? In short, we must glorify Him, obey Him, seek Him and His word, and be faithful to Him and His word. Obviously, not every person reading this would consider him or herself a Christian and thus obligated to follow these principles found in the Bible. However, as Thomas Jefferson (who did not even acknowledge that Jesus was the Savior of the world and God's Son) described, the Bible contains the principles to live a moral and upstanding life. Thus, for anyone who believes that God exists, it behooves you, as God's creation, to live a life as pleasing to God as possible.

Praise Him

King David says in Psalm 86:12, "I will praise thee, O Lord my God, with all my heart: and I will glorify thy name for evermore." The apostle Paul says in Romans 15:6, "That ye may with one mind and one mouth glorify God, even the Father of our Lord Jesus Christ." Glorifying God should be natural for the child of God who loves his father. What child who loves his parents refuses to "rise up and call [them] blessed"?[11] Of course, just as the feeling or emotion of love is not enough to sustain a marriage, so do we have more

---

10. Acts 5:29 (KJV).
11. Proverbs 31:28 (KJV).

responsibility to God than to love God, because we know this is love: that you "obey my commandments."[12] Thus, obedience is not only the expression of love; it is the essence of love to God and the responsibility of the child to his Heavenly Father.

Obey Him

The lawgiver Moses reflects the duty of obedience in Deuteronomy 6:24 (esv), "And the LORD commanded us to do all these statutes, to fear the LORD our God, for our good always, that he might preserve us alive, as we are this day." He further says in Deuteronomy 12:28 (esv), "Be careful to obey all these words that I command you, that it may go well with you and with your children after you forever, when you do what is good and right in the sight of the LORD your God." Likewise, in the New Testament the apostle Paul relates the following in Acts 5:28–29 (esv):

> "We strictly charged you not to teach in this name, yet here you have filled Jerusalem with your teaching, and you intend to bring this man's blood upon us." But Peter and the apostles answered, "We must obey God rather than men."

Obedience necessarily means that there are standards and rules prescribing and proscribing what is and what is not righteousness—in all areas of life. Obedience is not to be confused with one's subjective notions of right and wrong (which is the New Age philosophy of doing what is right according to one's own eyes), but rather it is a sort of universalistic approach to all decisions and beliefs.[13] The Bible clearly sets forth and God has indicated what His standards of obedience are relative to every area of life—including government.

Thus, it is our responsibility to seek those standards, the truth of God's word. Hugo Grotius puts it this way: "To the human race, the [Divine] Law has thrice been given by God; at the Creation; immediately after the Deluge,

---

12. John 5:3 (kjv).
13. "New Age," *Wikipedia.org,* http://en.wikipedia.org/wiki/New_Age (accessed May 5, 2009).

and at the coming of Christ. These three sets of Laws oblige all men, as soon as they acquire a sufficient knowledge of them."[14] Isaiah 26:2 (ESV) explains it this way: "Open the gates, that the righteous nation that keeps faith may enter in." And also in Deuteronomy 4:29 (ESV): "But from there you will seek the LORD your God and you will find him, if you search after him with all your heart and with all your soul."

And what motivation should we have to seek the truth? The Bible tells us that seeking the truth should be as precious as life itself, for "man cannot live by bread alone, but by every word of God."[15] The parable in Luke 15:8 (ESV) demonstrates: "What woman, having ten silver coins, if she loses one coin, does not light a lamp and sweep the house and seek diligently until she finds it?"

If man has nothing but head-knowledge of God but chooses to believe and live how he pleases without reference or regard to justice, righteousness, or responsibility to his fellow men, the affect of such conduct fails to comply with his responsibility to God. Similarly, one could acknowledge that he has a responsibility to help preserve the freedom and peace of society but at the same time allow his governmental administrators to conduct acts contrary to freedom and peace. His head-knowledge effectuates no freedom or peace in society. Bottom line: obedience is the only method by which responsibilities are affected.

Accept the Truth and Stay Faithful to the Truth

As discussed above, it is possible that you may find the truth yet reject it or ignore it. God warns that this is a damnable and cursed matter. To avoid the damnable repercussions of finding the truth and then rejecting it, faithfulness to the truth is required. First Timothy 6:12 (ESV) tells us to "fight the good fight of the faith. Take hold of the eternal life to which you were called and about which you made the good confession in the presence of many witnesses." After loving God, seeking the truth, obeying the truth, and being faithful to the truth, blessings result. Psalm 33:12 (ESV) says, "Blessed is the nation whose God is the LORD, the people whom he has chosen as his

---

14. Grotius, *Hugo Grotius on the Rights of War and Peace*, 6.
15. Luke 4:4 (KJV).

heritage!" Likewise Proverbs 14:34 (ESV) says, "Righteousness exalts a nation, but sin is a reproach to any people."

Christians—even notable Christian leaders—have claimed God's promises in these verses while simply praying and hoping that a certain abominable or liberal politician not get into the White House and praying that the lesser abominable politician get in instead. Let us be clear: since when did a lesser evil become righteousness? And since when did fear of a certain evil politician obtaining office ever qualify for living by faith and voting for someone known to be evil as well? These questions are more forcefully compelling when there are actually options available that are not evil but are in fact in compliance with God's standards of righteousness. Nowhere does God indicate that He will bless faithlessness in a person or a nation—even if such a decision appears to be pragmatic and the only thing to do. So what good are prayers that only have goals of keeping lesser evils in government administration?

History confirms that the "right of colonies was traced not merely to the charters, to the Magna Carta, and the English Constitution, but *to the law of God and nature;* to the common and primitive rights of mankind."[16] It has been recognized by historians that the U.S. Constitution was not a new set of progressive ideas (as many liberals would attempt to use to force their progressive policies and ideologies) but a compilation of truths recognized and compiled through Anglo-Saxon history. They have observed that "there is little in this Constitution that is absolutely new. There is much that is as old as Magna Carta."[17] Similarly stated, "At the base of that body of constitutional law was that part of Magna Carta...out of which grew the modern

---

16. John Quincy Adams and Charles Frances Adams, *The Life of John Adams,* vol. 1 (Philadelphia, Pennsylvania: J. P. Lippenscott & Co., 1874), 103.

17. "Out of England's fundamental statutes were fabricated the bills of rights by which the first state constitutions were prefaced, and out of those bills of rights were coined the first nine amendments to the Constitution of the United States." Hannis Taylor, *The Origin and Growth of the American Constitution,* (Boston and New York: Houghton Mifflin Co., 1911), 4, 223; "The colonial idea as expressed by [James] Otis and [Samuel] Adams was not new in America, for it will be recalled that, when the Puritan magistrates of Massachusetts Bay were asked (1683) to give up their charter which it was argued they had legally forfeited, the ministers who were consulted said that though according to some corrupt and unrighteous laws they

conception of 'due process of law.'"[18] These sources of common law have long been held as America's roots for liberty and came at a serious price, as reflected by Blackstone: "[Freedom obtained] by the great charter of liberties, which was obtained, sword in hand."[19] And likewise, Algernon Sidney said, "The intention of our ancestors was, without doubt, to establish this [liberty] amongst us by the Magna Carta, and other preceding or subsequent laws."[20] Thus, knowing, understanding, and applying the natural and revealed laws of God are vital to the preservation of freedom in America. America's founders, philosophers, statesmen, theologians, and politicians reflect that the natural and revealed laws of God are true, and that we have a responsibility relative to the truth. Therefore, it should be your purpose to inform and enlighten your mind regarding the natural and revealed laws of truth and the historical understanding of government and how it relates to American citizens—from government's relation to man to its formation, purpose, administration, power, and dissolution.

---

might have done so, yet according to laws of righteousness and equity they had not done so. These were the laws to which…the King was limited, not merely by acts of Parliament, 'but by eternal laws of truth, wisdom, and equity and the everlasting tables of right reason—tables that cannot be repealed, or broken like those of Moses.'" Halstead Van Tyne, *The Causes of the War of Independence*, 227–228.

18. Ibid., 222.

19. Blackstone and Lewis, ed., *Commentaries on the Laws of England,* 115.

20. Sidney, *Discourses on Government,* 329.

4

UNDERSTANDING
GOVERNMENT

O ne of the main causes contributing to problems in America today
is the lack of understanding of what government is, what it relates
to, and whom it relates to. The vast majority of Americans do not
know the whys, hows, and what fors of our government's formation. We hear
the word *constitution* thrown around like a baseball, but mostly we do not
know what it signifies, what it means, what it represents, what its effect is, or
how it relates to government activity, jurisdiction, or power. We hear phrases
like, "we need to get back to the Constitution," and we think we understand what it means. Unfortunately and apparently, the sovereigns ("we the
people") of the several (separate and distinct) states do not know the answers
to these questions regarding the Constitution; because it has been used in as
meaningless ways as the beaten-down and manipulated terms *conservative*
and *liberal.*

Anymore, the label of constitution is as a character in a cartoon—no
substance, not real, illusionary, and pretentious. If you disagree, pray tell, how
has America gone from what you probably refer to as a Christian nation to a
socialistic, communistic, globalist, abortion-performing, Christian-shunning,
homosexual-promoting, Constitution-rejecting, illegal-alien-accepting, lazy-
citizen-condoning, hand-out/bail-out-legislating, education-less, family-torn,
over-taxed, over-regulated nation? We, the people of the several states, are

seemingly powerless to make any changes, even when there are some 250 million self-proclaimed Christians in America with a history of tremendously brave and freedom-loving ancestors, and even when we have largely had a Republican-dominated Congress, White House, and judiciary for almost forty years! For the word *constitution* to have any bearing on not only our understanding of the government, but also our relation to it, one must obtain a fundamental grasp of the very nature of government as it relates to the citizens subjected to it.

THE STARTING POINT: UNDERSTANDING NATURE

To understand government is first to understand nature: the nature of God and mankind. Once again, philosophy shapes and forms the premises and conclusions of your mind. The fundamentals of understanding government are so necessary that if one does not have a strong grasp of this subject matter, every thought and rationale flowing from your mind is likely to be distorted by humanism, socialism, communism, globalism, secularism, hedonism, and every other philosophical creed that exists today. As a point of illustration: when you build a house, your preparation does not begin by constructing the roof on the fifth story. Rather, you actually begin by performing perk tests—the below-the-ground testing. It is testing what you cannot see on the surface, but it is what must take place before even laying the foundation. If the ground is not solid enough to stand on, you do not even consider building there. Likewise, to have a free nation you must know where to build before you actually build. Founding father Pelatiah Webster made a similar analogy as follows:

> It is as physically impossible to secure to civil society, good cement of union, duration, and security without a Constitution founded on principles of natural fitness and right, as to raise timbers into a strong, compact building, which have not been framed upon true geometric principles; for if you cut one beam a foot too long or short, not all the authority and all the force of all the carpenters can ever get it into its place, and make it fit with proper symmetry there.[1]

1. Hannis Taylor, *The Real Authorship of the United States Constitution Explained: James Madison and Pelatiah Webster Defended by Hannis Taylor Against Attacks Contained in Senate*

This understanding of where to build and how to build is the profound-yet-simple starting point that our founders were not only familiar with but also believed in and acted upon. To understand government, one must explore and understand the nature of man and God.

Consider the philosophers studied by America's founders, such as Hugo Grotius. Grotius wrote extensively and expounded thoroughly upon the understanding of the intrinsic nature of government. Grotius explains in simple and emphatic terms the reality that government's formation is directly and proportionally related to the natural laws of God. He starts with the very basic notion that humans are bound to submit themselves to the will of God, meaning that the Creator intended that certain natural laws exist in humans and on earth. Grotius illustrates that it is this basic understanding of God's nature that formulates the concept of justice and how government should function as well. He says, "We are brought to another origin of [Justice]... namely, the free will of God, to which, as our reason irresistibly tells us, we are bound to submit ourselves. But even the Natural Law of which we have spoken...although it does proceed from the internal principles of man, may yet be rightly ascribed to God; because it was by His will that such principles came to exist in us."[2]

Natural law does not proceed from man—the internal principles—but is "rightly ascribed to God; because it was by His will that such principles came to exist."[3] Natural law is not a subjective theory, whereby all concepts of justice derive from the opinions of man. It is based upon the independent creation of God and thus is immutable, unchangeable, constant, and absolute. Furthermore, Grotius connected justice to the will of God and then declared that to obtain justice man must submit to the will of God, because God ascribed and created natural law—the law to which nations are bound to submit. Thus, justice and government are simply reflections of the natural laws created by God as He intended.

Grotius further explained the notion of justice, which is one of the goals for government to obtain, in the following passage:

Document No. 402, Sixty-Second Congress, Second Session, (Washington D.C.: United States Government Printing Office, 1912), 48.

    2. Grotius, *Hugo Grotius on the Rights of War and Peace,* xxvi, xxvii.

    3. Grotius, *Hugo Grotius on the Rights of War and Peace,* xxvi.

For the Mother of Right, that is, of Natural Law, is *Human Nature;* for this would lead us to desire mutual society, even if it were not required for the supply of other wants; and the Mother of Civil Laws, is Obligation by mutual compact; and since mutual compact derives its force from Natural Law, Nature may be said to be the Grandmother of Civil Laws. The genealogy is, *Human Nature: Natural Law: Civil Laws.*[4]

The foundation of government, *first,* is rights derived from natural law, which is human nature; *secondly,* is civil laws derived from mutual society; and *thirdly,* is the obligations of the mutual compact (constitution), the enforcement of which derives from natural law. Grotius makes a full circle of all rights, laws, and justice being derived from natural law; and natural law is human nature. As stated earlier, Grotius also states that natural law—or the natural rules established by the nature and free will of God—are directly ascribed to God. Thus, Grotius believes that civil laws should reflect the constitution made by society, which should reflect the laws of human nature, all of which are a direct ascription to God Himself. Again, religion (in the commonly understood sense) is not the goal, but rather justice and freedom are the goals of creating a constitution and civil laws from natural law.

William Blackstone, the most influential lawyer, judge, law professor, and studier of jurisprudence to affect the philosophical and legal understanding of America's founding, writes in his *Commentaries on the Laws of England*—in no uncertain terms—regarding the source of all government formation, constitution, and action. He, too, expresses the direct correlation between natural law and government.

Man, considered as a creature, must necessarily be subject to the laws of his Creator, for he is entirely a dependent being. A being, independent of any other, has no rule to pursue, but such as he prescribes to himself, but a state of dependence will inevitably oblige the inferior to take the will of him on whom he depends as

---

4. Grotius, *Hugo Grotius on the Rights of War and Peace,* xxvii, (emphasis added).

the rule of his conduct…this will of his Maker is called the *law of nature.*

For as God, when he created matter, and endued it with a principle of mobility, established certain rules for the perpetual direction of that motion, so, when he created man, and endued him with free-will to conduct himself in all parts of life, he laid down certain *immutable laws of human nature,* whereby that free-will is in some degree regulated and restrained, and gave him also the faculty of reason to discover the purport of those laws.[5]

Blackstone establishes, first, the duty that the creation (mankind) has to comply with the will of the Creator (God). Then, Blackstone establishes that given the will of the Creator, as revealed by the order of His creation, there is in fact a natural law, which establishes certain rules and laws of conduct in all parts of life. Blackstone further confirms other revealed laws found in the Bible, such as, men have freedom of choice, men are given ability to reason, life comes from God, man has a responsibility to God, man is accountable to God for his actions, and God's laws are superior to man's laws. In short, Blackstone sets a foundation that a nation should conform its laws to the natural and revealed laws of God for the government to operate in compliance with the will of God. The goal: to establish justice and maintain freedom in society.

Many would likely agree with these statements—at least in theory or as it involves them individually—but likely have a hard time connecting the truth expressed by Grotius and Blackstone to America's modern society (partly because America has drifted so far from these concepts), especially as it concerns natural law. Why have these concepts been completely erased from public discussion, knowledge, acceptance, and consciousness? The concerns of conservatives, liberals, Republicans, and Democrats have been the focus of politics for many years; all the while, citizens do not even understand that most policies discussed and promoted do not even pass the perk test of freedom. Such shallow understanding and approaches to government would

---

5. Blackstone, *Commentaries on the Laws of England,* 28–29, (emphasis added).

not even have gotten America off the ground but would have crashed her into the soil of tyranny immediately after winning the War of Independence. So how far is America from hitting the ground today? I think I can actually hear the pilot screaming, "Mayday, Mayday!"

The fact is America's founding fathers believed that positive laws (human laws) must conform to the will of God as revealed in nature and the Bible, and they confirmed the truths expounded by Grotius and Blackstone. In "Federalist Paper #51," James Madison confirmed the notion that government should be a reflection of human nature, which formulates natural law.

> [The constitution] may be a reflection of human nature, that such devises should be necessary to control the abuses of government. But what is government itself, but the greatest of all reflections on human nature? If men were angels, no government would be necessary. If angels were to govern men, neither external nor internal controls on government would be necessary.[6]

If the United States government was formed on the basis of human nature as understood from a natural and revealed law perspective, what becomes of this nation when all of its governmental leaders—including conservatives— do not conform their lawmaking to these laws? And for those of you who are thinking that all of these politicians out there who claim to be pro-life, pro-family, pro-capitalism, and other conservative slogans are incorporating natural and revealed law principles, think again. The proof, as they say, is in the pudding. Indeed, what does it profit America to elect a Republican or conservative when they continue to advance agendas, laws, and policies that do not reflect the nature of God and the nature of man, the principles our Constitution reflected and mandated?

Indeed, understanding and applying the rudimentary fact that government should reflect the nature of man and God provides a litmus test for

---

6. James Madison, "Federalist Paper 51," in *The Federalist Papers: A Collection of Essays in Favour of the Constitution*, Hamilton, Jay, and Madison, 400–401.

every politician seeking your support and approval. In other words, if the politician does not believe that government should reflect this truth, it follows that all of his philosophies will produce laws that reflect principles to the contrary. One would not even need to inquire further about policy positions such as pro-life, pro-capitalism, and other issues, because without a fundamental understanding of human nature, the nature of God, and how it relates to justice and freedom, that politician offers little or no hope for America. Freedom lovers should be guided by the truths that have made America free in the past, not the misguided and deceptive issues on which the mainstream media politico would like for us to focus.

America's founders recognized the truth that the Enlightenment philosophers provided, and the founders accepted much of their guidance on the nature and the formation of government—as well as we should. One such philosopher was a Frenchman who wrote extensively on the nature of government and its relationship to man and who contributed greatly to our founders' understanding of the separation of powers, Charles Baron Montesquieu.[7] Montesquieu lived from 1689 to 1755, was "a French attorney and author, [and] was the most frequently invoked source during the Founding Era."[8] He wrote the book, *Spirit of Laws,* which "provided a powerful influence on the thinking of our founders."[9] Montesquieu expressed a similar theme to the one portrayed by Grotius and Blackstone: God is the Creator, man is the creature. God has created immutable laws, and man is obligated to follow those laws. Montesquieu understood that before one can understand government, he must understand man's nature, God, and man's relationship to God. He states,

> Laws in their most general signification, are the necessary relations arising from the nature of things...and laws are the relations subsisting between it and different things, and the relations of these to one another. God is related to the universe, as Creator and Preserver; the laws by which He created all things are those by which He preserves

---

7. Eidsmoe, *Christianity and the Constitution,* 54.
8. Barton, *Original Intent,* 214.
9. Ibid.

them. He acts according to these rules, because He knows them; He knows them, because He made them; and He made them, because they are in relation of His Wisdom and power.[10]

Given this maxim, as expressed by Montesquieu, that God created all things, and that He preserves them, and that God has created certain laws while He performed such acts of creation and preservation, what does that mean for government and the ability to create laws (known as positive laws)? After all, does it not make sense that government and laws should have a stable basis from which to build all principles, policies, and laws—using the perk test analogy again? What would become of a society whose laws were nothing more than what the majority of people thought to be right or wrong or what the politicians or elitists deemed to be right or wrong? Montesquieu wisely answers this question and offers the philosophy of American government: "The government most conformable to nature is that which best agrees with the humor and disposition of the people in whose favor it is established."[11] Thus, a political principle is established regarding the understanding of government: government should conform to the nature that best agrees with human nature and God's natural and revealed law. Government is not arbitrary; it is not party politics; it is not the will of the majority; it is not a living document. It is the establishment of justice, the protection of rights, and the provision for peace, all founded upon the principles established by the invariable laws of God Almighty.

An interesting dichotomy and contradiction of America's understanding of government reveals itself in the endless amount of literature and movies regarding the societies and governments of the Indians observed in early America. Such mediums portray the Indian way of life, society, and government structure to be superior to the American lifestyle, morality, and society, and inevitably portray American government and people as barbaric, unnatural, and undesired. The message sent is that the Indians possessed a greater way of life than we

10. Charles de Baron Montesquieu and Julian Hawthorne, ed., *The Spirit of Laws: The World's Great Classics*, vol. 1 (London: The London Press), 1.

11. Montesquieu and Hawthorne, ed., *The Spirit of Laws*, 6.

Americans did, and that Americans are morally culpable for the destruction of the Indian culture, society, and government system. While debating those issues is not the intent here, what must be noticed is that the Indians did not even operate under the governmental regulatory system as experienced in America's form of government: no written constitution, no separate branches of government, no democratic elections of public leaders, no rules of criminal procedure, etc. What was observed by America's founders was that the Indians lived in a sort of state of nature, whereby the people operated in a society and conducted themselves according to the natural laws of morality.

Thomas Jefferson even noted that living under such natural laws is preferable to government, where such government does not recognize natural laws: "Those societies (as the Indians) which live without government enjoy, in their general mass, an infinitely greater degree of happiness than those who live under the European governments...Among them, public opinion restrains morals as powerfully as laws ever did anywhere."[12] Such a view of the Indians is largely held to be true by many Americans today and is even used as political leverage regarding the treatment of minorities in America. But you cannot have it both ways: you cannot argue for the purity and superiority of the Indian lifestyle and government system while at the same time arguing for government regulation without reference to natural laws of God. Americans must decide and come to grips with the most fundamental understanding of what government is. Regarding America's foundation, however, our founding fathers accepted and incorporated the maxim that government should conform to the nature that best agrees with human nature and God's natural and revealed law.

Understanding this maxim, the question may be asked, "Since we have a Constitution that was created to secure freedom for the people of this nation, are not we in fact free?" Indeed, since 1787–89, the words of America's Declaration of Independence, Constitution, and Bill of Rights have not changed—with the exception of amendments. Such an assumption is dangerous and causes many to be lethargic towards their duty to preserve freedom, which is their natural and biblical responsibility towards

---

12. Simpson, *Notes on Thomas Jefferson*, 84.

man and God. Perhaps America has forgotten or is ignorant of the words of Montesquieu: "The constitution may happen to be free, and the subject not…It is the disposition only of the laws, and even of the fundamental laws, that constitutes liberty in relation to the constitution."[13]

It is clear, and it can be seen by the evidence of history, that the constitution of any nation may be free, but the people may be slaves. Relying on the brilliance, work, and wars of our founders will not ensure freedom for you and your posterity. Notice: a people will be free when the people enact laws that conform to a constitution that reflects natural laws. Thus, it is crucial for a society to insist that its government comply with the terms of its constitution (where such is based in the justice of natural law), or else the reasoning behind implementation of laws will not reflect the laws of God but will be based upon the agenda of people who care nothing of the effects on freedom.

Think about this: how has our nation changed so dramatically and drastically over the past one hundred, fifty, or even twenty years? Again, America's Constitution has not changed. Human nature has not changed. What is the difference? Perhaps it is because we have forgotten the following principles explained by Montesquieu, or worse, we ignore them:

> There is this difference between the nature and principle of government, that the former [the nature of government] is that by which it is constituted, the latter [the principle of government] by which it is made to act. One is its particular structure, and the other the human passions which set it in motion. Now, laws ought no less to relate to the principle than to the nature of each government.[14]

Montesquieu's understanding is clear: the laws of a nation ought not only to follow the *principle* of government, which is the constitution, but also the *nature* of government, which is derived from natural and revealed law, created by God. To suggest that America need not strictly follow the Constitution simply because the Constitution is not inerrant is meritless

---

13. Montesquieu and Hawthorne, ed., *The Spirit of Laws*, 183.
14. Montesquieu and Hawthorne, ed., *The Spirit of Laws*, 19.

and hypocritical—unless of course you desire to live in slavery. Even those who opposed the newly proposed United States Constitution in 1787 recognized that "perfection is not to be expected in any thing that is the production of man."[15] Regardless of not being able to obtain perfection on earth, Thomas Jefferson clearly states that America's Constitution must be literally and strictly followed, or else its meaning and impact is noneffectual, and you might as well not have a written constitution. Jefferson says, "Our peculiar security is in the possession of a written Constitution. Let us not make it a blank paper by construction."[16] Without a society's laws adhering to both the principles of the constitution and the natural laws of God (which forms the constitution), the idea of the *living constitution* takes root in the ignorant—or worse, deceitful—mind.

This living constitution approach advocates the idea that the constitution can and should change with every wind of philosophical change made in that society, causing the rights of man to be seriously jeopardized. More than that, the living constitution allows the government to perform actions that are strictly restricted or not allowed by the terms of the constitution. The living constitution application and ideology largely became a tool in the twentieth century for those who saw the constitution as a hurdle and obstacle to accomplish certain agenda, which could only be effectuated through a largely controlled and controlling federal government. Consider the following promotion of a living U.S. Constitution by Hannis Taylor in 1911:

Never in the constitutional life of any people has the organic development been so vast and rapid as that which has taken place here since the existing Federal Constitution went into effect. During the very short period in which the thirteen scattered communities that fringed our Atlantic seaboard toward the close of the seventeenth century have been expanding across the continent, the dissolving views of change have followed each other like the pictures in a panorama. In expanding

---

15. Brutus and Ralph Ketcham, ed., *The Anti-Federalist Papers and the Constitutional Convention Debates,* (New York: Signet Classic, 2003), 279–280.

16. Jefferson, *The Jeffersonian Cyclopedia,* 200.

with that expansion, in adapting itself to the changed relations resulting there-from, the American Constitution has developed elasticity, a
growing-power entirely beyond the cumbrous process of amendment
its terms provide…And yet during all that time [since 1804] it has
been passing rapidly, despite its rigid and dogmatic form, through a
marvelous process of unparalleled development, chiefly through the
subtle agency of judge-made law ever flowing from a generous foun-
tain, the Supreme Court of the United States…[T]here is no longer a
place for the withering legends of supernaturalism, or for myths and
traditions that defy the ordinary rules of common sense.[17]

As clearly expressed by the author, the U.S. Constitution contains too
many rigid forms which prevent the government from rapidly passing laws
and is full of supernaturalism and myths, such as inalienable rights deriving their source from nature and nature's God and other similar natural-law
principles. So instead of following the rigid and dogmatic form of government that *We the People of the United States* agreed to for over one hundred
years, the living constitution has been propagated, promulgated, and promoted with great success—so much so that we do not even require our public officials to adhere to it. This interpretation flies in the face of American
jurists who framed the judicial portrait of constitutional interpretation, such
as the following description from the late Joseph Story, U.S. Supreme Court
justice:

Every provision in the instrument [of the U.S. Constitution] may
therefore fairly be presumed to have reference to one or more of
these objects [named in the Preamble of the Constitution]. And consequently, if any provision is susceptible of two interpretations, that
[interpretation] ought to be adopted, and adhered to, which best
harmonizes with the avowed intentions and objects of the authors,
as gathered from their declarations in the instrument itself.[18]

17. Taylor, *The Origin and Growth of the American Constitution,* vii–ix.
18. Joseph Story, *A Familiar Exposition of the Constitution of the United States: Containing a
Brief Commentary,* (New York: Harper & Brothers, 1868), 38.

Contrarily, if in fact our Constitution should be living, then whose philosophical approach should be adopted in society—that of the majority, the minority, the government, or (God forbid) the United Nations? Whatever your choice, anything outside of constitutional provision denies the sovereigns of each state their compactual rights and takes the form of tyranny. The idea of a living or changing constitution was not accepted in America for the very reason that the Constitution was created and adopted: to secure natural rights. Consider the United States Supreme Court decision in *Mattox v. United States*. It stated the following:

> We are bound to interpret the Constitution in light of the law as it existed at the time it was adopted, not as reaching out for new guaranties of the rights of the citizen, but as securing to every individual such as he already possessed as a British subject—such as his ancestors had inherited and defended since the days of Magna Carta.[19]

Without the certainty of natural laws, the meaning of the constitution will change with each contemporary fad accepted in that society, or with the tyrannical agenda of the most powerful and elite, creating (once again) a monarchial and aristocratic government. Like the self-professing Christian "having a form of godliness, but denying the power thereof,"[20] America has for too long believed fallacious philosophy, ignored natural and revealed laws, and adopted flawed principles. Consequently, America has passed laws that pretentiously conform to the Constitution but completely disregard the nature, philosophy, and principle from which our Constitution was derived. It is time that we say of this ignorance of our nature and principle of government, "from such turn away."[21]

When the colonists analyzed the actions of Great Britain, they did not base their decision of revolution and resistance upon what Parliament ordered, but rather upon what the intention of the British constitution was, in light of natural law. Founding father Richard Bland wrote a response to

---

19. *Mattox v. United States*, 156 U.S. 237, 243 (1895).
20. Timothy 3:5 (KJV).
21. Ibid.

Great Britain's claim that it had the right to tax the colonies through an act of Parliament, in which he argued that any such act of Parliament was contrary to their constitution, stating:

> [W]e must recur to the civil Constitution of *England,* and from thence deduce and ascertain the Rights and Privileges of the People at the first Establishment of the Government, and discover the Alterations that have been made in them from Time to Time; and it is from the Laws of the Kingdom, *founded upon the Principles of the Law of Nature,* that we are to show the Obligation every Member of the State is under to pay Obedience to its Institutions.[22]

Bland simply held the common American view of freedom in government, which was government held to the constitutional limitations imposed upon it by the people and natural law. It cannot be overlooked that those who argue that the *living constitution* idea should be applied in American jurisprudence are in fact repeating history—American history—history that led to a revolutionary war. One of the very causes of the American Revolutionary War was the clash in philosophy of those who believed in the immutable laws of nature and nature's God and those who believed that the British Parliament could change the meaning of the constitution considering the *times,* circumstances, and other external observations. One author on this subject notes that this difference in constitutional philosophy was the cause of the War of Independence:

> The contrast cannot be too strongly insisted upon. Samuel Adams and many of his fellow countrymen, on the one hand, believed that the British Constitution was fixed by "the law of God and nature," and founded in the principles of law and reason so that Parliament could not alter it, but Lord Mansfield and his followers, on the other

---

22. Richard Bland, *An Inquiry Into the Rights of the British Colonies,* (Williamsburg, VA: Alexander Purdie & Co., 1766, Reprinted by Appeals Press, Inc., 1922), 6–7 (emphasis added). Note: I spelled some of the words, which were originally written in Old English, in modern English for reader convenience.

hand, asserted rightly that "the constitution of this country has been always in a moving state, either gaining or losing something," and "there are things even in Magna Charta which are not constitutional now" and others which an act of Parliament might change. Between two such conceptions of the powers of government compromise was difficult to attain... Such differences in ideals were as important causes of a breaking up of the empire [of Great Britain] as more concrete matters like oppressive taxation.[23]

As they say, history is bound to repeat itself. Thus, what we see in America today boils down to the same question that the colonies faced in 1776: are we going to limit government by the fundamental principles of natural law, or are we going to allow government to determine what law is without regard to the Creator of it? There is no middle ground.

THE NATURE OF MAN

The concept adopted by America's forefathers that to understand government is to understand natural law may not appear profound. However, it is profoundly significant to our nation's philosophical perspective and principles—so much that the authors discussing the matter abundantly reviewed these concepts and related them to governmental formation and affairs, which became the bedrock for America. In fact, it was the exploration and understanding of human nature that formed and shaped the very foundational and fundamental principles of American jurisprudence.[24] Then, if understanding the nature of man is crucial to understanding what government should be,

---

23. Claude Halstead Van Tyne, *The Causes of the War of Independence*, 235, 237.

24. "To understand political power right, and derive it from its original, we must consider, what state all men are naturally in, and that is, a state of perfect freedom to order their actions, and dispose of their possessions and persons, as they think fit, within the bounds of the law of nature, without asking leave, or depending upon the will of any other man... The state of nature has a law of nature to govern it, which obliges every one: and reason, which is that law, teaches all mankind, who will but consult it, that being all equal and independent, no one ought to harm another in his life, health, liberty, or possessions: for men being all the workmanship of one omnipotent, and infinitely wise maker; all the servants of one sovereign master, sent into

one should study the nature of man, specifically from the sourcebook of the One who created man—the Bible. As William Rawle[25] said, "A knowledge of human nature…dictated…the composition of our Constitution."[26]

Created in the Image of God

The first and primary truth that must be established about man is regarding his life. All other laws of God flow from it: liberty, property, feelings, emotions, children, and the pursuit of happiness. How can we describe the significance, impact, and importance of this notion and how it relates to government? Very simply put, if life is created by God, no one has the right to take it away, except as the Creator prescribes in His natural and revealed law. It means that as soon as life begins, no person, entity, or government has the ability to take away what that individual or organization did not have the ability to create. Thus, the fundamental idea of right-to-life comes directly from the fact that life is a precious gift of God. Alternatively, if life did not come from God but is somehow attributed to the random development of some sort of evolutionary processes independent of a Creator, making human beings just a higher form of animals, then life is not precious or

---

the world by his order, and about his business; they are his property, whose workmanship they are, made to last during his, not one another's pleasure: and being furnished with like faculties, sharing all in one community of nature, there cannot be supposed any such subordination among us, that may authorize us to destroy one another, as if we were made for one another's uses, as the inferior ranks of creatures are for our's." Locke and Macpherson, ed., *Second Treatise of Government*, 8, 9.

25. "Rawle was born in Philadelphia, where he studied at the Friends' Academy. He studied law in New York and at the Middle Temple, London, and was admitted to the bar in 1783. In 1791 President Washington appointed him United States district attorney for Pennsylvania, in which capacity he prosecuted the leaders of the Whiskey Insurrection. He was counsel for the First Bank of the United States and in 1830 assisted in revising the civil code of Pennsylvania. He took much interest in science, philanthropy, and education, being a founder and first president of the Pennsylvania Historical Society, president of the Pennsylvania Abolition Society, and for forty years a trustee of the University of Pennsylvania." Author Unknown, "Penn in the 18th Century," http://www.archives.upenn.edu/people/1700s/rawle_wm.html; "William Rawle," *Wikipedia.org*, http://en.wikipedia.org/wiki/William_Rawle, (accessed May 5, 2009).

26. William Rawle, *A View of the Constitution of the United States of America*, 2nd ed., (Wiggins, MS: Crown Rights Book Company, 1829), 284.

definitive at all and is subject to the authority of the strongest survive, which is currently presiding over a new life when he begins to exist.

The matter becomes an issue of property rights. Is the life the property of the individual or whoever is the strongest at the time? If life belongs to the individual, then the individual is always and will always be sovereign over the state. On the other hand, if life belongs to the state, then the individual is always and will always be the subject of the state, its control, and dominion. From life all other rights proceed, and if one does not have the right to life, independent of anyone or anything, then one does not have the right to liberty or property. If one has the right to life, then he necessarily has the right of liberty and property. What good would a right to life be without the right to protect life, secure life, advance life, and use life? Thus, the natural laws and rights of man begin to unfold from the understanding that life is a gift of God and belongs solely to the individual.

Life Given by God

Hundreds of millions would agree: life comes from God, whether considering the natural laws of God or the revealed laws of God. There are many biblical sources which specifically support the fact that God has created and granted life to the individual. The following Bible verses express this fact:

> The Spirit of God has made me, and the breath of the Almighty gives me life.[27]

> I perceived that there is nothing better for them than to be joyful and to do good as long as they live; also that everyone should eat and drink and take pleasure in all his toil—this is God's gift to man.[28]

> Behold, what I have seen to be good and fitting is to eat and drink and find enjoyment in all the toil with which one toils under the sun the few days of his life that God has given him, for this is his

---

27. Job 33:4 (ESV).
28. Ecclesiastes 3:12–13 (ESV).

lot. Everyone also to whom God has given wealth and possessions and power to enjoy them, and to accept his lot and rejoice in his toil—this is the gift of God.[29]

Look on life with the wife whom you love all the days of the life of your vanity, which He has given you under the sun, all the days of your vanity. For that is your share in this life, and in your labor which you labor under the sun. Whatever your hand finds to do, do it with all your might; for there is no work, nor plan, nor knowledge, nor wisdom, in the grave where you go.[30]

Every good gift and every perfect gift is from above and comes down from the Father of lights, with whom is no variableness nor shadow of turning.[31]

Lo, children are the inheritance of Jehovah; the fruit of the womb is a reward.[32]

The heavens are the LORD's heavens, but the *earth he has given to the children of man.*[33]

God created life and that life is a gift from God to the individual created. Now what? Well, notice the connection and relation that God has with every other area of life: work, family, property, industry, joy, and children. The exercise of every area of humanity is a gift of God. Thomas Jefferson observed this natural and revealed law principle, stating, "The Giver of life… gave it for happiness and not for wretchedness."[34] This is the inalienable right

---

29. Ecclesiastes 5:18–19 (ESV).

30. Ecclesiastes 9:9–10 (MJKV).

31. James 1:17 (MJKV).

32. Psalm 127:3 (MJKV).

33. Psalm 115:16 (ESV), (emphasis added); "God, who hath given the world to men in common, hath also given them reason to make use of it to the best advantage of life, and convenience. The earth, and all that is therein, is given to men for the support and comfort of their being." Locke and Macpherson, ed., *Second Treatise of Government,* 18.

34. Jefferson, *The Jeffersonian Cyclopedia,* 398.

referred to in the Declaration of Independence as *the Pursuit of Happiness.* Each of the aforementioned verses confirms that once God has granted life to an individual, He has also granted the rights of advancing that life. Why would God give life without the rights and freedoms of using life?

Thus, the essences of the gifts of God are the ability to enjoy life, use life, control life, and advance life. As simple as the notion of life may be, it is crucial to understand the implications and consequences that result from the fact that God created life. Starting with this maxim will serve as a foundation of government's role relative to man and as an understanding of its limitations of power over the life of man. The natural result of government's limitation of the power to create or destroy life is that the government also has limitations relevant to liberty and property—the natural springs from which life flows.

ATTRIBUTES OF THE LIFE OF MAN

Proceeding from the gift of life to man, one must observe the nature of life, because these natural laws of mankind set the parameters in which people operate their lives—the natural governmental factors built into the human body and mind. Some of these attributes are obvious and perhaps go without saying, but nonetheless they are important enough to identify and recognize in the continual effort to understand human nature (i.e., natural law) and the government that must, as closely as possible, resemble and conform to it—and not interfere with these rights.

Reason

One of the attributes of the life granted by God is the ability to reason. God expects us to use the reason built into humans to not only survive, live, and prosper but also to discover, understand, and know who God is. Isaiah 1:18 (KJV) says, "Come now, and let us reason together, says the LORD: though your sins be as scarlet, they shall be as white as snow; though they be red like crimson, they shall be as wool." Likewise, 1 Peter 3:15 (KJV) says, "But sanctify the Lord God in your hearts: and be ready always to give an answer to every man that asks you a reason of the hope that is in you with meekness and fear." No other creature on earth was given the ability to use reasoning in all of its decisions. The ability to put reason to one's decisions is inherent and gifted to human life. As the foundational philosophical statement says, "I think, therefore I am."[35] Of course, with the gift and ability to reason comes the responsibility of using your reason, because if those with life have reason, then the One who gave that reason expects us to use it. Therefore, with the God-given ability to reason, mankind is given the responsibility of using his reason to enjoy life, use life, control life, and advance life; individuals and governments have no right to interfere with this God-given gift, except as it conforms to their God-given and compact-given purpose and limitations (as will be discussed further herein).

To implement the natural law of reason into society and government, the form and system of government should expect that reason and rationalization attach to all the laws of that society. In other words, the laws should conform to the reasoning and understanding. Of course, this connection between laws and reason always has in mind reasoning as found in natural law. In other words, not all reasoning is sound and based upon principles of freedom found in natural law. Thus, one must incorporate sound reasoning using the source of true principles: natural and revealed law. William Blackstone confirmed this approach of using reason when he said,

> If our reason were always, as in our first ancestor before his transgression, clear and perfect, unruffled by passions, unclouded by prejudice, unimpaired by disease or intemperance, the task would be pleasant and easy; we should need no other guide but this. But every man now finds the contrary in his own experience; that his reason is corrupt, and his understanding full of ignorance and error.
>
> This has given manifold occasion for the benign interposition of divine providence; which, in compassion to the frailty, the imperfection, and the blindness of human reason, hath been pleased, at sundry times and in divers manners, to discover and enforce its laws by an immediate and direct revelation. The doctrines thus delivered we call the revealed or divine law, and they are to be found only in the holy scriptures.

---

35. René Descartes, *Discourse on the Method of Rightly Conducting the Reason, and Searching for Truth in the Sciences,* (1637), Part V.

These precepts, when revealed, are found upon comparison to be really a part of the original law of nature, as they tend in all their consequences to man's felicity. But we are not from thence to conclude that the knowledge of these truths was attainable by reason, in its present corrupted state; since we find that, until they were revealed, they were hid from the wisdom of ages. As then the moral precepts of this law are indeed of the same origin with those of the law of nature, so their intrinsic obligation is of equal strength and perpetuity. Yet undoubtedly the revealed law is (humanly speaking) of infinitely more authority than what we generally call the natural law.[36]

To suggest that laws are derived only by a purely human source is to deny truly that (1) God has established natural laws at His creation, (2) human laws derive their source from the Creator of man and the Creator of justice, and (3) there are laws of higher authority than the laws of man. Indeed, human reasoning, when flawed in its origin, can never be considered the source of the ultimate responsibilities concerning societal obligations and individual rights. Thus, when applying the reason that God gifted to man, society and government must consider the source of that reason: God.

Knowledge

Another attribute inherent in the life God has given is the capacity for knowledge—to learn, to expand the mind, to grow the capabilities of the mind, to memorize, to use reason in drawing conclusions: all are forms of knowledge. First Corinthians 1:5 (KJV) reflects this gift of knowledge from God: "That in every thing you are enriched by him, in all utterance, and in all knowledge." Knowledge is exclusively unique to the individual—no two people have the same knowledge or use their knowledge in the exact same manner. Like life itself, God has given to individuals the unique gifts of the mind—to use one's own personal knowledge to protect, promote, and prosper one's own life, including one's family, community, and nation.

---

36. Blackstone, *Commentaries on the Laws of England*, 31–32.

Again, with any gift given by God, the possessor of that gift is required and is responsible to use that gift and to apply the knowledge to one's own personal life. Consider the apostle Paul's rebuke to teachers who have a form of knowledge but do not apply the knowledge to their own personal lives. Paul says in Romans 2:20–21 (ESV), "An instructor of the foolish, a teacher of children, having in the law the embodiment of knowledge and truth—you then who teach others, do you not teach yourself? While you preach against stealing, do you steal?" God is clear: not only must you seek knowledge and teach knowledge, but you must also apply the knowledge, which is always associated with truth. Therefore, government must conform to the fact that God has given to man the natural right of knowledge and of using that knowledge to advance life. That is, do not suppress man's ability of using his knowledge to advance life. The effects of this natural law should be sought: capitalism, entrepreneurship, private school education, home school education, advanced and higher learning, freedom of speech, freedom of assembly, freedom of religion, freedom of information use (e.g., Internet), the right to redress government, sunshine laws, public debate, and other similar notions reflecting the desire for and advancement of knowledge and correction. Thus, any governmental actions, laws, regulations, or policies that suppress knowledge from the people—the government's sovereign and principal—are contrary to the natural laws of God and the structure of American government.

Choice

God has also instilled in the human life the ability to choose, and it is this God-given gift that forms the basis of much of American jurisprudence. While there are obvious components of God's sovereign will intervening in the lives of individuals and nations, finite and frail humanity cannot presume to know the mind of God when it comes to His directly influencing the decisions of individuals. Presuming such contradicts God's will. As the prophet Isaiah says, "For my thoughts are not your thoughts, neither are your ways my ways, declares the LORD. For as the heavens are higher than the earth, so are my ways higher than your ways and my thoughts than your thoughts."[37] Rather,

---

37. Isaiah 55:8–9 (ESV).

God has made clear in His word that mankind has a duty to follow and obey His word, to choose to serve Him, and not to "quench the Holy Spirit,"[38] that "whosoever will, let him come."[39] There is no spiritual or biblical basis in shirking commandments and obligations imposed by God because you proclaim yourself to be an exception to God's already-stated standard. Thus, theological positions concerning predestination and God's choice to bless this person, or this nation, do not relieve mankind's duty to obey God's natural and revealed laws. Why would God have given to the world the Bible if nothing we did actually influenced any results or consequences relative to nature or God? Such a position had little or even no bearing on America's founding, even while a large number of early American settlers were in fact Calvinists.[40]

CASE IN POINT

As a way of illustration concerning the importance of choice in American jurisprudence, history clearly reflects that America acknowledged the individual's right (found in natural law) to choose. America esteemed it so highly that our national and state laws even require *guardians*[41] to be appointed for such persons who are not able to make choices on their own for reasons like being mentally incompetent, being an infant, or being mentally retarded; meaning that "where action on behalf of an abnormal human being is taken in the courts, the will attributed to him is that of some other definite person."[42] America's laws did not accept the notion that God's allowing one to be in a more unfortunate or helpless situation revealed His will that such a person has no right of choice. In other words, America has historically believed that one's right to choose is so important that we will require substitutions of choice to make sure that the incompetent's choice is protected.

---

38. Theselonians 5:19.

39. Revelation 22:17.

40. "John Calvin was the virtual founder of America." E. W. Smith and Loraine Boettner, *The Reformed Doctrine of Predestination,* (Philadelphia: Presbyterian and Reformed, 1972), 389.

41. "Guardian—one who has the legal authority and duty to care for another's person or property, esp. because of the other's infancy, incapacity, or disability." Garner, *Black's Law Dictionary.*

42. John Chipman Gray and Roland Gray, *The Nature and Sources of the Law,* 2nd Edition, (New York: The MacMillan Company, 1921), 38.

Ironically and contrary to the use of guardianship, the freedom of choice ideology is used in America to advocate the mother's right to terminate the life of her unborn child. However, America's historical jurisprudence used the exact same principle of freedom of choice of the unborn child to protect the child from abortion, because had the child possessed an exercisable will, the child would protect his life and would thus be entitled to due processes of law. The unborn child's unspoken yet recognized will gave the unborn child the right to life. Thus, until 1973 with the United States Supreme Court decision in *Roe v. Wade,* "putting an end to the life of an unborn child [was] generally in this country an offence by statute against the State."[43]

Choice is so inherent and natural in humans that even God does not force Himself to be chosen by people. He gives to them a choice: whether or not to serve Him. This fact is even demonstrated in the first story in the Bible—the story of Adam and Eve. Unfortunately, they made the wrong choice. What other area in life should take preeminence over God that it would demand your loyalty, dedication, or even your life? Josiah 24:15 (ESV) says, "And if it is evil in your eyes to serve the LORD, choose this day whom you will serve, whether the gods your fathers served in the region beyond the River, or the gods of the Amorites in whose land you dwell. But as for me and my house, we will serve the LORD." John Meacham observed this fact in American history as well in his book, *American Gospel,* stating, "If the Lord himself chose not to force obedience from those he created, then who are men to try?"[44] The human attribute of choice is as important a consideration with regard not only to life but also to the nature of government. It applies to the choice of government form, administration, rulers, and dissolution.

Freedom

Another natural law reflected in human nature relative to this discussion is freedom. British philosopher John Locke[45] (who lived from 1632 to 1704

---

43. Ibid., 39.

44. Meacham, *American Gospel,* 5.

45. "Locke's little book on government is perfect as far as it goes." Jefferson, *The Jeffersonian Cyclopedia,* 392.

and was highly influential in our founders' philosophical understanding)[46] discusses God's gift of freedom given to every life, saying, "Scripture or reason I am sure do not any where say [that] we are all born slaves...as if divine authority hath subjected us to the unlimited will of another."[47] To the contrary, "THE *natural liberty* of man is to be free from any superior power on earth, and not to be under the will or legislative authority of man, but to have only the law of nature for his rule."[48] Again, America's philosophical founders appealed to both natural and revealed law concerning the understanding of government. Freedom was engrained into every fabric of American jurisprudence such that, "the freeman pays no tax, as the freeman submits to no law, but such as emanates from the body in which he is represented."[49] Did not the apostle Paul acknowledge and claim that he, too, was "free born"?[50]

Deep in philosophical meaning and implication God has granted to each individual a natural-born state of freedom, which is why Montesquieu observes: "In the state of nature, indeed, all men are born equal."[51] Freedom is not a grant or privilege from government, because government does not have the power to grant something that it did not possess in the first place. Just as it cannot create life, it cannot create freedom. Freedom can only come from God. "And I shall walk at liberty; For I have sought thy precepts,"[52] said King David—precepts that were given to all of mankind. Indeed, freedom—like life itself—cannot be given by government but can only be taken by government.

Moreover, it must be understood that government is literally nothing more than a system whereby justice should be sought, rights should be protected, and peace ought to be promoted—which will be discussed more thoroughly herein. Government has no power of itself, except as is granted to it by a legitimate source. First Timothy 6:17 (MJKV) illustrates the fact

---

46. Eidsmoe, *Christianity and Constitution*, 60.
47. John Locke, *Two Treatises on Government*, (London: Holborn-Bars, 1821), 3.
48. Locke and Macpherson, ed., *Second Treatise of Government*, 17.
49. Adams, *The Life of John Adams*, 108.
50. "And the chief captain answered, With a great sum obtained I this freedom. And Paul said, But I was free born." Acts 22:28 (MJKV).
51. Montesquieu and Hawthorne, ed., *The Spirit of Laws*, 111.
52. Psalm 119:45 (ASV).

that indeed God possesses all power and has given to all mankind the enjoyment of all things, and that none of it is naturally owned by government. "Charge the rich in this world that they be not high-minded, nor trust in uncertain riches, but in the living God, He offering to us richly all things to enjoy." This is clear: God alone has given to us *all* things—no exceptions. The natural law principle, then, is that particular persons do not have the inherent right to dictate to others their will, and that the power to control and advance the life of self belongs naturally to the individual—not to the government.

Ultimately, this issue of being born free is a matter of jurisdiction (a matter to be discussed later). Since man or government has not given us all things, man or government has no authority to take away these things. Just as your fellow man or group of men cannot take your freedom from you (without repercussion), neither can a community, and neither can a nation. King David puts it this way in Psalm 9:20 (ESV): "Put them in fear, O LORD! Let the nations know that they are but men!" If governments are but men, how can it be argued that government is somehow greater than the individual? To argue that a group of men (i.e., society) can take away freedom simply because they have agreed to do so does not consider the certainty of the natural law principle that freedom cannot be taken by anyone who did not create it in the first place.

Lest anyone be confused, however, regarding the right of the individual to do what he wants, when he wants, in whatever manner he wants, natural law does not suggest that anarchy is the correct form of government but rather reveals that self-responsibility is required so as not to interfere with the God-given rights of other men. Likewise, the Bible reveals that freedom is not the ability to do whatever we want when we want, for such conduct produces only chaos (because of man's sinful nature), as was acknowledged by our nation's ideological founders. Thus, the founding fathers did not accept the notion that freedom was simply no rules and no boundaries, but rather it was the ability to live responsibly in whatever manner natural and revealed laws allowed, without disturbing the rights of others in society.

Founding father John Jay understood the balance of freedom to form a harmonious community based upon the fact that God is the source of all things—including freedom—and that it is not the government alone or the individual alone whose will is sovereign but the will of God. In his autobiography, Jay says, "Let it be remembered that civil liberty consists, not in a right to every man to do just what he pleases, but it consists in an equal right to all the citizens to have, enjoy, and do, in peace, security, and without molestation, whatever the equal and constitutional laws of the country admit to be consistent with the public good."[53]

Likewise, Algernon Sidney, the lieutenant general and cavalry officer under Cromwell and the Puritan forces in the English Civil War and author of *Discourses on Government* (and who was beheaded for allegedly attempting to overthrow King Charles II[54]) understood the natural and revealed balance of freedom and responsibility on all men (including men in power) is set by God. He writes, "I desire it may not be forgotten, that the liberty asserted is not a licentiousness of doing what is pleasing to every one against the command of God; but an exemption from all human laws, to which they have not given their assent."[55]

America's founders believed that principles found in natural law and revealed law demonstrate that man should use his freedom to promote and advance life, should take responsibility for his actions, and should likewise respect the rights of his fellow man. For if his neighbor's rights are jeopardized then his rights are likewise jeopardized. Thus, when a society cannot govern itself because persons do not either recognize the rights of others or alternatively do not recognize their own rights, then this natural-law pillar upon which freedom rests will crumble.

It is this biblical understanding of the freedom of man that has been so instrumental in shaping and forming the essence of American society—from abolishing slavery[56] to forming a government with strict limitations. By way of example concerning the issue of freedom naturally inherent in life, this principle was the determining catalyst that served to abolish the slave trade and practice in America with the biblical understanding that all men are

---

53. Jay, *The Life of John Jay,* 276.

54. Eidsmoe, *Christianity and Constitution,* 68–69.

55. Sidney, *Discourses on Government,* 314.

56. "The West did not invent slavery; the West ended slavery." Buchanan, *The Death of the West,* 58.

free born. John Jay (who advocated for a formal constitutional provision to prohibit slavery in the United States) says,

> In my opinion every man…has a natural right to freedom and I shall ever acknowledge myself to be an advocate for the manumission of slaves, with the justice due to their masters, and with the regard due to the actual state of society. These considerations unite in convincing me that the abolition of slavery must necessarily be gradual.[57]

Of course, many are very critical of early America because slavery existed—for purposes of commerce. The vast majority of American perceptions on the subject are completely distorted by modern education and politics (but such is not for discussion herein). In fact, countries in Europe attempted to, and in fact did, force the American colonies to continue the slave trade because of the amount of capital they accumulated through slave labor.[58] Despite their efforts, many of the American colonies passed legislation to end the slave trade and importation. Europe and even some of the northern colonists did not like it. In his *The Jeffersonian Cyclopedia,* Thomas Jefferson notes such events as they took place in Virginia:

The first establishment [of slavery] in Virginia which became per-

---

57. Jay, *The Life of John Jay,* 285.

58. "[George III] has waged cruel war against human nature itself, violating its most sacred rights of life and liberty in the persons of a distant people who never offended him, captivating and carrying them into slavery in another hemisphere, or to incur miserable death in their transportation thither…[H]e has prostituted his negative for suppressing every legislative attempt to prohibit or to restrain this execrable commerce. And that this assemblage of horrors might want no fact of distinguished dye, he is now exciting those very people to rise in arms among us, and to purchase that liberty of which he has deprived them, by murdering the people upon whom he has obtruded them." Jefferson, *The Jeffersonian Cyclopedia,* 813; "The abolition of domestic slavery is the great object of desire in those Colonies, where it was, unhappily, introduced in their infant state. But previous to the enfranchisement of the slaves we have, it is necessary to exclude all further importations from Africa. Yet our repeated attempts to effect this by prohibitions, and by imposing duties which might amount to a prohibition, have been hitherto defeated by his Majesty's negative." Jefferson, *The Jeffersonian Cyclopedia,* 812; Kettell, *Southern Wealth and Northern Profits,* 14. It is no wonder why Great Britain opposed any of America's efforts to abolish slavery: Great Britain brought a capital (profit) of $5,600,000,000 as a result of the slave trade in just a short period of fifty years!

manent, was made in 1607. I have found no mention of negroes in the Colony until about 1650. The first brought here as slaves were by a Dutch ship; after which the English commenced the trade, and continued it until the Revolutionary war. That suspended, *ipso facto,* their further importation for the present…this subject was not acted on finally until the '78, when I brought in a bill to prevent their further importation. This passed without opposition, and stopped the increase of the evil importation, leaving to future efforts its final eradication.[59]

Do not be deceived regarding the matter: the South *and* the North *and* Africa[60] *and* Europe (among other nations, including Jamaica, Spain, and India) were involved in the slave trade and practice, despite post-modern America's sole attack on the South. Africa sold and used slaves, Europe sold and transported slaves, the North used and transported slaves, and the South used slaves. In fact, author Thomas Kettell reflects the North's involvement with slave trade and transportation in his book, *Southern Wealth and Northern Profits,* saying, "The employment of Northern ships was mostly the slave-trade, while the South, having daily less employment for the blacks, was determined to stop their arrival—a measure which the North regarded as depriving it of its legitimate business."[61] He was describing the condition of America twenty-seven years after 1776. Notice that when the South had less need for the North to transport slaves to the South, the North took offense, as it injured their profit margin. Indeed, the entire world used slave labor in all areas of commerce for thousands of years, including white slaves

---

59. Jefferson, *The Jeffersonian Cyclopedia,* 813.

60. "Negro slavery, which originated in Africa, spreading to Spain before the discovery of America, and to America soon after, made its appearance on this continent the year before the Mayflower brought the Pilgrims to Plymouth Rock." Taylor, *The Origin and Growth of the American Constitution,* 254; "The only way by which that [slave] trade could be ultimately destroyed was by teaching the African chiefs that the employment of their dependent people in the production of the raw materials of cotton, would be more advantageous than the selling them into slavery for transportation to other parts of the world." Kettel, *Southern Wealth and Northern Profits,* 37.

61. Kettell, *Southern Wealth and Northern Profits,* 3.

in England. Moreover, history is very clear that while there were slave-trade and slave-practice dissenters in America and Europe, the entire world was demanding cotton (and other commodities) at a never-before-seen rate in world history—whether using it for production, for retail sale, or for consumption—including America's northern states, Europe, India, and China. Thus, the paradox was noted in *Southern Wealth and Northern Profits* concerning those who so strongly dissented against the slave practice for commerce, recognizing, "It is neither just nor dignified to buy this raw material from the Americans, and to revile them for producing it."[62] In other words, you cannot proclaim the injustice of using slaves for commercial purposes and then turn around and demand the very commodity which the slaves produced.

Undoubtedly, there are still Americans who would judge and condemn to hell those evil slave-holding tyrants of the South. However, if you condemn the South for its use of slaves, you must simultaneously condemn those in the North and those other nations who used slave products to manufacture. If you did so, then you would condemn the entire world. Do you even give any thought to the fact that American corporations such as Walmart use the workforce of people enslaved in countries like China, Mexico, and India to manufacture cheap products in mass, so that they can make a profit in the United States? Yes, slavery is alive and well in the world. Consider this historical fact: "All the wealth or capital existing has been the result of slave-labor, or of the working of capital originally derived from slave-labor. The history of the wealth and power of nations is but a record of slave products."[63] The founding fathers recognized that every society operates under cheap labor, just as America does today. Oliver Ellsworth of Connecticut observed during the Constitutional Convention debates that "as population increases [in America] poor laborers will be so plenty as to render slaves useless. Slavery in time will not be a speck in our Country."[64] What business owner does not recognize and acknowledge this fact? If a business owner has the ability to pay an employee five dollars per hour versus fifteen dollars

---

62. Ibid., 42.
63. Ibid., 10.
64. Ketcham, ed., *The Anti-Federalist Papers and the Constitutional Convention Debates*, 162.

per hour, which do you think he will likely choose? Duh. Indeed, America sees similar feudal classes in its sociological structure today, as the disparity between rich and poor continues to rise, and more and more people sign up to be on the dole of government handouts. Another thing: why do you think American corporations send all of their jobs to foreign nations? The answer is clear: cheap or slave labor. Today's America, like the northern colonies of yesteryear, is simply profiting from slaves by not having to pay high prices for American-made products. We willingly participate in this cycle still without dissent—but I digress.

The fact remains, once America won her independence from Great Britain, slavery was very quickly on its way out—not because Abraham Lincoln freed the slaves, but because of the foundational and natural principles of freedom which undergirded her society,[65] as well as the invention of manufacturing devices such as the cotton gin. What Thomas Jefferson said became true: "After the year 1800 of the Christian era, there shall be neither slavery nor involuntary servitude in any of the said States."[66] America's founders recognized the God-given natural right that an individual is born with freedom, and that with life naturally comes freedom. Thomas Jefferson further expressed this fact when he stated, "The God who gave us life, gave us liberty at the same time [and] the hand of force may destroy, but cannot disjoin them."[67] Just as God did not create freedom for the individual to abuse his neighbor's rights, God did not create freedom for government to

---

65. "No person hereafter coming into this country shall be held within the same in slavery under any pretext whatever." Jefferson, *The Jeffersonian Cyclopedia*, 812; "The abolition of Slavery seemed to be going on in the United States and that the good sense of the several States would probably by degrees comple[te] it." Ketcham, ed., *The Anti-Federalist Papers and the Constitutional Convention Debates*, 161. The previous was noted by founding father Roger Sherman during the Constitutional Convention debates on August 21 and 22, 1787; "[E]very master of slaves is born a petty tyrant. They bring the judgment of heaven on a Country. As nations can not be rewarded or punished in the next world they must be in this. By an inevitable chain of causes and effects providence punishes national sins, by national calamities." Ibid. Likewise, during the debates on the same day, founding father George Mason made the previous observation.

66. Jefferson, *The Jeffersonian Cyclopedia*, 811.

67. B. L. Rayner, *The Life of Thomas Jefferson*, (Boston, MA: Lilly, Wait, Colman & Holden, 1834), 65.

abuse liberty by taking the freedom from the individual. Suffice it to say at this point that freedom is inherent in the life of an individual, and that such freedom is expected to be used in the furtherance of the gifts of God: life and liberty.

Self-preservation and Defense

Let us explore another intrinsic aspect of human nature. That is: self-preservation. Man will attempt to preserve his life before any other consideration instinctive or reasoned in his mind. Do you need someone to tell you this? Not likely, but this fact reflects, once again, the other natural laws built into the system God has created, such as being born free with the ability to reason, to know, to think, to perform industry, to enjoy the work of your hands, and to prosper in general. You do not have to teach your child that touching fire is not good, that jumping off a level too high will hurt, that cutting yourself with a knife is not smart, that not eating food or drinking water for days will have a detrimental effect on your mind and body. Why? Because it is natural. Thus, government should reflect this very basic natural law in its principles and laws—in more ways than you would initially think (taxes, regulations, commerce, education, etc.)—and should never compete with it.

This natural law of self-preservation starts with the basic notion that the individual has the right and should never be deprived of the ability to protect himself and others from physical harm—whether against individuals or from government. If man has a choice between preserving his life or supporting a government that is detrimental to his life, what choice do you think will be the natural loyalty of that person? Of course, when the person is overcome with fear, then his natural inclination of self-preservation may actually cause him to choose slavery over freedom, because choosing freedom necessarily means fighting for it; and since he is not willing to die, he chooses to be a slave—called voluntary slavery. Of course, to voluntarily become the slave of another (whether government or individual) completely contradicts the natural and revealed laws of God. Scripture reveals that we are not to become the slaves of men, because we are not our own but are God's, and as such, we should no more arbitrarily give our liberties to men than we should give our life. "You were bought with a price; do not become slaves of men."[68] What can be said of those who believe that God grants to them freedom, and yet the same person will voluntarily give that freedom to other men, outside of and contrary to God's stated purposes of government? Certainly, *godliness* does not come to mind.

In such a situation, government violates all principles of self-preservation by putting itself at odds with the natural rights of its citizens. If man thought he could live a more prosperous life to provide for himself and his family, would he entertain that option at the expense of the government having its power reduced or even abolished? Certainly the individual will consider the interests of self-preservation before just about any other natural inclination. Thus, where man chooses to accept slavery over less government, such a fact indicates the overreaching and oppressing power that the government exerts over the minds of the citizens. It is only when times are good that people do not feel the overburdensome hand of government upon society. But when times are bad, the grip feels ever tighter because of its incessant need to subsist itself and its power at the cost of the citizens.

What good is liberty or property without life? And the same can be said about liberty: what good is life without liberty—which was the very sentiment of Patrick Henry. "Give me liberty or give me death!"[69] Indeed, it was this very basic and fundamental truth that gave grounds to America's founders when they drafted their *"Declaration of the Causes of Taking Up Arms,* [which] was designed as a manifesto to the world, justifying a resistance to the parent government [of Great Britain]."[70] However, before America's founders declared their rights under God's natural and revealed laws to resist tyranny, Enlightenment philosophers had thoroughly articulated these

---

68. 1 Corinthians 7:23 (ESV); "This freedom from absolute, arbitrary power, is so necessary to, and closely joined with a man's preservation, that he cannot part with it, but by what forfeits his preservation and life together: for a man, not having the power of his own life, cannot, by compact, or his own consent, enslave himself to any one, nor put himself under the absolute, arbitrary power of another, to take away his life, when he pleases. No body can give more power than he has himself; and he that cannot take away his own life, cannot give another power over it." Locke and Macpherson, ed., *Second Treatise of Government,* 17.

69. Ed. Edward Archibald Allen, *The World's Best Orations,* Vol. 7, (St. Louis, MO, Ferd Kaiser, 1901), 2477.

70. Rayner, *The Life of Thomas Jefferson,* 73.

points, such that our founders were extremely familiar with them. One such philosopher was Montesquieu, and in his writing he phrases the natural law of self-preservation like this:

> The law which, impressing on our minds the idea of a Creator, inclines us towards Him, is the first in importance, though not in order, of natural laws. Man in a state of nature would have the faculty of knowing, before he had acquired any knowledge. Plain it is that his first ideas would not be of a speculative nature; he would think of the preservation of his being, before he would investigate its origin…There would, therefore, be no danger of their attacking one another; peace would be the first law of nature.[71]

Notice how his preface for acknowledging the law of self-preservation is that man is a created being with certain natural laws imparted. This is always the starting point: that God created life. Once again, the recognition of God in society and government has nothing to do with religion but everything to do with freedom, because without God no rights exist. Montesquieu recognizes that before man desires to seek his origin (i.e., God), he desires to preserve his current existence—he desires to preserve himself and his family. It is only after a man has established peace that he is able to stop looking inward and start looking outward from himself to others and to God. While man is forced to look inward (job, economy, income, taxes, etc.) just to survive, he is utterly useless to society, and as a result, government becomes more oppressive, expansive, controlling, and tyrannical, because the citizens are unable to look outward, given their condition.

Thus, there must be some measure for individuals in society to easily preserve and protect themselves so that there is no fear of being eliminated (e.g., physically, financially, politically, etc.) by the unsuspected—even the government itself. Montesquieu further expounds the natural law of self-preservation and its relationship to government and describes man's natural desire to protect life—even from the government.

---

71. Montesquieu and Hawthorne, ed., *The Spirit of Laws,* 3, 4.

The political liberty of the subject is a tranquility of mind arising from the opinion each person has of his safety. In order to have this liberty, it is requisite the government be so constituted as one man need not be afraid of another. When the legislative and executive powers are united in the same person, or in the same body of magistrates, there can be no liberty...There is no liberty, if the judicial power be not separated from the legislative and executive. Were it joined with the legislative, the life and liberty of the subject would be exposed to arbitrary control.[72]

Going beyond the observation that men have a natural desire to live and to preserve life, Montesquieu applies this nature to the principle of government. Again, laws should reflect the nature and the principle of government. The principle here is that, given the nature of men to have tranquility in society, the government should be formed and should proceed in such a way as to give men the peace of mind of such tranquility relative to other men and to the power of government. Government should never place its interests in competition with those of its citizens. By way of illustrating this natural law applied to principle of government, one will observe that a government best conformed to that nature will separate and limit its powers of making the laws, enforcing the laws, and interpreting the laws. The danger is that a citizen in such a society must and will naturally fear the one-government entity that can pass a law on one hand and execute it on the other and interpret its validity. This is similar to the Old Testament arrangement

---

72. Ibid., 151–152; "[B]ecause it may be too great a temptation to human frailty, apt to grasp at power, for the same persons, who have the power of making laws, to have also in their hands the power to execute them, whereby they may exempt themselves from obedience to the laws they make, and suit the law, both in its making, and execution, to their own private advantage, and thereby come to have a distinct interest from the rest of the community, contrary to the end of society and government: therefore in well ordered commonwealths, where the good of the whole is so considered, as it ought, the legislative power is put into the hands of divers persons, who duly assembled, have by themselves, or jointly with others, a power to make laws, which when they have done, being separated again, they are themselves subject to the laws they have made; which is a new and near tie upon them, to take care, that they make them for the public good." Locke and Macpherson, ed., *Second Treatise of Government*, 76.

of the prophet, priest, king, and judge: no one entity had more control over the other—each was bound to its jurisdictional limits. All their powers were limited to their function given by God. Thus, where a government has no checks unto itself, such a scenario provides no security of the people's rights over a power strong enough to pass, execute, and interpret all in the same place. This principle applies to many other circumstances as well and forms the basis of many positions regarding the size of government, the limits, the form, the power, the redress, and the philosophy of government. It forms the foundation of positions on matters such as the right to keep and bear arms (and not just for hunting purposes); the right to be free from unlawful searches and seizures; the right to amend, alter, and abolish the government; the right to remove oath-breaching politicians; and the right to be free from regulation without representation—among others.

CASE IN POINT: THE RIGHT TO KEEP AND BEAR ARMS

God, the author of life and giver of self-preservation instincts, reveals this natural law of self-preservation, not only to meet the needs of the individual, but also to obtain the goal of societal tranquility. Jesus says in Luke 22:36 (ESV) to his disciples, "But now let the one who has a moneybag take it, and likewise a knapsack. And let the one who has no sword sell his cloak and buy one." If you have never read and considered this verse, perhaps you have considered the fallacious arguments by many in governmental and social entities to ban guns or to highly regulate guns,[73] because guns are bad and cause many unnecessary deaths (as if cars, alcohol, and even medical doctors do not do the same).[74] Perhaps these people have not been faced with a situation of having to defend their lives or the lives of their families. Perhaps these people have never faced a situation where their government treats God-given

---

73. "Registration is only a step. The prohibition of private firearms is the goal," said Janet Reno. Alan Scholl, "Gun Controllers Target Ammunition," *The New American,* January 22, 2009.

74. "Gun Control: We Need Government Control Not Gun Control," *Hard Truth Alternative News,* http://www.theforbiddenknowledge.com/hardtruth/guncontrol.htm (accessed May 5, 2009). Number of physicians in the US = 700,000. Accidental deaths caused by physicians per year =120,000. Accidental deaths per physician = 0.171 (U.S. Dept. of Health &

rights like a play toy to be used however they please. Without a doubt, Adolf Hitler's regime would not have had the same affect had Hitler not disarmed the Jewish population. As Walter Williams noted, "Before we surrender our guns, we should remember that history's most barbaric people were also gun-ban advocates. Adolf Hitler sought a strict ban on gun possession by Jews."[75] The recent true-story film, *Defiance*,[76] reflects just how the use of firearms was the *only* viable tool used by those Jews who sought to live in freedom, resisting the efforts of Hitler's army to subdue their attempts. Undoubtedly, without the possession and use of their firearms, that Jewish community, which grew to 1,200 by the end of the War World II, would never have survived.

Of course, America's own history reveals the same attempt by Great Britain to disarm the colonies to further enslave them. This fact is noted by founding father George Mason's daughter Kate Mason Rowland in her book, *The Life of George Mason*. She says,

When the resolution of enslaving America was formed in Great Britain, the British Parliament was advised by an artful man [Sir William Keith] who was governor of Pennsylvania, to disarm the people; that it was the best and most effectual way to enslave them; but that they should not do it openly, but weaken them, and let them sink gradually, by totally disusing and neglecting the militia.[77]

Today, the strategy to steal freedom is the same: the gradual sink. Indeed, the use of a weapon may in fact be the only manner in which a person may preserve the gift of life that God has given him or her. What person, using

---

Human Services). Number of gun owners in the US = 80,000,000. Number of accidental gun deaths per year (all age groups) =1,500. Accidental deaths per gun owner = 0.0000188 (U.S. Bureau of Alcohol, Tobacco & Firearms). Therefore, doctors are approximately 9,000 times more dangerous than gun owners.

75. Walter Edward Williams, *Do the Right Thing: The People's Economist Speaks,* (Standford, CA: Hoover Press, 1995), 150.

76. Clayton Frohman and Edward Zwick (screenplay), *Defiance,* Director: Edward Zwick; (Release Date: January 16, 2009).

77. Kate Mason Rowland and General Fitzhugh Lee, intro., *The Life of George Mason, 1725–1792,* vol. 2, (New York: G. P. Putnam's Sons, 1802), 409.

any common sense and knowledge of history, cannot understand that without the ability to defend oneself using the commonly held manner of defense (i.e., guns), there is no equality of the defense of God-given rights? Perhaps those who advocate such regulation and confiscation of our ability to defend our rights and freedoms are those same individuals, like Sir William Keith, who advocate the ultimate goal of enslaving those who prevent their agenda. Thomas Jefferson rightly observes that "no freeman shall be debarred the use of arms [within his own lands]."[78] The fact is guns have done more to give power to the weak and defenseless than any other tool in human history.

Before the manufacturing and common possession of guns, one would have to be a skillful fighter with the sword, spear, knife, or hands to confront challengers of freedom. Today, all are equal in self-defending power and ability with access to and use of modern firearms. Thomas Jefferson recognizes the equalizing power of the manufacture of guns by stating, "Since the invention of gunpowder has armed the weak as well as the strong with missile death, bodily strength…has become but an auxiliary ground of distinction."[79] Make no mistake, America's founders were not a bunch of barbaric, redneck men, which is how many modern-day pundits would characterize them for their demand that we the people of the several states be an armed populous. To the contrary, they possessed more intellect, education, and understanding than the combination of thousands of modern men—even politicians. The following is noted about Thomas Jefferson:

> At college Jefferson was distinguished by his close application, and devoted…from twelve to fifteen hours a day to study. He became well versed…in Latin, Greek, Italian, French, and Spanish, making at the same time a respectable proficiency in his mathematical studies. After a five years' course of law under Judge Wythe, he was admitted to the bar in 1767. His success in the legal profession was remarkable; his fees for the first year amounted to nearly three thousand dollars.[80]

---

78. Jefferson, *The Jeffersonian Cyclopedia*, 51.

79. Ibid., 48.

80. Joseph Thomas, *Universal Pronouncing Dictionary of Biography and Mythology*, 4th ed., vol. 2, (Philadelphia, PA: J. B. Lippincott Company, original from Princeton University, 1915), 1376.

Jefferson was not the only intellectually successful founder. Most of America's founders were similarly studied men of the world, commerce, politics, philosophy, religion, science, and math. As a result of their study and knowledge, they understood the importance of what the firearm brought to society, placing more power in the hands of the people—a requirement in a republican form of government. Indeed, how can the eighty-five-year-old woman or twelve-year-old girl defend herself against the twenty-five-year-old man who is doped up on drugs? Moreover, what citizenry could defend its freedoms against an armed, tyrannical government without bearing arms? And of course the examples are endless. Do not be deceived. Police protection can only go so far, and in the first place was not intended to protect individuals from all harm and all pending and imminent assaults. What do you do when the police do not respect God-given rights and instead comply with demands from their superiors to confiscate firearms, take into custody resistors, search homes illegally, etc.? Where is the legal appeal? Where is the practical protection? Where is the likelihood of success? Every person has a natural right—and yes, duty—to protect himself and his family. Jesus Himsel confirmed this in the aforementioned passage as well as others.

Enlightenment philosophers and America's founders understood the principle reflected by Jesus. Hugo Grotius points out the following fact concerning Jesus's command to buy a sword and recognized, using inductive reasoning, that if weapons were not lawful to use against those who assault the freedom and rights of others, then possessing such weapons would not be lawful either. For how can it be said that it is lawful to possess a thing if it is not lawful to use the same? "It would not be lawful to carry a sword if it were not lawful under any circumstances to use it."[81] Who is the anti-gun advocate to demand and who is the government to require that this right of self-preservation be regulated to the point of being nonexistent? Jesus did not intend that His disciples buy a sword to hang it over the fireplace, unloaded, with a safety lock, out of reach to the point of being worthless. Instead, it was to be used when necessary, just as described in Luke 11:21 (ESV): "When a strong man, fully armed, guards his own palace, his goods are safe." Without the ability to protect yourself, your family, your community,

81. Grotius, *Hugo Grotius on the Rights of War and Peace,* 32.

and your nation, the fear of tyranny and death is—or should be if you care about freedom—heightened, and the possibility of tranquility among men is stifled. As a result, the government contradicts natural law and its purpose.

It truly is no wonder that the people of America and consequently America's founders insisted on incorporating the Second Amendment in the Constitution, knowing and understanding human nature and government's duty to conform to this natural law and right of man. Our founders knew that freedom cannot exist except when its citizens have the ability to resist tyrants. "A well regulated Militia, being necessary to the security of a free State, the right of the people to keep and bear Arms, shall not be infringed."[82] And in case you are wondering: no, this is not an outdated idea. It still applies today because human nature still applies today. While some anti-natural right proponents would suggest that this right to bear arms only applies to militias, which according to them only means the military, as defined by the United States Code, such an interpretation not only contradicts what the drafters of the Constitution stated but also contradicts the plain language of the amendment.

Understand, the Constitution does not change the definition of militia or even create a militia. Rather, the Constitution presumes that a militia of the several states already exists. Nowhere in the Constitution does it authorize a "militia of the United States."[83] It only recognizes the existence of the "militia of the several states,"[84] which existed prior to the Constitution's

----

82. U.S. Constitution, amend. 2.

83. Compare to 10 U.S.Code, sec. 311, which presumes or attempts to create a "Militia of the United States." Interestingly, the U.S. Code uses the word "militia" in the context of the "armies of the United States," thus creating the illusion that the Second Amendment would only apply to the militias created by the federal government, the effect of which is what many argue today, that the Second Amendment right does not belong to the individual citizen, but only the military:

(a) The militia of the United States consists of all able-bodied males at least 17 years of age and, except as provided in section 313 of title 32, under 45 years of age who are, or who have made a declaration of intention to become, citizens of the United States and of female citizens of the United States who are members of the National Guard.

(b) The classes of the militia are:

(1) the organized militia, which consists of the National Guard and the Naval Militia; and

2) the unorganized militia, which consists of the members of the militia who are not members of the National Guard or the Naval Militia.

84. The President shall be Commander in Chief of the Army and Navy of the United States, and of the *Militia of the several States.*" U.S. Constitution, amend. 2, art. 2, sec. 2.

ratification. Make no mistake, the Constitution authorizes Congress to only raise and support armies—not militias—and once a declaration of war is passed by Congress, the president becomes the commander in chief of the Army and Navy of the United States and of the militia of the several states. Very clearly, there is a difference between the armies raised and supported by Congress and the militia of the several states, which is under the sovereignty of the states and which existed independent of the Constitution and federal government. Clearly, there is no such thing as a militia of the United States in the Constitution, even though the United States Code attempts to do such an unconstitutional thing.

This understanding was recognized by author Hannis Taylor, who writes,

> The roots of [the Second Amendment] strike down in to the past until they reach the Assize of Arms of Henry II (1181), whereby the old constitutional force was reorganized by the duty being imposed upon every free man, for the defense of the state, to provide himself arms according to his means…The object of Henry Assize of Arms was to reorganize and rearm the ancient force as a body safer and more trustworthy for national defense than the feudal host. According to "The Federalist" this limitation indicates that the security of liberty against the tyrannical tendencies of power is only to be found in the right of the people to keep and bear arms with which to resist oppression.[85]

Taylor continued in his historical observations of the Second Amendment, pointing out the U.S. Supreme Court case regarding the security of the entire Republic. "In *Presser v. Illinois* [116 U.S. 252 (1886)] the Supreme Court—after holding that the provision, that 'the right of the people to keep and bear arms shall not be infringed,' is a limitation only on the powers of Congress and the National Government—declared that in view of the fact that all citizens capable of bearing arms constitute the reserved military force of the National Government as well as in view of its general powers,

---

85. Hannis Taylor, *The Origin and Growth of the American Constitution,* (Boston and New York: Houghton Mifflin Co., 1911), 232–233.

the states cannot prohibit the people from keeping and bearing arms, so as to deprive the United States of their rightful resource for maintaining the public security."[86]

Had the Second Amendment intended to create a right of only the military to keep and bear arms, the founders would have expressed such intent, because such an interpretation was totally contrary to historical and legal context of 1787 and to the plain reading of the Constitution and Second Amendment. However, the founders expressed no such intent but only confirmed the right that we the people of the several states had previously and perpetually possessed, and that is the right to keep and bear arms. "To the founding fathers, '[a] well regulated Militia' was organized, armed, disciplined, trained, and governed according to the precepts and practices of the pre-constitutional Colonial and State Militia Acts—for the Militia under those Acts were the only ones the Founders knew and in which most of them had actually served."[87] To suggest that we the people of the several states—individually and collectively—do not have the right to keep and bear arms makes the Second Amendment noneffectual and places the power of we the people of the several states into the hands of the armies of the United States and the unconstitutional creation of the militia of the United States, creating the fertile ground from which tyranny grows—a national police state—which was warned about by America's founders.

For hundreds of years prior to the adoption of the Constitution, the people of the colonies comprised the militia and were in fact very leery of standing armies per se, which was discussed thoroughly in the Anti-Federalist Papers and Federalist Papers.[88] "Moreover, no statute in that era ever gener-

---

86. Ibid., 233.

87. Edwin Vieira, *Constitutional Homeland Security: A Call for Americans to Revitalize "The Militia of the Several States," vol. 1: The Nation in Arms,* (Ashland, OH: BookMasters, Inc., 2007), 47–48.

88. "The liberties of a people are in danger from a large standing army, not only because the rulers may employ them for the purposes of supporting themselves in any usurpations of power, which they may see proper to exercise, but there is great hazard, that an army will subvert the forms of the government, under whose authority, they are raised, and establish one, according to the pleasure of their leader…We are informed, in the faithful pages of history, of such events frequently happening. Two instances have been mentioned in a former paper. They are so remarkable, that they are worthy of the most careful attention of every lover of freedom.

ally disbarred any free men or women from themselves possessing firearms in their homes, or from carrying them abroad for any legitimate reason unrelated to the Militia."[89] The drafters of our Constitution repeatedly confirmed the right of the individual to bear arms because of the tendency that men in power have to abuse their power and to contradict their people-given and God-given purpose in government. This is a common-sense and plain-reading understanding as well. How else can we retain power over the government without the means to ensure and protect that power? Of course, using the modernist and Darwinian philosophies of might makes right would even solidify the fact that we the people of the several states individually and collectively retain the right to keep and bear arms for the mere purpose of maintaining the might over government. Remember, the Second Amendment was designed to protect the freedom of the people of the several states from enemies, both *domestic* and foreign, as reflected by the Constitution. As such, we need a means to secure our liberty other than and outside the legal process, because men live in a state of nature when no redress or appeal can be made or is noneffectual—that is guns, ammunition, and other means of defense. Indeed, there may come a time when we must say, as Patrick Henry did, "An appeal to arms and to the God of Hosts is all that is left us!"[90] Without the people being equipped with arms, the security of a free state vanishes, and the natural law of self-preservation is contradicted.

They are taken from the history of the two most powerful nations that have ever existed in the world; and who are the most renowned, for the freedom they enjoyed, and the excellency of their constitutions: I mean Rome and Britain... As standing armies in time of peace are dangerous to liberty, and have often been the means of overturning the best constitutions of government, no standing army, or troops of any description whatsoever, shall be raised or kept up by the legislature, except so many as shall be necessary for guards to the arsenals of the United States, or for garrisons to such posts on the frontiers, as it shall be deemed absolutely necessary to hold, to secure the inhabitants, and facilitate the trade with the Indians: unless when the United States are threatened with an attack or invasion from some foreign power, in which case the legislature shall be authorised to raise an army to be prepared to repel the attack; provided that no troops whatsoever shall be raised in time of peace, without the assent of two thirds of the members, composing both houses of the legislature." Brutus and Ketcham, *The Anti-Federalist Papers and the Constitutional Convention Debates*, 287, 291.

89. Vieira, *Constitutional Homeland Security*, 44.

90. Compiled by a Member of the Philadelphia Bar, *American Oratory*, 15.

CASE IN POINT: THE WELFARE STATE

Of course, this matter of self-preservation extends much further than the ability to possess firearms, ammunition, and other tactical weapons. It includes facilitating self-responsibility, self-governance, and independence. It includes facilitating society's ability to contract freely; to retain the equally agreed to bargains; to receive the most return for one's efforts; to take risks and dare to explore and create; to work effectively, efficiently, and proficiently without undue burdens. It includes rewarding good behavior and repudiating bad behavior—both criminally and civilly. It includes creating a system and philosophy of laws that promotes self-reliance, wealth-creation, family and community unity, and care. It stays away from taking from those who have and giving to those who have not, especially where those who have not do nothing to earn what is redistributed to them. It keeps taxes at a minimum and promotes control over matters that should be handled by those who know the issues best: that is those who are mostly affected by its decisions and consequences.

To further promote tranquility and peace in a community, which is based upon the fundamental natural law of self-preservation, God set forth standards in His word of conduct conducive to such tranquility and peace. God tells us in Galatians 5:1 (ESV), "For freedom Christ has set us free; stand firm therefore, and do not submit again to a yoke of slavery." And furthermore in Galatians 5:13 (ESV), God tells us that we are "called to freedom… Only do not use your freedom as an opportunity for the flesh, but through love serve one another."

So if God requires that people use their freedom wisely and responsibly, how much less should a government use their power in the same manner? In 2 Thessalonians 3:10 (ESV), work ethic is demanded for the sake of peace. "For even when we were with you, we would give you this command: If anyone is not willing to work, let him not eat." The same is commanded in 2 Thessalonians 3:12 (ESV). "Now such persons we command and encourage in the Lord Jesus Christ to do their work quietly and to earn their own living." So what should be said of a government whose goal is wealth distribution—taking from some and giving to others? How can it be argued that government is complying with the natural law of self-preservation when it uses principles of injustice to take money from those who work for it and give it to those who do not? And please, spare us the argument that there are those in society who need help, and the federal government has to tax those who can afford it to give to those who cannot work.

The federal government's approach and the results prove that such an argument is not reality, and that the vast majority of those receiving welfare benefits have created their own plight through laziness, crimes committed, lethargy, indifference, and every other attitude that creates a lack of pride, motivation, entrepreneurship, achievement, or otherwise. Case in point: just look at the percentage of criminals who are appointed public defenders at taxpayers' cost. These (and others with similar character) are the same people for whom hard-working Americans provide food, shelter, and healthcare, as well. How does the government expect honest, self-sacrificing, hard-working Americans to respect the government when the government does not show the same respect to them! Shortly put, Americans are (or should be) sick and tired of the government violating the most basic and fundamental natural law of self-preservation by making it more and more difficult for the average Joe to provide for his own needs and those of his family. If the government is so concerned about treating people with equality, let us start with the basics: do not give special treatment to those leeches in society who do not deserve respect or honor, much less handouts.

It does not take a philosopher to see the problems that would be eliminated by citizens taking care of their own matters and not relying on the government to take care of them. By the same token, these same problems could be eliminated by the federal government getting out of the matters that belong to the families, the communities, and the states respectively to address and remedy. It is a simple matter of self-responsibility, which proceeds from self-preservation. In other words, I have a personal responsibility to ensure the well-being of myself and my family, and I have no right to insist that others take care of me. For the government to represent and advocate those who indulge in such an attitude contradicts natural law and the purpose of our government. Government's job is to implement the natural law of self-preservation by promoting self-responsibility, self-initiative, self-reliance, and self-security. The form and substance of government should reflect these self-governance principles and should refrain from socialistic and communistic agenda and policy, which take most of the control, ownership, and freedom of property and decisions from society and place them in the hands of government.

Unfortunately, America has been groomed to accept and cherish social-istic and communistic philosophies of government. It is so easy to see. Any time there is a government handout, the lines fill up faster than a theater showing a blockbuster movie. This applies to the poor and rich alike; to the small business and big business alike; and to the Christian and non-Christian alike. At any given opportunity, people seek government assistance, contri-bution, grants, and endorsements, including the very basics of life: finances, food, and shelter. Of course, it applies to banks, lending institutions, car manufacturers, and who knows what other industry will be next. These ideas are the very essence of socialism and communism—taking self-responsibility and God out of the picture for the family's sustenance and replacing them with the all-powerful, all-knowing state.

Of course, we hear a lot from our politicians telling us that they must bailout these failing companies, because if they do not, the economy will collapse. How convenient. The government gets to give taxpayer dollars to corrupt globalist corporates for events that their policies, laws, regula-tions, and philosophy have created. The effect: socialized economy and banks, depressed economic market, asset reduction, debt and inflation increase,[91] all making it more difficult on the average citizen to merely sur-vive.[92] In fact, consider how many of the goals presented in the *Communist*

---

91. "An eye-popping $1.75 trillion deficit for the 2009 fiscal year underlined the heavy blow the deep recession has dealt to the country's finances as Obama unveiled his first budget. That is the highest ever in dollar terms, and amounts to a 12.3 percent share of the economy—the largest since 1945. In 2010, the deficit would dip to a still-huge $1.17 trillion, Obama predicted." Caren Bohan and Jeff Mason, "Obama Budget Plan Forecasts Soaring Deficits," *NewsDaily,* (February 26, 2009), http://www.newsdaily.com/stories/tre51o6ja-us-obama-budget/ (accessed May 5, 2009).

92. "The German experience in the early 1920s provides a sobering object lesson as to the extensive and intensive damage hyperinflation can inflict on even a well-developed nation with a culturally sophisticated populace. For no historically literate person doubts that this disaster contributed significantly to the rise of Hitlerism, with all its horrific consequences. To expect cause and effect to differ markedly in the United States today would be imprudent to the level of recklessness." Vieira, *Constitutional Homeland Security,* 7.

Manifesto[93] (a movement that America vehemently opposed in years gone past) that America has apparently adopted and advanced:

1. Abolition of property in land and application of all rents of land to public purposes.
2. A heavy progressive or graduated income tax.
3. Abolition of all rights of inheritance.
4. Confiscation of the property of all emigrants and rebels.
5. Centralization of credit in the banks of the state by means of a national bank with state capital and an exclusive monopoly.
6. Centralization of the means of communication and transport in the hands of the state.
7. Extension of factories and instruments of production owned by the state; the bringing into cultivation of wastelands, and the improvement of the soil generally in accordance with a common plan.
8. Equal obligation of all to work. Establishment of industrial armies, especially for agriculture.
9. Combination of agriculture with manufacturing industries; gradual abolition of all the distinction between town and country by a more equable distribution of the populace over the country.
10. Free education for all children in public schools. Abolition of children's factory labor in its present form. Combination of education with industrial production, etc.

Contrary to the basic and fundamental nature of humans to preserve self, America's government has (among other atrocities) created several generations that do not attempt to preserve their self by the means commanded by God but rather by the ever-caring, ever-nurturing nanny state. Do we even realize that America is more communist than republican in philosophy and more globalist than independent in practice? Understand, this philosophy is contrary to natural and revealed law. "But if anyone does not provide for his

---

93. Karl Marx, Friedrich Engels, and Gareth Stedman Jones, ed., intr., *The Communist Manifesto,* (New York: Penguin Classics, 2002).

relatives, and especially for members of his household, he has denied the faith and is worse than an unbeliever."[94] Pretty strong and equally clear language. God expects the individual—not the government—to take care of his own matters and his own family. When the government creates policy that conflicts with this principle, it continually places its own interests and agenda at conflict with the sovereigns of the several states.

Speaking of unnatural, in no other forum could you demand or expect to be provided for than in a government that has taxed others excessively to provide for your needs. In other words, it is the "take from the rich and give to the poor" philosophy. There are circumstances, of course, where people need help. We have all been there. However, outside of the family or close-friend setting, most help is obtained through private contracts where the helper expects some return and performance from the person being helped. What is wrong with that? Otherwise, what incentive does the recipient of tax-funded care have to better himself? But again, human nature reveals that the individual should provide for himself, and God's word demands that we comply with that law. "But let each one test his own work, and then his reason to boast will be in himself alone and not in his neighbor."[95] Also, "It is the hard-working farmer who ought to have the first share of the crops."[96] Ask yourself: does America conform to this natural law of man and revealed law of God? Government bailout, social welfare, social security income tax, faith-based initiatives, Planned Parenthood, foreign aid, and federal programs galore should all ring a bell.[97] Today, what does not ring a bell is America's formerly accepted ideology concerning self-governance, as expressed by former United States Supreme Court justice Robert H. Jackson, when he stated in his legal opinion in *American Communications Association v. Douds*, "It is not the function of our Government to keep the citizen from falling into error; it is the function of the citizen to keep the Government from falling into error."[98]

---

94. Timothy 5:8 (ESV).

95. Galatians 6:4 (ESV).

96. Timothy 2:6 (ESV).

97. Compare to Thomas Jefferson's statement: "It is error alone which needs the support of government. Truth can stand by itself." Jefferson, *The Jeffersonian Cyclopedia*, 888.

98. *American Communications Association v. Douds*, 339 U.S. 382, 442 (1950).

CASE IN POINT: THE FIAT MONEY SYSTEM

Unfortunately, America's government has created laws, agencies, and policies that contradict the most fundamental notion of self-preservation, even with the most commonly used item in society: money. Make no mistake about it, America's current form of currency contradicts the natural law of self-preservation and furthermore violates Article 1, Sections 8 and 10 of the U.S. Constitution.[99] We currently operate our money system under the most vulnerable and fail-sure manner known to mankind. The system operates under fiat money, which is supported, backed, and secured by *nothing*! Proverbs 11:1 (ESV) comes to mind when considering that a fiat system devalues what every working person deserves and expects to possess when exchanging their services for currency: "A false balance is an abomination to the LORD, but a just weight is his delight." How can the people of the several states and their supposed representatives accept and advance a monetary system that has historically proven to be very vulnerable and jeopardous? Moreover, the system itself is unconstitutionally controlled by seven unelected persons, who are essentially and practically uncontrolled by Congress thanks to the unconstitutionally enacted Federal Reserve Act of 1913.[100] As noted by Professor John Holdsworth in 1914, "It is obvious that a board clothed with such powers can exercise an enormous influence either for good or ill upon the new system. Success or failure...will depend largely upon their ability, wisdom, and tact."[101] Reality check here: the entire nation's financial success is resting on the decisions of seven people, totally unaccountable to the people of the several states and in total contradiction to human history and natural law!

Most Americans do not even know the seriousness of the problem this fiat system causes. Unfortunately, most do not seem to care. If you think

---

99. "The Congress shall have Power to coin Money, regulate the Value thereof, and of foreign Coin, and fix the Standard of Weights and Measures." U.S. Constitution, art. 1, sec. 8. "No State shall...coin Money; emit Bills of Credit; make any Thing but gold and silver Coin a Tender in Payment of Debts." U.S. Constitution, art. 1, sec. 10.

100. "The [Federal Reserve] Act creates a Federal Reserve Board of seven members with sweeping powers of supervision and control over the new system." John Thom Holdsworth, *Money and Banking*, 6th Edition, (New York: Appleton, 1914), 351.

101. Ibid., 353.

differently, consider America's response to 2008 Republican presidential candidate Ron Paul as he attempted to inform America of the vulnerability of our fiat money system and that it was a necessity to get back to the gold standard money system that America once had when the value of America's money was secure and foundational. Today, not only is our money not secure, but it is controlled by seven unelected, uncontrolled people. Since when did the sovereigns of the several states give so much authority over our entire economic operation and stability to this group of seven? What a sham! This contradicts the very fundamental concepts of limited power, separation of powers, federalism, etc., because where so much power is placed in the hands of so few without the people retaining ultimate power, the people live in tyranny and are susceptible to many evils. If this principle is not true, then why does America not go ahead and allow the powers that be to choose their king to rule over us?

Think about the history lessons that we are ignoring: "Through a long period of evolution the great commercial nations have come to regard gold as the commodity best fitted to serve as a standard."[102] The most basic economics lesson reveals that money is simply a means of transferring and measuring commodities (with money itself being a commodity—e.g., gold). As such, the American people could once say with confidence, "At the present time the gold dollar is the money standard of this country."[103] Thus, the dollar (the means of transferring commodities and services) could actually be redeemed in gold (the value of transfer). "All parts of our circulating medium are in practice interchangeable, and are exchangeable directly or indirectly for gold coin, the legal standard."[104] Try turning in your dollar for gold today and see what happens; the bank tellers will laugh you out of the building. So if you cannot exchange your dollars for actual values of commodity, then what makes your dollar worth anything at all? What is the effect then? The effect is that the fiat money system has replaced sound money principles with that of unstable, unsound, and unreal principles. Even now, we see the collapse of the dollar taking place right before our eyes. Of course, most probably assume that a dip in the market always recovers. Oh really?

---

102. Ibid., 16.
103. Ibid., 14.
104. Ibid., 15.

Consider this as well: the word *dollar* is mentioned in the Constitution under Article 1, Section 9, Clause 1 and in the Seventeenth Amendment. Consider also that the word *dollar* is never defined in the Constitution. Why is it not? Because the definition of dollar already existed and had been in practice in the colonies years before the Constitution was even written. Alexander Hamilton, as the first secretary of treasury, reflects the founding fathers' understanding of what a dollar was in his writing, *On the Establishment of a Mint,* which Congress commissioned him to complete regarding the establishment of a uniform mint standard in the United States. In this writing, Hamilton answers the question: what ought to be the nature of the money unit of the United States? In his answer to that question, Hamilton acknowledges and confirms the fact that gold and silver were and should be the money standard in the United States. He never accedes that the dollar was anything other than the use of gold or silver coins. He says,

> A prerequisite to determining with propriety what ought to be the money unit of the United States, is to endeavor to form as accurate an idea as the nature of the case will admit, of what it actually is. The pound, though of various value, is the unit in the money account of all the States… There being no formal regulation on the point…it can only be inferred from the usage or practice[105]… An additional reason for considering the prevailing dollar as the standard of the present money unit, rather than the ancient one, is, that it will not only be conformable to the true existing proportion between the two metals [gold and silver] but will be more conformable to that which obtains in the commercial world generally.[106]

Additionally, notice that Hamilton observes the current market practices to make a determination of not only what a dollar was but also what its weights and measures should be. Thus, when the Constitution mentions the word dollar, it does not imply anything other than what was already

---

105. Alexander Hamilton and Henry Cabot Lodge, ed., *The Works of Alexander Hamilton in Twelve Volumes,* Volume 4, (New York: G. P. Putnam's Sons, 1904), 7.

106. Ibid., 10.

accepted. A dollar meant gold and silver coins as minted by the United States and the states respectively. James Madison confirms this pre-existing definition and understanding of dollar in Federalist Paper #42.

> All that need be remarked on the power to coin money, regulate the value thereof, and of foreign coin, is, that by providing for this last case, the Constitution has supplied a material omission in the articles of Confederation. The authority of the existing Congress is restrained to the regulation of coin STRUCK by their own authority, or that of the respective States. It must be seen at once that the proposed uniformity in the VALUE of the current coin might be destroyed by subjecting that of foreign coin to the different regulations of the different States. The punishment of counterfeiting the public securities, as well as the current coin, is submitted of course to that authority which is to secure the value of both. The regulation of weights and measures is transferred from the articles of Confederation, and is founded on like considerations with the preceding power of regulating coin.[107]

History confirms that the gold-and-silver-standard dollar existed prior to and is independent of the Constitution. It is just as the word *year* mentioned in the Constitution is independent of the Constitution and cannot be changed by the Constitution. In other words, a three-fourth majority of states cannot ratify a constitutional amendment, redefining year to mean one thousand days. Why? Because the term year has a predetermined and fixed meaning and understanding. The same is true for dollar. So where in the Constitution does it give authority to the federal government to replace the best money system in the world (the gold/silver standard) with the worst (the fiat dollar)? Nowhere! This fact is recognized by author Thomas F. Wilson in *The Power "To Coin" Money* when he states, "Specifically absent from the [U.S. Constitution]…are powers granted to the Congress for the emission

---

107. James Madison, "Federalist Paper 42," in *The Federalist Papers,* Hamilton, Jay, and Madison, 330, 331.

of paper money...and for the incorporation of a bank."[108] His observation is correct. That the founding fathers expressly disallowed the federal government and the states to emit paper is clear when considering that during the Constitutional Convention of 1787 the first drafts of the Constitution initially allowed Congress to "emit bills."[109] The words *emit bills* were subsequently removed after much opposition for purposes expressed by the founding fathers. Consider the following positions held by our founding fathers on the issue of Congress and the states issuing unfunded (fiat) paper money:[110]

> To emit an unfunded paper as the sign of value ought not to continue a formal part of the constitution, nor ever, hereafter, to be employed; being, in its nature, pregnant with abuses, and liable to be made the engine of imposition and fraud; holding out temptations equally pernicious to the integrity of government and to the morals of the people. (Benjamin Franklin)

> If the United States have credit, such bills will be unnecessary; if they have not, they will be unjust and useless. (Gouverneur Morris)[111]

> Morris on the fifteenth recited the history of paper emissions and the perseverance of the legislative assemblies in repeating them, though well aware of all their distressing effects, and drew the inference that, were the national legislature formed and a war to break out, this ruinous expedient [of issuing a fiat paper money], if not guarded against, would be again resorted to.

---

108. Thomas Frederick Wilson, *The Power "To Coin" Money: The Exercise of Monetary Powers by the Congress,* (Armonk, NY: M. E. Sharpe, 1992), 3.

109. Brutus and Ketcham, *The Anti-Federalist Papers and the Constitutional Convention Debates,* 138. The first draft of Article 7, Section 1, originally stated that "The Legislature of the United States shall have the power to borrow money, and emit bills on the credit of the United States." The final draft ratified by the Constitution states in part that Congress has the power "to borrow Money on the credit of the United States."

110. George Bancroft, *History of the United States of America: From the Discovery of the Continent [to 1789],* Volume 6, (New York: D. Appleton and Company, 1890), 301–303.

111. Ibid., 302.

[George] Mason of Virginia had a mortal hatred to paper money.

This is a favorable moment to shut and bar the door against paper money, which can in no case be necessary. The power may do harm, never good. Give the government credit, and other resources will offer. (Oliver Ellsworth)

Paper money can never succeed while its mischiefs are remembered; and, as long as it can be resorted to, it will be a bar to other resources. (James Wilson)

Rather than give the power [to Congress to emit bills] I would reject the whole plan [of the Constitution]. (John Langdon)

[Under the ratified version of the U.S. Constitution,] the pretext for a paper currency, and particularly for making the bills a tender, either for public or private debts, was cut off. (James Madison)

[Nathanial] Gorham favored striking the words [in the Constitution, allowing Congress to "emit bills"] without a prohibition inserted in the document, feeling that if the words were to stand, this could lead to the issuance of paper money.[112]

Pierce Butler remarked that paper money was a legal tender in no other country in Europe, and he wanted to disarm the government of such power.[113]

George Read stated that if the words [and emit bills] were not struck, it would be as alarming as the mark of the beast in Revelation.[114]

After reflecting on the views (as described herein) regarding the issuance of a fiat paper money, author George Bancroft summarizes the founding

---

112. Wilson, *The Power "To Coin" Money,* 80.
113. Ibid.
114. Ibid.

fathers' position on the Constitution's relation to paper money this way: "This is the interpretation of the [Article 1, Section 8] clause, made at the time of its adoption alike by its authors and by its opponents, accepted by all the statesmen of that age, not open to dispute because too clear for argument, and never disputed so long as any one man who took part in framing the constitution remained alive. History can not name a man who has gained enduring honor by causing the issue of paper money."[115] The founding fathers' views on this matter are simply reflections of what the world's lessons of economics concluded regarding the use of gold and silver as legal tender. Bancroft further describes the dangers of the use of fiat money this way:

> Paper money has no hold, and from its very nature can acquire no hold, on the conscience or affections of the people. It impairs all certainty of possession, and taxes none so heavily as the class who earn their scant possession by daily labor. It injures the husbandman by a twofold diminution of the exchangeable value of his harvest. It is the favorite of those who seek gain without willingness to toil; it is the deadly foe of industry. No powerful political party ever permanently rested for support on the theory that it is wise and right. No statesman has been thought well of by his kind in a succeeding generation for having been its promoter.[116]

Until 1913, such a view was understood and shared by most American citizens and politicians. To allow Congress to change the definition, meaning, and use of the dollar is to usurp power not granted to it by the Constitution. It is to change the meaning of dollar as reflected in the Constitution and effectively strip the value of the commodity and commercial reliability from the sovereigns of the several states. Moreover, using the fiat money system deprives all American citizens of their security in their labor, commodities, property, contracts, and commerce. An argument can be made that its use is criminal and fraudulent. Such a position has been accepted as fact by virtually

---

115. Ibid., 303.
116. Bancroft, *History of the United States of America*, 304.

every generation of every society in human history. However, current America ignores this fact. America has seen and is seeing the negative effects of our fiat money system take place—and it has been created by America's government.

So the question begs: does our government intend to facilitate sound money principles for the people? If the answer is yes, then another question begs: why does our government reject what has been proven to be the most reliable form of economic stability in human history? Certainly we elect educated-enough public officials in government who have studied economics and who realize that the fiat money system is without a doubt not conducive to economic stability. Given this presumed fact, the question begs: why does our government choose to set us up for economic failure? Even more basic than that question is why does our government refuse to obey the Constitution? After all, America's leaders were not always this way. Thomas Jefferson warned us of using fiat money when he said, "Admit none but a metallic circulation that will take its proper level with the like circulation in other countries."[117] And for years, we followed his advice. Not anymore.

Looking at the constitutional issue a little further, observe that Article 1, Section 10 mandates that the several states shall not "make any thing but gold and silver a legal tender in payment of debts." This means that the states cannot make or accept any other dollar commodity other than gold or silver as legal tender for debts. Thus, the federal government imposing upon the states the requirement that they accept legal tender in payment of debts other than gold and silver, such as the fiat money that is used today, violates the Constitution and assumes powers not granted to the federal government. Today, the federal government is assuming powers (not given to it in the U.S. Constitution) by creating national banks and emitting a fiat paper currency. The fact is, all powers not expressly given to the federal government are expressly reserved to the states and the citizens of the states. Well, since the states are prohibited from accepting or making anything but gold and silver as legal tender in payments of debts, since the Constitution does not expressly give Congress the power to create fiat paper currency, and since the Tenth Amendment reserves all powers not expressly granted to the federal

---

117. Jefferson, *The Jeffersonian Cyclopedia,* 579.

government to the states, then there is no, absolutely no constitutional way that the federal government possesses any such power to create a fiat paper currency. However, what do we see in America? We see the federal government assuming powers that do not exist in any shape, manner, or form. This legal and factual contradiction is noted by author Thomas Willet in *Political Business Cycles.*

> It is the official position of the U.S. Treasury that article 1, section 10 denies the states the power to issue fiat money, but that, since there is no clause in the Constitution which *explicitly* prohibits Congress from issuing it, Congress may do so! Note the inversion here of the Constitution's Tenth Amendment. Whereas the Tenth Amendment reserves to the states those powers not expressly granted to the federal government, the Treasury's position is that, though fiat money powers were denied to the states, the federal government has such powers.[118]

What a racket! The historical evidence on this matter is so overwhelming, yet it is almost ignored by most Americans and of course politicians (with few exceptions). The use of gold and silver as the value and transfer standard of money had been practiced in the colonies many years before the United States Constitution was ratified, and it was even provided for in the Articles of Confederation. It is worth noting that the United States Constitution did not change the Articles of Confederation regarding what money is but simply changed the source in which the minting of money was to take place from the individual states to Congress. This is confirmed in Federalist Paper No. 44.

> The right of coining money, which is here taken from the States, was left in their hands by the Confederation, as a concurrent right with that of Congress, under an exception in favor of the exclusive right of Congress to regulate the alloy and value. In this instance,

---

118. Thomas D. Willett, *Political Business Cycles: The Political Economy of Money, Inflation, and Unemployment,* (Durham, NC: Duke University Press, 1988), 428.

also, the new provision is an improvement on the old. Whilst the alloy and value depended on the general authority, a right of coinage in the particular States could have no other effect than to multiply expensive mints and diversify the forms and weights of the circulating pieces.

The latter inconveniency defeats one purpose for which the power was originally submitted to the federal head; and as far as the former might prevent an inconvenient remittance of gold and silver to the central mint for recoinage, the end can be as well attained by local mints established under the general authority... In addition to these persuasive considerations, it may be observed, that the same reasons which show the necessity of denying to the States the power of regulating coin, prove with equal force that they ought not to be at liberty to substitute a paper medium in the place of coin... The power to make any thing but gold and silver a tender in payment of debts, is withdrawn from the States, on the same principle with that of issuing a paper currency.[119]

Thus, the understanding and use of the dollar were not changed by the Constitution but were rather confirmed and reestablished by it. As such, the Constitution only provides for the use of gold and silver as the value of money and transfer standard. While the constitutionality issue is not necessarily the subject of discussion, noting the obvious and inherent fallacies within our money system reveals how far the people of the several states have come from the roots and foundation of America—from natural law. America's founders revered natural law and attempted to shape this nation around its principles. One such issue was the issue of money. America's founders relied upon the lessons of history to avoid the pitfalls that a fiat money system would create. Today, America's leaders are not that astute. Consequently, America stays at risk of more harm than we could imagine. Undoubtedly, history (even America's own history) proves that our current fiat money system is the least-stable, least-valuable, most-abused, most-manipulated, most-inflated, and

---

119. James Madison, "Federalist Paper 44," in *The Federalist Papers*, Hamilton, Jay, and Madison, 347–349.

most-destructive currency (as opposed to the other two forms of currency: *commodity*[120] and *trust*[121]). So why do we put up with this contradiction of good sense, constitutional provision, and natural law?

This principle of self-preservation is as basic as "1–2–3," but every fortress must have a foundation. Like a seed planted in the ground, from tiny matter to a tree with branches all around, it is the fundamentals that must be planted before the principles can blossom. Grotius quotes Cicero in the following:

> There is a First Principle of Self-preservation [with reference to Natural Law]…the first business of each is to preserve himself in the state of nature; the next, to retain what is according to nature, and

---

120. "[Gold] is subject to less fluctuation in value than most other commodities, however, and so is best suited to serve as standard money. Long experience has shown that gold and silver possess these desirable qualities in a larger measure than other commodities; consequently they have come into universal use as money… Gold and, to a lesser degree, silver have a greater stability of value than most other commodities because of the comparatively limited supply and the elasticity of demand for them." Holdsworth, *Money and Banking*, 9.

121. "Inconvertible or fiat currency. Inconvertible paper money consists of notes promising to pay money to the bearer, but not actually redeemable in specie. Such paper may be issued by banks as well as by governments. It is known as fiat money, because its use as money depends upon the fiat or command of the government. The essence of fiat money lies in the lack of expectation or intention of redeeming it in specie and in the artificial regulation of the amount issues. It circulates 'either because the people have no better money, and the quantity of it is so limited that its evils do not yet appear, or because the Government is strong enough to compel its citizens to accept the paper.' Usually governments in issuing this kind of paper seek to strengthen it by making it legal tender for debts and by making it receivable for taxes and other public dues. Inconvertible government notes have usually been resorted to only in times of great fiscal need, when the government has found it difficult to raise necessary funds by the usual methods of taxation or loans. *Many countries have had disastrous experiences with this form of currency.* Most of the American colonies issued 'bills of credit' to meet the expenses of the French and Indian Wars. This appeared to be such an easy method of raising money that some of the colonies used it to meet ordinary current needs. As larger and larger issues of these notes were authorized, without any provision being made for their redemption, they declined in value until they became practically worthless. A similar situation arose during the Revolutionary War, when both the separate colonies and the Continental Congress issued great quantities of irredeemable paper. Continental notes so depreciated that they were quoted in 1781 at 225 to 1 in coin. After the adoption of the Constitution they were made redeemable at the rate of one cent to the dollar." Ibid., 42–43, (emphasis added).

to reject what is contrary to it... The first Principle [of self-preservation] commends us to Right Reason... Hence in examining what agrees with Natural Law, we must first see what agrees with that first principle of self-preservation; and afterwards proceed to that which, though subsequent in origin, is of greater dignity; and must not only accept it, if it be offered, but seek it with all care.[122]

In other words, the nature and principle must comport with and begin with the basics. That is, man has the right to self-preservation, and government should facilitate independence and enable the individual to become as self-sufficient as possible. It should not condition an entire society with multiple generations to rely and depend on the government to replace what natural and revealed law has commanded the individual to be responsible for.

Live in Peace—Society

Government must also conform to humans' natural social connection and interaction, which actually derives from the previous discussion concerning self-preservation. With the natural desire and need for society and the natural law of self-preservation, the logical deduction follows that man desires to live in peace with his community. "Society has for its object, that every one may have what is his own in safety, by the common help and agreement... Therefore, it is not contrary to the nature of Society to take care of the future for one's self, so that the Rights of others be not infringed."[123] This law is the precondition basis for and germinating seed from which the formation of government springs. It is only man's desire to preserve self and the need to live in communities to enhance that desire of self-preservation that government is even needed from the perspective of natural law.

As Creator of man, God knew that man would congregate in communities and that governments would thus be formed, and God expects that man would live in peace with each other—so long as man follows the laws set forth in nature and by revelation. These laws of God are laws of justice (what is right and wrong) to establish peace, for "there can be no peace where

122. Grotius, *Hugo Grotius on the Rights of War and Peace,* 9.
123. Ibid., 10.

there is no justice,"[124] as Algernon Sidney proclaims. In Romans 12:18 (ESV), God tells us, "If possible, so far as it depends on you, live peaceably with all." Notice the very important condition placed on living in peace with men: *if possible.* God knows and expects that there are times when peace is not always possible—just ask Abel when his brother Cain committed the first murder. In other words, there are times when persons and governments put themselves at odds with others, creating a state of war[125] with such persons and placing the innocent person in a natural state of self-preservation. This principle applies to all persons (e.g., neighbor or government) who would usurp power over another without consent. Therefore, absolutely no person—or entity controlled by persons—has such a right to put another person into his own power without prior consent.[126]

---

124. Sidney, *Discourses on Government,* 335.

125. "The state of war is a state of enmity and destruction; and therefore declaring by word or action, not a passionate and hasty, but sedate, settled design upon another man's life puts him in a state of war with him against whom he has declared such an intention, and so has exposed his life to the other's power to be taken away by him, or any one that joins with him in his defence, and espouses his quarrel; it being reasonable and just I should have a right to destroy that which threatens me with destruction; for by the fundamental law of Nature, man being to be preserved as much as possible, when all cannot be preserved, the safety of the innocent is to be preferred, and one may destroy a man who makes war upon him, or has discovered an enmity to his being, for the same reason that he may kill a wolf or a lion, because they are not under the ties of the common law of reason, have no other rule but that of force and violence, and so may be treated as a beast of prey, those dangerous and noxious creatures that will be sure to destroy him whenever he falls into their power." Locke and Macpherson, ed., *Second Treatise of Government,* 14.

126. "And hence it is that he who attempts to get another man into his absolute power does thereby put himself into a state of war with him; it being to be understood as a declaration of a design upon his life. For I have reason to conclude that he who would get me into his power without my consent would use me as he pleased when he had got me there, and destroy me too when he had a fancy to it; for nobody can desire to have me in his absolute power unless it be to compel me by force to that which is against the right of my freedom—i.e. make me a slave. To be free from such force is the only security of my preservation, and reason bids me look on him as an enemy to my preservation who would take away that freedom which is the fence to it; so that he who makes an attempt to enslave me thereby puts himself into a state of war with me.

He that in the state of Nature would take away the freedom that belongs to any one in that state must necessarily be supposed to have a design to take away everything else, that freedom being the foundation of all the rest; as he that in the state of society would take away the freedom belonging to those of that society or commonwealth must be supposed to design to take away from them everything else, and so be looked on as in a state of war." Locke and Macpherson, ed., *Second Treatise of Government,* 14–15.

Unfortunately, the law of self-preservation is met with hostility with those stronger people who succumb to the sin of oppressing others. It is no wonder that God informs us that it is wise and prudent to pray for government rulers so that you may lead a quiet and peaceful life and be thankful for the ones that facilitate such peace. The apostle Paul says the following in 1 Timothy 2:1–2 (ESV):

> First of all, then, I urge that supplications, prayers, intercessions, and thanksgivings be made for all people, for kings and all who are in high positions, that we may lead a peaceful and quiet life, godly and dignified in every way.

While men come together in society in attempts to live in peace and tranquility, the government (or those in other positions of power) of that society may in fact be the very enemy of your peace and tranquility. Why else would there be the need to pray for your rulers that we may lead a quiet and peaceable life?

Again, the sin nature of man and the oppression that results from power-abusers are the biggest obstacles to man's natural desire for peace and tranquility, which sometimes makes living in peace with men impossible. For government to comply with this natural law of a desire for peace, the principles and laws of government should reflect this nature—in its own actions as well as by not usurping authority and acting outside of its compact with the people. Thus, to accomplish and avoid this conflict, the government should set up guards to prevent confrontation with the people, such as limited and separated powers, limited terms of office, and impeachment procedures, to name just a few.

Imperfect

For the same reason that men are not able to live in societies without government, governments are destructive to life, liberty, and freedom where there are no limitations and where the government does not comply with its limitations. The reason: the sin nature of man. Is this any wonder? After all, are not those who possess power also human flesh, bone, and mind? Consider these verses describing the natural state of man:

For all have sinned, and come short of the glory of God.[127]

The heart is deceitful above all things, and desperately wicked: who can know it?[128]

So I find it to be a law that when I want to do right, evil lies close at hand.[129]

What is man, that he can be pure? Or he who is born of a woman, that he can be righteous? Behold, God puts no trust in his holy ones, and the heavens are not pure in his sight; how much less one who is abominable and corrupt, a man who drinks injustice like water![130]

We see sin everywhere—all around us—and it affects every person, every family, every community, and every nation that exists, has existed, and will exist. The application of the sin nature on our government's substance and form is crucial and as significant as any other natural law to which the government must conform. Montesquieu acknowledges man's sin nature and incorporates this fact into his reasoning and rationale in *The Spirit of Laws*. He says,

Man, as a physical being, is like other bodies governed by invariable laws. As an intelligent being, he incessantly transgresses the laws established by God, and changes those of his own instituting. He is left to his private direction, though limited being, and subject, like all finite intelligences, to ignorance and error: even his imperfect knowledge he loses; and as a sensible creature, he is hurried away by a thousand impetuous passions. Such a being might every instant forget his Creator; God has therefore reminded him of his duty by the laws of religion.[131]

---

127. Romans 3:23 (KJV).
128. Jeremiah 17:9 (KJV).
129. Romans 7:21 (ESV).
130. Job 15:14–16 (ESV).
131. Montesquieu, *The Spirit of Laws*, 3.

Even with the gifts from God of life, reasoning, choice, knowledge, and freedom, man is not capable of using those gifts to perfectly follow the law of God. Our thousand impetuous passions cause man to err in judgment and action—a natural law that applies to government as well.

Accepting and realizing this fact should cause every person to analyze how government should reflect this natural law. Where come the notions of "we should trust our leaders" and "I believe our government leaders have good intentions" and "perceived bad decisions must be the result of our leaders knowing something that we do not know as ordinary citizens" when the evidence does not support such conclusions? Does a parent let just anyone babysit his child, not knowing the person's character, integrity, history, and capability? Of course not, and you do not simply place your trust in a politician who possesses characteristics, philosophies, and policies in contradiction to the natural laws of God. To do so would undercut our nation's foundation—a formation based upon literally thousands of years of history, experience, ideology, political struggle, and wars.

The understanding that all men—especially government administrators—are sinners prevailed in the minds and hearts of colonial citizens and leaders during the 1700s and 1800s. They held the following beliefs:

> Man, in his present state, appears to be a degraded creature; his best gold is mixed with dross, and his motives are very far from being pure and free from earth and impurity.[132]

> Political liberty is to be found only in moderate governments...when there is no abuse of power. But constant experience shows us that every man invested with power is apt to abuse it, and to carry his authority as far as it will go... To prevent this abuse, it is necessary from the very nature of things that power should be a check to power.[133]

---

132. Jay, *The Life of John Jay,* 346.
133. Montesquieu, *The Spirit of Laws,* 150.

Bad motives and abuse of power: what a thought! Dare we say conspiracies! To compare the difference in how the people of America guard against the abusers of power, consider that today those who propose that our government creates schemes of action, such as conspiracies, contrary to our Constitution are almost synonymous with kooks and wackos.[134] It is easy to see. Many mainstream media shows (including conservative television and talk radio) attempt to make such persons appear to be on the fringe of society, with no credibility given to them whatsoever. Indeed, anyone who would suggest that certain powerful governmental and commercial leaders would conspire to advance their own agenda at the cost of freedom is demonized and polarized. History proves otherwise. Indeed, our founders believed that governmental leaders were capable of conspiracies and were in fact involved in conspiracies! As an example, consider founding father James Wilson's warning against the artful and malicious design by their sovereign Great Britain "to degrade [the colonists] to a rank inferior."[135] He says the following in his speech to the Continental Congress in 1775:

> Lulled into delightful security, we dreamed contrived of nothing but increasing fondness and friendship, cemented and strengthened by a kind and perpetual communication of good offices. Soon, however, too soon, were we awakened from the soothing dreams! Our enemies renewed their designs against us, not with less malice, but with more art.[136]

Roscoe Conkling (a lawyer, politician, and strong supporter of Abraham Lincoln) confirms the efforts and conspiracies of governments throughout the ages to suppress freedom for the sake of the powerful and elite. "The right of free self-government has been in all ages the bright

---

134. William P. Grady, *How Satan Turned America Against God (Understanding the Times)*, vol. 1, (Swartz Creek, MI: Grady Publishing, Inc., 2005), 230–231. Consider Rush Limbaugh's assertion of who "kooks" are: you might be included, as certainly America's founders would have been included on Limbaugh's kook list.

135. Compiled by a member of the Philadelphia Bar, *American Oratory*, 2.

136. Ibid.

dream of oppressed humanity—the sighed-for privilege to which thrones, dynasties and power have so long blocked the way."[137] The reality is this: most abuses of power go unseen and undetected, as most people are lulled into false security. Think about it. What abuser of power broadcasts his ill-virtue, deceit, and vice to those who are detrimentally affected and whose trust has been given? Does not the Bible reveal that "men love darkness rather than light because their works are evil"?[138] What? You mean God believes in conspiracies too? Yes, He confirms their existence in all ages of men. Darkness is always used to hide evil deeds. Even a child understands this vice, as the unsuspected child will manipulate his parents behind their backs, turn them against each other, contrive plans to get his way, and will use whatever means necessary to accomplish his goal. Only the most astute and informed citizens would likely even become aware of such abuse, however, not by means of actual discovery of acts that took place behind closed doors, but by the long train of abuses evidenced by the apparent intentions of such leaders.[139]

It is this essential human nature of sin that has shaped our earlier form and substance of government (a republic), including the three branches of America's government (legislative, executive, and judicial). Likewise, it is this natural law that forms the rationale of limited government, separated powers of government, limited terms of government administrators, checks and balances, the power of government being in the hands of the citizens, and

---

137. Roscoe Conkling, *Speech of Roscoe Conkling at the Academy of Music, New York, September 17, 1880,* (New York: Cornwell Press, 1880), 3–4.

138. "And this is the judgment: the light has come into the world, and people loved the darkness rather than the light because their works were evil." John 3:19 (ESV).

139. Thomas Jefferson, *Declaration of Independence,* (See Appendix A); "[I]f a long train of actions shew the councils all tending that way; how can a man any more hinder himself from being persuaded in his own mind, which way things are going; or from casting about how to save himself, than he could from believing the captain of the ship he was in, was carrying him, and the rest of the company, to Algiers, when he found him always steering that course, though cross winds, leaks in his ship, and want of men and provisions did often force him to turn his course another way for some time, which he steadily returned to again, as soon as the wind, weather, and other circumstances would let him?" Locke and Macpherson, ed., *Second Treatise of Government,* 106.

other similar notions. Consider John Jay's thoughts on the matter of separated powers:

> Shall we have a king? Not in my opinion, while other expedients remain untried. Might we not have a governor-general, limited in his prerogatives and duration? Might not Congress be divided into an upper and lower house—the former appointed for life, the latter annually; and let the governor-general (to preserve the balance), with the advice of council, formed for that only purpose; of the great judicial officers, have a negative on their acts? Our government should, in some degree, be suited to our manners and circumstances, and they, you know, are not strictly democratical.[140]

Likewise, Sir William Rawle proposes that the separation of government powers derives from a moral order, meaning that it is found in the natural laws of man. He says,

> This natural division [of the powers of government is] founded upon moral order [and] must be preserved by a careful separation or distinction of the powers vested in different branches. If the three powers...are united in the same body, great dangers ensue.[141]

If human nature was not bent towards corruption, dishonesty, greed, selfishness, prejudice, and inequality, there would not be such a need for a government divided against itself through checks and balances to prevent such evil from affecting the very nature and principle of government's purpose. If natural law revealed that man was naturally good, honest, upright, humble, content, righteous, just, and fair, then why is there any need for three branches of government, checks and balances, limitations of powers, federalism, voting, term limits,[142] impeachment processes, and an oath of

---

140. Jay, *The Life of John Jay*, 256.

141. Rawle, *A View of the Constitution of the United States of America*, 12.

142. To implement such a concept of "limitation" into our nation's administration, our founders stressed the importance of limited terms of its administrators. Term limits have been

office? Such restrictions only hinder the efficiency of government and do not give to government the full power needed to serve best the interests of its subjects. And if all governments are ministers of God, with no regard for their actions, why not eliminate such inconveniences?

Why not propose to do away with the Constitution and Bill of Rights? Why not require all citizens to allow the government to decide for the parent what careers their children shall pursue, to distribute all wealth as they deem appropriate for the good of society, to require all people to register their DNA with the government upon birth, to put GPS monitoring systems in every new-born life, to have no restrictions on the ability to search your personal affects and homes regarding criminal evidence and prosecution, to confiscate all weapons of every sort, to form a world government, and to be controlled in every way? Why do we insist on having inalienable rights, freedoms, and privacies if natural law reveals that mankind and governments are naturally good? This is why:

---

incorporated into the framework of political administration, because our founders understood all of the natural tendencies already discussed herein—such as, the sin nature of man, the power-hungry proclivity of those who have been vested with power, and the effects of these tendencies on the citizens on the whole. This is why the proposal of a constitutional amendment allowing the President of the United States to serve unlimited terms is so dangerous. And although America's founders did not initially express term limits for the president, the exclusion of this limitation was very much resisted, even by the drafter of the *Declaration of Independence,* Thomas Jefferson, who said, "I disapproved also the perpetual re-eligibility of the President." Does America really think that highly of modern politicians? If so, it is just another proof that Americans have lost the understanding of what formed American government.

It must be noted, moreover, that America's founders understood that while term limits help limit the power of government, they do not completely prevent the abuse of power of those administrators who actively seek to acquire more of it, unlawfully and manipulatively so. Thus, the Constitution had to ensure many more checks on the usurpation of power by the government. To that end, the founders insisted upon the separation of powers among the three branches of government: legislative, executive, and judicial. Thomas Jefferson confirms this philosophy by stating, "Leave no authority not responsible to the people." To solidify their belief that the branches of government must not usurp the power of the people, the founders specifically framed the Constitution to place more power into the legislative branch of government, which is the direct representatives of the people. The founders wanted to ensure that the people were able to redress their government in the most effective and powerful way.

Certainty in political compacts…has ever been held by a wise and free people as essential to their security; as, on the one hand it fixes barriers which the ambitious and tyrannically disposed magistrate dare not overleap, and on the other, becomes a wall of safety to the community—otherwise stipulations between governors and governed are nugatory; and you might as well deposit the important powers of legislation and execution in one or a few and permit them to govern according to their disposition and will; but the world is too full of examples, which prove that to live by one man's will became the cause of all men's misery.[143]

Undoubtedly, America's formation reveals just how untrustworthy humans are, especially when given power, because natural law reveals that humans, when given the opportunity, will likely use power for objectives less than honorable. When government suggests otherwise by words or actions, watch out.

Oppressive in Power

"Bodies of men, as well as individuals, are susceptible of the spirit of tyranny," is a truth noted by Thomas Jefferson.[144] Given the natural law of human flaws and the tendency of men in power to abuse it, it necessarily follows that governmental leaders would actually use their power to oppress the citizens and to accomplish their selfish and evil agenda. It is apparent that many Americans are oblivious to the fact that America's leaders could be, and in fact are, corrupt on many levels and in many areas. Yes, even conservative politicians. What experience, what scripture, what author of reason can they cite that leads them to the conclusion that all, say, Republican Party leaders are virtuous? Human nature does not change, and what our political and philosophical founders experienced then is no different from what we experience now. Evidently, Algernon Sidney encountered those persons in his day who advocated the same ignorant ideology: namely, that no king can do wrong and that

---

143. Ketcham, ed., *The Anti-Federalist Papers*, 318.
144. Jefferson, *The Jeffersonian Cyclopedia*, 890.

he is a gift from God. Sidney asks his contemporaries who held such a belief "whether we have any promise from God, that all princes should forever excel in those virtues [of freedom]."[145] Likewise, regarding the presumption that rulers will act in good faith, with wisdom, virtue, and justice, many freedom lovers in America around 1787 would have said this to you:

> Is it because you do not believe that an American can be a tyrant? If this be the case you rest on a weak basis; Americans are like other men in similar situations...[and] your posterity will find that great power connected with ambition, luxury, and flattery, will as readily produce a Caesar, Caligula, Nero, and Domitian in America, as the same causes did in the Roman empire.[146]

Perhaps the disillusioned belief referred to herein results from indifference, reliance on our nation's Christian heritage and roots, taking for granted that things will always be this way, a belief that all men are inherently good, or sheer ignorance. Perhaps God has "sent them strong delusion, that they should believe a lie,"[147] or maybe the combination of several reasons cause such a belief. In case there are any readers who feel confident in the security that rulers provide, consider the following biblical examples and warnings concerning those in leadership over a nation or community—though there would not be enough time or paper to mention all of the tyrants and despots that have existed since the beginning of time.

Let us first look at the life of Lot in the cities of Sodom and Gomorrah, which took place before God revealed His law through Moses. The Bible reveals that Sodom and Gomorrah were extremely wicked and vile, and that God intended to destroy the cities because of their wickedness. It was God's intention to save the life of Lot and his family, because they were righteous in God's eyes. It is safe to presume and induce, given the implications and suggestions of the relevant verses, that the leaders of the cities were wicked

---

145. Sidney, *Discourses on Government,* 322.
146. Ketcham, ed., *The Anti-Federalist Papers,* 319.
147. Thessalonians 2:11 (KJV).

and evil in God's sight, and that the laws instituted were likewise evil and wicked. To assume that the laws were righteous when God describes the cities as wicked mocks common sense. (By the way, what classification would America fall in today when looking at its laws?) As a result, Lot suffered the consequences both physically and spiritually, even though he surely could pray to God silently and in private and worship God in his heart (a freedom many are content with, not understanding that civil rights are as equally important as religious rights. As James Madison said, "In a free government the security for civil rights must be the same as that for religious rights."[148])

To describe the effect on Lot, 2 Peter 2:7–8 (KJV) says, "Lot [was] vexed with the filthy conversation of the wicked; (for that righteous man dwelling among them, in seeing and hearing, vexed his righteous soul from day to day with their unlawful deeds.)" It is important to note the two different meanings of the word *vexed* in verse seven and then in verse eight. Verse seven tells us that Lot was vexed, meaning to wear down or to oppress.[149] The Bible describes Lot's circumstances as one would describe a slave (in a physical sense) who was being oppressed. This meaning is contrasted with the word vexed in verse eight, which means to torment[150] as it applies to his righteous soul. Thus, Lot was not only tormented spiritually by this wicked people but also physically, as he was oppressed by their unlawful deeds. Keep in mind that Lot was not a slave in the ordinary sense of the word as understood by modern Americans today. He could move around, shop, engage in commerce, etc. However, the effect of the wicked laws under which he lived caused Lot to be oppressed on a daily basis, meaning that the laws contradicted his way of life, his beliefs, his outlook, and his perspective. When a person lives in such conditions, he has to make a decision: (1) he must live in those conditions, knowing that he cannot live as he believes God wants him to, that he cannot raise his children in a godly environment, and that he must comply with laws that are evil; (2) he can resist the government and laws and face the consequences; or (3) he must remove himself and

---

148. James Madison, "Federalist Paper 51," in *The Federalist Papers,* Hamilton, Jay, and Madison, 403.

149. Strong, *Strong's Exhaustive Concordance of the Bible,* 40.

150. Ibid., 18.

his family from such an environment and seek a nation whose government facilitates the purpose of God.

How can it be argued that righteous people can live in a wicked society with a wicked government and there not be oppressive consequences both physically and spiritually to that person? The fact is God gives example after example of governments oppressing people who believe in true freedom and the vexing caused by that government. Sure, you could argue that it is God's will that people suffer, and this may in fact be the case. However, such a view does not take into consideration that God's will of oppression was always associated with punishment and judgment for unrighteous nations. God never imposed oppression just for the heck of it—this contradicts God's revelation of nations and governments. Why would any person desire not only to live in that environment (the judgment of God) but also to encourage the wicked government to create that environment? When a robber invades your home and threatens your family, do you presume it is God's will for you to suffer and let the invader do as he pleases? What a ridiculous thought process.

Furthermore, God describes the afore-referenced deeds of the cities as unlawful deeds, although they obviously complied with the government's laws controlling human behavior. God calls the deeds unlawful, because they were no doubt against God's natural laws. Indeed, no other revelation of God existed at that time, which is another biblical confirmation of natural law in both the Old and New Testaments. Any Christian or truth seeker should be able to recognize unlawful deeds when confronted by them, and failure to recognize and confront evil laws will result in what Lot experienced: oppression. Additionally, the apostle Peter warns of those people who promise liberty but who are in fact servants of corruption and slavery. These verses plainly warn us of those hypocrites who would bring us into bondage. Second Peter 2:18–19 (ESV) says, "For, speaking loud boasts of folly, they entice by sensual passions of the flesh those who are barely escaping from those who live in error. They promise them freedom, but they themselves are slaves of corruption. For whatever overcomes a person, to that he is enslaved."

Promising liberty but providing bondage—sounds familiar! Notice as well that where people are overcome by the enticements of others, they become slaves to those enticements. The enticements, of course, appear to be good on the surface but in fact are deadly. As Walter Williams says, "I know of no evil legislation written in explicitly evil language."[151] This is common sense. Think about it: what persons would be in the best position to promise liberty but bring bondage? Obviously, the best persons to bring anyone into bondage are those with the power to do so—that is, government. Do we really believe that such oppressors only existed during ancient times, as if human nature has changed since then? Any casual observer of humans today and reader of history will conclude that human nature is not improving; thus, persons in power have the same tendencies as they did when all the chapters of the Bible were written. The examples are plenteous.

We learn how the king of Egypt during the life of Moses used slavery to oppress the nation of Israel for the mere purpose of preventing their power from increasing and to prevent his power from being challenged. The Egyptian king obviously felt that the people of Israel were a serious threat to his power. So to control this threat, he enslaved them. The story is revealed as follows:

> Now there arose a new king over Egypt, who did not know Joseph. And he said to his people, "Behold, the people of Israel are too many and too mighty for us. Come, let us deal shrewdly with them, lest they multiply, and, if war breaks out, they join our enemies and fight against us and escape from the land." Therefore they set taskmasters over them to afflict them with heavy burdens.
>
> They built for Pharaoh store cities, Pithom and Raamses. But the more they were oppressed, the more they multiplied and the more they spread abroad. And the Egyptians were in dread of the people of Israel. So they ruthlessly made the people of Israel work as slaves and made their lives bitter with hard service, in mortar and brick, and in all kinds of work in the field. In all their work they ruthlessly made them work as slaves.[152]

The following verses give more explanation regarding the natural law of powerful people abusing the rights of man. This flawed character of human

---

151. Williams, *Do the Right Thing,* 150.
152. Exodus 1:8–14 (ESV).

nature is revealed and even magnified when the people lose their ability to prevent evil, the consequences of which result in the people becoming slaves. To illustrate this fact, God uses the simple, yet profound, analogy of salt, illustrating not only the human nature of sin but also the responsibility inherent in the citizens of society. We are told, "You are the salt of the earth, but if the salt loses its savor, with what shall it be salted? It is no longer good for anything, but to be thrown out and to be trodden underfoot by men."[153]

This analogy of salt is very significant, because it has some serious applications regarding one's interaction with society. The attributes of salt are the following. *First,* salt acts as a deterrent to natural decay of, say, meat. *Second,* salt gives flavor to foods. *Third,* salt is necessary in the human body to sustain life itself. Thus, we are to possess the same qualities as salt: (1) we are to function as a preventative of decay, meaning the decay of sin and corruption in every walk of life—including national and government issues;[154] (2) we should portray and demonstrate the full flavor of life given to us by God;[155] and (3) we must possess and use the gifts of life (knowledge, reason, choice, and freedom) given only from God.[156] The consequences of not possessing the salt quality are (1) you lose the essence of salt's functions (savor), (2) you are good for nothing, and (3) you shall live in tyranny, to be trodden under the foot of men. Again, who can better tread you under their feet than those who have the power to do so? That is government, the rich, the powerful. "Do not rich men oppress you, and draw you before the judgment seats?"[157]

God also warns us of those leaders who are too blind to lead their followers and who ultimately lead them into a pit. Obviously, the pit is not meant to be a good thing. Matthew 15:14 (MJKV) says, "Let them alone. They are blind leaders of the blind. And if the blind lead the blind, both shall fall into the ditch." How can a concerned, freedom-loving American accept the over-used, proven-

---

153. Matthew 5:13 (MJKV).

154. "Righteousness exalts a nation: but sin is a reproach to any people." Proverbs 14:34 (KJV).

155. "O taste and see that the Lord is good." Psalm 34:8 (KJV).

156. "I [Jesus] am come that they might have life, and that they might have it more abundantly." John 10:10 (KJV).

157. James 2:6 (KJV).

fallacious notion that we must elect the lesser of two evils? Where we are being led by those who head towards the pit, God tells us to leave them alone! Do you assume that God is proud of those who vote for leaders who lead us into the pit at a slower rate of speed? Right! God did not address the matter of the rate of speed at which the leaders lead you into the pit. Instead, God directly commands us to leave them alone—perhaps this would mean, *do not vote for them!* It is crucial for followers to know whom they are following and know whether or not the leader is even qualified. How can an informed citizen, who knows of the overwhelming trend of lesser of evils and even evils becoming the leaders of this nation, not realize that the negative effects are on their way and are in fact present? Can they expect "Change We Can Believe In" when they know that the only change being made is more of the same corrupt, evil, unconstitutional, and duplicitous acts? Such an approach is knowingly false and will inevitably lead you, your family, your community, and your nation into the pit. Ultimately, you get what you deserve and ask for.

King David (the "man after God's own heart"[158]) warns us of evil kings who, dare I say, conspire against God and God's work. He says in Psalm 2:2–3 (KJV), "The kings of the earth set themselves, and the rulers take counsel together, against the LORD, and against his anointed, saying, 'Let us break their bands asunder, and cast away their cords from us.'" Use a bit of common sense here: how do mortal beings conspire, contrive, and set out to take counsel together, against the Lord, and against his anointed? Can they gather an army and strike God the Father—who is a spirit[159]—with a sword or assault Him with a gun? Of course not. King David was not unfamiliar with the manner in which kings attempt this type of attack: through laws!—not all of which are blatantly evil. Consider King Nebuchadnezzar in the book of Daniel. Consider King Saul in the books of Samuel and Kings. Consider Prince Haman in the book of Esther. Consider King Herod in the Gospels. Consider King George in the 1700s. Consider Adolf Hitler in Germany. Consider Nero in Rome during the first century. Consider Queen "Bloody"

---

158. Samuel 13:14 (KJV).

159. "God is a Spirit: and they that worship him must worship him in spirit and in truth." John 4:24 (KJV).

Mary during the 1500s. Consider Joseph Stalin in Russia during the 1800s. Consider Caesar who allowed the crucifixion of Christ.[160]

The fact is America has been the exception to the rule of tyranny and despotism throughout the history of the world—although it has tasted the symptoms of such from rulers who have abused their power for unconstitutional purposes. Montesquieu observes the fact that the vast majority of nations that have ever existed have lived in tyranny:

> After what has been said [about despotic governments], one would imagine that human nature should perpetually rise up against despotism. But, notwithstanding the love of liberty, so natural to mankind, not withstanding their innate detestation of force and violence, most nations are subject to this very government.[161]

Think about it: is there any credible proof denying the maxim *power corrupts, and absolute power corrupts absolutely*? Perhaps the fact that some 170 million people have been killed by governments alone in the twentieth century will confirm this truth.[162] For those who are relying on the hope that God will spare judgment forever simply because there are righteous people in America, tell that to those suffering in China, Pakistan, Jerusalem, Indonesia, Africa, Sudan, and other nations throughout the world who are living under Christian-hating and freedom-rejecting governments and are being persecuted for their belief in Jesus Christ. Are Americans just *that* spiritual and right with God to live in this free nation? I dare not even suggest such a thought, and such a suggestion is a slap in the face to those innocent people and Christians killed, maimed, tortured, torn asunder, raped, sold into slavery, and God knows what else.[163] Again, are Christians in America any better

---

160. "But we speak the wisdom of God in a mystery, even the hidden wisdom, which God ordained before the world unto our glory: Which none of the princes of this world knew: for had they known it, they would not have crucified the Lord of glory." 1 Corinthians 2:7–8 (KJV).

161. Montesquieu, *The Spirit of Laws*, 62.

162. Rudolph J. Rummel, *Death by Government*, (New Brunswick, NJ: Transaction Publishers, 1994).

163. Hebrews 11 (ESV).

or have any special favor of God? Absolutely not, for "God shows no partial-ity."[164] All are equally important in God's sight, and yet none are distinctly more valuable. Nevertheless, millions suffer at the hands of tyrannical, des-potic, and unjust governments and receive no protection from them.

The Bible speaks of the hypocrite who "promises liberty but is a servant of bondage...for of whom a man is overcome, of the same is he brought in bondage"[165] through the writer of Job, who expresses the same sentiment and warning to those who are ensnared by such a hypocrite. Job says, "And He gives quietness, who then can condemn? And when He hides His face, who can behold Him? And it may be against a nation and a man together; from the reigning of ungodly men, from being snares for the people."[166]

Can this be any clearer? Evil leaders have no intention of protecting free-dom for their people only to ensnare them. Of course, for a citizen to spot such an evil leader the citizen must have a thorough knowledge of what free-dom is, from where it derives, how it is protected, and how the government is limited. If there is any motivation of evil persons to comply with natural laws and the Constitution, it is fear of being reprimanded and injured by the citizens. Without this fear factor, nothing will change their actions. Thomas Jefferson observes this fact when he says, "If once the people become inat-tentive to the public affairs, you and I, and Congress and Assemblies, Judges and Governors, shall all become wolves."[167] Jefferson and Job warn us not to let these wolves reign, because they will make trouble, they will hide their evil intent from the people, and they will enslave the citizens. The prophet Isaiah says the same thing in Isaiah 36:14–18 (MJKV):

So says the king, Do not let Hezekiah deceive you, for he shall not be able to deliver you. Nor let Hezekiah make you trust in Jehovah, saying, Jehovah will surely deliver us; this city shall not be delivered into the hands of the king of Assyria. Do not listen to Hezekiah; for

---

164. Romans 2:11 (ESV).
165. 2 Peter 2:19 (KJV).
166. Job 34:29–30 (MJKV).
167. Jefferson, *The Jeffersonian Cyclopedia*, 387.

so says the king of Assyria, Make a blessing with me by a present, and come out to me; and let everyone eat of his vine, and everyone of his fig tree, and everyone drink the waters of his own cistern, until I come and take you away to a land like your own land, a land of grain and wine, a land of bread and vineyards. Let not Hezekiah persuade you, saying, Jehovah will deliver us. Has any of the gods of the nations delivered his land out of the hand of the king of Assyria?

The prophet Isaiah did not believe in this modern notion of "politics is politics" and "all politicians lie—so what?" How absurd and how detrimental is such a belief. The Bible and history prove that "those who are in possession of power, generally strive to enlarge it for their own advantage in preference to the public good,"[168] and this was also expressed by William Rawle. Why would anyone who claims to love freedom granted by God not rise up in righteous indignation to persons who reject, not only the rights granted by God, but reject God as well? How could such leaders deserve any honor from those whose rights the leaders care nothing about, especially to the end of their own selfish agenda? Indeed, such leaders may advocate the rights of man, as long as it advances their own interests. However, they are merely "wolves in sheep clothing."[169] Does not Isaiah tell us not to let the king deceive you, because while the king promises you that the Lord shall deliver you if you do this or that, God will not deliver you, because this or that is contrary to God's word and revealed and natural law? Why will God not deliver you, good intentions not withstanding? Because God binds Himself to His standards, promises, consequences, and punishments already declared. God cannot bless what He has already declared to be evil.

Does America effectively have the same attitude that Israel had then? Even after knowing that judgment from God was inevitable because of the evil of the nation, they say, "There is no hope: but we will walk after our own devices."[170] Is there an attitude prevalent in America that suggests that we should simply

---

168. Rawle, *A View of the Constitution of the United States of America*, 282.

169. "Beware of false prophets, which come to you in sheep's clothing, but inwardly they are ravening wolves." Matthew 7:15 (KJV).

170. Jeremiah 18:12 (MJKV).

give up fighting for freedom because the tyrants have won the fight? Would the same person also say that he is going to allow those who would assault his family into his home? If not, then why say that you should allow evil to reign simply because you feel powerless to stop those nimrods? God forbid. While most may say that such a statement is not their attitude, does it appear that God is taking His hand of blessing off of America? Then, the question is why? Is it possible that so many people have given up, have been indifferent to the issues regarding their freedom, have forgotten the natural laws found in human nature, or have failed to recognize the tendency of sinful man to oppress those under their power? Is there perhaps an element of voluntary slavery?

When tyranny presents itself, voluntary slavery is possible. It happens every day and has occurred throughout history. God gives such an example of voluntary slavery in Jeremiah 27:11 (MJKV). "But the nations who bring their neck under the yoke of the king of Babylon, and serve him, those I will leave on their own land, says Jehovah. And they shall work it and dwell in it." Notice carefully that "the nations *bring their neck* under the yoke," revealing the voluntary nature of the people's slavery. As a result of this voluntary slavery, the people suffer, and their power is lost. A nation's lethargy, impotence, ignorance, and refusal to follow God's standards concerning national affairs can be deemed voluntary slavery, and there is never a shortage of persons who would assume the position (but never the title) of tyrant.

Moreover, God gives us further warnings of those who use their power for purposes of controlling people and property and of building their own empire by "gathering unto him nations" (i.e., globalism), as reflected in Habakkuk 2:5 (MJKV). "And also wine indeed betrays a proud man, and he is not content. He widens his soul like Sheol, and he is like death, and is not satisfied, but gathers all nations to himself, and heaps to himself all the peoples."

God portrays those people in power who have a hunger to nation build in a negative light (just as God destroyed Nimrod's attempts to nation build in Genesis), as does one of America's founders when he states, "I hope [America's] wisdom will grow with our power, and teach us, that the less we use our power the greater it will be."[171] Nation builders existed throughout

---

171. Jefferson, *The Jeffersonian Cyclopedia,* 601.

human history, and they exist today. Has there been any person born in this world that does not have the same sin nature? What makes the person born in America in the twenty-first century any different from the person born 1,000 BC in Egypt? If you think technology changes the heart of man, think again. If the writer of Habakkuk experienced nation gatherers from rulers who were never satisfied with what power they had and always had to have more, what person using any knowledge of the Bible, common sense, or human experience would not believe that the same tendencies exist today and are actually taking place? If one acknowledges these tendencies, would it not be wise to incorporate this natural law into government? America's founders did. The idea that government should remain small enough to retain an accurate perception of the nation's needs is expressed by Montesquieu in *Spirit of Laws,* when he says,

> It is natural to a republic to have only a small territory, otherwise it cannot long subsist. In a large republic there are men of large fortunes, and consequently of less moderation; there are trusts too great to be placed in any single subject; he has interest of his own; he soon begins to think that he may be happy, great and glorious, by oppressing his fellow citizens; and that he may raise himself to grandeur on the ruins of his country. In a large republic, the public good is sacrificed to a thousand views; it is subordinate to exceptions, and depends on accidents. In a small one, the interest of the public is easier perceived, better understood, and more within the reach of every citizen; abuses are of less extent, and of course are less protected.[172]

This concept is the opposite of the push for globalism, the accomplishment of which is spreading like wildfire. As well, Thomas Jefferson observes

---

172. Montesquieu, *The Spirit of Laws,* 120; "In a free republic, although all laws are derived from the consent of the people, yet the people do not declare their consent by themselves in person, but by representatives, chosen by them, who are supposed to know the minds of their constituents, and to be possessed of integrity to declare this mind." Brutus and Ketcham, *The Anti-Federalist Papers,* 276.

that nation gathering in fact is a principle contrary to the principles upon which America was founded. He says, "Conquest is not in our principles. It is inconsistent with our government."[173] Well, at least it *was* inconsistent with our principles. But then again, God's natural and revealed laws were the ground upon which our nation's foundation was laid. Unfortunately, generations have conducted careful excavation work to remove the solid ground of freedom and replace it with the shifty sand of slavery.

Certainly, God expresses more than once in His word His disgust with governments who suppress men and conspire and contrive in counsel against God and His anointed. Isaiah 10:1–4 (ESV) says the following:

> Woe to those who decree iniquitous decrees, and the writers who keep writing oppression, to turn aside the needy from justice and to rob the poor of my people of their right, that widows may be their spoil, and that they may make the fatherless their prey! What will you do on the day of punishment, in the ruin that will come from afar? To whom will you flee for help, and where will you leave your wealth? Nothing remains but to crouch among the prisoners or fall among the slain. For all this his anger has not turned away, and his hand is stretched out still.

Notice the reference to the decrees (laws) accomplishing unrighteousness against its citizens. The citizens living under such a government, as God says, have no justice done unto them by the government—the accomplishment of justice as the very essence of government's existence turns into the accomplishment of the desires of the powerful. What good is government where justice is not sought after, where the source of rightness (being the definition of justice) is rejected, and where the wisdom of modern-day man overshadows any wisdom of our outdated ancestors? Even more fundamental is this: what good are citizens who do not hold their government responsible for implementing natural laws which create justice? Should citizens be commended who do not resist tyranny because they do not believe they can

---

173. Jefferson, *The Jeffersonian Cyclopedia,* 185.

defeat the enemy? Those who are taking the battle on themselves would not dare.

Make no mistake, God views those rulers who use their position to oppress their subjects with contempt—and so should we. Isaiah 14:5–6 (ESV) says, "The LORD has broken the staff of the wicked, the scepter of rulers, that struck the peoples in wrath with unceasing blows, that ruled the nations in anger with unrelenting persecution." And what about the reference to the rich oppressors in James 2:6 (KJV)? "Do not rich men oppress you, and draw you before the judgment seats?" Even where the rulers of a nation are given the right environment to be just (say, America!), those who have rejected the truth and standards of righteousness will continue to deal unjustly, no matter how often citizens attempt to show favor and live uprightly—as if you can change a person's heart by being buddy-buddy with them. Isaiah 26:10 (ESV) confirms this. "If favor is shown to the wicked, he does not learn righteousness; in the land of uprightness he deals corruptly and does not see the majesty of the LORD." So what good does it do America for conservative leaders to dine at the table of kings in an attempt to change their hearts and change their policies, using positive-mental-attitude approaches, when God already tells us that wicked leaders *will not* do justly, love mercy, and walk humbly with God, no matter how much you butter them up?[174] God warns us not to cast our pearls before swine.[175] Maybe we should heed the warning and focus our energy elsewhere. That is right: maybe our focus should be on other places other than trying to elect a president who might appoint conservative judges.

Beyond that, King David revealed perfect hatred for such bloody men— bloody men who allowed millions of innocent and unborn lives to be killed. Consider King David's description of the unborn baby in the womb of his mother, the gift of life from God, the complexity of the human body, and God's account for each life conceived. Then consider David's request that God would slay those wicked men of blood who would destroy these innocent lives in the womb.

---

174. "He has told you, O man, what is good; and what does the LORD require of you but to do justice, and to love kindness, and to walk humbly with your God?" Micah 6:8 (ESV).

175. "Do not give dogs what is holy, and do not throw your pearls before pigs, lest they trample them underfoot and turn to attack you." Matthew 7:6 (ESV).

For you formed my inward parts; you knitted me together in my mother's womb. I praise you, for I am fearfully and wonderfully made. Wonderful are your works; my soul knows it very well. My frame was not hidden from you, when I was being made in secret, intricately woven in the depths of the earth. Your eyes saw my unformed substance; in your book were written, every one of them, the days that were formed for me, when as yet there was none of them. How precious to me are your thoughts, O God! How vast is the sum of them!

If I would count them, they are more than the sand. I awake, and I am still with you. Oh that you would slay the wicked, O God! O men of blood, depart from me! They speak against you with malicious intent; your enemies take your name in vain! Do I not hate those who hate you, O LORD? And do I not loathe those who rise up against you? I hate them with complete hatred; I count them my enemies. Search me, O God, and know my heart! Try me and know my thoughts! And see if there be any grievous way in me, and lead me in the way everlasting![176]

And lest you think that evil rulers and abusers of power are still ordained of God to rule in such a manner (a concept which will be further discussed herein), God clearly states in His word that there is no sin committed by man that is of God, but rather, evil results from man giving in to his own lusts. James 1:13–15 (ESV) says,

Let no one say when he is tempted, "I am being tempted by God," for God cannot be tempted with evil, and he himself tempts no one. But each person is tempted when he is lured and enticed by his own desire. Then desire when it has conceived gives birth to sin, and sin when it is fully grown brings forth death.

A powerful ruler whose lust is to acquire more power for the betterment of his own agenda is not of God, nor is ordained of God, but rather is

---

176. Psalm 139:13–24 (ESV).

a result of his own nation-gathering, power-hungry desires. How can God sanction actions in the name of government when the same actions are not sanctioned in God's word? If a child were to treat his parent with disobedience, a rebellious spirit, and contempt for authority, the parent would not allow the child to say, "God ordained my behavior because I am a Christian child." If a pastor committed adultery with the church piano player, the church would not let him excuse his actions by explaining (once caught), "I am God's man. I am ordained of God, and no repercussions are necessary or allowed." Likewise, a husband would not let his wife justify her adultery with another man by stating, "The bed is undefiled. I can do what I want." In each of those scenarios, the significant factor that exists in those relationships is that there is responsibility naturally or contractually imposed on the very position that the wrongdoer holds. Perhaps we are not going to be righteously indignant about neighbor Joe's excessive drinking, fornicating with countless women, and obsessive gambling, where you have no relationship with Joe, no contractual obligation, and no connection to Joe. Such is not the case, however, with government rulers. Why would you accept the abuse of power, ignorance of righteousness, and standards of truth from your rulers who have sworn an oath to uphold the Constitution (which is the contract/compact that America has with all its citizens) and who by apparent evidence have breached their obligation under, not only the Constitution, but also under standards of justice and morality as defined by God Himself?

Can any believer in the Bible or observer of history deny the temptation that man has to abuse his power, to be power hungry, to ignore the laws established by God, to take advantage of those under him, to manipulate the laws, and to implement the same in his or his beneficiaries' favor? Montesquieu observed that a nation living in freedom is rare and is the exception to the rule. Given the nature of man, how long do you think freedom would last when the citizens do not prevent that tendency from taking seed, germinating, and growing? Perhaps Americans are so lulled to sleep by prosperity and good times (which are in fact fleeting) that we cannot even identify oppressive rulers when we see them. And if you are expecting such rulers to come as a devil caricature with two horns, a pointed tail, and pitchfork in hand, you are deceiving yourself. For the American colonists, tyranny came in the form of commercial legislation—presumably with good intentions attached to the bill. Do you not understand that even Satan is transformed into an angel of light, as told in 2 Corinthians 11:14 (ESV)? "And no wonder, for even Satan disguises himself as an angel of light." Our founders understood the natural laws as revealed in nature, in history, in the Bible, and indeed from their own experiences, all of which gave them wisdom in the formation of the very nature of our Constitution and principles of government. A lack of understanding as to this reality leaves a gaping hole in one's understanding of his relationship to government and will likely result in government rulers taking advantage of and enslaving the citizens. The proof is in the works for even us to see.

THE NATURE OF GOD

To further explore the nature of government, one must not only understand the nature of man but also the nature of God, because understanding God will allow the creature to obtain the peace and tranquility expected by the Creator—the Creator of natural law and the Giver of revealed law to mankind. While it is not my purpose, nor is there a need, to set forth every conceivable facet of God's nature (as His nature is as enumerable as there are thoughts and ideas), there are some basic attributes that God possesses that reveal to His creation, His nature, what He expects, the laws set forth by His Creation, the consequences of contradicting His nature, and how to avoid detriment to ourselves for such contradictions.

It is very important to clarify this point, however, because while there are certain attributes that a righteous government must reflect, based upon the nature of God, this does not suggest that government is to become God or even attempt to take the place of God. Many people in America may actually put government in the place of God and expect that government should perform functions that only God should perform or functions that naturally belong to the individual. Thus, where government attempts to become all providing, all defending, all knowing, or all anything, that government has overstepped its limitations of jurisdiction, function, and purpose (as will be discussed further herein). Suffice it to say, there are certain elements of God's nature that suggest what government should strive for in relation to citizens to accomplish its natural and God-given purposes.

God has extended to man the observations and experiences of natural law: gravity, motion, force, dynamics, etc. God's natural laws help man understand His nature. God's natural laws, undoubtedly, extend much further than the laws of physics, although it is wise for anyone to take heed of such a law created by God, and even an atheist would agree that it is wise to understand the laws of nature. God's laws reach into every area of creation: from the seasons of the earth to the infinite universe around us; from the depths of the oceans to the heights of the heavens; from the force of a waterfall to the quietness of the darkness; all are given to use from God to understand and recognize who we are, who He is, and what our relationship is to Him and to each other. Once again, government must conform to natural law and the one that is the most conformable to it is the best form of government.

Knowledge and Wisdom

The first attribute of God to discuss is God's knowledge and wisdom. As humans are created in God's image with knowledge, we know that God Himself is the source of all knowledge, and only God can give knowledge. Ephesians 1:17 (ESV) says, "The God of our Lord Jesus Christ, the Father of glory, may give you a spirit of wisdom and of revelation in the knowledge of him." Only God could express and relate principles of law that will create and generate a society of quiet and peace, of tranquility and peace. Man's attempts are always disastrous. In the following Psalm 19:7–11 (KJV), King David expresses just how knowledgeable and wise the thoughts of God are:

> The law of the LORD is perfect, converting the soul: the testimony of the LORD is sure, making wise the simple. The statutes of the LORD are right, rejoicing the heart: the commandment of the LORD is pure, enlightening the eyes. The fear of the LORD is clean, enduring for ever: the judgments of the LORD are true and righteous altogether. More to be desired are they than gold, yea, than much fine gold: sweeter also than honey and the honeycomb. Moreover by them is thy servant warned: and in keeping of them there is great reward.

We see that the law of God is perfect, that it changes the soul. We are assured that whatever God says is certain, wise, and yet simple, "confounding the wise."[177] God's laws are right and cause the heart to rejoice. All commandments of God are pure and enlighten the eyes. And when you fear God, your fear is clean and endures forever. God's judgment is true and right. All of this is to be desired more than all of the wealth of the world, and in keeping these things, there is great reward.

Is it any wonder how America achieved its greatness? Our nation was saturated in the laws of God and the nature of man and God and attempted to form such a government on these natural laws—from the perspective of both man's sin nature and man's being created after God's image. America's initial government attempted to pass and execute laws that reflected not only the principle of natural law but also the nature of man and God. Is it any wonder there has been great reward in a land where peace and tranquility have been accomplished through seeking, acknowledging, and acting upon the very nature of God as revealed in natural law and in His revealed law?

Just as God's nature is composed of knowledge and wisdom, it is the duty of a society to form its government on the principle that laws must contain the knowledge and wisdom set forth by the Creator of all things. It is the duty of a society to explore, study, and seek wisdom from the greatest source of truth and life. It is the duty of a society to seriously consider the laws executed, the effects of such laws, and the nature and principle advanced by those laws. It is the duty of a society to never be guilty of those who "professing themselves to be wise...became fools"[178] and to acknowledge that God "made foolish the wisdom of this world."[179]

Righteousness

As knowledgeable and wise as God is, He is equally righteous: another attribute of God's nature. Psalm 11:7 (esv) says, "For the LORD is righteous; he loves righteous deeds; the upright shall behold his face." While this point is extremely obvious, one must acknowledge that since God is righteous

---

177. "But God has chosen the foolish things of the world to confound the wise; and God has chosen the weak things of the world to confound the things which are mighty." 1 Corinthians 1:27 (mjkv).

178. Romans 1:22 (kjv).

179. Corinthians 1:20 (kjv).

altogether, His standard of righteousness is correct, and any version of righteousness advanced by man "falls short of the Glory of God."[180] It is this righteousness that preserves nations, communities, families, and individuals. While many would agree with this thought in theory, it appears that many do not have the foggiest notion of how righteousness applies to government, and it has nothing to do with religion.

The fact is, government, as an institution created by man (which will be discussed in detail herein), is responsible to the people that created it. Does not this principle apply in every area of life? If you are an employer and your employee steals from you, lies to you, and competes against you, do you not fire that employee immediately? Of course! And you may even attempt to prosecute criminally or civilly your former employee. What if your pastor was embezzling tithe gifts and offerings, teaching false doctrine, and blaspheming God? Would you not fire him immediately and demand all embezzled money back? Without a doubt, most church members would certainly prosecute the pastor for such disgusting acts of unrighteousness. The samples in life go on and on, from children and parents, to doctors and patients; from husbands and wives, to lawyers and clients. All of life holds a standard of righteousness, the lineage or roots of which most people do not even realize or acknowledge. The same principle holds true for government and citizens: righteousness is the key to interrelations, blessings, and prosperity.

Justice

With knowledge, wisdom, and righteousness, God's nature must—and does—consist of justice. God is just: His ways, thoughts, laws, manners, actions, and judgments are just. Ecclesiastes 3:17 (MJKV) says, "I said in my heart, God shall judge the righteous and the wicked; for there is a time there for every purpose and for every work." God is just by judging wickedness and expects and demands that man do the same. Matthew 22:2–7 (ESV) gives an illustrative example of a king using his power to destroy those who would treat the law of God so lightly as to take away human life—where they made light of God's laws.

---

180. John 3:16 (KJV).

The kingdom of heaven may be compared to a king who gave a wedding feast for his son, and sent his servants to call those who were invited to the wedding feast, but they would not come. Again he sent other servants, saying, "Tell those who are invited, See, I have prepared my dinner, my oxen and my fat calves have been slaughtered, and everything is ready. Come to the wedding feast." But they paid no attention and went off, one to his farm, another to his business, while the rest seized his servants, treated them shamefully, and killed them. The king was angry, and he sent his troops and destroyed those murderers and burned their city.

Justice accomplished. The law of God is not something to be taken lightly on either side of the aisle. As nations are but men, justice is imparted on all men who break the laws of God—not just citizens, but the government as well. Why else would our system of government have impeachment avenues for the citizens to use against government administrators, as well as the right to alter, amend, or abolish the government? The justice of God is complete, thorough, without exception, and righteous altogether. Indeed,

[God] will render to every man according to his deeds: To them who by patient continuance in well doing seek for glory and honour and immortality, eternal life: But unto them that are contentious, and do not obey the truth, but obey unrighteousness, indignation and wrath.[181]

The LORD is known by the judgment which he executes: the wicked is snared in the work of his own hands.[182]

O LORD of hosts, that judges righteously, that tries the reins and the heart, let me see thy vengeance on them: for unto thee have I revealed my cause.[183]

---

181. Romans 2:6–8 (KJV).
182. Psalm 9:16 (KJV).
183. Jeremiah 11:20 (KJV).

[God the Father] has given [Jesus] authority to execute judgment also, because he is the Son of man.[184]

As God's nature is just, so too the government should strive to be just—as "ministers of God."[185] Understand that a cliché such as "justice for all" does not accomplish justice; in fact, there are times when constitutions are free, but the people are not. America's execution of and proclaimed belief in justice have been woven into the fabric of our Constitution, on both federal and state levels. However, the mark of justice will never be hit where those who create, execute, and interpret laws forget what justice is and where it comes from, for the wisdom of this world is made foolish by God.

Goodness

The next important attribute of God's nature is His goodness. "O taste and see that the LORD is good: blessed is the man that trusts in him."[186] God's nature of goodness should also be reflected in the government. A good government is one that possesses virtue—good intent—the intent, purpose, and goal to facilitate and provide its citizens with the best environment to conduct its affairs in accordance with the principles of natural law and revealed law. A government that cares more about its federal programs, tax revenue, power over the people, status with the nations of the world, global empire building, acquired properties, face saving, and scandal cover up than it does the life, liberty, and property of its citizens is void of virtue and goodness, will collapse, and should be resisted.

Impartial

God's nature is also impartial—a quality which should exist in the government in conformance to the nature of God. "For Jehovah your God is God of gods, and Lord of lords, a great God, the mighty, and a terrible God, who does not respect persons nor take a bribe."[187] "But he that does wrong shall receive for the wrong which he has done: and there is no respect of

---

184. John 5:27 (KJV).
185. Romans 13 (KJV).
186. Psalm 34:8 (KJV).
187. Deuteronomy 10:17 (MJKV).

persons."[188] This notion of impartiality is crucial to establish justice in any society: any government that executes wrath against those it does not agree with and mercy to those it does agree with does not conform to the nature of God. While judgment of a wicked act may have degrees of penalty, depending on the circumstance, the decision to execute judgment or not should not be persuaded or influenced by the unjust factor of prejudice and partiality. Thus, to accomplish the goal of impartiality, the government should incorporate measures to prevent it and even punish those government administrators who demonstrate partiality. Resisting a partial government shall also contribute to the peace and tranquility of society, as man would not fear destruction by others or the government as much, and thus, the need for self-preservation decreases, allowing man to further the gift of life more easily.

Sovereign

Perhaps the most important attribute of God's nature relative to government is the sovereignty of God, because defining and applying sovereignty forms the basis of all jurisdictions. It also forms the basis of all submission and resistance. The sovereignty of God forms the basis from which all other natures flow, for out of God's sovereignty all other gifts, rights, powers, and responsibilities derive. As John Jay says, "God governs the world, and we have only to do our duty wisely, and leave the issue to him."[189] If jurisdiction did not exist, there would be no right of man. Simply put, jurisdiction is a scope and limitation of authority.[190]

A simple example of the idea of jurisdiction is where, say, Bob murders a person in Alabama and is subsequently arrested in Alabama and charged under the laws of Alabama for murder. In this case, Florida has no jurisdiction to charge Bob for the same murder, because Florida has no jurisdiction. Another example is this: I (as, say, your neighbor) have no jurisdiction to enter your home and demand that you raise your children a certain way, because such a matter is outside my jurisdiction.

---

188. Peter 1:17 (KJV).

189. Jay, *The Life of John Jay*, 373.

190. "Jurisdiction—1. a government's general power to exercise authority over all persons and things within its territory. 2. a court's power to decide a case or issue a decree." Garner, *Black's Law Dictionary*.

How about this example, for those who see nothing wrong with the globalist movement: no foreign state or nation has any jurisdiction over America and the citizens of its respective states, because we the people of the several states have not consented to be subject to any other power or rule other than the Constitution of the United States of America.

While the issue of globalism has been presented, it must be acknowledged that globalism is alive and well,[191] despite many people's sheer ignorance on the subject, even to the point of denying its reality. While this subject is not the focus of this book, I believe it is crucial to at least highlight some notable comments on globalism by those who push for this realization. At this point I will say there is no need to take this author's word for it, but take it from the most powerful people in the world. Consider David Rockefeller's admission of the conspiracy of globalism in his book, *Memoirs.* Rockefeller says,

> Some even believe we (the Rockefeller family) are part of a secret cabal working against the best interests of the United States, characterizing my family and me as "internationalists" and of conspiring with others around the world to build a more integrated global political and economic structure—one world, if you will. *If that's the charge, I stand guilty, and I am proud of it.*[192]

Rockefeller is not alone—this is literally scratching the surface. The ideology of globalism/empire building has been confirmed over and over right before our very faces. Consider as well that the Council on Foreign

---

191. "Globalism is a known fact and is openly advocated by the most powerful in the U.S. and the world. Those who deny its existence are willfully ignorant." Buchanan, *The Death of the West,* 4; "The final surrender of national sovereignty to world government is now openly advocated. From Walter Cronkite to Strobe Talbott, from the World Federalist Association to the UN Millennium Summit, the chorus swells." The World Bank, *Advancing Sustainable Development: The World Bank and Agenda 21,* (Washington, D.C.: World Bank Publications, 1997); Boris Pleskovic and Nicholas Stern, eds., *Annual World Bank Conference on Development Economics 2000,* (Washington, D.C.: World Bank Publications, 2001); See Also Appendix D.

192. David Rockefeller, *Memoirs,* (New York: Random House, Inc., 2003), 405, (emphasis added).

Relations[193] has openly admitted to the same in the following: "We shall have world government whether or not you like it, by conquest or consent."[194] The president of the World Bank, Jim Wolfensohn, also openly admitted to the reality of global economy, politics, sociologics, finances, commerce, health, science, security, peace, and every other area of life. During his speech on April 2, 2001, Wolfensohn admitted the following: "We cannot turn back globalization. Our challenge is to make globalization an instrument of opportunity and inclusion—not of fear and insecurity. Globalization must work for all."[195] Wolfensohn further said, "Globalization is an opportunity to reach global solutions to national problems."[196] Former president Clinton's secretary of state, Strobe Talbot, demeaned national sovereignty and stated that the incorporation of globalism throughout the world is inevitable, saying, "In the next century, nations as we know it will be obsolete; all states will recognize a single, global authority. National sovereignty wasn't such a great idea after all."[197]

Just recently, Prime Minister Paul Martin, who signed the Trilateral Agreement between the United States, Canada, and Mexico known as the Security and Prosperity Agreement, gave a speech at the University of Ottawa regarding global governance, revealing once again this view towards global government and state interdependence. This is what he says:

---

193. "[Former CFR member and Advocate General of the U.S. Navy, Admiral Chester Ward] warned that the goal of the CFR is the 'submergence of US sovereignty and national independence into an all-powerful one-world government.' In the August 1978 issue of *W Magazine*, former CFR President Winston Lord is quoted as saying, 'The Trilateral Commission doesn't secretly run the world. The Council on Foreign Relations does that... Today the C.F.R. remains active in working toward its final goal of a government over all the world—a government which the Insiders and their allies will control... The goal of the C.F.R. is simply to abolish the United States with its constitutional guarantees of liberty. And they don't even try to hide it.'" Mark M. Rich, *The Hidden Evil: The Financial Elite's Covert War Against the Civilian Population,* (Morrisville, NC: Lulu Enterprises, Inc.), 19–20.

194. Berdj Kenadjian and Martin Zakarian, ill., *From Darkness to Light,* (Austin, Texas: Phenix & Phenix Literary Publicists, 2006), 266.

195. James Wolfensohn, "The Challenges of Globalization; The Role of the World Bank," (speech, Berlin, Germany, April 2, 2001).

196. Ibid.

197. John Tait, *Plain Truth,* (Longwood, FL: Xulon Press, 2008), 18–19.

[We must be] prepared to understand that in fact we're all going to have to give up a little of our sovereignty in order to make the world work... I think that we are really at the beginning of a very different era. [In] 1944, the great minds of the world...essentially laid the foundations for the...United Nations, and they built a system which functioned for over fifty or sixty years. I think that it's time to renew that vision—a very different world then when the day of independent nation states who simply came together but could ignore essentially what was going on inside those nations is over, that day is over... I think we got to take it one step further, and we got to say that in fact countries have responsibilities to their neighbors and their neighbors are in every nook and cranny of the world. And I believe that that is going to become the debate of our generation, and it is one that I am very happy to share with you.[198]

Former secretary of state Henry Kissinger openly admitted to the desire, plan, and goal of a new world order. Kissinger confirms this agenda in his own article, where he repeatedly refers to a new world order and specifically states, "The extraordinary impact of the president-elect [Obama] on the imagination of humanity is an important element in shaping a new world order. But it defines an opportunity, not a policy."[199] Globalism is a fact, and with its implementation and acceptance by America's government, so goes our national sovereignty, the Constitution, and our natural rights. One would have to be utterly devoid of America's history not to recognize that the ideology of globalism completely contradicts our nature, form, and substance of government. One of the underlying problems that most Americans do not realize is that this matter boils down to jurisdiction, founded in natural and revealed law. While the motives are numerous for those who believe, facilitate, and advance globalism, the end result will be global governance. Jeffrey Sachs says in his speech at the World Bank's Annual Conference on

---

198. Paul Martin, "Former Canadian Prime Minister: Give Up Your Sovereignty To Make The World Work," *CPAC* February 10, 2009, http://www.ronpaulwarroom.com/?p=19174.

199. Henry A. Kissinger, "The Chance for a New World Order," *The International Herald Tribune,* January 12, 2009, http://www.henryakissinger.com/articles/iht011209.html.

Economic Development in 2000, "I believe in shared global governance."[200] I shudder to think that there are supposed freedom-loving Americans who do not see a problem with this.

This matter of jurisdiction goes to what Jesus says, "Give unto Caesar the things that are Caesar's, and unto God, the things that are God's,"[201] because whatever is not Caesar's belongs to God or to other spheres of jurisdiction: individual, family, husband, wife, church, community, employer, etc. Without jurisdiction being complied with and understood, there are literally no limits to what the powerful may do to the weak. As Harvard University *cum laude* graduate and attorney, Herbert Titus, notes regarding Jesus's statements above, "Christ's answer was not…just an expedient way out of a political dilemma. Rather, it was a statement of legal principle affirming the general legitimacy of civil rule, while at the same time establishing jurisdictional limits to that rule."[202] If you believe that all matters relevant to the government belong to Caesar, then Algernon Sidney is addressing you when he says the following: "[You] confine the subject's choice to acting or suffering, that is, doing what is commanded, or lying down to have his throat cut, or to see his family and country made desolate. This [you] call giving to Caesar that which is Caesar's."[203] Sidney opposes such a view of Caesar's jurisdiction. Instead, Sidney says, "[You] ought to have considered, that the question is not whether that which is Caesar's should be rendered to him, for that is to be done to all men; but who is Caesar, and what doth of right belong to him."[204]

This matter should capture your mind and soul, because you have a duty to God, just as you have a duty to your family, your community, and your nation, but you must first understand the truth relative to what is Caesar's. It is important then to understand what God says about His own sovereignty by observing the following verses from scripture:

---

200. Jeffrey Sachs, Boris Pleskovic, and Nicholas Stern, eds., *Annual World Bank Conference on Development Economics 2000,* (Washington, D.C.: World Bank Publications, 2001), 47.

201. Luke 20:25 (KJV).

202. Herbert W. Titus, "A Reply to Professor Michael J. DeBoer," *Liberty University Law Review,* vol. 2, no. 2, (Lynchburg, VA: Liberty University School of Law, 2008), 407.

203. Sidney, *Discourses on Government,* 326.

204. Ibid.

For you are great and do wondrous things; you alone are God. (Psalm 86:10; ESV)

He who comes from above is above all. He who is of the earth belongs to the earth and speaks in an earthly way. He who comes from heaven is above all. (John 3:31; ESV)

There is only one lawgiver and judge, he who is able to save and to destroy. But who are you to judge your neighbor? (James 4:12; ESV)

Behold, the nations are as a drop of a bucket, and are counted as the small dust of the balance: behold, he takes up the isles as a very little thing. And Lebanon is not sufficient to burn, nor the beasts thereof sufficient for a burnt offering. All nations before him are as nothing; and they are counted to him less than nothing, and vanity. That brings the princes to nothing; he makes the judges of the earth as vanity. (Isaiah 40:15–17, 23; KJV)

May all kings fall down before him, all nations serve him! (Psalm 72:11; ESV)

He raises up the poor from the dust; he lifts the needy from the ash heap to make them sit with princes and inherit a seat of honor. For the pillars of the earth are the LORD's, and on them he has set the world. (1 Samuel 2:8; ESV)

He makes nations great, and he destroys them; he enlarges nations, and leads them away. (Job 12:23; ESV)

And Jesus came and said to them, "All authority in heaven and on earth has been given to me." (Matthew 28:18; ESV)

A person cannot receive even one thing unless it is given him from heaven. (John 3:27; ESV)

The Father [God] loves the Son [Jesus] and has given all things into his hand. (John 3:35; ESV)

With just the select verses considered, one can see the declaration that God is above all things, all people, all families, all communities, all governments, all nations, and above the entire universe. Every individual person, father, mother, pastor, judge, president, legislator, king, prince, and dictator will stand before Him one day and account for every thought and action they committed—whether or not in the name of authority. It is revealed as follows in Matthew 7:22–23 (ESV): "On that day many will say to me, 'Lord, Lord, did we not prophesy in your name, and cast out demons in your name, and do many mighty works in your name?' And then will I declare to them, 'I never knew you; depart from me, you workers of lawlessness.'"

Indeed, just because someone has the apparent authority to perform some act over another, such does not give this person authority under God to act as he chooses, nor does it relieve him of the consequences of his actions (here on earth or in heaven) if it be unlawful or evil.

God being the ultimate authority, natural and revealed law, common sense, and logic dictate that every other person, government, or otherwise is inferior to His commands and will. No person is exempt from the judgment and wrath of God simply because he holds a position giving him certain powers to act. Likewise, every person will answer for and be held accountable for actions or inactions contrary to God's will and commands, regardless of whether or not they were encouraged by friends, ordered by a judge, supported by a legislative body, or empowered by a president. This responsibility to the sovereign God creates a recognition and understanding that no person, other than God Himself, has complete authority over your life, and that any such person or government that attempts to subvert and contradict the sovereignty and will of God should be resisted. The apostle Peter proclaims, "I am to obey God rather than man,"[205] and Jesus commands, "Give unto Caesar the things that are Caesar's and unto God the things that are God's."

---

205. Acts 5:29 (KJV).

5

GOVERNMENT FORMATION

Like an inquisitive and thoughtful child asking the natural question to his parents "Where do babies come from?" so we, as American citizens, should be asking these basic questions regarding government: how does it come into existence, and what is its nature after formation? Understanding the answers to these questions is very fundamental to government, its purpose, powers, limits, and relation to its citizens and involves government formation. Most people take for granted the fact that a government even exists—similar to a child's lack of appreciation for having a house, food on the table, and medicine when he is sick. For many generations in America, our form of government and administration thereof has existed seemingly without our input, effort, work, or blood. Thus, one may have a tendency to believe that since the government has always existed, the government has a sort of preeminence or superiority over the person. Put another way, the government's existence is independent of the citizen's existence and has authority without the consideration of the people's consent, approval, or will. However, such an idea is contrary to logic and natural law and actually creates a slave mentality, rendering the citizens powerless over the government.

Lovers of freedom must have a deep and thorough understanding concerning the natural laws and principles of government formation. This is similar to a party maintaining the integrity of the contract by understanding the intent, terms, and obligations of each party. What good would the contract be without such an understanding? Sir William Rawle observes the seriousness of a compact (constitution) by stating in the following passage that a nation's very survival depends upon it:

> By a constitution we mean the principles on which a government is formed and conducted. On the voluntary association of men…the first step to be taken for their own security and happiness, is to agree on the terms on which they are to be united and to act. They form a constitution, or plan of government suited for their character, their exigencies, and their future prospects. They agree that it shall be the supreme rule of obligation among them.[1]

Rawle explains how impactful a constitution is on society and duly notes that both parties are bound to observe the constitution: citizen and government alike. Do Americans view our Constitution in the same light and with the same weight? I dare say, most do not. History, however, proves that without an appreciation for, understanding of, and compliance with a constitution, demanding governmental administrators to comply to the same is a lofty and pretentious thought. Additionally, to demand its compliance and thus ensure the freedoms protected by it one must (as Rawle says) understand the principles on which a government is formed and conducted. To understand the principles, one must first understand the nature of the thing, because "the perfection of a state, and its aptitude to fulfill the ends proposed by society, depend on its constitution."[2]

GOVERNMENT DOES NOT EXIST IN NATURE

What must first be recognized is that government does *not* exist in a state of nature. This fact is crucial to one's relationship to government. If government existed in a state of nature, then the power of the individual over such

---

1. Rawle, *A View of the Constitution of the United States of America*, 2.
2. Ibid., 16.

government would be subject to the natural powers vested in the government in a state of nature. However, if government does not exist in a state of nature, then the individual is—by nature—not controlled or limited by a government. When one discusses and contemplates existence in nature, it necessarily means created by God. Every other accepted entity of God following His creation would be God's ordination, or as literally interpreted in the Greek, God's *assignment* for specific and limited purposes.

A common misconception held by many is that God has created in nature the following entities: marriage, church, and government. Since no one was present at the time God created things and creatures, America's founders and Enlightenment philosophers referred to the Bible for their knowledge on this issue. That God created these entities and relationships is an incorrect belief and does not reflect the natural creation depicted in Genesis. Relative to the issue of whether or not government exists in a state of nature, John Chipman Gray observes, "Man was not made for the law, but the Law for man."[3] Likewise, even Thomas Paine (who apparently never admitted to any orthodox belief in religion) understands that there is a difference between the existence of society and government, stating, "Some writers have so confounded society with government, as to leave little or no distinction between them; whereas they are not only different, but have different origins. Society is produced by our wants, and government by our wickedness."[4] Put a different way, government never came into existence until the wickedness of man required its creation. Paine continues by reflecting on the notion that government would not even exist were it not for the sin nature of man. "Government even in its best state is but a necessary evil; in its worst state an intolerable one... Government, like [clothes], is the badge of lost innocence."[5]

The Bible confirms the fact that government does not exist in nature, as it is apparent that the only entity created by God is the life of the individual with the basic desire for companionship.[6] It cannot be said that God even

3. Gray, *The Nature and Sources of the Law*, 7.

4. Paine and Philip, ed., *Common Sense*, 5.

5. Ibid.

6. "Then the LORD God said, 'It is not good that the man should be alone; I will make him a helper fit for him.'" Genesis 2:18 (ESV).

created marriage per se, although God made Adam with the desire to be with the opposite sex. However, it is clear that not every man that has ever lived has always and without exception been married to a woman, for many men chose to live a single life, and such is not sinful.[7]

By comparison, it cannot be said that God created society, even though man has the desire to be in a community. Furthermore, God's creation of a desire cannot be equated to the creation of the thing itself. Nowhere does scripture indicate that God has created the institution of marriage or society, but only that such are natural outcomes of God's original creation of man, resulting from the desire of man. And out of the formation of societal relationships comes the need for government. Thus, one can see that God created only the individual, and that the individual has created society and government through his own natural power given by God.

The book of Genesis reveals much information regarding God's negative actions of government. In other words, the book reveals what God *did not* do regarding government more than it reveals what God did do regarding government. For centuries prior to America's independence, many societies had lived under a monarchy form of government, whereby one person embodies the executive, legislative, and sometimes even judiciary functions of government. One person will create law, enforce law, and interpret law. Throughout history, some have suggested and argued that a monarchy form of government is God's will and is the natural order of His creation; and they point to the lives of Adam, Noah, and Abraham to support their argument. However, the founders disagreed that natural or revealed law gave any one person such power and rather believed the opposite. "As the exalting one man so greatly above the rest cannot be justified on the equal rights of nature, so neither can it be defended on the authority of scripture; for the will of the Almighty…disapproves of government by kings,"[8] as Thomas Paine observed.

---

7. "Nevertheless, to avoid fornication, let every man have his own wife, and let every woman have her own husband. Art thou bound unto a wife? Seek not to be loosed. Art thou loosed from a wife? Seek not a wife." 1 Corinthians 7:2, 27 (KJV).

8. Paine and Philip, ed., *Common Sense,* 11–12; "Hence it is evident, that absolute monarchy, which by some men is counted the only government in the world, is indeed

Indeed, the scriptures reveal that God did not create one man to rule over all other men. But rather, God gave to *all mankind* the equal responsibility and authority to exercise dominion over the earth and all that is in it, and that God established nationalities and borders for men to maintain their society and government. Thomas Jefferson observes the same, stating, "The earth is given as a common stock for man to labor and live on."[9] If this is true, then the question of "Where does the power of government belong?" is seriously influenced and persuaded to the conclusion that the people possess power over the government, its formation, and its abolishing.

Observation of Government: Adam

If there were ever a time for God to establish the natural order (or God's will) of government, it would have been with Adam in the book of Genesis. But such an order does not exist. In fact, God created no form of government at all with any one of the patriarchs of scripture. Before God even created Adam, God revealed to us His intention to give to all mankind equal dominion and power of the earth. God says in Genesis 1:26–27 (ESV),

> "Let us make man in our image, after our likeness. And let them have dominion over the fish of the sea and over the birds of the heavens and over the livestock and over all the earth and over every creeping thing that creeps on the earth." So God created man in his

---

inconsistent with civil society, and so can be no form of civil-government at all: for the end of civil society, being to avoid, and remedy those inconveniencies of the state of nature, which necessarily follow from every man's being judge in his own case, by setting up a known authority, to which every one of that society may appeal upon any injury received, or controversy that may arise, and which every one of the society ought to obey; where-ever any persons are, who have not such an authority to appeal to, for the decision of any difference between them, there those persons are still in the state of nature; and so is every absolute prince, in respect of those who are under his dominion... For he being supposed to have all, both legislative and executive power in himself alone, there is no judge to be found, no appeal lies open to any one, who may fairly, and indifferently, and with authority decide, and from whose decision relief and redress may be expected of any injury or inconviency, that may be suffered from the prince, or by his order."
Locke and Macpherson, ed., *Second Treatise of Government*, 48.

9. Jefferson, *The Jeffersonian Cyclopedia*, 270.

own image, in the image of God he created him; male and female he created them.

Notice carefully that God says, "let *them* have dominion." God clearly did not intend that Adam—the individual—possess all powers of dominion, for He at least gave such power to Adam and Eve, which was the entire human population at the time. Even more clearly, God did not intend that Adam have dominion over other humans. God granted the following authority to Adam and Eve:

> And God blessed them. And God said to them, "Be fruitful and multiply and fill the earth and subdue it and have dominion over the fish of the sea and over the birds of the heavens and over every living thing that moves on the earth." And God said, "Behold, I have given you every plant yielding seed that is on the face of all the earth, and every tree with seed in its fruit. You shall have them for food. And to every beast of the earth and to every bird of the heavens and to everything that creeps on the earth, everything that has the breath of life, I have given every green plant for food." And it was so.[10]

It cannot be reasonably argued that God created a monarchy from this grant, because God clearly intended that Adam and Eve have dominion and control of the earth and the animals in it—not the people. Furthermore, common sense and contextual reading dictate that God's grant of power here referred to all of mankind (not just Adam and Eve), for it cannot be argued that God gave only Adam and Eve the commandment to be fruitful and multiply, and replenish the earth. Rather, all mankind has been given such power and authority. Thus, the remaining grants of power apply similarly. To suggest that God granted to Adam power over other humans necessarily suggests that God granted the same power to all of mankind, meaning each person born has power over every other person. Such an interpretation makes absolutely no sense and contradicts revealed and natural law.

---

10. Genesis 1:28–30 (ESV).

Indeed, America's founders possessed and shared this perspective and under-standing of God's ordination of government in Adam, as expressed by major Enlightenment philosophers like John Locke.[11]

To suggest that Adam and Eve had dominion over everything that creeps upon the earth, wherein there is life, meaning other humans, is without merit, "since all positive grants convey no more than the express words."[12] The clear meaning of this passage indicates that God granted to mankind the power of utilizing the earth and all that is within it. John Lock analyzes this matter in the following passage:

> Where [God] actually exercises this design, and gives him this dominion, the text mentions the fishes of the sea, and fowls of the air, and the terrestrial creatures in the words that signify the wild beasts and reptiles, though translated living thing that moveth…nor do these words contain in them the least appearance of any thing that can be wrested to signify God's giving to one man dominion over another.[13]

When God granted power to "them" to exercise dominion over the earth and all that is in it, God did not grant such power to one person, but to all mankind; and all of mankind shared in not only the authority but the responsibility. Likewise, God never granted any power to Adam to control and to have dominion over all other humans within any government. Thus,

---

11. "1. That Adam had not, either by natural right of fatherhood, or by positive donation from God, any such authority over his children, or dominion over the world, as is pretended: 2. That if he had, his heirs, yet, had no right to it: 3. That if his heirs had, there being no law of nature nor positive law of God that determines which is the right heir in all cases that may arise, the right of succession, and consequently of bearing rule, could not have been certainly determined: 4. That if even that had been determined, yet the knowledge of which is the eldest line of Adam's posterity, being so long since utterly lost, that in the races of mankind and families of the world, there remains not to one above another, the least pretence to be the eldest house, and to have the right of inheritance." Locke and Macpherson, ed., *Second Treatise of Government*, 7.

12. Locke, *Two Treatises on Government*, 26.

13. Ibid., 28.

no one person had any God-given power or authority to dictate and control others, and no monarchy or any other government was ever created by God. The deductive conclusion necessitates the fact that each person born has no inherent power granted by God to rule over others, but that mankind decides for himself as an individual and as a society (once formed) who rules and under what conditions.

Furthermore, observe that after Cain killed his brother Abel, Cain feared for his life at the hands of other men—and not just his father, Adam, per se (also contributing to the fact that Adam was not a monarchial power established by God). Cain says this to God after God tells him that he shall be a fugitive and a vagabond of the earth in Genesis 4:14 (ESV). "Behold, you have driven me today away from the ground, and from your face I shall be hidden. I shall be a fugitive and a wanderer on the earth, and whoever finds me will kill me." At this time, it was already known that there was a sense of justice regarding societal conduct, and there would be consequences for wrongdoing in society, not even necessarily from God Himself. [14] Even then, before any laws of God were revealed to man, government was to be used as the minister of God by punishing evil, not through the direct commandments of God, but through the natural laws of God. God reflects and confirms His standard of ministers of God to Noah and his sons after the flood. Regarding the sanctity of life God commands them to incorporate capital punishment into their existing societies in Genesis 9:6. [15] But such punishment was apparently already accepted and practiced in society, or else Cain would not have feared that punishment from other men. Thus, scriptures reveal that God did not establish government at creation, but rather man (through natural law) formed government in society by the powers vested in all of mankind by God.

---

14. "[U]pon this is grounded that great law of nature, whoso sheddeth man's blood, by man shall his blood be shed. And Cain was so fully convinced, that every one had a right to destroy such a criminal, that after the murder of his brother, he cries out, every one that findeth me, shall slay me; so plain was it writ in the hearts of all mankind." Locke and Macpherson, ed., *Second Treatise of Government,* 12.

15. "Whoever sheds the blood of man, by man shall his blood be shed, for God made man in his own image." Genesis 9:6 (ESV).

Observation of Government: Noah

Likewise, God did not grant or create in Noah a governmental authority or power to exercise over all of his inferiors. The following verses express God's grant and charge to Noah and his three sons after the flood destroyed the entire population of the earth, leaving only Noah, Ham, Shem, Japeth, and their wives:

> And God blessed Noah and his sons and said to them, "Be fruitful and multiply and fill the earth. The fear of you and the dread of you shall be upon every beast of the earth and upon every bird of the heavens, upon everything that creeps on the ground and all the fish of the sea. Into your hand they are delivered. Every moving thing that lives shall be food for you. And as I gave you the green plants, I give you everything. But you shall not eat flesh with its life, that is, its blood. And for your lifeblood I will require a reckoning: from every beast I will require it and from man. From his fellow man I will require a reckoning for the life of man. Whoever sheds the blood of man, by man shall his blood be shed, for God made man in his own image."[16]

Very clearly God gives a similar grant of power to Noah and his sons that He gave to "them." Here, God does not give any form of government to Noah and his sons. But rather, "God blessed Noah and his sons," as John Locke observes, "all the men then living, and not to one part of men over another."[17]

God's grant of power of the earth to all mankind is confirmed by the remaining portions of God's grant to Noah and his sons. He commands them to be fruitful and multiply; He reveals that all fishes of the sea are delivered in their hands; and that the fear and the dread of them shall be upon every beast of the earth; that for their lifeblood He will require a reckoning; from

---

16. Genesis 9:1–6 (ESV).

17. Locke, *Two Treatises on Government*, 23.

every beast He will require it and from man. It cannot be argued without abandoning all common sense and plain reading of the scriptures that sexual reproduction is given only to Noah and his sons; that the animals and fish were only to fear Noah and his sons; that meat was only given to Noah and his sons to eat; and that God would only protect the lives of Noah and his sons. It is obvious the grant of power and rules relative to man's interaction with animals and other men were universal to all men, just as it is revealed by the fact that God made a covenant to all humanity (and not just to Noah and his sons) not to flood the earth again.[18]

To further confirm God's ordination of the limited authority of Noah and his sons, after God gives the grants of authority above to Noah and his three sons, God divides Noah's posterity into nations, each having their own boundaries and independence from each other. Nowhere does God command others to obey Noah or his sons, but rather all of the descendants of Noah's sons are divided into their nations, without the reign or authority of a king:

CONCERNING JAPETH:

Now these are the generations of the sons of Noah, Shem, Ham, and Japheth. And sons were born to them after the flood. The sons of Japheth: Gomer and Magog and Madai and Javan and Tubal and Meshech and Tiras. And the sons of Gomer: Ashkenaz and Riphath and Togarmah. And the sons of Javan: Elishah and Tarshish and Kittim and Dodanim. *By these were the coasts of the nations divided in their lands, every one after his tongue, after their families, in their nations.*[19]

CONCERNING HAM:

And the sons of Ham: Cush and Mizraim and Phut and Canaan. And the sons of Cush: Seba and Havilah and Sabtah and Raamah

---

18. "I establish my covenant with you, that never again shall all flesh be cut off by the waters of the flood, and never again shall there be a flood to destroy the earth." Genesis 9:11 (ESV).

19. Genesis 10:1–5 (MJKV), (emphasis added).

and Sabtecha. And the sons of Raamah: Sheba and Dedan. And Cush fathered Nimrod. He began to be a mighty one in the earth. He was a mighty hunter before Jehovah. Therefore it is said, Even as Nimrod the mighty hunter before Jehovah. And the beginning of his kingdom was Babel, and Erech, and Accad, and Calneh, in the land of Shinar. Out of that land he went forth to Asshur. And he built Nineveh, and the city Rehoboth, and Calah, and Resen between Nineveh and Calah, which is a great city. And Mizraim fathered Ludim and Anamim and Lehabim and Naphtuhim, and Pathrusim and Casluhim (from whom came the Philistines) and Caphtorim. And Canaan fathered Sidon, his first-born, and Heth, and the Jebusite and the Amorite, and the Girgashite, and the Hivite, and the Arkite, and the Sinite, and the Arvadite, and the Zemarite, and the Hamathite. *And afterward the families of the Canaanites were spread abroad. And the border of the Canaanites was from Sidon (as you come to Gerar) to Gaza, as you go in towards Sodom and Gomorrah and Admah and Zeboim, even to Lasha. These were the sons of Ham, after their families, after their tongues, in their countries, and in their nations.*[20]

Concerning Shem:

The sons of Shem: Elam and Asshur and Arpachshad and Lud and Aram. And the sons of Aram: Uz and Hul and Gether and Mash, And Arpachshad fathered Salah; and Salah fathered Eber. And two sons were born to Eber. The name of the one was Peleg, for in his days the earth was divided. And his brother's name was Joktan. And Joktan fathered Almodad and Sheleph and Hazarmaveth and Jerah, and Hadoram and Uzal and Diklah, and Obal and Abimael and Sheba, and Ophir and Havilah, and Jobab. All these were the sons of Joktan. And their dwelling was from Mesha, as you go to Sephar, a mountain of the east. *These are the sons of Shem, after their families, after their tongues, in their lands, and after their nations.*[21]

---

20. Genesis 10:6–20 (MJKV), (emphasis added).
21. Genesis 10:22–31 (MJKV), (emphasis added).

As is clearly seen, God not only did not create a monarchy through Noah and his sons, but also God divided the families into nations, which were separated by borders and nationality. Scripture reveals even from the beginning of time that nationality is God's will. Once each son established his own nationality, subsequent attempts to circumvent what God ordained were destroyed by God, as is seen in the story of Nimrod and the city of Babel (see hereafter). Clearly, dictatorial rule and one-world government was rejected by God and never created by God.

Observation of Government: Abraham

Neither did God grant nor create a governmental authority in Abraham— Abraham's title being, "the father of the faithful,"[22] not the king of the faithful. Just the opposite: Abraham was told to leave his home, family, and country and go to a place that God would show him.

Algernon Sidney studiously observes that Noah was alive when Abraham was alive and commanded by God to depart from his country, establishing His covenant with him at that time, which confirms as well that no monarchial government existed.

> It is evident in scripture, that Noah lived three hundred and fifty years after flood... Abraham was born about two hundred and ninety years after the flood, and lived one hundred seventy-five years: he was therefore born under the government of Noah, and died under that of Shem: he could not therefore exercise a regal power whilst he lived, for that was in Shem: so that in leaving his country, and setting up of a family for himself that never acknowledged any superior, and never pretending to reign over any other, he fully shewed he thought himself free, and to owe subjection to none.[23]

---

22. "Walk in the footsteps of the faith that our father Abraham had before he was circumcised." Romans 4:12 (ESV). "Know then that it is those of faith who are the sons of Abraham." Galatians 3:7 (ESV).

23. Sidney, *Discourses on Government,* 345, 346.

When Abraham left as God had asked, Abraham took his wife, his nephew, all the substance that they had gathered, and the people that they had gotten in Haran, and they went forth to go into the land of Canaan.[24] After Abraham reached the land of Canaan, the following story unfolds in Genesis 13:5–9 (KJV):

And Lot also, which went with Abram, had flocks, and herds, and tents. And the land was not able to bear them, that they might dwell together: for their substance was great, so that they could not dwell together. And there was a strife between the herdmen of Abram's cattle and the herdmen of Lot's cattle: and the Canaanite and the Perizzite dwelled then in the land. And Abram said unto Lot, Let there be no strife, I pray thee, between me and thee, and between my herdmen and thy herdmen; for we be brethren. Is not the whole land before thee? Separate thyself, I pray thee, from me: if thou wilt take the left hand, then I will go to the right; or if thou depart to the right hand, then I will go to the left.

Abraham's reaction here to the problem presented is not that of a monarchial king but more of a land and property owner—a farmer or rancher. Indeed, Abraham made no demands to Lot but gave him preference of where to live. God did not establish a monarchial power in Abraham.

Observation of Government: Nimrod

The scripture, in fact, reveals the opposite of the notion that God created government and, moreover, reveals that God did not grant the power to govern to one person, naturally or otherwise. Rather, God gave power to all mankind to govern themselves. It is known in American history as self-government. Indeed, the first usurpation of the people's power was conducted by the mighty hunter Nimrod, as found in Genesis. We see in this story

---

24. "And Abram took Sarai his wife, and Lot his brother's son, and all their possessions that they had gathered, and the people that they had acquired in Haran, and they set out to go to the land of Canaan. When they came to the land of Canaan." Genesis 12:5 (ESV).

how God actually divests and destroys the power and government established by Nimrod and reestablishes power in the people. Thomas Paine duly notes that this type of government was in fact an evil one. "Government by kings was first introduced into the world by the Heathens… It was the most prosperous invention the Devil ever set on foot for the promotion of idolatry."[25]

In the scriptures it is apparent that neither Noah nor his sons exercised regal and monarchial authority over the people. On the other hand, Nimrod took advantage and acted as follows: "[Nimrod] turned into violence and oppression the power given to him by a multitude; which, like a flock without a shepherd, not knowing whom to obey, set him up to be their chief."[26] God conveys clearly that Nimrod "began to be a mighty one in the earth… And the beginning of his kingdom was Babel."[27] As God divided the nations through the nationalities of Ham, Shem, and Japeth, Nimrod attempted to combine the nations for his purposes and pleasure, as is reflected in scriptures. "And they said, Come, let us build us a city and a tower, and its top in the heavens. And let us make a name for ourselves, lest we be scattered upon the face of the whole earth."[28]

Nimrod did not accept God's ordination that nations be independent and sovereign, but instead desired to form a unity of nations, "lest they be scattered upon the face of the whole earth." Matthew Henry's *Commentaries on the Whole Bible* describes Nimrod's usurpation of power this way:

Whereas those that went before him were content to stand upon the same level with their neighbours, and though every man bore rule in his own house yet no man pretended any further, Nimrod's aspiring mind could not rest here; he was resolved to tower above his neighbours, not only to be eminent among them, but to lord it over them. The same spirit that actuated the giants before the flood (who became mighty men, and men of renown, Genesis 6:4), now revived

25. Paine and Philip, ed., *Common Sense,* 11.
26. Sidney, *Discourses on Government,* 346.
27. Genesis 10:8, 10 (KJV).
28. Genesis 11:4 (MJKV).

in him, so soon was that tremendous judgment which the pride and tyranny of those mighty men brought upon the world forgotten.[29]

Nimrod rejected God's ordination of nationality, borders, and self-governance, as he attempted to join the nations together under his control and dominion. As a result of the monarchial or dictatorial power wielded by Nimrod, God saw this wickedness and decided to end the reign of Nimrod by dividing the languages of this kingdom and by dispersing men into nations as He originally planned.

> And the LORD said, "Behold, they are one people, and they have all one language, and this is only the beginning of what they will do. And nothing that they propose to do will now be impossible for them. Come, let us go down and there confuse their language, so that they may not understand one another's speech." So the LORD dispersed them from there over the face of all the earth, and they left off building the city. Therefore its name was called Babel, because there the LORD confused the language of all the earth. And from there the LORD dispersed them over the face of all the earth.[30]

Whatever authority Nimrod acquired, God rejected his government, or authority over the people, by forcing his kingdom to separate and to be confused. After destroying Nimrod's attempts of building the mighty nation of Babel, God does not establish or require any form of government be instituted by men, but instead He reestablishes the grant of power to all the people as described to Adam and Eve and to Noah and his sons. Thus, the Bible reveals that God did not create any one person or any particular government to rule over others under any sort of rule of natural law.

Thomas Paine studied the Bible and concludes that "in the early ages of the world, according to the scripture chronology, there were no kings, the consequence of which was there were no wars; it is the pride of kings

---

29. Matthew Henry, *Matthew Henry's Commentary on the Whole Bible,* vol. 1, (Peabody, MA: Hendrickson Publishers, 1991).

30. Genesis 11:6–9 (ESV).

which throw mankind into confusion."[31] Observing and understanding that God did not create government but rather created individuals with an equal power and authority to occupy the earth; the only other alternative regarding the source of government formation is in the people.

GOVERNMENT IS SUBJECT TO THE WILL OF THE PEOPLE

Since the formation of government derives from the natural power of man, then the power of such government necessarily is subject to the will of its creator—the people. This fundamental principle is exactly what formed all of the individual states' constitutions, as well as the U.S. Constitution, which was a well-settled principle recognized by not only America's founders, but also by English philosophers and by the writers of scripture.[32] In other words, since the people created it, the people can amend, alter, or abolish it if they choose. Samuel Rutherford[33] in his classic philosophical dissertation *Lex Rex* concludes, "This power [given to a ruler] must have been virtually in [the citizens], because neither man nor community of men can give that which they neither have formally nor virtually in them."[34] Fellow philosopher Charles

---

31. Paine and Philip, ed., *Common Sense,* 11.

32. "Men being, as has been said, by nature, all free, equal, and independent, no one can be put out of this estate, and subjected to the political power of another, without his own consent. The only way whereby any one divests himself of his natural liberty, and puts on the bonds of civil society, is by agreeing with other men to join and unite into a community for their comfortable, safe, and peaceable living one amongst another, in a secure enjoyment of their properties, and a greater security against any, that are not of it." Locke and Macpherson, ed., *Second Treatise of Government,* 52.

33. "Samuel Rutherford (1600? – 1661) was a Scottish Presbyterian theologian and author. He was one of the Scottish Commissioners to the Westminster Assembly. Born in the village of Nisbet, Roxburghshire, Rutherford was educated at Edinburgh University, where he became in 1623 Regent of Humanity (Professor of Latin). In 1627 he was settled as minister of Anwoth in Galloway, from where he was banished to Aberdeen for nonconformity. His patron in Galloway was John Gordon, 1st Viscount of Kenmure. On the re-establishment of Presbytery in 1638 he was made Professor of Divinity at St. Andrews, and in 1651 Principal of St. Mary's College there. At the Restoration he was deprived of all his offices." "Samuel Rutherford," *Wikipedia,* http://en.wikipedia.org/wiki/Samuel_Rutherford (accessed May 5, 2009).

34. Samuel Rutherford, *Lex, Rex, or The Law and the Prince,* (Edinburgh: Robert Ogle and Oliver & Boyd, 1644), 6.

Montesquieu agrees with Rutherford, stating, "As in a country of liberty, every man who is supposed a *free agent* ought to be his own governor; the legislative power should reside in the whole body of the people."[35] Understand, this power that man has to form and institute government derives from the source of all power—God—just as the power to marry or to have children is from God. However, the actual formation and practical institution of the power is in the power of man. Rutherford describes the origination and structure of the people's power this way:

> That power of government in general be from God…because "there is no power but of God; the power that be are ordained of God." All civil power is immediately from God in its root; in that God hath made man a social creature. We fancied that government of superiors was only for the more perfect, but had no authority over or above the perfect…the kingly power is immediately and only from God, because it is not natural to us to be subject to government, but against nature for us to resign our liberty to a king, or any ruler or rulers.[36]

Out of God's creation of man comes the desire of man to be in a community (which is the essence of creating a society), just as the desire to be with the opposite sex causes men to form the marriage relationship through a contract with a woman, and likewise a woman with a man. As Thomas Jefferson puts it, "Every man, and every body of men on earth, possesses the right of self-government. They received it with their being from the hand of nature."[37] Therefore, out of man's desire to form society comes man's necessity to form government, even though it is "against nature for us to resign our liberty to a king, or any ruler or rulers."[38] This is the very principle precipitating George Washington's statement in his farewell address, where he states in part, "The basis of our political systems is the right of the people to make and to alter their Constitutions of Government. But the Constitution which

---

35. Montesquieu, *The Spirit of Laws,* 154.
36. Rutherford, *Lex, Rex,* 1, 2.
37. Jefferson, *The Jeffersonian Cyclopedia,* 609.
38. Rutherford, *Lex, Rex,* 2.

at any time exists, till changed by an explicit and authentic act of the whole people, is sacredly obligatory upon all."[39]

When man exercises and expands the natural gift of life and its natural by-products, he invariably places himself into societies, "which bound them together in a common cause."[40] As a result, "they will…point out the necessity, of establishing some form of government to supply the defect of moral virtue."[41] Consequently, "society is produced by our wants, and government by our wickedness; the former [society] promotes our happiness positively by uniting our affections, the latter [government] negatively by restraining our vices."[42] We see that God in fact ordains the existence of government, as is indicated in Genesis when God declares that "Whoever sheds the blood of man, by man shall his blood be shed, for God made man in his own image."[43] However, even more notable is that nowhere in Genesis does God command men to form a government, but God recognizes that men already formed a system of laws, whereby the peace and rights of people could be maintained.

It is important to distinguish the difference between the creation of power and the ordination of power. Again by comparison, a man has the power to create marriage by marrying a woman, but it is God that ordains the relationship and gives it divine legitimacy. Man possesses the power to marry, when to marry, whom to marry, and once married, exercises the powers natural to that marriage. Rutherford explained that government is also the exercise of man, suggesting that without man giving the prospect of government life, government is similar to a dream—nonexistent, imaginary, without substance—though possible to exist. "[Government] is an ordinance of men, not effectively, as if it were an invention and a dream of men, but subjectively, because exercised by man. Objectively…for the good of men, and for the external man's peace and safety especially."[44]

---

39. George Washington and William T. Peck, ed., *Washington's Farewell Address and Webster's Bunker Hill Orations,* (New York: Macmillan Co., original from Harvard University, 1919), 12.

40. Paine and Philip, ed., *Common Sense,* 6.

41. Ibid.

42. Ibid.

43. Genesis 9:6 (KJV).

44. Rutherford, *Lex, Rex,* 5.

Grotius explains it in light of natural law, saying (as also quoted in chapter 4), "For the Mother of Right, that is, of Natural Law, is Human Nature; for this would lead us to desire mutual society, even if it were not required for the supply of other wants; and the Mother of Civil Laws is Obligation by mutual compact; and since mutual compact derives its force from Natural Law, Nature may be said to be the Grandmother of Civil Laws. The genealogy is, Human Nature: Natural Law: Civil Laws."[45] Therefore, to put the concept into an analogy, government is the clay, and we the people of the states are its potter.

Establishing the fact that God did not create government, but that it is within the power of man to create government, one must acknowledge that government then has no power except what is given to it by the people who created it, and thus, the following is true:

> No right is to be acknowledged in any, but such as is conferred upon them by those who have the right of conferring, and are concerned in the exercise of the power, upon such conditions as best please themselves. No obedience can be due to him or them, who have not a right of commanding...[and] the law of every institution, as creatures are to do the will of their Creator, and in deflecting from it, overthrow their own being.[46]

Ultimately, with the power to create substance comes the power to create, amend, or abolish form. In other words, God has given to men the freedom to choose the form that best suits the needs and desires of that society—hopefully with the reflection of natural law and revealed law in the forefront of such a decision. Grotius observes the truth of this power to choose in the following passage:

> As there are many ways of living, one better than another, and each man is free to choose which of them he pleases; so each nation may choose what form of government it will: and its right in this matter is not to be measured by the excellence of this or that form...but by its choice.[47]

---

45. Grotius, *Hugo Grotius on the Rights of War and Peace,* xxvii.
46. Sidney, *Discourses on Government,* 385, 386.
47. Grotius, *Hugo Grotius on the Rights of War and Peace,* 38.

Therefore, the people have the power and freedom, as those whom God commanded to occupy and exercise dominion over the earth collectively, to create the form and substance of government. Government has no power in and of itself, either in nature or of God, and "is not an independent and irresponsible power, but the agent of the people, and controlled by their will."[48]

---

48. Rayner, *The Life of Thomas Jefferson*, x.

6

GOVERNMENT ADMINISTRATORS

Of, By, and For the People

Common sense, natural observation, logical reasoning, and God's revealed law all demonstrate that given the free nature of man and the power of man to formulate the form and substance of government, mankind also has the freedom and power to decide who administers government. The opposite of this assertion would be that certain people naturally possess a right to rule over others, inherent in some natural law observation, such as genetics, heredity, or fate. The right to rule argument has been made by many despots, kings, and tyrants throughout history, most of whom suppressed, oppressed, and destroyed individuals, families, communities, and nations. However, such a belief was rejected wholly by America's founders and framers, citing the natural and revealed laws of God.

William Blackstone was the "second most invoked political authority during the Founding Era [and] was also an English judge and law professor who authored the four-volume *Commentaries on the Laws of England (1765–69)*."[1] He offers the following insight on the power of the people to choose their leaders as they deem appropriate to secure the rights of man:

---

1. Barton, *Original Intent,* 216.

All mankind will agree that government should be reposed in such persons, in whom those qualities are most likely to be found, the perfection of which is among the attributes of Him who is emphatically styled the Supreme being; the three grand requisites...of wisdom, of goodness, and of power...and this authority is placed in those hands, wherein the qualities...are most likely to be found.[2]

Notice that Blackstone recognizes not only the qualifications government administrators should possess, "the attributes of Him who is emphatically styled the Supreme being," but also that such authority is placed in those hands by the people. Montesquieu reflects the same sentiment concerning the power of the people this way: "It is likewise a fundamental law in democracies, that the people should have the sole power to enact laws."[3] Likewise, Rutherford and Paine conclude respectively, "Civil power according to its institution is of God, and according to its acquisition and way of use is of man,"[4] and "a government of our own is our natural right."[5]

The power of the people to choose their governmental administrators is found in God's revealed word, as well. In fact, as was thoroughly discussed by our forefathers and philosophers, the Bible actually condemns the right-to-rule notion, as reflected by Thomas Paine when he says,

That the Almighty hath there entered his protest against monarchial government is true, or the scripture is false... To the evil of monarchy we have added that of hereditary succession; and as the first is a degradation and lessening of ourselves, so the second, claimed as a matter of right, is an insult and an imposition on posterity.[6]

The Bible confirms this power of the people. Perhaps one of the more well-known biblical cases on this point is where the nation of Israel desired

---

2. Blackstone, *Commentaries on the Laws of England,* 40.
3. Montesquieu, *The Spirit of Laws,* 13.
4. Rutherford, *Lex Rex,* 6.
5. Paine and Philip, ed. *Common Sense,* 34.
6. Ibid., 14–15.

to be led by a king, and not directly by God, through His prophets. This would have been the first time in its history that Israel would not be led by the direct word of God to His prophets. Even while their choice was not God's perfect will for them, Israel's power to choose was acknowledged and assented to by God Himself, further demonstrating the power of the citizenry to choose their leaders.

We find further events of the power in the people in 1 Samuel.

[And the people of Israel said,] "Behold, you, [Samuel], are old and your sons do not walk in your ways. Now appoint for [Israel] a king to judge us like all the nations."[7]

Then Samuel brought all the tribes of Israel near, and the tribe of Benjamin was taken by lot. He brought the tribe of Benjamin near by its clans, and the clan of the Matrites was taken by lot; and Saul the son of Kish was taken by lot. But when they sought him, he could not be found.

So they inquired again of the LORD, "Is there a man still to come?" And the LORD said, "Behold, he has hidden himself among the baggage." Then they ran and took him from there. And when he stood among the people, he was taller than any of the people from his shoulders upward. And Samuel said to all the people, "Do you see him whom the LORD has chosen? There is none like him among all the people." And all the people shouted, "Long live the king!"[8]

The power of the people to grant Saul the power of king was effectuated at the moment they agreed with God's choice with one voice, declaring, "Long live the king!" And so it was, not because God had chosen a leader for them, but because the people established Saul to be king over them.

Later in the same book, God confirms the fact that the people chose their governmental leader, and that God did not force such a leader upon the people. Furthermore, the foundational understanding of what *ordination*

---

7. Samuel 8:5 (ESV).
8. Samuel 10:20–24 (ESV).

of government means regarding the administrators that the people choose becomes more enlightened in the following verses:

> And when you saw that Nahash the king of the Ammonites came against you, you said to me, "No, but a king shall reign over us," when the LORD your God was your king. And now behold the king *whom you have chosen, for whom you have asked;* behold, the LORD has set a king over you. If you will fear the LORD and serve him and obey his voice and not rebel against the commandment of the LORD, and if both you and the king who reigns over you will follow the LORD your God, it will be well.[9]

The passage is clear: God placed the king over the nation, "whom you have chosen, for whom you have asked." God did not force the government or the administrator of government on the nation; He allowed them to choose. In other words, when the people expressed their will regarding the form of government and the administrator of government, God ordained their choice of both form and leader. Very importantly, however, God also limited the king's ability to rule outside of God's laws. Clearly, God prefers to use people to set nations up and down rather than His all-powerful sovereignty. However, notice that God promises to bless the people's choice of king only on the following conditions: "If you will fear the LORD and serve him and obey his voice and not rebel against the commandment of the LORD, and if both you and the king who reigns over you will follow the LORD your God," then will it be well with you. Put another way, God does not ordain all actions of government, even though He ordains the position of government. Thus, the people's choice of the administrator is not the final matter to God; but rather, God's laws and blessings remain absolute and consistent and apply to all people, including the king himself. This biblical understanding demonstrates just how important the people's choice of government leaders is for the blessing of God upon that nation.

---

9. Samuel 12:12–14 (ESV), (emphasis added).

Another demonstration of the biblical acknowledgment of the people's power to choose their administrator of government is found in the following verses, where God instructs the people of Israel regarding their appointment of government administrators:

> When you are come unto the land which the LORD thy God gives thee, and shall possess it, and shall dwell therein, and shall say, I will set a king over me, like as all the nations that are about me; You shall in any wise set him king over you, whom the LORD your God shall choose: one from among your brethren shall you set king over you: you may not set a stranger over thee, which is not your brother.[10]

Again, this verse clearly stands for the truth that the people actually have the practical and natural power to choose their leader. Subsequently, God ordains the leader whom the people choose. Why else would God give them the condition that the leader be "one from among your brethren" to be "king over you" and that "you may not set a stranger over you"? If God Himself chooses the leader directly, without regard to the people's choice, He would not need to give them any condition that the king be someone from their own nation. It is reasonably concluded then that God ordains the king whom the people choose. Once again, however, the element of limited power sheds understanding on the meaning of God's ordination of government. Specifically put, God limits the power and authority of their king this way:

> And it shall be with him, and he shall read therein all the days of his life: that he may learn to fear the LORD his God, to keep all the words of this law and these statutes, to do them: That his heart be not lifted up above his brethren, and that he turn not aside from the commandment, to the right hand, or to the left: to the end that he may prolong his days in his kingdom, he, and his children, in the midst of Israel.[11]

---

10. Deuteronomy 17:14–15 (KJV).
11. Deuteronomy 17:19–20 (KJV).

Therefore, it cannot be argued that once the people have made their will known and exercised their will by placing someone in power, that God is unconcerned with limitations of power, applications of laws, and responsibility of governmental leaders. Furthermore, it is clear that the people set such leaders only for their good, not for the good of the ruler. Similarly, the people are to keep God's conditions in mind when choosing a leader, because if that leader does not follow the conditions, God's judgment follows and blessing ceases.

God's standard is clear: the king must fear God, read God's laws and statutes, apply God's laws and statutes, not think of himself above his brethren, and not turn from God's commandments. Samuel Rutherford in fact comments on the aforementioned Bible verses regarding God's standards and the limitation of His ordination of the people's choice of ruler:

> Wherever God appointed a king he never appointed him absolute, as a sole independent angel, but joined always with him judges, who were no less to judge according to the law of God (2 Chron. 14:6) than the king, Deut. 17:15. And in a moral obligation of judging righteously, the conscience of the monarch and the conscience of the inferior judges are equally under immediate subjection to the King of kings; for there is here a co-ordination of consciences, and no subordination, for it is not in the power of the inferior judge to judge...as the king commandeth him, because the judgment is neither the king's, nor any mortal man's, but the Lord's, 2 Chron. 17:6, 7.[12]

In no way can one suggest that any ruler is exempt from the laws of God simply because the people have exercised their power to choose a leader, and such person has been placed in authority as an administrator of government, the power of which belongs to the people. In other words, merely becoming a leader through legitimate means does not give the administrator unlimited power and ordination from God. Consequently, such a person cannot auto-

---

12. Rutherford, *Lex, Rex,* 5.

matically and unconditionally obligate himself to obey the commands of the king (as one who is "ordained of God") simply because that person holds the power to command (a subject discussed further herein). Can a citizen concede more leeway and authority to a modern-day leader and expect that such an administrator of government not be bound by the limitations set forth by its creator—*the people*—any more than the kings chosen by Israel were limited by the laws of God given to the nation? With that said, however, God acknowledges the power of the people to choose their leaders.

Furthermore, concerning the power of the people to choose their government administrators, consider the example that Jesus, God's only begotten Son, gave us. Jesus does not require that the people choose Him to be their King. He accepts the freedom of man to choose. He knows this natural law principle of freedom of choice, because He created man with this gift of choice. While on earth, the people made it known and declared that they would not have Jesus to reign over them. Again, the people had the power to reject God's Son—the king and ruler of the world. "And he called his ten servants, and delivered them ten pounds, and said unto them, Occupy till I come. But his citizens hated him, and sent a message after him, saying, *We will not have this man to reign over us.*"[13] Can there be another man or woman on earth who can claim any power more than what Jesus did not demand Himself? Can a Christian give more loyalty, subjection, and submission to a finite, sinful, and even an evil man simply because such a person is in a position of administrator of government? No, because "the power of creating a man a king is from the people,"[14] as proclaimed by Rutherford.

Indeed our nation's founding reflects the biblical perspective of the natural law that men are born free and are thus able to choose their government's substance, form, and administrators. One such founding father who made such a declaration is John Jay, who said the following:

But let it be remembered that whatever marks of wisdom, experience, and patriotism there may be in your constitution, yet like the

---

13. Luke 19:13–14 (KJV), (emphasis added).
14. Rutherford, *Lex, Rex,* 6.

beautiful symmetry, the just proportion, and elegant forms of our first parents before their Maker breathed into them the breath of life, it is yet to be animated, and till then may indeed excite admiration, but will be of no use: from the people it must receive its spirit and by them be quickened.[15]

Using the analogy of the creation story found in Genesis, John Jay equated the people's power to create government to the power of God to create humans. Without the people breathing the breath of life into government, it does not exist. Without contradicting common sense, it naturally follows that since the people have the power to give the breath of life to government, the people have the power to take away the breath from government if they choose to do so, especially where the creature (government) defies the laws and parameters set forth by its creator (the people).

In a letter to George Washington, Jay further describes the power that the people have to establish their own government, for their own benefit. He says,

Providence has been pleased to bless the people of this country with more means of establishing their own government than any other nation has hitherto enjoyed; and for the use we may make of these means we shall be highly responsible to that Providence, as well as to mankind in general, and to our own posterity in particular.[16]

It cannot go without notice that John Jay not only reflected the power of the people to establish their own government, but also that the people are highly responsible to God for His blessings of allowing the people the ample means to do so. With this responsibility comes the need for citizens to educate themselves concerning the affairs of state. Without an understanding of their government and their leaders, the citizens will not know when to determine if and what actions of the government are null and void. John

15. Jay, *The Life of John Jay,* 82, 83.
16. Jay, *The Life of John Jay,* 276.

Jay expounded more on the subject. To the newly independent American nation, Jay proclaims the people's power to choose their government and their responsibility to maintain the integrity of the same in this statement:

> It certainly cannot be necessary to remind you, that your representatives here are chosen from among yourselves; that you are, or ought to be, acquainted with their several characters; that they are sent here to speak your sentiments, and that it is constantly in your power to remove such as do not. You surely are convinced that it is no more in their power to annihilate your money than your independence, and that any act of theirs for either of those purposes would be null and void.[17]

Similarly, Thomas Jefferson expresses in the Virginia and Kentucky resolutions that "the General Government was one of limited authority, granted originally by the States as the sovereign members of the Confederation, and that in case undelegated powers should be assumed, such became void and of no force, because unauthorized in the original constitutional compact." Jefferson further "declared that the General Government was not the 'exclusive or final judge of the extent of the powers delegated to itself, since that would have made its discretion and not the Constitution the measure of its powers; but as in all cases of compact among powers having no common judge, each party has an equal right to judge for itself, as well of infractions as of the mode and measures of redress.'"[18]

These proclamations not only reflect what is revealed in scripture, but they also mirror what had been previously discussed by Enlightenment writers—such as Algernon Sidney—all of whom were obviously very influential in the philosophical making of our nation. In the clearest of terms, Sidney discusses the power of the people in some depth in his *Discourses on Government*. Sidney proclaims the biblical and natural law premise that God created people—not government; that government is meant for the good of

---

17. Jay, *The Life of John Jay*, 487.

18. Alexander Harris, *A Review of the Political Conflict in America*, (New York: T.H. Pollock, 1876), 213–214.

the people—not for the good of government; that government is subject to the will of the people; and that the people have a right to abolish government when it becomes destructive to their good. He says,

> If disagreements happen between king and people, why is it a more desparate opinion to think the king should be subject to the censures of the people, than the people subject to the will of the king? Did the people make the king, or the king make the people? Is the king for the people, or the people for the king? Did God create the Hebrews, that Saul might reign over them? Or did they, from an opinion of procuring their own good, ask a king that might judge them and fight their battles?... The one tends to the good of mankind in restraining the lusts of wicked kings, the other exposes them, without remedy, to the fury of the most savage of all beasts.[19]
>
> Is there any absurdity in saying, that since God in goodness and mercy to mankind hath, with an equal hand, given to all the benefit of liberty, with some measure of understanding how to employ it, is it lawful for any nation, as occasion shall require, to give the exercise of that power to one or more men, under certain limitations and conditions; or to retain it to themselves if they think it good for them? If this may be done, we are at an end of all controversies concerning one form of government established by God, to which all mankind must submit; and we may safely conclude, that having given to all men, in some degree, a capacity of judging what is good themselves, he hath granted to all likewise a liberty of inventing such forms as please them best, without favouring one more than another.[20] He that institutes, may also abrogate; most especially when the institution is not only by, but for, himself.[21]
>
> [Natural liberty] remains to us whilst we form governments, that we ourselves are judges how it is good for us to recede from our natural liberty: which is of so great importance, that from thence

---

19. Sidney, *Discourses on Government*, 316–318.

20. Ibid., 333.

21. Ibid., 335.

only we can know whether we are freemen or slaves; and the difference between the best government and the worst, doth wholly depend upon a right or wrong exercise of that power. If men are born naturally free, such as have wisdom and understanding will always frame good governments; but if they are born under the necessity of a perpetual slavery, no wisdom can be of use to them; but all must forever depend on the will of their lords, how cruel, made, proud, or wicked soever they be.[22]

It was this type of understanding and explanation of the rights of man and the power of the people that shaped the philosophy of America's founders. America's founders studied these natural and revealed laws of God and implemented them into the formation of our nation—not for the purpose of promoting religion, but *freedom*. It is no wonder, then, why founding father James Madison states the following in Federalist Paper No. 37, when setting forth his argument on why the states should ratify the United States Constitution:

The genius of republican liberty seems to demand on one side, not only that all power should be derived from the people, but that those intrusted with it should be kept in independence on the people, by a short duration of their appointments; and that even during this short period the trust should be placed not in a few, but a number of hands.[23]

There can be no doubt that the power of the people to decide the administrators is not only natural and biblical but also overflows the cup of our history, both factually and philosophically. Thomas Jefferson confirms this notion when he states, "Unless the mass retains sufficient control over those entrusted with the powers of their government, these will be perverted to their own oppression, and to perpetuation of wealth and power in the individuals

22. Ibid., 352, 353.

23. James Madison, "Federalist Paper 37," in *The Federalist Papers*, Hamilton, Jay, and Madison, 278.

and their families selected for the trust. Whether our Constitution has hit
on the exact degree of control necessary, is yet under experiment."[24] Was
he a prophet? No, just a student of history and human nature. And in fact,
Jefferson's prediction has come true in America.

Obviously, where the people have created government under the limitations of the Constitution, it naturally follows that the people are responsible
to ensure that they retain sufficient control over their creation. Let us use just
a bit of common sense. How can the people retain sufficient control over
government, when the government is larger and more powerful than the
people can maintain? For crying out loud, for those who believe that a global
government is okay and does not jeopardize our rights and freedoms, please
explain how the people can retain control over a global government, when
history proves that the larger the government, the less control is retained by
the people and the more control is seized by the government. God save us
from those who are ignorant of those fallacies in thought. Furthermore, how
can a culture be preserved when it is controlled by persons who do not even
share the same philosophical understandings of right and wrong as you, your
community, your state, your region, or your nation? Do you really think that
there should be a global set of laws, rules, and regulations when our beliefs,
philosophies, understandings, religions, and standards contradict each other?
Conflict is most certainly the end result, and what do you think will happen
to those who contradict the all-powerful world government? To those who
see nothing inherently and fundamentally wrong with world government
I say, what absurdity, ignorance, lethargy, idiocy, and corruption! Jefferson
foresaw the problem that government imposes upon its citizens when the
citizens lose control over the government; and thus, Jefferson recognized that
the Constitution may not have exerted *enough* precise limitations to ensure
the people's control over their government—meaning, more provisions for
control may be needed. Boy, is that an understatement today!

The truth is, the nature of the relationship between the people and the
administrators of government is that the people are superior to the administrators. Since the people are superior to the government, it naturally fol-

---

24. Jefferson, *The Jeffersonian Cyclopedia*, 385.

lows that "[the people] may measure out, by ounce weights, so much royal power, and no more and no less…they may limit, moderate, and set banks and marches to the exercise…they give it out, conditionate, upon this and that condition, that they may take again to themselves what they gave out upon condition if the condition be violated,"[25] as John Locke said. This requires the people to become more responsible, however, because they must be aware of the actions of their government to know whether or not those actions comply with their conditions of service to the nation. Where the government administrators' actions do not comply, necessary action must be taken by the people—even if it means abolishing the government.

Let it be understood, the power to create also means the power to abolish or secede from such government, as is declared in America's Declaration of Independence. The post Civil War perception of secession appears to be completely misguided and twisted—and quite honestly, contrary to common sense and principles of freedom. However, secession from government was not only understood by America's founders and philosophers, but accepted—based upon natural law principles.[26] Founding father Richard Bland describes the natural law principle as follows: "[W]hen Men exercise

25. Locke, *Two Treatises on Government*, 6.

26. "All men, say they, are born under government, and therefore they cannot be at liberty to begin a new one. Every one is born a subject to his father, or his prince, and is therefore under the perpetual tie of subjection and allegiance. It is plain mankind never owned nor considered any such natural subjection that they were born in, to one or to the other that tied them, without their own consents, to a subjection to them and their heirs… For there are no examples so frequent in history, both sacred and profane, as those of men withdrawing themselves, and their obedience, from the jurisdiction they were born under, and the family or community they were bred up in, and setting up new governments in other places; from whence sprang all that number of petty commonwealths in the beginning of ages, and which always multiplied, as long as there was room enough, till the stronger, or more fortunate, swallowed the weaker; and those great ones again breaking to pieces, dissolved into lesser dominions. All which are so many testimonies against paternal sovereignty, and plainly prove, that it was not the natural right of the father descending to his heirs, that made governments in the beginning, since it was impossible, upon that ground, there should have been so many little kingdoms; all must have been but only one universal monarchy, if men had not been at liberty to separate themselves from their families, and the government, be it what it will, that was set up in it, and go and make distinct commonwealths and other governments, as they thought fit." Locke and Macpherson, ed., *Second Treatise of Government*, 61–62.

this Right, and withdraw themselves from their Country, they recover their natural Freedom and Independence: The Jurisdiction and Sovereignty of the State they have quitted ceases; and if they unite, and by common Consent take Possession of a new Country, and form themselves into a political Society, they become a sovereign State, independent of the State from which they separated."[27] Using this same principle of law, William Rawle describes the ability of states to secede from America's union as such:

> It is not to be understood, that [the Union's] interposition [on the states] would be justifiable, if the people of a state should determine to retire from the Union, whether they adopted another or retained the same form of government, or if they should, with the express intention of seceding, expunge the representative system from their code, and thereby incapacitate themselves from concurring according to the mode now prescribed, in the choice of certain public officers of the United States... The states, then, may wholly withdraw from the Union, but while they continue, they must retain the character of representative republic.[28]

Any state seceding from the union would likely experience initial hardship and impact (a consequence they have a right to live with), mostly because the federal government of America has attached so many strings to states' operation that one could hardly imagine not having the federal government in the way. However, the notion of secession is not sinful, unconstitutional, evil, strange, unfounded, or meritless. Rather, the natural right to secede was understood as fact by our founders and generations before and after. How do you think the United States came into existence? Was not America first a colony of Great Britain, whereby the governments established were initially done so by grant or charter of the king? Do you think King George thought it was okay for America to secede? Of course he did not; he

---

27. Richard Bland, *An Inquiry Into the Rights of the British Colonies*, 14. Note, author spelled the words, which were originally written in Old English, in modern English for reader convenience.

28. Rawle, *A View of the Constitution of the United States of America*, 296–297.

engaged in war against them because of their secession (just as the Union did against the Confederates). If the American colonies had the right to secede in 1776 when their governments were initially discovered and established under the authority of the king of the mother country, then how much more would the several states have a right to secede where they procured their own independence and were completely and wholly independent of any other government, including what did not even exist at the time—the federal government? If our founders did not have a right to secede from Great Britain, what justification do any of us have to be proud to be an American? But if they did, then why do we praise the Union for preventing the Confederate States from doing the same thing that our founding fathers did? And from where comes the critical judgment against any state who decides to secede today? The idea and concept of secession today is misunderstood, when it is so simple, especially when you understand the fundamental basis upon which the right rests. Every aspect of life, in fact, reflects this principle of power to secede.

For example, this relationship concept between the people and the government reflects very similarly to an employer-employee relationship, whereby the employer (the people) hires the employee (government administrator) under terms set forth in the contract. No one questions that the employee is a hireling of the employer and only has the authority granted while he complies with the terms of the contract. Likewise, a government administrator must comply with the terms set forth in the compact between the people and himself. Can it be said that the employer does not have the right to fire the employee even when the contract reserves the right to do so? Enlightenment philosophers purport that termination of employment (i.e., secession) to be enforceable by natural law, "since it is conformable to Natural Law to observe compacts (for some mode of obliging themselves was necessary among men, and no other natural mode could be imagined,) Civil Rights were derived from this source, mutual compact."[29] America produced an understanding of the right to secede from these Enlightenment philosophers, through the terms of a constitution or natural law itself. Thomas

---

29. Grotius, *Hugo Grotius on the Rights of War and Peace*, xxvii.

Paine recognizes the significance of compacts (charters) when he states, "A charter is to be understood as a bond of solemn obligation, which the whole enters into, to support the right of every separate part, whether of religion, personal freedom, or property[.] A firm bargain and a right reckoning make long friends."[30]

What person using common sense would suggest that the people are required to observe the terms of the Constitution and thus demand union, when the other party to the compact—the government—does not observe the bond of solemn obligation as well? You would not likely feel the same way if the government was prosecuting you for crimes with evidence procured from illegal searches and seizures in violation of the Fourth Amendment of the Constitution. The truth of the matter is that the people have a natural right to choose their leaders and use the natural means of the compact to ensure the protection of their God-given, natural rights.

What then shall be said of a people who shirk their responsibilities and allow their administrators (their employees, their inferiors) to violate the compact, when it is the people's job to oversee the inferior and ensure that he is following the terms of the compact? Is the employer any less liable for the actions of the employee simply because he chose not to monitor the employee? Are you aware that "vicarious liability"[31] is alive and well in the United States and is used as a basis for liability in numerous cases throughout this nation? This principle equally applies to our relationship to our employees—our governmental administrators. Moreover, the damage to society is no less impactful because we were ignorant of the null and void acts by the administrator, the laws of which impact the entire society (including their posterity) and not only those who were willfully ignorant. In other words, when you are ignorant of the unconstitutional acts of the government, your ignorance harms all of the citizens protected by the Constitution. What shall be said of a people who know what evil is, fail to derail the train leading to that evil, and have the power to correct it?

---

30. Paine and Philip, ed., *Common Sense*, 4 3.

31. "Vicarious liability: liability that a supervisory party (such as an employer) bears for the actionable conduct of a subordinate or associate (such as an employee) because of the relationship between the two parties." Garner, *Black's Law Dictionary.*

Man is naturally born free; has the natural power to create substance and form of government; may rightfully choose who the administrator of such government will be; and may condition, limit, and restrict the terms of the administrator's authority by compact. It does not stop there. The people furthermore have the right to terminate the administrators for violation of the compact and have the power and right to terminate any connection with the government they established, where the people deem the government to be destructive to the ends of securing their God-given rights of life, liberty, and property. There is nothing spiritual or inherently good about a union of peoples or states. What is worse: complying with the abuses of an illegitimate authority for the sake of the union, or seceding from the abuses of an illegitimate authority for the sake of freedom? Perhaps your posterity will be the judge.

7

GOVERNMENT'S PURPOSE

Have you ever wondered why people form governments? Most answers to that question would likely reveal that this subject is perhaps the most misunderstood and distorted truth regarding government today. Not knowing the purpose of government is as detrimental to society as just about any other matter. It would be like trying to navigate a ship without a compass or chartering an expedition without a map. If you do not know the direction you are supposed to go, you will not know whether or not you are off course—no matter how good you feel about where you are. Unfortunately, in today's political environment, America's citizens cannot even rely on—much less trust—their elected officials to align the direction of the nation with government's intended purpose. It is the biblical analogy of the blind leading the blind.

There are numerous reasons for this loss of vision that has developed over many generations. Regardless of the reasons, if the purpose of government is not understood, freedom can never be obtained or retained. God declares in no uncertain terms that

A divine sentence is in the lips of the king; His mouth shall not transgress in judgment. A just balance and scales are the LORD's; all the weights in the bag are his work. It is an abomination to kings to do evil, for the throne is established by righteousness.[1]

Will we the people of the states know if government is fulfilling this commandment of God if we do not know what is divine, what is just, what is evil, and what is righteous? Most certainly not. Be not mistaken, many people have the notion that the form of government (e.g., democracy) is the end or goal of government (the philosophy of which fails to consider the necessity of incorporating the natural and revealed laws of God to the principles and laws of government, which is why spreading democracy never works).[2] That is, as long as certain forms of government exist, so will freedom. Thomas Jefferson does not agree with such a statement but rather recognizes that even in democracies tyranny can reign. "Every government degenerates when trusted to the rulers of the people alone. The people themselves, therefore, are its only safe depositories. And to render even them safe, their minds must be improved to a certain degree."[3] Even in more certain terms, Jefferson says, "[While] certain forms of government are better calculated than others to protect individuals in the free exercise of their natural rights, and are at the same time themselves better guarded against degeneracy, yet experience hath shown that, even under the best forms, those entrusted with power have, in time, and by slow operations, perverted it into tyranny."[4] Very plainly, the form of government is not the *ends* to which society seeks.

Certain forms of government may be more destructive to obtaining or preserving freedom than one might imagine—this includes democracies. As an example, history reveals that monarchies are actually much easier to identify error of judgment (as opposed to democracies). This is what Thomas Paine identifies when he says, "Absolute [monarchy] governments (tho' the

---

1. Proverbs 16:10–12 (ASV).

2. "[T]o invade Iraq and overthrow her legitimate (if obnoxious) government was unjustifiable: simply to impose 'democracy' (or any other form of government) on the Iraqi people, even if this were imagined actually to be to *their* benefit as opposed merely to the advantage of the invaders and their allies." Vieira, *Constitutional Homeland Security,* 29–30.

3. Jefferson, *The Jeffersonian Cyclopedia,* 389.

4. Ibid.

disgrace of human nature) have this advantage with them, that they are simple; if the people suffer, they know the head from which their suffering springs, know likewise the remedy, and are not bewildered by a variety of causes and cures."[5]

Conversely, democracies have an intrinsic flaw: no one knows where the source of the problem is. Obviously, America today cannot be described with such simplicity as a monarchy would. Yet, I dare say that most Americans would shudder at the thought of living under a monarchy, only because we believe that being a democracy is good and is the end of our society. Although, I would venture to say that many would consent to a monarchy if a savior such as Barack Hussein Obama could retain such a position. However, it cannot be concluded that form alone is the end of society or government, because slavery can exist in a democracy just as well as it can in a monarchy. Whether you take a bus, train, plane, or car to your destination, the form may be insignificant if you reach your destination: freedom—being the gift of God, not the gift of man (assuming society even desires freedom).

However, it must be noted at this point that America's founders believed that natural and revealed law supported the republican form of government above all others, not for form's sake, but for freedom's sake. The following was a common understanding regarding the form of government, as explained by Thomas Paine:

> Near three thousand years passed away from the Mossaic account of the creation, till the Jews under a national delusion requested a king. Till then their form of government (except in extraordinary cases, where thy Almighty interposed) was a kind of republic administered by a judge and the elders of the tribes. Kings they had none, and it was held sinful to acknowledge any being under that title but the Lord of Hosts.
>
> And when a man seriously reflects on the idolatrous homage which is paid to the persons of Kings, he need not wonder, that the Almighty, ever jealous of his honor, should disapprove of a form of

---

5. Paine and Philip, ed., *Common Sense,* 8.

government which so impiously invades the prerogative of heaven… The children of Israel being oppressed by the Midianites, Gideon marched against them with a small army, and victory, thro' the divine interposition, decided in his favour.

The Jews elate with success, and attributing it to the generalship of Gideon, proposed making him a king, saying, "Rule thou over us, thou and thy son and thy son's son." Here was temptation in its fullest extent; not a kingdom only, but an hereditary one, but Gideon in the piety of his soul replied, "I will not rule over you, neither shall my son rule over you, THE LORD SHALL RULE OVER YOU."[6]

Putting the form of government aside, however, God has declared the purpose of government—from the Old Testament to the New. Anything outside of God's purpose of government exceeds the scope of God's ordination of that government. Similar to God's ordination of marriage essentially being to more fully and ably worship and glorify God, because it is "not good that man be alone."[7] God's ordination of government is threefold: (1) to facilitate the quiet and peace of society; (2) to provide justice; and (3) to punish evil and administer good. Not only does the Bible clearly state the purpose of government, but also America's founders expressed the same and literally framed a nation built upon those purposes. Consider what one of the most influential philosophers of American jurisprudence, John Locke, says concerning the purpose of government and perhaps more importantly, what government's purpose is *not*:

Absolute arbitrary power, or governing without settled standing laws, can neither of them consist with the ends of society and government, which men would not quit the freedom of the state of nature for, and tie themselves up under, were it not to preserve their lives, liberties and fortunes, and by stated rules of right and property to secure their peace and quiet. It cannot be supposed that they

---

6. Paine and Philip, ed., *Common Sense,* 12.
7. Genesis 2:18 (KJV).

should intend, had they a power so to do, to give to any one, or more, an absolute arbitrary power over their persons and estates, and put a force into the magistrate's hand to execute his unlimited will arbitrarily upon them. This were to put themselves into a worse condition than the state of nature, wherein they had a liberty to defend their right against the injuries of others, and were upon equal terms of force to maintain it, whether invaded by a single man, or many in combination.[8]

Very clearly, Locke rejects the thought that government's purpose (and consequently, the citizens' submission) should be anything less than what people in a state of nature have the power and purpose to accomplish: to preserve their lives, liberties, and properties based upon the natural laws of God. Suggesting that these purposes need not be met for government to be considered good ignores and contradicts the Bible and American history. By analogy, God does not ordain the abusive, manipulative, controlling, and selfish actions performed by a spouse towards another spouse in the ordained institution of marriage. To the contrary: God does not ordain actions performed outside God's ordained purposes from a spouse or a government. Neither should its citizens.

While many would agree with these preceding ideas in theory, experience and observation indicate that many do not know how to apply the purpose of government to today's America. Many figure, hey, I can still go to church, pray silently, go to the mall, watch TV, go to the baseball game on the weekend, and operate my business. Everything must be fine, and our government must be ordained of God, since they are punishing evil and promoting good (at least in their minds). Those with such an attitude do not understand that many proposed good laws passed and executed by our good leaders are depriving freeborn people of their natural liberties and compromising and subverting the contract between the people and the government—taking more and more control over what was never granted to the government in the first place. Thus, matters that appear to be insignificant now will have

---

8. Locke and Macpherson, ed., *Second Treatise of Government*, 72.

detrimental effects in the future, which is just what Patrick Henry says. "The object is now, indeed, small, but the shadow is large enough to darken all this fair land."[9] Again, this goes to government administrators not following the terms of the solemn obligation they bind themselves to when taking office. Thomas Paine described such a power-usurping government administrator this way: "A common murderer, a highwayman, or a housebreaker, has as good a pretence as he."[10]

Some would say, "Well, who cares if the government is not following the terms of their obligations under the Constitution; as long as they are doing *good*?" To such a person I say how would you feel if you were an employer and you had an employee who embezzled money from you for the sake of feeding poor children in India, Africa, or Chile? While the employee may have done a good thing, the employee usurped his authority and broke the contract of employment under which he operated. Such an employee should not be commended for great humanitarian work but should be fired for stealing, breaking trust, breaching the contract, and depriving the employer, stockholders, and other employees of monies that were rightfully theirs. Thus, the definition of *good* has to be defined and determined in light of jurisdiction, contract, and consent—all founded in natural and revealed law. Actions are not good when the means to accomplish the end are evil. Only a thorough recognition of godly and lawful government will equip a citizen with discernment regarding governmental affairs and knowledge of whether or not the government is as the employer (the people) described and is punishing evil and promoting good.

America's founders and those who influenced our founders had a very broad, deep, and knowledgeable understanding of the purpose of government, and quite frankly, America's governmental philosophy today does not closely resemble their understanding and implementation of such a government. The overwhelming trend in America (and most European nations) is the thought, "What can government do to help me?" The proof is overwhelming: taxes are out of sight; welfare dependence is outrageous; "our

---

9. Kettell, *Southern Wealth and Northern Profits*, 5.

10. Paine and Philip, ed., *American Crisis I*, 64.

rights [are] invaded by their regulation,"[11] which is passed more frequently than ever; government bailouts and socialization are common; retirement savings (that is, social security) are forced upon us through taxation; socialized medicine, insurance, and more are even demanded; socialized government education is considered a right; foreign aid monies are spent in the billions;[12] publicly financed abortions are readily available; the risks of failing corporations are socialized while profits privatized; banks are nationalized;[13] faith-based-initiative funds are readily accepted by Christian organizations; FEMA assistance is expected in any natural disaster; federal kickbacks to the states are status quo (conditioned, of course, upon federal mandates); federal land conservation programs continually grow; and the give-me, give-me, give-me goes on, solidifying the elitists' and government's socialist agenda.[14]

---

11. Compiled by a member of the Philadelphia Bar, *American Oratory*, 2.

12. "In 1998 U.S. foreign aid totaled $8.8 billion." Pleskovic and Stern, *Annual World Bank Conference on Development Economics 2000*, 39.

13. "Long regarded in the U.S. as a folly of Europeans, nationalisation is gaining rapid acceptance among Washington opinion-formers—and not just with Alan Greenspan, former Federal Reserve chairman. Perhaps stranger still, many of those talking about nationalising banks are Republicans. Lindsey Graham, the Republican senator for South Carolina, says that many of his colleagues, including John McCain, the defeated presidential candidate, agree with his view that nationalisation of some banks should be 'on the table.' Mr. Graham says that people across the U.S. accept his argument that it is untenable to keep throwing good money after bad into institutions such as Citigroup and Bank of America, which now have a lower net value than the amount of public funds they have received. 'You should not get caught up on a word [nationalization],' he told *The Financial Times* in an interview. 'I would argue that we cannot be ideologically a little bit pregnant. It doesn't matter what you call it, but we can't keep on funding these zombie banks [without gaining public control]. That's what the Japanese did.' Barack Obama, the president, who has tried to avoid panicking lawmakers and markets by entertaining the idea, has moved more towards what he calls the 'Swedish model'—an approach backed strongly by Mr. Graham. In the early 1990s Sweden nationalised its banking sector then auctioned banks having cleaned up balance sheets. 'In limited circumstances the Swedish model makes sense for the U.S.,' says Mr. Graham." Edward Luce and Krishna Guha, "Bank Nationalisation Gains Ground With Republicans," *The Financial Times Limited*, February 17, 2009.

14. "The U.S. government has already—under a conservative Republican administration—effectively nationalized the banking and mortgage industries. That seems a stronger sign of socialism than $50 million for art. Whether we want to admit it or not—and many, especially Congressman Pence and Hannity, do not—the America of 2009 is moving toward a modern

Such are not the purposes of government. The effect is like compiling leeches, one after the other, onto a host, sucking the blood of freedom out of the life of the host. Eventually, there is no life left.

Evidence shows that the function of government has even taken the place of God. Government's purpose has taken on an entirely new shape, form, drive, and purpose. Unfortunately, many Americans do not even seem to care about or understand the significance of this reality. The only thing they really know is: vote pro-life, vote for capitalism, and vote conservative. They don't understand that, where the government has lost its purpose, it no longer operates as a godly and constitutional nation, has lost the ordination of God, and (in the case of America specifically) has rejected the foundation upon which it was built, which leaves the entire society's rights and liberties at jeopardy. And people wonder how and why America is becoming (or already has become) a socialist/communist country—our Constitution notwithstanding.

This phenomenon has a cause. Likewise, our nation's vast freedom and independence had a cause, and that is, they acknowledged the true purposes

---

European state… [I]t was…under a conservative GOP administration that we enacted the largest expansion of the welfare state in 30 years: prescription drugs for the elderly. People on the right and the left want government to invest in alternative energies in order to break our addiction to foreign oil. And it is unlikely that even the reddest of states will decline federal money for infrastructural improvements. If we fail to acknowledge the reality of the growing role of government in the economy, insisting instead on fighting 21st-century wars with 20th-century terms and tactics, then we are doomed to a fractious and unedifying debate. The sooner we understand where we truly stand, the sooner we can think more clearly about how to use government in today's world. As the Obama administration presses the largest fiscal bill in American history, caps the salaries of executives at institutions receiving federal aid at $500,000 and introduces a new plan to rescue the banking industry, the unemployment rate is at its highest in 16 years… Whether we like it or not—or even whether many people have thought much about it or not—the numbers clearly suggest that we are headed in a more European direction. A decade ago U.S. government spending was 34.3 percent of GDP, compared with 48.2 percent in the euro zone—a roughly 14-point gap, according to the Organization for Economic Cooperation and Development. In 2010 U.S. spending is expected to be 39.9 percent of GDP, compared with 47.1 percent in the euro zone—a gap of less than 8 points. As entitlement spending rises over the next decade, we will become even more French." John Meacham and Evan Thomas, "We Are All Socialists Now," *Newsweek*, February 16, 2009, http://www.newsweek.com/id/183663.

of government: (1) promote peace among men, (2) secure absolute rights, and (3) execute justice—all within the jurisdictional limits imposed by the people in the Constitution. Before the false notion demonstrated today concerning government's purpose spread like wildfire across our nation, the following was well understood:

> In republican governments, justice ought to be the principle, the public good the object, and reason and virtue the life and spirit of their laws... The great end of civil government is social happiness; to induce us to respect the rights, interests, and feelings of others as our own, conformable to that great command in the law, which is the foundation of all relative duties from man to man; to love our neighbor as ourselves, and to do to all as we would they should do to us; knowing that the rights and enjoyments of others are the same to them as ours are to us, and that all men are brethren, have one father, who is God, created in his image, and connected in one great family under the government of their illustrious head the Prince of Peace and of the potentates and powers of the earth.[15]

Today, America largely reflects more of the notion that people are created in the image of the state. However, the above are the very purposes of government derived from natural and revealed laws of God and in reality are also interconnected—meaning you cannot have one without the other. How can there be justice without rights? How can there be peace without rights? How can there be rights without peace? How can there be peace without justice? How can there be justice without peace? A government attempting to provide more than this oversteps its authority and acts illegitimately and without ordination—even if it appears to be a good thing—like the kindhearted, embezzling employee.

Government's purpose is known, but the question is, are we willing to confront unauthorized and illegitimate government acts? Perhaps we are not because we feel the government advances our agenda—whether in business,

---

15. Root, *Reports of Cases*, xvi, xvii.

social, or political matters; or because such acts are proposed by our favorite political party; or because we feel good about the act; or because our pastor told us such-and-such candidate was a good, Christian man; or because Sean Hannity said this or that was the conservative thing to do; or because Rush Limbaugh proclaimed its constitutionality; or even because we are conquered by fear or similar feelings. These reasons should be insufficient to a Christian and a freedom lover. Moreover, the good intentions of the administrators or the promoters do not mitigate the damage caused to the nation and Constitution for every government act outside the actual purpose of government.

Securing the Peace of Society

One of the primary purposes of government is to help facilitate peace in society. The Bible reveals this purpose of government as promoting a quiet and peaceful life, which is a natural desire of people. However, history clearly proves that most people do not understand how to accomplish this end. Thus, to accomplish peace, society must understand what peace is and what it is not. In short, peace is not simply being free from conflict, but rather peace is being free from the unlawful intrusion by individuals or government on God-given rights. Government's purpose of peace does not involve making sure everyone has a roof over their head, money in their bank, a retirement account, health insurance, an education, a job, or any other necessity or convenience of life. Such needs and wants are the responsibility of the individual and the family, as is clearly stated in the natural and revealed laws of God. In 1 Timothy 2:1–3 (ESV), God reveals that government indeed can contradict the purposes of facilitating peace.

> First of all, then, I urge that supplications, prayers, intercessions, and thanksgivings be made for all people, for kings and all who are in high positions, that we may lead a peaceful and quiet life, godly and dignified in every way. This is good, and it is pleasing in the sight of God our Savior.

This passage of scripture strongly suggests that we will not lead a quiet and peaceable life where those in government authority interfere with what is good and acceptable in the sight of God, meaning his laws, justice, and righteousness. Thus, this passage clearly encourages Christians to get involved in government matters by praying for godly rulers to accomplish the purpose of their own quiet and peace. God knows the nature of man to abuse power and to become destructive to its intended purpose. Thus, wise people should pray not just for the decisions of the leaders but should pray for a government that will carry out God's intended purpose. Understand, this prayer is not for the sake of the government or its administrators (as you would pray for your family) but for the sake of the society. God did not create the government for people, but the people created government for the people, for their peace and happiness.

God never suggests—not once—that the government is to be sustained and endured above and at the expense of societal peace and quiet. Contrarily, the end result of living a quiet and peaceable life for the Christians results in the salvation of souls of men. "[God] desires all people to be saved and to come to the knowledge of the truth."[16] What could be more valuable to God than the souls of men? Notice too that being saved is not the only objective, but knowing the truth is the other objective. This confirms the truth that merely being a Christian will not save a nation from slavery and tyranny. If one does not know truth (even though he is saved), then what good will it do him, his family, his community, and his nation here on earth? God draws a direct correlation from the salvation of men's souls and knowing the truth to the peace and quiet of society. To support a government that does not advance, promote, and protect the natural laws created by God, which provide freedom, is to support an agenda contrary to God's will. If God desired that government exist for the sake of government existing, God would have created government in the first place and ordered all men to obey the will of all its rulers. Such a creation and command were never given. To the contrary, we are to obey God rather than man, and God does not command obedience to tyrants. Thus, there is a serious distinction between submission and obedience, as submission does not necessarily mean obedience.

Additionally, 1 Peter 2:13–17 (KJV) reflects and reiterates the purposes

---

16. Timothy 2:4 (ESV).

of government: to punish evil and promote good, which helps provide peace in society. It says,

> Submit yourselves to every ordinance of man for the Lord's sake: whether it be to the king, as supreme; Or unto governors, as unto them that are sent by him for the punishment of evildoers, and for the praise of them that do well. For so is the will of God, that with well doing ye may put to silence the ignorance of foolish men: As free, and not using your liberty for a cloke of maliciousness, but as the servants of God. Honour all men. Love the brotherhood. Fear God. Honour the king.

Like Romans 13, this passage clearly establishes the purpose of government: to provide peace in society by providing justice (which is another purpose of government). Also, notice that the submission referred to relates to the *ordinance* of man. An ordinance of man is what has already been described herein as a positive or man-made law. This positive law is to be contrasted to the laws of God—which God declares every person and every nation are subject unto. God clearly makes a serious distinction between the ordinances of man and the laws of God. In other words, they are not the same and should never be equated to each other. Just because man has made a law does not mean that the law has the authority of God's law, which are to be obeyed no matter what man says or what government orders. However, notice that God puts the same conditions and limitations on ordinances of man (laws) as He does to the higher powers (government) ordained of God in Romans 13. That is, they are to punish evil and promote good. One can clearly see that God expects the ordinances of man to serve the purposes of God, just as the form of government should serve God's purposes. This is confirmed in the Old Testament as well, where scripture declares, "When justice is done, it is a joy to the righteous but terror to evildoers."[17] Here, the Old Testament scripture mirrors Romans 13 and 1 Peter 2. The purpose of government: to punish evil and promote good—to provide justice. Thus, it

---

17. Proverbs 21:15 (ESV).

cannot be true that we are to subject ourselves both to the ordinance of man and to the laws and justice of God while the ordinance of man contradicts the laws of God and does not accomplish its purpose.

God conditions the duty of submission to be regulated and qualified by the intended purposes of government, and it is this godly government that is ordained by God and is the revealed will of God. Any other government, then, is not the will of God—just as the dictator Nimrod in Genesis 10 and 11 was not ordained of God when he intended to gather nations unto himself in Babel, which God destroyed. The same rule of limited government applied to King Saul, as he was not ordained of God when he contravened God's purpose for government, and as a result, God told Israel in 1 Samuel 12:25 (ESV), "But if you still do wickedly, you shall be swept away, both you and your king." Ultimately, as King Saul violated the laws of God, God removed him from his position of authority, establishing the truth that government is always limited to its purposes defined by God in His natural and revealed laws.

Government's limited purpose found in America's history in fact reflects the biblical purpose of government to maintain the peace of society. Grotius certainly understands that government's purpose was to protect the peace of society, as declared in the Bible. He recognizes that "if there were no public power, one man would swallow another alive."[18] Put another way, government should not allow one person, or even one group of people to become tyrants over others. "The State...is a perfect [that is, independent] collection of free men, associated for the sake of enjoying the advantages of [justice], and for common utility."[19] To accomplish this purpose of peace in society, government then should execute laws based upon the advantages of justice—and not the communistic idea of fairness. While I do not have the right to disturb the peace of society by simply doing what I want (which is another term for anarchy) regardless of whether it disturbs your rights or not, I do have the ability to exercise my absolute rights—the other purpose of government. Algernon Sidney says the same. "Common sense teaches, and all good men acknowledge, that governments are not set up for the advantage, profit,

---

18. Grotius, *Hugo Grotius on the Rights of War and Peace,* 54.
19. Ibid., 6.

pleasure, or glory of one or a few men, but for the good of the society."[20] This natural law proceeds from God's grant of power of dominion over the earth to all mankind—not just the chosen few.

If there are no restrictions on my ability to disturb your peace, then there are no restrictions on your ability to disturb my peace; and out of such a situation arises chaos and anarchy—and ultimately tyranny—because the strongest will always rise up over the ordinary citizens, just as Nimrod did in Genesis. The same principle applies to government: administrators have no more of a right to contravene the rights of the citizens than any other individual. Montesquieu puts it this way:

> It is true that in democracies the people seem to act as they please; but political liberty does not consist in an unlimited freedom. In governments, that is, in societies directed by laws, liberty can consist only in the power of doing what we ought to will, and in not being constrained to do what we ought not to will. We must have continually present to our minds the difference between independence and liberty. Liberty is a right of doing whatever the law permit, and if a citizen could do what they forbid he would no longer be possessed of liberty, because his fellow-citizens would have the same power.[21]

In short, self-responsibility coupled with liberty equals the peace of society. However, conflict arises when people or governments step outside of their jurisdiction and attempt to claim what is not rightfully theirs. Thus, a nation's constitution is crucial, because without expressing the terms of the natural rights of man, the powerful will inevitably trample on the rights of the weaker. How could a person who loves freedom and who understands that freedom only exists where a nation's constitution and citizens acknowledge, incorporate, and activate the natural and revealed laws of God be so willing to accept plans of action, laws, and associations that undermine the foundation of freedom? Without absolute rights secured by our Constitution, citizens, and politicians, the strongest shall surely obtain their prize, while the

---

20. Sidney, *Discourses on Government*, 451.
21. Montesquieu, *The Spirit of Laws*, 150.

ordinary, common, and weak of society must merely fall in line with their agenda or else suffer the consequences. Grotius recognizes this Nimrod tendency of some in society (the power hungry).

> A people which violates the Laws of Nature and Nations, beats down the bulwark of its own tranquility for future time... Laws were introduced from the fear of receiving wrong, and that men are driven to practice justice by a certain compulsion. For that applies to those institutions and laws on which were devised from the more easy maintenance of rights...to establish judicial authorities, and to uphold them by their common strength; that those who could not resist singly, they might, united, control.[22]

To promote peace, government must recognize the natural laws of man as well as the natural rights of man and then must implement its purpose to promote the natural law of peace, for it is the natural desire of man to live in peace for fear of receiving wrong. The sum of this purpose in fact reflects man's sin nature and man's natural rights simultaneously, because while man has the right to exercise his life, liberty, and property, he does not have the right to trample on the rights of others. Likewise, the government does not have the right to trample or deprive the citizens of rights secured by its compact with the people. How could it be said that government has a right to undermine rights that society collectively and persons individually do not have the right to undermine? Therefore, it should be recognized that government itself may be the worst enemy to the peace of man than any other person or persons, and as such, the citizens should be keenly aware of its action to prevent such.

This same underlying natural maxim—and its proceeding principle—apply to many areas of society. It is not just the fear of being killed by your neighbor that this principle of promoting peace applies. There are many other areas where government should promote peace and tranquility: finances, commerce, taxes, religion, foreign relations, wars, family, education, etc.

---

22. Grotius, *Hugo Grotius on the Rights of War and Peace, xxviii.*

Where government creates policy (which proceeds from principle) that creates a strain on society and ignores the rights of man, then men will have a fear of receiving wrong, not only from his neighbor, but also from the government itself. Therefore, when government does not act within the scope of its intended purpose, such a government is just as evil as the neighbor who uses his right to invade your rights and invades the peace of mankind.

PROTECTING ABSOLUTE RIGHTS OF MAN

As government intends and acts to secure the purpose of peace in society, it must simultaneously secure the purpose of protecting absolute rights. We hear a lot of talk about rights in America. We hear politicians say (as a ploy to gather votes on Election Day) that everyone has a right, say, to education, to a home, to a job, to privacy, to stability, to security, to safety, to retirement, to Medicare, to health, and the rights go on and on. While many of the proposed rights may be a good thing unto themselves, the means of accomplishing those goals are equally important. Of course, with the rights proposed by these politicians come more taxes, government agencies, regulations, and restrictions—all in the name of rights. These politicians essentially create rights out of thin air (not justified in jurisprudence) to purchase votes. It is similar to the way America's federal government pays for debts and obtains credits by borrowing money from the Federal Reserve System (a private bank, by the way),[23] which creates money out of thin air and secures the debt with nothing. It is worth noting that Thomas Jefferson warns us of the power possessed by these humungous corporate banks, saying, "I hope we shall…crush in its birth the aristocracy of our moneyed corporations, which dare already to challenge our government to a trial of strength and bid defiance to the laws of our country."[24] What a contrast is Jefferson's outlook to America's politicians today. Likewise, the views of America's founders on rights were strikingly different from politicians today. The approach of modern politicians to rights is similar to the way Great Britain attempted to

---

23. "Federal Reserve," *Wikipedia*, (accessed May 5, 2009), http://en.wikipedia.org/wiki/Federal_Reserve.

24. Jefferson, *The Jeffersonian Cyclopedia*, 49.

gain allegiance and loyalty from the colonists by stating that Great Britain was the parent country of America, "with a low papistical design of gaining an unfair bias on the credulous weakness of our minds."[25] Unfortunately, there are very few Patrick Henrys today saying, "Trust it not, sir; it will prove a snare to your feet. Suffer not yourselves to be betrayed with a kiss."[26] Do you really think that the government can create and provide all of the rights without it costing a pretty penny at our expense? When will Americans wake up to realize that politicians are buying our rights with our own money? But when the money runs out, beware of what they will use to fund their power to give you rights.

Surprisingly or not, many people buy into the bogus, government-given rights proclamations of most politicians. They begin believing that they have such rights (and as has been demonstrated already, actions always follow belief) and begin demanding their rights, which usually equates to, "Give me money." The following is what President Gerald Ford says (also attributed to Barry Goldwater): "If the government is big enough to give you every-thing you want, it is big enough to take everything you have."[27] Is America so ignorant of this truth? Do lawyers, judges, and politicians care anything about what Blackstone taught? After all, he was one of the most influential and widely used sources of commentary on law for 150 years in America and England. Do they care about Blackstone's idea that God has given to man certain inalienable rights? These rights do not include being taken care of by government, being bailed out just because you are in financially hard times, or taking what others have obtained through hard work and ingenuity. These natural rights granted by God include life, liberty, and property, which give you the ability to take control of your life and advance it accordingly while at the same time keeping government control out of your life. Of course, the natural follow up is self-responsibility, because the individual must pro-vide for his own needs and wants. Perhaps that is the problem today: self-responsibility is another outdated principle. Nowhere in nature, in the Bible,

25. Paine and Philip, ed., *Common Sense*, 22.

26. Compiled by a member of the Philadelphia Bar, *American Oratory*, 14.

27. Suzy Platt, *Respectfully Quoted: A Dictionary of Quotations*, (New York: Library of Congress, Congressional Research Service, Barnes & Noble Publishing, 1993), 140.

or in America's Constitution does the current notion of government's purpose and rights exist. So why does America continue to elect politicians who adopt this philosophy? Is it because the sovereigns, we the people, have accepted the notion that rights come from government and not God?

Blackstone clearly acknowledges that rights come from God—not government—and that government's purpose is to simply protect those rights. He says,

> The principal aim of society to protect individuals in the enjoyment of those absolute rights, which were vested in them by the immutable laws of nature, but which could not be preserved in peace without that mutual assistance and intercourse which is gained by the institution of friendly and social communities. Hence it follows, that the first and primary end of human laws is to maintain and regulate these absolute rights of individuals...and therefore, the principal view of human laws is, or ought always to be, to explain, protect, and enforce such rights as are absolute.[28]

Blackstone rightly notes that all purposes and laws of government should ultimately reflect the rights of man—that is, the purpose of peace and justice should mirror the purpose of protecting the rights of man. Before such a purpose can be established, however, the nation must acknowledge that these rights come from God and are derived by the immutable laws of nature. This is the reason why former Alabama Supreme Court chief justice Roy Moore declared to the federal prosecutor—when asked if he was going to acknowledge God again in his capacity as the chief judge of Alabama—that he must acknowledge God, even if it meant defying a federal court order. Many Christians criticized Judge Moore for his stance on the Creator of law and his defiance of the federal judge who ordered him not to acknowledge God in his public capacity. However, such persons are either ignorant of the entire context of Judge Moore's decision or have consciously rejected his reasoning. If you do not understand why Judge Moore did what he did and do

28. Blackstone, *Commentaries on the Laws of England,* 109.

not agree with him, then you are likely a part of the problem facing America, and you most certainly do not understand American history, American jurisprudence, and God's natural and revealed laws.

So why did Judge Moore insist on acknowledging God (through the use of the Ten Commandments) in his public capacity in defiance of a federal court order? Author Mark Sutherland describes the issue and Judge Moore's reason this way:

> In the Court record of the hearings, the presiding judge articulated the issue: "…the issue is can the state acknowledge God"…[T]o the question, "Can the state acknowledge God?" Judge Moore says not only, "Yes!" but, more importantly, "It must!" He realizes that to fail to do so wipes out hundreds of years of Western civilization based on the rule of law, and ushers in an age where the law is whatever the presiding judge says it is.[29]

Judge Moore did just as America's founders did when they acknowledged that "the God of public religion made all human beings in his image and endowed them, as Jefferson wrote, with sacred rights to life, liberty, and the pursuit of happiness. [They acknowledged that] what the God of public religion has given, no king, no president, no government can abridge—hence the sanctity of human rights in America."[30] In other words, without God granting rights, there are no rights. Thus, when the government suggests or demands that public officials not acknowledge God as the source of our rights, then rights are indeed in jeopardy, and government has assumed the role of rights giver, which of course means they are a *rights-taker* as well. What else would or could be the case? It would be like saying I have a right to breathe so that I can live, but I reject the oxygen that is in the air. The oxygen is in the air and is the life-giving component of breathing. You cannot breathe air and survive without there being a sufficient element of oxygen in the air. Likewise, you cannot have absolute and secured rights without a

---

29. Mark Sutherland, *Judicial Tyranny: The New Kings of America,* (St. Louis, MO: Amerisearch, Inc., 2005), 83.

30. Meacham, *American Gospel,* 22.

sufficient element of the One who created the rights. How can freedom lovers and, moreover, Christians, miss this? Thus, once again the issue here is not mixing religion and politics but rather maintaining freedom in society.

Think about it: what limits would government (or anyone else for that matter) have if man were not born with natural rights? If man were not born with rights, then rights would be that which the stronger party likes—just as Plato observed. This is essentially a Darwinian concept rooted in atheistic evolution and a survival of the fittest mentality.[31] Is this the ideology of our nation's founders? Absolutely not. As we have seen in previous discussions, God has created man with the right to life, liberty, freedom, and property. How can it be said that government can take away rights, when government itself is nothing more than a creation of man? It is like any other contract between parties: marriage or employment. How can the clay say, "I have created the potter"?[32]

Understand, your right to life, liberty, and property is as inviolable as the right to thought itself. If you have the right to think, then such a right comes from God. From the right of thought, which closely resembles the right to life, comes the other rights in life. John Jay revealed the primacy of conscience when he said, "Adequate security is also given to the rights of conscience and private judgment. They are by nature subject to no control but that of the Deity, and in that free situation they are now left. Every man is permitted to consider, to adore, and to worship his Creator in the manner most agreeable to his conscience. No opinions are dictated, no rules of faith prescribed, no preference given to one sect to the prejudice of others."[33]

Likewise, Thomas Paine (in a letter to Thomas Jefferson) notes that "the first kind [of rights] are the rights of thinking, speaking, forming and giving opinions, and perhaps all those which can be fully exercised by the individual without the aid of exterior assistance—or in other words, rights of personal competency."[34] But people are willing to accept the notion of, "well, as long

---

31. Grotius, *Hugo Grotius on the Rights of War and Peace*, xxviii.

32. "Hath not the potter power over the clay, of the same lump to make one vessel unto honour, and another unto dishonour?" Romans 9:21 (KJV).

33. Jay, *The Life of John Jay*, 82.

34. Paine and Philip, ed., *Common Sense*, 81.

as I can pray in my heart, that is all that matters," or "I have nothing to hide; these rights do not matter." Then trying to explain the concepts of natural rights from God—the rights of life, liberty, and property—is like trying to explain to an atheist the importance of acknowledging that the Bible is God's word, that man is a sinner in need of a Savior, that the consequence of sin is eternal damnation in hell, and that Jesus Christ died on the cross for their sins so they could escape the penalty of sin. But when judgment day arrives, you will wish that you took your rights more seriously—or maybe it will be your children or grandchildren who are the ones wishing.

STRIVING FOR JUSTICE

James Madison said, "Justice is the end of government. It is the end of civil society. It ever has been and ever will be pursued until it be obtained, or until liberty be lost in the pursuit."[35] While on earth, Jesus confirms the natural law and Old Testament[36] principles of the primacy of justice being administered by governmental leaders when He tells the Pharisees and Sadducees, "Woe to you, scribes and Pharisees, hypocrites! For you tithe mint and dill and cumin, and have neglected the weightier matters of the law: *justice* and mercy and faithfulness. These you ought to have done, without neglecting the others."[37] Interconnected to and interdependent on natural rights is justice, for what good are rights when the government is not bound to protect the essence of right and wrong? Justice simply means rightness, to do the right thing, or "law, right."[38] If government does not carry out justice or has the authority to decide what is right and wrong without foundation, then government would not accomplish its intended purpose of protecting peace and rights (its other two purposes). As God and nature reveal that

---

35. James Madison, "Federalist Paper 51," in *The Federalist Papers,* Hamilton, Jay, and Madison, 403.

36. "A divine sentence is in the lips of the king; His mouth shall not transgress in judgment. A just balance and scales are the LORD's; all the weights in the bag are his work. It is an abomination to kings to do evil, for the throne is established by righteousness." Proverbs 16:10–12 (ASV).

37. Matthew 23:23 (ESV) (emphasis added).

38. "Just: Latin, law, right." Garner, ed., *Black's Law Dictionary.*

man has certain rights, government's formation and constitution should and must reflect those natural rights granted by God, and all principles and laws derived from its nature and constitution should reflect and protect those rights, because we know that a "constitution can be free but its citizens not"[39] and that government should reflect both nature in its principles and laws.

Algernon Sidney states that "commonwealths were instituted for the obtaining of justice, he contradicts them not, but comprehends all in that word; because 'tis just, that whosoever receives a power, should employ it wholly for the accomplishment of the ends for which it was given.'"[40] This is exactly what the Bible says in Proverbs 16:10–12 (ASV). "A divine sentence is in the lips of the king; His mouth shall not transgress in judgment. A just balance and scales are the LORD's; all the weights in the bag are his work. It is an abomination to kings to do evil, for the throne is established by righteousness." Imagine advocating the idea that whoever receives the power of administering government should use all of his power to accomplish the ends of government, that being justice. There is no mention about welfare or government-sponsored grants and giveaways; not a word regarding the government fixing all the problems of the nation or investing in the stock market or bailing out failed banks; no suggestion that the citizens depend on the government to keep them safe and happy; no mention of the government giving money to churches for faith-based initiatives. Simply protect justice.

The Bible repeatedly confirms that government is not established to merely benefit those in power but to provide justice for society. First Kings 10:9 (MJKV) states with certainty that God established government for the benefit of the people, to do justice and provide judgment. "Blessed is Jehovah your God, who delighted in you, to set you on the throne of Israel. Because Jehovah loved Israel forever; therefore, He made you king to do judgment and justice." So unless you think God hates America, then His ordination of government is to accomplish judgment and justice. And of course, if you think God hates America, what are you doing still paying taxes to support it, because God only required us to pay taxes for this cause—meaning to sup-

---

39. Montesquieu, *The Spirit of Laws,* 183.
40. Sidney, *Discourses on Government,* 310.

port the government that accomplishes His purpose of justice. Speaking of such passages, in the New Testament God clearly states what government He ordains in Romans 13:1–6.[41] Unfortunately, regarding government, these verses are mostly and frequently misapplied, taken out of context, distorted, and even used by Christian leaders (in government, in churches, and in politics) to convince the citizens of falsehoods (which will be discussed further herein). Romans 13 was also used by Adolf Hitler to make dumb sheep and willing slaves out of millions of Christian-German citizens. Think about it![42]

Regardless of one's interpretation of submission in Romans 13, the Bible clearly portrays the purpose of government: to be a terror to evil and a minister of good. It is simple: for those who do evil, the government should punish them; for those who do good, the government should not hinder them and thus promote them. Not only does scripture require the government to administer justice, but also scripture expects and requires citizens to accept justice and to believe in it; otherwise, such a citizen is worthless to society. This means that the citizen must actively pursue, respect, and demand justice. As scripture says, "A worthless witness mocks at justice."[43] Thomas Paine reflects the same understanding. "[Government is] a punisher…for were the impulses of conscience clear, uniform, and irresistibly obeyed, man would need no other lawgiver."[44] Likewise, John Locke reflects a Biblical understanding of what government's purpose is, as government is

---

41. "Let every soul be subject to the higher authorities. For there is no authority but of God; the authorities that exist are ordained by God. So that the one resisting the authority resists the ordinance of God; and the ones who resist will receive judgment to themselves. For the rulers are not a terror to good works, but to the bad. And do you desire to be not afraid of the authority? Do the good, and you shall have praise from it. For it is a servant of God to you for good. For if you practice evil, be afraid, for it does not bear the sword in vain; for it is a servant of God, a revenger for wrath on him who does evil. Therefore you must be subject, not only for wrath, but also for conscience' sake. For because of this you also pay taxes. For they are God's servants, always giving attention to this very thing." Romans 13: 1–6 (MJKV).

42. Art Ross and Martha Stevenson, *Romans,* (Louisville, KY: Westminster John Knox Press, 1999), 68.

43. Proverbs 19:28 (ESV).

44. Paine and Philip, ed., *Common Sense,* 5.

merely made up of men (who are supposed to be ministers of God), held to godly standards:

> And thus, in the state of nature, one man comes by a power over another; but yet no absolute or arbitrary power, to use a criminal, when he has got him in his hands, according to the passionate heats, or boundless extravagancy of his own will; but only to retribute to him, so far as calm reason and conscience dictate, what is proportionate to his transgression, which is so much as may serve for reparation and restraint: for these two are the only reasons, why one man may lawfully do harm to another, which is that we call punishment.
>
> In transgressing the law of nature, the offender declares himself to live by another rule than that of reason and common equity, which is that measure God has set to the actions of men, for their mutual security; and so he becomes dangerous to mankind, the tye, which is to secure them from injury and violence, being slighted and broken by him. Which being a trespass against the whole species, and the peace and safety of it, provided for by the law of nature, every man upon this score, by the right he hath to preserve mankind in general, may restrain, or where it is necessary, destroy things noxious to them, and so may bring such evil on any one, who hath transgressed that law, as may make him repent the doing of it, and thereby deter him, and by his example others, from doing the like mischief. And in the case, and upon this ground, EVERY MAN HATH A RIGHT TO PUNISH THE OFFENDER, AND BE EXECUTIONER OF THE LAW OF NATURE.[45]

It cannot be said, implied, argued, suggested, or believed that these verses propose that any and all government is ordained of God and is a minister of God, no matter how evil the magistrates and rulers, no matter what laws are executed and enforced, or no matter how tyrannical the government is. To do so would imply that all purposes of government are ordained of God,

---

45. Locke and Macpherson, ed., *Second Treatise of Government,* 10.

which is clearly not true. God did not create government, but man creates government out of his natural right of freedom and out of the desire to live in a peaceful community and society.

Nowhere in scripture does God ordain government's unjust purposes: evil laws, evil kings, and evil intent. Contrarily, the Bible depicts that God judges all evil, and that all governments are subject to the laws of God. How can God ordain purposes, motives, intents, and actions that He has declared to be evil? It is impossible. Of course, this necessarily follows that God does not ordain those persons in charge of government's administration and execution, where such persons contradict the stated and revealed purpose of government. And if you are thinking the only matters God has declared to be evil are abortion and homosexuality, you are gravely mistaken, as has already been proven and will be further proven herein. Again, the entire Bible contains God's standard of righteousness with regard to government and its administrators. It should not have to be argued further that God clearly states that He has ordained government's purpose to punish evil and be a minister to good, but the following verses demonstrate a few of God's standards regarding government seeking justice:

Protect the Innocent

Surely this came upon Judah at the command of the LORD, to remove them out of his sight, for the sins of Manasseh, according to all that he had done, and also for the innocent blood that he had shed. For he filled Jerusalem with innocent blood, and the LORD would not pardon.[46]

They poured out innocent blood, the blood of their sons and daughters, whom they sacrificed to the idols of Canaan, and the land was polluted with blood. Thus they became unclean by their acts, and played the whore in their deeds. Then the anger of the LORD was kindled against his people, and he abhorred his heritage.[47]

---

46. Kings 24:3–4 (EJV).
47. Psalm 106:38–40 (ESV).

Protect Freedom

If you do not oppress the sojourner, the fatherless, or the widow, or shed innocent blood in this place, and if you do not go after other gods to your own harm, then I will let you dwell in this place, in the land that I gave of old to your fathers forever.[48]

Provide Justice

Thus says the LORD: Do justice and righteousness, and deliver from the hand of the oppressor him who has been robbed. And do no wrong or violence to the resident alien, the fatherless, and the widow, nor shed innocent blood in this place.[49]

For many nations and great kings shall make slaves even of them, and I will recompense them according to their deeds and the work of their hands... The clamor will resound to the ends of the earth, for the LORD has an indictment against the nations; he is entering into judgment with all flesh, and the wicked he will put to the sword, declares the LORD.[50]

You will repay them, O LORD, according to the work of their hands.[51]

Give to them according to their work and according to the evil of their deeds; give to them according to the work of their hands; render them their due reward.[52]

You shall appoint judges and officers in all your towns that the LORD your God is giving you, according to your tribes, and they shall judge the people with righteous judgment.[53]

---

48. Jeremiah 7:6–7 (ESV).
49. Jeremiah 22:3 (ESV).
50. Jeremiah 25:14, 31 (ESV).
51. Lamentations 3:64 (ESV).
52. Psalm 28:4 (ESV).
53. Deuteronomy 16:18 (ESV).

Give Fair Trials

The judges shall inquire diligently, and if the witness is a false witness and has accused his brother falsely, then you shall do to him as he had meant to do to his brother. So you shall purge the evil from your midst.[54]

Provide Due Process of Law and Fair Judgment

If there is a dispute between men and they come into court and the judges decide between them, acquitting the innocent and condemning the guilty, then if the guilty man deserves to be beaten, the judge shall cause him to lie down and be beaten in his presence with a number of stripes in proportion to his offense.[55]

A divine sentence is in the lips of the king; His mouth shall not transgress in judgment. A just balance and scales are the LORD's; all the weights in the bag are his work. It is an abomination to kings to do evil, for the throne is established by righteousness.[56]

Punish Evil

Whoever sheds the blood of man, by man shall his blood be shed, for God made man in his own image.[57]

When men strive together and hit a pregnant woman, so that her children come out, but there is no harm, the one who hit her shall surely be fined, as the woman's husband shall impose on him, and he shall pay as the judges determine. But if there is harm, then you shall pay life for life.[58]

---

54. Deuteronomy 19:18, 19 (ESV).
55. Deuteronomy 25:1, 2 (ESV).
56. Proverbs 16:10–12 (ASV).
57. Genesis 9:6 (ESV).
58. Exodus 21:22 (ESV). Notice that where the offender causes the death of the unborn baby, the offender shall be put to death—a life for a life.

These also are sayings of the wise. Partiality in judging is not good. Whoever says to the wicked, "You are in the right," will be cursed by peoples, abhorred by nations, but those who rebuke the wicked will have delight, and a good blessing will come upon them.[59]

A king who sits on the throne of judgment winnows all evil with his eyes.[60]

The Bible clearly reveals the purpose for government is to promote justice for all its citizens—the essence of such being advancing right and punishing wrong. Since God-given rights belong to each person born, it necessarily follows that justice does not belong to one race, one class, or one segment of society, but it belongs to every citizen in that government's jurisdiction. It was this principle incorporated into the foundation of our country that began the movement of slave abolition. While many people would like to criticize America for having slaves in the very early part of its existence, a study of history shows that America's notions of rights, peace, and justice—government's purposes—were the catalysts for ending the slave trade, even though the slave trade had been practiced for thousands of years in literally every continent of the world (including Africa, where slavery still exists) and upon every race of people to have ever existed. What an accomplishment and movement America made toward freedom for all! John Jay (who actually proposed a provision to eliminate slavery in the United States Constitution of 1787) expresses justice this way:

Justice is the same, whether due from one man to a million, or from a million to one man; because it teaches and greatly appreciates the value of our free republican national government, which places all our citizens on an equal footing, and enables each and every of them to obtain justice…and [justice] brings it into action and enforces this great and glorious principle, that the people are the sovereigns of this country.[61]

---

59. Proverbs 24:23–25 (ESV).
60. Proverbs 20:8 (ESV).
61. Jay, *The Life of John Jay*, 297.

What a concept: the people of a nation are sovereigns and all have equal justice, secured by the government! While slavery is an unacceptable vice, America's sense of justice for all produced a nation that made it possible for any person to excel and prosper, to the point that America has elected (to be fair and honest regarding ethnicity) a half-black/half-white man to be president of the United States, Barack Hussein Obama. And while the mention of Obama has arisen, may it be noted that it is very interesting how society chooses to acknowledge the African race in Obama and utterly ignore the white race in Obama. What would happen if someone suggested that Obama was a white person, totally ignoring his black race? Such a person would be sacrificed at the stake of political correctness—but I digress.

Conservatives across America demonstrated an almost stifling fear of the policies that president-elect Barack Obama proposed, thinking that America's rights were *now* at risk. Perhaps the fear is misplaced. Perhaps what they should fear is God's judgment on our nation for abandoning our responsibility of making sure that government serves its God-stated purpose—including when Republican and conservative politicians run for and take office. How is it that we think America has somehow, all of a sudden, and overnight gotten to a place where America could vote for a socialist like Obama, when we had a wonderful, Christian president in the White House just before Obama? Did America change overnight, really? Absolutely not, and such a thought proves the ignorance of people who have lost sight of the purpose of government as described by God and our ancestors, who have already fought these battles and formed this nation in response to the tyranny imposed on them by similar illegitimate governments. Are we ready to lay down so easily what they fought for? God forbid.

Have you not wondered from what sources and from what ideology our nation's founding derived? You can be assured they were not the sources used in modern public education in America. Unfortunately, most public school education undermines the truth and wisdom advocated by our founding generation. In all reality, these men did not just come up with a new idea on their own without any direction, study, knowledge, or contemplation. It was not like cramming for a biology exam the night before the test by sitting down and memorizing a bunch of definitions and rules. It was not an experiment of hodgepodge thrown together by ignorant men. It was not like a group of children at a playground attempting to play a new game invented out of the head of one of the creative young minds, and all of the children say, "What the heck; sounds fun."

The fact is this nation's founding was an amazing point in history when a generation of leaders and citizens were largely—some extremely—familiar with the experience and knowledge derived from thousands of years of politics, religion, theology, spiritual reformation, philosophical enlightenment, wars, and battles, all of which were studied, explored, debated, and expressed by our founders and those who were before them. Former senator Charles Mathias, Jr. confirms that America came into existence because of the accumulated wisdom and knowledge of the founders and their vast familiarity with history. Mathias says, "The intellectual creativity of the authors of the Constitution was not invention, but the application of historical lessons in a rational, coordinated, and successful system."[62] In addition, America's founders did not just simply understand and incorporate historical lessons, but moreover they understood and incorporated principles directly from the oldest laws known to man: the Bible and natural law. Indeed, natural and revealed laws of God were applied to areas of religion, morals, philosophy, and politics of their day and were used as the very foundation of our existence. Is America so ignorant of the significance, impact, meaning, enlightenment, and wisdom of the words found in our Declaration for Independence?

We hold these **truths** to be **self-evident**, that all men are **created equal**, that they are **endowed by their Creator** with certain **unalienable Rights**, that among these are **Life, Liberty and the pursuit of Happiness**—That **to secure these rights**, Governments are **instituted among Men, deriving their just powers from the consent** of the governed—That whenever any Form of Government becomes destructive of these ends, it is the **Right of the People to alter or to abolish it,** and to institute new Government, **laying its foundation on such principles** and **organizing its powers in such form**, as to them shall seem **most likely to effect their Safety and Happiness.**[63]

---

62. The United States, *The Constitution of the United States of America,* (New York: Barnes and Noble Books, 1995), 86.

63. Thomas Jefferson, *Declaration of Independence,* (See Appendix A), (emphasis added).

This short paragraph in the Declaration of Independence reflects much of the truths concerning justice: that God has created men; that men have certain unalienable and inviolable rights; that men have the power to create and abolish government; and that government's purpose is to protect the peace, rights, and justice of society. The Declaration of Independence was a mere reflection of natural and revealed law and what had been discussed and explored for hundreds of years in Europe and the colonies by people such as Reverend John Calvin, Reverend Martin Luther, Samuel Rutherford, Algernon Sidney, John Winthrop, Reverend John Cotton, Reverend Thomas Hooker, William Blackstone, John Locke, Thomas Paine, Baron Montesquieu, Hugo Grotius, Samuel de Pufendorf, Emmerich de Vattel, Sir Edward Coke, John Milton, notable philosophers such as Plato and Cicero, and many other invaluable thinkers of their day and history. Can the history, education, knowledge, and wisdom of so many men and so many generations be ignored and forgotten so quickly by a few generations of ignorant, indifferent, and lazy Americans? Take a look at America, and answer the question.

8

GOVERNMENT'S ADMINISTRATION

O nce government has been established by the power of the people, its operation mostly consists of administrators, the oversight of which belongs to the people (either directly or through their repre-sentatives). There are many ways to administer government, just as there are many vehicles that could get you from point A to point B, but natural law, revealed law, and history reveal to people with eyes wide open the better ways and means. The most basic forms of government are these: monarchy—the rule of one; aristocracy—the rule of a few; and democracy—the rule of many. Whatever administrative form is chosen, those creating it should and must be aware of the significance and consequences of the choice made. As Blackstone observes, "Having…considered the three usual species of govern-ment…I proceed to observe, that, as the power of making laws constitutes the supreme authority in any state resides, it is the right of that authority to make laws."[1]

Of course, where the supreme authority is in one person or a few per-sons, that authority to make laws will still impact all citizens. Conversely,

---

1. Blackstone, *Commentaries on the Laws of England*, 44.

those making laws must be equipped with the necessary components of making laws designed actually to meet the purposes of government. Abuses of power by the authority in a monarchy or an aristocracy affect the masses, but the masses have little ability or power to redress and control such outcomes and effects.

Likewise, where the power of government is in the whole people, their lack of virtue, love of country, and education will result in laws being passed that do not achieve the purpose of government and have a similar effect as those monarchs or aristocrats who abuse their powers. The end result is still illegitimate government and tyranny. Is this so surprising? This principle applies to everyday life, and after all, did not God command Christians to grow in virtue, love, and knowledge?

> Jesus said unto him, "You shall love the Lord your God with all your heart and with all your soul and with all your mind."[2]

> His divine power has granted to us all things that pertain to life and godliness, through the knowledge of him who called us to his own glory and excellence, by which he has granted to us his precious and very great promises, so that through them you may become partakers of the divine nature, having escaped from the corruption that is in the world because of sinful desire. For this very reason, make every effort to supplement your faith with virtue, and virtue with knowledge.[3]

Even the Christian walk with God requires virtue, love, and knowledge. Faith alone can and will lead a Christian into the pit where he is following a blind leader. Both he and the leader will end up falling. Moreover, the same requirements of virtue, love, and knowledge are required to avoid falling into the pit on a national level and in the sense of governmental affairs.

Many—if not most—of Americans believe that America is a pure democracy, mostly because modern education and media describe our government

---

2. Matthew 22:37 (ESV).

3. Peter 1:3–5 (ESV).

as such. Even though America is not strictly a democracy (and for good reason), it has some elements of a democracy. Our founders were very familiar with Montesquieu's description of a quasi-democracy.

> When the body of the people is possessed of the supreme power, it is called a democracy. In a democracy the people are in some respects the sovereign, and in others the subject. There can be no exercise of sovereignty but by their suffrages, which are their own will… The people, in whom the supreme power resides, ought to have the management of everything within their reach: that which exceeds their abilities must be conducted by their ministers.[4]

In this description, Montesquieu recognizes the impossibility that the people of a democracy would be able to manage everything presented in a nation, just as Blackstone notes in his commentaries that "popular assemblies are frequently foolish in their contrivance, and weak in their execution."[5] Thus, there would be a need to appoint administrators to attend to the matters that exceed their ability and that are outside their reach. Therefore, America's form is not an absolute democracy, because administration is not conducted directly by the people but is entrusted in the hands of other administrators, on behalf of the people.

The founders understood the lack of practicable reality in using an absolute democracy and furthermore did not agree with its principles. The founders believed that the administration should not be conducted merely by the will of the majority but by principles found in nature and in the Bible, to ensure that government would achieve the purposes of government reflected in natural law and revealed law. As such, the founders formed a constitutional republic—a mixture of different forms well-known throughout human history—the best of all worlds, so to speak—based upon natural and revealed laws of God. Thomas Jefferson says this concerning their choice of America's government formation: "The republican is the only form of government which is not eternally at open or secret war with the rights of

---

4. Montesquieu, *The Spirit of Laws*, 8, 9.
5. Blackstone, *Commentaries on the Laws of England*, 42.

mankind."[6] The founders of America observed the advantages and disadvantages of all forms of government and actually were careful to incorporate an element of each one into our nation's formation, attempting to use the strengths and eliminate the disadvantages of each. But the form alone was not the masterpiece, but rather the principles that the form represented (based upon natural laws of God) created the most superior form of government the world had known. Thomas Jefferson reflects this sentiment. "With all the defects of our Constitution, whether general or particular, the comparison of our governments with those of Europe, is like a comparison of heaven and hell. England, like the earth, may be allowed to take the intermediate state."[7] Their formation demonstrates the most knowledgeable and wisest planning, as the structure of our Constitution had a form of democracy, aristocracy, and monarchy—a republic where sovereignty, power, and oversight rested with the people, but the administration was entrusted to a few, and the execution was entrusted to one.

However, while America's founders wisely chose America's form of government, they also recognized the inherent flaw in the formation: that is, if the people of the states lacked certain character, philosophy, and understanding, that freedom could not be retained, and America's greatness would fall. Undoubtedly, our founders enumerated the following requirements to be prevalent in society for freedom to exist in America: virtue, love of country, and education.

VIRTUE

One thing is certain, our founders recognized that since the sovereignty and power belonged to the people, such a society could not exist in freedom without the existence and indeed dominance of virtue in that society, just as Montesquieu recognizes, "The natural place of virtue is near to liberty."[8] Blackstone expresses the same sentiment in his *Commentaries,* stating, "In a democracy, where the right of making laws resides in the people at large,

6. Jefferson, *The Jeffersonian Cyclopedia,* 390.

7. Ibid., 571.

8. Montesquieu, *The Spirit of Laws,* 111.

public virtue, or good of intention, is more likely to be found."[9] It was never suggested that the survival of America was the modern idea of diversity of thought and multiculturalism (which is the dominant view of many politicians today). To the contrary, one of the stated purposes for ratifying the Constitution was commonality, not diversity.

> With equal pleasure I have as often taken notice that Providence has been pleased to give this one connected country to one united people—a people descended from the same ancestors, speaking the same language, professing the same religion, attached to the same principles of government, very similar in their manners and customs, and who, by their joint counsels, arms, and efforts, fighting side by side throughout a long and bloody war, have nobly established general liberty and independence.[10]

America no longer possesses such unity and commonality, just as was recognized by former president G. W. Bush when he states in his first inaugural speech, "Sometimes [America's] differences run so deep, it seems we share a continent, but not a country."[11] The evidence proves that the ideals of

---

9. Blackstone, *Commentaries on the Laws of England,* 42.

10. "In a republic, the manners, sentiments, and interests of the people should be similar. If this be not the case, there will be a constant clashing of opinions; and the representatives of one part will be continually striving, against those of the other. This will retard the operations of government, and prevent such conclusions as will promote the public good." "The United States includes a variety of climates. The productions of the different parts of the union are very variant, and their interests, of consequence, diverse. Their manners and habits differ as much as their climates and productions; and their sentiments are by no means coincident. The laws and customs of the several states are, in many respects, very diverse, and in some opposite; each would be in favor of its own interests and customs, and, of consequence, a legislature, formed of representatives from the respective parts, would not only be too numerous to act with any care or decision, but would be composed of such heterogeneous and discordant principles, as would constantly be contending with each other." Brutus, *The Anti-Federalist Papers,* 277; John Jay, "Federalist Paper 2," in *The Federalist Papers,* Hamilton, Jay, and Madison, 18. The Anti-Federalists did not see America as having the necessary common ingredient to ensure success as a union.

11. George W. Bush, "Text of Bush's Inaugural Speech," *Associated Press,* January 20, 2001.

Americans are about as diverse as the number of people. However, with this diversity America does not become stronger: it becomes weaker. America was not always such. Author John Meacham recognizes that America's foundation was built upon substance of character and philosophy. "What separated us from the Old World was the idea that books, education, and the liberty to think and worship as we wished would create virtuous citizens who cherished and defended reason, faith, and freedom."[12] To suggest that all cultures, all opinions, all religions, all languages, all ways of life be accepted in America, and that such acceptance will give America strength, is ludicrous and has been proven fallacious.

Obtaining and preserving freedom has nothing to do with voting into public office a minority race, which supposedly and somehow proves that the people are noble and enlightened. Since when did the color of one's skin or ethnicity determine any value in that person? A person is no more qualified for public office because he is black than because he is white. And as a side note, now that America has elected its first minority president, what excuse do minorities have of not being able to rise to the occasion, and that "whitey" is holding them back? Indeed, a large percentage of voters who voted for Obama were white—what issue is there of racism being discussed as relevant to being held back in America today? The necessary ingredient for freedom's success has nothing to do with race and everything to do with values.

John Jay declares to the citizens of America that virtue (among other characteristics) is a must, without which the environment for freedom would be hostile. He says,

> Let virtue, honor, the love of liberty and of science be and remain the soul of this constitution, and it will become the source of great and extensive happiness to this and future generations. Vice, ignorance, and want of vigilance will be the only enemies able to destroy it. Against these be ever jealous.[13]

Can any honest person deny the existence of those signs in America that John Jay prophetically declares to be the destructive cause of freedom?

---

12. Meacham, *American Gospel*, 7, 8.
13. Jay, *The Life of John Jay*, 83.

Vice: meaning moral depravity. *Ignorance:* meaning the lack of knowledge or awareness. *The lack of vigilance:* meaning the lack of alertly watching for danger. These enemies are here and now and are in fact destroying what was established by these great men and women of our history.

Even George Washington feared that his generation of Americans (after independence had been won) would destroy what had been fought for and conquered with blood, tears, and lives by the lack of virtue he discerned in the nation. He says, "[V]irtue, I fear, has in a great degree taken its departure from our land, and the want of disposition to do justice is the source of the national embarrassments."[14] If George Washington feared that the constitutional republic could be destroyed during his lifetime, how much better do we think America is today? Indeed, most would agree it is worse today and has been for some time. Sidney also recognizes that government cannot obtain its end (that is, justice) without the existence of virtue, and moreover that virtue be exalted. "[The accomplishment of the ends of government, meaning justice] could be performed only by such as excelled in virtue: but lest they should deflect from it, no government was thought to be well constituted."[15] One might wonder how these statesmen could be so dogmatic in their prophetic declarations concerning the rise and fall of nations, given the existence of virtue or not. However, it is clear that these men studied not only the history of nations but also the Bible and incorporated the revelations of God into their analysis and conclusions. Maybe America could resolve its problems if it did the same; but it does not appear that we will.

Sidney continues his discourse regarding the necessity of virtue in a free democracy by rejecting the following suggestion made by a contemporary commentator on government:

> Whether virtue be exalted or suppressed; whether he that bears the sword be a praise to those that do well and a terror to those that do evil, or a praise to those that do evil and a terror to those as do well, it concerns us not; for the king must not lose his right, nor have his power diminished, on any account.[16]

---

14. Ibid., 244.
15. Sidney, *Discourses on Government,* 311.
16. Ibid.

Sidney responds to that statement by stating, "I have been sometimes apt to wonder, how things of this nature could enter into the head of any man."[17] In other words, to Sidney, whether or not virtue exists in a nation absolutely matters, and whether or not the government is a terror to good works absolutely matters, referring to Romans 13. Sidney recognized that before a government can fulfill its Romans 13 purpose, the nation must exalt virtue, or else, as John Jay declared, these enemies will destroy the nation.

Montesquieu also believes that the lack of virtue in a democracy would destroy it from within. He puts it this way:

> In a popular (democratic) state, one spring more is necessary, namely, virtue…but when, in a popular government, there is a suspension of the laws, as this can proceed only from the corruption of the republic, the state is certainly undone… When virtue is banished, ambition invades the minds of those who are disposed to receive it, and avarice possesses the whole community.
>
> The objects of their desires are changed; what they were fond of before has become indifferent; they were free while under the restraint of laws, but they would fain now be free to act against the law; and as each citizen is like a slave who has run away from his master, that which was a maxim of equity he calls rigor; that was a rule of action he styles constraint; and to precaution he gives the name of fear.[18]

Very interestingly, America demonstrates the following prediction made by Thomas Jefferson: "Our government will remain virtuous for many centuries; as long as…[the people] are chiefly agricultural, and this will be as long as there shall be vacant lands in any part of America. When they get piled upon one another in large cities, as in Europe, they will become corrupt as Europe."[19] Wow! It is as if Jefferson was able to see America today for what it has become. Indeed, Jefferson was right. When society lacks virtue,

---

17. Ibid.
18. Montesquieu, *The Spirit of Laws*, 20, 21.
19. Jefferson, *The Jeffersonian Cyclopedia*, 393.

corruption follows; and from corruption, the nation becomes undone and citizens become slaves, not knowing the original desires, understandings, ambitions, and purposes that originally formed the nation. Thus, while it is important to understand and know the purpose of government, it is equally important that the nation exalt virtue to maintain the purpose of government and in fact to accomplish it. For without the prevalence of virtue, the enemies of freedom prevail.

LOVE OF COUNTRY

Author Edmond Burke says in his *Reflections of the Revolution in France,* "To make us love our country, our country ought to be lovely."[20] However, for a nation even to obtain the character of "lovely," its citizens must take an active part in making it such. Essentially, a nation being lovely and a citizen's love of country are bi-conditional, very similar to many other relationships in life— such as husband and wife. Thus, another element that must exist in a republican nation for freedom to exist is the love of country. This matter of loving your country is another distorted sound bite, metaphor, and idea presented in America—and is actually used against those citizens who would question a politician or idea that is contrary to the principles of freedom (such as a suggestion that some of America's wars are fought illegally and unjustly). The phrase *love of country* is used so flippantly and without substance that it is like the subconsciously and monotonously used phrase, "How's it going?" The response to which is usually, "Pretty good; how about you?" The words are used and are proposed to have meaning, but in reality they mean nothing and have no substance. They are in fact more of a reflex than a response. Even worse, people equate being patriotic with loving your country. In fact, they are not the same. What is truly sad about patriotism is that most governments of the world use patriotism against their own citizens by making them feel good about being enslaved by their own government. Being patriotic simply means that you are loyal to your country. Virtually every citizen in the world is loyal to his country and is thus patriotic. Therefore, being

---

20. Edmund Burke, *Reflections on the Revolution in France, and on the Proceedings in Certain Societies in London Relative to that Event,* 10th Edition, (London: Pall-Mall), 116.

patriotic is not enough and does not equate to love of country. This concept is very similar to the person who claims to love God but does nothing more than say it and does nothing to show it. But we know more proof is needed, for "loving God is keeping His commandments."[21]

Similarly, loving your country is keeping its commandments, which are found in the principles of its constitution and in the nature upon which those principles were founded. Remember, laws must reflect both nature and the principles of the constitution. Furthermore, loving your country should never contradict natural and revealed law and reason (the pillars of freedom). Thomas Paine recognizes that regarding the prejudices being suffered by Englishmen during his day. "The prejudice of Englishmen, in favour of their own government by king, lords, and commons, arises as much or more from national pride [or from being patriotic] than reason."[22] Many in America have a disillusioned perspective concerning the leaders in American government, believing that no serious harm can come to us because, "We are Americans!" However, such a view of mere men was not the perspective of the men who made America. Rather, it is this thought that colors the lenses of their perspective:

> Are we [Americans] so much better than the people of other ages and of other countries, that the same allurements of power and greatness, which led them aside from their duty, will have no influence upon men in our country? Such an idea, is wild and extravagant—Had we indulged such a delusion, enough has appeared in a little time past, to convince the most credulous, that the passion for pomp, power and greatness, works as powerfully in the hearts of many of our better sort, as it ever did in any country under heaven.[23]

If your government administrators commit wrong and possess fallacious philosophy, your patriotic pride should not prevent you from recognizing fallacies and evils in your own government and attempting to correct them.

---

21. John 5:3 (KJV).
22. Paine and Philip, ed., *Common Sense,* 10.
23. Brutus, *The Anti-Federalist Papers,* 289.

Being willfully ignorant does not exempt you for this flaw either. To correct is to love: to love is to correct. What parent does not understand this? Of course, looking at the way most parents correct their children today, it is no wonder why citizens do not correct their government. Moreover, Montesquieu also connects virtue to the love of country, stating, "Virtue in a republic is a most simple thing; it is a love of the republic."[24] Thus, without virtue there is no love, and without love, there is no virtue. They are interdependent, and the existence of both produce in the citizen a sense of devotion to the very ideas and principles that make the nation what you love. If it is true that we love the purposes of our nation, purposes like "capital punishments and just wars [that] arise from our love of the innocent,"[25] then what is to be said of the people in a nation who allow that nation's very foundation, form, and substance, which provide the security of those purposes (which Americans supposedly love),[26] to be destroyed? In other words, how can one say they possess virtue and love for America when they do not stand on the principles that formed it and vote for those who do not comply with those principles? It sounds like the biblical notion of "faith without works is dead."[27]

An analogy of this love of country requirement can be seen in a husband and wife relationship. When a man falls in love with a woman (and vice versa) and they marry each other, they marry for the qualities possessed by each and for the expectation that the other will possess those qualities for life. The husband will love his wife throughout the many years of marriage, as she maintains the qualities and characteristics that he loved at the beginning, yea, even before the marriage agreement began. Even when the marriage suffers from different struggles in life, perhaps causing the wife not to demonstrate the qualities the husband loved in her beforehand, the marriage will continue and will succeed where the husband believes the wife still possesses those original qualities and is willing to suffer evil while evils are sufferable from his wife, because he believes she still possesses those qualities. However,

---

24. Montesquieu, *The Spirit of Laws,* 40.

25. Grotius, *Hugo Grotius on the Rights of War and Peace,* 23.

26. "Lest innocent blood be shed in your land that the LORD your God is giving you for an inheritance, and so the guilt of bloodshed be upon you." Deuteronomy 19:10 (ESV).

27. James 2:17 (ESV).

when the wife demonstrates a long train of abuses of abandoning the qualities and characteristics that the husband loved for an extended period of time, when the intent of the wife is clear that she no longer possesses those qualities loved by the husband, the husband rightfully and naturally loses his affection for his wife, or at least the desire to support her behavior. The same analogy applies to a citizen's love of country.

A citizen's love of country will create many emotional and physical reactions, even to the detriment of the citizen. Paine describes that many citizens are willing to do as Grotius suggests. "The vices of Princes are to be tolerated like bad seasons."[28] Bad seasons come and go, but what of the abuses with design? What of the perpetrated philosophy that contradicts natural and revealed laws of God? What should be said of the citizen who, while loving his country, facilitates government's abuse of not just himself, but also his family, neighbors, community, and nation? By comparison, what shall be said of the husband who will deny the reality that his wife has abandoned the marriage and will continue to claim his undying love for her, while he personally, emotionally, psychologically, and financially suffers; while she cheats on him, curses him, diminishes him, harms him, and even fights against him; and while she abuses his children as well? At some point, denial is unhealthy and promotes slavery. The feeling of love is natural where the wife once loved the husband and possessed the characteristics of a good wife, but the wife's abandonment of the marriage relationship is reality nonetheless, and the husband will never escape the tortures of that relationship until he realizes he loves a devil.

These emotional and physical reactions can actually be good, in that they should cause you to attempt to preserve the thing that you love (e.g., redressing the government). Therefore, the citizen's love of country should create the desire to know, understand, study, become involved, reprove, correct, and engage the nation. Blind love for your country is no nobler than is sacrificing freedom in the future for comfort in the present. All of these acts of love lead us to the next necessity of a free republican democracy: education.

---

28. Grotius, *Hugo Grotius on the Rights of War and Peace*, 41.

EDUCATION

Without a doubt, a free nation cannot exist without the people being educated. As Judge Jess Root puts it, "Whatever his rank, character, occupation, or business, may be in the community; without [wisdom and knowledge, or knowledge and virtue] in the community…although possessed of every other advantage, he will be wretched as an individual; and as a member of society will be wanting in cordiality to its true interest."[29] To be clear, education does not mean the indoctrination of the federal (and even state) education systems America knows today, which are actually destroying the true education needed to preserve a free society. The education needed for a nation to be free of course includes the basic education of being able to read, write, and perform basic scholastic skills; but more importantly, the nation must possess the education of philosophically understanding its history, ideology, religion, culture, nature, foundations, principles, and how they all relate to current political, cultural, legal, and moral affairs. As Thomas Jefferson astutely observes, "Education is the true corrective of abuses of constitutional power."[30] This is why America has historically emphasized foundational, meaningful, and advanced education, so that the individual citizen can maintain the virtue and knowledge needed to preserve a free society. It is a fact that in early America "protestant societies strongly encouraged universal [meaning complete] education, and it was the Bible largely that was used to teach children to read, write and understand literature."[31] Indeed, Blackstone takes the need for education to another level and says that without a thorough desire to study jurisprudence (meaning "the fundamental elements of a particular legal system")[32] *and* its consequential laws, such persons may not even possess ethical behavior. He says, "Jurisprudence, or the knowledge of those laws, is the principal and most perfect branch of ethics."[33]

---

29. Root, *Reports of Cases,* ii.
30. Jefferson, *The Jeffersonian Cyclopedia,* 2.
31. Eidsmoe, *Christianity and the Constitution,* 22–23.
32. Garner, ed., *Black's Law Dictionary.*
33. Blackstone, *Commentaries on the Laws of England,* 27.

The demand for education serves many purposes, one of which is to secure the God-given rights of mankind by the citizens of a government. The Enlightenment philosophers wrote extensively on the need for education to keep government in check and to prevent the abuse of government upon the citizens. Grotius describes the importance of education this way:

> Passages of history are of twofold use to us; they supply both examples of our arguments, and judgments upon them. With regard to examples, in proportion as they belong to better times and better nations, they have the more authority.[34]

Is there any better nation that has more authority than America to use as an example of freedom—especially America's founding generation? Never in history was there a freer, more industrious, more innovative, and more powerful nation than America. Maybe America was so successful because the founders "placed the study of history at the heart of the undertaking, partly on the grounds that examples from the past would illuminate morality and religion."[35] Learning from those who provided the understanding, ways, and means to create America would indeed be a noteworthy education. What good is the power that the people of America possess without a proper understanding of how to use it and in what manner it is to be used? What good are our minds, logic, and reasoning if we do not study the matters relevant to that which affects us most?

Without an active study of the matters of state, we fail our responsibilities as the sovereign of America to preserve the freedom secured by we the people of the states in our Constitution. With freedom comes great responsibility and obligation. With lethargy, indifference, and ignorance comes great slavery. Undoubtedly, our posterity will feel the effects of our decisions one way or the other. Enlightenment philosophers understand this truth and agree on the following:

> Such as have reason, understanding or common sense, will, and ought to make use of it in those things that concern themselves

---

34. Grotius, *Hugo Grotius on the Rights of War and Peace,* xxxvi.
35. Meacham, *American Gospel,* 21.

and their posterity, and suspect the words of such as are interested in deceiving or persuading them not to see with their own eyes, that they may be more easily deceived. This rule obliges us so far to search into matters of state, as to examine the original principles of government in general, and of our own in particular. We cannot distinguish truth or falsehood, right from wrong, or know what obedience we owe to the magistrate, or what we may justly expect from him, unless we know what he is, why he is, and by whom he is made to be what he is.[36]

It is absolutely essential that the citizens dig deeply into the matters of state to inquire into the important questions regarding our administrators and to rightly divide the issues, so we can know what he is, why he is, and by whom he is made to be what he is, all of which is predicated upon the natural law precept that all men are sinners and those in power tend to abuse their power, as well as the power of the government is in the hands of the people. To suggest that America can stay free while the people are ignorant of the truths that make them free would be like placing a five-year-old child as the king of a monarchy nation; the lack of education on the child's part would utterly destroy the nation. You might as well make your decisions through a lottery process. Your chances of success would be as great, if not greater.

To be certain, a complete and transformative education must be emphasized and encouraged, because without it a nation cannot maintain its freedom. Montesquieu confirms this fact by saying,

It is in a republican government that the whole power of education is required. The fear of despotic governments naturally arises of itself amidst threats and punishments; the honor of monarchies is favored by the passions, and favors them in its turn; but virtue is a self-renunciation, which is ever arduous and painful. The virtue may be defined as the love of the laws and of our country...this love is peculiar to democracies.

---

36. Sidney, *Discourses on Government*, 321.

In these alone the government is intrusted to private citizens. Now, a government is like every thing else: to preserve it we must love it... Every thing, therefore, depends on establishing this love in a republic; *and to inspire it ought to be the principle business of education:* but the surest way of instilling it into children is for parents to set them an example.[37]

Notice that Montesquieu places the responsibility on the citizens to educate themselves concerning the matters of state, and yes, he even suggests that it is the parents' responsibility to educate the children on such matters. Just as the Bible says, "Train up a child in the way he should go: and when he is old, he will not depart from it."[38] Montesquieu essentially connects a person's love of country with their education, meaning without a desire to educate oneself regarding the matters of state, there can be no real love of country, and when there is no education and love of country, freedom ceases.

Is this any different from what the Bible describes regarding the necessity of remembering history to understand the nature and reality of one's current state? Consider the following verses: "Therefore I will not neglect to put you always in remembrance of these things, though you know them and are established in the present truth."[39] And furthermore, "But I intend to remind you, you once knowing these things, that the Lord having delivered a people out of the land of Egypt, in the second place destroyed the ones not believing."[40] God reveals to us the importance of educating oneself in history and to remember and understand the past so that one can know and understand the present and future. Without education, there is no remembering; without recollection, there is no application; and without (correct) application, there is no (correct) execution. This principle applies to individuals *and* nations, without which destruction always follows.

Education is designed and intended to have a long term so that the student will become an independent-minded, free-thinking, wise, and dis-

---

37. Montesquieu, *The Spirit of Laws,* 34, (emphasis added).
38. Proverbs 22:6 (KJV).
39. Peter 1:12 (MJKV).
40. Jude 1:5 (KJV).

cerning citizen to help preserve the natural gifts of God—life, liberty, and property. Blackstone confirms the reality that a free nation cannot exist unless the citizenry is educated about the nature of God and man, their government, the principles of government, and the laws of government. He says in his *Commentaries,*

> For I think it an undeniable position, that a competent knowledge of the laws of that society in which we live, is the proper accomplishment of every gentlemen and scholar; an highly useful, I had almost said essential, part of liberal and polite education.[41]

Interestingly, Blackstone classifies the education of laws of society as an undeniable position that every gentlemen and scholar should accomplish, because it is essential to education. The education of laws, of course, necessarily means that the citizen must understand the source of all laws, which is God, and must apply the natural laws created by God to understand how government relates to those laws and how the citizen relates to his government and positive law.

Another reason that education of the citizens is required for a republican nation to maintain freedom is because its leaders are chosen by society; and citizens from society become governmental leaders. Without an education of laws, both citizens and leaders would be led and would lead others into the ditch and would ultimately lead the nation into slavery. Blackstone reveals the reality that nations suffer harms caused by uneducated citizens and leaders, saying,

> The mischiefs that have arisen to the public from inconsiderate alterations in our laws, are too obvious to be called in question; and how far they have been owing to the defective education of our senators, is a point well worthy of public attention.[42]

---

41. Blackstone, *Commentaries on the Laws of England,* 2.
42. Ibid., 5.
43. Ibid., 7.

Blackstone further shares his disgust with those who choose to be ignorant of the laws by saying, "Ignorance of the laws of the land hath ever been dishonorable in those who are intrusted by their country to maintain, to administer and to amend them."[43] Blackstone dogmatically states that government administrators should have the most extensive and intense knowledge of the Constitution even to be worthy of our vote. "It is necessary for a senator to be thoroughly acquainted with the constitution; and this is a knowledge of the most extensive nature; a matter of science, of diligence, of reflection; without which no senator can possibly be fit for his office."[44]

Indeed, how long can freedom last when the citizens are so ignorant of the nature and principles of laws, and the politicians are either ignorant of the same or corrupt in their implementation? The fact is this: America would never have existed had it not been for the arduous study (concerning theology, philosophy, political science, government, etc.) of the generations before, during, and after our nation's fight for independence. How presumptuous for Americans to think and accept the idea that the freedoms and liberties long enjoyed by our nation will perpetually continue without the complete education required to preserve them! It is very apparent that our nation's educational philosophy is utterly failing—and with it, our nation.

From the decision of whether or not to secede from Great Britain; from the discussions of what form of government American should incorporate; to the first day our Constitution was framed by our founders, education and the knowledge of history played as important a role as just about any other factor. Those who drafted its substance and form recognized that America would fall without active preservation. Before the sovereigns of the states even ratified the newly proposed Constitution of the United States, the framers recognized that the form of government proposed would indeed fail without the people's preservation of it. In fact, when Benjamin Franklin is asked by an inquiring lady about whether or not the new America has a monarch or a republican form of government, Franklin says, "A Republic, Madam, if you can keep it."[45]

---

44. Ibid., 4.

45. Michael P. Riccards, *A Republic, If You Can Keep It: The Foundation of the American Presidency, 1700–1800,* (Westport, CT: Greenwood Press, Inc., 1987), 41.

By way of analogy: consider a house left unattended for even a short period of time. Before too long, the house deteriorates and becomes uninhabitable. A nation is no different, and Franklin gave warning to his listeners and to his posterity that this republic may be kept alive and well only by the active participation of its citizens. This necessarily requires an adequate education of the people, which is another reason that government (especially federal) education is so dangerous to America's society.

Contemplate this: when you send a child to a Christian school, what agenda do you expect the school to teach? Christianity. If you send your child to a Jewish school, what agenda do you expect the school to teach? Judaism. If you send your child to a government school, what agenda do you expect the school to teach? In today's America expect socialism, evolutionism, humanism, secularism—anything but the nature and principles of God's natural and revealed law.[46] What effect do you think that has on generations of people and their understanding of freedom? The answer to that question is already revealed. Freedom-loving Americans cannot expect that their children will be fully and completely educated on the salient matters of freedom in our nation by simply sending their children off to public school, and in most cases private school, or even taking them to church (a sad commentary upon our nation). The necessary education needed today must come from independent sources (and I do not mean Rush Limbaugh, Sean Hannity, and the like) and certainly from the parents and other family members, who are ultimately responsible for the education of their children.

It is very apparent to see just how education contributed to the freest nation to have ever existed. After the Constitution was drafted, there was much debate as to whether or not to ratify it by the states, and there were a few key participants in the advocating of the Constitution: James Madison, John Jay, and Alexander Hamilton. These men wrote newspaper articles,

---

46. "Under the new catechism, the use of public schools to indoctrinate children in Judeo-Christian beliefs is strictly forbidden. But public schools can and should be used to indoctrinate children in a tolerance of lifestyles, an appreciation of reproductive freedom, respect for all cultures, and the desirability of racial, ethnic, and religious diversity… [T]hese schools shall be converted into learning centers of the new religion." Buchanan, *The Death of the West*, 53.

known as the *Federalist Papers*,[47] for all of America to read, expounding the reasons why the sovereigns (the people) of the state of New York (as well as the remaining states) should ratify the Constitution. These *Federalist Papers* were extremely influential in what became the ratification of the Constitution of the United States of America. When advocating the states' ratification of the newly proposed Constitution, James Madison observes the significant part that education played in the framing of the Constitution. He says,

> The history of almost all the great councils and consultations held among mankind for reconciling their discordant opinions, assuaging their mutual jealousies, and adjusting their respective interests, is a history of factions, contentions, and disappointments, and may be classed among the most dark and degraded pictures which display the infirmities and depravities of the human character.[48]

Likewise, without knowledge of the history of almost all the great councils and consultations, America will simply become like the abandoned house, only to deteriorate with the corruption of vagabonds, dust, weather, invaders, and pests.

Clearly, our form of government, which was designed to facilitate freedom, is merely a house built on sand when its citizens and even leaders are uneducated, not only with regard to classical education, but also with regard to the history and articulations of freedom. By ignoring its foundational principles, precepts, and maxims; by voting for those who are proven, known, or even suspected of being less than honorable, less than knowledgeable of natural laws, less than educated in America's history, and less than proponents of freedom's principles, the Constitution, and all of the history that formed it; and by believing (which is revealed through action) that this nation shall remain free simply because you vote Republican reveals just how uneducated and ignorant the American people truly are. Praying for God to

---

47. "Descending from theory to practice, there is no better book than the *Federalist.*" Jefferson, *The Jefferson Cyclopedia,* 392.

48. James Madison, "Federalist Paper 37," in *The Federalist Papers,* Hamilton, Jay, and Madison, 282, 283.

spare the nation of tyranny and oppression from a known socialist who happens to wear the title of Democrat, and praying for God to work a miracle by putting a Republican in office who is known to be anything but an advocate of freedom is a slap in the face of any spirituality, patriotism, and common sense. Why should God spare any nation the evil it deserves, and indeed asks for, by relying on the lesser of two evils to preserve freedom? Such an approach to preserving freedom is absurd and insulting to those who risked and sacrificed their lives, fortunes, and sacred honor by fighting King George and his army for the freedoms we have enjoyed!

Our founders handed freedom to their posterity on a silver platter, but for them, it cost much. Their sacrifice included not only many thousands of lives, riches, families, properties, homes, torments, and tortures, but it also included their diligent search for virtue, love of country, and education. Without all of these combining factors, America may not have succeeded in winning their war for independence and may not have created the freest nation the world has known, making it almost too easy for their posterity to succeed and prosper in the blessings and promises of God. However, this is clear: each generation has the same responsibility to maintain freedom, without which the nation will surely fall into tyranny.

9

GOVERNMENT ADMINISTRATORS

Their Qualifications

If someone were to ask the average American (or even the above-average American) what qualifications do you look for in a governmental administrator, the answer would likely reveal horrific conclusions about the state of America. Without an understanding of what qualifications are necessary to preserve freedom, freedom will not last. This is common sense and applies to everyday life and relationships, to which all can relate. The frightening reality of today is that even the ignorant citizens realize that something is terribly wrong in and with America, and that most politicians are not worthy of support, which creates an attitude of distrust towards our leaders. Such a distrust and lack of confidence is not only telling of the state of our nation but also reveals the fact that the citizens have allowed politics to become this way.

George Washington, the father of our country, thought that the better kind of people would not accept rulers who did not reflect and enforce the Constitution, and as a result of their lack of confidence in such rulers, faith and belief that liberty could exist in this nation would cease. He says,

What I fear most is, that the better kind of people, by which I mean
the people who are orderly and industrious, who are content with
their situations, and not uneasy in their circumstances, will be led
by the insecurity of property, the loss of confidence in their rulers,
and the want of public faith and rectitude, to consider the charms of
liberty as imaginary and delusive.[1]

Washington believed that people in society who are orderly and industrious with their lives would actually pay attention to the philosophy and performance of their leaders and would react appropriately. Indeed, what citizen
enjoys and accepts being lied to by politicians?—as if being trustworthy is
not a mandatory requisite to government leadership.[2] The fact that even a
portion of Americans still have faith in the government administrators who
have, with apparent design, proven themselves advocates of nothing more
than quasi-freedom, would likely shock and disgust Washington. And how
can we prove that many Americans still have faith in such leaders? Because
they continue to play their games, vote for their rhetoric, pander their lies,
and patronize their campaigns, all the while most of them complaining that
our government is corrupt and untrustworthy.

What is even more amazing is this idea prevalent in America that we expect
change from politicians who have proven or even admit to not believing in the
natural laws, principles, and ideology of America's founding. This misconception contradicts common sense and human nature. Blackstone clearly explains
that when governmental leaders do not understand—first and foremost—the
principles of law, then such administrators are dangerous to freedom.

If practice [of law] be the whole he is taught, practice must also be
the whole he will ever know; if he be not instructed in the elements
and first principles upon which the rule of practice is founded, the
least variation from established precedents will totally distract and
bewilder him.[3]

---

1. Jay, *The Life of John Jay,* 246.

2. "The whole art of government consists in the art of being honest." Jefferson, *The
Jeffersonian Cyclopedia,* 410.

3. Blackstone, *Commentaries on the Laws of England,* 22.

To believe that a politician—a person who implements and influences law!—who does not accept, understand, or promote the principles of free government will provide positive change for America not only contradicts common sense and human nature but actually encourages the destruction of our republic, which we are guaranteed under the U.S. Constitution.[4] The same principle applies in every other area of life. Think about it: would you ask a doctor to operate on your or your child's body when the doctor does not understand the nature of biology? Or, when you consider marrying a mate for life, do you expect that the prospective mate will become a wonderful and desirable spouse when such person proves to be selfish, abusive, hateful, jealous, manipulative, and arrogant before marriage? Most people with common sense who care anything about the person who is about to embark on the marriage journey would vehemently warn him or her about what the future holds with that prospective spouse. Such is a common experience of life. How is it then that the same principle does not apply to government administrators?

When inspecting a candidate for public office, citizens should analyze their qualifications based upon not what they say they are going to do but what they have already done. Our selection criteria should be based upon the facts, in other words. Algernon Sidney believes that such selection criteria should exist regarding government administrators and puts it this way: "Good and wise counselors do not grow up like mushrooms; great judgment is required in choosing and preparing them."[5] This short, insightful statement contradicts the approach of many Americans today and exposes the fallacious belief that a candidate will mushroom into a great leader once he has taken office, when he (the politician) has not proven such character before taking office. Furthermore, Sidney expresses the requirement not only that leaders be qualified but also that the people possess great judgment in choosing and preparing them, all of which require virtue, love of country, and education on the part of the citizens. It is only when citizens approach voting in this fashion that truly credible and qualified politicians can be elected as ministers of God and not terrors of freedom.

---

4. "The United States shall guarantee to every State in this Union a Republican Form of Government." U.S. Constitution, art. 4, sec. 4.

5. Sidney, *Discourses on Government,* 324.

It is common sense to know that a government administrator does not become honorable and trustworthy, uplifting and upholding the purpose for which he was entrusted with power, simply because he says he will or simply because he has been given power to do so. Assume for the moment that you were a plaintiff in a lawsuit where you sued another person (called the defendant) for conspiring to damage your business reputation and good will (for which you have worked years to develop). Assume that the defendant had been telling your clients that you were involved in illegal activities, that you were involved in price fixing, that you absconded with clients' money, that you knowingly used illegal aliens for cheap labor, and many other false accusations. When you went to trial and the defendant took the witness stand, would you not want the jury to know about his past conduct of, say, being convicted for theft, giving contradictory statements at a previous deposition, and of having the motive to steal your business clients away? Of course you would, and you would be very upset if your attorney did not attempt to bring those facts to light. This common understanding and approach goes to the credibility and veracity of the witness. How does this same principle not apply to those who want us to give them our power of government administration and who have the ability to steal freedoms from us and our posterity? To believe that a person would all of a sudden rise to the occasion, as a mushroom all of a sudden expands from its stem, is ludicrous, without merit, and mocks common sense. Yet, Americans repeatedly prove that they believe their politicians are mushrooms, ripe for explosive power to move our nation in the right direction. What is even more perplexing is that after being elected into office and after proving to America that there is in fact nothing fundamentally different about the politician, Americans vote them back into office! This begs the question of whether or not most Americans even know what the right direction is, going back to our knowledge of the purpose of government.

How can our administrators be expected to protect, defend, and preserve the Constitution (which they swear before God and the people of the states to do) when the citizens, the sovereigns, do not even understand what that means? They do not understand the following:

[A]ll magistrates are equally the ministers of God, who perform the work for which they were instituted; and that the people which institutes them, may proportion, regulate and terminate their power, as to time, measure, and number of persons, as seems most convenient to themselves, which can be no other than their own good…this shows the work of all magistrates to be always and every where the same, even the doing of justice, and procuring the welfare of those that create them.[6]

The concept that citizens wisely choose their leaders and that the leaders possess certain qualifications does not fly in the face of common sense, and most people would agree with that. If most people would agree with that theory, where is the theory put into practice? Indeed, such a choice affects the freedoms of the citizens more than just about any other decision. However, the application of this concept is extremely confused and misapplied across America, to the point that citizens do not even care about the most fundamental issue regarding political leadership, which is faithfully carrying out his oath of office to defend, preserve, and protect the Constitution with virtue and within jurisdictional limits. Be sure, the oath of office (which is required under the Constitution of the U.S. of America, Article 2, Section 1) is rooted in natural and revealed law (as discussed further herein), the violation of which is enforceable by natural, revealed, and compact law, as discussed by Hugo Grotius.

It is made a question whether that which is contrary to an oath is only unlawful, or also void. For this we must distinguish: if good faith alone be engaged, an act done against the oath is valid; as a testament, a sale. But not, if the oath be so expressed that it contains at the same time a full abdication of power to do the act… The act of a superior cannot effect that an oath, so far as it was obligatory, is not to be performed; for that it is to be so, is a matter of Natural and of Divine Law.[7]

---

6. Sidney, *Discourses on Government,* 420.

7. Grotius, *Hugo Grotius on the Rights of War and Peace,* 173; "[I]t is to be observed, that tho' oaths of allegiance and fealty are taken to him, it is not to him as supreme legislator, but as supreme executor of the law, made by a joint power of him with others; allegiance being nothing

The terms of the oath of office taken by our public officials are very specific—they are spelled out in the Constitution. Thus, as Grotius indicated that oaths are enforceable by natural and revealed law, when the oath taker violates his oath, his acts have no effect and are void. Is this not the same thing that Jesus said regarding the truthfulness and binding of your speech and actions? "But let your speech be, Yea, yea; Nay, nay: and whatsoever is more than these is of the evil one."[8] Certainly, public officials are nothing more than the agents—as opposed to the principals—of the citizens in their jurisdiction. Since the citizens have no authority to breach the Constitution—the agreement that all of society must live by—then it necessarily and absolutely follows that the agents may not breach the Constitution as well, because the agents can have no more power than the principal (the citizens). To allow otherwise is to place the public officials in the status of principal and the citizens as agents—that is, it creates tyrants.

What is even more disturbing is that many Americans do not even understand the significance of that matter but instead focus on forcing religion or morality into politics by simply voting pro-life and the like. However, they completely ignore the salient fact that without constitutional government, policy implementation may change as often as the administrator changes every two to four years, leaving society with nothing but relativism, no absolute rights, and tyranny. Again, this goes back to the question to the citizen, "What is your goal?" If your goal is to ensure the use of natural and fundamental laws in society, then the citizen must do his part in virtue, love of country, and education and must insist that his leaders do the same.

---

but an obedience according to law, which when he violates, he has no right to obedience, nor can claim it otherwise than as the public person vested with the power of the law, and so is to be considered as the image, phantom, or representative of the common-wealth, acted by the will of the society, declared in its laws; and thus he has no will, no power, but that of the law. But when he quits this representation, this public will, and acts by his own private will, he degrades himself, and is but a single private person without power, and without will, that has any right to obedience; the members owing no obedience but to the public will of the society." Locke and Macpherson, ed., *Second Treatise of Government*, 79.

8. Matthew 5:37 (ASV); "When I therefore was thus minded, did I show fickleness? Or the things that I purpose, do I purpose according to the flesh, that with me there should be the yea yea and the nay nay?" 2 Corinthians 1:17 (ASV).

Politicians, of course, recognize the blindness of most Americans and in fact feed the flame of ignorance by dwelling on issues that seem important and will offer promises to fix this or that or to implement this program or that program. Meanwhile, they divert the little focus retained by citizens and trample on all of the fundamental concepts that make a people free. After being hypnotized into a frenzy, the citizens vest more and more power into those who, with purpose and design, lie to them, having motives other than what they have sworn an oath to do. It is a vicious cycle and must be broken—the price of which may become more expensive as the years pass by. These shallow approaches of simply voting Democrat or Republican, or even pro-life and the like, may seem spiritual and right on the surface but in fact fail to consider the whole picture of America's problems and the true solutions to those problems. The only solutions considered by most Americans today are what the politicians chant with excitement every two to four years that they will affect and change—but change never takes place. While focusing on the theatrical politicians on the stage, citizens do not see what is happening behind the stage screen, which is purposefully hidden from their view through diversion. This flawed approach to choosing administrators proves that the current generations of Americans are ignorant of the standards proposed by our founders and the Bible.

It cannot be ignored that the Bible has a lot to say about choosing government leaders, which creates a duty and expectation to those who believe in the Bible to follow certain principles and rules in this regard. A Christian, especially, has to acknowledge and accept the fact that God will hold him accountable for his choice of who will administer government, because government administrators are ministers of God.[9] This is not for the purposes of pleasing men or acquiring power, but for the purpose of punishing evil and promoting good within its jurisdictional limitations. How can it be said that a government is doing a good thing by ignoring the Constitution, by usurping its authority granted by the people, by presenting falsehoods to the people, by attempting to become God to the people, by nation-gathering, and by transforming its intended, limited purpose into an all-knowing, omnipotent

---

9. Romans 13.

provider for all? It has been well accepted in English and American history and well stated in the Bible that actions taken outside of jurisdictions are evil and should be resisted. Where are the people hiding who believe this principle? Where are the politicians who would conform their actions and policies to this principle?

The verses described in the following paragraphs are just a sample of God's standard for choosing government administrators. These principles should form the guidelines for every Christian and freedom lover's choice for governmental leadership. Very interestingly, these biblical principles seem to be ignored by most Christian leaders with regard to voting for governmental leaders. To them, what seems to be more important is that he is a Republican or he claims to be pro-life, which shows the utter depravity of the condition of conservative America. And if you are thinking that most are voting for leaders who exhibit these biblical qualifications, why is America in the condition it is in? After all, has God not promised to exalt the righteous nation? And does God not keep His promises? The problem is not God—the problem is the people of the states.

Starting with the very basics of qualifications, before a leader deserves the loyalty of his followers, he must fear God. Do not be confused. This matter has very little to do with being a Christian or being religious. Thomas Jefferson was neither an evangelical Christian nor a religious person, but he contributed as much as any one person to the freedom of this nation, because he understood the principles of freedom derived from natural and revealed law. This goes to the truth of God's word being applied (whether by a Christian or not). "So shall my word be that goes out from my mouth; it shall not return to me empty, but it shall accomplish that which I purpose, and shall succeed in the thing for which I sent it."[10] Fearing God is the simple notion that my opinion regarding any matter is not the ultimate authority, and that the Almighty Judge will hold me accountable for my decisions in all aspects of life. It causes one to search the Source of laws from a place other than the wisdom of man. In other words, one who fears God believes that he has a responsibility to the One who has created right and wrong. One who

---

10. Isaiah 55:11 (ESV).

does not fear the Creator of rights certainly (or at least very likely) has no respect for rights itself. Genesis 42:6, 18 (KJV) tells of Joseph's qualifications expressed to the people in Egypt, of whom he was second in command. "And Joseph was the governor over the land. And Joseph said unto them the third day, This do, and live; for I fear God." Here, Prince Joseph appealed and pointed to his allegiance to God and did not expect the people simply to comply with his order because he was a prince over Egypt. Rather, he wanted them to recognize his good intent, morals, and virtue, derived from his fear of God in addition to his authority as a prince.

Beyond the fear of God, a government leader must possess understanding of the laws of God, or else he will be a great oppressor, as described in Proverbs 28:16 (ESV). "A ruler who lacks understanding is a cruel oppressor." The Bible of course informs us of what a "cruel oppressor" is, stating that he is one who perverts the rights of man. "[I]t is not for kings to drink wine, or for rulers to take strong drink, lest *they drink and forget what has been decreed and pervert the rights of all the afflicted.*"[11] There is, by necessity of the language of this verse, a presumption that a king's decrees will conform to the rights of all, because the warning here is that a king should avoid perverting those rights by making sure he is thinking clearly, not as a person who is diluted with internal or external intoxications. By inductive reasoning then, a cruel oppressor is one whose judgment distorts, perverts, and deprives the citizens of their natural rights. Indeed, such a ruler who perverts judgment and justice will, "as a roaring lion, and a ranging bear,"[12] in fact destroy the rights of the citizenry.

God further instructs us to choose leaders who are able, truthful, and who hate covetousness (greed). "Moreover you shall provide out of all the people able men, such as fear God, men of truth, hating covetousness; and place such over them, to be rulers of thousands, and rulers of hundreds, rulers of fifties, and rulers of tens."[13] Of course, this is just the starting point. The following verses shed more light on God's expectations regarding our

---

11. Proverbs 31:4–5 (ESV), (emphasis added).
12. Proverbs 28:15 (KJV).
13. Exodus 18:21 (KJV).

vote. Administrators must fear God, know the laws of God, be a brethren, keep the words of the law, not be arrogant or conceited (as if he is better than those who chose him to be the leader), and not to turn from God's commandments.

> Thou shalt in any wise set him king over thee, whom the LORD thy God shall choose: one from among thy brethren shalt thou set king over thee: thou may not set a stranger over thee, which is not thy brother. And it shall be with him, and he shall read therein all the days of his life: that he may learn to fear the LORD his God, to keep all the words of this law and these statutes, to do them: That his heart be not lifted up above his brethren, and that he turn not aside from the commandment, to the right hand, or to the left: to the end that he may prolong his days in his kingdom, he, and his children, in the midst of Israel.[14]

Before you say, "Amen!" do you hold the same standard when voting every two years? Most elections reveal that either no one is qualified to run for public office any longer, or no one is voting for those who are actually qualified. Let us consider more biblical authority on the subject, observing King David's view. "David also commanded all the princes of Israel to help Solomon his son, saying, now set your heart and your soul to seek the LORD your God."[15] Recent elections have already proven that most Christians would not vote for a candidate who truly sought the Lord if they thought that such a leader did not have a chance of winning. They would rather vote for a candidate they thought would win and who was a lesser of two evils. And we wonder why God has withheld His hand of blessing from our land, our family, our government, our economy, our churches, and our communities. It cannot be said of America what was once said of the Hebrew midwives who "did not as the king of Egypt commanded them,"[16] because they violated the king's order. "Therefore, God dealt well with the midwives:

---

14. Deuteronomy 17:15, 19–20 (KJV).
15. Chronicles 22:17, 19 (KJV).
16. Exodus 1:17 (KJV).

and the people multiplied, and waxed very mighty."[17] A faithless and God-rejecting approach to choosing leaders only shortens the time before God's wrath is unleashed.

Let us ask the question bluntly: do people really want the blessing of God on themselves, their families, their community, and their nation? The vast majority would automatically answer, "Of course we do!" Well, God has already revealed to us the formula for His blessing regarding the choosing of leaders:

> And thus did [King] Hezekiah throughout all Judah, and wrought that which was good and right and truth before the LORD his God. And in every work that he began in the service of the house of God, and in the law, and in the commandments, to seek his God, he did it with all his heart, and prospered.[18]

King Hezekiah gave more than lip service to the laws of God: he believed them, acted upon them, and implemented them. As a result, "[h]e displayed the qualities of a *constitutional king,* in restoring and upholding the ancient institutions of the kingdom; while his zealous and persevering efforts to promote the cause of true religion and the best interests of his subjects entitled him to be ranked with the most illustrious of his predecessors."[19] Consequently, Israel prospered. For these same reasons, America once prospered.

How can a person who cares about preserving freedom civilly and religiously compromise the revelation of God by accepting those who have no discernment regarding matters of justice—not as defined by the United States Supreme Court, but by the Supreme Court of the Universe—God Almighty. God has revealed that the quality of discernment is necessary for a nation to preserve the peace and freedom of society. "The word of my lord the king shall now be comfortable [or peaceful]: for as an angel of God, so is

---

17. Exodus 1:20 (KJV).
18. Chronicles 31:20–21 (KJV).
19. Robert Jamieson and A.R. Fausset, *A Commentary, Critical and Explanatory, on the Old and New Testaments,* Volume 1, (New York: S.S. Scranton and Co., 1875), 283, (emphasis added).

my lord the king to discern good and bad: therefore the LORD thy God will be with you."[20] Juxtaposed against itself, this verse also states that where the king does not discern good and bad, God will *not* be with us.

God also expects that we choose leaders who judge and rule in the fear of God. "The Spirit of the LORD spoke by me, and his word was in my tongue. The God of Israel said, the Rock of Israel spoke to me, He that rules over men must be just, ruling in the fear of God."[21] Additionally, God further demands that we choose wise men who have understanding and who share sound philosophy. "How can I myself alone bear your cumbrance, and your burden, and your strife? Take you wise men, and understanding, and known among your tribes, and I will make them rulers over you."[22] Also, God expects the leaders you choose to judge righteously without bias or prejudice. "And I charged your judges at that time, saying, hear the causes between your brethren, and judge righteously between every man and his brother, and the stranger that is with him."[23]

Are you getting the picture? Get this picture too: God has revealed to us the consequences of choosing leaders who do not follow God's laws. "And Samuel said unto Saul, I will not return with you: for you have rejected the word of the LORD, and the LORD has rejected you from being king over Israel."[24] Yes, Israel sinned against God when they declared, "God save the king." Saul was presented to the people to be king over them instead of the prophet of God—most assuredly because he appeared (in all physical terms) to be superior to all other people in Israel (a more winnable candidate)—and Israel suffered the consequences as a result. Judging candidates in error and supporting them shall not spare a nation. Do you expect to be ignorant on the matter and then wait for God just to swoop in and save you from your lack of righteous judgment? The Bible repeatedly reveals how God deals with nations and further reveals that a government itself cannot be judged in the world to come (in heaven or hell), but only individuals can. Moreover, the

20. Samuel 14:17 (KJV).
21. Samuel 23:2–3 (KJV).
22. Deuteronomy 1:12–13 (KJV).
23. Deuteronomy 1:16 (KJV).
24. Samuel 15:26 (KJV).

Bible reveals that God expects all actions of evil to receive their retribution on earth, even when committed by the righteous. So how much more shall the wicked be judged here on earth for their evil actions? "If the righteous is repaid on earth, how much more the wicked and the sinner!"[25] God expects nations to maintain the standard of righteousness on earth as ministers of God. Thus when considering that "righteousness exalts a nation, but sin is a reproach to any people,"[26] one has to conclude that God does not judge nations in heaven or hell but here on earth, making time of the essence to ensure that citizens and leaders judge righteously and that our government complies with the natural and revealed laws of God.[27] And of course, when ministers of God become ministers of evil, it behooves we the people of the states to stand on our authority as creators of government, act as ministers of God, do what it takes to reinstate righteousness in a nation, and punish those who sought to accomplish evil.

CASE IN POINT

This criterion of judging righteously brings us to a case in point relevant to the matter of qualifications of government administrators. One of the main arguments that is proposed by many conservatives and Christians imploring others to vote for a lesser-of-two-evils president is that the lesser would appoint conservative judges to the Supreme Court, who will in turn render rules of law in favor of conservative principles (as if a rule of law can be changed with simply the vote of five Supreme Court judges). Such an argument mocks common sense and overwhelming historical data and has proven to be fallacious in application (though I am certain many such proponents are well intentioned). It also shows an ignorance of the fact that

---

25. Proverbs 11:31 (ESV); "The eyes of the LORD are in every place, keeping watch on the evil and the good." Proverbs 15:3 (ESV). Most certainly God has an interest in how leaders in government conduct the affairs, laws, and policies of a nation and keeps a watch out for their action, whether they are just or unjust.

26. Proverbs 14:34 (ESV).

27. "As nations can not be rewarded or punished in the next world they must be in this." Mason, *The Anti-Federalist Papers,* 162.

America was formed to make the legislative branch (the people's representatives) of government more powerful than the judicial and executive branches. James Madison reflects this fact when he says, "It is not possible to give each department an equal power of self-defense. In a republican government, the legislative authority necessarily predominates."[28]

So, how is it that abortion has been legalized for over thirty-five years in America without any action from Congress (the federal legislators) and without the realization that the appointment of conservative judges has done nothing to give the right to life back to the unborn? America's conservative citizens and the leaders themselves have proven not to judge righteously. Understand, the issue of abortion is just one of the many that reveal the utter depraved condition of logic, philosophy, and character possessed by many citizens and politicians today.

Here is the straight talk that conservatives need to observe and consider. Many believe that the Republican politician will advocate pro-life issues and will make changes in favor of pro-life regulations and laws, and the Democrat will not. However, the fact remains that since 1972 (the year in which *Roe v. Wade* was decided), not one Republican president (and the same could be said for our congressman, with little exception) has done one substantial thing to overturn *Roe v. Wade.* Since 1972, abortion deaths have continually and consistently numbered over 1 million per year. In fact, the evidence shows that any reduction in abortions has actually been caused by sex education, increased access to birth control, and more advanced forms of science regarding birth control.[29] That fact alone should actually cause a life-saving citizen to vote for a Democrat who pushes sex education and birth control measures, because it has proven to be more successful than pro-life politicians (as previously discussed).[30]

---

28. James Madison, "Federalist Paper 51," in *The Federalist Papers,* Hamilton, Jay, and Madison, 401; "Though in a constituted common-wealth, standing upon its own basis, and acting according to its own nature, that is, acting for the preservation of the community, there can be but one supreme power, which is the legislative, to which all the rest are and must be subordinate." Locke and Macpherson, ed., *Second Treatise of Government,* 77.

29. Nicholas D. Kristof, "Abortions, Condoms, and Bush," *The New York Times,* (November 5, 2006), http://select.nytimes.com/2006/11/05/opinion/05kristof.html?_r=1.

30. Ibid.

Furthermore, if citizens really cared about actually eliminating abortions through politicians, why did they not throw their support to Congressman Ron Paul (a medical doctor—an obstetrician and gynecologist), who has actually put his money where his mouth is on the abortion subject by repeatedly drafting and introducing legislation in the House of Representative, such as the Sanctity of Life Act,[31] defining life as beginning at conception, giving the child due process of law protection under the United States Constitution, and thus ending the right to demand an abortion in America? Literally, this would have saved millions of lives almost instantaneously. Oh, wait, you could not vote for him, because he was against unconstitutional wars. Of course, America's War on Terror is a so-called holy war of God, and anyone who dares not support it is not patriotic and deserves to be strung up on the nearest tree—even though they do not understand that "the formal conditions of victory—whether through armistice, surrender, or treat of peace—cannot be obtained."[32] I get it. There is always a convenient reason not to vote for someone who actually demonstrates real change and anti-status-quo, establishment politics. Apparently, these citizens really do not

---

31. *The Sanctity of Life Act,* HR 2597, 2007, 110th Congress; Author Unknown, "ND House Passes Abortion Ban," reported on KXMC TV Minot, February 17, 2009, http://www.kxmc.com/getArticle.asp?ArticleId=333726, (accessed May 5, 2009). See also *The Personhood of Children Act* (House Resolution 1572), introduced by State Representative Dan Ruby. North Dakota state legislators effectively accomplished the same thing by passing a state bill, in a 51-41 vote, defining life as being a fertilized egg, which consequently protects the rights of the unborn child and which complies with *Roe v. Wade,* where the U.S. Supreme Court does not attempt to define life. As such, the state of North Dakota did define life.

32. "The constant hysterical harping by politicians and the big media on fighting 'the war on terrorism' at any cost, rather than on preserving America's traditional way of life in every way possible, stirs up primitive emotions and stifles analytical thought—contributing more to mass panic than to a rational solution of that problem—just when cold, deliberate, and careful calculation is necessary. The official line on 'the war on terrorism' demands that common Americans suspend their own independent judgment, and instead rely in the manner of robots on directives 'from the top down,' the factual support for which 'the authorities' refuse to reveal on the grounds that disclosure of the evidence would supposedly compromise 'national security.' In such wise, Americans are being systematically indoctrinated that they are helpless and hopeless without 'the authorities'—and therefore that they must depend upon, believe, and above all obey 'the authorities' in all things, without investigation, demur, skepticism, or (least of all) criticism." Vieira, *Constitutional Homeland Security,* 9–10.

consider such a man worthy of support and prove that the abortion issue is not as important as they make it appear. The evidence becomes more overwhelming, proving the fact that ending abortion is not the primary goal of those who blow that trumpet's horn so often.

To advocate the need to vote for lesser evils in hopes of getting a conservative judge into office, in hopes that his court will hear a legal issue directly on the point of reversing abortion, in hopes that he will vote with a majority in favor of ending abortion, again shows ignorance and a gambling-style approach to change. Such an approach clings onto a proven non-effectual and ineffective plan of action—talk about not being pragmatic and choosing a non-winnable solution! America's founding fathers previously told us that the judiciary branch of government would have the *least* possibility of power usurpation, "because it will be least in a capacity to annoy or injure them."[33] In other words, the judiciary is not the branch of government that we the people of the states need to focus on relative to policy change. Consider what Alexander Hamilton says on the subject.

> If there should happen to be an irreconcilable variance between [the Legislative and Judiciary branches], that which has the superior obligation and validity ought, of course, to be preferred; or, in other words, the Constitution ought to be preferred to the statute, [and] the intention of the people to the intention of their agents. Nor does this conclusion by any means suppose a superiority of the judicial to the legislative power. It only supposes that the power of the people is superior to both.[34]

And how do the people voice their will? Through their legislatures—through the constitutional amendment process if necessary! Supreme Court judges do not represent the people, so why do conservatives continue to focus on the judicial branch of government (indirectly through the executive branch

---

33. Alexander Hamilton, "Federalist Paper 78," in *The Federalist Papers,* Hamilton, Jay, and Madison, 594.

34. Alexander Hamilton, "Federalist Paper 78," in *The Federalist Papers,* Hamilton, Jay, and Madison, 596–597.

appointments) to implement fundamental change? Moreover, recent history proves that U.S. Supreme Court judges largely do not even intend to issue rulings consistent with the nature, principles, and intent of the Constitution.[35] Will abortion be overruled until another liberal judge is placed on the bench, only to help form a majority rule on the other side of the issue, and now we are back to square one?! And then how long would you have to wait again until a pro-life judge is appointed, etc. It is like playing a game of how many people are on your side, and how many are on our side. It becomes a game of pure numbers—so much for fundamental law. Fundamental law has nothing to do with numbers of the judiciary and everything to do with we the people of the states knowing and implementing and demanding sound natural law principles in government through the constitutional process. Unfortunately, many well-intended people are distracted and are wasting their resources in the thought that the Supreme Court is just out of control, and our nation's demise is all contributed to the U.S. Supreme Court.[36] If that is true, it makes it extremely inconvenient and virtually impossible to make any changes in the rule of law, because the judiciary branch has absolutely no connection democratically to we the people of the states, thereby creating a virtual wall of separation between government and people, which of course is tyranny. While this perspective regarding the U.S. Supreme Court is true to a degree, freedom-loving Americans must realize that the judiciary is not where the

---

35. "I do not believe that the meaning of the Constitution was forever 'fixed' at the Philadelphia Convention. Nor do I find the wisdom, foresight, and sense of justice exhibited by the framers particularly profound. To the contrary, the government they devised was defective from the start, requiring several amendments, a civil war, and momentous social transformation to attain the system of constitutional government, and its respect for the individual freedoms and human rights, that we hold as fundamental today." Mark R. Levin, *Men In Black: How the Supreme Court is Destroying America,* (Washington, D.C: Regnery Publishing, Inc., 2005), 9. U.S. Supreme Court Justice Thurgood Marshall expressed his feelings on the U.S. Constitution in that speech delivered at the Annual Seminar of the San Francisco Patent and Trademark Law Association in Maui, Hawaii, on May 6, 1987.

36. The typical thought from conservatives today is the following: the Supreme Court, more than any other branch or entity of government, is the most radical and aggressive practitioner of unrestrained power. And while this may be true, the effect should not be what it has been. In other words, we the people have the power to reign in the Supreme Court through our legislators.

battle rages. America's founders foresaw such a tyrannical situation and created a government whereby the power of the judiciary is never to exceed the power of the sovereigns of the United States.

To prevent this type of tyranny, America's founders did not create the judiciary to have such a power and control over the people but instead created a system whereby the people had control over the judiciary. William Rawle confirms the people's power over the judiciary by stating,

> On the whole, it seems that with the right to new model all the inferior tribunals, and thereby to vacate the commissions of their judges, and with the power to impeach all judges whatever, a sufficient control is retained over the judiciary power for every useful purpose.[37]

William Blackstone proclaims the same principle when he says, "[W]henever a question arises between the society at large and any magistrate vested with powers originally delegated by that society, it must be decided by the voice of the society itself; there is not upon earth any other tribunal to resort to."[38] Despite the inherent power of the people to make real changes, all that seems to matter is voting for a self-proclaimed pro-lifer in hopes that a conservative judge will overturn *Roe v. Wade*. You might as well go gambling at a casino, because your chances would be better.

Our founders understood that supreme authority does not rest with one particular body of government—not even the Supreme Court of the United States, despite what many conservative (or dare I say, Christian) politicians would have their constituents believe, especially regarding their power to do anything of substance about the enslaving *Roe v. Wade* decision. The idea that a group of five out of nine justices could dictate to the American people what the rule of law is regarding the life of an unborn child is unnatural and ignorant.[39] Even the late Joseph Story, U.S. Supreme Court justice, acknowledges that the

---

37. Rawle, *A View of the Constitution of the United States of America*, 281.

38. Blackstone, *Commentaries on the Laws of England*, 212.

39. "The Constitution [of Spain] proposed has one feature which I like much; that which provides that when the three coordinate branches differ in their construction of the Constitution, the opinion of two branches shall overrule the third. Our Constitution has not sufficiently solved this difficulty." Jefferson, *The Jeffersonian Cyclopedia*, 197.

Supreme Court is not the final authority on matters of the Constitution. He says in his *Exposition on the Constitution of the United States,*

> [The Constitution] is the language of the people... It is not an instrument for the mere private interpretation of any particular men. The people have established it and spoken their will; and their will, thus promulgated, is to be obeyed as the supreme law. Every department of the Government must, of course...in the exercise of its own powers and duties, necessarily construe the instrument. But, if the case admits of judicial cognizance, every citizen has a right to contest the validity of that construction before the proper tribunal; and to bring it to the test of the Constitution. And, if the case is not capable of judicial redress, still the people may, through the acknowledged means of new elections, or proposed amendments, check any usurpation of authority, whether wanton, or unintentional, and thus relieve themselves from any grievances of a political nature.[40]

Not only does the United States Constitution grant power to the legislative branch (the branch most controlled by the people) to remove any subject matter from the U.S. Supreme Court's appellate jurisdiction,[41] but also historical review reveals that the opinion of courts (no matter how high) is never the supreme law of the land. Indeed, Sir Matthew Hale, in his *History of the Common Law,* which was first published in 1713, duly explains that the following:

> The decisions of courts of justice...do not make a law properly so called...yet they have a great weight and authority in expounding, declaring and publishing what the law...is...and though such decisions are less than a law, yet they are a great evidence thereof, than the opinion of any private persons.[42]

---

40. Story, *A Familiar Exposition of the Constitution,* 37.

41. "[Under the Judiciary Act of 1789,] [t]o the Supreme Court of the United States was likewise given 'appellate jurisdiction from the Circuit Courts and courts of the several states, in the cases hereinafter specifically provided for.'" Taylor, *The Origin and Growth of the American Constitution,* 227.

42. Gray, *The Nature and Sources of the Law,* 218, 219.

And of course, if courts are in fact obligated with the responsibility of simply and only declaring the established rule of law, how is it that American jurisprudence accepted and instituted the notion that it must protect the life of the unborn baby (as established by hundreds of years of precedence from judicial, executive, and legislative branches of government not only in America but also in England and throughout Europe), and then all of a sudden the rule of law is that the freedom of choice of the mother supersedes the freedom of choice of the unborn child? Enlightenment forefather Sir Francis Bacon[43] has a thing or two to say about the kind of judges we see in America today. He recognizes that "above all things, integrity is their portion and proper virtue. Cursed (saith the law) is he that removeth the land-mark.[44] The mislayer of a mere stone is to blame. But it is the unjust judge that is the capital remover of land-marks, when he defineth amiss of lands and properties."[45] In other words, judges have no authority or right to remove fundamentally held customs and traditions of society derived from the natural laws of God. They are simply to "interpret law, and not to make law, or give law."[46] Moreover, most Americans, including United States Supreme Court justices (mostly appointed by Republican presidents) do not understand what Blackstone says about the role of a judge. Judges are to

abide by former precedents...as well as keep the scale of justice even and steady, and not [be] liable to waver with every new judge's

---

43. "Francis Bacon, 1st Viscount St Alban KC (22 January 1561–9 April 1626) was an English philosopher, statesman, scientist, lawyer, jurist, and author." "Francis Bacon," Wikipedia, (accessed May 5, 2009), http://en.wikipedia. org/wiki/Francis_Bacon#Philosophy_and_works.

44. "Thou shalt not remove thy neighbour's landmark, which they of old time have set in thine inheritance, which thou shalt inherit in the land that the LORD thy God giveth thee to possess it." Deuteronomy 19:14 (KJV). "Cursed be he that removeth his neighbour's landmark. And all the people shall say, Amen." Deuteronomy 27:17 (KJV). "Remove not the ancient landmark, which thy fathers have set." Proverbs 22:28 (KJV). "Remove not the old landmark; and enter not into the fields of the fatherless." Proverbs 23:10 (KJV). Bacon is referring to the previous Bible verses.

45. Francis Bacon and Walter Worrall, ed., *The Essays or Counsels Civil and Moral,* (New York: E.P. Dutton & Co., 1597, 1625), 232.

46. Ibid.

opinion…because the law in that case being solemnly declared and determined, what before was uncertain, and perhaps indifferent, is now become a permanent rule, which it is not in the breast of any subsequent judge to alter or vary from, according to his private sentiments, he being sworn to determine, not according to his own private judgment, but according to the known laws and customs of the land; not delegated to pronounce a new law, but to maintain and expound the old one.[47]

These issues and questions all go back not only to an understanding of America's jurisprudence, form, and substance of government and history but also to a proper and accurate perspective relative to choosing government administrators. Abortions (or any other injustice) *could* be ended in relative short order if Congress would use their greater power over the executive and judicial branches by removing the jurisdiction of the issue from federal jurisdiction (under Article 3, Section 2 of the United States Constitution), which is confirmed by Alexander Hamilton in Federalist Paper No. 80 when he says,

If some partial inconveniences should appear to be connected with the incorporation of any of [the subject matter jurisdiction of the United States Supreme Court], it ought to be recollected that the national legislature will have ample authority to make such exceptions, and to prescribe such regulations as will be calculated to obviate or remove these inconveniences. The possibility of particular mischiefs can never be viewed, by a well-informed mind, as a solid objection to a general principle, which is calculated to avoid general mischiefs and to obtain general advantages.[48]

Again, in Federalist Paper No. 81 Hamilton states, "In all cases of federal cognizance, the original jurisdiction would appertain to the inferior tribunals;

---

47. Gray, *The Nature and Sources of the Law,* 219, 220.

48. Alexander Hamilton, "Federalist Paper 80," in *The Federalist Papers,* Hamilton, Jay, and Madison, 614.

and the Supreme Court would have nothing more than appellate jurisdiction, 'with such exceptions and under such regulations as the Congress shall make.'"[49] Instead of taking the necessary action to make real change in the lives of millions of lives and in America's culture and society as a whole, most Americans are waiting for the magic year when another conservative judge will be appointed to the Supreme Court by a conservative president—as if that has made any difference over the past forty years and will make any difference over the next forty years. How naïve.

Sir Francis Bacon's words ring true regarding pro-lifers' all-talk-but-no-action approach to protecting the unborn life. "There is no trusting to the force of nature nor to the bravery of words, except it be corroborate by custom."[50] In other words, no force and bravery exist in one's talk where the talk is not supported by actions (custom). It appears that the only force and bravery that most conservatives and Christians display is the custom of voting for people who do nothing about what they claim to believe in. All the talk in the world notwithstanding, "insomuch as a man would wonder to hear men profess, protest, engage, give great words, and then do just as they have done before; as if they were dead images and engines moved only by the wheels of custom."[51] What are we waiting for—the return of Christ or the destruction of America? Perhaps whichever comes first.

Observe, too, what your legislators are doing to reverse the federal adjudication of *Roe v. Wade* through their power under Article 2, Section 3 of the Constitution. Did your legislator support Congressman Paul's Sanctity of Life Act? Do we hear any discussion from pro-life politicians to remove federal jurisdiction over the matter? After all, it has long been established that, even where the United States Supreme Court has no appellate jurisdiction, "the courts and the judges of every state possess…the right to decide on the constitutionality of a law of their own state and of the United States."[52] Thus, when the power to rule on issues of abortion is removed from federal jurisdiction, the states would be given the chance once again to protect the

49. Ibid., 623.
50. Bacon, *The Essays or Counsels Civil and Moral*, 169.
51. Ibid.
52. Rawle, *A View of the Constitution of the United States of America*, 276.

life of the unborn through their own sovereign means. This is a concept that is even accepted today by proponents of a federalist society: namely, allowing states to offer *more* rights and protection of rights than the federal constitution provides. Apparently, this concept does not apply to the protection of the unborn life, and as such, states cannot offer more protection to unborn life than the United States Supreme Court has opined as constitutional. How long will pro-lifers believe that the incremental approach to getting conservative judges will save one life, make changes to the philosophy and nature of our fundamental understandings, and hold back the judgment of God?— especially when nothing has changed in over thirty-five years, and over 1 million babies are killed each year without fail! Have the circumstances not proven to require different action from pro-life citizens?

While there are myriad of issues that should demand our attention, abortion seems to be one that most conservatives determine to be the most important. However, is there any issue more telling that demonstrates the hype and hope of change are misplaced in politicians or the political party we have been told for decades will make the necessary changes to protect the life of the unborn? Perhaps there was a time when the approach proposed by many conservative leaders was appropriate, but as Thomas Paine says, "there is a proper time for it to cease"[53] and to begin a new course of action.

The circumstances surrounding real change seem too familiar. Today, America suffers from the same time-delayed nature of redress that America's colonists faced when they sent petition after petition to King George regarding the injustices perpetrated against America. Objective observers of America's condition realize that "every quiet method for peace ha[s] been ineffectual"[54] regarding so many government acts that Christians and conservatives would declare to be evil and contrary to the God's natural and revealed laws. So at what point do such persons say enough is enough, depart from the wisdoms that have proven to be ineffectual for generations, and say as King David says, "I hate vain thoughts: but thy law do I love"?[55] This question is what America's founders faced as well.

---

53. Paine and Philip, ed., *Common Sense*, 27.
54. Ibid.
55. Psalm 119:113 (KJV).

As to government matters, it is not in the power of Britain to do this continent justice. The business of it will soon be too weighty, and intricate, to be managed with any tolerable degree of convenience, by a power, so distant from us, and so very ignorant of us; for if they cannot conquer us, they cannot govern us. To be always running three or four thousand miles with a tale or a petition, waiting four or five months for an answer, which when obtained requires five or six more to explain it in, will in a few years be looked upon as folly and childishness. There was a time when it was proper, and there is a proper time for it to cease.[56]

Is preserving and protecting not only God's laws but also the lives of the most innocent a noble object worth the expense of trying a different course of action (from a course that has proven ineffectual), even if it means you have to make a decision you are not accustomed to with a risk of inconvenience? Is the goal of saving millions of lives not important enough to pay even a small price of voting outside your comfort zone? Thomas Paine's answer would likely have been yes. "The object contended for, ought always to bear some just proportion to the expence."[57] If the abortion issue is not worth contending for, then there are a host of other issues that should be. If the price is too high or the goal not worthy enough, then perhaps the love of what America stands for (justice and absolute rights) does not truly exist, and the love for the innocent is merely a political ploy to advance political parties and not legitimate government or justice.

Being a self-proclaimed conservative does not exempt you from this error in philosophy, where you do not know and implement the principles derived from God's natural and revealed law. Even God's prophet, Moses, was rejected by Israel—God's chosen people—after Moses was used by God to deliver them from slavery in Egypt (proving that citizens must *want* freedom actually to obtain it). The people were more content with being slaves than following God's man to live in freedom, and they even suggested that

56. Paine and Philip, ed., *Common Sense*, 27.
57. Ibid., 28.

Moses was attempting to become a tyrant or dictator over Israel—despite God using Moses to deliver them out of slavery. God had actually to perform numerous miracles to convince the people to show any loyalty to Moses after the pharaoh finally let God's people go. This was the people's attitude towards their deliverer: "Is it a small thing that you have brought us up out of a land flowing with milk and honey, to kill us in the wilderness, that you must also make yourself a prince over us?"[58] Are we any less susceptible to this attitude? Would we really prefer slavery over a truly godly leader to lead us out of slavery? The answer has likely already been answered.

Many repeatedly refer to the following statement of Benjamin Franklin: "God governs in the affairs of men. And if a sparrow cannot fall to the Ground without his Notice, is it probable that an Empire can rise without his Aid?" The implication that the responsibility of choosing a qualified leader as pre-scribed by God does not rest solely on the shoulders of each individual is absurd. It is as if the Christian leaders and people have no responsibility to inform others and advocate for administrators who actually possess biblical and freedom attributes, hoping and praying that God will just grant them a godly leader despite their faithless decisions. Again, ignorance—and even hypocrisy—is apparent, for even Thomas Paine understands the flaw in this approach to choosing leaders.

> If the setting up and putting down of kings and governments is God's peculiar prerogative, he most certainly will not be robbed thereof by us; wherefore, the principle itself leads you to approve of every thing, which ever happened, or may happen to kings as being [God's] work.[59]

Selecting leaders is not like throwing your cards to the wind, hoping God will deal you a good hand. The Bible is replete with verse after verse revealing that in fact governmental leaders are chosen by the people, and that it is the responsibility of the people to make wise choices. Can you gamble

---

58. Numbers 16:13 (ESV).

59. Paine and Philip, ed., *Common Sense*, 57.

all of your income at the Biloxi casinos and then pray that God will meet all your needs? Similarly, holding your nose and voting for the lesser of two evils while praying that God will work a miracle by granting to America a godly leader is faithless, naïve, and downright hypocritical. Approaching decisions in this manner is similar to the attitude described by Paine, where it leads one to conduct oneself without regard to truth, duty, and character. Such a person merely acts without foundation in hopes that God will approve his actions, ignoring truth and the principles of freedom. In other words, your decisions concerning how to vote, how to engage government, how to submit to government, or how to resist government are based not upon the principles of truth, but rather upon the expedient and convenient theory that no matter what you decide to do, God will work it out for your good.

Indeed, the consequences of these decisions will have their day of harvest. Here were the consequences that Israel suffered for choosing a leader who cared nothing about following God's laws:

> This will be the manner of the king that shall reign over you: He will take your sons, and appoint them for himself, for his chariots, and to be his horsemen; and some shall run before his chariots. And he will appoint him captains over thousands, and captains over fifties; and will set them to ear his ground, and to reap his harvest, and to make his instruments of war, and instruments of his chariots. And he will take your daughters to be confectionaries, and to be cooks, and to be bakers.
>
> And he will take your fields, and your vineyards, and your olive-yards, even the best of them, and give them to his servants. And he will take the tenth of your seed, and of your vineyards, and give to his officers, and to his servants. And he will take your menservants, and your maidservants, and your goodliest young men, and your asses, and put them to his work. He will take the tenth of your sheep: and ye shall be his servants. And ye shall cry out in that day because of your king which ye shall have chosen you; and the LORD will not hear you in that day.[60]

---

60. Samuel 8:11–18 (KJV).

While the methods of slavery are different in America today, the effects are the same as in the day of Israel. And Americans scratch their heads and wonder why we are getting more of the same politics as usual from our government administrators when we continue to place people in those positions who care nothing about securing and advocating the constitutional form of government that secured our freedoms to begin with.

While the biblical references to the qualifications of governmental administrators could be expounded more thoroughly, to do so would seem almost superfluous, because the Bible is so very clear on God's requirements and the blessings and curses resulting from our following or rejecting these standards. The only question is whether or not we choose to believe the Bible and obey His word in faith, knowing that God rewards those who do His commandments. And in case you have not read them for yourself, here are some additional biblical standards on the subject. The following are taken from the King James Version:

And wisdom and knowledge shall be the stability of thy times, and strength of salvation: the fear of the LORD is his treasure. (Isaiah 33:6)

Hate the evil, and love the good, and establish judgment in the gate: it may be that the LORD God of hosts will be gracious unto the remnant of Joseph. (Amos 5:15)

Praise the LORD...Kings of the earth, and all people; princes, and all judges of the earth. (Psalm 148:7–11)

Be wise now therefore, O ye kings: be instructed, ye judges of the earth. Serve the LORD with fear, and rejoice with trembling. Kiss the Son, lest he be angry, and ye perish from the way, when his wrath is kindled but a little. Blessed are all they that put their trust in him. (Psalm 2:10–12)

My son, if you will receive my words and hide my commandments with you, so that you attend to wisdom, you shall extend your heart to understanding; yea, if you cry after knowledge and lift up your voice for understanding; if you seek her as silver, and search for her as for hidden treasures, then you shall understand the fear of Jehovah and find the knowledge of God. For Jehovah gives wisdom; out of His mouth come knowledge and understanding. He lays up sound wisdom for the righteous; He is a shield to those who walk uprightly. He keeps the paths of judgment, and guards the way of His saints. (Proverbs 2:1–8)

The fear of the LORD is the instruction of wisdom; and before honour is humility. (Proverbs 15:33)

A king that sits in the throne of judgment scatters away all evil with his eyes. (Proverbs 20:8)

Woe unto them that call evil good, and good evil; that put darkness for light, and light for darkness; that put bitter for sweet, and sweet for bitter! Woe unto them that are wise in their own eyes, and prudent in their own sight! (Isaiah 5:20–21)

Counsel is mine, and sound wisdom: I am understanding; I have strength. By me (wisdom) kings reign, and princes decree justice. By me (wisdom) princes rule, and nobles, even all the judges of the earth. (Proverbs 8:14–16)

These things also belong to the wise. It is not good to have respect of persons in judgment. He that says unto the wicked, "Thou art righteous," him shall the people curse, nations shall abhor him. (Proverbs 24:23–24)

And thou, Ezra, after the wisdom of your God, that is in your hand, set magistrates and judges, which may judge all the people that are beyond the river, all such as know the laws of thy God; and teach ye them that know them not. (Ezra 7:25)

Judge not according to the appearance, but judge righteous judgment. (John 7:24)

Can there be any argument about what God expects regarding choosing government leaders? From where come the notions that politicians always lie, corruption is just a part of politics, every person who is elected has to change, and other notions accepting that politicians justifiably possess the depravities of the sinful nature of man while being accepted by the citizens who feel the effects of their depravity? Can it be said that such a notion is biblical? Absolutely not. Choosing government administrators who do not possess the knowledge, understanding, belief, and conviction of freedom's principles derived from God's natural and revealed laws only adds fuel to the fire destroying our nation. Until America revives the notion of choosing truly qualified leaders, not based upon experience alone, but based upon their philosophical understanding of freedom and its source, all else matters little.

10

GOVERNMENT ADMINISTRATORS

Their Limits

PHILOSOPHICAL UNDERSTANDING OF GOVERNMENTAL LIMITS

O ne of the fundamental concepts discussed for generations before and after America's founding is the concept of limited government—meaning, the limited authority, scope, power, and jurisdiction of government. America's founders, in the Declaration of Independence, confirm the expressed limitations on the powers of government by stating, "Governments are instituted among Men, deriving their just powers, from the consent of the governed."[1] What the founders did *not* say was deriving their powers. Instead, the governments' powers must be just or right, as expressed in the Constitution of the United States, because the Constitution contains the consented-to powers of the federal government (not state governments). The fact is, America's founders placed numerous limitations on the federal government specifically and expressed these limitations in a variety of ways, such as term limits, separation of powers, the power of government

---

1. Thomas Jefferson, *Declaration of Independence,* (See Appendix A).

in the people, impeachment procedures, limited powers of each branch of government, protection of the people's rights in the Bill of Rights, the reservation of all powers to the states and people not expressly granted to the federal government, and others. They did this for good reason, based upon natural law. Thomas Jefferson confirms the old adage give them an inch, and they'll take a mile—actually a thousand miles—when he says, "To take a single step beyond the boundaries thus specifically drawn around the powers of Congress, is to take possession of a boundless field of power, no longer susceptible of any definition."[2] Indeed, these limitations were expressed by the copious writings of the founding fathers in philosophy, jurisprudence, and maxims, as found in foundational, historical, legal, casual, and contractual documents surrounding the formation of this nation.

Consider the following fundamental understanding of government's limitations and the people of the states' retention of the ultimate power to govern ourselves:

> THOUGH in a constituted common-wealth, standing upon its own basis, and acting according to its own nature, that is, acting for the preservation of the community, there can be but one supreme power, which is the legislative, to which all the rest are and must be subordinate, yet the legislative being only a fiduciary power to act for certain ends, there remains still in the people a supreme power to remove or alter the legislative, when they find the legislative act contrary to the trust reposed in them: for all power given with trust for the attaining an end, being limited by that end, whenever that end is manifestly neglected, or opposed, the trust must necessarily be forfeited, and the power devolve into the hands of those that gave it, who may place it anew where they shall think best for their safety and security. And thus the community perpetually retains a supreme power of saving themselves from the attempts and designs of any body, even of their legislators, whenever they shall be so foolish, or so wicked, as to lay and carry on designs against the liberties and properties of the subject.[3]

---

2. Jefferson, *The Jeffersonian Cyclopedia*, 193.
3. Locke and Macpherson, ed., *Second Treatise of Government*, 78.

This philosophy presented by one of America's founders' favorite philosophers, John Locke, was what predominated American ideology and understanding in government and society, and was that which ultimately formed the framework of the U.S. Constitution. "We the People of the United States, in Order to form a more perfect Union, establish Justice, insure domestic Tranquility, provide for the common defence, promote the general Welfare, and secure the Blessings of Liberty to ourselves and our Posterity, do ordain and establish this Constitution for the United States of America." Separated powers in government in fact were intended to "bind the king as much as the meanest subject"[4] against usurpations of power, but admittedly they did not wholly prevent it. James Madison says,

> In a single republic, all the power surrendered by the people is submitted to the administration of a single government; and the usurpations are guarded against by a division of the government into distinct and separate departments... Hence a double security arises to the rights of the people. The different governments will control each other, at the same time each will be controlled by itself.[5]

Thus, while the constitutional form can attempt to prevent the evils of government, the form itself does nothing without its citizens choosing administrators who uphold the Constitution and the nature and principles the Constitution reflects. Indeed, the choosing of qualified government administrators who understand government's limitations is just another pillar upon which our freedom rests.

APPLICATION OF LIMITATIONS

There seems to be such confusion and misguidance in America today concerning what qualifications a leader must possess to be considered worthy of our vote and support. Many people look for determining factors such

---

4. Compiled by a member of the Philadelphia Bar, *American Oratory,* 8.

5. James Madison, "Federalist Paper 51," in *The Federalist Papers,* Hamilton, Jay, and Madison, 402.

as these: military experience, political experience, legal experience, business experience, educational experience, etc. While these criteria are good in one sense, there seems to be a major component missing, and that is: what is the person's philosophical and foundational understanding of government's constitutional limitations, and what is he or she willing to do to uphold it? Thomas Jefferson says, "An unprincipled man…ought never to be employed [for public office]."[6] What principles would Jefferson be referring to? The principles of freedom through nature and nature's God—i.e., natural law. Romans 13:4 confirms this perspective by clearly stating that government is the "servant of God."[7] Since when do servants have the autonomous power to do anything except what they are told to do by their masters? Today, politicians supposedly worthy of America's support act like masters over us and mirror more and more the hereditary right to rule that only certain privileged individuals acquire through mere birth. They act as if governments are instituted among men to secure the power of the state, to ensure corporate tranquility, and to provide for the welfare of elitists. This thought was abhorred by our founders—as it should be by the people of the states, since it is a direct attack on our natural rights, secured by the Constitution. Thomas Paine notes that such leaders "contribute nothing towards the freedom of the state."[8] Likewise, Thomas Jefferson warns, "Our young Republic…should guard against hereditary magistrates."[9]

Obviously, America's government does not openly place hereditary rulers into government administration. However, America seems deceived into thinking that there are only certain acceptable choices for candidates every two to four years. In fact, former president George W. Bush reflects on the fallacious philosophy America possesses today regarding who is qualified to be a government administrator, by stating in his State of the Union Address in 2006, "In a system of two parties, two chambers, and two elected

---

6. Jefferson, *The Jeffersonian Cyclopedia,* 647.

7. "For he is God's servant for your good. But if you do wrong, be afraid, for he does not bear the sword in vain. For he is the servant of God, an avenger who carries out God's wrath on the wrongdoer." Romans 13:4 (ESV).

8. Paine and Philip, ed., *Common Sense,* 8.

9. Jefferson, *The Jeffersonian Cyclopedia,* 387.

branches, there will always be differences and debate."[10] First of all, to suggest that there are differences between the Republicans and Democrats is laughable. Sure, there may be different approaches to their goals. One may be a wide receiver and the other a running back, but they play for the same team. Back to the point at hand, to suggest that America is a system of two parties is either ignorant or deceitful. Our founders despised the thought of political party loyalty taking priority over the principles of freedom. In fact, George Washington warns of political party loyalty in his Farewell Address.

> I have already intimated to you the danger of parties in the state, with particular reference to the founding of them on geographical discriminations. Let me now take a more comprehensive view, and warn you in the most solemn manner against the baneful effects of the spirit of party, generally. This spirit, unfortunately, is insepa-rable from our nature, having its root in the strongest passions of the human mind. It exists under different shapes in all governments, more or less stifled, controlled, or repressed; but, in those of the popular form, it is seen in its greatest rankness, and is truly their worst enemy.[11]

Washington's attitude towards party loyalty is the opposite of what we see today in America. How does America so quickly forget the wise counsel of the father of our nation? We hear politicians continually stress the existence of only two parties, as if those who belong to another party other than Republican or Democrat are not worthy of national attention and are wackos, have nothing to offer America, or are not qualified. Likewise, the major media networks insist on ignoring viable candidates belonging to a third party, even though their views, ideas, and direction for America mirror or closely resemble those of our founders. Even the supposed independents and extreme conservatives

---

10. George W. Bush, "State of the Union Address by the President," (Washington, D.C., January 31, 2006), http://stateoftheunionaddress.org/2006-george-w-bush (accessed May 5, 2009).

11. George Washington and William T. Peck, ed., *Washington's Farewell Address and Webster's Bunker Hill Orations,* (New York: Macmillan Co., 1919), 1.

on national media programs give no time of day for such candidates—guys like Lou Dobbs, Glenn Beck, and Neal Boortz. Shoot, Sean Hannity threw down on Congressman Ron Paul (who contradicted those in his own party) during his presidential campaign in 2008—mostly and apparently because Congressman Paul did not support an unconstitutional war. (Note: there is a difference between war and constitutional war.) Indeed, Congressman Paul speaks out against House Joint Resolution 114 in the 107th Congress in 2002. One of the reasons he did so was based upon the clear and plainly stated constitutional provisions of the war power.

> I welcome the opportunity to speak out in opposition to this reso-
> lution… We are giving the president the authority to defend the
> national security of the United States against the continuing threat
> posed by Iraq. In other words, we are transferring the power to
> declare war to the president. He can declare the war and fight the
> war when he pleases… In this bill that we are working on, they men-
> tion the United Nations…twenty-five times. They never mention
> Article 1, Section 8, once… The constitutional process, I think, has
> been sadly neglected. It is very clear in the Constitution and it is very
> clear in our history about where this power to wage war and declare
> war resides. And it resides in the U.S. Congress.[12]

Apparently, such a congressman so worried about following the Constitution is unworthy of support. Do the people of the states not realize that the Constitution was written for our benefit to secure our rights and free-doms? I thought conservatives were those people who actually cared about our government sticking to the original intentions of our Constitution and understood the importance of complying with the Constitution![13] America's

---

12. Ron Paul, "Authorization For Use Of Military Force Against Iraq Markup Before The Committee On International Relations House Of Representatives One Hundred Seventh Congress," 107th Congress, 2nd Session, October 2–3, 2002, H.J. Res. 114, *Congressional Record* 107–116, (Washington D.C., U.S. Government Printing Office, 2002), 30.

13. "The voters will know I'll put competent judges on the bench, people who will strictly interpret the Constitution and will not use the bench to write social policy. I believe in strict

view on this one particular matter simply reflects their lack of appreciation for our Constitution; and it completely contradicts our founders' views on the subject. Consider Thomas Jefferson's views on the issue of the power to engage war.[14]

> We have already given…one effectual check to the dog of war, by transferring the power of declaring war from the Executive to the legislative body, from those who are to spend to those who are to pay.
>
> The question of declaring war is the function equally of both Houses.
>
> The question of war, being placed by the Constitution with the Legislature alone, respect to that made it my duty to restrain the operations of our militia to those merely defensive; and considerations involving the public satisfaction, and peculiarly my own, require that the decision of that question, whichever it may be, should be pronounced definitely by the Legislature themselves.
>
> I oppose the right of the president to declare anything future on the question, "Shall there or shall there not be war?"
>
> As the Executive cannot decide the question of war on the affirmative side, neither ought it to do so on the negative side, by preventing the competent body from deliberating on the question.
>
> If Congress are to act on the question of war, they have a right to information.
>
> We had reposed great confidence in that provision of the Constitution which requires two-thirds of the Legislature to declare war.

---

constructionists." Levin, *Men In Black,* 176. Compare the verbiage of the Republican party's lead politician—the former president G.W. Bush—and his unconstitutional (admitted to by Congressman Henry Hyde) actions of engaging war without a declaration of war by Congress and in violation of his express grants of power in the Constitution. I guess if the word *strict* means loose as a goose, then Bush does believe in strict constructionists, because he surely did not use strict construction interpretation of the Constitution to fulfill his duties as the executive branch.

14. Jefferson, *The Jeffersonian Cyclopedia,* 918–919.

> We see a new instance of the inefficiency of constitutional guards. We had relied with great security on that provision which requires two-thirds of the Legislature to declare war.
>
> The power of declaring war being with the Legislature, the Executive should do nothing necessarily committing them to decide war.

It appears that Jefferson and Congressman Paul's views on the matter are equivalent. The principles behind Jefferson's view (the constitutional view) on this matter have long been held as true because of the dangers of prolonged war—not only regarding finances but also foreign and national concerns, the consequences of which are felt by Americans for generations. In the sixth century BC, Sun Tzu recognized this fact in *The Art of War*. "There is no instance of a country having benefited from prolonged warfare."[15] At one time, the United States Supreme Court confirmed that the president has no powers other than what is expressly granted by the Constitution—even if an emergency existed in the nation.

> Emergency does not create power. Emergency does not increase granted power or remove or diminish the restrictions upon power granted or reserved. The Constitution was adopted in a period of grave emergency. Its grants of power to the Federal Government and its limitations of the power of the States were determined in the light of emergency and they are not altered by emergency.[16]

Also in 1862, the United States Supreme Court recognized as well that the president has absolutely no authority or right to make, cause, or declare war even during times of war or during times of an emergency. "To say that [the President] can 'declare war,' because in the event of war he commands the Army, Navy and Militia in service, when war is declared, under the Constitution, *is absurd*."[17]

---

15. Sun Tzu and Lionel Giles, trans., *The Art of War*, (Charleston, SC: Forgotten Books, 1963), 6.

16. *Home Building & Loan Assn v. Blairsdell*, 290 U.S. 398, 425 (1934).

17. *Preciat, et al. v. U. S.*, 67 U.S. 459, 462 (1862), (emphasis added).

Indeed, our Constitution was created during times of great emergency, yet the Constitution makes absolutely no provision for or exceptions to the duty and obligation of Congress to declare a just war, even in times of emergency. Think about it: any situation calling for war would be deemed an emergency. Thus, if Congress is allowed to convey power to the executive branch in violation of the terms of the Constitution, because they deem the circumstances an emergency, then they make the Constitution non-effectual and convert our nation from a constitutional republic to an oligarchy despot. Keep in mind, as well, that the historical and legal context of Congress' ability to declare war is that there were many in the colonies who did not believe the federal government should be able to create standing armies except during times of actual war or invasion—period. "As standing armies in time of peace are dangerous to liberty, and have often been the means of overturning the best constitutions of government, no standing army, or troops of any description whatsoever, shall be raised or kept up by the legislature."[18] Make no mistake, not only did many not want the executive branch to hold the power of engaging war, but they wanted to deny the legislative branch the power to have standing armies during times of peace. To this concern, the writers of the *Federalist Papers* responded to ease the fears of their fellow colonists in Federalist Paper No. 24.

A stranger to our politics, who was to read our newspapers at the present juncture, without having previously inspected the plan reported by the [constitutional] convention, would be naturally led to one of two conclusions: either that [the proposed constitution] contained a positive injunction, that standing armies should be kept up in time of peace; or that it vested in the EXECUTIVE branch the whole power of levying troops, without subjecting his discretion, in any shape, to the control of the legislature…

[N]either the one nor the other was the case; that the whole power of raising armies was lodged in the *legislature,* not in the *executive;* that this legislature was to be a popular body, consisting of the representatives of the people periodically elected; and that instead of the provisions he had supposed in favor of standing armies, there was

18. Brutus, *The Anti-Federalist Papers,* 291.

to be found, in respect to this object, an important qualification even of the legislative discretion, in that clause which forbids the appropriation of money for the support of an army for any longer period than two years a precaution which...will appear to be a great and real security against the keeping of troops without evident necessity.[19]

To convince those jealous of freedom and those who saw the danger of standing armies in the hands of the federal government, Hamilton clearly acknowledged that not only was the declaration of war only in the hands of Congress, but also the power to fund standing armies during times of peace was in the power of Congress—not the executive branch. Consider that these arguments made by the writers of the *Federalist Papers* were used to urge strongly the states to ratify the Constitution. These were the purposes and intents of the Constitution, if you will. By analogy, these arguments in support of the new Constitution were the offer to the sovereigns of the individual states to form a contract, which the states had to accept to form a binding agreement. So the states ratified the Constitution—the contract—and if the terms are subsequently breached, the people of the states have every right to terminate the contract. How can it be reasonably argued that the states should be bound to accept the notion that the Constitution should be fudged here and there, when the proponents of the Constitution explicitly gave reasons for its adoption and the federal government now violates those reasons? That is called bait and switch and is illegal in all of the states in the union. It is fraudulent and criminal. Use a bit of simple logic. How can the executive branch possess power that is not only not granted to it but was argued not to belong even to the legislative branch?

Alexander Hamilton continues his discussion on the issue of standing armies and the power to engage and declare war in subsequent papers. Hamilton notes,

The power of raising armies at all...can by no construction be deemed to reside anywhere else, than in the legislatures themselves...

---

19. Alexander Hamilton, "Federalist Paper 24," in *The Federalist Papers,* Hamilton, Jay, and Madison, 183–184.

The legislature of the United States will be obliged, by this provision, once at least in every two years, to deliberate upon the propriety of keeping a military force… They are not at liberty to vest in the executive department permanent funds for the support of any army, if they were even incautious enough to be willing to repose in it so improper a confidence.[20]

Even Alexander Hamilton, who was one of the most pro-national-government advocates, acknowledges that the legislative branch was to maintain control over the war power at all times, and that they should not—ever—give the executive branch the use of the army without their control. To do so would be an improper confidence. Hamilton recognizes that there would perhaps be a time when the war power would be abused by the federal government, and the freedoms of the citizens would be jeopardized. However, Hamilton also notes that even where such abuses take place, there may be a majority of people who accept the abuse at the expense of freedom and constitutional liberty. To this situation, Hamilton recognizes the power of the people of the several states to claim their independence and sovereignty over the unconstitutional acts of the federal government and to resist such tyrannical acts.

The provision for the support of a military force will always be a favorable topic for declamation. As often as the question comes forward, the public attention will be roused and attracted to the subject, by the party in opposition; and if the majority should be really disposed to exceed the proper limits, the community will be warned of the danger, and will have an opportunity of taking measures to guard against it. Independent of parties in the national legislature itself, as often as the period of discussion arrived, the State legislatures, who will always be not only vigilant but suspicious and jealous guardians of the rights of the citizens against encroachments from the federal government, will constantly have their attention awake to the conduct of the national rulers, and will be ready enough, if any thing

20. Alexander Hamilton, "Federalist Paper 26," in *The Federalist Papers,* Hamilton, Jay, and Madison, 200, 201.

improper appears, to sound the alarm to the people, and not only to be the VOICE, but, if necessary, the ARM of their discontent.

Schemes to subvert the liberties of a great community REQUIRE TIME to mature them for execution. An army, so large as seriously to menace those liberties, could only be formed by progressive augmentations; which would suppose, not merely a temporary combination between the legislature and executive, but a continued conspiracy for a series of time. Is it probable that such a combination would exist at all? Is it probable that it would be persevered in, and transmitted along through all the successive variations in a representative body, which biennial elections would naturally produce in both houses? Is it presumable, that every man, the instant he took his seat in the national Senate or House of Representatives, would commence a traitor to his constituents and to his country? Can it be supposed that there would not be found one man, discerning enough to detect so atrocious a conspiracy, or bold or honest enough to apprise his constituents of their danger? If such presumptions can fairly be made, there ought at once to be an end of all delegated authority. The people should resolve to recall all the powers they have heretofore parted with out of their own hands, and to divide themselves into as many States as there are counties, in order that they may be able to manage their own concerns in person.

If such suppositions could even be reasonably made, still the concealment of the design, for any duration, would be impracticable. It would be announced, by the very circumstance of augmenting the army to so great an extent in time of profound peace. What colorable reason could be assigned, in a country so situated, for such vast augmentations of the military force? It is impossible that the people could be long deceived; and the destruction of the project, and of the projectors, would quickly follow the discovery.[21]

After recognizing the duty of the states to protect the freedom of their citizens, Hamilton acknowledges the conspiracy that would have to take

---

21. Alexander Hamilton, "Federalist Paper 26," in *The Federalist Papers,* Hamilton, Jay, and Madison, 201.

place between the legislative and executive branch for such a usurpation to take place. Quite frankly, Hamilton had a hard time foreseeing that so many public officials would conspire in these unconstitutional actions. However, we see in America today how that same unconstitutional conspiracy has in fact come to pass. The United States Congress—with the exception of Congressman Ron Paul—has completely conceded the power granted to them by the sovereigns of the states to the executive branch and has done the very things that our founders warned us about. They have, either implicitly or expressly, shirked their constitutional responsibilities as agents of the people under the terms of the Constitution, and they have violated their oath of office and jeopardized the nation's freedoms secured by the Constitution, which they swore to protect, defend, and support. The well-known United States Supreme Court justice and former professor of Harvard University Joseph Story also confirms the aforementioned description of the power of war and recognizes the danger in allowing the executive branch the power to declare war in his *Exposition of the U.S. Constitution.* He says,

> The power to declare war, if vested in the General Government, might have been vested in the president, or in the Senate, or in both, or in the House of Representatives alone. In monarchies, the power is ordinarily vested in the Executive. But certainly, in a republic, the chief magistrate ought not to be clothed with a power so summary, and, at the same time, so full of dangers to the public interest and public safety. It would be to commit the liberties, as well as the rights of the people, to the ambition, or resentment, or caprice, or rashness of a single mind.[22]

Of course, if declaring war is no longer accepted by the states and the people, then the Constitution should be amended—not ignored![23] But any such proposal would be deserving of great public debate and analysis (as would any provision of the Constitution to be amended by the states). America's father, George Washington, proclaims that unless the states amend

---

22. Story, *A Familiar Exposition of the Constitution of the United States,* 120–121.
23. U.S. Constitution, art. V.

the Constitution, all of its provisions *must* be followed. "Let the reins of government then be braced and held with a steady hand, and every violation of the constitution be reprehended. If defective, let it be amended, but not suffered to be trampled upon whilst it has an existence."[24] But I suppose there are some Americans who would rather believe Congressman Henry Hyde (who is a Republican, by the way) who states the following in response to Ron Paul's comments (previously cited about obeying our Constitution):

> There are things in the Constitution that have been overtaken by events, by time. Declaration of war is one of them. There are things no longer relevant to a modern society. Why declare war if you don't have to? We are saying to the president, use your judgment. So, to demand that we declare war is to strengthen something to death. You have got a hammerlock on this situation, and it is not called for. Inappropriate, anachronistic, it isn't done anymore.[25]

In other words, Hyde believes the Constitution should not get in the way of how the government wants to act, when they want to act, and to what extent they want to act. No other interpretation of statement is possible. So much for the Constitution being the supreme law of the land, and so much for the people being governed by consent. Wow, what champions for constitutional government Hyde and his like are! I feel so much better about sending thousands of American soldiers halfway around the world to—for argument's sake—protect (though such military acts of aggression—as opposed to defense—never secure rights but only jeopardize them) the freedoms in America secured by the Constitution, knowing that our congressmen do not care whether we follow the Constitution, and knowing that they will decide for us which provisions are outdated. How reassured and

---

24. Albert Bushnell Hart, ed. and Mabel Hill, comp., *Liberty Documents: With Contemporary Exposition and Critical Comments Drawn from Various Writers,* (New York: Longmans, Green, 1903), 218.

25. James T. Bennett, *Homeland Security Scams,* (Piscataway, NJ: Transaction Publishers, 2006), 133.

safe I feel. (Do you sense the sarcasm?) No doubt, Congressman Hyde would not agree with this commonly held view during the framing of our nation:

> Before the existence of express political compacts it was reasonably implied that the magistrate should govern with wisdom and justice, but mere implication was too feeble to restrain the unbridled ambition of a bad man, or afford security against negligence, cruelty, or any other defect of mind... Therefore, a general presumption that rulers will govern well is not a sufficient security.[26]

The truth is, people holding the "Hyde-constitutional" view have a good reason not to bring these issues to the people of the states for debate and consideration, because most certainly history, truth, law, philosophy, and logic defeat their slave-producing view and expose it for what it is: evil and corrupt. Without a doubt, people holding Congressman Hyde's view of constitutional government would have had serious problems with American founders such as John Dickinson who says, "[W]ho are a free people? Not those over whom Government is reasonably and equitably exercised, but those, who live under Government, so constitutionally checked and controlled that proper provision is made against its being otherwise exercised."[27] Yes, Samuel Adams would have likely consider people like Congressman Hyde to be enemies of a free nation, considering Adam's point of view of the Constitution: "There are fundamental rules of the Constitution, which it is humbly presumed neither the supreme legislature nor the supreme executive can alter. *In all free states the Constitution is fixed.*"[28]

Whom do these congressmen think they are giving power to the executive branch that they do not have the lawful authority to give? What are the people of the states doing allowing these tyrants to hold public office? We must be ignorant of the American philosophy and natural law principle that "Where-ever law ends, tyranny begins...and whosoever in authority exceeds

---

26. Brutus and Ketcham, ed., *The Anti-Federalist Papers*, 318.
27. Halstead Van Tyne, *The Causes of the War of Independence*, 230.
28. Ibid., (emphasis added).

the power given to his command…may be opposed, as any other man, who by force invades the right of another."[29] Did the sovereigns of the states grant this power to the executive branch? Absolutely not! Do we not care about the constitutional limitations of government? Do we not care about the rule of law and the consent of the governed? The Declaration of Independence (which is the legal and philosophical foundation for the Constitution) clearly states that "governments are instituted among Men, deriving their just powers from the consent of the governed."[30] Powers are not derived from bureaucrats, politicians, or elitists. In fact, as John Locke puts it, the powerful and rich in society have a greater duty to bind themselves to the law than does the weak, poor, and insignificant.[31] Why? Because the powerful have a much greater ability to harm those lesser in society! How much more does this apply to the government—the institution formed and trusted among men—possessing the brute power to take away life, liberty, and property from the very people that formed it? In fact, Locke describes anyone who attempts to overturn the constitution and its framework as the greatest criminal in society:

> [W]hoever, either ruler or subject, by force goes about to invade the rights of either prince or people, and lays the foundation for overturning the constitution and frame of any just government, is highly guilty of the greatest crime.[32]

Notice Locke's criminal accusation applies to *anyone*—whether prince or people—who tries to overturn the constitution and invade the rights of man. America's jurisprudence has long held that Congress cannot delegate powers

---

29. Locke and Macpherson, ed., *Second Treatise of Government,* 103.

30. Jefferson, *Declaration of Independence,* (See Appendix A).

31. "[T]he exceeding the bounds of authority is no more a right in a great, than in a petty officer; no more justifiable in a king than a constable; but is so much the worse in him, in that he has more trust put in him, has already a much greater share than the rest of his brethren, and is supposed, from the advantages of his education, employment, and counsellors, to be more knowing in the measures of right and wrong." Locke and Macpherson, ed., *Second Treatise of Government,* 103.

32. Locke and Macpherson, ed., *Second Treatise of Government,* 116.

to another branch of government,[33] no more than they can delegate power to a foreign government. Do Americans even care? Do Americans care that we specifically took away the power to create war from the executive branch? If they do not, why go through the formality of an oath of office to uphold the Constitution, if we do not require that our public officials conform to it? Why pretend that we care about the Constitution at all? If you take this cavalier approach to the Constitution, what refrains the government from ignoring constitutional provisions on, say, your right of free speech; or your right to be free from unlawful searches and seizures; or your right to be tried by a jury of your peers; or your right to keep and bear arms if they can simply ignore the constitutional provision concerning wars? But I guess you have nothing to hide, so you are not at risk of having your rights violated. And of course, our government would never do anything to oppress *you*. Right.

Are these people who refuse to insist on strict and full compliance with the terms of the Constitution the same people who would concede to the federal government's attempts to impede the First Amendment restriction on Congress to regulate speech, such as in the reinstitution of the Fairness Doctrine[34] proposed by Representative Maurice Hinchey (Democrat from New York), which without a doubt regulates speech?[35] Of course right-wingers jump up and down shouting that this is a violation of the First Amendment of the Bill of Rights which states, "Congress shall make no law respecting an establishment of religion, or prohibiting the free exercise thereof; or abridging

---

33. "That Congress cannot delegate legislative power to the President is a principle universally recognized as vital to the integrity and maintenance of the system of government ordained by the Constitution." *Marshall Field & Co. v. Clark,* 143 U.S. 649, 692, (1892).

34. "The Fairness Doctrine had two basic elements: It required broadcasters to devote some of their airtime to discussing controversial matters of public interest, and to air contrasting views regarding those matters. Stations were given wide latitude as to how to provide contrasting views: It could be done through news segments, public affairs shows, or editorials. The doctrine did not require equal time for opposing views but required that contrasting viewpoints be presented." Steve Rendall, "The Fairness Doctrine: How We Lost it, and Why We Need it Back," *Common Dreams,* February 12, 2005.

35. Dick Uliano, "Dems Target Right-Wing Talk Radio," *CNNPolitics.com,* February 13, 2009, http://politicalticker.blogs.cnn.com/2009/02/13/dems-target-right-wing-talk-radio/ (accessed May 5, 2009).

the freedom of speech, or of the press; or the right of the people peaceably to assemble, and to petition the Government for a redress of grievances." And yes, they are correct. Any attempt by Congress to regulate speech is unconstitutional (even though some—even conservatives and libertarians like Neal Boortz—argue that public airwaves are not subject to the First Amendment restrictions). Using the rationale that Congress has the power to regulate speech because the medium for that speech is a public utility perverts the Constitution and assumes power that the Constitution did not grant to it.[36] How can Congress assume powers from the sovereigns of the states and from their delegated agents (the state governments) when Congress did not even come into existence until the formation of the Constitution, and when its powers to regulate speech—regardless of what form of medium—have been denied by the people of the United States? America's founders did not create "situation law," whereby the Constitution changes its meaning and application with each change in circumstances. Rather, the sovereigns of the states created the terms of agreement under which the government is to operate. To suggest otherwise only facilitates the continual usurpation of unconstitutional power and increases tyranny.

To demand that companies who pay for the use of airwaves present both sides of public-related issues is preposterous. The fact is, the issues presented today do not take the shape of a coin but the shape of a prism, with multi-faceted perspectives and issues to be addressed. However, like all other politics in America today, the government and mainstream media insist on presenting the controlled Republican-Democrat racket. Here is a proposal: if the government is going to require that public airwaves be used to present fairness to the debate, then they should require those independent and third-party perspectives to be presented to the public—the so-called "you can't

---

36. "In denouncing that monstrous proposal [of regulating the postal mail distribution], [Daniel] Webster said that 'the bill conflicted with that provision in the Constitution which prohibited Congress from passing any law to abridge the freedom of speech or of the press.' What was the liberty of the press? He asked. It was the liberty of printing as well as the liberty of publishing, in all the ordinary modes of publication." Taylor, *The Origin and Growth of the American Constitution,* 231. The position has been long held that Congress may not restrict the channels by which speech is communicated.

win" opinions. After all, are not those who propose victory in Iraq proud of the fact that the Iraqi elections contain some 400 political parties running for election?[37] So why are there only two parties worth considering in America, if a sign of democracy at work is the plethora of political parties presented for public discussion? Let us be honest: the Fairness Doctrine proposed would only benefit those within the control of the elitists and political powers. There is a reason for this: control and manipulation.

The bottom line analysis is not about public airwaves, but it is about the protection of freedom. Freedom is so important that Thomas Jefferson even said, "Were it left to me to decide whether we should have a government without newspapers, or newspapers without a government, I should not hesitate a moment to prefer the latter."[38] Matters of freedom are ultimately left to the states, pursuant to Amendments Nine and Ten of the Bill of Rights. If indeed the Constitution did not foresee public airwaves to be a consideration for federal regulation, then the Constitution needs to be amended, not ignored. Otherwise, the first amendment is clear: Congress shall make NO law abridging the freedom of speech. However, the analysis of the Fairness Doctrine is for another discussion.

The point to be made is this: do those same critics of the Fairness Doctrine jump up and down shouting that going to war without a declaration from Congress is unconstitutional and evil? Evidently not—and the death grip of party politics continues. Use a bit of common sense. If you allow Congress to violate systematically their oath of office to uphold the Constitution regarding a matter that you think benefits you or your cause, then how shocking is it that Congress will violate the Constitution on matters that harm you or your cause? The Constitution is not an à la carte menu from which to choose which provisions are to be followed and which ones

---

37. "Preoccupied as it was poring over Tom Daschle's tax returns, Washington hardly noticed a near-miracle abroad. Iraq held provincial elections. There was no Election Day violence. Security was handled by Iraqi forces with little U.S. involvement. A fabulous bazaar of 14,400 candidates representing 400 parties participated, yielding results highly favorable to both Iraq and the United States." Charles Krauthammer, "Iraq: Good News is No News," *The Washington Post,* February 13, 2009, http://www.washingtonpost.com/wp-dyn/content/article/2009/02/12/AR2009021203012.html (accessed May 5, 2009).

38. Simpson, *Notes on Thomas Jefferson,* 80.

are not. But recent history seems to indicate that such an approach is exactly what Americans feel is appropriate.

To explain this concept of the certainty of the Constitution, consider that the Constitution was created when certain words were understood and accepted by the people of the sovereign states at the time of its creation. For example, read the following provision from Article 1, Section 2: "The House of Representatives shall be composed of members chosen every second *year* by the people of the several states, and the electors in each state shall have the qualifications requisite for electors of the most numerous branch of the state legislature. No person shall be a Representative who shall not have attained to the age of *twenty-five years,* and been *seven years* a citizen of the United States, and who shall not, when elected, be an inhabitant of that state in which he shall be chosen." Now, the following words were emphasized: year, twenty-five years, and seven years. Who can argue that the term year should mean month, and the term twenty-five years should mean thirty years, and that the term seven years should mean ten years. These terms are clearly understood and explicitly stated. If the Constitution is to be read as a situation law document, to be changed in meaning as the circumstances change, then why not change these and similar terms also? After all, a person at the age of twenty-five today does not display nearly the intelligence, maturity, and life experience that a person at the age of twenty-five displayed in 1787.[39] So should we not simply read twenty-five to mean thirty or forty? Let us be fair and honest, if the phrase "Congress shall make no law" can be changed, then why cannot the term "year" be changed? And if you suggest that only certain provisions can be changed and not others, then you will have a challenge to decide which provisions will be changed and which ones will not and who will change them (if not through the amendment process).

Indeed, who is going to be the person to decide which provisions of the Constitution to follow, if all of the Constitution is not to be followed because certain provisions are outdated? Will it be you? Will it be Congress?

---

39. "Madison, then thirty-two, and Hamilton, then twenty-six, were actually present in Philadelphia, as Members of Congress, in which Charles Pinckney, then twenty-five, took his place not long afterwards." Hannis, *The Real Authorship of the United States Constitution Explained,* 19.

Will it be the majority of the people? Will it be the president? Will it be the Supreme Court? Will it be the United Nations? Will it be the Council on Foreign Relations? Will it be the global bankers? Whoever decides which provisions of the Constitution do not need to be followed without the legal means of amendment, such persons are tyrants and deserve no support from the people. Indeed, such persons are the domestic enemies from whom our public officers swear an oath to refute.

Apparently, Americans do not think that much of the Constitution—conservatives included. How do we know? We know by the number of Americans (at least initially) who supported an unconstitutional, power-usurping war and did not care enough about the Constitution to require their representatives to comply with its expressed terms. Congress and the president completely reversed hundreds of years of lessons learned from world history—lessons which reveal that war powers were erroneously given to kings (because of their abuse). Our founders learned those lessons and expressed in the Constitution that the war power went to Congress *alone*. Bottom line: our politicians have proven to be less than worthy of public office and have rejected the Constitution in practice, nature, theory, substance, and meaning. They have violated their oath of office. Yet, they continue to get elected—amazing.

This deliberate exclusionary approach of worthy candidates is dangerous to freedom. It creates a death grip around the minds of Americans, such that there is virtual control over whom the voters will be allowed to see and thus vote for, creating the perception of "I have to vote for a candidate who can win; otherwise, I am wasting my vote." America's system of government undeniably considers a government administrator's duty to be very simple. It has nothing to do with party politics or any other unfounded, nonsensical notion; and it has everything to do with complying with the Constitution. When an administrator of government takes office, he will take one oath alone, and that is the following:

> I do solemnly swear that I will support and defend the Constitution of the United States against all enemies, foreign and domestic; that I will bear true faith and allegiance to the same; that I take this obligation freely, without any mental reservation or purpose of evasion;

and that I will well and faithfully discharge the duties of the office on which I am about to enter. So help me God.[40]

This oath is sworn to before God and the people of America to ensure that the government administrators maintain the integrity of the office and the trust of the people, because the founders knew that it was possible for the Constitution to be free but not the people. Indeed, it used to be accepted as truth that "the people are entitled to the utmost purity and integrity in the conduct of their representatives."[41] Now, that is debatable. So what does the citizen do when the administrator breaches their oath and promise? What effect occurs upon the power that the administrator holds? And what happens to the ordination of God upon that administrator? Does the administrator maintain his status as a minister of God?

Today, that oath seems almost meaningless and evidently has no or little effect on any administrator's actual performance of his duties—and that is one of the reasons for the difference in American today, as compared to our founding generation. What good is a constitutional government (and oath to it) without administrators who understand the limitations expressed therein, to uphold it and allow the people to oversee it? What freedoms are secure without a government administration to execute the principles upon which those freedoms are secured? How long will our unalienable rights be secure while the administrators of government pass, execute, and interpret laws contrary to the superior natural and revealed laws and principles from which those rights exist? The apparent attitude that many Americans have today concerning our government administrators reflects the approach of two steps forward and four steps back. That is, as long as the administrators possess—or even claim to possess—just a smidgen of conservative ideology, that candidate is somehow worthy of our support. All the while, he rejects the principles that allow those ideals to exist. How naïve.

Power can be detrimental, yet it can be very useful, all depending on how it is used. Given its tendency to be abused, a biblical and historical

---

40. Henry H. Smith, ed., *Constitution of the United States with the Amendments Thereto*, 2nd Edition, (Washington D.C.: Government Printing Office, 1879), 270.

41. Rawle, *A View of the Constitution of the United States of America*, 47.

perspective of power must be understood to perceive and discern when it is being abused beyond its constitutional limits. Then we will know how and when to repeal or abolish it—for the very preservation of the life and society from whom the power was vested. It has been established that no power in government can exist without the consent of the people. This is confirmed in nature and in the Bible. Furthermore, when the power is limited by the people, any extension or usurpation of that power is unlawful and without merit, for how can a legitimate power exist if it does not comply with the terms of its creator? America's founders largely and substantially understood the nature, creation, limits, and applications of power relative to government, and they incorporated those concepts into the United States Constitution.

Observation of historical and natural law reveals that power is in fact and is most likely a burden on mankind because of the power-hungry tendency of sinful man when vested with power. Algernon Sidney astutely observes that "an absolute power over the people is a burden, which no man can bear; and that no wise or good man ever desired it; from thence conclude, that it is not good for any to have it, nor just for any to affect it, thought it were personally good for himself; because he is not exalted to seek his own good, but that of the public."[42] This fear of corrupt power permeated our founding generation, and the founders who authored the *Federalist Papers* reflect that fear.

> Where the whole power of the government is in the hands of the people, there is the less pretense for the use of violent remedies in partial or occasional distempers of the State. The natural cure for an ill-administration, in a popular or representative constitution, is a change of men.[43]

---

42. Sidney, *Discourses on Government,* 454; "For he that thinks absolute power purifies men's blood, and corrects the baseness of human nature, need read but the history of this, or any other age, to be convinced of the contrary." Locke and Macpherson, ed., *Second Treatise of Government,* 49.

43. Alexander Hamilton, "Federalist Paper 21," in *The Federalist Papers,* Hamilton, Jay, and Madison, 159.

Alexander Hamilton simply states here the accepted and understood principle of his time: that power of government is in the hands of the people and that men in power have a tendency to violate their constitutionally granted or otherwise granted limits of power. The fact is, we should be very concerned about any government administrator who believes that the Constitution need not be strictly followed, because the Constitution was written for our benefit and security. We should shun any suggestion that we ignore the Constitution and just give discretionary power to wage war or otherwise. How much more fundamental can securing freedom possibly be than to make sure that our Constitution is followed properly, contextually, and strictly? No matter how many times we elect or reelect politicians, this error in judgment and philosophy continually works against the freedom secured by our Constitution.

Hamilton proposed that a change of men is a natural cure of ill administrators—those who would ignore the Constitution and supreme law of our land. The question then becomes what do citizens do when generations of administrators possess and advocate philosophy contrary to their constitutional limitations? What actions must be taken to secure the constitutional form of government, which is the security of our natural rights from God? What happens when the lesser of two evils continually usurps authority, reconstructs and subverts the Constitution, ignores the will of the people, obtains power unto himself that was not granted by the people, and barely reflects any semblance of the American ideology that was fought and died for by our founders?

While the answer to the this question is not the focus of this chapter, observe what John Chipman Gray (citing Austin) says regarding the ideal of limited powers and administrators breach of those limits.

> When political power is vested in a number of persons, not only may their mode of action be limited, but the objects to which their action can be directed may also be limited. Certain matters may be excluded from those upon which they can issue commands that will be obeyed...in the United States the sovereignty of each of the states, and also of the larger state arising from the federal union, resides in the states' governments, as forming one aggregate body...

but the powers of the United States—that is, of all the states' governments…are very limited over the individual citizens of a particular State—are very limited in character; they are defined by the Constitution, and commands by such aggregate body on matters outside of the Constitution would not be obeyed by the individual citizens.[44]

Did that sink in? He said the federal government was limited in powers, limited in character, defined by the Constitution, and not to be obeyed by citizens when it acts outside the Constitution. This understanding was confirmed by the United States Supreme Court in 1886, in the case of *Norton v. Shelby County*, where the court ruled, "an unconstitutional act is not a law; it confers no rights; it imposes no duties. It is, in legal contemplation, as inoperative as though it had never been passed."[45] This legal position is no surprise when studying American history, because it was addressed long before specific legal issues were raised in America's courts of law, through philosophical discussions of freedom and America's proposed form and substance of government. James Madison recognizes the limited nature of the federal government's authority in Federalist Paper No. 40, stating, "We have seen in the new government, as in the old (Articles of Confederation), the general powers are limited; and that the States, in all unremunerated cases, are left in the enjoyment of their sovereign and independent jurisdiction."[46] Of course, state sovereignty is a joke today, and the thought of the federal government being limited is likewise hilarious. This is predicted by the author of Anti-Federalist Paper No. 1. "This disposition, which is implanted in human nature, will operate in the federal legislature to lessen and ultimately to subvert the state authority, and having such advantages, will most certainly succeed, if the federal government succeeds at all."[47] Maintaining the integrity of state independence and sovereignty had always been a concern

44. Gray, *The Nature and Sources of the Law*, 76, 77.

45. *Norton v. Shelby County*, 118 U.S. 425, 426 (1886).

46. James Madison, "Federalist Paper 40," in *The Federalist Papers*, Hamilton, Jay, and Madison, 307.

47. Brutus, *The Anti-Federalist Papers*, 275.

of those involved in the Constitutional Convention debates, as is expressed
by Pelatiah Webster.[48]

> But now the great and most difficult part of this weighty subject
> remains to be considered, viz., how these supreme powers [of the
> federal government] are to be constituted in such manner that they
> may be able to exercise with full force and effect the vast authori-
> ties committed to them, for the good and well-being of the United
> States, and yet be so checked and restrained from exercising them to
> the injury and ruin of the states, that we may with safety trust them
> with a commission of such vast magnitude.[49]

To secure this end of freedom, Webster further offers the resolution of
limiting the federal government in the following manner:

> The powers of Congress, and all the other departments, acting under
> them, shall all be restricted to such matters only of general necessity
> and utility to all the states as cannot come within the jurisdiction
> of any particular state, or to which the authority of any particu-
> lar state is not competent: so that each particular state shall enjoy
> all sovereignty and supreme authority to all intents and purposes,
> excepting only those high authorities and powers by them delegated
> to Congress, for the purposes of the general Union.[50]

In response to this prediction and concern, Alexander Hamilton attempts
to appease the negative views that many had regarding the Constitution and
the interposition on the states' rights and sovereignty. "The State governments would clearly retain all the rights of sovereignty which they before had,
and which were not, by that act, exclusively delegated to the United States."[51]

---

48. "He formulated…the novel principles which they were to translate into a working
system of government." Taylor, *The Real Authorship of the United States Constitution Explained*,
19. Webster has been credited as the real author of the U.S. Constitution.

49. Taylor, *The Origin and Growth of the American Constitution*, 224.

50. Ibid.

51. Alexander Hamilton, "Federalist Paper 32," in *The Federalist Papers,* Hamilton, Jay, and
Madison, 238.

Very plainly, Hamilton acknowledges the sovereignty that each state retained through the ratification of the U.S. Constitution. To ensure further that the rights and freedoms of the people were secure against federal government encroachment, the Bill of Rights was added to the Constitution, including an amendment whereby the states retained all sovereignty and rights not specifically delegated to the federal government.[52] However, it must be acknowledged that while the Bill of Rights was added as a sort of insurance policy against federal government tyranny, some founders believed that such an inclusion was not necessary, because the U.S. Constitution would not have granted the federal government powers to violate our freedoms anyway. Alexander Hamilton says,

> I…affirm that bills of rights…are not only unnecessary in the proposed Constitution, but would even be dangerous. They would contain various exceptions to powers not granted; and, on this very account, would afford a colorable pretext to claim more than were granted. For why declare that things shall not be done which there is no power to do? Why, for instance, should it be said that liberty of the press shall not be restrained, when no power is given by which restrictions may be imposed.[53]

In other words, Hamilton believes that instead of the scope of federal government being controlled by their enumerated powers in the Constitution, it would conversely be controlled by whatever actions were not expressly limited in the Bill of Rights.[54] Of course, Hamilton's approach confirmed the strict constructionist interpretation that the federal government has absolutely no power to do any act unless it is expressly granted to it by the U.S.

---

52. "As the Convention did not see fit so to limit the powers of the new system [as Webster had proposed] it is very natural that…it should be restrained by a bill of rights… [A]mendments had been offered by [John Hancock] and others…embracing the general declaration which reserved to the states or the people the powers not delegated to the United States." Taylor, *The Origin and Growth of the American Constitution,* 224–225.

53. Taylor, *The Origin and Growth of the American Constitution,* 444.

54. Taylor, *The Origin and Growth of the American Constitution,* 245. The concept was explained by U.S. Supreme Court justice, Joseph Story, who said a negation in particular cases implies an affirmation in all others.

Constitution, and that any such powers that were not expressly enumerated would be completely within the sovereignty of the states. To be absolutely certain regarding the limitations that the people of the several states placed upon the federal government and the sovereignty and independence retained by the states to govern themselves, it is recorded fact that the Bill of Rights did not even apply to the states, but rather only to the federal government.

> The fact was fixed in the record that the proposed amendments [Bill of Rights] were intended simply to prevent misconstruction or abuse of powers by declaratory and restrictive limitations. It has been settled from the outset by a long list of authorities that the ten amendments actually adopted are to be regarded as limitations on the powers of the Federal Government and not upon the powers of the states.[55]

This position has in fact been confirmed by the United States Supreme Court numerous times.[56] Even after the ratification of the fourteenth amend-

---

55. Taylor, *The Origin and Growth of the American Constitution,* 229.

56. *United States v. Cruikshank,* 92 U.S. 542 (1875). This decision held that the First Amendment was not intended to limit the powers of the state governments in respect to their own citizens but to operate upon the national government only; "The clause of the Constitution which confers upon Congress the power 'to regulate commerce among the several States,'…is specific and limited, both in its spirit and letter; and does not authorize that body to interfere in any way with the internal trade of the several States, or to prescribe regulations…within their respective limits; all which, as matters of internal police, remain solely and exclusively with the States themselves." *Silliman v. The Hudson River Bridge Co.,* 66 U.S. 81, 82 (1861); "The construction of the state constitution and statutes and the common law on the subject of reading depositions of witnesses in criminal trials is not a federal question, and this Court is bound in such cases by the construction given thereto by the state court. The Sixth Amendment does not apply to proceedings in a state court, nor is there any specific provision in the federal Constitution requiring defendant to be confronted with the witnesses against him in a criminal trial in the state courts." *West v. Louisiana,* 194 U.S. 258 (1904); "This Court is bound by the decision of the highest court of a state that a state statute does not violate any provision of the state constitution, and is valid so far as that instrument is concerned. The first ten amendments to the federal Constitution operate on the National government only, and were not intended to, and did not, limit the powers of the states in respect to their own people." *Jack v. Kansas,* 199 U.S. 372 (1905).

ment, the United States Supreme Court held that the first eight amendments of the Bill of Rights were applicable only against the federal government based upon the applications of jurisdiction.[57] That is, the sovereigns of all government (that is, the people) entered into an agreement both with the federal government through the U.S. Constitution and amendments and with each respective state through each individual state constitution. Therefore, two contracts are needed. This is why the state governments have separate constitutions from the federal constitution: they are separate jurisdictions. For those who would be scared that the states would be able to get by with depriving their citizens of their natural rights, keep in mind that the issues regarding jurisdiction between federal government and state government do not involve the right of the state to do whatever it pleases contrary to natural law and their constitution (because we know that the state governments are limited to the same natural law principles that the federal government is). But rather, the issue is a matter of jurisdiction based upon the respective contracts that the sovereigns entered into with their respective state and federal governments. Ultimately, each state citizen would have the duty to ensure that his state is protecting the freedoms and rights that it wants the federal Constitution to protect and secure. However, to blindly hand over to the federal government jurisdiction over issues that do not belong to the

---

57. "It is well settled that the first ten articles of Amendment to the Constitution of the United States were not intended to limit the powers of the states in respect of their own people, but to operate on the national government only... That the first ten articles of amendment were not intended to limit the powers of the state governments in respect to their own people, but to operate on the national government alone, was decided more than a half century ago, and that decision has been steadily adhered to since." *Spies v. Illinois,* 123 U.S. 131, 166 (1887); "Is any one of the rights secured to the individual by the Fifth or by the Sixth Amendment any more a privilege or immunity of a citizen of the United States than are those secured by the Seventh? In none are they privileges or immunities granted and belonging to the individual as a citizen of the United States, but they are secured to all persons as against the Federal Government, entirely irrespective of such citizenship. As the individual does not enjoy them as a privilege of citizenship of the United States, therefore, when the Fourteenth Amendment prohibits the abridgment by the States of those privileges or immunities which he enjoys as such citizen, it is not correct or reasonable to say that it covers and extends to certain rights which he does not enjoy by reason of his citizenship, but simply because those rights exist in favor of all individuals as against Federal governmental powers." *Maxwell v. Dow*, 176 U.S. 587, 595, 596 (1899).

federal government, based upon our contract with it through the federal
Constitution, is to do more damage to the structure of government and
society by placing power into the hands of a power that has the greatest
ability to deprive all state citizens of the freedoms that so many Americans
say they believe in.

However, many Americans likely do not understand the reason why the
Bill of Rights applied to the federal government, and why America's founders
insisted on such. But the reason is very simple: the states were independent,
sovereign states and their body politic (that is, the people) already had existing constitutions, securing and protecting the rights of their own citizens, and
the U.S. Constitution in no way devolved the rights, powers, and jurisdictions derived under such state constitutions. Thus, since the states retained
their own sovereignty and independence under the U.S. Constitution, the
Bill of Rights was designed to protect the people of the several states from
power usurpation by the federal government. It is clear how far America has
gone from these principles. Whatever attempts were made to maintain state
sovereignty and to prevent the federal government's usurpation of constitutional freedoms have largely been lost, even though there was a time when
the people and politicians largely believed this principle and conformed their
actions to it in America.

You cannot ignore this fact: America was birthed in the philosophy of
limited government and individual rights and freedoms. They studied and
learned from those who believed the same—those very sources contained
herein. They studied philosophers like Algernon Sidney regarding usurpations of authority and manipulations of acquiring it, who says,

> What name can be fit for those, who have no other title to the places
> they possess, than the most unjust and violent usurpation, or being
> descended from those who for their virtues were, by the people's
> consent, duly advanced to the exercise of a legitimate power; and
> having sworn to administer it, according to the conditions upon
> which it was given, for the good of those who gave it, turn all to their
> own pleasure and profit, without any care of the public?
>
> These may be liable to hard censures; but those who use them
> most gently, must confess, that such an extreme deviation from the

end of their institution, annuls it; and the wound thereby given to the natural and original rights of those nations cannot be cured, unless they resume the liberties, of which they have been deprived, and return to the ancient custom of choosing those to be magistrates, who for their virtues best deserve to be preferred before their brethren, and are endowed with those qualities that best enable men to perform the great end of providing for the public safety.[58]

It is clear: where there are usurpations of authority by government administrators, such administrators are not worthy of support, and their actions should be annulled by the citizenry. Sidney also recognized that the usurped power would not be overthrown until, first, the people resume the liberties of which they have been deprived. The question arises again, how do Americans expect to take back their freedom by voting for people who do not implement the principles derived from natural and revealed law, regardless of whether or not that person is a lesser of two evils? It is now apparent that a different course of action is necessary in America, and we must be willing to lose now for the sake of winning later. Otherwise, the same extreme deviations will continue, and freedoms will be lost. But again, who actually cares now?

Interestingly—or perhaps better described as disturbingly—many Americans believe that the governmental administrators prevalent today are acting within the scope of limited authority as prescribed and proscribed by our Constitution (just as Henry Hyde), not because they have studied the issues necessarily, but for shallow reasons such as the administrators have been voted into office; they have been ordained by God; they are pro-life; they are working with what they have; they are conservatives; they are trying to protect us; they are family oriented; and similar unfounded or ineffectual explanations. The fact is the federal government's limited power has been overstepped and distorted, and has evolved into what is essentially a gigantic corporation, where we, the voters, are nothing more than silent shareholders in the corporation and are simply collateral to whatever decisions the board decides to implement.

---

58. Sidney, *Discourses on Government,* 389.

If we begin to think that we are losing money, we vote for a new board of directors, who just happen to be friends of the guys we just voted out and have the same philosophy and agenda. Also, it must be acknowledged that many Americans do not actually believe or trust in the politicians they vote for, but they simply vote for them because there are no better alternatives. Consequently, many likely think that they are powerless and subordinate to the government (which is why they revert to nothing but prayer and voting for the lesser of two evils). But such a philosophy is completely contrary to what America's government is, and if one is going to comply with America's true form of government, then love of country, education, knowledge, freedom, and activism are required from each patriotic citizen—even if it means not voting for a Republican or Democrat.

Do most Americans really even understand the absolute and substantial significance of the limited powers of government in America? Would most Americans compare the limitations placed on government regarding local, state, and national matters to the limitations placed on other individuals regarding personal, business, and family matters? In other words, do you expect that when you visit the grocery store with your twelve-year-old female child that you should not be harassed by a perverted seventy-year-old man who gets his kicks out of touching hot moms? Moreover, do you expect that person not to ask your twelve-year-old daughter out on a date? Why? Because your personhood, your body, and your family are possessions that belong to you, and you have an *inviolable* right to be left alone by those who would step outside of the limitations that our laws place on them. You do not accept the stranger's reasoning that you looked like you wanted it or that your daughter looks much older than twelve. That is absolutely not acceptable. Well then, you should understand what James Madison clearly states in Federalist Paper No. 39—the national government possesses only limited powers as expressed in the Constitution, and in all other areas of life the several states retain *inviolable sovereignty.* The matter is clear: the national (federal) government is very limited, and any powers not expressly vested to it are completely off limits to the federal government.

> The idea of a national government involves in it, not only an authority over the individual citizens, but an indefinite supremacy over all persons and things, so far as they are objects of lawful government...

In this relation, then, the proposed government cannot be deemed a national one; since its jurisdiction extends to certain enumerated objects only, and leaves to the several States a residuary and inviolable sovereignty over all other objects.[59]

Is this what we see today? Is it that hard to understand? To suggest that our national government has complied with this rule is laughable. Of course, the states have shirked their responsibility to protect the rights of their citizens and have preferred money over freedom and sovereignty.

Madison's term *inviolable*, used to describe state sovereignty, serves a very important and significant meaning, and its application is fitting to such meaning. Inviolable means "impregnable to assault or trespass" and "not to be violated."[60] This is the same legal term used in English and American jurisprudence to describe the right an individual has to be left alone from violations of assault, battery, and harassment from others. In other words, no one has the right to disturb the most sacredly held rights of individual autonomy. So just as the seventy-year-old pervert should be arrested for violating you and your daughter's inviolable rights to be free from assaults and batteries, so too the power-usurping, constitutional-law-breaking government administrator should be not be supported by the people. Madison used this description to articulate the power the states possess in all matters not expressly granted to the national government (as seen in the Ninth and Tenth Amendments in the Bill of Rights). Without this understanding of our and the state's inviolable rights secured in the Constitution, we will repeatedly and continually be manhandled by those political and constitutional perverts who laugh in the face of inviolable rights. The same principle can be applied to the individual states, in that the states have no more power than what the citizens have granted.[61] To summarize such a concept of limited power, governments are limited by jurisdiction—a concept that can be

---

59. James Madison, "Federalist Paper 39," in *The Federalist Papers,* Hamilton, Jay, and Madison, 301.

60. Ehrlich, Carruth, Hawkins, and Flexner, *Oxford American Dictionary.*

61. "The Constitution of the United States was not framed, in this respect, on ground new to us. The principle had been previously inserted in all the state constitutions then formed." Rawle, *A View of the Constitution of the United States of America,* 275.

easily envisioned in relation to heads of home, parents to children, employers to employees, and nation to nation. However, it is somehow misunderstood and misapplied with regard to the federal government's limited powers[62] over states and individuals and state governments' limited powers over citizens.

In fact, Enlightenment philosophers used such day-to-day relationships in explaining the concept of limited governmental power. Grotius stated, "Among men…our parents are a sort of gods to us, to whom obedience is due; not infinite indeed, but an obedience of its own proper kind."[63] Similarly, John Locke recognizes that "[t]he affection and tenderness which God hath planted in the breast of parents towards their children, makes it evident, that this is not intended to be a severe arbitrary government, but only for the help, instruction, and preservation of their offspring."[64] Even parental power is not indefinite or infinite, nor does parental obedience require absolute obedience, as such power is not infinite indeed. Similarly, our obedience to government is not absolute but is an obedience of its own proper kind. Given the sin nature of mankind, understanding this concept should be easy.

Furthermore, applying this concept is simple—as simple as understanding fire. In fact, our founders compared government power to the element of fire. Fire can serve a great purpose, or it can serve great evil. A fire kept in a fireplace can be used to heat a home or cook a meal, both of which provide the means and ability to have shelter and substance for the inhabitants in the home. However, once the fire escapes the boundaries of the fireplace, the house and all its occupants are in danger, and unless squelched, the fire will take control of everything. George Washington is attributed to the following quote: "Government is not reason; it is not eloquence; it is force. Like fire, it

---

62. "I see with the deepest affliction, the rapid strides with which the Federal branch of our government is advancing towards the usurpation of all the rights reserved to the States, and the consolidation in itself of all powers, foreign and domestic and that too, by constructions which, if legitimate, leave no limits to their power… [I]t is but too evident, that the three ruling branches of that department are in combination to strip their colleagues, the State authorities, of the powers reserved by them, and to exercise themselves all functions foreign and domestic." Jefferson, *The Jeffersonian Cyclopedia*, 132. Compare the modern American acceptance of federal authority to Thomas Jefferson's quote.

63. Grotius, *Hugo Grotius on the Rights of War and Peace*, xxvii.

64. Locke and Macpherson, ed., *Second Treatise of Government*, 88.

is a dangerous servant and a fearful master."[65] So it is with the power abused by government, which is why a free nation should never be foolish enough to "shut and lock a door against absolute monarchy…[while] at the same time…[putting] the crown in possession of the key."[66] What good is it to place our freedoms in a safe room and lock the door to keep the government from stealing them, only to give government a key to the door? How does this make any sense? Why pretend that the constitutional limitations even matter? Why do we not just open the door to our rights and freedoms and say to the government (as Congressman Hyde said regarding Congressman Paul's bill to declare war), "Here they are; use them as you deem appropriate in your discretion. Make me happy, make me comfortable, take care of me, and protect me, oh, great state of mine!" How ludicrous.

NATURAL LAW CONFIRMS LIMITATIONS

It is interesting how laws of nature can be so widely and commonly believed, accepted, respected, and observed relating to physical nature, but the laws of nature regarding human relationships with government are virtually unknown, despite the fact that our founders used the laws of nature as proof of the laws of human nature relating to government. Just as human conduct

---

65. John V. Denson, *Reassessing the Presidency: The Rise of the Executive State and the Decline of Freedom,* (Auburn, AL: Ludwig von Mises Institute, 2001), xv.

66. Paine and Philip, ed., *Common Sense,* 10; "I easily grant that civil government is the proper remedy for the inconveniences of the state of Nature, which must certainly be great where men may be judges in their own case, since it is easy to be imagined that he who was so unjust as to do his brother an injury will scarce be so just as to condemn himself for it. But I shall desire those who make this objection to remember that absolute monarchs are but men; and if government is to be the remedy of those evils which necessarily follow from men being judges in their own cases, and the state of Nature is therefore not to be endured, I desire to know what kind of government that is, and how much better it is than the state of Nature, where one man commanding a multitude has the liberty to be judge in his own case, and may do to all his subjects whatever he pleases without the least question or control of those who execute his pleasure? And in whatsoever he doth, whether led by reason, mistake, or passion, must be submitted to? Which men in the state of Nature are not bound to do one to another? And if he that judges, judges amiss in his own or any other case, he is answerable for it to the rest of mankind." Locke and Macpherson, ed., *Second Treatise of Government,* 12–13.

must conform to the laws of gravity, motion, and thermodynamics, government and human conduct must conform to the laws of nature. Montesquieu
argues the point that all rules of nature must be observed, and that it is
the duty of the creation to respect and conform to the laws of the Creator,
because such is the motion set in place by the Creator. He says,

> These rules [of nature] are fixed and invariable relation. In bod-
> ies moved, the motion is received, increased, diminished, or lost,
> according to the relations of the quantity of matter and velocity;
> each diversity is uniformity, each change is constancy.[67]

Thus, a natural principle can be derived from the maxim that power
of government is derived from the people (as has already been established
herein), because government never exists in a state of nature but only by
agreement and formation of men, the concept of which is explained by
Algernon Sidney as follows: "[The people] who give a being to [their rulers],
cannot but have a right of regulating, limiting, and directing them as best
pleaseth themselves."[68] How then can it be said that a government ignoring
its limitations is ordained of God or good? To suggest such simply shows an
ignorance of America's history, philosophy, and foundation.

One may, of course, argue that no such natural laws exist with regard
to human conduct and its relationship to government, but such a person
would have to reject that there is a Creator who set certain laws into motion
when He created the earth and its inhabitants. At the same time, however,
you also have to accept that such a philosophy is destructive to every right
that most Americans would claim to possess. Furthermore, such a philosophy would embrace Congressman Hyde's view of complying with the
Constitution: it does not really matter; it is not necessary to secure freedom;
and as long as I am comfortable and happy, you can do what you want with
the Constitution.

Indeed, without the acceptance of natural law, all certainty of rights van-

---

67. Montesquieu, *The Spirit of Laws*, 2.
68. Sidney, *Discourses on Government*, 353–354.

ishes. This is no novel concept but has been digested and regurgitated for centuries. Hugo Grotius puts it the following way: "It is most true [as Cicero says] that everything loses its certainty at once, if we give up the belief in rights."[69] Thus, those who would argue that one should never mix religion with politics would have been scolded by all of the thinkers who influenced and contributed to the founding of America, including thinkers that literally revolutionized the western world. The fact is America's system of government would never have existed had it not been for the realization that rights come from God, not government. It is the philosophy expressed by Grotius on the subject of limiting government that shaped our nation's form and substance.

> Before laws were made, there were relations of possible justice. To say that there is nothing just or unjust but what is commanded or forbidden by positive laws, is the same as saying that before the describing of a circle all the radii were not equal. We must therefore acknowledge relations of justice antecedent to the positive law by which they are established.[70]

Certain natural laws existed even before government existed, just as a circle's radius was the same at all points before any mathematician discovered such a maxim. To suggest that certain understood laws of government did not exist prior to the establishment of government is to deny the "Laws of Nature and of Nature's God," as Thomas Jefferson wrote in the Declaration of Independence. Both of them existed prior to man or government. As a result of the existence of immutable and natural laws, all men and governments are bound by such, and none have the right to take from another what naturally belongs to that person—without prior agreement—including government.

Grotius agrees. "Natural Law itself shows that it is unlawful for me to take what is yours against your will."[71] Again, how can government possess

---

69. Grotius, *Hugo Grotius on the Rights of War and Peace,* xxix.
70. Ibid., 2.
71. Ibid., 4.

what is yours without your consent? Put another way, how can the government ignore the Constitution when that is the agreement that we all decided to live by? Would the government allow you, a mere citizen, to breach the agreement? Try it and see what happens. And if America has gotten to the point where individuals feel they have no power regarding their consent (or even knowledge) of laws, then it is just further proof that the federal government has become too big, that states have lost their sovereignty, and that the people of the states have no control over their agent—the government. Consequently, slavery will be the end result. Do you think that the circumstances would get better by making the government bigger or by merging our system of laws and society with other countries, such as Canada, Mexico, and Europe? Well, consider that those plans are already being arranged and have been for quite some time.[72]

A nation that is built on the natural and revealed laws of God cannot exist simultaneously with a culture of people and politicians who reject such foundations of law. It would be like trying to keep a body alive by removing the blood. Sidney explains that the acceptance and implementation of natural law regarding limitations on government is necessary for the preservation of the entire nation (which of course allows the individual to conduct his life more freely in relation to his Creator). Sidney says,

---

72. "The Security and Prosperity Partnership of North America (SPP) was launched in March of 2005 as a trilateral effort to increase security and enhance prosperity among the United States, Canada and Mexico through greater cooperation and information sharing." http://www.spp.gov/ (accessed May 5, 2009), *Associated Press,* "McCain 'League of Democracies' Gains Support: Does the world have an appetite for a U.S.-led coalition of countries?" *www. msnbc.com,* http://www.msnbc.msn.com/id/24891134 (accessed May 5, 2009); Mobin Pandit, "Former US commerce official seeks change at IMF, World Bank," *The Peninsula,* May 5, 2009. Former US commerce official says that US should enter into the "global economic system and surrender some of its authority as part of a reform of the global financial system," http://www.thepeninsulaqatar.com/Display_news.asp?section=Business_News&subsection =Local+Business&month=May2009&file=Business_News2009050574910.xml; "Full U.S. engagement on human rights issues is an important step toward realizing the goal of an inclusive and vibrant intergovernmental process to protect rights around the globe."Author Unknown, "U.S. Applies For UNHRC Membership," *VOA News.com,* May 4, 2009,), http://www. voanews.com/uspolicy/2009-05-04-voa8.cfm; Dan Weil, "Obama Warms Up to Joining World Court," *NewsMax.com,* April 30, 2009, http://www.newsmax.com/insidecover/obama_world_ court/2009/04/30/209347.html. This is the tip of the iceberg.

It must be acknowledged, that the whole fabric of tyranny will be much weakened, if we prove, that nations have a right to make their own laws, constitute their own magistrates; and that such as are constituted owe an account of their actions to those by whom, and for whom, they are appointed.[73]

Of course, any society can choose the route of tyranny, where there are no absolute rights. (China would be a good place for such people to live.) That is your choice. Indeed, Sidney revealed that tyranny would be rampant and uncontrolled if it were not for the acknowledgement that laws derive their source from the God of nature and from those who appoint magistrates, and that the power of magistrates is not absolute or inherent but is conditioned upon, limited, and controlled by the creator of such power: the people. The explanation of this conditional power of magistrates, indeed, mirrors not the animals and brute beasts of nature, where only the strongest survive, but rather the power reflects both the nature of man and the nature of God—both of which are unchangeable. For without the unchanging sources of nature, everything loses its certainty at once. Again, America's foundation reflects the understanding of government's limitations found in natural law. That is why William Rawle points out that America's Constitution reflects the limited nature of government. "The first paragraph [of the Article 1 of the United States Constitution] evinces that it is a limited government. The term 'all legislative powers herein granted,' remind both the Congress and the people, of the existence of some limitation."[74]

Blackstone, as well, proposes the essential influence that natural law has in the implementation of limited governmental structure, administration, and laws. He is quoted in the following passages:

Law...signifies a rule of action...which is prescribed by some superior, and which the inferior is bound to obey. Thus, when the Supreme Being formed the universe, and created matter out of nothing, he impressed certain principles upon that matter.[75]

---

73. Sidney, *Discourses on Government*, 320.
74. Rawle, *A View of the Constitution of the United States of America*, 33.
75. Blackstone, *Commentaries on the Laws of England*, 27.

But laws…denote the rules, not of action in general, but of human action or conduct; that is, the precepts by which man…a creature endowed with both reason and free-will, is commanded to make use of those faculties in the general regulation of his behavior.[76]

Man, considered as a creature, must necessarily be subject to the laws of his Creator, for he is entirely a dependent being…a state of dependence will inevitably oblige the inferior to take the will of him on whom he depends as the rule of his conduct.[77]

And consequently, as man depends absolutely upon his Maker for everything, it is necessary that he should, in all points, conform to his Maker's will.[78]

This will of his Maker is called the law of Nature. Just as man (the creature) must conform to the rules of conduct prescribed by God (his creator), so too must government (the creature) conform to the rules of conduct prescribed by the people (its creator). There are the eternal immutable laws of good and evil, to which the Creator himself, in all his dispensations, conforms; and which he has enabled human reason to discover, so far as they are necessary for the conduct of human actions.[79]

This law of nature…is superior in obligation to any other.[80]

If it is true (and our founders believed it to be) that limitations of government exist in natural law, then government's *positive law* (defined as "law established by human authority"[81]) is not the final authority of law but

---

76. Ibid., 28.
77. Ibid., 28–29.
78. Ibid., 29.
79. Ibid., 29.
80. Ibid., 31.
81. Garner, ed., *Black's Law Dictionary.*

rather should reflect what has already been revealed by God in nature and in His word—including the limitation of government. The criteria used to judge our government administrators is not how much good are they doing, because even when the government appears to be doing good but steps outside of its jurisdiction and prescribed authority, it violates the law that all must follow: the Constitution. Rather, the criteria are listed in the supreme law of the land: the Constitution. Of course, it is also true that when the people are ignorant of their rights, the source of their rights, and their duties relative thereto, all the theories in the world would not stop a tyrant. You might as well tie a piece of thread around the neck of an untrained, in-heat Rottweiler and put him in a fenceless yard to keep him contained.

BIBLICAL CONFIRMATION OF LIMITATIONS

While America's founders understood and accepted the concept that natural law limited government, many of the influential leaders of our nation agreed that the even better source of law was the direct revelation of God (the Bible), because man's interpretation of natural law may be distorted, given the finite capacity of man's reasoning. Blackstone expresses the notion that natural law's authority exists, but that God's revealed law is a more accurate source of natural law than man's observation of natural law. He states the following:

> [Man's corrupt reasoning and understanding] has given manifold occasion for the benign interposition of divine Providence...the doctrines thus delivered we call the revealed or divine law, and they are to be found only in the holy scriptures. These precepts, when revealed, are found upon comparison to be really a part of the original law of nature.[82]

> Yet undoubtedly the revealed law is of infinitely more authenticity than...the natural law.[83]

---

82. Blackstone, *Commentaries on the Laws of England*, 31.
83. Ibid., 32.

Upon these two foundations, the law of nature and the law of revelation, depend all human laws; that is to say, no human laws should be
suffered to contradict these.[84]

The Bible confirms that government is not a god unto itself—having no
limits or boundaries or jurisdiction. Time after time, God confirms that He
alone is the source of all law, and that human laws and conduct contradicting His laws are not blessed by Him, nor are they to be obeyed by man. The
Bible always connects man's laws to the laws of God, revealing the connection between government's obligation to conform to natural and revealed
laws of God and the limitation of power and authority over other persons.
Second Chronicles 30:12 (ESV) states, "The hand of God was also on Judah
to give them one heart to do what the king and the princes commanded by
the word of the LORD." Notice, the people were to obey the commandments of kings and princes when such was accomplished by the word of the
Lord. The king's executive authority was limited by the word of the Lord.
In other words, commandments demanded outside of or in contradiction
to the word of the Lord did not contain authority, and God did not command or expect the people to obey such commandments. While the subject
is raised, it does not appear that God is giving America one heart to do what
the government says, despite Obama's claim of being able to unite America.
America's disparity in philosophy, culture, ideology, beliefs, goals, and religion would prevent any unity that it was once capable of.

The Bible's description of Joshua's authority over the Israelites (which
became effective after Moses died) also confirms this principle of limited
power. Specifically, Joshua 1:16–17[85] shows how the people of Israel would

---

84. Ibid., 32. And to think, Blackstone was the most influential commentator in English
and American jurisprudence from the 1700s to the late 1800s, and his *Commentaries* were used
as legal authority, advocating the natural and revealed laws of God as the basis for all positive law
in America. I wonder, do Christians even believe that all governmental laws and administration
are revealed in the scriptures? The polls, leaders, and philosophy of the day do not seem to
indicate such.

85. "And they answered Joshua, saying: We will do all that you command us, and wherever
you send us we will go. Just as we listened to Moses in all things, so we will listen to you. Only
may Jehovah your God be with you as He was with Moses." Joshua 1: 16–17 (MJKV).

submit to the reign of Joshua, so long as he followed God's laws (as Moses did) and consequently possessed the blessing of God on his authority over the nation. Infamous Bible commentator Matthew Henry rightly describes these verses as a "limitation of their obedience" to Joshua.[86] It is very clear that the Israelites would not have submitted themselves to the authority of Joshua if they believed (given the prior and current conduct of Joshua) that his authority was not ordained of God, that Joshua did not follow the laws of God, and that Joshua was not blessed of God. In other words, "[a] reason is here intimated why [the Israelites] would obey [Joshua] as they had obeyed Moses, because they believed (and in faith prayed) that God's presence would be with him as it was with Moses."[87] Without these conditions being satisfied, Joshua would have had no authority over the people of Israel—and rightly so.

Again, in Nehemiah 5, God reveals that government is limited by the natural laws of justice. Nehemiah, who was the governor of Israel and became the instigator to rebuilding the wall around Jerusalem, had to confront the rich and oppressive members of society when they began lending money to the poor of society just for the simple purpose of survival—oh yes, and to pay the king's taxes.[88] The problem was, the lenders were charging interest on the monies lent to the poor, to the point that the poor had to mortgage their lands, houses, and crops—and even sell their children into servanthood—to pay the debts to the rich. Of course, this was in direct violation of Deuteronomy 23:19.[89] Nehemiah challenged the nobles and rulers, gathered a great assembly against them, and as a result, the creditors rescinded the debts and entered into a binding contract to restore to the debtors all that they had unlawfully taken from them. Nehemiah recognized that for leaders to be held to their word and to be held responsible to act justly, an oath and

---

86. Matthew Henry, George Burder, Joseph Hughes, Samuel Palmer, and Archibald Alexander, *An Exposition of the Old and New Testaments,* (New York, NY: H.C. Sleight, 1833), 504.

87. Ibid.

88. Nehemiah 5:1–5 (MJKV).

89. "You shall not charge interest on loans to your brother, interest on money, interest on food, interest on anything that is lent for interest." Deuteronomy 23:19 (ESV).

contract should be imposed upon the promising party (just as our politicians do today). In other words, their words alone were not enough, but a binding contract would be a safeguard against their abuse of the people.

Afterwards, Nehemiah informs us that the governors before him did not operate under the same limitations as he did, with the same character, nor with similar integrity. He states, "The former governors who were before me laid heavy burdens on the people and took from them for their daily ration forty shekels of silver. Even their servants lorded it over the people. But I did not do so, because of the fear of God."[90] After having rectified the unlawful actions of the rulers and nobles, Nehemiah compares and contrasts the rule of right verses the rule of wrong, necessarily implying that government must administer justice according to the creator of it (God). Nehemiah's predecessors created a heavy burden on the citizens, taking advantage of them, ruling arbitrarily, using their position for personal gain, and forsaking the laws of justice in their administration. Contrarily, Nehemiah ruled over his people under the laws of God, because he knew that he if did not rule accordingly, he would be judged accordingly. Thus, he prays, "Remember for my good, O my God, all that I have done for this people."[91] Why would Nehemiah expect God to bless him if he had not acted according to the principles of God's laws? Very clearly, the Bible describes the difference between an unjust ruler and a just ruler, the differences of which are found in how they follow and carry out the laws of God.

The same types of limitations are seen in the Bible regarding judicial authority. Second Chronicles 19:5–6 (ESV) reflects the limitations that judges have when ruling a case. "[King Jehoshaphat] appointed judges in the land in all the fortified cities of Judah, city by city, and said to the judges, 'Consider what you do, for you judge not for man but for the LORD. He is with you in giving judgment.'" God declares that the authority of judges (who actually served as checks and balances to the kings and princes) was limited by their purpose, which was to judge for the Lord, or in other words, for justice—what is right and wrong. These judges did not perform their

90. Nehemiah 5:15 (ESV).
91. Nehemiah 5:19 (ESV).

government administration for man's sake alone but for the sake of doing the will of God. Thus, it necessarily means that God's will for mankind is that they live under a just and righteous government for the expressed purpose of being able to follow the laws and commandments of God in peace, just as King David prays in Psalms 119:134 (ESV), saying, "Redeem me from man's oppression, that I may keep your precepts." Anything outside of God's will was beyond their judicial authority—for good reason. Once again, God establishes that the government is not independent of or autonomous to God's established law.

It could never be reasonably argued that the Bible supports the theory that citizens are to comply with human authority independent of God's established natural and revealed laws. The Bible confirms the thought that God's kingdom rules above all kingdoms, and all are to hearken unto the King of kings and Lord of lords. Psalm 103:19–22 (ESV) states it this way:

> The LORD has established his throne in the heavens, and his kingdom rules over all. Bless the LORD, O you his angels, you mighty ones who do his word, obeying the voice of his word! Bless the LORD, all his hosts, his ministers, who do his will! Bless the LORD, all his works, in all places of his dominion. Bless the LORD, O my soul!

Clearly, God's kingdom rules over all other kingdoms, and only His ministers that do His will are blessed and ordained. It is the responsibility of all kingdoms and ministers—meaning governments—to comply with His commandments—not the other way around. Their authority is limited to what God has revealed His will to be, and they are charged with the instructions He sets forth, as His ministers—not the other way around.

How can it be said that all governmental action is authorized and ordained of God? There is not one verse in the Bible to even suggest that, but rather the Bible overflows with examples, principles, and verses demanding the opposite: that all governments who contradict the ultimate authority of God are illegitimate and not ordained by God, because they have violated the purpose established by God. In fact, scriptures repeatedly reveal how God judges those nations who ignore the natural laws of God—known as justice. God abhors those nations (Gentile and Jewish) which abuse justice, use government as a ploy for individual gain, and oppress the citizens.[92] If natural laws of God did not exist, by what standard were all the nations of the earth judged? To suggest that the government is not limited and may pass and execute any laws under any circumstances, and that the citizen is bound to comply and obey in the name of submission, advocates the proposition that God has no standard or interest in what government does and how the individual responds and actually places the positive law of man above the natural and revealed law of God. It is as if the government is not accountable to God and to the people. To suggest that also advocates the existence of government over the existence of family and freedom.

A government that violates the terms of its limited powers granted by the people cannot be considered to be ordained of God. God says, give "honor to whom honor is due,"[93] which clarifies and gives condition to the following verse in 1 Peter 2:17 (KJV): "Honour all men. Love the brotherhood. Fear God. Honour the king." God would not command that men give all honor to all kings without limitation and then contradict Himself by saying, "Give honor to whom honor is due." So the question is, do *all* men deserve honor? When a person breaches a contract with another person and then demands that the non-breaching party comply with the contract, does the non-breaching party owe a duty to the breaching party to comply with the terms of the contract? In other words, does the breaching party deserve honor from the non-breaching party? Of course not. In fact, the Bible confirms that a *just* [94] human contract is as enforceable as any other compact or

---

92. "But as for me, I am filled with power, with the Spirit of the LORD, and with justice and might, to declare to Jacob his transgression and to Israel his sin. Hear this, you heads of the house of Jacob and rulers of the house of Israel, who detest justice and make crooked all that is straight, who build Zion with blood and Jerusalem with iniquity. Its heads give judgment for a bribe; its priests teach for a price; its prophets practice divination for money; yet they lean on the LORD and say, 'Is not the LORD in the midst of us? No disaster shall come upon us.' Therefore because of you Zion shall be plowed as a field; Jerusalem shall become a heap of ruins, and the mountain of the house a wooded height." Micah 3:8–12 (ESV).

93. Romans 13:7 (KJV).

94. "Because you have said, 'We have made a covenant with death, and with Sheol we have an agreement, when the overwhelming whip passes through it will not come to us, for we have made lies our refuge, and in falsehood we have taken shelter'; therefore thus says the Lord GOD,

law on earth. The apostle Paul puts it this way: "even with a man-made covenant, no one annuls it or adds to it once it has been ratified."[95] In fact, the use of man-made contracts is used to show the significance of contracts as related to man and God (e.g., the "Abrahamic covenant"). The Bible is filled with example after example of the just nature of enforcing private contracts and the repercussions to those who do not perform as promised. Similarly, if I am employed by ABC Corporation, but I do not show up for work without cause, am I due honor from my employer by virtue of simply being an employee? Of course not. With position comes certain responsibility, and where responsibility is shirked, honor is not due. It has nothing to do with simply being alive or with personality, but it has everything to do with duty, character, and principle.

Likewise, God does not demand that we give honor to government actions when they do not comply with the terms of the contract entered into between the people and the government. If God expects us to give honor to whom honor is due, God also does *not* expect that we give honor to whom honor is *not* due. Grotius describes this concept of lawful authority when he says, "An act done against the promise becomes unjust, because…a legitimate promise gives a Right to the promisee."[96] Grotius recognizes that a citizen is not required to give honor to a government act done against a promise made to the one who is supposed to give honor. Understand this: America does not operate under a despotic government where "we never hear of a constitution."[97] Rather, America operates under the Constitution of the United States—the contract forming the supreme law of the land, which is constructed to describe the nature, scope, and limitations of the government itself.[98]

'Behold, I am the one who has laid as a foundation in Zion, a stone, a tested stone, a precious cornerstone, of a sure foundation: "Whoever believes will not be in haste." And I will make justice the line, and righteousness the plumb line; and hail will sweep away the refuge of lies, and waters will overwhelm the shelter.' Then your covenant with death will be annulled, and your agreement with Sheol will not stand; when the overwhelming scourge passes through, you will be beaten down by it." Isaiah 28:15–18 (ESV).

95. Galatians 3:15 (ESV).
96. Grotius, *Hugo Grotius on the Rights of War and Peace*, 45.
97. Rawle, *A View of the Constitution of the United States of America*, 10.
98. Ibid., 2.

The fact is it is not even Christian ideology or American ideology to excuse the corrupted actions of government. While some would use certain Bible verses such as "turn the other cheek"[99] and "walk the extra mile"[100] to suggest that we excuse the unlawful acts of government and submit and obey regardless of what it does, God does *not* command that when someone slaps you, give your life or limbs, or if someone asks you to walk one mile, walk five hundred. Furthermore, God did not command that we obey man rather than God. In other words, there is a limit to Christian compliance (based upon the principle of jurisdiction) to any person or government, because God has declared that "if a man not provide for his family, he is worse than an infidel."[101] God does not command that we give our life for our government or our enemies. Rather, "by this we know love, that he laid down his life for us, and we ought to lay down our lives for the *brothers*."[102] God does not command that we sacrifice our lives, our limbs, our families' lives, our friends' lives, and our nations' life for the sake of compliance with a government that has usurped not only the powers created and granted by the people but also the purposes God has expressed. And while we are commanded to love our enemies,[103] we are not commanded to sacrifice our lives, families, and liberties for the sake of evil that is done against us. Indeed, God has established government for the very specific purpose of punishing evil here on earth so that "His will may be done on earth as it is in Heaven."[104] If God expected that we be like grass, only to be trampled on and cut down by the powerful or by government, then why did God ordain government to begin with for the

---

99. Matthew 5:39 (KJV).

100. Matthew 5:41 (KJV).

101. Timothy 5:8 (KJV); "Much food is in the plowed ground of the poor, but when there is no justice, it is swept away," Proverbs 13:23 (MKJV). Scriptures reveal that even poor persons would have the means to provide for their own, but when government does not operate under the natural laws of God, the poor are not able to provide for their own and end up depending on government and others. How can a man provide for his family (without living like an animal) without a society operating under just laws?

102. John 3:16; John 15:13 (KJV), (emphasis added).

103. Matthew 5:44 (KJV).

104. Luke 11:2 (KJV).

expressed purpose of punishing evil? How superfluous and noneffectual would God's ordination be if we were to submit to tyrannical government? By sacrificing your freedom, your family, and your friends because of your love for your enemies, you deny the love that God commands you to give to your family and neighbors. Would you allow your neighbor to pillage your house, rape your wife, and sell your children as sex slaves in Mexico because you are to love your neighbor? God's will on earth is not that evil governments or people become tyrants over citizens. To the contrary, God desires that people choose to live by the laws of God that they may live. First Corinthians 7:21 (KJV) tells us, "Art thou called being a servant? care not for it: but if thou mayest be made free, use it rather."[105] This verse expresses plainly that Christian people should not desire to be slaves but rather should search to be free so that they may use their freedom to serve Christ. God only allows tyranny to take place as a form of judgment and punishment against wicked people and a wicked nation.[106] (Who in the world wants God's judgment?) This New Testament truth that God does not want people to live in slavery is reflected numerous times in the Old Testament as well, including in Psalm 103:6 (ESV), stating that "The LORD works righteousness and justice for all who are oppressed." Clearly, the nature of God is to deliver nations from slavery and tyranny, and thus, it is certainly and biblically plain that righteous people should not desire

---

105. "The Spirit of the Lord GOD is upon me, because the LORD has anointed me to bring good news to the poor; he has sent me to bind up the brokenhearted, *to proclaim liberty to the captives, and the opening of the prison to those who are bound,*" (emphasis added), Isaiah 61:1; "*For you were called to freedom,* brothers. Only do not use your freedom as an opportunity for the flesh, but through love serve one another," (emphasis added), Galatians 5:13 (ESV).

106. "And the people will oppress one another, every one his fellow and every one his neighbor; the youth will be insolent to the elder, and the despised to the honorable... For Jerusalem has stumbled, and Judah has fallen, because their speech and their deeds are against the LORD, defying his glorious presence. For the look on their faces bears witness against them; they proclaim their sin like Sodom; they do not hide it. Woe to them! For they have brought evil on themselves. Tell the righteous that it shall be well with them, for they shall eat the fruit of their deeds. Woe to the wicked! It shall be ill with him, for what his hands have dealt out shall be done to him. My people—infants are their oppressors, and women rule over them. O my people, your guides mislead you and they have swallowed up the course of your paths. The LORD has taken his place to contend; he stands to judge peoples." Isaiah 3:5, 8–13 (ESV).

tyranny and most definitely should not condone it, nor facilitate it, which necessarily means that the citizens must actively resist tyranny, because tyranny most certainly will come without resistance—only a fool would deny this. A righteous and just people should demand that justice be the focus of government, as Christ's government itself is based upon justice.[107] In fact, scriptures are filled with verses like these, confirming the importance—and yes, the insistence—of justice:

> Woe to those who decree iniquitous decrees, and the writers who keep writing oppression.[108]

> Blessed are they who observe justice, who do righteousness at all times![109]

> It is not good to be partial to the wicked or to deprive the righteous of justice.[110]

> When justice is done, it is a joy to the righteous but terror to evildoers.[111]

> Evil men do not understand justice, but those who seek the LORD understand it completely.[112]

> [L]earn to do good; seek justice, correct oppression; bring justice to the fatherless, plead the widow's cause.[113]

---

107. "Of the increase of his government and of peace there will be no end, on the throne of David and over his kingdom, to establish it and *to uphold it with justice and with righteousness* from this time forth and forevermore. The zeal of the LORD of hosts will do this," (emphasis added), Isaiah 9:7 (ESV).

108. Isaiah 10:1 (ESV).

109. Psalm 106:3 (ESV).

110. Proverbs 18:5 (ESV).

111. Proverbs 21:15 (ESV); Romans 13 (ESV).

112. Proverbs 28:5 (ESV).

113. Isaiah 1:17 (ESV).

Behold, a king shall reign in righteousness, and rulers shall rule in judgment.[114]

For I the LORD love justice; I hate robbery and wrong; I will faithfully give them their recompense, and I will make an everlasting covenant with them.[115]

If a man is righteous and does what is just and right...does not oppress anyone, but restores to the debtor his pledge, commits no robbery, gives his bread to the hungry and covers the naked with a garment, does not lend at interest or take any profit, withholds his hand from injustice, executes true justice between man and man, walks in my statutes, and keeps my rules by acting faithfully—he is righteous; he shall surely live, declares the Lord GOD.[116]

Thus says the Lord GOD: "Enough, O princes of Israel! Put away violence and oppression, and execute justice and righteousness. Cease your evictions of my people," declares the Lord GOD.[117]

Hate evil, and love good, and establish justice in the gate; it may be that the LORD, the God of hosts, will be gracious to the remnant of Joseph.[118]

He has told you, O man, what is good; and what does the LORD require of you but to do justice, and to love kindness, and to walk humbly with your God?[119]

---

114. Isaiah 32:1 (MJKV).
115. Isaiah 61:8 (ESV).
116. Ezekiel 18:5–9 (ESV).
117. Ezekiel 45:9 (ESV).
118. Amos 5:15 (ESV).
119. Micah 6:8 (ESV).

God tells us that governments that operate contrary to His laws deserve punishment and judgment as they do not comply with His purpose for government as described in Romans 13 and in other scriptures—Old and New Testament. It is only when government operates as Nehemiah did (as demonstrated in Nehemiah 5) that we the people of the United States subject ourselves unto their power not for fear's sake but rather for conscience sake, because righteous men understand justice and judgment, as created by God. Indeed, were it not for God, there would be no justice—period. "Many seek the face of a ruler, but it is from the LORD that a man gets justice."[120] Since justice comes from God alone, then it naturally follows that it is not for government to decide whether or not men deserve justice. Rather, it is a requirement of God that government implement justice, as expressed throughout scripture, including Romans 13.

To somehow suggest that we must allow evil to take place because it is God's will is ludicrous and dangerous in all regards. Scriptures confirm this fact, stating in Job 37:23 (KJV), "Touching the Almighty, we cannot find him out: he is excellent in power, and *in judgment, and in plenty of justice: he will not afflict*,"[121] (emphasis added). In other words, since God possesses perfect judgment and justice, He does not afflict us out of His perfect will. Thus, it should be the desire of every person that righteous justice and judgment be executed in a nation, so that we can pray as King David does: "I have done what is just and right; do not leave me to my oppressors."[122] Certainly David understands the connection between executing justice and freedom for the citizens of such a nation. Thus, where government perverts justice and becomes tyrannical, it is the duty of the righteous man to resist and strive against such tyranny. Why? The reason why it is the duty of righteous people to resist tyranny is because God is the author of justice and expects that justice be executed by all governments and peoples of the earth. It is His will that justice be implemented in society through government.[123] Proverbs 28:4 (ESV) demonstrates this fact,

---

120. Proverbs 29:26 (ESV).

121. "[F]or [God] does not willingly afflict or grieve the children of men." Lamentations 3:33 (ESV).

122. Psalms 119; 121 (ESV).

123. "But let him who boasts boast in this, that he understands and knows me, that *I am the LORD who practices steadfast love, justice, and righteousness in the earth. For in these things I delight, declares the LORD,*" (emphasis added), Jeremiah 9:24 (ESV).

reflecting the character of the righteous person—that he is to strive against those rulers who do not keep the law. "Those who forsake the law praise the wicked, but those who keep the law strive against them." Conversely, scripture states that if you forsake the law, then you are praising the wicked. In fact, if righteous people do not insist that their government operate under the natural laws of God, beware. "O house of David! Thus says the LORD: 'Execute justice in the morning, and deliver from the hand of the oppressor him who has been robbed, lest my wrath go forth like fire, and burn with none to quench it, because of your evil deeds.'"[124] How then can a so-called Christian accept that its rulers govern outside of their God-imposed and we-the-people-imposed limits and forsake the law? Such a Christian literally praises the wicked and proves that he is not willing to follow the law and strive against the wicked. About Proverbs 28:4, Matthew Henry states:

> Those that do indeed make conscience of the law of God themselves will, in their places, vigorously oppose sin, and bear their testimony against it, and do what they can to shame and suppress it. They will reprove the works of darkness, and silence the excuses which are made for those works, and do what they can to bring gross offenders to punishment, that others may hear and fear.[125]

Jesus also confirms the fact that evil is to be judged, regardless of God's will, when He says about His betrayer, "Woe to that man by whom the Son of Man is betrayed! It would have been better for that man if he had not been born."[126] Was it prophesied that Judas Iscariot was to betray Christ? Of course.[127] However, Judas' actions are to be judged by man and certainly will be judged by God, as Jesus confirms. Certainly, these things must come to pass as scriptures declared. However, nothing could be further from the

---

124. Jeremiah 21:12 (ESV).

125. Matthew Henry, John Stoughton, and John Rickerton Williams, *An Exposition of the Old and New Testament,* vol. 3, (Funk and Wagnalls, 1886). Commentary on Proverbs 28:4.

126. Matthew 26:24 (ESV).

127. "And as they were eating, [Jesus] said, 'Truly, I say to you, one of you will betray me.'" Matthew 26:21 (ESV); "For it is written in the Book of Psalms, 'May his camp become desolate, and let there be no one to dwell in it'; and 'Let another take his office.'"Acts 1:20 (ESV).

truth than to say that one must participate in evil or condone evil or not resist evil because you think that these things must come to pass. Jesus already condemned the evil that was to take place and declared it would be better for those evil ones not to have been born. The same is true for those who rule contrary to God's laws. Woe unto them. So why would it be better that these persons not be born? Because they are to be judged for their evil actions. Thus, to comply with the evil and unlawful actions of government or to somehow argue that being neutral is in fact spiritual or commanded by God denies the truth of God and only prevents God's expressed purpose of government from being accomplished on earth: to promote good and punish evil.

COMPACT LIMITATIONS

Not only does America's history confirm the principle of limitations based upon compact, but as referred to herein, the Bible itself confirms that men are bound to and limited by their compacts (i.e., agreements, contracts, covenants). Beyond the natural and revealed laws of God regarding government's limitations, the Constitution is the states' and people's compact (agreement) with the federal government. It is ratified by the states, because the states existed before the federal government. Thus, before a federal government could exist, its power had to be consented to and created out of the sovereigns—the states.[128] There was good reason why our forefathers expressed

---

128. "The Constitution thus became the result of a liberal and noble sacrifice of partial and inferior interests, as citizens of the Union, yet still remaining distinct, as citizens of the different states, created a new government, without destroying those which existed before, reserving in the latter, what they did not surrender to the former, and in the very act of retaining part, conferring power and dignity on the whole." Rawle, *A View of the Constitution of the United States of America,* 18. See Also, "[T]he Constitution is to be founded on the assent and ratification of the people of America, given by deputies elected for the special purpose; but, on the other, that this assent and ratification is to be given by the people, not as individuals composing one entire nation, but as composing the distinct and independent States to which they respectively belong. It is to be the assent and ratification of the several States, derived from the supreme authority in each State, the authority of the people themselves. The act, therefore, establishing the Constitution, will not be a NATIONAL, but a FEDERAL act." James Madison, "Federalist Paper 39," in *The Federalist Papers,* Hamilton, Jay, and Madison, 298–299. "[The United States Constitution] will therefore require the concurrence of thirteen States." Alexander Hamilton, "Federalist Paper 85," in *The Federalist Papers,* Hamilton, Jay, and Madison, 669.

the terms of the federal, state, and the people's power in the Constitution. Have you not wondered why our founders spent the time debating, discussing, arguing, and finally writing out the terms of the Constitution? In fact, our founders learned from great Enlightenment philosophers, such as Hugo Grotius, who says, "If any people intended to share the power of government with the king…such limits ought to be assigned to the power on each as might easily be recognized by distinctions of places, persons, and matters."[129] They also learned from great thinkers, such as John Locke, who describes the nature of political power and its limitations this way:

> Political power is that power, which every man having in the state of nature, has given up into the hands of the society, and therein to the governors, whom the society hath set over itself, with this express or tacit trust, that *it shall be employed for their good, and the preservation of their property:* now this power, which every man has in the state of nature, and which he parts with to the society in all such cases where the society can secure him, is to use such means, for the preserving of his own property, as he thinks good, and nature allows him; and to punish the breach of the law of nature in others, so as (according to the best of his reason) may most conduce to the preservation of himself, and the rest of mankind.
>
> So that the end and measure of this power, when in every man's hands in the state of nature, being the preservation of all of his society, that is, all mankind in general, *it can have no other end or measure, when in the hands of the magistrate, but to preserve the members of that society in their lives, liberties, and possessions;* and so cannot be an absolute, arbitrary power over their lives and fortunes, which are as much as possible to be preserved; but a power to make laws, and annex such penalties to them, as may tend to the preservation of the whole, by cutting off those parts, and those only, which are so corrupt, that they threaten the sound and healthy, without which no severity is lawful. And *this power has its original only from compact and agreement, and the mutual consent of those who make up the community.*[130]

---

129. Grotius, *Hugo Grotius on the Rights of War and Peace,* 42.
130. Locke and Macpherson, ed., *Second Treatise of Government,* 89, (emphasis added).

What good is writing down the Constitution (the agreement) if we do not intend to hold the public officers to it? Do you treat your civil contracts in the same manner? If so, watch out; your fall is coming (and by the way, I have something to sell you). Similarly, the states could not exist, nor could they possess power, without the power of the people who created them. Thus, it was we the people of the states who created the contract of our federal governmental and its terms. We set forth our contract with the government, granting it certain specific and limited powers and stated the following to that effect:

> We the People of the United States, in Order to form a more perfect Union, establish Justice, insure domestic Tranquility, provide for the common defence, promote the general Welfare, and secure the Blessings of Liberty to ourselves and our Posterity, do ordain and establish this Constitution for the United States of America.[131]

How can the federal government say that its power is greater than that of the sovereigns of the states united, when the state sovereigns created it? The Constitution clearly states in Amendment 10, "The powers not delegated to the United States by the Constitution, nor prohibited by it to the States, are reserved to the States respectively, or to the people." Also in Amendment 9 it says, "The enumeration in the Constitution, of certain rights, shall not be construed to deny or disparage others retained by the people." In other words, how can the creature say that it is greater than the creator? We the people clearly set limits of government in the Constitution, and all government administrators are limited to the powers vested in the general government by the Constitution. Of course, the philosophical basis for this limitation was set forth in the Declaration of Independence, stating that governments derive their *just* powers from the consent of the governed. From this understanding, America's form and substance of government, as delineated in the Constitution, expressly conditions the power of government on (1) justice (consistent with the laws of nature and nature's God)

---

131. U.S. Constitution, Preamble.

and (2) the consent of the people in the states. Likewise, the states' powers are limited to those vested and granted to it by the people of that state. Thus, the concept of jurisdiction and federalism deeply indwell our nation and jurisprudence, all deriving their source from the concepts declared by natural law and revealed law, which were the underlying rationalizations for the philosophers and founders who formed our nation. Unfortunately, the practice of a true Republican form of government, whereby the federal government is limited to the *expressed* grants of power in the Constitution,[132] whereby the states retain sovereignty in *all* matters not expressly granted to the federal government, and whereby the people of the states retain ultimate control over all government as enforcers of the supreme law of the land (the Constitution), is virtually lost, ignored, and forgotten.

Let this be clear and understood, to contradict this understanding and implementation of limitations on our government (both federal and state) is to fail to submit ourselves unto the higher powers (Romans 13:1; KJV). Why? Because in America the government administrators are not the higher power, but rather it is we the people of the several sovereign states who formed a more perfect union; it is we the people of the states who retain the power of the government; it is we the people of the states who even created the state and federal governments; it is we the people of the states who retain the rights to amend, alter, or abolish the government we established; it is we the people of the states who set forth the limitations of our administrators. Gray observes and confirms this understanding about America, stating the following:

> The existence of governments with written constitutions has familiarized us, at least in the United States, with frequent and strict limitations upon the powers of the highest ordinary legislative bodies.[133]

---

132. "From the accepted doctrine that the United States is a government of delegated powers, it follows that those not expressly granted, or reasonably to be implied from such as are conferred, are reserved to the states, or to the people. To forestall any suggestion to the contrary, the Tenth Amendment was adopted. The same proposition, otherwise stated, is that powers not granted are prohibited." *United States v. Butler*, 297 U.S. 1, 68 (1936).

133. Gray, *The Nature and Sources of the Law*, 154. See Also, "The kings of the Gentiles exercise lordship over them; and they that exercise authority upon them are called benefactors.

Thus, the higher powers as referred to in Romans 13 are not George W. Bush, Bill Clinton, or Barack Hussein Obama; but rather, the higher powers are the sovereigns of the states united as defined by the Constitution of the United States, and if there are any people who still use those verses (after reading all of the evidence to the contrary herein) as an excuse not to resist, speak out, or criticize politicians who do not comply with the Constitution, then such persons are truly not being obedient to Romans 13. Our government administrators are not the higher powers; it is ultimately the Constitution of the United States that is the higher power. To suggest otherwise is to deny even the very existence of our Republican form of government; it is to deny America's heritage, where God's natural and revealed laws were the very foundation of our Constitution. It is, in fact, to reject the government that God has ordained in America.

Consider as well the inherent limitations of the United States' form of government, specifically that our government's expressed purpose is to secure justice—meaning to secure what is right and wrong. While many would suggest that governmental power is defined as a set of rules commanding citizens to maintain certain and specific conduct of prescription and proscription without reference to right and wrong, such a concept is not what founded this nation. In other words, if our government is not complying with its expressed purposes, it is acting outside of its scope and authority.

But ye shall not be so: but he that is greatest among you, let him be as the younger; and he that is chief, as he that doth serve." Luke 22:25–26 (KJV). "God's warning [to Israel concerning their asking for a king] was directed at more than monarchy: It is a warning against big government generally, a warning of what happens when God's model government [in 1 Samuel 8], a republic of limited powers, is rejected... The American notion that government ought to be the servant of the people, not exercise dominion over them, may be traced directly to 1 Samuel 8 and Luke 22." John W. Robbins, *Freedom and Capitalism: Essays on Christian Politics and Economics,* (Unicoi, TN, The Trinity Foundation, 2006), 33. See Also, God has established His constitution in writing as well and will judge everyone according to the written constitutin of God. "And if any man shall take away from the words of the book of this prophecy, God shall take away his part out of the book of life, and out of the holy city, and from the things which are written in this book." Revelation 22:19 (KJV). "And Jesus answered him, saying, 'It is written, That man shall not live by bread alone, but by every word of God.'" Luke 4:4 (KJV). "I will worship toward thy holy temple, and praise thy name for thy lovingkindness and for thy truth: *for thou hast magnified thy word above all thy name.*" Psalms 138:2 (KJV) (Emphasis added).

Indeed, William Blackstone deduced that municipal government derives its power from the people, who have a natural right to form a government that preserves and protects the natural rights granted to each individual from God. He defined it as follows: "Municipal law is a rule of civil conduct prescribed by the supreme power in a state commanding what is right, and prohibiting what is wrong."[134]

Notice that according to Blackstone government must consider what is right and what is wrong, not as ordained by man, but as ordained by God. It was discussed throughout Blackstone's *Commentaries*. How else can rights be established where there is no absolute right or wrong as defined by some source other than human whim? Consider that America's dictionaries once reflected Blackstone's definition of *tyranny* as an "arbitrary or despotic exercise of power; the exercise of power over subject and others with a rigor not authorized by law or justice, or not requisite for the purposes of government."[135] That is opposed to the modern definition of tyranny being "government by a tyrannical ruler,"[136] without any reference to authority, justice, or the purposes of government. Such a small observation is indeed descriptive and telling of America's outlook of government. Furthermore, Blackstone acknowledged that the government *must* comply with the compact (the Constitution) created by the people. "A compact is a promise proceeding from us...in compacts we ourselves determine and promise what shall be done, before we are obliged to do it."[137] Therefore, government is bound by the terms of its compact with the people, according to the limits of the Constitution, to do that which is right and punish that which is wrong. Again, these are America's higher powers.

It is very important to take a moment to expound further this concept of *compact*, as used by William Blackstone. Black's Law Dictionary (the most widely recognized and used legal dictionary in America)[138] defines a compact

---

134. Blackstone, *Commentaries on the Laws of England,* 45.

135. Noah Webster, *An American Dictionary of the English Language,* Third Edition, Abridged from the Quarto Edition of the Author, (New York: S. Converse, 1830), 865.

136. Ehrlich, Carruth, Hawkins, and Flexner, *Oxford American Dictionary,* 998.

137. Blackstone, *Commentaries on the Laws of England,* 35.

138. "Black's Law Dictionary," *Wikipedia,* (accessed May 5, 2009), http://en.wikipedia.org/wiki/Black%27s_Law_Dictionary.

as "an agreement or covenant between two or more parties, esp. between governments or states."[139] Many business persons can relate to this concept because of the number of contracts entered into between parties in business. Throughout America, courthouse dockets are filled with civil lawsuits where a non-breaching party sues the breaching party for breach of a contract and resulting damages. But to address this matter elementary one must understand that there are certain inherent elements to a compact: (1) an agreement must be made, (2) the agreement creates an obligation (or duty) to one or both parties, (3) the terms must be complied with by both parties, and (4) both parties have the right to terminate the contract or enforce the compliance of such against the other party. The states who formed the Constitution have all rights and powers to ensure that the other party (the federal government) complies with the terms set forth therein. Thus, as founding father James Wilson states,

> The measures of this power, and the limits, beyond [the Constitution] he cannot extend it, are circumscribed and regulated by the same authority, and with the same precision, as the measures of the subject's obedience; and limits, beyond which he is under no obligation to practice it, are fixed and ascertained. Liberty is, by the constitution, of equal stability, of equal antiquity, and of equal authority, with prerogative. The duties of the king and those of the subject are plainly reciprocal: they can be violated on neither side, unless they be performed on the other.
>
> Of this great compact between the king and his people, one essential article to be performed on his part is, that, in those cases where provision is expressly made and limitations set by the laws, his government shall be conducted according to those provisions, and restrained according to those limitations.[140]

Can a person violate the laws and, say, kill his neighbor without repercussion? No. And why not? Because the states' body politic (that is, the people) have entered into a compact to establish government through the Constitution to protect their rights. Thus, when someone violates the rights of a citizen, the

---

139. Gardner, Ed., *Black's Law Dictionary.*
140. Compiled by a member of the Philadelphia Bar, *American Oratory,* 8.

state is obligated to punish the wrongdoer. There is an obligation on the citizen to comply with the laws that conform to the Constitution, and there is an obligation on the state to comply with the laws that conform to the Constitution. The obligation is bi-conditional. The government can no more violate the Constitution than a citizen can. No person (government administrator or not) has a right to violate the contract that all agreed to follow. Would anyone doubt the existence of such rights in business terms or private terms? Why then would there be any doubt relating to governments and the people? Certainly our founders did not accept the powerless notion many have today, but rather the very nature of a compact necessarily means that the party who created the compact has the power to ensure its compliance and enforce its terms.

COMPACTS BIND EVEN GOD

For those who are looking for additional biblical reasons to require the strict compliance of the Constitution, let us consider that God binds Himself to compacts—covenants—not because the covenant was a natural law or command of God, but because He and another party entered into the agreement. He has complied with the terms set forth and agreed upon by Himself and Abraham, Israel, the body of Christ, and even mankind in general (e.g., the flood). If our government administrators are not bound by the terms of America's compact, what sense can be made of the fact that even God holds Himself to compacts? Would not a Christian who believes that God binds Himself to His promises of, say, allowing you to enter into heaven by receiving the gift of salvation through His Son, Jesus Christ, expect God to keep that promise? How disappointing for you if He did not.

So on what grounds do you expect God to keep His covenant with you? After all, God is the Creator of all things and all powerful—the ultimate authority; can He not decide to throw you in hell, even though you have complied with what He has promised would save you from hell? Who are you to demand that God comply with His promises? Well, you might respond with, "God is just and righteous, and He cannot contradict what He promised to do." Rightly put. And for this reason we are to demand even more fervently the compliance of our compacts with government, because government administrators are not inherently just and righteous, as God is, but are disposed to and susceptible to evils—all the more reason that you should require them to follow the agreement. Thus, applying the same principle to mere humans, all of whom are born equal with no right to rule over others, does it not make even more sense that requiring government to comply with their promise is in fact natural and even biblical?

Look at the following verses revealing the numerous times that God binds His actions to the covenant (compact) He made with certain persons and nations:

> And I will remember my **covenant**, which is between me and you and every living creature of all flesh; and the waters shall no more become a flood to destroy all flesh. (Genesis 9:15; kjv)

> And I will establish my **covenant** between me and you and your seed after you in their generations for an everlasting **covenant**, to be a God unto you, and to your seed after you. (Genesis 17:7; kjv)

> And the LORD said to Moses, "Write these words, for in accordance with these words I have made a **covenant** with you and with Israel." So he was there with the LORD forty days and forty nights. He neither ate bread nor drank water. And he wrote on the tablets the words of the **covenant**, the Ten Commandments. When Moses came down from Mount Sinai, with the two tablets of the testimony in his hand as he came down from the mountain, Moses did not know that the skin of his face shone because he had been talking with God. (Exodus 34:27–29; esv)

> And if you shall despise my statutes, or if your soul abhor my judgments, so that you will not do all my commandments, but that you break my **covenant**. (Leviticus 26:15; kjv)

> (For the LORD thy God is a merciful God) he will not forsake you, neither destroy you, nor forget the **covenant** of your fathers which he sware unto them. (Deuteronomy 4:31; kjv)

> Keep therefore the words of this **covenant**, and do them, that you may prosper in all that you do. (Deuteronomy 29:9; kjv)

And an angel of the LORD came up from Gilgal to Bochim, and said, I made you to go up out of Egypt, and have brought you unto the land which I swore unto your fathers; and I said, I will never break my **covenant** with you. (Judges 2:1; KJV)

And the anger of the LORD was hot against Israel; and he said, "Because that this people hath transgressed my **covenant** which I commanded their fathers, and have not hearkened unto my voice." (Judges 2:20; KJV)

But when Christ had offered for all time a single sacrifice for sins, he sat down at the right hand of God, waiting from that time until his enemies should be made a footstool for his feet. For by a single offering he has perfected for all time those who are being sanctified. And the Holy Spirit also bears witness to us; for after saying, "This is the **covenant** that I will make with them after those days, declares the Lord: I will put my laws on their hearts, and write them on their minds." (Hebrews 10:12–16; ESV)

Clearly, God takes His compacts seriously and actually and literally binds His own conduct to those compacts—quite an amazing thought. Is government greater than God? To suggest that America's Constitution is nothing more than a mortal, outdated, and errant document and thus not worthy of strict compliance is to ignore the natural law and biblical principle established by God Himself that all compacts are to be complied with and enforced. Again, if it is flawed, then the Constitution provides a way for the people of the states to amend it.

God binds Himself to compacts just as fervently and strictly as He binds Himself to the laws of nature. When God created matter, earth, the universe, animals, and humans, He created certain immutable laws of nature, which He has bound Himself to since the beginning of creation. Grotius observes this when he states, "natural Law is so immutable that it cannot be changed by God himself... God himself allows himself to be judged of by this rule."[141]

---

141. Grotius, *Hugo Grotius on the Rights of War and Peace*, 4–5.

With the same adherence, God does not breach His covenants. So should government be allowed to conduct its actions with more authority, autonomy, and affinity than God the Creator of all there is? How absurd is the thought or even the suggestion. After all, are not government administrators ministers (or agents) of God? How can an agent of God be given more authority, discretion, and leeway than God Himself demonstrates? If the Creator (who is able to destroy both the soul and body)[142] observes limitations of authority by natural law and by compact, even while He possesses all authority in all that exists, how much more or less should individuals, communities, and nations observe the compacts that they have entered into?

It must be concluded then that government (specifically America's government) and its administrators are indeed limited in scope, authority, and action and must comply with all limitations as set forth in the Constitution, which was created by the sovereign states' body politic. Actions outside of their lawful and prescribed authority are null and void, and it is the right and duty of Americans to enforce the terms of the contract designed for the security of our unalienable rights, not only for our current generation, but also for our posterity.[143] The only question is do we care enough to do anything about it?

---

142. Matthew 10:28 (KJV).

143. "[The legislative power] is not, nor can possibly be absolutely arbitrary over the lives and fortunes of the people: for it being but the joint power of every member of the society given up to that person, or assembly, which is legislator; it can be no more than those persons had in a state of nature before they entered into society, and gave up to the community: for no body can transfer to another more power than he has in himself; and no body has an absolute arbitrary power over himself, or over any other, to destroy his own life, or take away the life or property of another. A man, as has been proved, cannot subject himself to the arbitrary power of another; and having in the state of nature no arbitrary power over the life, liberty, or possession of another, but only so much as the law of nature gave him for the preservation of himself, and the rest of mankind; this is all he cloth, or can give up to the common-wealth, and by it to the legislative power, so that the legislative can have no more than this. Their power, in the utmost bounds of it, is limited to the public good of the society. It is a power, that hath no other end but preservation, and therefore can never have a right to destroy, enslave, or designedly to impoverish the subjects. The obligations of the law of nature cease not in society, but only in many cases are drawn closer, and have by human laws known penalties annexed to them, to inforce their observation. Thus the law of nature stands as an eternal rule to all men, legislators as well as others. The rules that they make for other men's actions, must, as well as their own and other men's actions, be conformable to the law of nature, i.e. to the will of God, of which that is a declaration, and the fundamental law of nature being the preservation of mankind, no human sanction can be good, or valid against it." Locke and Macpherson, ed., *Second Treatise of Government*, 70.

11

ORDINATION OF
GOVERNMENT

Most Christians are familiar with words from Romans 13 (KJV), "Let every soul be subject unto the higher powers. For there is no power but of God: the powers that be are ordained of God." In modern America, these verses are perhaps the most highly referred to biblical support for being passive or compliant towards matters of state. Unfortunately, the distorted and misapplied conclusions derived from these verses have created much indifference, lethargy, and harmful attitudes about a citizen's duty concerning freedom. Indeed, such interpretations are not biblically accurate. Also, such an approach was not the understanding of the vast majority of Christians during America's founding (with the exception of conscientious objectors, such as the Quakers). The question is what does *ordained* mean, and how does it apply? The understanding of what is ordained should influence one's response to and interaction with government, for when certain government administrators or government actions contradict the ordination of God, there would be no command or duty to submit.

The first logical starting point of discussion would be to define *ordained* according to its original language. The actual Greek meaning of *ordained* is "to arrange in an orderly manner; to addict, appoint, determine, ordain, set."[1] The way some refer to God's ordination of government would suggest that God has conveyed to all government a free, simple, absolute title to power, regardless of natural rights and justice. However, this is not true in the slightest degree. There are essentially three possible applications of this meaning. First, that God arranges all government, including its administrators, with no conditions, limitations, or standards. Second, that God arranges government and its administrators when such government follows certain conditions, limitations, or standards. Third, that God arranges the institution of government, or in other words, the form of government. (The application of such interpretation actually conforms more to the literal meaning of the words *arrangement* or *form*.) Essentially for sake of argument, the second and third proposed approaches to *ordained* can be consolidated into one approach (that is God's ordination of government is limited and conditional), leaving only two main proposed approaches or interpretations of *ordained*.

Once the responsible citizen has come to grips with the truth of this matter, two possibilities result in the life of the citizen: (1) the citizen has an inherent duty to engage and correct government and to ensure that government operates within its natural and compact limitations, or (2) the citizen should not be involved in government whatsoever and should suffer whatever evils the government distributes to the citizens. There is no middle ground. Thus, you must analyze and reach a conclusion about these two interpretations of ordination of God, because they are likely to be the crux of the issue facing many Christian-Americans.

OPTION 1—GOD'S ORDINATION OF GOVERNMENT IS LIMITED AND CONDITIONAL

To reach the conclusion that government is limited, another truth must exist: someone or something else must be superior to government. That someone or something else must possess authority above and independent of government. This premise must be established, because without a higher

---

1. Strong, *Strong's Exhaustive Concordance of the Bible,* 71.

authority over government, there is no higher authority than government; it is the strong arm of the law. If you disagree, commit a few crimes and see what happens to you. Or alternatively, there would be no authority on earth higher than whoever is the strongest at the time—whether it be a mob, gang, or otherwise. As to the first premise, the Bible repeatedly and clearly states that *all* power belongs to God—no other person or persons possess this title. Second Corinthians 5:18 (KJV) states, "All things are of God, who has reconciled us to himself by Jesus Christ, and has given to us the ministry of reconciliation." Matthew 28:18 (KJV) states, "Jesus came and spoke unto them, saying, *All power is given unto me in heaven and in earth*" (emphasis added). God affirms that all power is His and His alone. Thus, if there are any authorities whatsoever on earth, they must necessarily derive their authority from the One who possesses that authority to begin with. Such an acknowledgment was made by the Roman centurion (military leader) who recognized the authority that Jesus possessed while He was on earth; and in fact, the centurion used the analogy of his position as a military leader to communicate to Jesus that he understood that Jesus possessed authority over life and death. The conversation is as follows:

> The centurion answered [Jesus] and said, Lord, I am not worthy that thou shouldest come under my roof: but speak the word only, and my servant shall be healed. *For I am a man under authority, having soldiers under me: and I say to this man, Go, and he goeth; and to another, Come, and he cometh; and to my servant, Do this, and he doeth it.*[2]

The key theme thus to understanding the ordination of something is to understand the authority to do something. Here, we see that the Roman centurion recognized that Jesus possessed not only the power to heal, but also the authority to heal, just as the centurion possessed the power to command his soldiers because he had the authority to command his soldiers. Certainly the Roman centurion would not have used such an analogy to communicate

---

2. Matthew 8:8–9 (KJV), (emphasis added).

the understanding of authority where there was not the understanding that before a military leader can command orders he has to have the authority to command the orders. Of course, there can be no argument that scriptures reveal that God is the ultimate and complete authority over all there is, both in heaven and in earth:

The LORD will reign forever and ever.[3]

O LORD, God of our fathers, are you not God in heaven? You rule over all the kingdoms of the nations. In your hand are power and might, so that none is able to withstand you.[4]

The LORD is king forever and ever; the nations perish from his land.[5]

For kingship belongs to the LORD, and he rules over the nations.[6]

For the LORD is a great God, and a great King above all gods.[7]

To the King of ages, immortal, invisible, the only God, be honor and glory forever and ever. Amen.[8]

And they sing the song of Moses, the servant of God, and the song of the Lamb, saying, "Great and amazing are your deeds, O Lord God the Almighty! Just and true are your ways, O King of the nations!"[9]

Thus, it necessarily and shortly follows that all power derives from the All-Powerful, the Creator God, and that no authority or ordination exists

---

3. Exodus 15:18 (ESV).
4. 2 Chronicles 20:6 (ESV).
5. Psalms 10:16 (ESV).
6. Psalms 22:28 (ESV).
7. Psalms 95:3 (ESV).
8. 1 Timothy 1:17 (ESV).
9. Revelation 15:3 (ESV).

in any person or persons without a direct assignment of that power from God. To suggest otherwise would be like saying the Roman centurion has authority to order his soldiers to fight for the enemy simply because he has the power to order them in the field of battle. To the contrary, the Roman centurion would have the authority to order his soldiers to do this or that for the expressed purpose of achieving justice—the proper scope of his authority passed down by the ultimate Superior—God. Therefore, the proper and true understanding of ordination and power is to understand proper authority, in that, the inferior has no more power than what the superior grants to him, under the conditions, scope, and limits set forth by the superior. This is a legal principle that has been overwhelmingly accepted as fact throughout the ages of history, and certainly cannot be denied today.

Most people who believe in God at all have no problems accepting the fact that God is all powerful with all authority, and stemming from such a belief, would likely concede that the inferior (e.g., government) must comply with the limitations of power and authority granted to it by the One who possesses all authority and all power (i.e., God). Thus, the next premise to be established is whether or not God assigns unlimited authority and power to any and all government and its administrators. This premise is necessary because if all power comes from God, then it must be established in what manner, in what scope, and to what degree God conveys His authority to others. In other words, it must be determined if God places limitations and conditions on His conveyance of authority. If God does not place limitations on government and simply ordains any and all actions of government as if all government is of God, then serious problems result. In conjunction with this determination is also the determination of God's commands regarding the submission of that authority—that is, does God command absolute obedience without regard to justice, or does God limit submission to the purposes expressed by God.

It must first be noted that nowhere in Romans 13 does God require the absolute or unconditional obedience to all government. Such a commandment would completely defy all biblical understanding and reference to God being the all-powerful and all-authority. Rather, God only commands that citizens be subject unto the higher powers, acknowledging that (1) submission does not necessarily equate to obedience, and (2) the higher powers are not the Highest power. Furthermore, God qualifies His command that citizens submit to the higher powers in that the higher powers must (1) be ordained of God, (2) be ministers of God, and (3) accomplish the natural law purposes of promoting good and punishing evil—*justice*. The apostle Paul is simply regurgitating what is confirmed throughout the Old Testament (of which he was *very* familiar) in verses like Proverbs 16:12 (ESV), where it states, "It is a hateful thing for kings to commit wickedness; for the throne is established by righteousness." Already, it is clear that submission does not mean absolute obedience but is conditioned on the qualifiers of God.

The reality that God limits both the authority of government and the submission of the citizen is further established by additional language in Romans 13 conditioning the citizen's duty to submit upon certain qualifying factors noted herein. After reviewing the proper authority, purpose, and scope of the higher powers, God (through the apostle Paul) tells us that it is *for this cause* that we pay tribute (taxes). The phrase "for this cause" places a clear condition on paying tribute. This conditional phrase has the context of the legal application of the term, *condition subsequent,* which means this: "a condition that, if it occurs, will bring something else to an end."[10] Thus, put another way, as long as government is ordained of God, you should pay tribute. Clearly, God expects that citizens should support a government that qualifies as ordained of God, because God's will is that mankind live in peace. However, this rule of law would require the opposite to be true. God does not command that a citizen submit to a government that contradicts God's ordination and arrangement of government. Thus, using inductive reasoning as described herein, if government is *not* ordained of God, then there is no duty to support or submit to that government.

God gives an even more descriptive scope of the limits of the submission to higher powers, because God reveals in addition to all of the other qualifications of submission and authority that all of this is to be governed by our conscience, meaning that submission to government should not be based upon fear (unless of course you are a citizen who is doing evil).[11] But rather,

---

10. Garner, ed., *Black's Law Dictionary.*

11. "For rulers are not a terror to good conduct, but to bad. Would you have no fear of the one who is in authority? Then do what is good, and you will receive his approval, for he is God's servant for your good. *But if you do wrong, be afraid,* for he does not bear the sword in vain. For

submission to government should be based upon the internal and external acknowledgement of accomplishing justice, knowing that when government is ordained of God, it accomplishes its God-given purposes. Given the plain reading and understanding of all of scripture and a study of Romans 13, it cannot be reasonably argued that God demands that all citizens (Christian or not) pay tribute and submit to a government that is punishing good and promoting evil; a government that is unauthorized to act with its power; a government that violates its agreement with the people; or a government that oppresses and rules arbitrarily.

So how can a Christian person—in good conscience (an element of submission required by God)—support a government that contradicts the expressed purpose and authority of the higher powers and that punishes good and promotes evil? How can a Christian person declare with conviction—in good conscience—that we must submit ourselves to those who claim authority over us—as so-called ministers of God—when in belief, practice, philosophy, and application they are ministers of evil? Did God anticipate that the Romans 13 minister of God would be an antichrist, an abomination of God, or a despiser of justice? Absolutely not. God cannot ordain both good and evil at the same time. God has already stated His purpose of government in Romans 13 (as in other New Testament scriptures) as well as throughout the Old Testament. "So says Jehovah, Keep judgment and do justice; for My salvation is near to come, and My righteousness to be revealed."[12]

Did God expect that the Romans 13 minister of God would be one who blasphemes the thought of natural laws established by God? Absolutely not. God cannot create laws of right and wrong for all men to live by and then command men to submit themselves under man's laws which contradict God's laws. Talk about confusion, and we know that God is not the author of confusion.[13] God cannot proclaim that one thing is righteous on one hand and then condemn it as evil on the other. Did Romans 13 intend

---

he is the servant of God, an avenger who carries out God's wrath on the wrongdoer," (emphasis added). Romans 13:3–4 (ESV).

12. Isaiah 56:1 (ESV).

13. "For God is not the author of confusion, but of peace, as in all churches of the saints." 1 Corinthians 14:33 (KJV).

to nullify all of the other biblical references to resisting evil—even if that evil is derived from government? Absolutely not. Did Romans 13 intend to void verses of scripture like Proverbs 28:4 (ESV), which states, "Those who forsake the law praise the wicked, but those who keep the law strive against them"? Absolutely not. To the contrary, just (or righteous) persons have no choice but to insist that their government follow the laws that God created all men to follow. Such is the basis of justice, and such is the commandment of God.

Grotius makes a similarly analogous and compelling argument when applying the meaning of ordination of government. He claims that if the means of government, that is paying taxes, is good, (which Romans 13 claims it is), then the end of taxes (government) must also be good. Therefore, it cannot be concluded that any evil government is ordained of God, because God would not have us do a good thing (paying taxes) to support an evil thing (government). He says the following:

> If a thing be good and right, the end to which it tends cannot be otherwise than good and right. Now to pay taxes is right, and is a thing even binding on the conscience, as the apostle Paul explains: but the end to which taxes are subservient, [that is, one end among others] is that the government may be able to maintain forces for the purpose of defending good citizens and restraining bad men.[14]

This is the very reason why Romans 13:5 interconnects the reasoning of "for this cause do we pay tribute" with "we do this for conscience sake." In other words, citizens should support their government when their government is performing its God-mandated function of punishing evil and promoting good. However, if its government is not fulfilling its God-mandated purpose, then in good conscience we cannot submit and also pay tribute to a government that promotes evil and punishes good. What kind of conscience would one have that would consider his godly duty fulfilled and satisfied by supporting a government that contradicts and punishes the very acts that

---

14. Grotius, *Hugo Grotius on the Rights of War and Peace*, 19.

God deems righteous and just? And please, spare me the argument that God hardens the hearts of princes and government leaders for His will, so who are we to question God's will? Do I dare classify such a position as completely and utterly stupid? Do you not consider that maybe God is hardening their hearts so that they can be destroyed by righteous and just people for righteousness sake, so that evil people may fear the punishment and righteousness of God here on earth, as they most certainly would at the judgment seat of God in heaven, and so that true ministers of God can effectuate a Romans 13 government? God has done it before, and He can do it again. "For it was the LORD's doing to *harden their hearts that they should come against Israel in battle, in order that they should be devoted to destruction and should receive no mercy but be destroyed,* just as the LORD commanded Moses."[15] To suggest somehow that God would have everyone suffer at the hands of tyrants, and that such a sacrifice pleases God, ignores the truth that "to do justice and judgment is more pleasing to Jehovah than sacrifice."[16] Are not justice and judgment the very reasons why God ordains government and why the people establish government? Certainly God did not establish government for sacrifice—that would be the role of individuals and churches, and there is not one verse (Old or New Testament) even to suggest that government was instituted to make sure people sacrifice for the sake of others. However, the Bible repeatedly confirms that government is ordained by God to do justice and judgment. Thus, according to Proverbs 21:3, God sees more righteousness in a nation that makes certain that its government implements justice and judgment than a nation that is all sacrifice (dare we say, religious), but its government is tyrannical.

Jesus in fact confirms this Proverbs 21:3 understanding when He addresses the Pharisees and Sadducees and accuses them of focusing on the less important matters of life (that is, sacrifice) and ignoring more important matters of life (that is, justice). Jesus says, "Woe unto you, scribes and Pharisees, hypocrites! For ye pay tithe of mint and anise and cummin, and have omitted the weightier matters of the law, judgment, mercy, and faith:

---

15. Joshua 11:20 (ESV). (emphasis added).
16. Proverbs 21:3 (MJKV).

these ought ye to have done, and not to leave the other undone."[17] Again, America will not be spared God's judgment because there are millions of Christians going to church, giving their money to church, and performing all of these sacrificial deeds in the name of God. But rather, America will only be spared when it does what God commands it to do within its God-established authority, scope, and limits.

Grotius certainly would agree with this, concluding that the government which maintains its purpose of defending good citizens and retraining bad men is the government God intended that we pay tribute to and that He ordains. Any other government is not ordained of God, does not have ministers of God, and should not be supported by the citizens. This argument implies and concludes that where government does not comport to its God-ordained role, then citizens would not be required to be subject unto it by obeying unlawful commands and paying taxes to support such an unordained government. In other words, those men who possess power under the authority of government are limited—limited by natural laws of God, the good and evil described in Romans 13. We must be willing to hold them accountable to this standard. Anything short is ungodly and unscriptural and unnatural. Of course, the Bible and history itself are clear that even while governments do not comply with their God-ordained functions, their citizens mostly submit to their laws for the sake of self-preservation (fear) or peace of society (convenience). The Bible is clear that we are to pray for peace and live peaceable as much as possible, just as our founders state in the Declaration of Independence that we should "suffer evils while evils are sufferable" (words described by John Locke in *Treatises on Government*).[18] However, such an obligation to pray for peace and to live in peace does not contradict the philosophy and understanding of God's ordination of limited government proposed during America's founding era. "Civil Society is the result, not of Divine precept, but of the experience of the weakness of separate families to protect themselves; and is thus called by Peter an ordinance of man, though it is also an ordinance of God, because He approves it."[19]

17. Maatthew 23:23 (KJV)
18. Locke, *Treatises on Government*, 386.
19. Grotius, *Hugo Grotius on the Rights of War and Peace*, 56.

When government contradicts the purposes revealed by God (to promote good and punish evil), He is not obligated to ordain such a government. Again, God does not sanction evil. To the contrary, God must judge that government (or more specifically those persons in power in the name of government) as He must judge all evil. As a result, such government does not possess God's ordination or arrangement of its authority—no more than a car thief holds title to it simply because he is in the driver's seat with the engine on driving down the road. Possession of a thing (yes, even the power to possess a thing) does not give right to the thing. Consequently, the citizens are not legally, morally, ethically, or spiritually bound to be subject unto those illegal and illegitimate powers. Furthermore, God's desire that we pray for peace and live in peace does not create an unconditional duty to obey government at all cost to the citizen. Rather, the Bible clearly expresses the same sentiment as Hugo Grotius noted previously: government is not a result of God's creation but is a result of man's creation; and for the sake of obtaining justice, God ordains government so that man may live in peace on earth, not so that men may live in tyranny on earth. In other words, we do not create government for the sake of putting people in power to enslave us for their benefit. We put them in power for the benefit and sake of society. Hence, "For the rulers are not a terror to good works, but to the bad. And do you desire to be not afraid of the authority? Do the good, and you shall have praise from it. For it is a servant of God to you for good. For if you practice evil, be afraid, for it does not bear the sword in vain; for it is a servant of God, a revenger for wrath on him who does evil."[20] This is the same concept that was long ago expressed in Proverbs 17:26 (MJKV). "[I]t is not good to punish the just, nor to strike princes for uprightness." For a person to strike a prince because of his uprightness—or justice, equity, and judgment—is evil and works contrary to the ordination of God; that is, to promote good and punish evil—to do justice. Conversely, for a person to strike a prince because he is not doing justice, equity and judgment—well, that is a different matter altogether, as clearly indicated by the language of that verse.

By way of comparison, most Christians do not have a hard time understanding that God has ordained the civil institution of marriage. So would

---

20. Romans 13:3–4 (MJKV).

you agree that God ordains every act of the spouse within the marriage, if you believe that God ordains all actions of government? Or would you, rather, state that God ordains the marriage union itself, but individual actions are judged independently of God's ordination of the institution of marriage? God ordained, or arranged, the act of marriage because "it was not good for man to be alone."[21] God knew that man would serve Him better with a help-meet. Can it be said that God ordains the actions of a husband who beats his wife, degrades her, and cheats on her? If not, why? Is it perhaps because God has set the criteria and conditions of a godly marriage? For example, "husbands, love your wives, and be not bitter against them"[22] and "love [your] wives as [your] own bodies. He that loves his wife loves himself."[23] If a man does not love his wife, and if he performs sinful acts upon her, would any reasonable person suggest that the wife (by God's command) is spiritually, morally, or physically bound to obey his commands and submit to all his demands, actions, or even to the marriage itself? The same principle applies to government.

To further discuss the matter relative to the limitations of authority and submission, one must recognize that there is a very important distinction and connection (as noted by Grotius prior) between God's ordaining (1) government in general (as described in Romans 13, where God gives His approval of the arrangement of government for the purposes expressed); and (2) the ordinances of man (as described in 1 Peter 2:13–14).[24] Put in another way, there are two types of ordinations described in the Bible: the ordination of form of government and laws of government. Thus, the scriptures depict two types of government ordinations that we are to submit to: the form of government found in Romans 13 and the laws of man found in 1 Peter 2—where those forms of government and laws of government comply with the stated purpose of God's ordination. Understand, scriptures do

---

21. Genesis 2:18 (KJV).
22. Colossians 3:19 (KJV).
23. Ephesians 5:28 (KJV).
24. "Submit yourselves to every ordinance of man for the Lord's sake: whether it be to the king, as supreme; Or unto governors, as unto them that are sent by him for the punishment of evildoers, and for the praise of them that do well." 1 Peter 2:13–14 (KJV).

not equate the form of government or the ordinances of man to the natural and revealed laws of God, as is clearly seen by the phrases "higher powers" and "ordinances of man," which are obviously not God's laws. Both passages of scripture give the command of submission as well as the conditions of submission relevant to both form and power. Moreover, in both references to submission to government, God reveals the qualifying factor of submission: promote good and punish evil—or in other words, to enforce *justice,* as all definitions of right and wrong come from God. Thus, even in the verses that some use to argue slave-like submission, God explicitly explains that the form of government and the laws of government are not above God's laws, which necessarily means that they are subordinate to God's laws. The implications are numerous, but suffice it to say, God expressly does not ordain illegitimate government for illegitimate purposes. Illegitimate government cannot legally possess form, title, and laws to promote good and punish evil, which are the expressed conditions of God's ordination.

Very obviously, the command to submit interdependently relates to: (1) the *laws* of God, (2) the *authority* of God, and (3) the *purposes* of God. As a result, God has conditioned our submission and support to government based upon the God-given laws (natural and revealed), authority, and purposes (the justice of God). No inference is even suggested in the previously mentioned verses that submission is mandatory to any person who has power (the mere possession or otherwise) without reference to any conditions, limitations, or standards. Rather, these verses clearly demonstrate that submission to ordinances and higher powers are required where the powers are legitimate and fulfill their lawful and God-ordained purpose. To suggest otherwise is to make ineffective the words plainly used in scripture. Therefore, the concept of ordained government is not simply any person in power of government but is rather government that has legitimately established form and authority to accomplish the purposes of God.

OPTION 2—GOD'S ORDINATION OF GOVERNMENT IS UNLIMITED AND UNCONDITIONAL

Accepting the alternative explanation of "submission to any government in power" leads to the conclusion that blind and unconditional submission is required for any governmental demand, no matter what. To conclude such, a statement has to be admitted: there is no authority superior to government on earth—not even God's authority—and no one has a right to resist (passively or actively) such authority. However, even if one accepts the notion of submission stated heretofore, the inquiry of ordination does not stop at who has power, because such a citizen must make a determination of whether or not that particular governmental power obtained such power lawfully. How can it be reasonably asserted that unconditional submission is required to that person or persons where they did not acquire the power within natural laws or within limits (assuming that you are interested in laws and limits) of a compact? That would be equivalent to saying that mere possession of a thing gives the right of title to the thing; such as when a thief steals a car, the possession of the car would give the thief ownership of the car. No one with any sense of justice would argue that such is true.[25] This matter of acquiring title and authority lawfully is common sense and has been accepted as a true principle that power must derive from a proper source. It is acknowledged by America's founders "to prove…that those acts are unconstitutional and void, is…altogether unnecessary… It rests upon plain and indubitable truths."[26] Since brute power alone is not (or should not be) the ultimate criteria for the determination of authority (and thus submission), the question then becomes how does one know what governmental power was acquired lawfully and thus ordained of God? In other words, how does one determine which particular authority in power is ordained of God?

The significance of this question is this: since the citizen must submit to the ordained government of God, he must know whether that particular government administration is indeed lawful and legitimate. After all, Jesus acknowledged the most important aspect of government—that being jurisdiction—and commanded that we are to render unto Caesar the things that are Caesar's and unto God the things that are God's. There is an element of not only position but also title. In other words, proper jurisdiction—meaning, legitimacy. To voluntarily submit to an illegitimate and unlawful power is to

---

25. "If also a man contend in the games, he is not crowned, except he have contended lawfully." 2 Timothy 2:5 (ASV).

26. Compiled by a member of the Philadelphia Bar, *American Oratory,* 7.

submit to be a slave. If you believe otherwise, would you submit to a military general from China who ordered you to fight on behalf of Muslim terrorists? Why not? After all, he is a general with authority and power. Obviously, the answer to this question is (1) the Chinese general has no jurisdiction in America, and (2) the cause for war is unjust. This refers to America's founding and the biblical principle of jurisdiction. From the beginning of time, those who believed in the natural and revealed laws of God recognized and acknowledged that actions conducted outside of proper jurisdiction are void and voidable.[27] Thus, an inquiry into the relevant factors to reach the conclusion of whether or not the person in power has legitimate authority is necessary. Ask the following questions: is submission required to the government power that takes control by force, by approval, by manipulation, by inheritance, and/or by transfer? All proposals are ways that government administration can be had—history proves this. For the sake of discussion, however, the polarized options in this list are *by force*—without consent of the people and without rights established by natural law (such as by a despot), and *by approval*—with consent of the people (such as by constitutional amendment approved by the states or people). The answer to this question should affect one's interpretation and relation to what "ordained of God" means and how it affects the issue of ordination and thus, submission.

If one accepts the interpretation of *ordained* to be governmental administration taken by force, he (1) ignores the obvious conditions and purposes God placed on ordained government; (2) accepts the fact that no person

---

27. "I doubt not but this will seem a very strange doctrine to some men: but before they condemn it, I desire them to resolve me, by what right any prince or state can put to death, or punish an alien, for any crime he commits in their country. It is certain their laws, by virtue of any sanction they receive from the promulgated will of the legislative, reach not a stranger: they speak not to him, nor, if they did, is he bound to hearken to them. The legislative authority, by which they are in force over the subjects of that commonwealth, hath no power over him. Those who have the supreme power of making laws in England, France or Holland, are to an Indian, but like the rest of the world, men without authority: and therefore, if by the law of nature every man hath not a power to punish offences against it, as he soberly judges the case to require, I see not how the magistrates of any community can punish an alien of another country; since, in reference to him, they can have no more power than what every man naturally may have over another." Locke and Macpherson, ed., *Second Treatise of Government,* 10.

living on this earth has any absolute, secured rights, as given by God; (3) accepts the fact that no one has any right to resist, change, petition, or participate in governmental change or action whatsoever, (4) accepts the notion that might makes right, for whoever wins power obtains the ordination of God; and (5) voluntarily puts himself into slavery, or alternatively, puts himself at war with the existing powers that be (if he chooses to conquer them and become the ordained power of God by virtue of his victory).[28]

If you disagree with these conclusions, which are based upon the position posed, then you necessarily advocate that the Chinese general previously referenced would have the authority to require you to aid Muslim terrorists were the Chinese government to take over the United States through whatever means, and your refusal to comply with such a demand would be sinning against God and your community. After all, would the Chinese general not be your higher power at that point? If you say no, then the only grounds upon which you can justify your argument is on the bases of jurisdiction, authority, or the natural laws of God. And of course, as soon as you do so, you must then admit that such a truth applies to all governments, and not just foreign. The fact is clear that America's forbearers rejected this slavish philosophy and understanding of ordination and submission, and they would not have considered your submission argument to be a friend of freedom.[29] Specifically, Algernon Sidney completely disagrees (as do our founding fathers, as expressed in the Declaration of Independence and U.S. Constitution) with this slave-producing philosophy and sheds light on what ordained government is and the fallacy of the position of might makes right. He says,

> But if it were possible, it could not be justifiable; and whilst our dispute is concerning right, that which ought not to be is no more

---

28. "[I]t is plain, that he that conquers in an unjust war can thereby have no title to the subjection and obedience of the conquered." Locke and Macpherson, ed., *Second Treatise of Government*, 92.

29. "Whosoever uses force without right, as every one does in society, who does it without law, puts himself into a state of war with those against whom he so uses it; and in that state all former ties are cancelled, all other rights cease, and every one has a right to defend himself, and to resist the aggressor." Ibid., 116.

to be received than if it could not be. No right can come by conquest, unless there were a right of making that conquest... No man
can justly impose any thing upon those who owe him nothing...[30]
Whosoever...grounds his pretensions of right upon usurpation and
tyranny, declares himself to be...an usurper and a tyrant, that is, an
enemy to God and man, and to have no right at all.

That which was unjust in its beginning, can of itself never
change its nature... He that persists in doing injustice, aggravates it,
and takes upon himself all the guilt of his predecessors. But if there
be a king in the world that claims a right by conquest, and would
justify it, he might do well to tell whom he conquered, when, with
what assistance, and upon what reason he undertook the war; for he
can ground no title upon the obscurity of an unsearchable antiquity;
and if he does it not, he ought to be looked upon as an usurping
Nimrod.[31]

Most people do not want to accept the notion that might makes right
(because it is contrary even to the conscience within us) but somehow are
not able to grasp the concept that government has limitations set forth by
God *and* by the people, and any such usurpations of those limits are evil
(even if apparently done with good intentions).[32] How can a person have it

---

30. Sidney, *Discourses on Government,* 354.

31. Ibid; "Though governments can originally have no other rise than that before
mentioned, nor polities be founded on any thing but the consent of the people; yet such have
been the disorders ambition has filled the world with, that in the noise of war, which makes so
great a part of the history of mankind, this consent is little taken notice of: and therefore many
have mistaken the force of arms for the consent of the people, and reckon conquest as one of the
originals of government. But conquest is as far from setting up any government, as demolishing
an house is from building a new one in the place. Indeed, it often makes way for a new frame of
a common-wealth, by destroying the former; but, without the consent of the people, can never
erect a new one." Locke and Macpherson, ed., *Second Treatise of Government,* 91.

32. "As conquest may be called a foreign usurpation, so usurpation is a kind of domestic
conquest, with this difference, that an usurper can never have right on his side, it being no
usurpation, but where one is got into the possession of what another has right to. This, so far as
it is usurpation, is a change only of persons, but not of the forms and rules of the government:
for if the usurper extend his power beyond what of right belonged to the lawful princes, or
governors of the commonwealth, it is tyranny added to usurpation." Ibid., 100.

both ways, stating that we must submit to government no matter how the governmental authority was acquired (e.g., by forceful conquest) while at the same time demanding and declaring that people have absolute rights, such as the right to life? And how can one claim that Christians should not meddle in politics, but at the same time he himself vote for the godly candidate who will uphold Christian values? Is his vote merely a gesture, or does he really believe in his right to change and affect government? Furthermore, who is such a person to require government administrators to follow only certain provisions (in the Constitution) of their limitations but not other provisions? Or even more drastically put, who is the person to demand that citizens are to submit to and pay tribute to a higher power that has no legitimate authority, promotes evil, and punishes good? Do not the scriptures warn against any person who adds or takes away from the Bible?[33] Who made such a person prophet, priest, king, and final authority on the matter? Who granted him the ability to waive governmental limitations at the expense of other citizens' rights? To participate in government in any way necessarily implies that such a person claims interest in governmental affairs, and moreover that he has the personal right to influence what government does, and that there are certain matters worth being involved in for the purpose of protecting what he believes to be valuable or a right.

Rights of man and limitations of government are not based upon opinions; they are based upon human nature as revealed in natural and revealed law. Put another way, if the people have the right to vote—or the right to life for that matter—and participate in government, then the right must be based upon some fundamental concept independent from the government and citizen itself, such as what our founders declared: God is the author and giver of life, liberty, and property, and that government does not have ultimate authority on the matter. What authority does a citizen have to persuade government somehow, if that person believes that all government is ordained of God and that all citizens must submit to all government actions? Such a position is hypocritical, contradictory, and cowardly. By enforcing and

---

33. "And if anyone takes away from the Words of the Book of this prophecy, God will take away his part out of the Book of Life, and out of the holy city, and from the things which have been written in this Book." Revelation 22:19 (MJKV).

implementing rights, by voting and getting involved in government, that person is demonstrating that government is not God, and that the power of the people should matter and should make a difference in governmental affairs. If such a person believed that all government was ordained, and that citizens should submit themselves to every ordinance of government and man, then to suggest that the government must respect rights given by God would contradict their proposal of ordination and submission; and furthermore, such a person (whether knowingly or not) accepts the description of right as the following: "what [the] stronger party likes."[34]

LIMITATIONS OF GOVERNMENT CONFIRMED

The fact is natural law, revealed law, human history, and American history all reveal that God does not ordain all government and all ordinances of man and does not give to government all authority. Rather, God Himself retains all power, and certain power is delegated to certain jurisdictions to accomplish His will as has already been proven. He has given limited authority to the husband, to the wife, to the father, to the mother, to the pastor, to the employer, to the church, and to the government. All power is subject to the ordinances of God relative to the rights granted by God to individuals, relative to the limitations of government found in nature and revealed law and relative to the constitution/compact set forth by the people of a nation. Just as a child is not obligated to submit to a kidnapper, a wife is not obligated to submit to an abusive husband, a church member is not obligated to submit to an infidel pastor, or an employee is not obligated to submit to an embezzling employer, so too the citizen is not obligated to submit to the abusive, power-usurping, illegitimate government. If you disagree, on what basis do you distinguish the wife's ability to resist an abusive husband, a child's ability to resist a kidnapper, or a church member's ability to resist an infidel pastor? They are all based upon the same principles: authority and jurisdiction.

For those who would argue that God ordains all government regardless of the natural and contractual limitations imposed by God and by the people,

---

34. Grotius, *Hugo Grotius on the Rights of War and Peace,* 18, xxvi.

would they argue as well that no person has a right to defend his home or protect his family from the outside invader who comes in to destroy it? After all, does not the Bible teach us to love our enemies?[35] Does not the Bible tell us to turn the other cheek?[36] Does not the Bible command us to sell what we have and give to the poor?[37] Of course, many Christians feel they can justify the personal self-defense application, because it involves physical threat, and of course God allows us to resist physical threat! However, would they not also accept the notion that a person can preemptively resist and oppose an invader who has the apparent and imminent ability and intent to harm him or his family? Likewise, would they not accept the notion that a nation can preemptively cause a defensive war against another nation that has demonstrated the apparent and imminent ability and intent to shoot nuclear missiles on the nonaggressive nation? How then can they not accept the notion that a citizen can preemptively resist a government's apparent and imminent ability and intent to take away God-given rights other than life, such as property or liberty? If God ordained your government to circumvent your rights (as you propose), how much less did God ordain the foreign government to do the same? Using the example above, how do you know that God did not ordain that Chinese military general to command you to become a terrorist? Who are you to pick and choose which governments God ordains to take away rights? If you presume to know, on what basis do you make your determination? And if you in fact make such a determination, what sources control your determination? Are those sources independent from your own personal opinion, and do they rest on the immutable and natural laws of God? If not, then what makes your opinion better than the Chinese military general's opinion? Are you the determiner of which nations have jurisdiction to trample on rights? Heck, do you even think there are such things as rights? Do you accept that *all* laws are justified and lawful (under

---

35. "But I say to you who hear, love your enemies, do good to those who hate you." Luke 6:27 (ESV).

36. "But I say to you, do not resist the one who is evil. But if anyone slaps you on the right cheek, turn to him the other also." Matthew 5:39 (ESV).

37. "Jesus said to him, 'If you would be perfect, go, sell what you possess and give to the poor, and you will have treasure in heaven; and come, follow me.'" Matthew 19:21 (ESV).

man *and* God), where the purpose, scheme, and pattern of laws deteriorate notions of fundamental rights and freedom as found in human nature? Do you accept that citizens should become slaves first before taking any action to preserve the right to life or property? Understand this historical, legal, and philosophical fact: the rationalization of self-defense against individuals or governments or foreign nations is the same regardless of whether or not the attack focuses on life, property, liberty, or whether or not the attack is foreign or domestic.[38] Rights are all gifts from God, and every individual is entitled to them without unlawful intrusion from anyone or any government. Without the equally vigorous protection of all freedoms and rights, all rights are equally subject to destruction. This is why all constitutional provisions are indeed important and crucial to the survival of freedom in a nation.

Fortunately, in America it is very easy to use the above approach of being subject unto the higher powers against the person who refuses to demand governmental compliance to God's purposes and to its constitutional limits, because America's philosophy, form, and substance of government necessarily requires that the government's action comply with the Constitution, and that we retain the power of government and oversee its administrators. America is not a monarchy, aristocracy, or oligarchy. America is a constitutional republic—a luxury that most generations throughout human history were not blessed to experience, and as a result, many died at the hands of their own government. Some Christians would suggest that God's sovereignty will take care of all of that, as if the deaths of millions are the price we should bear for the sake of submission—how indifferent and ludicrous. Thomas Paine reflects the understanding that America has no king but the supreme law of the Constitution founded in the natural and revealed laws of God, saying,

---

38. "I do solemnly swear (or affirm) that I will support and defend the Constitution of the United States against all enemies, *foreign and domestic;* that I will bear true faith and allegiance to the same; that I take this obligation freely, without any mental reservation or purpose of evasion; and that I will well and faithfully discharge the duties of the office on which I am about to enter. So help me God." Smith, *Constitution of the United States with the Amendments Thereto,* 270, (emphasis added).

But where says some is the King in America? I'll tell you friend, he reigns above, and doth not make havock of mankind like the Royal Brute of Britain. Yet that we may not appear to be defective even in earthly honors, let a day be solemnly set apart for proclaiming the charter; let it be brought forth placed on the divine law, the word of God; let a crown be placed thereon, by which the world may know, that so far as we approve of monarchy, that in America THE LAW IS KING. For as in absolute governments the King is law, so in free countries the law *ought* to be King; and there ought to be no other.[39]

Indeed, America's higher powers do not belong to any person, but rather they belong to the foundational laws of our country detailed in the Constitution of the United States of America, which recognizes the right of the people to maintain their republican form of government, that the power of government rests in the people, and that the Constitution is supreme. There is no person above it. Government administrators are simply the ministers of God and the people, servants of the Constitution, and answerable to God and the people under the Constitution for all their actions. Moreover, the Constitution itself is founded on the principles of natural and revealed laws and rights from God, and it attempts as much as humanly possible to protect and secure those rights for the people—not for the government. It is for this reason that these indifferent and submissive Christians are able to peaceably enjoy society without being destroyed by their own government. Indeed, they are reaping the benefits of the arduous labor of their forbearers, who if alive would likely want to either tar and feather them or take them to the nearest tree with a short rope, treating them as traitors to the ideals that thousands bled and died to secure and protect. Ultimately, we have a duty and right to abolish, alter, or destroy any form, substance, or administration of government that becomes destructive to these ends, because "that which can ratify, can destroy."[40] This is the country we live in. This is the form of govern-

---

39. Paine, *Common Sense*, 34.
40. Compiled by a member of the Philadelphia Bar, *American Oratory*, 8.

ment we live under. These are the requirements given to us by our founders. If you do not accept this, then you do not accept the ordination of God.

This understanding of American government begs the question which was raised earlier regarding how you determine which government is ordained by God or has acquired power lawfully. The question essentially becomes a matter of choosing this day whom you will serve instead. In other words, how can a person choose to submit to a manipulated form of government that contradicts the original form of American government, which was created to secure God-given rights? How can a citizen consciously choose to obey and submit to a government that steps outside of the parameters set forth by the sovereign body politic and secured by its form and substance of government in contradiction to Romans 13, "for this cause do we pay tribute"? The question is relevant because one who believes that all government is ordained by God—without limitation—still has to determine whether or not the current government has lawful power and not hijacked power. One's choice to ignore this matter brands himself lethargic and lazy relative to God and to government administration; he ignores the duty to submit to the higher powers; and he proves that the matter of submission is not one of conviction but convenience—and as such, is not worthy of being listened to. If submitting to ordained government is really so important to the point of allowing an entire nation to become slaves, then a deep understanding of the subject is required, and a choice of whom you will serve presents itself to you and your posterity. You may try to point to a different time and place when a group of Christians did not take up arms against their government (not to say that they did not have the right to—under God), but you do not live in the Middle East or Rome or China. You live in the United States of America, where God has ordained this government for this purpose under the authority granted in the natural and revealed laws of God. Who are you to take us back two thousand years into human history and demand that we invert the scripture that says, "To whom much is given much is required,"[41] and instead say, "to whom much is given, much lethargy is required"? Without question, it was the persecution of early Christians that caused a massive migration of people

---

41. Luke 12:48 (KJV).

out of those torturous regimes and into places of respite, if they were that fortunate. Do you not think that those people would not have given all they had to be under the higher powers of the United States of America, a nation established on the laws of God? Yet, there are some who act like a contestant on a game show regarding how they treat submission to government, as if no matter what their choice, no real harm can come from it. Undoubtedly, history confirms that America's higher power is the Constitution of the United States, and any power acted outside of the Constitution falls outside of the lawfully acquired power necessary to be ordained of God. So what does the submit-to-all-government person do with that fact?

If such persons lived in Iraq, China, Sudan, Chile, North Korea, or Afghanistan,[42] perhaps their opinion on governments ordained of God would be different. Perhaps they would not be so indifferent about the actions and intentions of their government administrators. Only in America, where freedom is assumed, do people hold the position that getting involved in politics is not Christian, because freedom was already paid for by other people's blood. What a disgrace. The fact remains, however, when the citizens fail to require that the government administration uphold, support, and defend the Constitution, they violate Romans 13 and 1 Peter 2, because our Constitution is the supreme law of the land. It is our higher power, and "all attempts to alter the charter or constitution…unless by the authority of its own legislature, are violations of its rights, and illegal,"[43] as James Wilson so plainly stated. If such a person has determined that the current distorted government administrators are ordained of God without reference to history, the Bible, jurisdiction, and the Constitution, then such a person automatically concludes that the original foundation of our government is to be refuted and buried with time and with those who created our original government. He personally and voluntarily chooses to determine which government was in fact ordained of God. So what makes such a person any better than the one who chooses to follow the mandates set forth by the sovereign states'

---

42. Michelle A. Vu, "Top 10 Worst Places to Live as a Christian," *The Christian Post,* (February 5, 2008), http://www.christianpost.com/article/20080205/top-10-worst-places-to-live-as-a-christian.htm.

43. Compiled by a member of the Philadelphia Bar, *American Oratory,* 9.

body politic—the true form of American government—and chooses to hold the agents of the people accountable to the terms of the Constitution that we all agreed to follow? Posterity will no doubt make the judgment of who is better.

If the view that we must submit to unlawful government is correct, then what right does that person have to insist that its government administrators follow any parameters set forth in the Constitution at all? Or what right does that person have to demand the right to vote, the right to a jury trial, the right to be free from unreasonable searches and seizures, the right to freedom of speech and religion, the right to be free from unusual punishment, or the right to keep and bear arms? Without the Constitution to secure them, the rights of American citizens are subject to the strongest will and wishes, and they become the rules of law that the citizen must follow. According to their definition of *ordained,* such government would be the ordination of God. God save us from anyone accepting such a philosophy and approach to government, for what would such a person do to another person who disturbs the ordination of God? Would they turn their neighbor in to the Gestapo for being a dissenter?[44] Would they spy on their community to ensure that all comply with the rule of law? Would they obey the command from their government to report all persons who voice an opinion opposing their government? And if that person is not willing to protect and promote the ordination of God by supporting its government, then what kind of biblical conviction does that person have to begin with? And who are they to judge others who have a conviction more certain than theirs, which produces action instead of just talk?

Do those who take such a view believe the following statement?

These great essential rights, are derived from a source above all that is human; are holden by tenure superior to what any power on earth can create or give; it is the Magna Charta of the Deity, the supreme ruler and governor, which grants and confirms these rights to man;

---

44. "It is the old practice of despots, to use a part of the people to keep the rest in order." Jefferson, *The Jeffersonian Cyclopedia,* 254.

they are therefore justly called natural rights, and the violation of a crime against the law of nature.[45]

If they believe this, then how can citizens be obligated by God to obey and submit to people who abuse power, government, and law, where such abuse violates the very rights that the power, government, and law were designed to protect and secure? That makes absolutely no sense. Apparently, these persons would prefer "the government of tyrants, savages, and brutes"[46] over "the reign of God, of enlightened reason and love."[47] To such persons, the honorable founding father, Daniel Webster, rhetorically asks the following questions, as he describes the settlement of America and the foundations of its settlement:

> More than all, a government, and a country, were to commence, with the very first foundations laid under the divine light of Christian religion. Happy auspices of a happy futurity! *Who would wish that his country's existence had otherwise begun?—Who would desire the power of going back to the ages of fable?—Who would wish for an origin obscured in the darkness of antiquity? Who would wish for other emblazoning of his country's heraldry,* or other ornaments of her genealogy, than to be able to say, that her first existence was intelligence; her first breath the inspirations of liberty; her first principle of truth of divine religion?[48]

Unfortunately, so many Americans are willing to revert back to tyranny for anything but godly reasons, instead of doing their duty to God and man and actively ensuring that freedom is maintained in a country where millions

---

45. Root, *Reports of Cases,* xvii.

46. Ibid., xlv, xlvi.

47. Ibid; "[W]hich is best [government] for mankind, that the people should be always exposed to the boundless will of tyranny, or that the rulers should be sometimes liable to be opposed[?]" Locke and Macpherson, ed., *Second Treatise of Government,* 115.

48. Jedidiah Morse, *Annals of the American Revolution,* (Hartford, CT: Publisher Unknown, 1824), 2, (emphasis added).

have paid the price to procure such freedom. There is no question about it. Without taking active measures to prevent tyranny, tyranny will inevitably prevail, and your ungodly submission only supports its success.

It must be observed and acknowledged that there are politicians who hope that America would consist of citizens who believe that absolute or blind submission is required for all ordained governments, because that mentality would simply make their quest to acquire and usurp power that much easier. Again, history proves this. Specifically regarding America's history, Thomas Paine recognizes this tendency of power-hungry leaders. He declares,

> Men who look upon themselves born to reign, and others to obey, soon grow insolent; selected from the rest of mankind their minds are early poisoned by importance; and the world they act in differs so materially from the world at large, that they have but little opportunity of knowing its true interests, and when they succeed to the government are frequently the most ignorant and unfit of any throughout the dominions.[49]

With the combination of blind submitters and power-hungry politicians, freedom does not last. Where such politicians have a large percentage of citizens who believe that all government actions are ordained of God, what inhibitors exist to prevent the unlawful usurpation of power? The damaging and evil consequences in such a case could be divulged without exhaust.

Regardless of how one interprets *ordained*, it is likely safe to say that most people believe that government is not the ultimate authority, and that it should be limited. If one does in fact believe in the limits of government according to the Bible and/or the Constitution and believe that not all government is ordained of God, then the belief should translate into action, for what good is faith without works? In other words, the citizen should be actively engaged to ensure that its government follows Romans 13 and 1 Peter 2 and the contractual obligations set forth in the United States

---

49. Paine, *Common Sense*, 17.

Constitution and state constitutions. Does it appear that America is getting better in these regards? Most Americans in general would likely say that America is in serious trouble, and that America is not the same as it was when it was created or even fifty years ago. Our economy is suppressed; we fight unconstitutional wars; our politicians openly admit that they do not follow the outdated portions of the Constitution; our government spies on its own citizens; our government persists in attempts to circumvent the Constitution and Bill of Rights; our government admits to torture tactics; our military is used within our own borders for citizen control; our politicians are corrupt without question; taxes are too burdensome and spent frivolously; morality is animal-like; children are fatherless; unborn children are killed with federal government sanction; and freedoms dangle by a thread over the flames of tyranny. Of course, all the while politicians promise that they will provide answers, change, or that things are getting better—deceiving all those who believe them.

With the understanding that America's integrity and values are declining, what is the cause, and why are people not demanding that the government administration on all levels comply with natural, revealed, and contractual laws? Whatever the reason, they are flawed and shirk the commandment to stand fast in liberty given by God. For as soon as one acknowledges the limitation of government and the purpose set forth by God, by America's Constitution, and by history; and as soon as he recognizes that our government was established to put the power in the hands of the people, then education, responsibility, duty, and action are all required. But that may be too high of a price to pay for many. Of course, as they say, you get what you pay for.

12

SUBMISSION TO GOVERNMENT

For those Christians or persons who believe that unconditional obedience and submission is required to any and all government that imposes its power, however acquired, not much can be said in discussion of the issues of submission to government, because they have mentally, spiritually, and physically surrendered their God-given rights in exchange for slavery. Quite frankly, to attempt to convince them otherwise would be wasting valuable time, resources, and breath. I say, save it for someone who has sense—a sense of freedom, right and wrong, justice, and equity. These antagonists to freedom have done as many loyalists to Great Britain did in 1776 and have "blend[ed] the tyrannical acts of administration with the lawful measures of government,"[1] which is duly noted by founder James Wilson. To describe such persons, do I dare use the same verbiage Thomas Paine uses to describe those who believed that inherent allegiance was due to hereditary kings?

---

1. Compiled by a member of the Philadelphia Bar, *American Oratory*, 6.

It is needless to spend much time in exposing the folly of hereditary right, if there are any so weak as to believe it, let them promiscuously worship the ass and lion, and welcome.[2]

But for those persons who believe that government is limited by certain sources—natural law, revealed law, or by compact of the people—then the issue of submission to government requires discussion relative to the points of when submission is required or when submission is no longer required. The discussions of natural rights, limited government, purpose of government, and ordination of government all relate to the issue of submission and obedience, because all of them define the boundaries of government, the rights of man, and their interrelation to each other.

The Quandary

John Locke articulates what history and human nature demonstrate concerning the tyranny of government versus the natural right of man to self-govern and to be free:

> To tell people they may provide for themselves, by erecting a new legislative, when by oppression, artifice, or being delivered over to a foreign power, their old one is gone, is only to tell them, they may expect relief when it is too late, and the evil is past cure. This is in effect no more than to bid them first be slaves, and then to take care of their liberty; and when their chains are on, tell them, they may act like freemen. This, if barely so, is rather mockery than relief; and men can never be secure from tyranny, if there be no means to escape it till they are perfectly under it: and therefore it is, that *they have not only a right to get out of it, but to prevent it.*[3]

---

2. "Nature disapproves it, otherwise she would not so frequently turn it into ridicule by giving mankind as ass for a lion." Paine, *Common Sense,* 16. Ass and lion refer to the proof alledgely found in nature that right of power is hereditary.

3. Locke and Macpherson, ed., *Second Treatise of Government,* 110–111, (emphasis added).

History and human nature demonstrate that the discussion of submission to government is perplexing. As America's founders learned, while the people may have the right not to submit to government action or demand, "all experience hath shewn that mankind are more disposed to suffer, while evils are sufferable than to right themselves by abolishing the forms to which they are accustomed."[4] Patrick Henry takes it a step further at a Continental Congress meeting, when the Colonies were deciding whether or not to resolve to form an army to defend themselves against the encroachments of Great Britain. He says, "It is natural to man to indulge in the illusions of hope. We are apt to shut our eyes against a painful truth, and listen to the song of that siren, till she transforms us into beasts."[5] Recognizing and dealing with tyranny can be a laborious task, but such a task was taken on by America's founders, for as John Dickinson says, "A free people can never be too quick in observing nor too firm in opposing the beginnings of alteration either in form or reality, respecting institutions formed for their security. The first kind of alteration leads to the last."[6] Thus, Americans are not (or should not be) unfamiliar with the problems inherent in allowing evils to be suffered without resistance from citizens.

A serious problem presents itself, however, because while the people choose to maintain false hope and suffer the evils that are knowingly in violation of the government's limited authority, their compliance to such evils only validates the unlawful actions, and thus implied consent[7] is given. Just as the writer of Anti-Federalist Paper No. 1 says, "When the people once part with power, they can seldom or never resume it again but by force."[8] How right he is. While this implied consent may not actually give the usurped power legitimacy legally,[9] it gives the usurped power intensity factually.

---

4. Jefferson, *The Declaration of Independence*.

5. Compiled by a member of the Philadelphia Bar, *American Oratory*, 13, 14.

6. Halstead Van Tyne, *The Causes of the War of Independence*, 237.

7. "Implied consent—consent inferred from one's conduct rather than from one's direct expression." Garner, ed., *Black's Law Dictionary*.

8. Cato, *The Anti-Federalist Papers*, 271.

9. "When the meaning and scope of a constitutional provision are clear it cannot be overthrown by legislative action, although several times repeated and never before challenged." *Fairbank v. United States*, 181 U.S. 283, 311 (1901).

Thomas Jefferson notes this fact by stating, "It is a dangerous lesson to say to the people 'whenever your functionaries exercise unlawful authority over you, if you do not go into actual resistance, it will be deemed acquiescence and confirmation.' How long had we acquiesced under usurpations of the British parliament? Had that confirmed their right, and make our Revolution a wrong?"[10] However, Jefferson also admits that implied consent eventually gives right to a power usurper. "The government of a nation may be usurped by the forcible intrusion of an individual into the throne. But to conquer its will, so as to rest the right on that, the only legitimate basis, requires long acquiescence and cessation of all opposition."[11] Thus, while it could not be argued that usurped power is legitimized by implied consent, this implied consent naturally causes the unlawful authority to grow in power, force, and intensity, given the purely practical considerations. Eventually, the right to rule exists by virtue of default.

Implied consent given to unlawful authority creates an even bigger problem because of the very nature of government. Thomas Paine observes this problem: societies suffer more at the hands of government (tyranny) than at the hands of no government (being in a state of nature). He states, "Our calamities are heightened by reflecting that we furnish the means [the power] by which we suffer."[12] Using the analogy of giving power to a beast,

---

10. Jefferson, *The Jeffersonian Cyclopedia*, 65.

11. Ibid., 185.

12. Paine, *Common Sense*, 5; "Whereas by supposing they have given up themselves to the absolute arbitrary power and will of a legislator, they have disarmed themselves, and armed him, to make a prey of them when he pleases; he being in a much worse condition, who is exposed to the arbitrary power of one man, who has the command of 100,000, than he that is exposed to the arbitrary power of 100,000 single men; no body being secure, that his will, who has such a command, is better than that of other men, though his force be 100,000 times stronger. And therefore, whatever form the common-wealth is under, the ruling power ought to govern by declared and received laws, and not by extempory dictates and undetermined resolutions: for then mankind will be in a far worse condition than in the state of nature, if they shall have armed one, or a few men with the joint power of a multitude, to force them to obey at pleasure the exorbitant and unlimited decrees of their sudden thoughts, or unrestrained, and till that moment unknown wills, without having any measures set down which may guide and justify their actions: for all the power the government has, being only for the good of the society, as it ought not to be arbitrary and at pleasure, so it ought to be exercised by established

the chances of resistance become slimmer and slimmer, because the beast's power becomes that much harder to resist. Eventually, there will come a point when the people will not be able to say confidently in defense of freedom, as Patrick Henry does, "We are not weak, if we make a proper use of those means which the God of nature hath placed in our power."[13] Thomas Jefferson uses the following analogy to describe this quandary: "The time to guard against corruption and tyranny is before they shall have gotten hold of us. It is better to keep the wolf out of the fold, than to trust to drawing his teeth and talons after he shall have entered."[14] Thus, giving implied consent to unlawful power is more detrimental to freedom than not giving any power at all to government and having a form of anarchical government (that is, no government). This is why Benjamin Franklin says that America will be a republic, "if we can keep it."

Eventually, the government's long train of abuses becomes so invasive that the power of the people virtually ceases to exist, and as a result, the people become slaves. And what powers do slaves have after relinquishing their rightful and natural power to a government that now has all control? Can it be said that submission to government should only cease after its citizens have become slaves? What good does the power of the people do anyone if it is not used to resist unlawful authority and usurpation of power? Does not the Bible state, "You were bought with a price; do not become slaves of men"?[15] As has been repeatedly observed, God does not desire that people be the slaves of government or more powerful men, but rather desires that we live in freedom so that we may more fully serve Him and live a life that was intended for human beings—God's creation. Does not the Bible also tell us that "whether you eat or drink, or whatever you do, do all to the

---

and promulgated laws; that both the people may know their duty, and be safe and secure within the limits of the law; and the rulers too kept within their bounds, and not be tempted, by the power they have in their hands, to employ it to such purposes, and by such measures, as they would not have known, and own not willingly." Locke and Macpherson, ed., *Second Treatise of Government*, 72–73.

13. Compiled by a member of the Philadelphia Bar, *American Oratory*, 15.

14. Jefferson, *The Jeffersonian Cyclopedia*, 210.

15. 1 Corinthians 7:23 (ESV).

glory of God"?[16] This verse clearly states that we are to conduct all areas of life in a manner that pleases God. Does one think that executing natural and revealed laws of God would not please Him? Some attempt to shirk their civic responsibility of being the workmen of God for His purposes. They become workmen for evil purposes by quoting a Bible verse such as, "The LORD has made everything for its purpose, even the wicked for the day of trouble."[17] Their logic ultimately leads to a conclusion that since evil exists, and since God is in control, there is nothing we can do about it, should do about it, or could do about it. However, observe that the very next verse says, "Everyone who is arrogant in heart is an abomination to the LORD; be assured, he will not go unpunished."[18] Clearly, God does not create evil but punishes evil—yes, on earth. We see one of the ways God punishes evil: through government (Romans 13). Therefore, you cannot logically argue that God's will is that we allow government to become evil, when its very purpose is to punish evil—the thing which God hates. And if in fact God creates evil for His pleasure and for His will's sake, then who are you to suggest that God would not raise up a group of people or states in a nation to perform an evil (i.e., resistance) against those in power who perpetrate evil?

Very likely, those who would suggest that citizens submit to government in all things and to render the things that are Caesar's to Caesar are the same people who would be the first to submit to government's requirement regarding matters belonging to God and His church; whether it be getting a license to preach; forming a corporation under the laws of the state to operate a church; complying with state and federal regulations to educate students or provide day care for children in that church; filing for tax-exempt status under the IRS Code and complying with all of its federally mandated policies to maintain such a privileged status; collecting taxes for Caesar from its church employees and in return giving all of the money collected to Caesar—all this, despite the fact that scriptures are abundantly clear that such matters belong only to God, and that no man (government) has any right or authority to impose civil or criminal prescriptions or proscriptions

16. Corinthians 10:31 (ESV).
17. Proverbs 16:4 (ESV).
18. Proverbs 16:5 (ESV).

(with threat of fine, penalty, imprisonment, etc.) regarding matters of the church.[19] But I guess the Romans 13 command to "submit yourselves unto the higher powers" in civil government applies to matters that belong only to God. Indeed, you would be hard pressed to find any Baptist, Methodist, Lutheran, Catholic, Pentecostal, or any other denomination that does not follow all state and federal regulations just to be able to keep the church doors open. So much for give unto God the things that are God's. This small description only demonstrates the utter lack of understanding concerning the proper jurisdictions of government—all government—including individual, family, business, church, and society.

If a simple and physical matter of eating and drinking requires that we use responsibility, wisdom, and prudence, then how much more are we in America (who have been given one of the greatest gifts of freedom the world has ever known) responsible to use our knowledge and freedom—what is left of it—to implement the natural and revealed laws in society and government? If eating and drinking are spiritual matters to God, then so are matters of state. Is the same attitude of indifference applied to the matters of maintaining employment, providing for family, pursuing education, securing retirement, maintaining health, or raising children? If so, then such a person's life is undoubtedly a wreck—or will soon be—and will be an example to all around of what *not* to do. Even organizing a matter as unimportant as a little league baseball team

---

19. "Jesus answered, 'My kingdom is not of this world. If my kingdom were of this world, my servants would have been fighting, that I might not be delivered over to the Jews. But my kingdom is not from the world.'" John 18:36 (ESV); "And I tell you, you are Peter, and on this rock [meaning, Jesus Himself] I will build my church, and the gates of hell shall not prevail against it. I will give you the keys of the kingdom of heaven, and whatever you bind on earth shall be bound in heaven, and whatever you loose on earth shall be loosed in heaven." Matthew 16:18–19 (ESV); "Now, the power here delegated is a spiritual power; it is a power pertaining to the kingdom of heaven, that is, to the church, that part of it which is militant here on earth, to the gospel dispensation; that is it about which the apostolical and ministerial power is wholly conversant. It is not any civil, secular power that is hereby conveyed, Christ's kingdom is not of this world; their instructions afterward were in things pertaining to the kingdom of God, Acts 1:3." Matthew Henry's Commentary on Matthew 16:18–19; "For no one can lay a foundation other than that which is laid, which is Jesus Christ."1 Corinthians 3:11 (ESV); "[The Household of God is] built on the foundation of the apostles and prophets, Christ Jesus himself being the cornerstone." Ephesians 2:20 (ESV).

takes practice, diligence, training, correction, planning, execution, instruction, understanding, and discipline. Very likely, there are many who are more concerned about how well their son plays in a meaningless little league baseball game than what kind of government they are bequeathing to their son.[20]

To suggest that matters of government are simply left to God's sovereignty and that we must therefore submit to government—no matter how tyrannical—mocks biblical understanding, American history, and common sense. The Bible clearly establishes the fact that we, as the creature, must do all that we can to accomplish God's will on earth. Many verses confirm this fact, one of which is Proverbs 16:9 (ESV). "The heart of man plans his way, but the LORD establishes his steps." When God created Adam, He expected him to work in the garden. It is a part of God's natural laws. No peace in society (which is God's will) can be accomplished by allowing tyrants and tyranny to reign. Of course, many of those who advocate submission so righteously claim that resistance is right, pure, just, and holy when the tyrannical government attempts to regulate or suppress spreading the gospel, as if God has established only one law in the entire universe worth fighting and dying for. Such an approach to submission to government contributes nothing to God's intended and expressed purpose of government in Romans 13 and 1 Peter 2. To wait until one becomes a slave to resist evil would be like a person claiming to be rich after giving all of his money away—he may have been rich at one time, but the act of giving it away deprives him of his power to use his money. Furthermore, how much harm will be done when you let the wolf into the fold; how many of the fold must suffer and die at the attack of the wolf; and how many of the fold will it take to subdue the wolf? The United States appears to be a nation with a multitude of sheep, and wolves are taking over and suppressing the sheep.[21] Thus, the question becomes at what point is a citizen required to submit, or conversely, to resist?

---

20. "A good man leaves an inheritance to his children's children." Proverbs 13:22 (ESV). God expects parents to leave not only their children an inheritance materially, but also to their grandchildren. Knowing that material possessions are of the least value in God's estimation, how much more should American parents leave to their children an inheritance of freedom?

21. "Who would not think it an admirable peace betwix the mighty and the mean, when the lamb, without resistance, yielded his throat to be torn by the imperious wolf?" Locke and Macpherson, ed., *Second Treatise of Government,* 115.

SUBMISSION'S CONSIDERATIONS

Before a citizen can ascertain the relative bearings to answer this question, foundational precepts must be established, in addition to the matters already discussed herein. Just as demonstrated beforehand, an individual has the natural right of self-preservation against individuals and governments. A person being attacked and whose life, limbs, and livelihood are threatened apparently and imminently has no appeal to the channels of justice whilst the threat pursues: the sheriff, the police, the court system and even the state can (and should) be great tools to redress these types of harms caused to citizens but are worthless to the imminently threatened individual.[22] The individual is not required to use legal procedures to protect himself from any person who would intentionally or even negligently do him harm. Thus, the individual has a right of self-defense, regardless of legal process. It is a shoot now, ask questions later approach, founded in natural and revealed law. The law clearly requires, however, that the circumstances surrounding the apparent threat be sufficient enough to cause a reasonable person to believe that the threat was real and imminent. Where such facts satisfy this burden, no reasonable person would critically judge the threatened person for taking the life of another or for resisting another to prevent the imminent harm. It should be observed that the threatened person need not wait until an actual battery (unlawful touching) take place, which he has an inviolable right against; but rather such person may rely on the circumstances to accurately judge whether or not he should defend himself before being physically harmed.

Our founders used the same principles regarding laws of nations, determining that citizens are able to defend themselves where a "long train of abuses and usurpations, pursuing invariably the same Object evinces a design to reduce them under absolute Despotism."[23] Where the circumstances show

---

22. "But force, or a declared design of force upon the person of another, where there is no common superior on earth to appeal to for relief, is the state of war; and it is the want of such an appeal gives a man the right of war even against an aggressor, though he be in society and a fellow-subject... force without right upon a man's person makes a state of war both where there is, and is not, a common judge." Locke and Macpherson, ed., *Second Treatise of Government*, 15.

23. Jefferson, *Declaration of Indepedence*.

such an intention of abuses, "it is their right, it is their duty, to throw off such Government, and to provide new Guards for their future security."[24]

The citizen must understand and realize that God sees nations as nothing more than men. In other words, there is nothing spectacular and special about a nation, because as King David noted in Psalm 9:20 (KJV), "Put them in fear, O LORD: that the nations may know themselves to be but men." Nations are nothing more than men, operating under an arrangement ordained by God, as described in Romans 13. God did not create man so that man could create government so that government could undermine the natural order and laws of God—laws created not only for God's glory but for our benefit. Also, God Himself cannot allow any acts contrary to His laws to be condoned by Himself or His ministers (i.e., government).[25] The scriptures are abundantly clear that God has created natural law and order, and that God expects all men, including government, to comply with His laws. Furthermore, God's perfect will is that human government be possessed of those people who acknowledge God's laws, who love justice, and who implement the same.

> For according to the work of a man [God] will repay him, and according to his ways [God] will make it befall him. Of a truth, God will not do wickedly, and the Almighty will not pervert justice. Who gave him charge over the earth, and who laid on him the whole world?... If you have understanding, hear this; listen to what I say. Shall one who hates justice govern? Will you condemn [God] who is righteous and mighty, who says to a king, "Worthless one," and to nobles, "Wicked man," who shows no partiality to princes, nor regards the rich more than the poor, for they are all the work of his hands?[26]

Very clearly, this scripture puts government's relationship to natural and revealed laws in perspective by proclaiming that God judges kings and

---

24. Ibid.
25. Romans 13 (KJV).
26. Job 34:11–13, 17–19 (ESV).

princes and governments according to their works (i.e., laws, regulations) and that God shows no partiality to them, even calling them wicked when they are wicked. God consequently repays and befalls them according to their actions in relation to God's established laws. This passage of scripture is explained further as follows:

> If the world were not God's property, as having been made by Him, but committed to His charge by some superior, it might be possible for Him to act unjustly, as He would not thereby be injuring Himself; but as it is, for God to act unjustly would undermine the whole order of the world, and so would injure God's own property (Job 36:23). Can even He who (in thy view) hateth right (justice) govern? The government of the world would be impossible if injustice were sanctioned. God must be just, because He governs (2 Samuel 23:3).[27]

Using just a little common sense reveals that human governments would not even be capable of justice were it not for the natural laws and order which God established and demands from His creation. Thus, since God ordains government as a minister of God to establish and secure justice on earth, any government which contradicts its role as God's minister also contradicts its Superior's purpose of justice and righteousness. In such a matter, God's ministers would become something other than the established government. They would become those who *resist* the injustice and tyranny of those in charge of government who act not as ministers of God but ministers of evil.

How can God ordain something that is opposed to God and His laws? Does not the Bible say that a house divided against itself cannot stand?[28] Does not Jesus Himself condemn governmental leaders for not executing justice? Jesus confirms that one of the weightiest matters concerning the law is justice—that is, what is right and what is wrong.[29] Law does not stand

---

27. Jamieson and Fausset, *A Commentary, Critical and Explanatory, on the Old and New Testaments,* 337.

28. Mark 3:25.

29. Matthew 23:23 (ESV).

alone on man's word, but rests in the fundamental creations of God. Indeed, everything regarding the application of government's authority rises and falls on God's authority. Even Jesus recognized that His will was not His own, but was based upon the authority of God and that any actions outside of such authority would not be valid.[30] Jesus recognizes that God's authority is the final authority on all matters, and though Jesus came to earth as God, He also came to earth as man, and set the example to humans that all humans (including those in government leadership) must act within the authority of God.

Similar in concept would be a corporation where the thing proposed to exist does not exist at all, except men agree to form a fictitious entity and operate under its operating agreements. Indeed, there is nothing sacred about a nation unto itself. Governments do not exist in nature, and God did not create government at all. Since God is no respecter of persons,[31] how can it be said that God is a respecter of governments, where governments are the creation of persons? In fact, all power of government remains in the people—as demonstrated in natural law, revealed law, and in America's compact (the Constitution). While the government may appear to be powerful unto itself, such appearance only derives from the usurpation of powers not properly granted to it by the states and people and by intimidation and fear tactics. This fact is confirmed by Thomas Jefferson, as he says, "When governments fear the people, there is liberty. When the people fear the government, there is tyranny."[32]

America's founding fathers went to great lengths to ensure that their posterity would not only realize that the power of government was in their hands but would also use the power they have to ensure that their rights were secured, as reflected in the Constitution, Bill of Rights, and Declaration of Independence. Thus, a proper perspective of what government is and where the power lies would perhaps give to the citizens a more healthy respect for their own power and the limitation that the government should be held to.

---

30. "If anyone's will is to do God's will, he will know whether the teaching is from God or whether I am speaking on my own authority." John 7:17 (ESV).

31. "For there is no respect of persons with God." Romans 2:11 (KJV).

32. Williams, *Do the Right Thing*, 149.

Of course, the modern American government today would not have the citizens realize that the power of government is completely in their hands—as the creators of the government itself—and would have the citizens ignorant that they have the complete and absolute power "to alter or to abolish it, and to institute new Government, laying its foundation on such principles and organizing its powers in such form, as to them shall seem most likely to effect their Safety and Happiness."[33] This very issue of submission to power was actually one of the main struggles in the War Between the States, commonly known as the Civil War. The notion that the states are required to be bound by a union of the United States insults common sense, common understanding of contract law, natural law, revealed law, America's Declaration of Independence, and the Constitution. Is the ultimate goal of the United States union or freedom? To insist that a body of people be required to feed or suffer at the hand of a government without their consent is called slavery. Is this not how America even came to exist? This power struggle has been felt for thousands of years and existed during the days Jesus walked the earth.

While Jesus performed His ministry, He ruffled quite a few feathers, mostly the influential, rich, powerful, princes, governors, and kings. Those who hated Him and what His message declared saw no better way to destroy Him than to put Him in competition with the power of government. One of their attempts to subdue and condemn Jesus is found in Luke 23:1–2 (KJV). Here is the transaction in part: "And the whole multitude of them arose, and led him unto Pilate. And they began to accuse him, saying, we found this fellow perverting the nation, and forbidding to give tribute to Caesar, saying that he himself is Christ a King."

God forbid that a citizen pervert the nation by not giving tribute to the government and by saying that the power of government is in the people! Jesus's condemners knew that the quickest way to trap Him into the iron grips of trouble would be to put the government against Him—and that they did. Of course, Jesus did not mind putting government in its place (just before they crucified Him), as is revealed in John 19:10–11 (ESV). "So Pilate said to Him, 'You will not speak to me? Do you not know that I have

---

33. Jefferson, *Declaration of Independence.*

authority to release you and authority to crucify you?' Jesus answered him, 'You would have no authority over me at all unless it had been given you from above. Therefore he who delivered me over to you has the greater sin.'" And of course, nowhere in scripture does God give carte blanche power to government, except as it fulfills His purpose of promoting good and punishing evil and where the people have chosen their leaders in conformance with God's standards set forth throughout scripture, including the limitations imposed upon government by compact and by natural law.

Thus, when considering the citizen's duty to submit, he must consider all relevant factors of natural law, revealed law, and compact law to gauge fully his understanding and his standing. Without a proper exploration of these historical, philosophical, political, and biblical concepts, a citizen will not likely stand on the principles of truth but of convenience and will likely cower in fear of government reprisal or commit rage in frustration of government oppression. Neither approach will produce lasting results for our posterity.

Submission's Limits

Pat Buchanan correctly observes that "God-and-country people are raised to respect and obey their rulers… As long as Americans believe that their government is acting constitutionally, they will obey. By definition, conservatives are not rebels. But neither were the founding fathers until pushed to the wall."[34] (Buchanan is clearly not referring to those we-must-submit-to-tyranny believers.) Being pushed to the wall means reaching the point of no longer being willing to suffer evils while evils are sufferable. To America's founders, *evil* meant any government actions not authorized by their Constitution under the monarchy of Great Britain and contrary to natural law. It may then be asked, what is the effect upon the freedom-loving citizens when the government acts outside of its lawful authority? If you believe in constitutional government, then you must know the answer to this question. Fortunately, these questions have already been discussed, argued, and debated for thousands of years, which gave America's founders

---

34. Buchanan, *The Death of the West*, 214.

the philosophical and spiritual understanding of submission to government. One such philosopher who had a major influence on this discussion was Algernon Sidney. This is what he says regarding submission to unlawful acts (notice the language used directly from scriptures):

> He [the powers over thee] therefore, and he only, is the servant of God, who does the work of God; who is a terror to those that do evil, and a praise to those that do well; who beareth the sword for the punishment of wickedness and vice, and so governs, that the people may live quietly in all godliness and honesty. The order of his institution is inverted, and the institution vacated, if the power be turned to the praise of those that do evil, and becomes a terror to such as do well; and that none who live honestly and justly can be quiet under it.
>
> If God be the fountain of justice, mercy, and truth, and those his servants who walk in them, no exercise of violence, fraud, cruelty, pride, or avarice, is patronized by him: and they who are the authors of those villanies, cannot but be the ministers of him, who sets himself up against God; because it is impossible, that truth and falsehood, mercy and cruelty, justice and the most violent oppression, can proceed from the same root.[35]

Sidney concludes that a power-usurping government does not receive God's blessing, ordination, sanction, or approval but rather works against His will, and as such does not deserve the approbation, praise, condolence, or support of any citizen. This is the same philosophy that formed the basis of resistance during the American Revolutionary War. A similarly accepted philosophy is that of Hugo Grotius, who concludes the following:

> It is beyond controversy among all good men, that if the persons in authority command anything contrary to Natural Law or the Divine Precepts, it is not to be done. For the apostles, in saying that "we

---

35. Sidney, *Discourses on Government*, 421, 422.

must obey God rather than man" appealed to an undoubted rule, written in the minds of all.[36]

In the same way, scripture reveals that where no honor exists, no honor is due. Grotius used scripture as well to denote that "the Jewish Law [in the Old Testament] shows that what is commanded by that law is not contrary to Natural Law. For Natural Law being...perpetual and immutable, God, who is never unjust, could not command anything against that Law."[37] Thus, where government contradicts the precepts of natural law, revealed law, the constitutional compact, and the purposes of government as demonstrated in those foundational sources, such a government cannot be considered just, and God cannot be said to support that government or command a person to submit to it. How can it be said that God expects a person to submit to evil government where a nation be but men and where God ordained government for the expressed purpose of punishing evil? Indeed, if God demands that governments punish evil, but governments inflict evil, who then shall punish the government? If the answer is God then, pray tell, if God directly punishes evil actions on earth, then why did God even ordain government to punish evil of citizens, since He could directly punish evil Himself? The fact that God established government (who be but men) to punish evil necessarily means that government must also be punished by its superiors for its evil, which in America is we the people of the states united!

What appears to have been lost is the very basic understanding of jurisdiction and limitations of power—which extend and apply to every area of life (not just government). The fact is, our founders and previous generations thoroughly understood this topic and wrote extensively on the subject. The prevailing philosophy of limited authority and jurisdiction gave confidence to all of the Colonies in 1776 to resist the greatest governmental power on earth at that time—Great Britain. They knew they were standing on a solid foundation, with philosophers such as Hugo Grotius articulating the following concepts: "By Natural Law, all have the Right of repel-

---

36. Grotius, *Hugo Grotius on the Rights of War and Peace*, 52.
37. Ibid., 8.

ling wrong. But civil society being instituted to secure public tranquility, the State acquires a Superior Right over us and ours, as far as is necessary for that end."[38] This was exactly what God told us in Romans 13 and 1 Peter 2. Submit to governments as long as it is punishing evil and promoting good. These same principles were used by the writers of the *Federalist Papers* and are specifically explained by Alexander Hamilton in Federalist Paper No. 27. "The legislatures, courts, and magistrates, of the respective members, will be incorporated into the operations of the national government as far as its just and constitutional authority extends."[39] Again, jurisdiction is the key word and key principle here.

Thus, where authority ends, submission ends. If Hamilton believed that governments were to be submitted to without regard to limitations, what need would there have been to explain the limitations of the national government, or what need would there have been to even write a constitution, or declare independence for that matter, and fight and die for such a declaration? Similarly, if God expected all people to submit to all governments, then why place the conditions of promoting good and punishing evil on the ministers of God?

These limitations on government were accepted by America's founders as maxims and truths established in God's natural and revealed laws. They simply acknowledge that God is sovereign and that all other authorities in life must be maintained within their proper sphere and contained therein. Any usurpation of such authority violates the other spheres of authority established by God, such as the individual, the family, the church, etc. Duties to obey authorities in life relate first and foremost to jurisdiction, because where no authority exists, no jurisdiction exists and vice versa. Where authority or jurisdiction exists, then a citizen must do as Jesus commanded and render unto Caesar the things that are Caesar's. Jesus did not say, "Render unto Caesar all things." If Caesar does not have jurisdiction over a certain matter, then there is no command to render any honor or tribute to him, because a

---

38. Grotius, *Hugo Grotius on the Rights of War and Peace,* 53.

39. Alexander Hamilton, "Federalist Paper 27," in *The Federalist Papers,* Hamilton, Jay, and Madison, 208.

government can no more usurp powers granted by God than the individual can usurp the power of another individual or another family. Similarly, one nation has no authority to control or interfere with the affairs of a foreign nation. Indeed, governments are bound by God's laws, just as the citizen is bound by God's laws. Neither party has a superior right to violate the laws that all humanity must observe.

In case there is still doubt, confusion, or even resistance to the thought that citizens must not blindly submit themselves to their respective government, even a casual study of the Bible will reveal that God never commanded blind obedience. Rather, God's commandment of submission to government is limited to God's purposes, just as in any other area of life. To begin, let us analyze all of the verses in the Bible where the Romans 13 phrase *be subject* is used. A Bible concordance shows that this Greek word *hupotasso* is used in different English forms in the scriptures, such as *submit, submission,* or *be subject.* This Greek word literally means to subordinate,[40] and in the verses listed shortly, God uses the word hupotasso to describe relationships where a certain party must be subordinate to another. It must be acknowledged that the same word is used to describe the relationship between (1) wives and husbands, (2) church members and pastors, (3) citizen and government, (4) younger and older, (5) servants and masters, and (6) children and parents. In other words, the same word is used in about every major relationship of life. The following examples are from the King James Version of the Bible:

Wives and Husbands

Wives, submit yourselves unto your own husbands, as unto the Lord. (Ephesians 5:22)
Wives, submit yourselves unto your own husbands, as it is fit in the Lord. (Colossians 3:18)

Therefore as the church is subject unto Christ, so let the wives be to their own husbands in every thing. (Ephesians 5:24)

---

40. Strong, *Strong's Exhaustive Concordance of the Bible,* 75.

Church Members and Pastors

That ye submit yourselves unto such, and to every one that helps with us, and labors. (1 Corinthians 16:16)

Citizen and Government

Submit yourselves to every ordinance of man for the Lord's sake: whether it be to the king, as supreme. (1 Peter 2:13)

Let every soul be subject unto the higher powers. For there is no power but of God: the powers that be are ordained of God. (Romans 13:1)

Younger and Older

Likewise, you younger, submit yourselves unto the elder. Yea, all of you be subject one to another, and be clothed with humility: for God resisteth the proud, and give grace to the humble. (1 Peter 5:5)

Servants and Masters

Servants, be subject to your masters with all fear; not only to the good and gentle, but also to the froward. (1 Peter 2:18)

Children and Parents

And [Jesus] went down with them, and came to Nazareth, and was subject unto them: but his mother kept all these sayings in her heart. (Luke 2:51)

Ironically enough, many Americans today argue that this phrase *be subordinate to* means something like show respect to, show reverence to, give honor to, and other similar meanings that do not necessarily require obedience. This is mainly because it is not politically correct to suggest that a wife submit to her husband or a church member submit to his pastor or a younger submit to his elder. However, you cannot have it both ways. You cannot argue that God does not command wives to obey their husbands and then argue that citizens must obey their government in all things. Why? Because the exact same word is used in all of these scenarios. Neither can you argue that a church member is free to act as he pleases relative to church affairs without obedience to the pastor while at the same time arguing that the same person must submit to his government because God commands him to. Such approaches to scripture show ignorance and hypocrisy (which begs the question of what is the motive behind such conflicting applications of God's revealed law).

Even the apostle Paul does not lay down with passiveness when arrested by the Jewish government on false charges. In fact, he uses his knowledge of the laws and legal procedures of Israel and Rome to prevent the Jews from killing him. He says to the government,

> I am standing before Caesar's tribunal, where I ought to be tried. To the Jews I have done no wrong, as you yourself know very well. If then I am a wrongdoer and have committed anything for which I deserve to die, I do not seek to escape death. But if there is nothing to their charges against me, no one can give me up to them. I appeal to Caesar.[41]

Paul in essence declares to the Jewish government that they have no jurisdiction over him, and that even if they did have jurisdiction over him, since he did no wrong act, then they did not have the authority to judge him. Paul's defense related to (1) jurisdiction/authority and (2) justice/rightness. If Paul accepted the notion that citizens must demonstrate absolute submission and obedience to government, then why did he prevent the Jewish government from pursuing their prosecution instead of simply turning the other cheek or not resisting evil?[42] Was he not resisting their efforts to prosecute him as he appealed to Caesar? Yes, he was. He denied the Jewish government what they sought and thus did not submit. Let us be clear, the word *submission* does not necessarily mean to obey, though there is obviously a component of obedience in submission. Rather, unconditional obedience can only be attributed

---

41. Acts 25:10–11 (ESV).

42. "But I say to you, Do not resist the one who is evil. But if anyone slaps you on the right cheek, turn to him the other also." Matthew 5:39 (ESV).

to God, just as the apostles declared, "We are to obey God rather than man."[43] It is as author John Meacham states, "If the Lord himself chose not to force obedience from those he created, then who are men to try?"[44] Thus, there is a very important distinction between submission and obedience; they are not equivalent.

Think of this: does it make any sense that God would require Christians to show the same amount of obedience to a husband, a pastor, an elder, a parent, a master, or a government that they render to God? Of course not! Any person who believes in God would likely concur. However, notice that the same Greek word hupotasso is used in the following verses with respect to man submitting to God as is used in all other civil and human relationships:

> Submit yourselves therefore to God. Resist the devil, and he will flee from you.[45]

> For they being ignorant of God's righteousness, and going about to establish their own righteousness, have not submitted themselves unto the righteousness of God.[46]

Since the same word is used to describe man's duty to submit to God as is used to submit to other men and government, and since we know that we are to obey God rather than man, it cannot be reasonably argued that all men and governments have the same authority and power that only God possesses. Again the issue goes back to jurisdiction, and scripture thoroughly defines the jurisdiction of each of the human relationships; truly, scripture reveals that no superior has any jurisdiction outside of what God has provided their purpose to be.

Let us be absolutely clear on this matter of submission to government.

---

43. Acts 5:29 (KJV).
44. Meacham, *American Gospel,* 5.
45. James 4:7 (KJV).
46. Romans 10:3 (KJV).

The submission requirements (as expressed by God) in Romans 13 can accurately be stated as follows: citizens are to submit themselves to a government whose authority and power is ordained of God for the expressed purposes of punishing evil and promoting good, and citizens should support (pay tribute, pay taxes) such a government, not for the sake of fear of being punished by that government, but for the sake of their conscience. Let us invert this truth. Citizens are not to submit themselves to a government whose authority is not ordained of God, for their purposes contradict the punishment of evil and promotion of good. Such a government should not be supported by citizens for the sake of conscience and not for the sake of fear. Thus, there are many levels of consideration that Romans 13 reflects: (1) the higher powers—legitimacy of authority, (2) promoting good and punishing evil—purpose of government, (3) for this cause—limitation of submission, and (4) not for fear, but for conscience—pure and just purposes and intents of submission.

If God commands submission to this Romans 13 type of government, He necessarily does not command submission to an antithetical type of government. This is confirmed over and over again in scripture. God does not ordain, condone, or promote evil. Since this is true, there is absolutely no way that God would or could command that we pay tribute for this cause when this cause includes illegal and improper authority, power, and purpose. God clearly sets forth the criteria of government's authority, limitations, and purpose, and He further limits the citizen's obligation to submit and even to support government. Thus, when government does not fulfill its Romans 13 ordination of God as ministers of God, the citizen is not obligated to pay tribute or submit to such an illegitimate government. Unfortunately, in the name of Romans 13 some argue that you must submit yourself to a government that not only contradicts the higher powers (the U.S. Constitution) but also the Highest power (the natural and revealed laws of God), declaring further that we must not only submit but also give support by paying tribute (taxes) to a government whose authority and power contradict the higher powers, whose limitations are ignored, and that punishes good and promotes evil. While declaring this position, these persons would dare to argue that they promote such a position of submission not for the sake of fear but for the sake of conscience—all the while shaking in their boots at the thought of government retribution. This application completely contradicts and is the antithesis of Romans 13.

The first and foremost truth that God establishes regarding priority of submission is found in the very first commandment given to Moses: "Thou shalt have no other gods before me."[47] That means our allegiance to God must take priority over anything, anyone, and any government—and to do otherwise is committing idolatry. Thus, since God's jurisdiction supersedes all others, that would be the first and foremost act to follow. Following from there, the submitter must then analyze the different jurisdictions as described by the ordainer of those jurisdictions to determine the limits of their jurisdiction. This is why the Constitution of the United States of America is so important to understand. No one should ever equate the Constitution to an inerrant, holy document. However, in America it should be observed that the Constitution sets forth the limits placed on government, which God has ordained in form and in power and which has been agreed upon by the states' sovereign.

SUBMISSION TO THE PRINCIPLES OF SLAVERY OR FREEDOM

Scripture is clear that there may be circumstances where submission is not possible. *"If it be possible,* as much as lieth in you, live peaceably with all men."[48] Indeed, there are times where not only is submission out of the question, but resistance is required. "Submit yourselves therefore to God. Resist the devil, and he will flee from you."[49] The devil can come in many forms, and sometimes as an angel of light,[50] but scriptures reveal where the devil is most effectively at work: in government. Scores of examples from the Bible could be discussed proving this fact. How else can one resist a force that does not physically reveal itself (i.e., a spirit)? As Paul said, the Christian race is

---

47. Exodus 20:3 (KJV).

48. Romans 12:18 (KJV), (emphasis added).

49. James 4:7 (KJV).

50. "For such men are false apostles, deceitful workmen, disguising themselves as apostles of Christ. And no wonder, for *even Satan disguises himself as an angel of light.*" 2 Corinthians 11:13–14 (ESV), (emphasis added).

not one of beating the air,[51] but rather it should have substance to it. So how can we resist the evil one without seeing him? Can it be said that Satan uses husbands, pastors, employers, and elders to cause harm to people—Christians included? Of course. Scripture reveals this. America's founders understood that these forces of evil must be resisted. "Resistance to tyrants is obedience to God" was one of the mottos of our founding generation.[52] Once evil is identified, resistance is required. King David said, "Who will rise up for me against the evildoers? Or who will stand up for me against the workers of iniquity? Unless the LORD had been my help, my soul had almost dwelt in silence."[53]

In fact, David proved the application of resisting evil government when he overthrew the governmental power of his son, Absalom.[54] The power Absalom acquired was not lawful, as no right can come by conquest, unless there was an existing right undergirding the conquest. David, the "man after God's own heart,"[55] did not submit to unlawful authority, and when given the right opportunity, he overthrew the unlawful government and reestablished lawful government. So which government was ordained of God, David's or Absalom's? Who would you have followed after Absalom took control of David's kingdom, when David was out in the wilderness being hunted like an animal? You would have had to make a decision about which government was ordained of God. The same decision must be made today in America.

Indeed, not submitting to evil government was accepted and expected in earlier generations before, during, and after our nation's founding. Grotius expresses this common philosophy of that day, appealing to the revealed law of God:

> We are commanded to love our enemies by the example of God, who makes his sun to rise on the unjust. Yet the same God punishes some

---

51. "I do not run aimlessly; I do not box as one beating the air." 1 Corinthians 9:26 (ESV).

52. Rayner, *The Life of Thomas Jefferson,* 31; Jefferson, *The Jeffersonian Cyclopedia,* 890.

53. Psalm 94:16–17 (KJV).

54. Samuel 13–16.

55. "But now thy kingdom shall not continue: the LORD hath sought him a man after his own heart, and the LORD hath commanded him to be captain over his people, because thou hast not kept that which the LORD commanded thee." 1 Samuel 13:14 (KJV); "And when he had removed him, he raised up unto them David to be their king; to whom also he gave testimony, and said, I have found David the son of Jesse, a man after mine own heart, which shall fulfil all my will." Acts 13:22 (KJV).

evil deeds in this evil, and will hereafter punish them in the heaviest manner. And the same argument solves what is said this subject about the injunction to Christians to be merciful. For God is called merciful, gracious, longsuffering…and yet Scripture everywhere speaks of his wrath, that is, his intention to punish…and of this wrath, the magistrate is constituted minister.[56] Moses is praised for his extreme gentleness; yet Moses inflicted punishment, even capital punishment, on the guilty. We are everywhere commanded to imitate the gentleness and patience of Christ. Yet Christ it was who inflicted the most severe punishment on those disobedient Jews; Matt 12:7.[57]

Grotius continues in the same vein of thought, appealing to natural law this time:

That private war may be lawful, so far as Natural Law goes, I conceive is sufficiently apparent from what has been said above, when it was shown, that *for any one to repel injury, even by force, it is not repugnant to Natural Law.* But perhaps some may think that after judicial tribunals have been established, this no longer lawful: for though public tribunals do not proceed from nature, but from the act of man, yet equity and natural reason dictate to us that we must conform to so laudable an institution.

Since it is much more decent and more conducive to tranquility among men, that a matter should be decided by a disinterested judge, than that men, under the influence of self-love, should right themselves according to their notions of right… It is not to be doubted, indeed, that the license which existed before the establishment of public justice is much restricted. Yet still it continues to exist; namely when public justice ends: for law which forbids us to seek our own by other than judicial proceedings, must be understood to apply only when judicial aid can be had.[58]

---

56. Romans 13:4 (KJV).
57. Grotius, *Hugo Grotius on the Rights of War and Peace,* 23.
58. Ibid., 30, (emphasis added).

Common sense reveals that individuals do not sacrifice their rights of life, liberty, and property granted by God simply because an institution of government exists, just as Grotius explained that a person does not give up the right of self-defense simply because there are courts of justice. Thomas Jefferson recognized this common sense understanding of natural rights when he said, "The idea is quite unfounded that on entering into society we give up any natural rights."[59]

At some point when a person submits to an unlawful authority of government, such a person becomes a slave and becomes virtually powerless to enforce any rights once secured by the constitution of that state. Of course, there are levels of slavery, which America is experiencing even today. Slavery does not necessarily mean you are in chains and shackles. Slavery may be that the citizens fear their government to the point that the citizens do not resist even when such actions are unlawful. Montesquieu states, "As virtue is necessary in a republic, and in a monarchy honor, so fear is necessary in a despotic government."[60] Such fear will allow the government to accomplish the same ends without the use of chains and shackles, because the minds of the citizens are enslaved already. Where there is no will to resist, there will be no resistance. Slavery may also be that the citizens have no meaningful means of redress, no effective means of change, and no substantive power over the government. Slavery may also be when the citizens believe lies and manipulations intended to acquire the approval of the people[61] (just as Absalom did in 2 Samuel 15), thus creating an allusion of legitimacy in government. This legal term is called fraud in the inducement or fraud in the fact. Under contract law, when such frauds take place the contract is null and void by the harmed party.[62] Suffice it to say, slavery exists in many forms and involves more than the physical movement of persons—just

---

59. Jefferson, *The Jeffersonian Cyclopedia*, 609.

60. Montesquieu, *The Spirit of Laws*, 26.

61. "Through its capture of the institutions that shape and transmit ideas, opinions, beliefs, and values—TV, the arts, entertainment, education—this elite is creating a new people. Not only ethnically and racially, but culturally and morally, we are no longer one people or 'one nation under God.'" Buchanan, *The Death of the West*, 5.

62. Garner, *Black's Law Dictionary*.

as Samuel Adams observes in 1702 concerning the colonists' condition in New England, "[T]he King's subjects in New England did not differ much from slaves, and that the only difference was, that they were not bought and sold."[63] Thus, to understand where a nation falls on the scale of freedom and slavery, one must know the difference between the two and study the elements of both. Again, education is key to a free, democratic republic where the power of government is in the people.

Even a casual observer of America's current condition would reveal that freedom is a thing *not* to be desired in America—not because freedom is so abundant, but because the demand is virtually unseen and unfelt. Many citizens today reduce their response to government to mostly passive obedience—especially when the powers that be claim to be Christian, conservative, or Republican—even in the face of blatant and unconstitutional usurpation of authority. Where such leaders usurp authority and actually gain compliance by their followers, such leaders act unlawfully and with despot effect. (Regardless of intentions, the apostle Peter did not think he was doing Satan's work either when he told Jesus, "Far be it from thee, Lord.")[64] What consequently follows is that citizens living under such usurped authority become voluntary slaves, for where can rights be secured if the power designed to protect those rights is unlawfully used? Consider Montesquieu's description of passive obedience:

> In despotic states, the nature of government requires the most passive obedience; and when the prince's will is made known, it ought infallibly to produce its effect. In a country like this they are no more allowed to represent their apprehensions of a future danger than to impute their miscarriage to the capriciousness of fortune. Man's portion here, like that of beasts, is instinct, compliance, and punishment. Little does it then avail to plead the sentiments of nature, filial respect, conjugal or paternal tenderness, the laws of honor, or want of health; the order is given, and that is sufficient.[65]

---

63. Halstead Van Tyne, *The Causes of the War of Independence*, 38.
64. Matthew 16:22, 23 (KJV).
65. Montesquieu, *The Spirit of Laws*, 27.

While most Americans would never admit that they live in slavery of any sort, the evidence does support such a position, and there are many references of such. Take into consideration the fears that most Americans face daily from their government. These would include items such as an individual's fear of being audited by the IRS; a church's fear of losing tax-exempt status for preaching against certain politics; fear of what a Democrat president will do during a short four-year term; fear of terrorist attacks by people who hate America; fear of being placed in prison for doing your job as a border patrol agent; fear of supporting a fringe political leader and being deemed a terrorist;[66] fear of disturbing a political power structure ordained of God; fear of being investigated by Family and Children Services for spanking your child; fear of the economy collapsing, losing your job, and not being able to provide for your family; fear of operating a business without the proper licensing; fear of crimes being committed against you; fear of being continually monitored by the government;[67] fear of saying the politically incorrect thing and being prosecuted by the government or fired by your employer; fear of proclaiming politically incorrect speech in public forums and experiencing media reprisal; fear of being fired from public school teaching for stating that evolution is false; fear of losing retirement benefits from the military for preaching in Jesus's name as a chaplain; fear of family values

66. "The MIAC [Missouri Information Analysis Center] report specifically describes supporters of presidential candidates Ron Paul, Chuck Baldwin, and Bob Barr as 'militia' influenced terrorists and instructs the Missouri police to be on the lookout for supporters displaying bumper stickers and other paraphernalia associated with the Constitutional, Campaign for Liberty, and Libertarian parties." Kurt Nimmo, "Secret State Police Report: Ron Paul, Bob Barr, Chuck Baldwin, Libertarians are Terrorists," *Infowars.com,* March 11, 2009, http://www.infowars.com/secret-state-police-report-ron-paul-bob-barr-chuck-baldwin-libertarians-are-terrorists/ (accessed May 5, 2009).

67. "Privacy advocates are issuing warnings about a new radio chip plan that ultimately could provide electronic identification for every adult in the U.S. and allow agents to compile attendance lists at anti-government rallies simply by walking through the assembly. The proposal, which has earned the support of Janet Napolitano, the newly chosen chief of the Department of Homeland Security, would embed radio chips in driver's licenses, or 'enhanced driver's licenses.'" Bob Unruh, "Radio Chip Coming Soon To Your Driver's License? Homeland Security Seeks Next-Generation REAL ID," *World Net Daily,* February 28, 2009, http://wnd.com/index.php?fa=PAGE.view&pageId=90008 (accessed May 5, 2009).

being demised by politicians; fear of the devalued and depreciated dollar; fear of Social Security funds being spent away by the government; fear of being imprisoned for not paying taxes; fear of illegal immigrants taking advantage of your own country;[68] and the list goes on.

These fears of course do not even consider the hundreds of federal executive orders, laws, and regulations that have serious negative effect upon the rights of citizens—and citizens do not even have knowledge or awareness of them. Furthermore, it does not take into consideration the manipulation of extremely powerful people (not necessarily politicians) over the affairs of governments and nations. In this regard, those who would use such unlawful powers would have the citizens be ignorant and blissful, but of course "this tranquility cannot be called a peace."[69] And what of the cultural cleansing that has turned America upside down—from abortion to widespread moral degradation; from ungodly governmental dependence to the dumbing down of American education; from political corruption to church impotency; from historical ignorance to undying support for a lesser of two evils; from family collapse to unruly and violent children; and from interdependence on foreign governments to the sacrifice of American independence. The factors keep adding up to produce slavery. Is this so surprising, since the slave mentality already exists?

Moreover, there are many causes for the debasement of American society and government, but the effect is a slave mentality of the people and a slave effect upon their lives. Montesquieu takes note of the slave mentality in society:

> In despotic governments its aim is to debase it…excessive obedience supposes ignorance in the person that obeys… As education, therefore, consists chiefly in social converse, it must be here very much limited; all it does is to strike the heart with fear, and to imprint on the understanding a very simple notion of a few principles of

---

68. "Uncontrolled immigration threatens to deconstruct the nation we grew up in and convert America into a conglomeration of peoples with almost nothing in common." Buchanan, *The Death of the West*, 3; "I must add that the Congress have nothing to do with this matter [of immigration]. It belongs to the legislatures of the several states." Jefferson, *The Jeffersonian Cyclopedia*, 415.

69. Montesquieu, *The Spirit of Laws*, 58–59.

religion. Learning here proves dangerous, emulation fatal; and as to virtue, Aristotle cannot think that there is any one virtue belonging to slaves; if so, education in despotic countries is confined with a very compass. Here, therefore, education is in some measure needless: to give something, one must take away every thing, and begin with making a bad subject in order to make a good slave.[70]

One could argue that America is quickly working its way to making good slaves, where citizens are ignorant, fearful, powerless, overtaxed, deceived, distracted, uneducated, living hand to mouth,[71] and virtually unable to make any difference in our society and government. Consider what constitutional law expert and attorney Edwin Vieira, Jr. describes as happening in America today:

> That any free people would acquiesce in, let alone accede to, such a scheme [of a national police-state apparatus] is unbelievable. Nonetheless, the necessary and sufficient framework is being erected (by default, if not actual intention), with everyone aware of, many vocalizing their anxiety over, and even some unabashedly approving what is happening, but with vanishingly few dissenters apparently willing or able to do much of anything to thwart or even slow down these developments, or to eliminate or even mitigate the dangers they pose.[72]

Does this not make sense, though? After all, what citizen can redress government when his life is in disarray; his finances consume his thoughts; his own family contradicts and disrespects him; his children stress him out; his wife battles against him daily; his employees steal from him; his debt overwhelms him; and his spiritual leader tickles his ears with truths inapplicable to the battles confronting him? He becomes virtually powerless and thus gladly passes the burden of overseeing government to the politicians, who gladly receive the power given to them by the manipulated, beaten-down citizens.

---

70. Montesquieu, *The Spirit of Laws*, 32–33.

71. Ibid., 63.

72. Vieira, *Constitutional Homeland Security*, 36.

Has America reached the point where liberty itself has been abused to the point of becoming a slave? Is there such a thing as abused liberty? Consider Montesquieu's concept of abused liberty:

> To these great advantages of liberty it is owing that liberty itself has been abused. Because a moderate government has been productive or admirable effects, this moderation has been laid aside; because great taxes have been raised, they wanted to carry them to excess; and ungrateful to the hand of liberty, of whom they received this present, they addressed themselves to slavery who never grants the least favor.
>
> Liberty produces excessive taxes; the effect of excessive taxes is slavery.[73] The Freedom of every citizen constitutes a part of the public liberty, and in a democratic state is even a part of the sovereign. To sell one's freedom is so repugnant to all reason as can scarcely be supposed in any man.[74]

When one citizen voluntarily enslaves his mind and body to the government, he jeopardizes the entire public liberty of every citizen. Such an approach to government is repugnant to all reason and does not take into consideration God's commandment that we "love our neighbors as ourselves."[75] It does not even take into consideration the natural law of peace. The evidence overflowing from America's cup indicates that we, in fact, possess certain qualities of slavery, and such a reality does not even cross the minds of most American citizens.

A pointed fact demonstrating the slavish mentality of America is the ignorance that most citizens and administrators possess regarding the influence and bearing of natural and revealed laws on government. Freedom cannot exist in such a state. As soon as you lose understanding of the natural rights granted by God, you have accepted and adopted the mindset of slavery. Algernon Sidney puts it this way:

---

73. Montesquieu, *The Spirit of Laws*, 216.

74. Ibid., 236.

75. Matthew 5:43 (KJV).

[For a citizen to deny that you] can proceed from the laws of natural liberty, or any other root than the grace and bounty of the prince, [you] declare they can have none at all. For as liberty solely consists in an independency upon the will of another, and by the name of slave, we understand a man who can neither dispose of his person or goods, but enjoys all at the will of his master: there is no such thing in nature as a slave.[76]

Thus, where a person denies that natural law is the root of authority, slavery follows. Likewise, where natural law is not even considered in the discussion and application of authority, slavery follows. Look at America today. The concept of natural rights relative to governmental action is virtually nonexistent in public forums or even in church pulpits. Citizens are bombarded with party politics from CNN, MSNBC, Fox News, talk radio, and even from supposed Christian leaders. All the while, citizens think that voting for a certain candidate is going to change the course of America—when recent history has already proven that such is not the case. What most are missing is that America's overall philosophy is drastically wrong, and if it is not changed, it will cause America to continue down the road of slavery.

The End of Submission or the End of Freedom

Many people claim that once and if the government passes a certain point of tyranny, they will resist that government—by force if necessary. While this may in fact be true, the reality of this statement must be compared to established actions, for courage does not blossom like a mushroom but rather is produced by a genuine belief in a principle superior to the life of the individual. By way of illustration, many of these people are the same ones who feel that voting for the lesser of two evils is the only way to keep evil politicians out of office. At the same time they admit that the lesser does not follow the Constitution, is corrupt, lies to the people, and does not hold

---

76. Sidney, *Discourses on Government,* 327, 328.

the philosophy that made America great. Still, the lesser receives their vote, because he is the only one who can win. Unfortunately, the voter forsakes all elements of faith, principle, and courage and is motivated mainly by the fear of what will result if the greater evil takes office.

The obvious question begged is this: how do you expect to resist government that crosses the line when fear of imprisonment, loss of income, or even death will affect your decision at that point? Why are you not willing simply to vote for a person who *does* in fact hold your beliefs and whose ideas conform to the Constitution? Is it because to do so may mean a greater of two evils will get into office? In other words, if you are not willing to suffer the lesser inconvenience of the greater evil getting into office, what makes you think you are going to suffer the greater inconvenience of bankruptcy, imprisonment, or death? This truth is similar to the example given to us in Jeremiah 12:5.[77] "If you have run with the footmen, and they have wearied you, then how can you contend with horses? And if in the land of peace, wherein you trustedst, they wearied you, then how will you do in the swelling of Jordan?"

Similar to those who talk about defeating the horses yet are beaten in the footrace, many conservatives proclaim their devotion to resisting evil when it becomes too great yet continually and repeatedly put aside all principles and truth regarding their support for lesser evils. Anyone who approaches the lesser decisions based upon anything other than the laws of nature and nature's God will make greater decisions based upon the same mistaken rational.[78] Is this so shocking? No. Common sense and understanding dictates this truth. Just as a leader cannot administer government with principle, truth, and character when he did not possess such qualities before being placed in such a position, so too a citizen cannot rise to the occasion of resisting evil based upon principle, when pragmatism, convenience, and fear controlled his decisions before the evil was presented. How ludicrous to

---

77. Combination of KJV and MJKV.

78. "By faith Moses, when he was grown up, refused to be called the son of Pharaoh's daughter, choosing rather to be mistreated with the people of God than to enjoy the fleeting pleasures of sin. He considered the reproach of Christ greater wealth than the treasures of Egypt, for he was looking to the reward." Hebrews 11:24–26 (ESV).

think that citizens with the mindset that they have to vote for a lesser for fear of a certain politician getting into office would actually and physically resist government made up of lesser evils. Montesquieu observes the same contradiction in philosophy during his day.

> After what has been said [about despotic governments], one would imagine that human nature should perpetually rise up against despotism. But, notwithstanding the love of liberty, so natural to mankind, notwithstanding their innate detestation of force and violence, most nations are subject to this very government. This is easily accounted for.
>
> To form a moderate government, it is necessary to combine the several powers; to regulate, temper, and set them in motion; to give, as it were, ballast to one, in order to enable it to counterpoise the other. This is a master-piece of legislation, rarely produced by hazard, and seldom attained by prudence. On the contrary, a despotic government offers itself, as it were, at first sight; it is uniform throughout; and as passions only are requisite to establish it, this is what every capacity may reach.[79]

To truly possess the requisite elements of a freedom lover, you must also possess the elements of a freedom believer. To truly possess the requisite elements of a freedom believer, your approach and actions towards freedom are not the pragmatism of modern day politics. Instead, you must internalize what truly produces freedom (that is, the natural laws of God) and act in accordance, regardless of whether or not you believe such an approach is the winning way.

Considering Montesquieu's observation that most nations that exist and have ever existed live under despotic government, the causes must be explored to hopefully equip statesmen, pastors, religious leaders, and even politicians who actually care about freedom with knowledge to address these cases. As the Bible tells us, "There is nothing new under the sun."[80] Thus,

---

79. Montesquieu, *The Spirit of Laws*, 62.
80. Ecclesiastes 1:9 (KJV).

every generation faces the same causes for the attitudes detrimental to freedom. In fact, Thomas Paine similarly found these reasons to affect those who were loyalists to Great Britain:

> I am included to believe, that all those who espouse the doctrine of reconciliation [with Great Britain], may be included within the following descriptions. Interested men, who are not to be trusted; weak men who cannot see; prejudiced men who will not see; and a certain set of moderate men, who think better of the European world than it deserves.[81]

There are a number of reasons history reveals certain common and glaring causes for a citizen's detrimental attitude towards freedom, namely these: fear of losing one's comfort and familiarity; rejection of principles of natural and revealed law; deterioration of philosophical understanding; ignorance; and lethargy.

Fear of Losing Comfort and Familiarity

Fear: one of the most damaging mindsets a person can experience. Fear is stifling in every way. It causes a person to cower from the object of their fear; it creates emotional and physical anxiety in a person, derived from a person's self-preservation nature; and it forces him to rearrange his thinking (even if it means believing lies) to avoid any confrontation with the object of his fear, as if he is living in a fairy tale and everything is okay. The Bible is full of such examples of fear (applicable to the issue of freedom and slavery), but perhaps there is none better than in Numbers 11:1–6 (ESV), when Moses led Israel from their slavery in Egypt and was leading them to the Promised Land, directed by God. This passage reveals a lot about what fear will do to the mind of a person, even to the point that the person would desire to be a slave rather than to face his fear. Numbers 11:1–6 (MJKV) reveals this story:

> And the people complained in the hearing of the LORD about their misfortunes, and when the LORD heard it, his anger was kindled, and the fire of the LORD burned among them and consumed some

---

81. Paine and Philip, ed., *Common Sense*, 25.

outlying parts of the camp. Then the people cried out to Moses, and Moses prayed to the LORD, and the fire died down. So the name of that place was called Taberah, because the fire of the LORD burned among them. Now the rabble that was among them had a strong craving. And the people of Israel also wept again and said, "Oh that we had meat to eat! We remember the fish we ate in Egypt that cost nothing, the cucumbers, the melons, the leeks, the onions, and the garlic. But now our strength is dried up, and there is nothing at all but this manna to look at."

Even while living in slavery, the Israelites enjoyed the blessings of food and comfort. No doubt, the Egyptians gave a certain amount of freedom to the Israelites to make them just comfortable enough not to want to rebel against Egypt. Indeed it worked, for as soon as the Israelites experienced some discomfort, they reverted back to what they were comfortable with: slavery. It is no wonder that Grotius says, "A man may by his own act make himself the slave of any one."[82] America's founders new this concept to be called *voluntary slavery.*

As human experience has shown, the fear of losing comfort can distort a person's philosophy regarding resistance towards government's unlawful actions. Patrick Henry recognizes this flaw in human nature and recognizes that the fear of losing comfort may actually cause voluntary slavery. He says, "Is life so dear, or peace so sweet, as to be purchased at the price of chains and slavery? Forbid it, Almighty God! I know not what course others may take; but as for me, give me liberty, or give me death!"[83] Do we really want to be placed in a situation where the only choices are to live as a slave or die free? Do citizens think that God desires that we live in a state of comfort until such a decision of slavery or death must be made? Perhaps God uses certain incidences of economic recession and depression to awaken the motivation and values of the citizens and their responsibilities in a free nation. Perhaps God will take away the comforts of America so we might say what Thomas

---

82. Grotius, *Hugo Grotius on the Rights of War and Peace,* 38.
83. Compiled by a member of the Philadelphia Bar, *American Oratory,* 15.

Paine says before the Declaration of Independence was signed, "Thousands are already ruined... Those men have other feelings than us who have nothing suffered. All they now possess is liberty, what they before enjoyed is sacrificed to its service, and having nothing more to lose, they disdain submission."[84] Then, when all comforts have vanished, the only matter left to address is freedom.

America's founders, who supported independence from Great Britain, faced the same hurdle to motivate many of the colonists in support of independence from Great Britain. Thomas Paine keenly notices that the plan of present convenience in fact caused many "passive tempers [to] look somewhat lightly over the offenses of Britain, and, still hoping for the best...and to call out, 'Come we shall be friends again for all this.'"[85] I can hear the loyalists saying, "Oh, come on. It is not that bad; we can still do what we want for the most part. So our government isn't perfect; so what? Things will get better." Paine brings reality to the table, however, and responds to such an attitude by stating the following:

> But examine the passion and feelings of mankind. Bring the doctrine of reconciliation to the touchstone of nature, and then tell me, whether you can, hereafter love, honour, and faithfully serve the power that hath carried fire and sword into your land?
>
> If you cannot do all these, then are you only deceiving yourselves, and by your delay bringing ruin upon posterity. Your future connection with Britain, who you can neither love nor honour, will be forced and unnatural, and being formed only on the plan of present convenience, will in a little time fall into a relapse more wretched than the first.[86]

Had there not been enough people to support the defiance against Great Britain, and had America insisted on this unfounded reconciliation, many of

---

84. Paine and Philip, ed., *Common Sense*, 31.
85. Ibid., 25.
86. Ibid.

us in America would be saying this today to such persons: "The blood of his children shall curse his cowardice, who shrinks back at a time when a little might have saved the whole and made them happy."[87] Similarly, Americans who believe that they will resist government when it crosses the line are only deceiving themselves. Those same people do not simply vote for persons they know to be the best-qualified candidates, because they fear the greater evil candidate—which is a faithless and slavish mentality.

Fear of losing comfort creates a slavish mentality to the point that when faced with mere hunger, citizens will gladly give themselves to slavery in exchange for knowing that they have a meal to eat and a place to sleep. Translating this into modern terms, decisions—whether by individuals, businesses, or governments—regarding freedom versus slavery are made out of fear: fear of economic collapse;[88] fear of financial depression; fear of not having the lifestyle they so thoroughly enjoy; fear of higher taxes; fear of losing status quo; fear of social repercussions; fear of media predators; fear of foreign nation backlash; fear of political correctness; fear of political parties; fear of losing one's seat at the king's table; fear of losing voluntary contributions; fear of going against the flow; fear of losing church members (and thus tithes and offerings, and thus income); fear of family in-laws; and fear of a decrease in business. Decisions made out of these fears will never produce freedom but only more slavery.

The fact is fear should never influence the decisions of persons with character—especially those who believe in a greater power than themselves and

---

87. Paine and Philip, ed., *American Crisis I,* 69.

88. "The commerce and industry when suspended on the Daedalian wings of paper money, as on the solid ground of gold and silver; and that in time of war, the insecurity is greatly increased, and great confusion possible where the circulation is for the greater part in paper." Jefferson, *The Jeffersonian Cyclopedia,* 571; "By the Constitution, Congress may regulate the value of foreign coin; but if they do not do it, the old power revives to the state, the Constitution only forbidding them to make anything but gold and silver tender in payment of debts." "I deny the power of the General Government to making paper money, or anything else, a legal tender." Jefferson, *The Jeffersonian Cyclopedia,* 574; "We have no metallic measure of values at present, while we are overwhelmed with bank paper. The depreciation of this swells nominal prices, without furnishing any stable index of real value." Jefferson, *The Jeffersonian Cyclopedia,* 575.

in the duties and responsibilities that we have towards our posterity. Thomas Jefferson tells us, "Renounce your domestic comforts for a few months, and reflect that to be a good husband and good father at this moment, you must also be a good citizen."[89] The Bible, too, has much to say about fear. "There is no fear in love; but perfect love casts out fear: because fear hath torment. He that fears is not made perfect in love."[90] "For God has not given us the spirit of fear; but of power, and of love, and of a sound mind."[91] The Bible reveals story after story of people who did not fear the world or those in the world but rather only feared God. As such, they stood against kings and governments. Consider the Hebrew midwives who were commanded by the Egyptian Pharaoh, in an effort to control the population (and thus power), to kill all of the male Hebrew babies who were born of the Israelites. The story follows:

> [The king of Egypt said], "When you serve as midwife to the Hebrew women and see them on the birthstool, if it is a son, you shall kill him, but if it is a daughter, she shall live." But the midwives feared God and did not do as the king of Egypt commanded them, but let the male children live. So the king of Egypt called the midwives and said to them, "Why have you done this, and let the male children live?" The midwives said to Pharaoh, "Because the Hebrew women are not like the Egyptian women, for they are vigorous and give birth before the midwife comes to them." So God dealt well with the midwives. And the people multiplied and grew very strong.[92]

The apostle Paul says of those women in Hebrews 11:23 (KJV), "By faith Moses, when he was born, was hid three months of his parents, because they saw he was a proper child; and they were not afraid of the king's commandment." So what is to be said of those who fear consequences of actions

---

89. Ibid., 268.
90. John 4:18 (KJV).
91. Timothy 1:7 (KJV).
92. Exodus 1:16–20 (ESV).

taken in faith? Is defiance of government based upon belief and faith in the natural and revealed laws of God left only to those who lived in generations before, as if we are too sophisticated to do so now? Perhaps such persons do not possess the love of country that must exist for a free nation to exist, as Montesquieu described.[93] Consider as well that politicians conduct themselves reflecting fear—only it is their fear of losing power, just as the Pharisees did during Jesus's life. "Then gathered the chief priests and the Pharisees a council, and said, What do we? For this man doeth many miracles. If we let him thus alone, all men will believe on him: and the Romans shall come and take away both our place and nation."[94] What did the Pharisees do to control their fear of losing power? They killed Jesus Christ, the main threat to their establishment. Are things really any different today in America? I think not.

Compare the attitude of comfort before freedom, however, to America's founders and their philosophical mentors. Look at how they despised slavery and despotism and how they were willing to suffer infinite pains and labors to secure freedom. They understood what is required to secure freedom—it was and is no easy task. Founding father John Jay expresses that fear should never influence the actions of a citizen who is complying with the will of God when he states, "Whatever may be the characters, the prejudices, the views, or the arts of our opponents, we have only to be faithful to our Great Leader. They who march under the banners of Emmanuel with God with them; and consequently have nothing to fear."[95] Obviously, John Jay agrees with the following words from Montesquieu: "If by some revolution the state has happened to assume a new form, this seldom can be effected *without infinite pains and labor,* and *hardly ever by idle and debauched persons.*"[96] It is a fact that "all the luxuries, and many of the comforts of life were sacrificed at once on the altar of colonial liberty."[97] But even in the face of such extreme difficulties, our founders possessed a Christ-like courage, stating as Thomas

93. Montesquieu, *The Spirit of Laws,* 34.

94. John 11:47, 48 (KJV).

95. Jay, *The Life of John Jay,* 506.

96. Montesquieu, *The Spirit of Laws,* 47, (emphasis added).

97. Rayner, *The Life of Thomas Jefferson,* 41.

Paine does, "I thank God that I fear not. I see no real cause for fear. I know our situation well, and can see the way out of it."[98] So have American citizens of recent and current generations proven to be willing to affect freedom with infinite pains and labor, or have we proven to be ever idle and debauched persons? Perhaps self-reflection would reveal that America is far from what America's founders were. The state of our nation reflects it.

Observe the mindset demonstrated by John Jay in his attempts to awaken the citizenry to their current state of slavery under Great Britain and Jay's confirmation of what Montesquieu states regarding idle and debauched persons being inconsistent with freedom and liberty:

> Whereas certain inhabitants and subjects of this State, either seduced by the arts or corrupted by the bribes of the enemy, or influenced by unmanly fear, profess to owe allegiance to the King of Great Britain, although the said king had denied them his protection, absolved them from their allegiance, and by force of arms attempted to reduce them from subjects to vassals, and from freemen to slaves.
>
> And whereas others, from the like or similar motives, or with design to maintain an equivocal neutrality, and ungenerously avoid the dangers incident to those who nobly stand forth for the liberties of their country, pretend to hold for true the exploded and ridiculous doctrine of passive obedience and non-resistance to any power, however tyrannical, unconstitutional, oppressive, and cruel.[99]

Jay recognizes that there were many who failed to take action because of different fears. Not only did Jay possess the knowledge to address this fallacious reason to resist tyranny, but he possessed the courage to sign his name on the Declaration of Independence (a certain death sentence for himself and his family); to serve as a general of the Continental Army against Great Britain; to become an ambassador to Spain and France in efforts to obtain

---

98. Paine and Philip, ed., *American Crisis I*, 70.

99. Jay, *The Life of John Jay*, 49.

financial assistance in their fight for independence; to pledge his own personal money as security for any loans; and to be a New York state congressman and the first United States Supreme Court chief justice. Jay further
recognized that it was his duty to resist tyranny, and that being neutral on
the matter was as wrong as it was dishonorable. He says, "I joined myself to
the first assertors of the American cause, because I thought it my duty; and
because I considered caution and neutrality, however secure, as being no less
wrong than dishonorable."[100] Try to find this kind of dedication to freedom
in the face of inevitable and infinite pains and labors in America today. Most
leaders simply attempt to secure their interest and security, forsaking their
posterity and sacrificing their freedom for the sake of caution, practicality,
and fear.

CASE IN POINT
Perhaps very reflective of the spirit of fear is a political flier supporting Senator
John McCain's bid for president published in *Focus on the Family Action* in
October 2008.[101] Let me make this clear, while I understand and recognize
that *Focus on the Family* has accomplished good, and while I do not attempt
to undermine their positive influence in many people's lives, I feel compelled
to reflect on the error in philosophy they demonstrated, which contributes
to the destruction of America's freedom and is relevant to this discussion.
This critique and observation is similar in nature to Thomas Paine's appeal
to his fellow colonists to rise to the call of freedom. "This is not inflaming or
exaggerating matters, but trying them by those feelings and affections which
nature justifies, and without which, we should be incapable of discharging
the social duties of life, or enjoying the felicities of it." Moreover, the following criticism is not "mean[t] to exhibit horror for the purpose of provoking
revenge, but [is] to awaken us from fatal and unmanly slumbers, that we may
pursue determinately some fixed objects. It is not in the power [of those who
destroy freedom] to conquer America, if she do not conquer herself by delay
and timidity."[102]

---

100. Ibid., 95.

101. James Dobson, *Focus on the Family Action,* Issue 10, October 2008, http://www.gwu.
edu/~action/2008/interestg08/dobson102008newsletter.pdf (accessed May 5, 2009).

102. Paine and Philip, ed., *Common Sense,* 26.

Earlier in the Republican primaries, Dr. James Dobson stated absolutely and unequivocally that he would not support Senator John McCain, because he disagreed with most of John McCain's positions. In fact, James Dobson is quoted as saying, "Speaking as a private individual, I would not vote for John McCain under any circumstances."[103] To be certain on Dobson's position, the interviewer had Dobson listen to a quote from McCain regarding homosexual marriage. The quote is, "I think that gay marriage should be allowed if there's a ceremony kind of thing, if you want to call it that...I don't have any problem with that."[104] Dobson's response again is that he would not support McCain. "That came from McCain, and the McCain Feingold Bill kept us from telling the truth right before elections...and there are a lot of other things. He's not in favor of traditional marriage, and I pray that we won't get stuck with him."[105]

This was not the first time Dobson threatened not to support a Republican. "Dobson noted he'd been interviewed by *U.S. News and World Report* after the 2004 elections and warned if Republicans squandered their opportunity, they would pay a price at the polls in either 2008 or 2006." Oh, really? This is certain: Dobson's actions have been nothing but supportive of Republican (and Republican only) candidates. Only God knows his heart, but we must observe the error of the philosophy behind his statements and actions. If he does truly believe what he says, what motivates him to immediately turn an about face and publish the following material nationwide?

In his address, Dobson starts off by stating, "I'd like to take a few moments to consider what is at stake in this year's election, particularly for those of us who embrace a biblical worldview. Please understand that I will share these thoughts under the umbrella of Focus on the Family Action, which has supported the preparation and distribution of this letter."[106] Interestingly, Dobson makes it known that the political position about to be

---

103. Bob Unruh, "Dobson Says 'No Way' to McCain Candidacy," *World Net Daily Exclusive,* (January 13, 2007), http://www.worldnetdaily.com/news/article.asp?ARTICLE_ID=53743 (accessed May 5, 2009).

104. Ibid.

105. Ibid.

106. James Dobson, *Focus on the Family Action,* Issue 10, October 2008, http://www.gwu.edu/~action/2008/interestg08/dobson102008newsletter.pdf (accessed May 5, 2009).

advocated was Focus on the Family's baby and not his personal view (perhaps to save face, knowing what he previously said about not supporting McCain under any circumstances). So are we to believe that what he says he does not believe, or that Focus on the Family paid him to say what he said? Regardless, he speaks with passion as he continues. "Let's start with the need to elect a pro-family, pro-life president."[107] Stop right there! Is Dobson speaking of the same person whom he recently and dogmatically insisted he would not support and about whom he says, "I pray that we won't get stuck with him"? He already dogmatically stated that McCain was not an advocate of traditional marriage. How can he declare that McCain is now pro-family? This statement already reveals contradiction, manipulation, and desperation.

Of course (as was the case with most conservatives who supported John McCain), one of the only matters to be addressed as a reason to support McCain is this: "Between 2009 and 2012 there will likely be two or more opportunities for the president to nominate new justices to the Supreme Court."[108] As if any Republican appointed Supreme Court judge has changed the course of this nation for the good! This fallacy has already been discussed herein, but again, *Roe v. Wade* was decided by seven Republican judges, and for the past forty years abortions have been performed at a rate of over 1 million every year—despite the fact that Republican judges have dominated the Supreme Court.[109] This is a known fact and is not deniable. How can Dobson expect any different from 2009 to 2012, especially from a person who is one of the weakest pro-family, pro-life candidates in Republican history? Even the so-called Christian president, G. W. Bush, made nominal efforts to reduce the number of abortions performed each year during his eight year administration! In fact, as has been studied and revealed, abortion reduction must be attributed to sex education, condom access, and government supported Planned Parenthood.[110]

---

107. Ibid.

108. Ibid.

109. Thomas J. Reese, "Abortion: Rhetoric or Results," *The Washington Post,* September 24, 2008, http://newsweek.washingtonpost.com/onfaith/thomas_j_reese/2008/09/abortion_rhetoric_or_results.html (accessed May 5, 2009).

110. Nicholas D. Kristof, "Abortions, Condoms, and Bush," *The New York Times,* (November 5, 2006), http://select.nytimes.com/2006/11/05/opinion/05kristof.html?_r=1 (accessed May 5, 2009).

Dobson continues his appeal to those who embrace a biblical worldview. He says, "It's probably obvious which of the two major party candidates' views are most palatable to those of us who embrace a pro-life, pro-family worldview."[111] Perhaps the answer is not as obvious as Dobson would have those who embrace a biblical worldview think. Is Dobson even considering the fact that Obama actually has a great track record for family values compared to McCain? Obama has been married to one wife; has two children who have a close connection to their parents; has never been caught cheating on his wife or even suspected of such; and actually possesses a traditional American family, as defined even by Christians.

What about McCain? Does he exemplify a person with pro-family views? Consider John McCain's well-known extramarital affairs with several women during his first marriage, including with the woman he is married to today. Consider McCain is admittedly pro-homosexual marriage. Consider that McCain introduced the McCain Feingold Bill, one of the goals of which was to put judges into office who were not pro-life, as Dobson already recognized. Of course, no one is perfect, but how can Dobson make a declaration that McCain is a better candidate than Obama on these family issues, when the evidence and facts do not support this? He admitted it himself just months prior. When Bill Clinton was in office, the Christians were crying out with righteous indignation about Clinton's extramarital affair with Monica Lewinsky, crying out for impeachment. When asked why, one of the responses was rightfully claimed, *because we expect better from our president.* I guess standards are different for Democrats than they are for Republicans. Even Clinton has been married to the same woman his entire adult life and has a claim of faith in Jesus Christ.[112] Why criticize only the Democrats for their flaws and embrace the Republicans despite their flaws? What makes McCain a champion of our freedom?

Dobson further says, "I have agonized at times during this election process and have been strongly critical of Senator McCain and the Republican

---

111. James Dobson, *Focus on the Family Action,* Issue 10, October 2008, http://www.gwu. edu/~action/2008/interestg08/dobson102008newsletter.pdf (accessed May 5, 2009).

112. Author Unknown, "Church Leaders Praise Bill Clinton's 'Spirituality'," *Christian News,* http://www.jesus-is-savior.com/church_leaders_praise_bill_clinton.htm (accessed May 5, 2009).

Party on numerous occasions. My concern is for the biblical and moral values that I and millions of Americans hold dear. I will gladly support politicians of any stripe who are willing to defend the sanctity of human life, support the institution of traditional marriage, protect the country from terrorism, and advance the cause of religious liberty."[113] This assertion is almost hilarious but yet very sad, knowing that thousands of people read and heed what Dobson says. Dobson already established in previous interviews that McCain is not a defender of the sanctity of human life; is not a supporter of traditional marriage; and is not an advancer of religious liberty. If he were any of these things and notably so, Dobson would have already and gladly given his support to McCain and would not have said that he would not vote for McCain under any circumstances.

In further effort to justify his position to support McCain, Dobson focused on an Obama statement that said knowing when life begins is above his pay grade. Dobson responded with, "If this question is above your pay grade, then so is the job attached to it."[114] Well, the fact is Obama was right. It is not the job of the president to decide when life begins. That has already been decided by God Almighty and has been revealed in scriptures. And if you do not accept that source, then our government was formed to put the power of such decisions in the hands of the people—through their legislatures. Indeed, that matter is above his pay grade, and perhaps Obama admitting that such a matter is not for a president to decide will open the door for abortion issues to be placed back into the state arena and into the people's hands (which if done, would likely be extremely positive for pro-lifers, given the 250 million Christians in America). Again, jurisdiction applies. Since when do we place such a decision regarding abortion into the hands of one person? And since when has any Democrat or Republican president made any difference regarding the number of abortions in America? For the same reason we do not put the ultimate decision in the hands of the Supreme Court judges, we do not put the decision in the hands of the president. The

---

113. James Dobson, *Focus on the Family Action,* Issue 10, October 2008, http://www.gwu.edu/~action/2008/interestg08/dobson102008newsletter.pdf (accessed May 5, 2009).

114. Ibid.

president of the United States is not the answer to all problems, nor was he ever meant to be—even on matters that we all would consider important. Would this not be the opportune time for Dobson to declare and promote the limited constitutional form of government that protected the unborn life for 200 years in America prior to 1972? Instead, it is politics as usual and a thorough lack of understanding of jurisprudence and jurisdiction—not to mention courage to step outside the mainstream Republican-Democrat racket.

The other reason Dobson promoted McCain was because the Republican platform is a remarkably conservative document, as if Republicans were the only politicians who "could draw strength and standing from God."[115] So what? And what about other truly viable third parties that have, not only the conservative platform, but also the true and actual conservative candidates? Furthermore, since when has title changed the philosophy of a politician or been the criteria for support? Is Dobson not familiar with Thomas Paine's observation that "men do not change from enemies to friends by the alternation of a name"?[116] Dobson himself recognized that Republicans have strayed from the faith, which is why he threatened not to support them in 2004. Has not Dobson observed over the past forty years what Republicans have done to America, including the legalizing of abortion and the removal of God from the public forum? Any objective observer would have to admit that Republicans and Democrats are way off line from the straight and narrow path of freedom, and that both have contributed to our slavery. The reasoning that the Republican platform is conservative is as deep as a fish bowl and as thoughtful as a Hallmark card, and using such a reason only shows that Dobson was grasping for anything to give his readers to support McCain. It also reveals the Republicans are good and Democrats are bad mentality that is enslaving the minds of Americans, thanks to leaders like Dobson.

Dobson's third reason for promoting McCain was that McCain selected an astonishingly strong pro-life, pro-family running mate in Governor Sarah Palin, as if Dobson was placing all bets on the fact that maybe McCain would

---

115. Meacham, *American Gospel,* 7.
116. Paine and Philip, ed., *Common Sense,* 30.

die, and Palin would become president. Of course, it is a fact that many Christians all over America were very excited that McCain picked Palin as his running mate, as if there was now a justifiable reason to vote for McCain. Are Dobson and other conservatives not aware that McCain knew he did not have the support of many Christians and conservatives for the same reasons that Dobson earlier expressed that he would not support him under any circumstances? Did Dobson believe that McCain would promote true freedom in America simply because Palin claims to be pro-life and pro-family? Is this the reason that Dobson even claimed that McCain is a defender of family values and the unborn? Does it not cross Dobson's mind that such a pick for vice president is more strategic in nature than substantive, in an effort to capture the vote and support through deceit? Like the person who believes people mushroom into good leaders despite the evidence, Dobson seems to think that McCain mushroomed into a worthy candidate because he nominated Palin. In fact, most of what Dobson says in promotion of McCain actually was his promotion of Palin. "I'll discuss Governor Palin's candidacy in greater detail in a moment."[117] Indeed he did, because that was all he could do.

Dobson's last reason for promoting McCain was that he (Dobson) had "become [concerned] with Barack Obama's liberal views."[118] Since when has a conservative *not* been concerned with the liberal views of any Democrat? What radio talk show host has not criticized every possible Democrat for their liberal views? The real question is why are not these same people concerned about the liberal views of the Republicans? Or is this just about party politics? Dobson already expressed his utter dissatisfaction with McCain, and even the Republican Party. But then he saw the light and started to support McCain, as if all would be lost if McCain did not get into office. The fact is McCain would likely do more damage to the nation than Obama, because (as during the Bush administration) Christians and conservatives fell asleep and stood back, idle and debauched. They actually believed that their president was securing freedom in America, looking more at the person enacting policy than the principle behind the policy. Maybe with Obama in office

117. Ibid.
118. Ibid.

Christians and conservatives will at least pay attention to what is being done and actually resist. Maybe it will light a fire in their pants to get off of their lounger and learn about the issues affecting America and our posterity.

So what was Dobson saying essentially? Bottom line: Dobson was saying that McCain was a lesser of two evils, and that we (Christians) have more to fear if Obama gets into office than if McCain gets into office. This approach of righteousness only keeps America "low and humble as possible [and] instead of going forward we…go backward."[119] This approach does not even compare to America's founders like John Jay, who makes the bold proclamation to his generation to reject the "ridiculous doctrine of passive obedience and non-resistance to any power, however tyrannical, unconstitutional, oppressive, and cruel,"[120] regardless of personality or party politics.

While many of America's current conservative leaders fear certain liberal candidates, the more pertinent questions are as follows: Where is the fear of slavery? Where is the fear that our posterity is going to live under a despotic government? Where is the fear that all knowledge of what freedom is will be lost to the supporting of the lesser of two evils? Where is the fear that the lesser of two evils will still be evil and will still reject all understanding of American freedom as procured by our founders (both in England and America)? Where is the fear that the power of the people will no longer be effective, and that after becoming slaves, any power once held will have disappeared? Where is the fear that your children will be subjects completely and solely to the state, without any semblance of liberty granted by God? Where is the fear of God, who has promised to destroy any nation that rejects Him and His laws? Where is the fear that God will in fact turn America over to slavery where the people have voluntarily subjected themselves to evil powers? Indeed, there is a lot of submission going on, but it is misplaced. The submission to God, to fellow men, to family, and to posterity is nonexistent.

Rejecting Natural and Revealed Laws of God

Another reason for the detrimental attitude of American citizens towards government is their rejecting the natural and revealed laws of God. History and

---

119. Paine and Philip, ed., *Common Sense*, 29.
120. Jay, *The Life of John Jay*, 49.

the Bible are replete with examples of the negative consequences of citizens not following natural and revealed laws relative to government. Consider the following from the Bible: "He destroys you, O Israel, for you are against me, against your helper. Where now is your king, to save you in all your cities? Where are all your rulers—those of whom you said, 'Give me a king and princes'? I gave you a king in my anger, and I took him away in my wrath."[121] Notice that when God's people said give me a king, God—in anger—gave them just what they wanted, to their detriment. Woe to such a people where God gives them in anger what they want.

For decades Americans have received exactly what they wanted: lesser evils (but still evil) and dependence on government—just as Israel did in Hosea. Dobson says the following in the previously mentioned political address: "Regardless of your political views, I want to urge Christians everywhere to be in prayer about this election."[122] But may I ask what good is prayer when the people reject the very basic and fundamental principles derived from natural and revealed laws? Jesus already addressed that question when He was on earth. "You are wrong, because you know neither the Scriptures nor the power of God."[123] The answer is not our lack of prayer, for many people likely pray about elections (especially on a national level). May I dare ask, what good has it done?

Can there be any excuse for not knowing the principles found in natural and revealed laws regarding government and the citizens' duty to it? America is perhaps the only nation in human history founded on these principles and specifically on Christian ideology, where the Bible has been preached on every corner of almost every street for hundreds of years. As Jesus says, where much has been given, much will be required—no excuses.[124] Blackstone agrees with this principle when he says,

121. Hosea 13:9–11 (ESV).

122. James Dobson, *Focus on the Family Action,* Issue 10, October 2008, http://www.gwu.edu/~action/2008/interestg08/dobson102008newsletter.pdf (accessed May 5, 2009).

123. Matthew 22:29 (ESV).

124. "For to whomever much is given, of him much shall be required. And to whom men have committed much, of him they will ask the more." Luke 12:48 (ESV).

It is incumbent upon every man to be acquainted with those [laws] at least with which he is immediately concerned; lest he incur the censure, as well as the inconvenience, of living in society without knowing the obligations which it lays him under. And thus much may suffice for persons of inferior condition, who have neither time nor capacity to enlarge their views beyond that contracted sphere in which they are appointed move.

But those, on whom nature and fortune have bestowed more abilities and greater leisure, cannot be so easily excused. These advantages are given them, not for the benefit of themselves only, but also of the public.[125]

The result of not following the natural and revealed laws of God can be found in Romans 11:7–10 (ESV):

What then? Israel failed to obtain what it was seeking. The elect obtained it, but the rest were hardened, as it is written, "God gave them a spirit of stupor, eyes that would not see and ears that would not hear, down to this very day." And David says, "Let their table become a snare and a trap, a stumbling block and a retribution for them; let their eyes be darkened so that they cannot see, and bend their backs forever."

Without a heart that is willing to "ask, seek, and knock"[126] for truth found in natural and revealed laws regarding every aspect of life and acknowledge God in His paths,[127] such a person fails to walk in the light as Jesus is in the light.[128] Indeed, God's paths comprise every walk and area of life—including government and our interaction with it.

Solomon explains to his son the rewards of searching for God's wisdom regarding not only one's personal life, but also a nation's life. Solomon says,

---

125. Blackstone, *Commentaries on the Laws of England*, 3, (emphasis added).
126. Matthew 7:7 (KJV).
127. Psalm 23:3 (KJV).
128. John 2 (KJV).

My son, if you receive my words and treasure up my commandments with you, making your ear attentive to wisdom and inclining
your heart to understanding; yes, if you call out for insight and raise
your voice for understanding, if you seek it like silver and search
for it as for hidden treasures, then you will understand the fear of
the LORD and find the knowledge of God. For the LORD gives
wisdom; from his mouth come knowledge and understanding; he
stores up sound wisdom for the upright; he is a shield to those who
walk in integrity, guarding the paths of justice and watching over
the way of his saints. Then you will understand righteousness and
justice and equity, every good path; for wisdom will come into your
heart, and knowledge will be pleasant to your soul; discretion will
watch over you, understanding will guard you, delivering you from
the way of evil, from men of perverted speech, who forsake the paths
of uprightness to walk in the ways of darkness.[129]

How can a person say that these principles would apply to government
any less than they apply to an individual's life? To suggest that such a verse
does not apply to government would be foreign to our founding fathers and
their mentoring philosophers.

Our founding and Enlightenment fathers understood that when a nation
possessed knowledge of natural and revealed laws and implemented the same
into society, that nation would be as free as possible while here on earth
(understanding that no government is perfect, because men are not perfect).
Consider what Grotius says regarding a nation's implementation of these
principles into government.

What we Gentiles have gained by the coming of Christ is, not that
we are freed from the law of Moses; but that, wherever formerly we
could only have obscured hope founded on the goodness of God,
we now have a Covenant, and may be gathered into one Church
with the descendants of the Patriarchs, the being taken away, which

---

129. Proverbs 2:1–13 (ESV).

was the partition-wall between us…it is now lawful for the Ruler of Christian states to make laws of the same purport as the laws of Moses.

Except those Mosaic Laws of which the whole substance belonged to the time when Christ was expected, and the Gospel not yet revealed; or except has commanded contrary generally; or specially. With these three exceptions [just mentioned], there cannot be devised any case in which that which was formerly instituted by the Law of Moses should not be within the lawful sphere of instated law at present…whatever is commanded by the law of Moses, connected with the virtues which Christ required from his disciples, that, at least, if not more, is due from Christians.[130]

Imagine a modern-day politician—or even a pastor—stating this and suggesting that America incorporate the laws of Moses into our government! I believe such a suggestion would be rejected outright even by most Christians today in America, because after all, we have a separation of church and state (all the while, these same people receive or would agree with those who receive federal and state monies for faith-based programs—and of course, accepting the restrictions attached to the money). Are not all laws based upon some principle, some theory, something higher than the law itself? Of course they are. But America has proven that it does not prefer what Grotius suggested.

Here is another example of our Enlightenment father's expectation that government use God's natural and revealed laws as principles establishing its own modern-day laws. Algernon Sidney says,

It hath been ever hereupon observed, that they who most precisely adhere to the laws of God, are least solicitous [anxious] concerning the commands of men, unless they are well grounded; and those who most delight in the glorious liberty of the sons of God, do not only subject themselves to him, but are most regular observers of

---

130. Grotius, *Hugo Grotius on the Rights of War and Peace*, 7–8.

the just ordinances of man, made by the consent of such as are concerned, according to the will of God.[131]

In other words, men who are familiar with the laws of God are the best citizens, knowing what laws are well grounded and knowing what ordinances of man are just according to the will of God, because having such knowledge equips you to know what laws are according to the will of God. Simultaneously, men with knowledge of God's principles would be the first to resist evil in government, knowing which laws are not well grounded and what laws are not just. This knowledge is the reason why a free nation cannot exist without the education of its citizens. Education of what? The education of justice as described by natural and revealed laws—the will of God. And while Dobson suggests that "it is time for Christians everywhere to turn to Him for guidance and wisdom,"[132] perhaps Christian leaders would do well to adhere to their own words and dig into already established natural and revealed laws of God. Perhaps they would find more pleasing results regarding all matters of freedom by stepping outside of their hypnotic approach to electing the lesser of two evils. Perhaps they will realize that their approach has accomplished nothing for freedom, and as a result, shed the worldly fears associated with truly standing and standing truly.

Deterioration of Philosophy and Principle

Perhaps coming full circle in this discussion, a deterioration of philosophical understanding contributes greatly to the demise of the attitude of citizens towards government. Many Christians believe that God will spare America from judgment, because America has millions of Christians occupying its territory. Many refer to the scripture in the Old Testament where God tells Abraham that he is going to destroy the city of Sodom because "their sin [was] very grievous."[133]

---

131. Sidney, *Discourses on Government*, 315.

132. James Dobson, *Focus on the Family Action,* Issue 10, October 2008, http://www.gwu.edu/~action/2008/interestg08/dobson102008newsletter.pdf (accessed May 5, 2009).

133. Genesis 18:20 (KJV).

"Then Abraham drew near and said, 'Will you indeed sweep away the righteous with the wicked?'"[134] God took Abraham up on the question and told Abraham that He would spare the cities if Abraham could find fifty righteous people, meaning lawful and just. Abraham went on his journey to find fifty righteous people, but he could not do so. So God dropped the number down to forty-five, then to thirty, then to twenty, and then to ten, but Abraham was not able to find even ten righteous people in the city. The principle here is that God would spare an entire nation whose sin is grievous where there are a certain percentage of people—or even just one person—that is righteous.

First of all, to presume that God will not actively destroy a nation assumes that the nation cannot destroy itself. Betting on the presumption that God will not actively destroy a nation neglects the biblical principle that it "rains on the just and the unjust alike"[135] according to certain natural law principles such as "you reap what you sow."[136] But assuming this argument that God obligates Himself to spare an evil nation where there are a few righteous people present is true, there is a certain element of righteousness that must be explored (although only God knows the hearts of men and can judge who is righteous). It must be furthered explored within the context of current observation of evil nations and whether or not there are righteous people therein. In other words, what fruits do we look for when determining whether or not a citizen is righteous for purposes of sparing a nation judgment? God's word gives direction on this matter, especially regarding the citizen in relation to government.

In 1 Kings 19, God gives a story of the prophet Elisha who becomes depressed because his government is out to kill him. He feels he is the only person who is a man of God, and that all others have forsaken God. "But he himself went a day's journey into the wilderness and came and sat down under a broom tree. And he asked that he might die, saying, 'It is enough; now, O LORD, take away my life, for I am no better than my fathers.'"[137]

---

134. Genesis 18:23 (ESV).
135. Matthew 5:45 (KJV).
136. Galatians 6:7 (KJV).
137. Kings 19:4 (ESV).

However, God shed some light on just how many righteous people there were that lived in that nation. God says to Elisha, "Yet I will leave seven thousand in Israel, all the knees that have not bowed to Baal, and every mouth that has not kissed him."[138] It is interesting to observe that the righteous people described here by God are those who do not give their allegiance to the evil king and who have resisted showing him honor. This is similar to so many Old and New Testament people who demonstrated the same kind of resistance to ungodly government: Daniel, Shadrach, Meshach, Abednego, Paul, Peter, John the Baptist, Jesus, Esther, Stephen, Elisha, David, midwives in Egypt, and others. Can it be concluded that America is full of righteous Christians who refuse to bow their knee to unlawful government? There are even professing Christians who have verbally acknowledged that they will not resist what they know to be evil in government. How many more have bowed their knee to Baal in their hearts or actions?

Despite the independent will and sovereignty of God to spare nations for the sake of the righteous, God's word is clear that God will judge a nation— righteous or unrighteous alike—that rejects Him and His word, which contain God's philosophy. A Christian nation cannot expect the sparing of judgment and certainly should expect to suffer the natural consequences of their actions when the people have turned from the commandments of God found in natural and revealed laws. Can a person who jumps off a hundred-story building expect not to get hurt because he is righteous? Being a Christian no more spares God's judgment and the natural consequences of rejecting natural and revealed laws than being a Jew automatically saves that person from hell—all must comply with God's natural and revealed laws for God to save and bless them. The apostle Paul tells us, "See to it that no one takes you captive by philosophy and empty deceit, according to human tradition, according to the elemental spirits of the world, and not according to Christ."[139] God knows that being a Christian does not automatically mean that such a person will not accept and adopt and even implement worldly philosophy. Thus, we are to die daily to worldly philosophy[140] and study to

---

138. Kings 19:18 (ESV).

139. Colossians 2:8 (ESV).

140. "I protest, brothers, by my pride in you, which I have in Christ Jesus our Lord, I die every day!" 1 Corinthians 15:31 (ESV).

show ourselves approved unto God.[141] For we know that anyone who adopts a worldly philosophy chooses to be judged by God.[142]

History also reveals that a corrupted philosophy will ultimately destroy a nation. Our founders were aware of this and read about this from philosophers such as Montesquieu. Our founders observed and believed that "the corruption of every government generally begins with that of its principles."[143] A *principle* is a "basic truth or a general law or doctrine that is used as a basis of reasoning or a guide to action or behavior."[144] Every person, community, family, and nation accepts and believes certain principles, because all action or behavior proceeds from there. It controls your premises, assumptions, rationale, and conclusions. A bad principle leads to bad conclusions and bad behavior—in an individual's life and a nation's life. Montesquieu likewise observed that principle controls everything in a nation, saying, "Once the principles of government are corrupted, the very best laws become bad and turn against the state."[145] This is why a nation's "constitution [may be] free, but not the people,"[146] because the accepted principle, the accepted truth, and the accepted doctrine have more effect on the implementation of laws and on society's behavior than any other factor. America may have the freest Constitution in the world but may have a people in slavery. Thus, the act of preserving freedom takes place every day and requires much work and labor—there is no finish line.

---

141. "Do your best to present yourself to God as one approved, a worker who has no need to be ashamed, rightly handling the word of truth." 2 Timothy 2:15 (ESV).

142. "And Samuel said to Saul, 'I will not return with you. For you have rejected the word of the LORD, and the LORD has rejected you from being king over Israel.' As Samuel turned to go away, Saul seized the skirt of his robe, and it tore. And Samuel said to him, 'The LORD has torn the kingdom of Israel from you this day and has given it to a neighbor of yours, who is better than you.'" 1 Samuel 15:26-28 (ESV). Unfortunately for the people of Israel, the damage had been done while King Saul ruled over the nation. People were killed, people were enslaved, taxes were raised, wars were raged, fear was prevalent, and God's blessing was absent. But the tyranny began when the people of Israel adopted the worldly philosophy that they had to have a king. Indeed, God gave them what they wanted.

143. Montesquieu, *The Spirit of Laws*, 109.

144. Ehrlich, Carruth, Hawkins, and Flexner, *Oxford American Dictionary*.

145. Montesquieu, *The Spirit of Laws*, 116.

146. Ibid., 183.

Montesquieu portrays an enlightening example of how principle can change a person's belief and behavior when he describes a man who was once industrious and innovative and subsequently became a leech on society because of the way the government treated the individual's innovation and industry.

> Content I am because of my poverty. When I was rich, I was obliged to pay my court to informers, knowing I was more liable to be hurt by them than capable of doing them harm. The republic constantly demanded some new tax of me; and I could not decline paying.
>
> Since I have grown poor, I have acquired authority; nobody threatens me; I rather threaten others. I can go or stay where I please. The rich already rise from their seats and give me the way. I am king, I was before a slave: I paid taxes to the republic, now it maintains me: I am no longer afraid of losing: but I hope to acquire.[147]

The individual first possessed and believed the principle that self-responsibility was a good way of life and worth living. However, after the government punished his good behavior, he adopted a new principle—a doctrine of government reliance not self-responsibility or initiative. It is easy to see how the corrupted philosophy possessed by this man would destroy a nation if accepted by many in the nation. The same could be said in every area of society.

Likewise, many other philosophies will destroy a nation, regardless of whether or not the nation has Christians in it, because God has established His standards, which if rejected brings judgment. There are Christians living in despotic and tyrannical governments today—even despite apparent spiritual revivals taking place. As John Jay says, "the Almighty will not suffer slavery and the gospel to go hand in hand."[148] It must be noted that "where the Spirit of the Lord is, there is liberty."[149] Thus, no Christian can live in tyr-

---

147. Ibid., 109–110.
148. Jay, *The Life of John Jay*, 56.
149. Corinthians 3:17 (KJV).

anny and slavery without it bothering and disturbing the freedom he has in Christ, just as Lot's soul was vexed daily because of the unlawful and ungodly government he lived in. This fact has already been established. Slavery and freedom cannot coexist without a state of war between those who advocate slavery and those who advocate freedom. Thomas Jefferson puts it this way: "Time indeed changes manners and notions, and so far we must expect institutions to bend them. But time produces also corruption of principles, and against this it is the duty of good citizens to be ever on the watch, and if the gangrene is to prevail at last, let the day be kept off as long as possible."[150] So where persons adopt a philosophy that is okay with living in slavery, do they really possess the biblical philosophy and belief that God gives freedom, life, and property? Any person who decides to live voluntarily in slavery will likely have some explaining to do to his Maker one day.

Ignorance

Perhaps the most applicable reason for the freedom-damaging attitude that American citizens possess is the vice of ignorance. While ignorance may be bliss, bliss will only last so long, for sin's pleasure lasts only for a season.[151] Eventually such citizens will be trodden under the foot of men for failing to be salt and light of the earth. Ignorance causes more pain and damage than most would care to know. Ignorance will also destroy a nation, because ignorance of citizens produces those Nimrods who seek to take advantage of their ignorance. America's founders recognized this historical fact and warned against it. George Washington knew this better than most. Notice his observation as he writes to John Jay.

> Ignorance and design are difficult to combat. Out of these proceed illiberality, improper jealousies, and a train of evils which oftentimes in republican governments must be sorely felt before they can be removed. The former, that is ignorance, being a fit soil for the latter to work in, tools are employed which a generous mind would disdain

---

150. Jefferson, *The Jeffersonian Cyclopedia,* 210.
151. Hebrews 11:25 (KJV).

to use, and which nothing but time and their own puerile and wicked
productions can show the inefficacy and dangerous tenancy of.[152]

Going back to an earlier discussion regarding the sin nature of man
and the power hungry and abusive tendency of those in power, such a sin is
exacerbated when those who are being abused do not even know the warning signs of such abuse or the preventative measures to be taken to prevent
the abuse. Unfortunately, many (if not most) do not know what warnings
signs to look for, nor do they understand the natural laws and principles
to apply regarding power and the abuse of it. Their ignorance is truly a
conduit for tyrants to control the mass of citizens and to manipulate the
economies of social function to assert their will upon others—masterfully,
no doubt.

People shake their heads in wonderment of how tyrants like Adolf Hitler
could ever perform their terror without resistance from the masses. After
all, was not Germany the same nation where Reverend Martin Luther performed his cultural-changing ministries of God that even made their way
into America? Were there not millions of Christians living in Germany at
that time (just as in America today)? Were there not millions of patriotic
Germans who had Bibles sitting on their tables and dressers and bookshelves?
Were there not churches established in every city? The fact is Christianity in
Germany was extremely popular and accepted; so much so that Hitler himself
used Christianity as a means to acquire the support of most Germans.

The book, *My New Order,* contains many of Hitler's statements, and
among them you find Hitler's declaration of a personal relationship with
Jesus Christ, his strong support for traditional morality, and an ardent attack
against atheism. Is it shocking that Hitler says, "My feeling as a Christian
points me to my Lord and Savior as a fighter"?[153] Do you think the citizens
believed him? Do you think Hitler would have professed such a faith if he
did not believe it would help him acquire more power? Hitler also rallied the

---

152. Jay, *The Life of John Jay,* 244.

153. Adolf Hitler and Raoul de Roussy de Sales, ed., *My New Order,* (New York: Reynal &
Hitchcock, 1941), 26.

German citizens against the movement of atheism in Germany, declaring, "We were convinced that the people needed and required this faith. We have therefore undertaken the fight against the atheistic movement, and that not merely with a few theoretical declarations; we have stamped it out."[154] Hitler also proclaims a belief in strong moral values, stating, "The advantages of a personal and political nature that might arise from compromising with atheistic organizations would not outweigh the consequences which would become apparent in the destruction of general moral basic values."[155] Hitler sounded great!

The fact is Hitler's speeches were filled with Christian lingo. Obviously most Christians, pastors, and churches in Germany believed Hitler. And why would Hitler need to portray himself in such a light? Perhaps for the same reason that American politicians do today: to gain the undeserved support of the majority of citizens—especially in a Christian nation like Germany was during Hitler's days. But did Hitler truly believe and act upon his proclaimed ideals? Absolutely not! Disturbingly so, many Americans have the same attitude towards politicians (as long as they are in their favorite party) that as long as the politician says it, he must believe it; and if he believes it, he will most certainly act in conformity to his belief. Have we not learned lessons from the slavery and deaths of others? God remove the blindness from such persons' eyes.

Two things must be observed then from this history lesson: (1) millions of Christians in a nation did not prevent evil from causing devastating results to society, and (2) evil took place in this Christian nation, because the people were ignorant of the unlawful authority assumed by Hitler and were convinced that his actions were good. Algernon Sidney understood the deception of Nimrods as well and described how such evil can take place—even with the consent of the people. He says,

A people, from all ages in love with liberty, and desirous to maintain their own privileges, could never be brought to resign them,

154. Selwyn Duke, "Hitler and Christianity," *The New American*, (June 9, 2008), 35.
155. Hitler, *My New Order*, 153.

unless they were made to believe, that in conscience they ought
to do it; which could not be, unless they were also persuaded that
there was a law set to all mankind, which none might transgress,
and which put the examination of all those matters out of their
power.[156]

Why would America be exempt from this fact of life? In fact, America
faces a very similar notion even today, specifically regarding the alleged
War on Terror.[157] Many conservatives believe that, first of all, the War on
Terror is a legitimate and even godly war, not even considering the historical and constitutional implications and concerns involved. But let us put
that matter aside and discuss the other side to the War on Terror, and that
is governmental intrusion of rights long established in America in the name
of fighting the War on Terror.[158] The misnamed legislation the Patriot Act
passed with flying colors in both houses of Congress and was immediately
signed into law by the president in 2001, while most who voted for it did
not even read the bill. This law as well as many others (including numerous executive orders signed by President Bush from 2001–2008) seriously
jeopardizes the rights of Americans, including the right of habeas corpus, the
right to be free from unreasonable searches and seizures, the right to be free

---

156. Sidney, *Discourses on Government,* 312.

157. "'The war on terrorism' is fundamentally a misnomer because 'War' is a constitutional
term of art; and 'the war on terrorism' has not been, and due to the diffuse nature of the
enemy and the indefinable character of the conflict cannot be, 'declare[d]' as the Constitution
prescribes. Constitutionally speaking, 'War' is a specific set of legal relations between two or
more independent nations. For the most obvious example, in an actual 'War' soldiers of one
nation may, within certain limits, intentionally kill soldiers of another nation without thereby
being guilty of murder under the law of any nation. According to strict constitutional logic,
then, a 'war on terrorism' is an existential impossibility—if only because 'terrorism' is a set of
typically *para*-military tactics, not a country or even a political ideology; and because 'terrorists'
do not constitute one or more independent nations, but, outside the context of international
war, are at most mere bands of private criminals." Vieira, *Constitutional Homeland Security,* 8.

158. "'The war on terrorism' provides a peculiarly plastic precedent under color of which
public officials can manufacture ever-more-extensive, ever-more-abusive 'emergency powers', on
the basis of the metaphor of waging 'war'." Vieira, *Constitutional Homeland Security,* 11.

from cruel and unusual punishment, the right to counsel, the due process requirement of judge-reviewed warrants, and the right to be tried by a jury of peers—all of which have been learned about, demanded, and fought for by literally scores of generations of English and American citizens, and all of which were sanctified by our Constitution and Bill of Rights. As a result, the Department of Homeland Security has been created, but the freedoms of our homeland have been ignored, as if security can ever be accomplished when liberty has been shunned. United States Supreme Court Justice Robert Jackson acknowledges this type of irony when he said, "Implicit in the term 'national defense' is the notion of defending those values and ideas which set this Nation apart…It would indeed be ironic if, in the name of national defense, we would sanction the subversion of…those liberties…which make the defense of the Nation worthwhile."[159] Yet, many Americans do not even seem to consider the tyrannical implications of giving those rights up so easily in the name of fighting terrorism. A free society cannot exist when the citizens so easily give up their powers and rights and hand them over to the government for the sake of security. As Benjamin Franklin says, "Those who give up their liberty for more security neither deserve liberty nor security."[160] It boils down to the philosophical and historical understanding that "liberty is necessary to achieve security, and indeed is the most important of the defining characteristics of security."[161]

To suggest that America would never experience what Germany did with Hitler or Russia did with Stalin or Italy did with Mussolini is absurd, because every ignorant nation teeters and toys with and even asks for slavery. In the end, they will likely get just that if they do not become educated with the knowledge of freedom's principles and nature and actually implement into government those principles. The founders were aware that "acquiescence in such an encroachment, would give it the force of precedent, and precedent would soon establish the right"[162]—i.e., implied consent. To

159. Andrew Napolitano, *A Nation of Sheep*, (Nashville, TN: Thomas Nelson Inc, 2007), 3.
160. Ibid.
161. Vieira, *Constitutional Homeland Security*, 37.
162. Rayner, *The Life of Thomas Jefferson*, 42.

preserve freedom in any nation, the citizens must be aware of the current state of affairs as applied to the laws of nature and nature's God and their constitution. To be ignorant of these freedom producers and sustainers does not produce bliss. It produces slavery. Such ignorance will give no guidance on issues regarding jurisdiction, unlawful usurpation of power, the necessary limits of power, the God-given rights of man, the power of the people, proper actions by government, which candidates to support, which politicians to reject, what consequences to expect, when to obey, and when to resist.

Lethargy

One of the most disturbing reasons for the indifference of Americans is lethargy—or put differently, laziness. Proverbs 27:23–24 (MJKV) demonstrates the necessity of being diligent in personal matters and matters of state. It says, "Know well the face of your flocks; set your heart on your herds. For riches are not forever; nor the crown from generation to generation." In other words, good government (or any other matter in life) does not just happen or exist, but rather, it takes due diligence to ensure that the crown endures from generation to generation.

Compare good government's need for diligence to evil government's need: lethargy. This is confirmed in scriptures repeatedly, and no less in the following verse: "When a land transgresses, it has many rulers, but with a man of understanding and knowledge, its stability will long continue."[163] Again in Proverbs 12:24 (ESV) we see how lethargy's end result is slavery. "The hand of the diligent will rule, while the slothful will be put to forced labor." Unfortunately, Americans today demonstrate anything but due diligence when it comes to matters of protecting freedom, and it is catching up with us. They act as "the sluggard [who] says, 'There is a lion outside! I shall be killed in the streets!'"[164] Indeed, there is a lion outside in the streets of America, but most choose to stay inside, and the lion goes around to and fro, seeking whom he may devour—namely, freedom. Lethargy comes in different forms, such as the following:

---

163. Proverbs 28:2 (ESV).
164. Proverbs 22:13 (ESV).

At least my generation does not have to deal with slavery.

America's destruction is inevitable.[165]

I want to enjoy my retirement years not worrying about politics.

God's will is that the world accepts the Antichrist.

Each form of lethargy has its own unique disgust. Such an attitude is not of the Bible, is not Christian,[166] and is not what created and prospered America. Thomas Jefferson proclaimed that eternal vigilance is the price of freedom.[167] Unfortunately, the prosperity of America has created generations of noneffective citizens. With regard to the most common forms of lethargy, that is, "at least my generation does not have to deal with slavery" and "God's will is that the world accepts the Antichrist," I feel the need to address them specifically.

The "It's Not My Generation" Fallacy

Many Americans, and in fact Christians, have the mindset that they are grateful that their generation is not the generation to endure the difficult task of battling against slavery (of course believing that (1) slavery is inevitable, and (2) they do not already live in slavery). They see the handwriting on the wall; yet they choose to let another generation suffer because of their indifference. Such an attitude is directly contradictory to the Bible. "Rescue those who are being taken away to death; hold back those who are stumbling to the slaughter."[168] Indeed, America is being taken away to death and to the slaughter.

---

165. "Many have given in to defeatism and despair and whine like Hollywood stars and starlets who threaten to leave the country rather than live in George Bush's America. So, Christians save their protest for the privacy of the voting booth, but those they elect often have no more stomach for this battle than they do." Buchanan, *The Death of the West*, 213.

166. Colossians 3:23 (KJV).

167. C. S. Bezas, "The Founding Father's Voter's Guide," *Bella Online, The Voice of Women*, (November 2, 2008), http://www.bellaonline.com/articles/art59263.asp (accessed May 5, 2009).

168. Proverbs 24:11 (ESV).

The matter is direct and simple: what caring, loving, and interested father, grandfather, uncle, mother, grandmother, or any family member would desire that their posterity be one of the unfortunate souls that must face slavery or be born into it?[169] Such an approach to the known evils confronted at the present time actually seals the fate of their posterity without a chance of being born into a government that recognizes God-given freedom.[170] There will come a point when their posterity will say, "There is no retreat, but in submission and slavery! Our chains are forged!"[171] The posterity of such persons would undoubtedly curse their name and their existence if they were to know the attitude exemplified by their ancestors. This lethargic attitude actually disgusted Thomas Paine and would disgust anyone else who sacrificed life, liberty, or property for the cause of freedom for one's posterity. Paine tells of this shameful demonstration of lethargy during his day.

> A noted one, who kept a tavern at Amboy, was standing at his door, with as pretty a child in his hand, about eight or nine years old, as most I ever saw; and after speaking his mind as freely as he thought was prudent, finished with this unfatherly expression, "Well, give me peace in my days." Not a man lives on the continent, but fully believes that separation [with Great Britain] must some time or other finally take place, and a generous parent would have said, "if there must be trouble, let it be in my days, that my child may have peace;" and this single reflection, well applied, is sufficient to awaken every man to duty.[172]

Does America reflect Paine's sentiment that the desire for our children and our posterity to live in freedom creates a duty to resist unlawful government? Do the current generations of America truly care about the sacrifices made by our ancestors? If so, why shirk our responsibility to ensure freedom for our posterity, and why let our posterity pay for the debts we have created

---

169. Proverbs 11:29 (ESV), "Whoever troubles his own household will inherit the wind."
170. Paine and Philip, ed., *American Crisis I*, 69.
171. Compiled by a member of the Philadelphia Bar, *American Oratory*, 15.
172. Paine and Philip, ed., *American Crisis I*, 67.

(speaking not only financially, of course, but in every other way)? How can America celebrate freedom on the Fourth of July every year and then in reality consent to every material principle contrary to what produces freedom? Such lip service defines hypocrisy, and America's founders likely would not even have made their sacrifices had they known of our actions (or better put, inactions) today. Consider what John Adams says regarding the price his generation paid to preserve freedom for his posterity:

> Posterity, you will never know how much it cost the present generation to preserve your freedom. I hope you will make good use of it. If you do not, I shall repent in heaven that ever I took half the pains to preserve it.[173]

Our founders did not believe or adopt the philosophy of "let my posterity deal with fighting slavery." However, they also expected that their posterity would appreciate the price they paid to procure it. In fact, they believed the opposite of such lethargy. John Jay says,

> Everybody will agree that we have received great and undeserved mercies, as a society, from our Creator; and that it is fit and proper we should, as a society, acknowledge and implore the continuance of them.[174]

Our founders would likely not have paid such a cost for freedom had they known what their posterity would do with their highly purchased prize. But they fought for the prize with the hope and expectation that their posterity would do their part in preserving freedom. In fact, one of the express reasons for resistance to the tyranny of Great Britain was the vision of freedom for America's posterity. Thomas Paine says,

---

173. John Adams, Abigail Adams, and Charles Francis Adams, *Familiar Letters of John Adams and His Wife Abigail Adams, During the Revolution: With a Memoir of Mrs. Adams,* (New York: Hurd and Houghton, 1876), 265.

174. Jay, *The Life of John Jay,* 387.

[America's War for Independence] is not the concern of a day, a year, or an age; posterity are virtually involved in the contest, and will be more or less affected, even to the end of time, by the proceedings now. Now is the seed time of continental union, faith and honor.[175]

Can you blame our founding fathers for their ill thoughts of anyone who would sacrifice freedom at the altar of comfort and ease and at the expense of their posterity no less? Samuel Adams says,

If you love wealth more than liberty, the tranquility of servitude better than the animating contest of freedom, depart from us in peace. We ask not your counsel nor your arms. Crouch down and lick the hand that feeds you. May your chains rest lightly upon you and may posterity forget that you were our countrymen.[176]

Indeed, they understood what Montesquieu says regarding the cost of freedom. It was paid with infinite pains and labor, and they shuddered to think that a generation of Americans would prefer slavery over freedom for the sake of remaining lazy and lethargic in their minds and bodies. Perhaps John Adams has already repented of the great cost he and his generation paid for freedom, seeing what America has become.

For America's founders, freedom was not mere verbiage; they fought and died for it. They looked at the state of affairs in their nation and reached the following conclusion: "As parents, we can have no joy, knowing that this government is not sufficiently lasting to ensure any thing which we may bequeath to posterity."[177] For this reason, the founders feel the need to point out,

Our cause is just. Our union is perfect. Our internal resources are great…we gratefully acknowledge, as signal instances of the Divine

---

175. Paine and Philip, ed., *Common Sense,* 20.

176. Oak Norton, "Educating All Parents To Ensure The Future Of Our Republic: Founding Fathers Quotes," *Norton News,* http://www.oaknorton.com/foundingfatherquotes.cfm (accessed May 5, 2009).

177. Paine and Philip, ed., *Common Sense,* 25.

favor towards us, that his Providence would not permit us to be called into this severe controversy, until we were grown up to our present strength, had been previously exercised in warlike operation, and possessed of the means of defending ourselves.

With hearts fortified with these animating reflections, we most solemnly, before God and the world, declare, that, exerting the utmost energy of those powers, which our beneficent Creator hath graciously bestowed on us, the arms we have been compelled by our enemies to assume, we will, in defiance of every hazard, with unabating firmness and perseverance, employ for the preservation of our liberties; being with one mind resolved to die freeman, rather than to live as slaves.[178]

Compare this courage to the attitude of those who think "well, at least it is not my generation," and who "[leave] the sword to our children, and [shrink] back at a time, when, a little more, a little farther, would…render this [nation] the glory of the earth."[179] I do not think more words are needed to explain the shamefulness of the latter expression.

The "Antichrist is Inevitable" Fallacy

As to the other disgusting lethargic attitude regarding going along with the corruption of government—"God's will is that the world accept the Antichrist"—such an attitude is devilish in its very roots, and arguably such persons have accepted the mark of the beast in their hearts already. Furthermore, the proponents of such an attitude offer the most illogical and harmful argument. As an illustration, is it not a fact that all living creatures die? Then why not go ahead and kill yourself? After all, it is inevitable. Such logic is flawed, fallacious, and contradicts God's command to occupy until He comes. Additionally, it contradicts the biblical principle of preparing for the battle against your enemy. "The horse is made ready for the day of battle, but the victory belongs to the LORD."[180]

---

178. Rayner, *The Life of Thomas Jefferson,* 75, 76.
179. Paine and Philip, ed., *Common Sense,* 28.
180. Proverbs 21:31 (ESV).

While ultimately God gives victory, it only comes to those who pre-pare themselves in every way possible for victory. If one approached other life events (work, family, finances, social duties, education, etc.) in the same lethargic way they treat evil in government, they would be rightly labeled a loser, because nothing of any positive value results from being lazy. Evil is never defeated by sitting back and watching it happen.

The Bible is clear that while the Antichrist shall appear towards the end of the world as we know it, the earth previously contained and currently contains antichrists[181] who possess the same spirit of the Antichrist and who push the same agenda. These persons have existed since Nimrod in Genesis and will continue to exist until the Antichrist is revealed. How can it be said that the only antichrist to worry about is *the* Antichrist found in the book of Revelation? As if antichrist-type evil cannot prevail in society. Is the Christian who claims that there is nothing you can do about the Antichrist going to go along with every other antichrist until the one in Revelation appears? And who are they to know that they have or have not already followed him? Are Christians who accept the evils performed by those who share the same phi-losophy as the Antichrist less evil than those who we read about in Revelation 13:15–17 who took the mark of the beast?

Does God excuse our lethargy because the Antichrist would one day acquire power over most of the world? Why would God tell us to resist the devil, and he will flee from us? And do you think the following verses con-gratulate you for having your eyes wide shut?

> For you yourselves are fully aware that the day of the Lord will come like a thief in the night. While people are saying, "There is peace and security," then sudden destruction will come upon them as labor pains come upon a pregnant woman, and they will not escape. But you are not in darkness, brothers, for that day to surprise you like a

---

181. "Children, it is the last hour, and as you have heard that antichrist is coming, so now many antichrists have come. Therefore we know that it is the last hour." 1 John 2:18 (ESV). "For many deceivers have gone out into the world, those who do not confess the coming of Jesus Christ in the flesh. Such a one is the deceiver and the antichrist." 2 John 1:7 (ESV).

thief. For you are all children of light, children of the day. We are not of the night or of the darkness. So then let us not sleep, as others do, but let us keep awake and be sober.[182]

And what of God's commandments in 2 Peter 3:10–18 to prepare for the day of the Lord?

But the day of the Lord will come like a thief, and then the heavens will pass away with a roar, and the heavenly bodies will be burned up and dissolved, and the earth and the works that are done on it will be exposed. Since all these things are thus to be dissolved, what sort of people ought you to be in lives of holiness and godliness, waiting for and hastening the coming of the day of God, because of which the heavens will be set on fire and dissolved, and the heavenly bodies will melt as they burn! But according to his promise we are waiting for new heavens and a new earth in which righteousness dwells.

Therefore, beloved, since you are waiting for these, be diligent to be found by him without spot or blemish, and at peace. And count the patience of our Lord as salvation, just as our beloved brother Paul also wrote to you according to the wisdom given him, as he does in all his letters when he speaks in them of these matters. There are some things in them that are hard to understand, which the ignorant and unstable twist to their own destruction, as they do the other Scriptures. You therefore, beloved, knowing this beforehand, take care that you are not carried away with the error of lawless people and lose your own stability. But grow in the grace and knowledge of our Lord and Savior Jesus Christ. To him be the glory both now and to the day of eternity. Amen.[183]

Contrary to the attitude that "there is nothing I can do to stop the Antichrist" and the corruption in government leading to his control, God

---

182. Thessalonians 5:2–6 (ESV).
183. Peter 3:10–18 (ESV).

requires the Christian to be steadfast in the truth of God's word and to be vigilant, faithful, obedient, the salt, the light, and the soldier of Christ, putting on the whole armor of God.

Consistent in spirit with those who physically accept the mark of the beast in Revelation 14, those who have accepted the mark of the beast in their hearts have accepted the philosophy which God condemns. "And another angel, a third, followed them, saying with a loud voice, 'If anyone worships the beast and its image and receives a mark on his forehead or on his hand, he also will drink the wine of God's wrath, poured full strength into the cup of his anger, and he will be tormented with fire and sulfur in the presence of the holy angels and in the presence of the Lamb.'"[184] God save us from such an attitude of supposed Christians.

---

184. Revelation 14:9–10 (ESV).

13

RESISTANCE TO UNLAWFUL GOVERNMENT

The United States Army defines the *nature of resistance* as follows: "Resistance, rebellion, or civil war begins in a nation where political, sociological, economic, or religious division has occurred. Divisions of this nature are usually caused by a violation of rights or privileges, the oppression of one group by the dominant or occupying force, or the threat to the life and freedom of the populace."[1] However, most Americans today likely do not even consider, much less understand, the fundamental concepts of securing freedom and resisting tyranny, because they do not even understand the fundamentals of God-given rights and how they relate to government usurpations of those rights. Although, it must be acknowledged that many more Americans are awakening to the idea as we continue further into tyranny, which creates more caution in the minds of citizens, as the government's policies violate the natural law of self-preservation.

In general, Americans have not even come close to the realization of resistance towards the status quo (much less the federal government), which is

---

1. Department of the Army Field Manual, *Guerrilla Warfare and Special Forces Operations,* FM 31–21, September 1961, 5.

evident by the presidential election in 2008. The vast majority of Americans demonstrated their belief that they will be able to "further their cause by peaceful and legal means"[2] when they voted for one of the two major parties. There are likely hundreds of thousands of Americans who have reached the nature of resistance, but most Americans do not relate resistance to their own personal circumstances.

Certainly, Americans have heard the stories of America's founders who died during our war for independence and have heard about America's fallen soldiers who have died on foreign soil fighting wars against other nations. They likely sympathize with those who have sacrificed their lives for the cause of freedom. However, most Americans project the concepts of fighting for freedom to the third person and foreign nations, never even thinking that fighting for freedom applies to them currently and personally. Even further from their mind is the thought that fighting for freedom applies to enemies both foreign *and* domestic. Of course, human nature desires to avoid life-threatening conflicts and desires to live in peace. Unfortunately, such a desire has created cowardice in some and ignorance in others. They would rather live in peace than live in freedom. Such an attitude strangles the neck of freedom such that it can barely breathe at all. Furthermore, such an approach contributes to the voluntary slave state of any nation. Thus, the further resistance is from the minds of the citizens, the harder it becomes for citizens to be willing to enact real change in government and force administrators to comply with the terms of the compact. The fact is for freedom to exist, the citizens must fight for it—no exceptions—which explains why many find any excuse to use God as an excuse *not* to resist, such as the Romans 13 argument.

Before a citizen will resist a government based upon unconstitutional acts, he must understand what America's founders understood, for as the United States Army recognized, resistance comes when the government has violated rights. When the citizens do not have a fundamental understanding of rights, resistance is unlikely and improbable. The American citizen must acknowledge that all things, including rights, freedoms, responsibilities, lim-

---

2. Ibid.

its, jurisdiction, and power come from God; that no government has the authority to remove what God has given; that government is a minister of God, not a minister of itself; and that unlawful and unconstitutional actions of the government must be resisted. He must have an ideological conviction in his heart, as Thomas Jefferson does.

> Can the liberties of a nation be thought secure when we have removed their only firm basis, a conviction in the minds of the people, that these liberties are the gift of God? That they are not to be violated but with his wrath? Indeed, I tremble for my country, when I reflect that God is just; that his justice cannot sleep forever: that considering numbers, nature and natural means only, a revolution in the wheel of fortune, an exchange of situation is among possible events; that it may become probably by supernatural interference! The Almighty has no attribute which can take side with us in such a contest.[3]

Indeed, God is just, and His mercy will not last where a nation continually rejects His natural and revealed laws and sells their freedom for a mess of pottage. Jefferson's understanding of divine justice has vanished with history. Americans no longer demonstrate an understanding of divine justice or recognition that God is the author of all rights. If you consider yourself a freedom lover, do you believe as Thomas Jefferson did? Moreover, are you willing to take action upon the belief that you say you have? Do your convictions translate into action that steps outside of what Fox News, CNN, ABC, MSNBC, and talk radio tell you?

It is this type of conviction as expressed by our founders that produces actions and not just words. Compare their actions to the mindset many Christians in America possess that God will grant or perform whatever it is that the Christian demands and speaks[4] without reference to our complying with the laws of God revealed in scriptures and in natural law. Do these

---

3. Rayner, *The Life of Thomas Jefferson*, 37.
4. Matthew 7:11 (KJV); Matthew 16:19 (KJV); Matthew 17:20 (KJV); Matthew 21:22 (KJV); John 14:13 (KJV).

people who believe that speaking it into existence is a reality believe that the same principle applies to a nation, because God sets nations up and puts them down? If so, why is America still continuing down the road to slavery? Why is God not answering their prayers? Perhaps their words do not produce actions. Perhaps they believe that God can only heal bodies from cancer; save marriages from collapse; remove addictions from the mind; and deliver souls from hell; but God cannot deliver a nation from bondage and can only work through the lesser of two evils, or else America is doomed! What a paradox. And what of those who believe that God's will is that you live in success, wealth, and riches? Certainly such an opportunity does not present itself in a tyrannical government, unless of course you sell yourself to the state and take the mark. Thus, the only way for God to provide wealth, riches, and success in a material way, while at the same time giving liberty to the citizen who is not willing to sell his soul for the sake of making money, is for society to insist on a free society *and* government. By the way, try making the argument that God will still make you rich even in a despotic government to those Christians in China who are being persecuted and killed for their defiance of tyrannical, despotic, arbitrary, and ungodly laws.

The truth is actions always speak louder than words, and actions are the only way to secure freedom, no matter how much prayer or talk is exerted. George Washington sees the need to act and not only to think it. He says,

> What astonishing changes a few years are capable of producing! I am told even respectable characters speak of a monarchical form of government without horror. From thinking proceeds speaking; thence to acting is often but a single step. But how irrevocable and tremendous! What a triumph for our enemies, to verify their prediction! What a triumph for the advocates of despotism, to find that we are incapable of governing ourselves; and that systems, founded on the basis of equal liberty, are merely ideal and fallacious; would to God that wise measures may be taken to avert the consequences we have but too much reason to apprehend.[5]

5. S. G. Arnold, *The Life of George Washington, the First President of the United States,* (New York: T. Mason and G. Lane, 1840), 186.

Washington understands the necessity of actually placing your actions where your mouth is. How can God answer prayers to heal America when America continues to reject His will as revealed in nature and the Bible? It is impossible. Such persons who believe only in speaking things into existence ignore the remaining instructions from God's word that we reject the vain philosophies of the world and obey His laws.

During America's struggle for independence, Patrick Henry believed that action was necessary to preserve freedom and so nobly and with conviction stated, "If we wish to be free—we must fight!"[6] Fighting, of course, may come in different forms. As has been quoted for hundreds of years, "The pen is mightier than the sword." So hopefully fighting for freedom will not require physical resistance and force. However, regardless of what form it takes, fighting for freedom is not only our duty but our right. Just as U.S. Supreme Court Justice William Douglas says, "The right to revolt has sources deep in our history."[7] Founding father James Wilson confirms the truth that free men have a natural right to resist tyranny.

Have not British subjects, then, a right to resist force—force acting without authority—force employed contrary to law—force employed to destroy the very existence of law and of liberty? They have, sir, and this right is secured to them both by the letter and the spirit of the British constitution... The British liberties, sir, and the means and the right of defending them, are not the grants of princes; and of what our princes never granted they surely can never deprive us.[8]

Wilson understood that where there is the right to freedom there is the right to defend it, because freedoms are not granted by government but by

---

6. Compiled by a member of the Philadelphia Bar, *American Oratory,* 15.

7. Bill Swainson, ed., *Encarta Book of Quotations: 25,000 Quotations from Around the World,* Revised Edition, (New York: Macmillan, 2000), 283.

8. Compiled by a member of the Philadelphia Bar, *American Oratory,* 9; "It is the glory of the British Prince and the happiness of all his subjects, that their constitution hath its foundations in the immutable laws of nature, and as the supreme legislature as well as the supreme executive that are repugnant to any essential law in nature." Halstead Van Tyne, *The Causes of the War of Independence,* 225.

God. Governments have no authority to deprive what only God can give. Of course, America's founders simply adopted and carried a legacy passed onto them by their forefathers—the settlers of America in the seventeenth century—when the citizens and chartered governments of the newly established colonies resisted the efforts of Great Britain to control their natural rights of self-government.[9]

Understand, however, the philosophy behind resistance to government is not taken lightly.[10] Rather, such a decision takes extreme discipline intellectually, politically, emotionally, and in every other way. In other words, the level of resistance should be in proportion to the level of harm to one's freedom. Additionally, human nature reveals that when a nonviolent form of resistance is possible, such an approach should and must be considered and

---

9. "One of the first cases of colonial defiance of the English Government was (1664) when Charles II sent commissioners to 'regulate' New England. At the mere hint that Massachusetts was to be asked to permit the substitution of a new charter establishing a royal colony in place of their corporate charter with its self-rule, the Puritan rulers put their charter in safe hands, manned the harbor fort, set new guns on its ramparts, and petitioned the King to let their 'laws and liberties live.' Fearing lest they were to lose their charter, they spoke humbly of being in that case ready to perish or at least to seek new habitations... The next serious attempt to take the Massachusetts charter was in 1681 when Randolph appeared with a legal demand that the corporation appear in London before the Court of the King's Bench to defend their right to their charter... [The magistrates' and deputies'] unanimous advice was that it was the undoubted duty of the authorities of Massachusetts Bay 'to abide by what rights and privileges the Lord our God in his merciful providence hath bestowed upon us.' They argued that it was better to obey the God of their fathers than to put their trust in princes. To sin by giving away the inheritance of their fathers 'would be to incur the high displeasure of the King of Kings.'" Halstead Van Tyne, *The Causes of the War of Independence,* 33–35.

10. "[R]evolutions happen not upon every little mismanagement in public affairs. Great mistakes in the ruling part, many wrong and inconvenient laws, and all the slips of human frailty, will be born by the people without mutiny or murmur. But if a long train of abuses, prevarications and artifices, all tending the same way, make the design visible to the people, and they cannot but feel what they lie under, and see whither they are going; it is not to be wondered, that they should then rouze themselves, and endeavour to put the rule into such hands which may secure to them the ends for which government was at first erected; and without which, ancient names, and specious forms, are so far from being better, that they are much worse, than the state of nature, or pure anarchy; the inconveniencies being all as great and as near, but the remedy farther off and more difficult." Locke and Macpherson, ed., *Second Treatise of Government,* 113.

used. America's history reveals this. Indeed, America's founders believed that the level of resistance should be in proportion to the nature of the unlawfulness of the government. "As the invasions of our rights have become more and more formidable, our opposition to them has increased in firmness and vigor, in a just, and in no more than a just, proportion."[11] No reasonable person would suggest that citizens and states should take up arms against the government when the encroachments against freedom are light, without apparent purpose, and sporadic. By the same token, when the encroachments rise in intensity, so should the resistance. Indeed, scriptures reveal that citizens should never perform violence against their government when it is performing equity (that is, justice). However, the same command is not given where government is perverting justice and is instead administering injustice: "[T]o punish the just is not good, nor to strike princes *for equity*."[12] To be certain of understanding this verse, the following words have the following literal meanings: *strike* (nâkâh)—to beat, kill, punish, slaughter, slay, smite, or wound; *equity* (yôsher)—right, upright (-ness).[13] Notice that scriptures do not prohibit the striking of the prince where the prince *does not* administer equity, justice, and righteousness. Of course, any time such a striking takes place, much guidance, consideration, and wisdom must go into such a decision, as scriptures reveal. "Plans are established by counsel; by wise guidance wage war."[14] Furthermore, anytime citizens strike their government because of the usurpation of power or because of tyrannical power perpetrated against the people, "[i]f any mischief come in such cases, it is not to be charged upon him who defends his own right, but on him that invades his neighbours' [rights]."[15]

Again, before one can even begin to understand the truth concerning the right to resist and the proportion of resistance, one must understand the natural laws that create the right, as well as the Constitution which reflects

---

11. Compiled by a member of the Philadelphia Bar, *American Oratory,* 6.

12. Proverbs 17:26 (ESV), (emphasis added).

13. James Strong, *Strong's Exhaustive Concordance of the Bible,* (Peabody, MA: Hendrickson Publishers), 78, 53.

14. Proverbs 20:18 (ESV).

15. Locke and Macpherson, ed., *Second Treatise of Government,* 115.

and secures the right. When citizens are ignorant of natural and revealed laws and of the Constitution which secures the rights of man, the subject of resistance against government would be like talking to a five year old about trigonometry. The level of understanding regarding the matter would be so utterly out of proportion. Think about it. What person would feel the need to sacrifice their life, their family, their property, their career, their future, and all they know simply because their government did not comply with a Constitution that was created over 200 years ago? What citizen would sacrifice so much by resisting the government when he does not even know why the Constitution was written, what the purpose of the Constitution is, and what the Constitution reflects? Would such a citizen even contemplate what Alexander Hamilton says in Federalist Paper No. 85?

> [The] fundamental principle of republican government...admits the right of the people to alter or abolish the established Constitution, whenever they find it inconsistent with their happiness, yet it is not to be inferred from this principle, that the representatives of the people...would...be justifiable in a violation of those provisions.[16]

They would likely read such a statement from our founders and justify their passivity by saying, "Well, there is no reason for me to resist the government when they violate the Constitution, because I am happy. As long as I am happy, there is no reason to abolish anything. Why fix what's not broken?" Sadly, most Americans today do not even know that our nation (societal and governmental) is largely broken; and if they do know it is broken, they do not know why it is broken or how to fix it. They think that electing a socialist or a lesser of two evils will spare our nation and set us on the right track. The fact is, once a society dissolves, the government dissolves directly and proportionally as well.[17] Freedom is never secure in a society whose philosophy runs contrary to freedom's principles. So where would that leave us today? Scary thought.

---

16. Alaexander Hamilton, "Federalist Paper 78," in *The Federalist Papers,* Hamilton, Jay, and Madison, 599.

17. "Whenever the *society is dissolved,* it is certain the government of that society cannot remain." Locke and Macpherson, ed., *Second Treatise of Government,* 107.

Yes, Hamilton rightly observed that the right to alter or abolish the Constitution is the right of the people, and that government administrators must absolutely follow the terms of the Constitution. But when citizens have no concept of what that means, it means nothing. So what good does it do any American citizen to address constitutional matters, when the people do not understand the Constitution?

Compare this to the colonists in America when they appealed to the English constitution to address their right to resist Great Britain's tyrannical acts. They said, "We behold, sir, with the deepest anguish we behold, that our opposition has not been as effectual as it has been constitutional."[18] Even when Great Britain had a monarchial form of government, justice still applied, and their constitution formed the supreme law of the land. Even the king had no right to violate the laws that all were bound to obey. America's history provides ample proof that only an informed and properly educated citizenry can know the line in the sand regarding matters of resistance of government.

Today, America's government would have the people believe that the citizens *must* comply with all laws (constitutional or not), but at the same time the government has the power to interpret the meaning and application of the Constitution as it deems appropriate to administer its agenda. It is comparable to Pat Buchanan's statement, "Where the other side [the government] is always making demands, and…is always ready to fight, this translates into endless retreats and eventual defeat."[19]

Do you feel pushed around, ignored, lied to, and deceived by your government? If you do, you are not alone. This political environment creates a ripe environment for slavery, because once again, the power shifts from the people to the government, creating a state of war between the government and its citizens.[20] When nothing is certain, certainly nothing matters. This applies to government, the Constitution, freedom, politics, society, and

---

18. Compiled by a member of the Philadelphia Bar, *American Oratory,* 6.

19. Buchanan, *The Death of the West,* 214.

20. "[F]or wherever violence is used, and injury done, though by hands appointed to administer justice, it is still violence and injury, however coloured with the name, pretences, or forms of law, the end whereof being to protect and redress the innocent, by an unbiassed application of it, to all who are under it; wherever that is not bona fide done, war is made upon the sufferers, who having no appeal on earth to right them, they are left to the only remedy in

especially resistance. In other words, when the people do not understand the absolute rights and certainties expressed in the Constitution, and when the people do not enforce the terms of the Constitution, the meaning of it all vanishes. The effect is that citizens lose the will and the knowledge to resist unlawful governmental actions. At that point, unconditional submission would be required of all citizens, for who is to say that the government's actions are wrong?

America's founders possessed the opposite belief of relativism and unconditional submission. They believed in the natural law principles of absolute rights and government limitations. Thus, when faced with the situation of unconstitutional acts, they had a choice: submit and live as slaves, or resist and live or die as free men. History reveals which choice they took, and their choice would not have been made had they not understood where the line in the sand was. Their decision to resist tyranny was a well thought out and articulated process, which deserved much weight and response. In the end, Thomas Jefferson articulates the duty to resist evil and secure the blessings of liberty to their posterity.

> We are reduced to the alternative of choosing an unconditional submission to the tyranny of irritated ministers, or resistance by force—

---

such cases, an appeal to heaven." Locke and Macpherson, ed., *Second Treatise of Government,* 16; "[U]sing force upon the people without authority, and contrary to the trust put in him that does so, is a state of war with the people...[and] the people have a right to remove [such a force] by force. The use of force without authority, always puts him that uses it into a state of war, as the aggressor, and renders him liable to be treated accordingly." Ibid., 80–81; "[W]henever the legislators endeavour to take away, and destroy the property of the people, or to reduce them to slavery under arbitrary power, they put themselves into a state of war with the people, who are thereupon absolved from any farther obedience, and are left to the common refuge, which God hath provided for all men, against force and violence. Whensoever therefore the legislative shall transgress this fundamental rule of society; and either by ambition, fear, folly or corruption, endeavour to grasp themselves, or put into the hands of any other, an absolute power over the lives, liberties, and estates of the people; by this breach of trust they forfeit the power the people had put into their hands for quite contrary ends, and it devolves to the people, who have a right to resume their original liberty, and, by the establishment of a new legislative, (such as they shall think fit) provide for their own safety and security, which is the end for which they are in society." Ibid., 111.

the latter is our choice. We have counted the cost of this contest, and find nothing so dreadful as voluntary slavery. Honor, justice, and humanity, forbid us tamely to surrender that freedom which we received from our gallant ancestors, and which our innocent posterity have a right to receive from us. We cannot endure the infamy and guilt of resigning succeeding generations to that wretchedness which inevitably awaits them, if we basely entail hereditary bondage upon them.[21]

Do current Americans even think about what their posterity will inherit—whether freedom or slavery? It does not appear that they think about it much. Apparently, Americans are willing to sell their birthright for a mere mess of pottage, as Esau was willing to sell his birthright to his brother Jacob for such a cheap price in Genesis.[22] Perhaps our nation should be called The United States of *Edom*.[23]

As has been established herein, every person has the God-given right of life, liberty, and property. As a result, they have a God-given right to defend them. Can it be said that God requires His creation to defend and protect their rights, placing a duty on man? If you were to ask founder John Jay, he would answer yes. He so succinctly explained our duty to resist tyranny in the following: "The great Sovereign of the universe has given us independence, and to that inestimable gift has annexed the *duty of defending it.*"[24] This is the same principle articulated by James Wilson afore-cited. Furthermore, this duty in fact complies with the principles established in the Bible that we are to do the following:

Occupy until [Jesus] comes.[25]

---

21. Rayner, *The Life of Thomas Jefferson*, 75.

22. Genesis 25 (KJV).

23. "And Esau said to Jacob, 'Let me eat some of that red stew, for I am exhausted!' (Therefore his name was called Edom.) Jacob said, 'Sell me your birthright now.' Esau said, 'I am about to die; of what use is a birthright to me?' Jacob said, 'Swear to me now.' So he swore to him and sold his birthright to Jacob. Then Jacob gave Esau bread and lentil stew, and he ate and drank and rose and went his way. Thus Esau despised his birthright." Genesis 25:30–34 (ESV).

24. Jay, *The Life of John Jay*, 405, (emphasis added).

25. Luke 19:13 (KJV).

Be watchful, stand firm in the faith, act like men, be strong.[26]

Take courage, and be men…lest you become slaves.[27]

For freedom Christ has set us free; stand firm therefore, and do not submit again to a yoke of slavery.[28]

Submit yourselves therefore to God. Resist the devil, and he will flee from you.[29]

In all circumstances take up the shield of faith, with which you can extinguish all the flaming darts of the evil one; and take the helmet of salvation, and the sword of the Spirit, which is the word of God.[30]

Stand therefore, having fastened on the belt of truth, and having put on the breastplate of righteousness.[31]

We "wrestle not against flesh and blood, but against principalities, against powers, against the rulers of the darkness of this world, against spiritual wickedness in high places."[32] Most Americans believe that the War on Terror is the war to focus on today. However, the War on Tyranny in America is where the battle wages.

In modern America, resistance towards government may be a foreign concept to most, because it is never debated, contemplated, or even suggested by most all sources of public media and discussion, from television to church meetings. But the idea and contemplation of resistance to unlawful author-

---

26. Corinthians 16:13 (ESV).
27. Samuel 4:9 (ESV).
28. Galatians 5:1 (ESV).
29. James 4:7 (ESV).
30. Ephesians 6:16, 17 (ESV).
31. Ephesians 6:14 (ESV).
32. Ephesians 6:12 (ESV).

RESISTANCE TO UNLAWFUL GOVERNMENT

ity was often discussed before, during, and even for a period after (i.e., The War Between the States) our founder's declared independence from Great Britain. It is hard to believe that any person who does not even consider not voting for a lesser of two evils would actually consider resisting a lesser of two evils, when the person they voted for actually exercised unlawful power and authority and ignored the compact he swore to bind himself to when he was elected into office. As was discussed earlier, fears of resisting such a power far outweigh any fears of a greater of two evils being elected into office. So what likelihood would there be of such a person actually standing up with fellow citizens (or alone) to resist governmental power? Not likely.

Perhaps a question weighing on the minds of many citizens is, "Why do our nation's leaders continue their corruption and deceit of America?" After all, have we not elected Republican candidates a majority of the time for the past forty years? So why do our leaders have so many faults? Why have we become communistic in philosophy? Grotius gives the answer and explains the notion of nonresistance to unlawful authority. He presents an understanding of why the faults of kings go unpunished in the following passage: "People are described as being punished for the faults of kings: for that does not happen because the people did not punish the king or control him, but because it consented…to his transgressions."[33] In other words, do not complain about the faults of the king when you consent to his actions.

The conclusion reached from this logical deduction is that the only way a nation can relieve itself of the evils of government is not to consent to its transgressions—which can be done civilly (through the political process) or in a state of war (as described by Enlightenment philosophers and our founders). Does it appear that the political process relieves America of the transgressions of its government? Not hardly. That begs the question do the people of America truly have an appeal to redress the grievances enslaving them?

Think about the reasons that our founders resisted, which largely had to do with Great Britain not considering the rights of the colonies regarding tax issues, and that bled into commerce and property issues as well. During

---

33. Grotius, *Hugo Grotius on the Rights of War and Peace,* 41.

that time, Great Britain passed the Stamp Act, and here is a short, general description of it.

> The Stamp Act of 1765 was the fourth Stamp Act to be passed by the Parliament of Great Britain but the first attempt to impose such a direct tax on its American colonies. The act required all legal documents, permits, commercial contracts, newspapers, wills, pamphlets, and playing cards in the colonies to carry a tax stamp. It was part of an economic program directly affecting colonial policy that was initiated in response to Britain's greatly increased national debt incurred during the British victory in the Seven Years War.[34]

So this involved taxes and commerce. So what? Most Americans today would not think twice about what Great Britain did. But the colonists were outraged and jointly formed a committee to respond to the king's act. Have you not wondered why they became so indignant about what really would be a minor infraction by American standards today? Still, they believed that Great Britain's actions were unconstitutional, unlawful, and deserved resistance. The standing chairman of the congressional committee addressing this matter, James Otis, believed that the actions of Great Britain deserved a response more than words from the colonies because of Great Britain's unconstitutional (and thus, tyrannical) acts.

In *The Life of John Adams,* we have a glimpse of the response Otis felt was necessary.

> As the acting chairman of the committee, appointed to prepare an answer…he saw that a discussion with the governor [for Great Britain] about the duty of submission to the decrees of Parliament, and the happiness of acquiescing in perfect confidence that the rights of the colonies would be safe in the hands of the "supreme legislature" and the "patriot king," would be a superfluous and worse than

---

34. "Stamp Act 1765," *Wikipedia,* http://en.wikipedia.org/wiki/Stamp_Act_1765 (accessed May 5, 2009).

useless waste of time. The act of Parliament was a grievance. But the principles in the concluding paragraph of [Great Britain governor's] speech required an answer other than of words... *The popular resistance...soon displayed itself with energy beyond the law.*[35]

Otis would not likely be well received by most in America today—especially by most politicians—even though Otis was one of the most influential statesmen during the Revolutionary period. Otis' conclusion resulted from the recognition that (1) actions outside of a constitution are to be resisted, and (2) trusting in superfluous means of redress would no doubt be worthless. Otis did not suggest that the colonists comply with Great Britain's laws until a new king would sit on the throne, thus giving America the opportunity of a new conservative king—maybe, just maybe. Otis did not hold on to the hope that maybe change would be affected if only they could get some conservative judges to rule that the king's actions were unlawful. Contrarily, he and many others saw Great Britain's actions for what they were: tyrannical. It was this spirit of freedom that produced the energy to resist tyranny, because they understood that the king himself did not possess absolute power, and that the king must comply with the constitution of Great Britain just like every other person under its jurisdiction.[36] It was this spirit of freedom that produced America. It was not a spirit of rebellion that (as some would falsely suggest) intoxicated the minds of America's founders, but rather America's founders resisted unlawful authority with honor and respect towards Great Britain's government. They attempted resolution through civil and amenable means and ends first, recognizing the following:

We are its best friends: this friendship prompts us to wish, that the power of the crown may be firmly established on the most solid basis: but we know, that the constitution alone will perpetuate the former, and securely uphold the latter. Are our principles irreverent to majesty? They are quite the reverse: we ascribe to it perfection

---

35. Adams, *The Life of John Adams,* 95, (emphasis added).
36. Ibid., 174.

almost divine. We say, that the king can do no wrong: we say, that
to do wrong is the property, not of power, but of weakness. We feel
oppression, and will oppose it; but we know, for our constitution
tells us, that oppression can never spring from the throne.[37]

In the end, however, the spirit of freedom necessarily meant resistance
to tyranny. It also meant choosing which side of the fence you were on.
It did not afford the luxury of neutrality. Our founders strongly believed
that the fight for freedom required people to choose which side they were
on. Neutrality during the War for Independence was not acceptable; you
were either for freedom or against it. This feeling was so strong that the
Continental Congress passed the following legislation during America's War
for Independence in 1776:

> To put an end to this state of things, the Convention appointed
> a Committee for inquiring into, detecting and defeating all con-
> spiracies which may be formed in this State, against the liberties
> of America. Whereas certain inhabitants and subjects of this State,
> either seduced by the arts or corrupted by the bribes of the enemy,
> or influenced by unmanly fear, profess to owe allegiance to the King
> of Great Britain, although the said king had denied them his pro-
> tection, absolved them from their allegiance, and by force of arms
> attempted to reduce them from subjects to vassals, and from free-
> men to slaves.
>
> And whereas others, from the like or similar motives, or with
> design to maintain an equivocal neutrality, and ungenerously avoid
> the dangers incident to those who nobly stand forth for the liberties
> of their country, pretend to hold for true the exploded and ridicu-
> lous doctrine of passive obedience and non-resistance to any power,
> however tyrannical, unconstitutional, oppressive, and cruel. And
> whereas it is not only just, but consonant to the usage of all civilized
> states, to withdraw their protection from, and punish such of their

---

37. Compiled by a member of the Philadelphia Bar, *American Oratory,* 11.

subjects as refuse to do their duty in supporting the liberties and constitutional authority of the state of which they are members.

Resolved, that the committee appointed by the Convention of this State for the purpose of inquiring into, detecting, and defeating all conspiracies, &c. have full power and authority to disfranchise and punish all such unworthy subjects of this State, as shall profess to owe allegiance to the king of Great Britain, and refuse to join with their countrymen in opposing his tyranny and invasion.[38]

Indeed, every person must choose this day whom you will serve, and being neutral is simply implied consent to the aggression of another—whether an individual or government. The question always comes down to "whether we are subjects of absolute unlimited power, or of a free government formed on the principles of the [American] Constitution."[39]

While America's system ingenuously provides for the change of leaders every two to four years, the change of leaders accomplishes no effect when the leaders continue to lead the people into slavery. Today, America simply exchanges one member of the Moose Club for another. The direction remains consistent and purposeful. This same noneffectiveness of the change of leaders was seen by America's founders. They knew and understood that a change of leaders was not the answer to secure freedom, but rather a change of power was the answer—putting the power of government into the people's hands. Thus, America's founders believed this:

Stopping at the point at which many, who were the boldest at the outset, evidently wished [the Revolution] to stop, and with honest motives, the Revolution would have been nothing more, in effect, than transferring the government to other hands, without putting it into other forms; and no change would have been wrought in the political condition of the world.

It would have been merely a spirited and successful rebellion,

---

38. Jay, *The Life of John Jay,* 49–50.
39. Adams, *The Life of John Adams,* 179.

or rather a struggle for power, like that which long embroiled the royal races of the Plantagenets, Tudors, and Stuarts, terminating at best in a limited medication of the old system, and most likely in its entire adoption, substituting George or John the First in the place of George the Third.[40]

Even during the American Revolution, there were people who believed that the cure was putting different people into the same positions of power. The reality was that changing leaders would not solve the problem—the problem was where the power lay. The people did not possess the power; the government did. Thus, expatriation was their choice, because the founders deemed such philosophy and action to be "a natural right, and acted upon as such, by all nations, in all ages."[41]

Is America in any different a position today? I think not. Most Americans worry about which candidate takes office, while most of the nation and both major political parties—Republican and Democrat—paddle along in the same boat leading them all over a cliff. When will freedom-loving Americans remove their faith from politics and put their faith in the proven principles of truth? If the founders possessed the philosophy of this generation (and many generations past), America would be called Great Britain's "female dog" today, and without a doubt, no resistance towards King George would ever have been made.

Understanding the concepts of jurisdiction and resistance to unlawful authority is essential for freedom lovers. Any freedom-loving citizen should contemplate this topic from a biblical (especially for a Christian) and historical point of view, because understanding when to submit and when to resist and the variations in between will form the citizen's conduct, his leadership in his family, his community, and his nation, and his choice to follow others in leadership positions. Our founders were very familiar with this discussion, which equipped them with the knowledge of whether or not to secede from Great Britain and declare independence. From such resources of understanding the founders studied the following concepts written by Grotius:

---

40. Rayner, *The Life of Thomas Jefferson*, 32.
41. Ibid., 57.

On this rule of non-resistance [against the state], there are some remarks to be made. First, those Rulers who are subject to the people, whether original institution or by subsequent convention, if they transgress against the laws and the State, may not only be resisted, but put to death. Secondly, if the king or other ruler has abdicated his power, or manifestly regards it as derelict, lost to him, he may thenceforth be treated as a private citizen...

Fourthly, if the king act, with a really hostile mind, with a view to the destruction of the whole people, Barclay says that the kingdom is forfeited; for the purpose of governing and the purpose of destroying cannot subsist together... Sixthly, if the king have a party only of the Sovereignty, another part being in the Senate or the people, and if the king invade the part which is not his, he may justly be opposed by force, because in that part he has not authority... Since each party has its portion of the Sovereign, it must also have the right defending that part.[42]

Again, Grotius' explanation of lawful and unlawful conduct of the king boils down to jurisdiction; and his explanation of the citizens' response to such acts boils down to jurisdiction.

The authors of the *Federalist Papers* discussed these very concepts of resistance when they published their writings in America. Their understanding of resisting unlawful government showed that even with the formation of the new America, the founders recognized the right of the citizens and the states to resist such unlawful powers. Moreover, America's founders expected the states to play an active role in protecting individual rights against the federal government's encroachment. The states were to protect these rights by *voice* and *arms*. In fact, most every state in the union had a state guard designed to protect the rights of citizens.[43] Unfortunately, many state guards have been

---

42. Grotius, *Hugo Grotius on the Rights of War and Peace,* 57–58.

43. "State Defense Forces ("SDF") (also known as State Guards, State Military Reserves, or State Militias) in the United States are military units that operate under the sole authority of a state government, although they are regulated by the National Guard Bureau through the Army National Guard of the United States. State Defense Forces are authorized by state and federal

federalized, once again stripping the states of their independence and ability to protect their interests. However, America's founders knew that the states would be the main catalysts to prevent tyranny of the federal government, as expressed by Alexander Hamilton in the following:

> Independent of parties in the national legislature...the State legislatures who will always be not only vigilant but suspicious and jealous guardians of the rights of the citizens against encroachments from the federal government, will constantly have their attention awake to the conduct of the national rulers, and will be ready enough, if any thing improper appears, to sound the alarm to the people, and not only to be the VOICE, but, if necessary, the ARM of their discontent.[44]
>
> If the representatives of the people betray their constituents, there is then no resource left but in the exertion of that original right of self-defense which is paramount to all positive forms of government...it may safely be received as an axiom in our political system, that the State governments will, in all possible contingencies, afford complete security against invasions of the public liberty

---

law and are under the command of the governor, as State Defense Forces are distinct from their state's National Guard in that they cannot become federal entities (all National Guard units can be federalized under the National Defense Act of 1933) with the creation of the National Guard of the United States. The federal government recognizes State Defense Forces under 32 U.S.C. § 109 which provides that State Defense Forces as a whole may not be called up, ordered into service for the armed forces of the United States, thus preserving their separation from the National Guard. However, 32 U.S.C. § 109 further states that individual members of the state defense force are not exempt from service in the armed forces allowing individuals to be conscripted or volunteer for service into the armed forces. Although every state has laws authorizing State Defense Forces, approximately twenty-three states, to include Puerto Rico, currently have active State Defense Forces, each with different levels of activity, state support, and strength. SDFs generally operate with emergency management and homeland security missions. Most SDFs are organized as Army units, but Air Force and Maritime units also exist." "State Defense Forces," *Wikipedia,* http://en.wikipedia.org/wiki/State_Defense_Forces (accessed May 5, 2009).

44. Alexander Hamilton, "Federalist Paper 26," in *The Federalist Papers,* Hamilton, Jay, and Madison, 201, 202.

by the national authority. Projects of usurpation cannot be masked under pretenses so likely to escape the penetration of select bodies of men, as of the people at large.[45]

Remember, these papers were actually published in *The New York Times* and read by the public at large. Thus, the people were largely educated regarding these issues, and freedom was able to exist for a longer period of time after America's independence was won. Can you imagine current politicians suggesting that each state be a guard against the federal government's encroachment on the rights of citizens and advocating that the states take up arms in response to such conduct? Such a suggestion today would likely cause that person to lose their job, ruin their reputation, and even face treason charges under the Patriot Act, the Homegrown Terrorism Act, and other similar laws supposedly meant to protect us. Shoot, most politicians (and many citizens) advocate the notion that America should join world government in military, economic, criminal, and environmental prescription and proscriptions. History cannot be denied, however. Our founders understood the natural right given by God to resist unlawful powers exercised by government, because they understood that "God has put all things in subjection under [Jesus's] feet. For in that [God] put all in subjection under [Jesus], he left nothing that is not put under him."[46]

Consider the beautiful and motivating statement to follow made by John Jay to the people of America after they declared independence from Great Britain, and it became time to defend their independence. The words, philosophies, and truths presented by this founding father are perhaps the most astounding of any statements made during this time. Without the statement being read by thousands of colonists, America's War for Independence may never have been fought; for there was much fear in the hearts and minds of

---

45. Alexander Hamilton, "Federalist Paper 28," in *The Federalist Papers,* Hamilton, Jay, and Madison, 213–215. See Also, "Attempts of [the states to actively resist the federal government] would not often be made with levity or rashness, because they would seldom be made without danger to the authors, unless in cases of a tyrannical exercise of the federal authority." Alexander Hamilton, "Federalist Paper 16," in *The Federalist Papers,* Hamilton, Jay, and Madison, 126.

46. Hebrews 2:8 (KJV).

the people. They were facing the biggest government power of their time, and they were likely to fail if they resisted it. However, the truths, the passion, the motivation, and the principles of John Jay's words penetrated hundreds of thousands of hearts across America and stirred in them a fire of freedom. Those words also planted the seeds of freedom in their souls for years.

Never before was there a more necessary time for the people to decide if they indeed desired freedom and were willing to sacrifice for it. Jay's appeal cut across borders, differences, ideas, motives, conceptions, and fears, enlightening their eyes to the seriousness of the matter and bringing them to the awareness that *now* was the time to act in an effort to preserve freedom for them and their posterity, no matter how grim the chances looked. There can be no greater demonstration of an American's consideration and duty to himself, his family, his nation, and his Creator than the appeal of John Jay to his fellow countrymen regarding the state of nations, freedom, government, and man's duty relative to each.

> Under the auspices and direction of Divine Providence, your fore-fathers removed to the wilds and wilderness of America. By their industry, they made it a fruitful—and by their virtue, a happy country. And we should still have enjoyed the blessings of peace and plenty, if we had not forgotten the source from which these blessings flowed; and permitted our country to be contaminated by the many shameful vices which have prevailed among us. It is a well-known truth that no virtuous people were ever oppressed; and it is also true, that a scourge was never wanting to those of an opposite character. Even the Jews, those favourites of Heaven, met with the frowns, whenever they forgot the smiles of their benevolent Creator. By tyrants of Egypt, of Babylon, of Syria, and of Rome, they were severely chastised; and those tyrants themselves, when they had exe-cuted the vengeance of Almighty God, their own crimes bursting on their own heads, received the rewards justly due to their viola-tion of the sacred rights of mankind. You were born equally free with the Jews, and have as good a right to be exempted from the arbitrary domination of Britain, as they had from the invasions of Egypt, Babylon, Syria, or Rome. But they, for their wickedness, were

permitted to be scourged by the latter; and we, for our wickedness, are scourged by tyrants as cruel and implacable as those.

Our case, however, is peculiarly distinguished from theirs. Their enemies were strangers, unenlightened, and bound to them by no ties of gratitude or consanguinity. Our enemies, on the contrary, call themselves Christians. They are of a nation and people bound to us by the strongest ties. A people, by whose side we have fought and bled; whose power we have contributed to raise; who owe much of their wealth to our industry, and whose grandeur has been augmented by our exertions... The enemy with greater strength again invade us—invade us, not less by their arts than their arms. They tell you, if you submit, you shall have protection—that their king breathes nothing but peace—that he will revise (not repeal) all his cruel acts and instructions, and will receive you into favour. But what are the terms on which you are promised peace? Have you heard of except absolute, unconditional obedience and servile submission? If his professions are honourable—if he means not to cajole and deceive you, why are you not explicitly informed of the terms; and whether parliament mean to tax you hereafter at their will and pleasure? Upon this and the like points, the military commissioners of peace are silent; and, indeed, are not authorized to say a word, unless a power pardon implies a power to adjust claims and secure privileges; or unless the bare possession of life is the only privilege which Americans are to enjoy... If peace were not totally reprobated by him, why are those pusillanimous, deluded, servile wretches among you, who, for present ease or impious bribes, would sell their liberty, their children, and their souls; who, like savages, worship every devil that promises not to hurt them; or obey any mandates, however cruel, for which they are paid?

How is it that these sordid, degenerate creatures, who bow the knee to this king, and daily offer incense at his shrine, should be denied the peace so repeatedly promised them? Why are they indiscriminately abused, robbed, and plundered, with their more deserving neighbors? But in this world, as in the other, it is right and just that the wicked should be punished by their seducers. And why all this desolation, bloodshed, and unparalleled cruelty? They tell you, to reduce you to obedience. Obedience to what? To their sovereign will and pleasure. And what then? Why, then you shall be pardoned, because you consent to be slaves. And why should you be slaves now, having been freemen ever since the country was settled? Because, forsooth, the king and parliament of an island, three thousand miles off, choose that you should be hewers of good, and drawers of water for them. And is this the people who proud domination you are taught to solicit? Is this the peace which some of you so ardently desire? For shame! For shame… The King of Heaven is not like the king of Britain, implacable. If we turn from our sins, He will turn from his anger. Then will our arms be crowned with success, and the pride and power of our enemies, like the arrogance and pride of Nebuchadnezzar, will vanish away.

Let a general reformation of manners take place—let universal charity, public spirit, and private virtue be inculcated, encouraged, and practiced. Unite in preparing for a vigorous defense of your country, as if all depended on your own exertions. And when you have done all things, then rely upon the good Providence of Almighty God for success, in full confidence that without his blessing, all our efforts will inevitably fail… Cease, then, to desire the flesh-pots of Egypt, and remember her task-masters and oppression. No longer hesitate about rejecting all dependence on a king who will rule you with a rod of iron: freedom is now your power—value the heavenly gift: remember, that if you dare to neglect or despise it, you offer an insult to the Divine bestower—nor despair of keeping it… Blush, then, ye degenerate spirits, who give all over for lost, because your enemies have marched through three or four counties in this and a neighboring State—ye who basely fly to have the yoke of slavery fixed on your necks, and to swear that you and your children shall be slaves for ever. Rouse, brave citizens! Do your duty like men; and be persuaded that Divine Providence will not permit this western world to be involved in the horrors of slavery.

Consider, that from the earliest ages of the world, religion, liberty, and reason have been bending their course towards the setting sun. The holy gospels are yet to be preached to these western regions; and we have the highest reason to believe that the Almighty will not suffer slavery and the gospel to go hand in hand. It cannot, it will not be. But if there by any among us, dead to all sense of honor, and love of their country; if deaf to all the calls of liberty, virtue, and religion; if forgetful of the magnanimity of their ancestors, and the happiness of their children; if neither the examples nor the success of other nations—the dictates of reason and of nature; or the great duties they owe to their God, themselves, and their posterity, have any effect upon them—if neither the injuries they have received, the prize they are contending for, the future blessings or curses of their children—the applause or reproach of all mankind—the approbation or displeasure of the Great Judge—or the happiness or misery consequent upon their conduct, in this and a future state, can move them—then let them be assured, that they deserve to be slaves, and are entitled to nothing but anguish and tribulation.

Let them banish from their remembrance the reputation, the freedom, and the happiness they have inherited from their forefathers. Let them forget every duty, human and divine; remember not that they have children; and beware how they call to mind the justice of the Supreme Being: let them go into captivity, like the idolatrous and disobedient Jews; and be a reproach and a by-word among nations. But we think better things of you—we believe and are persuaded that you will do your duty like men, and cheerfully refer your cause to the great and righteous Judge. If success crown your efforts, all the blessings of freemen will be your reward. If you fall in the contest, you will be happy with God in heaven.[47]

To echo what Jefferson says, "My God! How little do my countrymen know what precious blessings they are in possession of, and which no other people on earth enjoy." To have leaders such as him in a time like this would truly reform the nation. Unfortunately, our possession is ever so slight and

47. Jay, *The Life of John Jay*, 51–57.

with just the right amount of force can be easily taken from us. Thus, we are faced with decisions similar to our founders—decisions that require action in one form or another.

I believe Pat Buchanan is close to being accurate when he says the following: "We traditionalists who love the culture and country we grew up in are going to have to deal with this question: Do we simply conserve the remnant, or do we try to take the culture back? Are we conservatives, or must we also become counterrevolutionaries and overthrow the dominant culture?"[48] His questions were relevant when written, but our situation has worsened exponentially since then. The question is now more defined and focused. Evidence overwhelmingly proves that America's national culture cannot be reclaimed with counterrevolutionary action—the differences are too vast, the goals too different, and the philosophies too irreconcilable. America's national culture is rotting as we speak with no signs of restoration. The old saying goes, "Why throw good money after bad?" In other words, where are freedom lovers going to focus their time, attention, money, motivation, energy, and concern?

Do you really want to raise your children in this corrupted, decadent, and divergent society? Since the national factor seems to be out of the equation, the question is what are freedom-loving Americans willing to do to retake freedom in their *state* under the Ninth and Tenth Amendments[49] of the Constitution? If you think differently, I challenge you to show what good the conservative, family morals, Christian, right-wing movements have done over the past one hundred years on a national level? The only viable conclusion is that our resources must be focused at the state level. This of course has many implications concerning not only the citizen's outlook and approach to government, but also the states' role in this republican form of government—this federalist system, under which we operate.

Thomas Jefferson correctly observes the role that states should play in the federal government's usurpation of power and unconstitutional acts.

---

48. Buchanan, *The Death of the West,* 215.

49. "The enumeration in the Constitution, of certain rights, shall not be construed to deny or disparage others retained by the people." U.S. Constitution, amend 10; "The powers not delegated to the United States by the Constitution, nor prohibited by it to the States, are reserved to the States respectively, or to the people." U.S. Constitution, amend 9.

Jefferson admits that it would not be wise for society to take up arms against the government for every violation of the Constitution, because we would be doing so at least once a year.[50] Jefferson believes that "we must be patient... and give them time for reflection and experience of consequences."[51]

However, time is a luxury that freedom lovers can barely afford today. Jefferson would likely agree. He says, "We must...separate from our companions only when the sole alternatives left, are the dissolution of our Union with them, or submission to a government without limitation of powers."[52] Arguably, we have reached such a time. Very arguably, we are passed such a time. So what are the states doing about it? Jefferson positions that "in the meanwhile, the States should be watchful to note every material usurpation on their rights; denounce them as they occur in the most peremptory terms; to protest against them as wrongs to which our present submission shall be considered, not as acknowledgments or precedents of right, but as a temporary yielding to the lesser evil, until their accumulation shall overweigh that of separation."[53] Unfortunately, there are very few states *not* shirking this responsibility—although there is without a doubt a fast-growing movement

---

50. Jefferson, *The Jeffersonian Cyclopedia,* 133.

51. Ibid.

52. Ibid.

53. Jefferson, *The Jeffersonian Cyclopedia,* 133. See Also, "[I]n a confederacy the people, without exaggeration, may be said to be entirely the masters of their own fate. Power being almost always the rival of power, the general government will at all times stand ready to check the usurpations of the state governments, and these will have the same disposition towards the general government... It may safely be received as an axiom in our political system, that the State governments will, in all possible contingencies, afford complete security against invasions of the public liberty by the national authority. Projects of usurpation cannot be masked under pretenses so likely to escape the penetration of select bodies of men, as of the people at large. The legislatures will have better means of information. They can discover the danger at a distance; and possessing all the organs of civil power, and the confidence of the people, they can at once adopt a regular plan of opposition, in which they can combine all the resources of the community. They can readily communicate with each other in the different States, and unite their common forces for the protection of their common liberty." Alexander Hamilton, "Federalist Paper 28," in *The Federalist Papers,* Hamilton, Jay, and Madison, 214–215. "[The states] would be signals of general alarm [against encroachments of the federal government]. Every government would espouse the common cause. A correspondence would be opened. Plans of resistance would be concerted." James Madison, "Federalist Paper 46," in *The Federalist Papers,* Hamilton, Jay, and Madison, 369.

amongst the states to reclaim their sovereignty (thank God!).[54] For years, the states have looked to the federal government for as many handouts and programs as the federal government would offer. For many years, the states have been nothing but the yes man of the federal government, acting merely as their agent and not as an independent state looking out for the interests and freedoms of its citizens. As a result, the states are powerless. That is the fault of many generations. Now, their posterity is reaping the consequences. Without a complete about-face from the states, there is no hope to reclaiming freedom and constitutional government. It may be a grim, pessimistic outlook, but history confirms this fact.

Will there be any states remaining in the union to protect the rights of their citizens? Will there be any states that understand the Constitution was created and ratified by the states, and that they have the power to reclaim a constitutional government anytime they please? Will the citizens demand that their states begin taking the job of protector of rights seriously? Will there be any states that once again implement the Jeffersonian principles reflected in the Virginia and Kentucky resolutions that "the General Government was simply the representative of the delegated authority of the sovereign States of the Union, and was authorized to execute its civil mandates upon the people of every State, so far as its authority extended"?[55] Without a doubt, time is running out and decisions are soon to be made: decisions regarding voluntary slavery and freedom. Perhaps most states and citizens will revert to unconditional submission to an unlimited federal government, but the choice is still yours. Just as certain, however, there will be states and citizens who will not go along as such.

While most of the options do not look promising relative to the national level, reclaiming freedom on a state and local level appears to be the most vital and promising—and indeed exciting—alternative. It is clear that there are still thousands of freedom lovers in America. However, it is also clear that

---

54. Jerome R. Corsi, "Lawmakers In 20 States Move To Reclaim Sovereignty: Obama's $1 Trillion Deficit-Spending 'Stimulus Plan' Seen As Last Straw," *World Net Daily,* February 6, 2009, http://www.worldnetdaily.com/index.php?fa=PAGE.view&pageId=88218 (accessed May 5, 2009).

55. Harris, *A Review of the Political Conflict in America,* 214.

their influence is virtually unfelt on the national level. Thus, each of you must consider all of the truths concerning freedom and America's current state and condition. You must decide whether or not you will step outside of your comfort zone and begin blazing a trail of freedom outside of what the federal government and controlled media would have you believe is reality—for the sake of not only yourself but also your posterity. Undoubtedly, the answers and means are available to the truth seeker. When philosophy produces ideology and ideology produces belief and belief produces action, freedom lovers in America will reach their goal.

May freedom lovers in America dedicate themselves once again to knowing, understanding, and implementing the principles of freedom found in the natural and revealed laws of God. May they be willing to set aside the lusts and desires for comfort and convenience and consider their duties to God, family, community, nation, and posterity in all things. May they take it upon themselves to fight for the good cause of freedom as if the results depended solely upon them.

Appendix A

THE DECLARATION OF INDEPENDENCE

IN CONGRESS, July 4, 1776

The unanimous Declaration of the thirteen United States of America

When in the Course of human events it becomes necessary for one people to dissolve the political bands which have connected them with another, and to assume among the powers of the earth, the separate and equal station to which the Laws of Nature and of Nature's God entitle them, a decent respect to the opinions of mankind requires that they should declare the causes which impel them to the separation.

We hold these truths to be self-evident, that all men are created equal, that they are endowed by their Creator with certain unalienable Rights, that among these are Life, Liberty and the pursuit of Happiness.—That to secure these rights, Governments are instituted among Men, deriving their just powers from the consent of the governed,—That whenever any Form of Government becomes destructive of these ends, it is the Right of the People to alter or to abolish it, and to institute new Government, laying its foundation on such principles and organizing its powers in such form, as to them shall seem most likely to effect their Safety and Happiness. Prudence, indeed, will dictate that Governments long established should not be changed for light and transient causes; and accordingly all experience hath shewn that mankind are more disposed to suffer, while evils are sufferable than to right themselves by abolishing the forms to which they are accustomed. But when a long train of abuses and usurpations, pursuing invariably the same Object evinces a design to reduce them under absolute Despotism, it is their right, it is their duty, to throw off such Government, and to provide new Guards for their future security.—Such has been the patient sufferance of these Colonies; and such is now the necessity which constrains them to alter their former Systems of Government. The history of the present King of Great Britain is a history of repeated injuries and usurpations, all having in direct object the establishment of an absolute Tyranny over these States. To prove this, let Facts be submitted to a candid world.

He has refused his Assent to Laws, the most wholesome and necessary for the public good.

He has forbidden his Governors to pass Laws of immediate and pressing importance, unless suspended in their operation till his Assent should be obtained; and when so suspended, he has utterly neglected to attend to them.

He has refused to pass other Laws for the accommodation of large districts of people, unless those people would relinquish the right of Representation in the Legislature, a right inestimable to them and formidable to tyrants only.

He has called together legislative bodies at places unusual, uncomfortable, and distant from the depository of their public Records, for the sole purpose of fatiguing them into compliance with his measures.

He has dissolved Representative Houses repeatedly, for opposing with manly firmness his invasions on the rights of the people.

He has refused for a long time, after such dissolutions, to cause others to be elected, whereby the Legislative powers, incapable of Annihilation, have returned to the People at large for their exercise; the State remaining in the mean time exposed to all the dangers of invasion from without, and convulsions within.

He has endeavoured to prevent the population of these States; for that purpose obstructing the Laws for Naturalization of Foreigners; refusing to pass others to encourage their migrations hither, and raising the conditions of new Appropriations of Lands.

He has obstructed the Administration of Justice by refusing his Assent to Laws for establishing Judiciary powers.

He has made Judges dependent on his Will alone for the tenure of their offices, and the amount and payment of their salaries.

He has erected a multitude of New Offices, and sent hither swarms of Officers to harass our people and eat out their substance.

He has kept among us, in times of peace, Standing Armies without the Consent of our legislatures.

He has affected to render the Military independent of and superior to the Civil power.

He has combined with others to subject us to a jurisdiction foreign to our constitution, and unacknowledged by our laws; giving his Assent to their Acts of pretended Legislation:

For quartering large bodies of armed troops among us:

For protecting them, by a mock Trial from punishment for any Murders which they should commit on the Inhabitants of these States:

For cutting off our Trade with all parts of the world:

For imposing Taxes on us without our Consent:

For depriving us in many cases, of the benefits of Trial by Jury:

For transporting us beyond Seas to be tried for pretended offences:

For abolishing the free System of English Laws in a neighbouring Province, establishing therein an Arbitrary government, and enlarging its Boundaries so as to render it at once an example and fit instrument for introducing the same absolute rule into these Colonies:

For taking away our Charters, abolishing our most valuable Laws and altering fundamentally the Forms of our Governments:

For suspending our own Legislatures, and declaring themselves invested with power to legislate for us in all cases whatsoever.

He has abdicated Government here, by declaring us out of his Protection and waging War against us.

He has plundered our seas, ravaged our Coasts, burnt our towns, and destroyed the lives of our people.

He is at this time transporting large Armies of foreign Mercenaries to compleat the works of death, desolation, and tyranny, already begun with circumstances of Cruelty & perfidy scarcely paralleled in the most barbarous ages, and totally unworthy the Head of a civilized nation.

He has constrained our fellow Citizens taken Captive on the high Seas to bear Arms against their Country, to become the executioners of their friends and Brethren, or to fall themselves by their Hands.

He has excited domestic insurrections amongst us, and has endeavoured to bring on the inhabitants of our frontiers, the merciless Indian Savages whose known rule of warfare, is an undistinguished destruction of all ages, sexes and conditions.

In every stage of these Oppressions We have Petitioned for Redress in the most humble terms: Our repeated Petitions have been answered only by repeated injury. A Prince, whose character is thus marked by every act which may define a Tyrant, is unfit to be the ruler of a free people.

Nor have We been wanting in attentions to our British brethren. We have warned them from time to time of attempts by their legislature to extend an unwarrantable jurisdiction over us. We have reminded them of the circumstances of our emigration and settlement here. We have appealed to their native justice and magnanimity, and we have conjured them by the ties of our common kindred to disavow these usurpations, which would inevitably interrupt our connections and correspondence. They too have been deaf to the voice of justice and of consanguinity. We must, therefore, acquiesce in the necessity, which denounces our Separation, and hold them, as we hold the rest of mankind, Enemies in War, in Peace Friends.

We, therefore, the Representatives of the united States of America, in General Congress, Assembled, appealing to the Supreme Judge of the world for the rectitude of our intentions, do, in the Name, and by Authority of the good People of these Colonies, solemnly publish and declare, That these United Colonies are, and of Right ought to be Free and Independent States, that they are Absolved from all Allegiance to the British Crown, and that all political connection between them and the State of Great Britain, is and ought to be totally dissolved; and that as Free and Independent States, they have full Power to levy War, conclude Peace, contract Alliances, establish Commerce, and to do all other Acts and Things which Independent States may of right do.—And for the support of this Declaration, with a firm reliance on the protection of Divine Providence, we mutually pledge to each other our Lives, our Fortunes and our sacred Honor.

The fifty-six signatures on the Declaration appear in the positions indicated:

COLUMN 1

Georgia:
  Button Gwinnett
  Lyman Hall
  George Walton

COLUMN 2

North Carolina:
  William Hooper
  Joseph Hewes
  John Penn

South Carolina:
  Edward Rutledge
  Thomas Heyward, Jr.
  Thomas Lynch, Jr.
  Arthur Middleton

COLUMN 3

Massachusetts:
  John Hancock

Maryland:
  Samuel Chase
  William Paca
  Thomas Stone
  Charles Carroll
    of Carrollton

Virginia:
  George Wythe
  Richard Henry Lee
  Thomas Jefferson
  Benjamin Harrison
  Thomas Nelson, Jr.
  Francis Lightfoot Lee
  Carter Braxton

COLUMN 4

Pennsylvania:
  Robert Morris
  Benjamin Rush
  Benjamin Franklin
  John Morton
  George Clymer
  James Smith
  George Taylor
  James Wilson
  George Ross

Delaware:
  Caesar Rodney
  George Read
  Thomas McKean

COLUMN 5

New York:
  William Floyd
  Philip Livingston
  Francis Lewis
  Lewis Morris

New Jersey:
  Richard Stockton
  John Witherspoon
  Francis Hopkinson
  John Hart
  Abraham Clark

COLUMN 6

New Hampshire:
  Josiah Bartlett
  William Whipple

Massachusetts:
  Samuel Adams
  John Adams
  Robert Treat Paine
  Elbridge Gerry

Rhode Island:
  Stephen Hopkins
  William Ellery

Connecticut:
  Roger Sherman
  Samuel Huntington
  William Williams
  Oliver Wolcott

New Hampshire:
  Matthew Thornton

Appendix B

THE CONSTITUTION OF THE UNITED STATES OF AMERICA

We the People of the United States, in Order to form a more perfect Union, establish Justice, insure domestic Tranquility, provide for the common defence, promote the general Welfare, and secure the Blessings of Liberty to ourselves and our Posterity, do ordain and establish this Constitution for the United States of America.

ARTICLE I

Section 1

All legislative Powers herein granted shall be vested in a Congress of the United States, which shall consist of a Senate and House of Representatives.

Section 2

The House of Representatives shall be composed of Members chosen every second Year by the People of the several States, and the Electors in each State shall have the Qualifications requisite for Electors of the most numerous Branch of the State Legislature.

No Person shall be a Representative who shall not have attained to the Age of twenty five Years, and been seven Years a Citizen of the United States, and who shall not, when elected, be an Inhabitant of that State in which he shall be chosen.

Representatives and direct Taxes shall be apportioned among the several States which may be included within this Union, according to their respective Numbers, which shall be determined by adding to the whole Number of free Persons, including those bound to Service for a Term of Years, and excluding Indians not taxed, three fifths of all other Persons. The actual Enumeration shall be made within three Years after the first Meeting of the Congress of the United States, and within every subsequent Term of ten Years, in such Manner as they shall by Law direct. The Number of Representatives shall not exceed one for every thirty Thousand, but each State shall have at Least one Representative; and until such enumeration shall be made, the State of New Hampshire shall be entitled to chuse three, Massachusetts eight, Rhode-Island and Providence Plantations one, Connecticut five, New-York six, New Jersey four, Pennsylvania eight, Delaware one, Maryland six, Virginia ten, North Carolina five, South Carolina five, and Georgia three.

When vacancies happen in the Representation from any State, the Executive Authority thereof shall issue Writs of Election to fill such Vacancies.

The House of Representatives shall chuse their Speaker and other Officers; and shall have the sole Power of Impeachment.

Section 3
The Senate of the United States shall be composed of two Senators from each State, chosen by the Legislature thereof for six Years; and each Senator shall have one Vote.

Immediately after they shall be assembled in Consequence of the first Election, they shall be divided as equally as may be into three Classes. The Seats of the Senators of the first Class shall be vacated at the Expiration of the second Year, of the second Class at the Expiration of the fourth Year, and of the third Class at the Expiration of the sixth Year, so that one third may be chosen every second Year; and if Vacancies happen by Resignation, or otherwise, during the Recess of the Legislature of any State, the Executive thereof may make temporary Appointments until the next Meeting of the Legislature, which shall then fill such Vacancies.

No Person shall be a Senator who shall not have attained to the Age of thirty Years, and been nine Years a Citizen of the United States, and who shall not, when elected, be an Inhabitant of that State for which he shall be chosen.

The vice president of the United States shall be president of the Senate, but shall have no Vote, unless they be equally divided.

The Senate shall chuse their other Officers, and also a president pro tempore, in the Absence of the vice president, or when he shall exercise the office of president of the United States.

The Senate shall have the sole Power to try all Impeachments. When sitting for that Purpose, they shall be on Oath or Affirmation. When the president of the United States is tried, the Chief Justice shall preside: And no Person shall be convicted without the Concurrence of two thirds of the Members present.

Judgment in Cases of Impeachment shall not extend further than to removal from Office, and disqualification to hold and enjoy any Office of honor, Trust or Profit under the United States: but the Party convicted shall nevertheless be liable and subject to Indictment, Trial, Judgment and Punishment, according to Law.

Section 4

The Times, Places and Manner of holding Elections for Senators and Representatives, shall be prescribed in each State by the Legislature thereof; but the Congress may at any time by Law make or alter such Regulations, except as to the Places of chusing Senators.

The Congress shall assemble at least once in every Year, and such Meeting shall be on the first Monday in December, unless they shall by Law appoint a different Day.

Section 5

Each House shall be the Judge of the Elections, Returns and Qualifications of its own Members, and a Majority of each shall constitute a Quorum to do Business; but a smaller Number may adjourn from day to day, and may be authorized to compel the Attendance of absent Members, in such Manner, and under such Penalties as each House may provide.

Each House may determine the Rules of its Proceedings, punish its Members for disorderly Behaviour, and, with the Concurrence of two thirds, expel a Member.

Each House shall keep a Journal of its Proceedings, and from time to time publish the same, excepting such Parts as may in their Judgment require Secrecy; and the Yeas and Nays of the Members of either House on any question shall, at the Desire of one fifth of those Present, be entered on the Journal.

Neither House, during the Session of Congress, shall, without the Consent of the other, adjourn for more than three days, nor to any other Place than that in which the two Houses shall be sitting.

Section 6

The Senators and Representatives shall receive a Compensation for their Services, to be ascertained by Law, and paid out of the Treasury of the United States. They shall in all Cases, except Treason, Felony and Breach of the Peace, be privileged from Arrest during their Attendance at the Session of their respective Houses, and in going to and returning from the same; and for any Speech or Debate in either House, they shall not be questioned in any other Place.

No Senator or Representative shall, during the Time for which he was elected, be appointed to any civil Office under the Authority of the United States, which shall have been created, or the Emoluments whereof shall have been encreased during such time; and no Person holding any Office under the United States, shall be a Member of either House during his Continuance in Office.

Section 7

All Bills for raising Revenue shall originate in the House of Representatives; but the Senate may propose or concur with Amendments as on other Bills.

Every Bill which shall have passed the House of Representatives and the Senate, shall, before it become a Law, be presented to the president of the United States: If he approve he shall sign it, but if not he shall return it, with his Objections to that House in which it shall have originated, who shall enter the Objections at large on their Journal, and proceed to reconsider it.

If after such Reconsideration two thirds of that House shall agree to pass the Bill, it shall be sent, together with the Objections, to the other House, by which it shall likewise be reconsidered, and if approved by two thirds of that House, it shall become a Law. But in all such Cases the Votes of both Houses shall be determined by yeas and Nays, and the Names of the Persons voting for and against the Bill shall be entered on the Journal of each House respectively. If any Bill shall not be returned by the president within ten Days (Sundays excepted) after it shall have been presented to him, the Same shall be a Law, in like Manner as if he had signed it, unless the Congress by their Adjournment prevent its Return, in which Case it shall not be a Law.

Every Order, Resolution, or Vote to which the Concurrence of the Senate and House of Representatives may be necessary (except on a question of Adjournment) shall be presented to the president of the United States; and before the Same shall take Effect, shall be approved by him, or being disapproved by him, shall be repassed by two thirds of the Senate and House of Representatives, according to the Rules and Limitations prescribed in the Case of a Bill.

Section 8

The Congress shall have Power To lay and collect Taxes, Duties, Imposts and Excises, to pay the Debts and provide for the common Defence and general Welfare of the United States; but all Duties, Imposts and Excises shall be uniform throughout the United States;

To borrow Money on the credit of the United States;

To regulate Commerce with foreign Nations, and among the several States, and with the Indian Tribes;

To establish an uniform Rule of Naturalization, and uniform Laws on the subject of Bankruptcies throughout the United States;

To coin Money, regulate the Value thereof, and of foreign Coin, and fix the Standard of Weights and Measures;

To provide for the Punishment of counterfeiting the Securities and current Coin of the United States;

To establish Post Offices and post Roads;

To promote the Progress of Science and useful Arts, by securing for limited Times to Authors and Inventors the exclusive Right to their respective Writings and Discoveries;

To constitute Tribunals inferior to the supreme Court;

To define and punish Piracies and Felonies committed on the high Seas, and Offences against the Law of Nations;

To declare War, grant Letters of Marque and Reprisal, and make Rules concerning Captures on Land and Water;

To raise and support Armies, but no Appropriation of Money to that Use shall be for a longer Term than two Years;

To provide and maintain a Navy;

To make Rules for the Government and Regulation of the land and naval Forces;

To provide for calling forth the Militia to execute the Laws of the Union, suppress Insurrections and repel Invasions;

To provide for organizing, arming, and disciplining, the Militia, and for governing such Part of them as may be employed in the Service of the United States, reserving to the States respectively, the Appointment of the Officers, and the Authority of training the Militia according to the discipline prescribed by Congress;

To exercise exclusive Legislation in all Cases whatsoever, over such District (not exceeding ten Miles square) as may, by Cession of particular States, and the Acceptance of Congress, become the Seat of the Government of the United States, and to exercise like Authority over all Places purchased by the Consent of the Legislature of the State in which the Same shall be, for the Erection of Forts, Magazines, Arsenals, dock-Yards, and other needful Buildings;—And

To make all Laws which shall be necessary and proper for carrying into Execution the foregoing Powers, and all other Powers vested by this Constitution in the Government of the United States, or in any Department or Officer thereof.

Section 9

The Migration or Importation of such Persons as any of the States now existing shall think proper to admit, shall not be prohibited by the Congress prior to the Year one thousand eight hundred and eight, but a Tax or duty may be imposed on such Importation, not exceeding ten dollars for each Person.

The Privilege of the Writ of Habeas Corpus shall not be suspended, unless when in Cases of Rebellion or Invasion the public Safety may require it.

No Bill of Attainder or ex post facto Law shall be passed.

No Capitation, or other direct, Tax shall be laid, unless in Proportion to the Census or enumeration herein before directed to be taken.

No Tax or Duty shall be laid on Articles exported from any State.

No Preference shall be given by any Regulation of Commerce or Revenue to the Ports of one State over those of another; nor shall Vessels bound to, or from, one State, be obliged to enter, clear, or pay Duties in another.

No Money shall be drawn from the Treasury, but in Consequence of Appropriations made by Law; and a regular Statement and Account of the Receipts and Expenditures of all public Money shall be published from time to time.

No Title of Nobility shall be granted by the United States: And no Person holding any Office of Profit or Trust under them, shall, without the Consent of the Congress, accept of any present, Emolument, Office, or Title, of any kind whatever, from any King, Prince, or foreign State.

Section 10

No State shall enter into any Treaty, Alliance, or Confederation; grant Letters of Marque and Reprisal; coin Money; emit Bills of Credit; make any Thing but gold and silver Coin a Tender in Payment of Debts; pass any Bill of Attainder, ex post facto Law, or Law impairing the Obligation of Contracts, or grant any Title of Nobility.

No State shall, without the Consent of the Congress, lay any Imposts or Duties on Imports or Exports, except what may be absolutely necessary for executing its inspection Laws: and the net Produce of all Duties and Imposts, laid by any State on Imports or Exports, shall be for the Use of the Treasury of the United States; and all such Laws shall be subject to the Revision and Controul of the Congress.

No State shall, without the Consent of Congress, lay any Duty of Tonnage, keep Troops, or Ships of War in time of Peace, enter into any Agreement or Compact with another State, or with a foreign Power, or engage in War, unless actually invaded, or in such imminent Danger as will not admit of delay.

Article II

Section 1

The executive Power shall be vested in a President of the United States of America. He shall hold his Office during the Term of four Years, and, together with the Vice President, chosen for the same Term, be elected, as follows:

Each State shall appoint, in such Manner as the Legislature thereof may direct, a Number of Electors, equal to the whole Number of Senators and Representatives to which the State may be entitled in the Congress: but no Senator or Representative, or Person holding an Office of Trust or Profit under the United States, shall be appointed an Elector.

The Electors shall meet in their respective States, and vote by Ballot for two Persons, of whom one at least shall not be an Inhabitant of the same State with themselves. And they shall make a List of all the Persons voted for, and of the Number of Votes for each; which List they shall sign and certify, and transmit sealed to the Seat of the Government of the United States, directed to the President of the Senate. The President of the Senate shall, in the Presence of the Senate and House of Representatives, open all the Certificates, and the Votes shall then be counted. The Person having the greatest Number of Votes shall be the President, if such Number be a Majority of the whole Number of Electors appointed; and if there be more than one who have such Majority, and have an equal Number of Votes, then the House of Representatives shall immediately chuse by Ballot one of them for President; and if no Person have a Majority, then from the five highest on the List the said House shall in like Manner chuse the President. But in chusing the President, the Votes shall be taken by States, the Representation from each State having one Vote; A quorum for this purpose shall consist of a Member or Members from two thirds of the States, and a Majority of all the States shall be necessary to a Choice. In every Case, after the Choice of the President, the Person having the greatest Number of Votes of the Electors shall be the Vice President. But if there should remain two or more who have equal Votes, the Senate shall chuse from them by Ballot the Vice President.

The Congress may determine the Time of chusing the Electors, and the Day on which they shall give their Votes; which Day shall be the same throughout the United States.

No Person except a natural born Citizen, or a Citizen of the United States, at the time of the Adoption of this Constitution, shall be eligible to the Office of President; neither shall any Person be eligible to that Office who shall not have attained to the Age of thirty five Years, and been fourteen Years a Resident within the United States.

In Case of the Removal of the President from Office, or of his Death, Resignation, or Inability to discharge the Powers and Duties of the said Office, the Same shall devolve on the Vice President, and the Congress may by Law provide for the Case of Removal, Death, Resignation or Inability, both of the President and Vice President, declaring what Officer shall then act as President, and such Officer shall act accordingly, until the Disability be removed, or a President shall be elected.

The President shall, at stated Times, receive for his Services, a Compensation, which shall neither be increased nor diminished during the Period for which he shall have been elected, and he shall not receive within that Period any other Emolument from the United States, or any of them.

Before he enter on the Execution of his Office, he shall take the following Oath or Affirmation:—"I do solemnly swear (or affirm) that I will faithfully execute the Office of President of the United States, and will to the best of my Ability, preserve, protect and defend the Constitution of the United States."

Section 2

The President shall be Commander in Chief of the Army and Navy of the United States, and of the Militia of the several States, when called into the actual Service of the United States; he may require the Opinion, in writing, of the principal Officer in each of the executive Departments, upon any Subject relating to the Duties of their respective Offices, and he shall have Power to grant Reprieves and Pardons for Offences against the United States, except in Cases of Impeachment.

He shall have Power, by and with the Advice and Consent of the Senate, to make Treaties, provided two thirds of the Senators present concur; and he shall nominate, and by and with the Advice and Consent of the Senate, shall appoint Ambassadors, other public Ministers and Consuls, Judges of the supreme Court, and all other Officers of the United States, whose Appointments are not herein otherwise provided for, and which shall be established by Law: but the Congress may by Law vest the Appointment of such inferior Officers, as they think proper, in the President alone, in the Courts of Law, or in the Heads of Departments.

The President shall have Power to fill up all Vacancies that may happen during the Recess of the Senate, by granting Commissions which shall expire at the End of their next Session.

Section 3

He shall from time to time give to the Congress Information of the State of the Union, and recommend to their Consideration such Measures as he shall judge necessary and expedient; he may, on extraordinary Occasions, convene both Houses, or either of them, and in Case of Disagreement between them, with Respect to the Time of Adjournment, he may adjourn them to such Time as he shall think proper; he shall receive Ambassadors and other public Ministers; he shall take Care that the Laws be faithfully executed, and shall Commission all the Officers of the United States.

Section 4

The President, Vice President and all civil Officers of the United States, shall be removed from Office on Impeachment for, and Conviction of, Treason, Bribery, or other high Crimes and Misdemeanors.

ARTICLE III

Section 1

The judicial Power of the United States shall be vested in one supreme Court, and in such inferior Courts as the Congress may from time to time ordain and establish. The Judges, both of the supreme and inferior Courts, shall hold their Offices during good Behaviour, and shall, at stated Times, receive for their Services a Compensation, which shall not be diminished during their Continuance in Office.

Section 2

The judicial Power shall extend to all Cases, in Law and Equity, arising under this Constitution, the Laws of the United States, and Treaties made, or which shall be made, under their Authority;—to all Cases affecting Ambassadors, other public Ministers and Consuls;—to all Cases of admiralty and maritime Jurisdiction;—to Controversies to which the United States shall be a Party;—to Controversies between two or more States;—between a State and Citizens of another State;—between Citizens of different States;—between Citizens of the same State claiming Lands under Grants of different States, and between a State, or the Citizens thereof, and foreign States, Citizens or Subjects.

In all Cases affecting Ambassadors, other public Ministers and Consuls, and those in which a State shall be Party, the supreme Court shall have original Jurisdiction. In all the other Cases before mentioned, the supreme Court shall have appellate Jurisdiction, both as to Law and Fact, with such Exceptions, and under such Regulations as the Congress shall make.

The Trial of all Crimes, except in Cases of Impeachment, shall be by Jury; and such Trial shall be held in the State where the said Crimes shall have been committed; but when not committed within any State, the Trial shall be at such Place or Places as the Congress may by Law have directed.

Section 3

Treason against the United States, shall consist only in levying War against them, or in adhering to their Enemies, giving them Aid and Comfort. No Person shall be convicted of Treason unless on the Testimony of two Witnesses to the same overt Act, or on Confession in open Court.

The Congress shall have Power to declare the Punishment of Treason, but no Attainder of Treason shall work Corruption of Blood, or Forfeiture except during the Life of the Person attainted.

Article IV

Section 1

Full Faith and Credit shall be given in each State to the public Acts, Records, and judicial Proceedings of every other State. And the Congress may by general Laws prescribe the Manner in which such Acts, Records and Proceedings shall be proved, and the Effect thereof.

Section 2

The Citizens of each State shall be entitled to all Privileges and Immunities of Citizens in the several States.

A Person charged in any State with Treason, Felony, or other Crime, who shall flee from Justice, and be found in another State, shall on Demand of the executive Authority of the State from which he fled, be delivered up, to be removed to the State having Jurisdiction of the Crime.

No Person held to Service or Labour in one State, under the Laws thereof, escaping into another, shall, in Consequence of any Law or Regulation therein, be discharged from such Service or Labour, but shall be delivered up on Claim of the Party to whom such Service or Labour may be due.

Section 3

New States may be admitted by the Congress into this Union; but no new State shall be formed or erected within the Jurisdiction of any other State; nor any State be formed by the Junction of two or more States, or Parts of States, without the Consent of the Legislatures of the States concerned as well as of the Congress.

The Congress shall have Power to dispose of and make all needful Rules and Regulations respecting the Territory or other Property belonging to the United States; and nothing in this Constitution shall be so construed as to Prejudice any Claims of the United States, or of any particular State.

Section 4

The United States shall guarantee to every State in this Union a Republican Form of Government, and shall protect each of them against Invasion; and on Application of the Legislature, or of the Executive (when the Legislature cannot be convened), against domestic Violence.

ARTICLE V

The Congress, whenever two thirds of both Houses shall deem it necessary, shall propose Amendments to this Constitution, or, on the Application of the Legislatures of two thirds of the several States, shall call a Convention for proposing Amendments, which, in either Case, shall be valid to all Intents and Purposes, as Part of this Constitution, when ratified by the Legislatures of three fourths of the several States, or by Conventions in three fourths thereof, as the one or the other Mode of Ratification may be proposed by the Congress; Provided that no Amendment which may be made prior to the Year One thousand eight hundred and eight shall in any Manner affect the first and fourth Clauses in the Ninth Section of the first Article; and that no State, without its Consent, shall be deprived of its equal Suffrage in the Senate.

ARTICLE VI

All Debts contracted and Engagements entered into, before the Adoption of this Constitution, shall be as valid against the United States under this Constitution, as under the Confederation.

This Constitution, and the Laws of the United States which shall be made in Pursuance thereof; and all Treaties made, or which shall be made, under the Authority of the United States, shall be the supreme Law of the Land; and the Judges in every State shall be bound thereby, any Thing in the Constitution or Laws of any State to the Contrary notwithstanding.

The Senators and Representatives before mentioned, and the Members of the several State Legislatures, and all executive and judicial Officers, both of the United States and of the several States, shall be bound by Oath or Affirmation, to support this Constitution; but no religious Test shall ever be required as a Qualification to any Office or public Trust under the United States.

ARTICLE VII

The Ratification of the Conventions of nine States, shall be sufficient for the Establishment of this Constitution between the States so ratifying the Same.

The Word, "the," being interlined between the seventh and eighth Lines of the first Page, the Word "Thirty" being partly written on an Erazure in the fifteenth Line of the first Page, The Words "is tried" being interlined between the thirty second and thirty third Lines of the first Page and the Word "the" being interlined between the forty third and forty fourth Lines of the second Page.

Attest William Jackson Secretary

Done in Convention by the Unanimous Consent of the States present the Seventeenth Day of September in the Year of our Lord one thousand seven hundred and Eighty seven and of the Independence of the United States of America the Twelfth In witness whereof We have hereunto subscribed our Names,

George Washington
President and deputy from Virginia

New Hampshire
John Langdon
Nicholas Gilman

Massachusetts
Nathaniel Gorham
Rufus King

Connecticut
William Samuel Johnson
Roger Sherman

New York
Alexander Hamilton

New Jersey
William Livingston
David Brearley
Wm. Paterson
Jonathon Dayton

Pennsylvania
B. Franklin
Thomas Mifflin
Robert Morris
Geo. Clymer

Thomas Fitz Simons
Jared Ingersoll
James Wilson
Gouvenor Morris

Delaware
George Read
Gunning Bedford, Jr.
John Dickinson
Richard Bassett
Jacob Broom

Maryland
James McHenry
Dan of St Thos. Jenifer
Daniel Carroll

Virginia
John Blair
James Madison, Jr.

North Carolina
Wm. Blount
Richard Dobbs Spaight
Hugh Williamson

South Carolina
J. Rutledge
Charles Cotesworth Pinckney
Charles Pinckney
Pierce Butler

Georgia
William Few
Abraham Baldwin

Appendix C

THE BILL OF RIGHTS

THE PREAMBLE TO THE BILL OF RIGHTS

Congress of the United States
*begun and held at the City of New-York, on
Wednesday the fourth of March, one thousand seven
hundred and eighty nine.*

THE Conventions of a number of the States, having at the time of their adopting the Constitution, expressed a desire, in order to prevent misconstruction or abuse of its powers, that further declaratory and restrictive clauses should be added: And as extending the ground of public confidence in the Government, will best ensure the beneficent ends of its institution.

RESOLVED by the Senate and House of Representatives of the United States of America, in Congress assembled, two thirds of both Houses concurring, that the following Articles be proposed to the Legislatures of the several States, as amendments to the Constitution of the United States, all, or any of which Articles, when ratified by three fourths of the said Legislatures, to be valid to all intents and purposes, as part of the said Constitution; viz.

ARTICLES in addition to, and Amendment of the Constitution of the United States of America, proposed by Congress, and ratified by the Legislatures of the several States, pursuant to the fifth Article of the original Constitution.

Note: The following text is a transcription of the first ten amendments to the Constitution in their original form. These amendments were ratified December 15, 1791, and form what is known as the "Bill of Rights."

Amendment I

Congress shall make no law respecting an establishment of religion, or prohibiting the free exercise thereof; or abridging the freedom of speech, or of the press; or the right of the people peaceably to assemble, and to petition the Government for a redress of grievances.

Amendment II

A well regulated Militia, being necessary to the security of a free State, the right of the people to keep and bear Arms, shall not be infringed.

Amendment III

No Soldier shall, in time of peace be quartered in any house, without the consent of the Owner, nor in time of war, but in a manner to be prescribed by law.

Amendment IV

The right of the people to be secure in their persons, houses, papers, and effects, against unreasonable searches and seizures, shall not be violated, and no Warrants shall issue, but upon probable cause, supported by Oath or affirmation, and particularly describing the place to be searched, and the persons or things to be seized.

Amendment V

No person shall be held to answer for a capital, or otherwise infamous crime, unless on a presentment or indictment of a Grand Jury, except in cases arising in the land or naval forces, or in the Militia, when in actual service in time of War or public danger; nor shall any person be subject for the same offence to be twice put in jeopardy of life or limb; nor shall be compelled in any criminal case to be a witness against himself, nor be deprived of life, liberty, or property, without due process of law; nor shall private property be taken for public use, without just compensation.

Amendment VI

In all criminal prosecutions, the accused shall enjoy the right to a speedy and public trial, by an impartial jury of the State and district wherein the crime shall have been committed, which district shall have been previously ascertained by law, and to be informed of the nature and cause of the accusation; to be confronted with the witnesses against him; to have compulsory process for obtaining witnesses in his favor, and to have the Assistance of Counsel for his defence.

Amendment VII

In Suits at common law, where the value in controversy shall exceed twenty dollars, the right of trial by jury shall be preserved, and no fact tried by a jury, shall be otherwise re-examined in any Court of the United States, than according to the rules of the common law.

Amendment VIII

Excessive bail shall not be required, nor excessive fines imposed, nor cruel and unusual punishments inflicted.

Amendment IX

The enumeration in the Constitution, of certain rights, shall not be construed to deny or disparage others retained by the people.

Amendment X

The powers not delegated to the United States by the Constitution, nor prohibited by it to the States, are reserved to the States respectively, or to the people.

Appendix D

A VERY REAL
NEW WORLD ORDER

By Chuck Baldwin
January 27, 2009

It is hard to believe, but a majority of Americans (including Christians and conservatives) seem oblivious to the fact that there is a very real, very legitimate New World Order (NWO) unfolding. In the face of overwhelming evidence, most Americans not only seem totally unaware of this reality, they seem unwilling to even remotely entertain the notion.

On one hand, it is understandable that so many Americans would be ignorant of the emerging New World Order. After all, the mainstream media refuses to report, or even acknowledge, the NWO. Even "conservative" commentators and talk show hosts such as Rush Limbaugh, Sean Hannity, Michael Savage, or Joe Scarborough refuse to discuss it. And when listeners call these respective programs, these "conservative" hosts usually resort to insulting the caller as being some kind of "conspiracy kook." One host even railed that if anyone questions the government line on 9/11, we should "lock them up and throw away the key." So much for freedom of speech!

This is an area—perhaps the central area—where liberals and conservatives agree: they both show no patience or tolerance for anyone who believes that global government (in any form) is evolving. One has to wonder how otherwise intelligent and thoughtful people can be so brain dead when it comes to this issue. It makes one wonder who is really pulling their strings, doesn't it?

The list of notable personalities who have openly referenced or called for some kind of global government or New World Order is extremely lengthy. Are all these people "kooks" or "conspiracy nuts"? Why would world leaders—including presidents, secretaries of state, and high government officials; including the media, financial, and political elite—constantly refer to something that doesn't exist? Why would they write about, talk about, or openly promote a New World Order, if there is no such thing?

Many of us recall President George Herbert Walker Bush talking much about an emerging New World Order. For example, in 1989, Bush told the students of Texas A&M University, "Perhaps the world order of the future will truly be a family of nations."

Later, Bush, Sr. said, "We have before us the opportunity to forge for ourselves and for future generations a new world order... When we are successful, and we will be, we have a real chance at this new world order, an order in which a credible United Nations can use its peacekeeping role to fulfill the promise and vision of the U.N.'s founders." Bush, Sr. also said, "What is at stake is more than one small country, it is a big idea—a new world order." Bush, Sr. further said, "The world can therefore seize the opportunity to fulfill the long-held promise of a new world order."

What was President G. H. W. Bush talking about, if there is no such thing as an emerging New World Order? Was he talking out of his mind? Was he hallucinating? England's Prime Minister, Tony Blair, said, "We are all internationalists now, whether we like it or not." He continued saying, "On the eve of a new Millennium we are now in a new world. We need new rules for international co-operation and new ways of organizing our international institutions." He also said, "Today the impulse towards interdependence is immeasurably greater. We are witnessing the beginnings of a new doctrine of international community."

In 1999, Tony Blair said, "Globalization has transformed our economies and our working practices. But globalism is not just economic. It is also a political and security phenomenon." What is Tony Blair talking about, if there is no emerging New World Order? What does he mean by "a new doctrine of international community"? What does he mean by "new world"? How can one have globalism, which includes "a political and security phenomenon," without creating a New World Order? Is Tony Blair hallucinating?

Likewise, former President George W. Bush penned his signature to the Declaration of Quebec back on April 22, 2001, in which he gave a "commitment to hemispheric integration and national and collective responsibility for improving the economic well-being and security of our people." By "our people," Bush meant the people of the Western Hemisphere, not the people of the United States. Phyllis Schlafly rightly reminded us that G. W. Bush "pledged that the United States will 'build a hemispheric family on the basis of a more just and democratic international order.'"

Remember, too, that it was G. W. Bush who, back in 2005, committed the United States to the Security and Prosperity Partnership (SPP), which is nothing more than a precursor to the North American Community or Union, as outlined in CFR member Robert Pastor's manual, "Toward a North American Community." If there is no such thing as an emerging New World Order, what was G. W. Bush talking about when he referred to "a hemispheric family" and an "international order"? The public statements of notable world leaders regarding an emerging New World Order are copious. Consider the statements of former CBS newsman, Walter Cronkite.

In his book, *A Reporter's Life,* Walter Cronkite said, "A system of world order—preferably a system of world government—is mandatory. The proud nations someday will see the light and, for the common good and their own survival, yield up their precious sovereignty..." Cronkite told BBC newsman Tim Sebastian, "I think we are realizing that we are going to have to have an international rule of law." He added, "We need not only an executive to make international law, but we need the military forces to enforce that law." Cronkite also said, "American people are going to begin to realize that perhaps they are going to have to yield some sovereignty to an international body to enforce world law."

If there is no emerging New World Order, what is Walter Cronkite talking about? Can there be any doubt that Cronkite is talking about global government? Absolutely not! Now, when Bush, Sr. talks about fulfilling "the promise and vision of the U.N.'s founders," he was talking about the same thing former UN Secretary-General Boutros Boutros-Ghali was talking about when he said, "The time for absolute and exclusive sovereignty…has passed."

The United Nations has been on the forefront of promoting the New World Order agenda since its very inception. In 1995, the UN released a manual entitled, *Our Global Neighborhood.* It states, "Population, consumption, technology, development, and the environment are linked in complex relationships that bear closely on human welfare in the global neighborhood. Their effective and equitable management calls for a systematic, long-term, global approach guided by the principle of sustainable development, which has been the central lesson from the mounting ecological dangers of recent times. Its universal application is a priority among the tasks of global governance."

If there is no emerging New World Order, what is "global governance" all about? "Who are the movers and shakers promoting global government?" you ask. Obviously, it is the international bankers who are the heavyweights behind the push for global government. Remember, one cannot create a "global economy" without a global government to manage, oversee, and control it.

In a letter written to Colonel E. Mandell House, President Franklin D. Roosevelt said, "The real truth of the matter is, as you and I know, that a financial element in the large centers has owned the government of the U. S. since the days of Andrew Jackson." "Old Hickory" did his best to rid the United States from the death grip that the international bankers were beginning to exert on this country. He may have been the last president to actually oppose the bankers. In discussing the Bank Renewal bill with a delegation of bankers in 1832, Jackson said, "Gentlemen, I have had men watching you for a long time, and I am convinced that you have used the funds of the bank to speculate in the breadstuffs of the country. When you won, you divided the profits amongst you, and when you lost, you charged it to the bank. You tell me that if I take the deposits from the bank and annul its charter, I shall ruin ten thousand families. That may be true, gentlemen, but that is your sin! Should I let you go on, you will ruin fifty thousand families, and that would be my sin! You are a den of vipers and thieves. I intend to rout you out, and by the eternal God, I will rout you out."

Unfortunately, the international bankers proved themselves to be too formidable for President Jackson. And in 1913, with the collaboration of President Woodrow Wilson, the bankers were given charge over America's financial system by the creation of the Federal Reserve. Ever since the CFR and Trilateral Commission were created, they have filled the key leadership positions of government, big media, and of course, the Federal Reserve.

In his book, *With No Apologies,* former Republican presidential nominee Barry Goldwater wrote, "The Trilateral Commission is intended to be the vehicle for multinational consolidation of the commercial and banking interests by seizing control of the political government of the United States. The Trilateral Commission represents a skillful, coordinated effort to seize control and consolidate the four centers of power—political, monetary, intellectual and ecclesiastical. What the Trilateral Commission intends is to create a worldwide economic power superior to the political governments of the nation-states involved. As managers and creators of the system, they will rule the future." Was Goldwater a prophet or what?

And again, the goals of the global elite have been publicly stated. Back in 1991, the founder of the CFR, David Rockefeller praised the major media for their complicity in helping to facilitate the globalist agenda by saying, "We are grateful to *The Washington Post, The New York Times, Time Magazine* and other great publications whose directors have attended our meetings and respected their promises of discretion for almost forty years... It would have been impossible for us to develop our plan for the world if we had been subjected to the lights of publicity during those years. But, the world is now more sophisticated and prepared to march towards a world government. The supranational sovereignty of an intellectual elite and world bankers is surely preferable to the national auto-determination practiced in past centuries."

How could Rockefeller be any plainer? He acknowledged the willful assistance of the major media in helping to keep the elitists' agenda of global government from the American people. To this day, the major media has not deviated from that collaboration. And this includes the aforementioned "conservative" talking heads. They know if they want to keep their jobs, they dare not reveal the New World Order. The NWO, more than anything else, is the "Third Rail" to the national media.

Is it any wonder that President Barack Obama has stacked his government with numerous members of the CFR? Among these are Robert Gates,

Janet Napolitano, Eric Shinseki, Timothy Geithner, and Tom Daschle. Other CFR members include CFR President Richard Haass, CFR Director Richard Holbrooke, and founding member of the Trilateral Commission and CFR member Paul Volcker. Obama even asked a CFR member, Rick Warren, to deliver the inaugural prayer.

Still not convinced? Just a few days ago, when asked by a reporter what he thought the most important thing was that Barack Obama could accomplish, former Secretary of State Henry Kissinger said, "I think his task will be to develop an overall strategy for America in this period when, really, a New World Order can be created. It's a great opportunity; it isn't just a crisis."

This is the same Henry Kissinger, you will recall, who said back in 1991, "Today, America would be outraged if UN troops entered Los Angeles to restore order. Tomorrow, they will be grateful! This is especially true if they were told that there were [sic] an outside threat from beyond, whether real or promulgated, that threatened our very existence. It is then that all peoples of the world will plead to deliver them from this evil. The one thing every man fears is the unknown. When presented with this scenario, individual rights will be willingly relinquished for the guarantee of their well-being granted to them by the World Government."

Even Gideon Rachman, the chief foreign affairs commentator for the *Financial Times,* wrote an editorial expressing his support for world government. In his column he said, "I have never believed that there is a secret United Nations plot to take over the US... But, for the first time in my life, I think the formation of some sort of world government is plausible.

"A 'world government' would involve much more than co-operation between nations. It would be an entity with state-like characteristics, backed by a body of laws. The European Union has already set up a continental government for twenty-seven countries, which could be a model. The EU has a supreme court, a currency, thousands of pages of law, a large civil service and the ability to deploy military force.

"So could the European model go global? There are three reasons for thinking that it might." Rachman then goes on to explain the reasons why he believes world government is plausible. Do you now see why it does not matter to a tinker's dam whether it is a Republican or Democrat who resides at 1600 Pennsylvania Avenue? For the most part, both major parties in Washington, D. C., have been under the dominating influence of the international bankers who control the Federal Reserve, the CFR, and the Trilateral Commission. And this is also why it does not matter whether one calls himself conservative or liberal. For the most part, both conservatives and liberals in Washington, D. C., are facilitating the emerging New World Order. It is time we wake up to this reality.

Presidents Bush, Sr., Bill Clinton, and Bush, Jr. have thoroughly set the table for the implementation of the NWO, as surely as the sun rises in the east. All Obama has to do is put the food on the table—and you can count on this: Barack Obama will serve up a New World Order feast like you cannot believe!

That a New World Order is emerging is not in question. The only question is what will freedom-loving Americans do about it? Of course, the first thing they have to do is admit that an emerging New World Order exists! Until conservatives, Christians, pastors, constitutionalists, and others who care about a sovereign, independent United States acknowledge the reality of an emerging New World Order, they will be incapable of opposing it. And right now, that is exactly what they are not doing.

MORE ON THE
NEW WORLD ORDER

By Chuck Baldwin
January 30, 2009

In my last column, I attempted to wake up my fellow Americans, who are either currently slumbering through the collapse of our constitutional republic or in a protracted state of denial regarding a very real—and very dangerous—burgeoning New World Order. The information that I need to disseminate on this matter is so plentiful that it is extremely difficult to condense into one column. Therefore, I must at least attempt to provide a little more information on this subject. I will use this column to do just that.

I already quoted former President George Herbert Walker Bush in my previous column. Here are more of his quotes. In 1991, Bush, Sr. said, "My vision of a New World Order foresees a United Nations with a revitalized peacekeeping function." In 1992, he said, "It is the sacred principles enshrined in the United Nations charter to which the American people will henceforth pledge their allegiance." Wow! I thought U. S. Presidents, as well as all civil magistrates and military personnel, swore an oath to uphold the U. S. Constitution. Not in Bush's mind, obviously. On January 25, 1993, Warren Christopher, the new Secretary of State under Bill Clinton, told

CNN: "We must get the New World Order on track and bring the U. N. into its correct role in regards to the United States."

In 1958, Cleon Skousen, a former FBI agent (a man I was fortunate enough to get to know before his death), wrote a book entitled *The Naked Communist.*

In it, he outlined the long-term communist agenda. Since then, the movers and shakers of the New World Order have successfully achieved many of these goals within the U.S. Here are some samples of those goals:

- Permit free trade between all nations regardless of Communist affiliation and regardless of whether or not items could be used for war.
- Provide American aid to all nations regardless of Communist domination.
- Promote the U. N. as the only hope for mankind.
- Capture one or both of the political parties in the United States.
- Get control of the schools.
- Infiltrate the press.
- Gain control of key positions in radio, TV, and motion pictures.
- Break down cultural standards of morality.
- Infiltrate the churches and replace revealed religion with social religion.
- Discredit the American Constitution by calling it inadequate, old-fashioned, out of step with modern needs, a hindrance to cooperation between nations on a worldwide basis.

Is there anyone who cannot see that the purveyors of the New World Order have largely achieved most of their goals? All they need to do now is tie it all together under one governmental umbrella. One of the organizations that is at the forefront of promoting the New World Order is the Council on Foreign Relations (CFR). In my last column, I showed how the CFR dominates the Presidencies of both Republican and Democratic administrations (including the current one), as well as the Federal Reserve. I would even go so far as to say that the CFR is a very "clear and present danger" to the sovereignty and independence of the United States.

For example, CFR member and UN spokesman, Walt Rostow, said,

"It is, therefore, an American interest to see an end to nationhood." The American people need to wake up to the fact that the international banking interests that dominate our political and financial entities are working tirelessly to "see an end to nationhood." I am talking about the Rothschilds and Warburgs of Europe, and the houses of J. P. Morgan, Kuhn, Loeb, Schiff, Lehman, and Rockefeller.

Rear Admiral Chester Ward, who was the Judge Advocate General of the Navy from 1956–1960 and a former member of the CFR who pulled out after realizing what they were all about, warned the American people about the dangers of this and similar organizations (such as the Trilateral Commission). He said, "The most powerful clique in these elitist groups have one objective in common—they want to bring about the surrender of the sovereignty and the national independence of the United States. A second clique of international members in the CFR...comprises the Wall Street international bankers and their key agents. Primarily, they want the world banking monopoly from whatever power ends up in the control of global government."

Admiral Ward also said, "The main purpose of the Council on Foreign Relations is promoting the disarmament of U. S. sovereignty and national independence and submergence into an all powerful, one world government." Remember, the CFR was incorporated in 1921 and is currently comprised of only about 4,000 members. The CFR was co-founded by Edward Mandell House and John D. Rockefeller. Colonel (an honorary title—he was not a military colonel) House had been the chief advisor of President Woodrow Wilson. Historians often call House "Wilson's alter ego" due to the powerful influence he held over the president. House was a rabid Marxist, whose goal was to socialize the United States. In his book, *Philip Dru: Administrator*, House said he was working for "socialism as dreamed of by Karl Marx."

House's stated goals were to incorporate a gradual income tax upon the backs of the American people for the purpose of establishing a state-controlled central bank. Both of these goals were accomplished in 1913, the very first year of the House-dominated Wilson administration.

House's blueprint became the foundation for the CFR. What was not accomplished by the proposed League of Nations at the end of World War I was realized with the formation of the United Nations at the end of World

War II. Not by accident, much of the original funding for the CFR came from Rockefeller and J. P. Morgan. President Franklin D. Roosevelt gave CFR members much authority in his administration, and they have pretty much dominated the foreign and financial policies of the United States ever since.

In the April, 1974 edition of the CFR publication, *Foreign Affairs,* Columbia University Professor and CFR member Richard Gardner wrote a column entitled, "The Hard Road to World Order." In it, he called for "an end run around national sovereignty, eroding it piece by piece." He named the following organizations that would help fulfill that objective: the International Monetary Fund, the World Bank, the General Agreement on Tariffs and Trade (GATT), the Law of the Sea Conference, the World Food Conference, the World Population Conference, and of course, the United Nations. I would also include NAFTA, the World Trade Organization (WTO), the Security and Prosperity Partnership (SPP), CAFTA, etc.

The CFR has a sister organization called the Trilateral Commission (TC). This group was co-founded by the Marxist, Zbigniew Brzezinski, and David Rockefeller. Like Gardner, Brzezinski calls for a piecemeal "movement toward a larger community of the developed nations...through a variety of indirect ties and already developing limitations on national sovereignty." (Source: Brzezinski, *Between Two Ages,* p. 296.) Brzezinski is also a major proponent (along with CFR member Robert Pastor) of the North American Community (or Union), whose construction began during the second term of President George W. Bush and continues today under President Barack Obama. Here is a sample list of the notable dignitaries in and out of government who hold (or held) membership in the CFR or TC (and sometimes both):

George Schultz
Alan Greenspan
Madeleine Albright
Roger Altman
Bruce Babbitt
Howard Baker
Samuel Berger
Michael Dukakis

Elaine Chao
Dianne Feinstein
Ruth Bader Ginsburg
Chuck Hagel
Gary Hart
John McCain
George Mitchell
Bill Moyers
Jay Rockefeller
Al Gore
Donna Shalala
Strobe Talbott
Fred Thompson
Robert Zoellick
Richard Nixon
Hubert H. Humphrey
George McGovern
Gerald Ford
Jimmy Carter
John Kerry

It is absolutely essential that we stop looking at potential leaders as either Democrats or Republicans, or as conservatives or liberals. Those monikers mean very little today. We must start identifying people as either Americans or globalists. Either they believe in an independent, sovereign, self-governing United States of America, or they believe in supranational government and internationalism. Either they believe in devotion to the U. S. Constitution, Bill of Rights, and Declaration of Independence, or they believe in the goals and objectives of the United Nations. We must rid ourselves of the propensity to support those who classify themselves as "conservatives," and we must stop blindly supporting the GOP "because it is a 'conservative' party." If they do not understand AND OPPOSE the New World Order, they do not deserve our support or our vote!

George W. Bush, Bill Clinton, and George H. W. Bush laid the foundation for everything that Barack Obama is doing to facilitate the New World

Order. That two of these Presidents are Democrats and two are Republicans only proves my point: both the Democratic and Republican parties have succumbed to New World Order ideology. There is more that we can do, of course, but I will save the bulk of that discussion for another day. In the meantime, we need to realize that the New World Order exists, to understand that both major parties are collaborating to facilitate its creation, to start looking at leaders as either Americans or globalists, and to refuse to support the latter in any shape, manner, or form.

Pastors need to start warning their people about the New World Order (and the biblical principles relating to it) from their pulpits—loud and often! People need to start warning their family members and friends. We need to start searching out like-minded patriots—who understand what's going on—for information and encouragement. And remember this: WE CAN DEFEAT THE NEW WORLD ORDER. Yes, we can! The fatalistic view that we are helpless is a bunch of baloney! Our forefathers defeated the New World Order in their day. The globalists have been stymied many times through the years. The fact that they have not yet totally achieved their globalistic objectives shows us that it is possible to stop them, or at the very least, set their agenda backward.

I also urge my Christian brothers and sisters to rid themselves of the propensity to say, "This is God's will; there is nothing we can do about it." That, too, is hooey! Christians are to be the "salt of the earth." Salt is a preservative, a retardant against decay. We are instructed to be faithful "unto death." In Romans chapter 3, the apostle Paul made it clear that we must never support evil that good may come. I would remind my brethren that refusing to resist evil is the same as supporting it. Sitting back complacently and saying, "This must happen so Jesus can come," borders on blasphemy. It runs counter to everything the Bible teaches. We Christians have a duty, an obligation to do right with no regard to outcome or consequences.

When asked when He would establish His Kingdom on the earth, the first thing out of Jesus's mouth was, "It is not for you to know." Yet, many Christians presume to know the times and seasons of Christ's return. But let's be honest with ourselves and admit that we do NOT know. To sit back and say that we have full understanding of Bible prophecy and can say for certain what God does or does not want to accomplish in and through our country is the height of arrogance and pride. Only God knows those things. It's time we let God be God and start doing what is ours to do.

What we do know is any attempt at establishing global government is as wicked now as it was at the Tower of Babel. As Christians, we are instructed to resist the wicked one. We must oppose him and his work. We are told to "occupy" until Christ returns, whenever that is. To "occupy" means to "take care of business." God expects us to follow His teaching and do what is ours to do. To use Christ's coming as an excuse to not "take care of business" is itself inexcusable!

As John Quincy Adams said, "Duty is ours; results are God's." If we would truly do our duty, who knows what God would do to help us defeat (for the sake of our children and grandchildren) this devilish New World Order? As for me and my house, we will fight for a free, independent and sovereign United States—so that we might walk, work, and worship in freedom—as long as we have breath in our being. How about you?

P.S. Several readers informed me that Michael Savage began acknowledging the New World Order on his radio show last year. Some said he has even spoken against it. This is good news. If only the rest of the so-called "conservative" talking heads would do the same thing—but in a more aggressive fashion: you know, like America's freedom depended on it, because it does.

P.P.S. Dennis Cuddy wrote a good chronological history of the New World Order, which covers its progression through the twentieth century. It can be viewed at http://www.constitution.org/col/cuddy_nwo.htm.